Dear Reader,

What you have in your hand are two of my favorite books I've had the privilege to write. They were certainly two of the more emotional books I've written. They're very different stories in some ways, but at their core, they're both about finding love and redemption.

A Hunger for the Forbidden, is the final book in the Corretti Dynasty series (if you've been following the whole series, that's amazing. And I hope this is a satisfying conclusion!) Fair warning, Matteo and Alessia have a hard road ahead. Forbidden desire, family feuds, an unexpected pregnancy and dark secrets are all in the way of their happily-ever-after.

In *The Highest Price to Pay* Blaise and Ella don't have secrets between them. Or so they think. They believe they already know the worst about each other. But it's not about the pain on the surface, or Ella's physical scars, it's about the deep pain they hide from the world.

Matteo and Blaise both feel beyond redemption for very different reasons, but with the same result.

I think that everyone needs love. And who better to appreciate the beauty of love than a man who's resigned himself to living without it? A man who believes he isn't worthy of it?

These stories are about the real power of love. About how love can pull a person from the darkest of places and bring them into the light.

I hope you enjoy my two damaged heroes as much as I did.

All the best,

Maisey

The more powerful the family...the darker the secrets!

Introducing the Correttis—Sicily's most scandalous family!

Behind the closed doors of their opulent palazzo,
ruthless desire and the lethal Coretti charm are alive and well.

We invite you to step over the threshold and enter the
Correttis' dark and dazzling world....

The Empire

Young, rich and notoriously handsome, the Correttis'
legendary exploits regularly feature in Sicily's tabloid pages!

The Scandal

But how long can their reputations withstand the glaring heat
of the spotlight before their family's secrets are exposed?

The Legacy

Once nearly destroyed by the secrets cloaking their thirst for
power, the new generation of Correttis are riding high again—
and no disgrace or scandal will stand in their way....

Sicily's Corretti Dynasty

A LEGACY OF SECRETS—Carol Marinelli
AN INVITATION TO SIN—Sarah Morgan
A SHADOW OF GUILT—Abby Green
AN INHERITANCE OF SHAME—Kate Hewitt
A WHISPER OF DISGRACE—Sharon Kendrick
A FACADE TO SHATTER—Lynn Raye Harris
A SCANDAL IN THE HEADLINES—Caitlin Crews
A HUNGER FOR THE FORBIDDEN—Maisey Yates

8 volumes to collect—you won't want to miss out!

Maisey Yates

A Hunger for the Forbidden

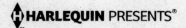

Recycling programs
for this product may
not exist in your area.

ISBN-13: 978-0-373-23964-1

A HUNGER FOR THE FORBIDDEN

First North American Publication 2013

Copyright © 2013 by Harlequin Books S.A.

Printed in U.S.A.

All about the author...
Maisey Yates

MAISEY YATES knew she wanted to be a writer even before she knew what it was she wanted to write.

At her very first job she was fortunate enough to meet her very own tall, dark and handsome hero, who happened to be her boss, and promptly married him and started a family. It wasn't until she was pregnant with her second child that she found her very first Harlequin Presents® book in a local thrift store—by the time she'd reached the happily-ever-after, she had fallen in love. She devoured as many as she could get her hands on after that, and she knew that these were the books she wanted to write!

She started submitting, and nearly two years later, while pregnant with her third child, she received The Call from her editor. At the age of twenty three, she sold her first manuscript to the Harlequin Presents line, and she was very glad that the good news didn't send her into labor!

She still can't quite believe she's blessed enough to see her name on, not just any book, but on her favorite books.

Maisey lives with her supportive, handsome, wonderful, diaper-changing husband and three small children, across the street from her parents and the home she grew up in, in the wilds of southern Oregon. She enjoys the contrast of living in a place where you might wake up to find a bear on your back porch, then walk into the home office to write stories that take place in exotic, urban locales.

Other titles by Maisey Yates available in ebook:

HIS RING IS NOT ENOUGH
THE COUPLE WHO FOOLED THE WORLD
HEIR TO A DARK INHERITANCE *(Secret Heirs of Powerful Men)*
HEIR TO A DESERT LEGACY *(Secret Heirs of Powerful Men)*

To the fabulous editors at the M&B office.
You push me to be better and to take risks.
And you make my job fun. Thank you.

CHAPTER ONE

ALESSIA BATTAGLIA ADJUSTED her veil, the whisper-thin fabric skimming over the delicate skin of her neck. Like a lover's kiss. Soft. Gentle.

She closed her eyes, and she could feel it.

Hot, warm lips on her bare flesh. A firm, masculine hand at her waist.

She opened her eyes again and bent down, adjusting the delicate buckles on her white satin heels.

Her lover's hands on her ankle, removing her high heels. Leaving her naked in front of him, naked before a man for the first time. But there was no time for nerves. There was nothing more than the heat between them. Years of fantasy, years of longing.

Alessia swallowed and took the bouquet of bloodred roses from the chair they were resting on. She looked down at the blossoms, some of them bruised by the way she'd laid them down.

Brushing her fingertips over the crushed velvet petals brought another wave of memory. A wave of sensation.

Her lover's mouth at her breast, her fingers woven through his thick dark hair.

"Alessia?"

Her head snapped up and she saw her wedding coordinator standing in the doorway, one hand covering her headset.

"Yes?"

"It's time."

Alessia nodded, and headed toward the doorway, her shoes loud on the marble floor of the basilica. She exited the room that had been set aside for her to get ready in, and entered the vast foyer. It was empty now, all of the guests in the sanctuary, waiting for the ceremony.

She let out a long breath, the sound loud in the empty, high-ceilinged room. Then she started her walk toward the sanctuary, past pillars inlaid with gold and stones. She stopped for a moment, hoping to find some comfort, some peace, in the biblical scenes depicted on the walls.

Her eyes fell to a detailed painting of a garden. Of Eve handing Adam the apple.

"Please. Just one night."

"Only one, cara mia?"

"That's all I have to give."

A searing kiss, like nothing she'd ever experienced before. Better than any fantasy.

Her breath caught and she turned away from the painting, continuing on, continuing to the small antechamber outside of the sanctuary.

Her father was there, his suit crisp and pressed. Antonioni Battaglia looked every inch the respectable citizen everyone knew he was not. And the wedding, so formal, so traditional, was another statement of his power. Power that he longed to increase, with the Corretti fortune and status.

That desire was the reason she was here.

"You are very much like your mother."

She wondered if there was any truth to the words, or if it was just the right thing to say. Tenderness was something her father had never seemed capable of.

"Thank you," she said, looking down at her bouquet.

"This is what's right for the family."

She knew it was. Knew that it was the key to ensuring that her brothers and sisters were cared for. And that was, after all, what she'd done since her mother died in childbirth. Pietro, Giana, Marco and Eva were the brightest lights in her existence, and she would do, had done, whatever she could to ensure they had the best life possible.

And still, regret settled on her like a cloak, and

memory clouded the present. Memories of her lover. His hands, his body, his passion.

If only her lover, and the man waiting behind the doors to the sanctuary, waiting to marry her, were the same.

"I know," she said, fighting against the desolation inside of her. The emptiness.

The double doors parted, revealing an impossibly long aisle. The music changed, everyone turned to look at her—all twelve hundred guests, who had come to watch the union of the Battaglia family and their much-hated rivals, the Correttis.

She held her head up, trying to breathe. The bodice of her dress threatened to choke her. The lace, which formed a high collar, and sleeves that ended in a point over her hands, was heavy and scratched against her skin. The yards of fabric clung to her, heat making her feel light-headed.

It was a beautiful dress, but it was too fussy for her. Too heavy. But the dress wasn't about her. The wedding wasn't about her.

Her father followed her into the sanctuary but didn't take her arm. He had given her away when he'd signed his agreement with the late Salvatore Corretti. He didn't need to do it again. He didn't move to take a seat, either, rather he prowled around the back of the pews, up the side of the church, his steps parallel to hers. That was Antonioni Battaglia all over. Watching proceedings, ensuring all went well. Watching her. Making sure she did as she was told.

A drop of sweat rolled down her back and another flash of memory hit her hard.

His sweat-slicked skin beneath her fingertips. Her nails digging into his shoulders. Her thighs wrapped around lean, masculine hips...

She blinked and looked up at Alessandro. Her groom. The man to whom she was about to make her vows.

God forgive me.

Had she not been holding the roses, she would have crossed herself.

And then she felt him. As though he had reached out and put his hands on her.

She looked at the Corretti side, and her heart stopped for a moment. Matteo.

Her lover. Her groom's enemy.

Matteo was arresting as ever, with the power to draw the breath from her lungs. Tall and broad, his physique outlined to perfection by his custom-made suit. Olive skin and square jaw. Lips that delivered pleasure in beautiful and torturous ways.

But this man standing in the pews was not the man who'd shared her bed that night a month ago. He was different. Rage, dark and bottomless, burned from his eyes, his jaw tight. She had thought, had almost hoped, that he wouldn't care about her being promised to Alessandro. That a night of passion with her would be like a night with any other woman.

Yes, that thought had hurt, but it had been better than this. Better than him looking at her like he hated her.

She could remember those dark eyes meeting hers with a different kind of fire. Lust. Need. A bleak desperation that had echoed inside of her. And she could remember them clouded by desire, his expression pained as she'd touched him, tasted him.

She looked to Alessandro but she could still feel Matteo watching her. And she had to look back. She always had to look at Matteo Corretti. For as long as she could remember, she'd been drawn to him.

And for one night, she'd had him.

Now…now she would never have him again.

Her steps faltered, her high heel turning sideways beneath her. She stumbled, caught herself, her eyes locking with Matteo's again.

Dio, it was hot. Her dress was suffocating her now. The veil too heavy on her head, the lace at her throat threatening to choke her.

She stopped walking, the war within her threatening to tear her to pieces.

* * *

Matteo Corretti thought he would gag on his anger. Watching her walk toward Alessandro, his cousin, his rival in business and now, because of this, his enemy.

Watching Alessia Battaglia make her way to Alessandro, to bind herself to him.

She was Matteo's. His lover. His woman. The most beautiful woman he had ever seen in his life. It wasn't simply the smooth perfection of her golden skin, not just the exquisite cheekbones and full, rose-colored lips. It was something that existed beneath her skin, a vitality and passion that had, by turns, fascinated and confused him.

Her every laugh, every smile, every mundane action, was filled with more life, more joy, than his most memorable moments. It was why, from the first time he'd sneaked a look at her as a boy, he had been transfixed.

Far from the monster he'd been made to believe the Battaglias were, she had been an angel in his eyes.

But he had never touched her. Never breached the unspoken command issued by his father and grandfather. Because she was a Battaglia and he a Corretti, the bad blood between them going back more than fifty years. He had been forbidden from even speaking to her and as a boy he had only violated that order once.

And now, when Salvatore had thought it might benefit him, now she was being traded to Alessandro like cattle. He tightened his hands into fists, anger, anger like he hadn't felt in more than thirteen years, curling in his gut. The kind of rage he normally kept packed in ice was roaring through him. He feared it might explode, and he knew what happened when it did.

He could not be held responsible for what he might do if he had to watch Alessandro touch Alessia. Kiss her.

And then Alessia froze in place, her big, dark eyes darting from Alessandro, and back to him. Those eyes. Those eyes were always in his dreams.

Her hand dropped to her side, and then she released her hold on her bouquet of roses, the sound of them hitting the stone floor loud in the sudden silence of the room.

Then she turned, gripping the front of her heavy lace skirt, and ran back down the aisle. The white fabric billowed around her as she ran. She only looked behind her once. Wide, frightened eyes meeting his.

"Alessia!" He couldn't stop himself. Her name burst from his lips, and his body burst from its position in the pews. And he was running, too. "Alessia!"

The roar of the congregation drowned out his words. But still he ran. People were standing now, filing into the aisle, blocking his path. The faces of the crowd were a blur, he wasn't aware of who he touched, who he moved out of his way, in his pursuit of the bride.

When he finally burst through the exterior doors of the basilica, Alessia was getting into the backseat of the limo that was waiting to carry her and her groom away after the ceremony, trying to get her massive skirt and train into the vehicle with her. When she saw him, everything in her face changed. A hope in her eyes that grabbed him deep in his chest and twisted his heart. Hard.

"Matteo."

"What are you doing, Alessia?"

"I have to go," she said, her eyes focused behind him now, fearful. Fearful of her father, he knew. He was gripped then by a sudden need to erase her fears. To keep her from ever needing to be afraid again.

"Where?" he asked, his voice rough.

"The airport. Meet me."

"Alessia…"

"Matteo, please. I'll wait." She shut the door to the limo and the car pulled out of the parking lot, just as her father exited the church.

"You!" Antonioni turned on him. "What have you done?"

And Alessandro appeared behind him, his eyes blazing with fury. "Yes, cousin, what have you done?"

* * *

Alessia's hands shook as she handed the cash to the woman at the clothing shop. She'd never been permitted to go into a store like this. Her father thought this sort of place, with mass-produced garments, was common. Not for a Battaglia. But the jeans, T-shirt and trainers she'd found suited her purpose because they were common. Because any woman would wear them. Because a Battaglia would not. As if the Battaglias had the money to put on the show they did. Her father borrowed what he had to in order to maintain the fiction that their power was as infinite as it ever was. His position as Minister for the Trade and Housing department might net him a certain amount of power, power that was easily and happily manipulated, but it didn't keep the same flow of money that had come from her grandfather's rather more seedy organization.

The shopgirl looked at her curiously, and Alessia knew why. A shivering bride, sans groom, in a small tourist shop still wearing her gown and veil was a strange sight indeed.

"May I use the changing room?" she asked once her items were paid for.

She felt slightly sick using her father's money to escape, sicker still over the way she'd gotten it. She must have been quite the sight in the bank, in her wedding gown, demanding a cash advance against a card with her father's name on it.

"I'm a Battaglia," she'd said, employing all the self-importance she'd ever heard come from Antonioni. "Of course it's all right for me to access my family money."

Cash was essential, because she knew better than to leave a paper trail. Having a family who had, rather famously, been on the wrong side of the law was helpful in that regard at least. As had her lifelong observation of how utter confidence could get you things you shouldn't be allowed to have. The money in her purse being a prime example.

"Of course," the cashier said.

Alessia scurried into the changing room and started tugging off the gown, the hideous, suffocating gown. The one chosen by her father because it was so traditional. The virgin bride in white.

If he only knew.

She contorted her arm behind her and tugged at the tab of the zip, stepping out of the dress, punching the crinoline down and stepping out of the pile of fabric. She slipped the jeans on and tugged the stretchy black top over her head.

She emerged from the room a moment later, using the rubber bands she'd purchased to restrain her long, thick hair. Then she slipped on the trainers, ruing her lack of socks for a moment, then straightened.

And she breathed. Feeling more like herself again. Like Alessia. "Thank you," she said to the cashier. "Keep the dress. Sell it if you like."

She dashed out of the store and onto the busy streets, finally able to breathe. Finally.

She'd ditched the limo at the bank, offering the driver a generous tip for his part in the getaway. It only took her a moment to flag down a cab.

She slid in the back, clutching her bag to her chest. "Aeroporto di Catania, *per favore.*"

"Naturalmente."

Matteo hadn't lingered at the basilica. Instead, he'd sidestepped his cousin's furious questions and gotten into his sports car, roaring out of the parking lot and heading in the direction of the airport without giving it any thought.

His heart was pounding hard, adrenaline pouring through him.

He felt beyond himself today. Out of control in a way he never allowed.

In a way he rarely allowed, at least. There had been a few breaks in his infamous control, and all of them were tied to Alessia. And they provided a window into just what he could become if the hideous cold that lived in him met with passionate flame.

She was his weakness. A weakness he should never have allowed and one he should certainly never allow again.

Dark eyes clashing with his in a mirror hanging behind the bar. Eyes he would recognize anywhere.

He turned sharply and saw her, the breath pulled from his lungs.

He set his drink down on the bar and walked across the crowded room, away from his colleagues.

"Alessia." He addressed her directly for the first time in thirteen years.

"Matteo." His name sounded so sweet on her lips.

It had been a month since their night together in New York City, a chance encounter, he'd imagined. He wondered now.

A whole month and he could still taste her skin on his tongue, could still feel the soft curves of her breasts resting in his palms. Could still hear her broken sighs of need as they took each other to the height of pleasure.

And he had not wanted another woman since.

They barely made it into his hotel room, they were far too desperate for each other. He slammed the door, locking it with shaking fingers, pressing her body against the wall. Her dress was long, with a generous slit up the side, revealing her toned, tan legs.

He wrapped his fingers around her thigh and tugged her leg up around his hip, settling the hardness of his erection against her softness.

It wasn't enough. It would never be enough.

Matteo stopped at a red light, impatience tearing at him. Need, need like he had only known once before, was like a beast inside him, devouring, roaring.

Finally, she was naked, her bare breasts pressing hard against his chest. He had to have her. His entire body trembling with lust.

"Ready for me, cara mia?"

"Always for you."

He slid inside of her body, so tight, much more so than he'd expected, than he'd ever experienced. She cried out softly, the bite of her nails in his flesh not due to pleasure now.

A virgin.

His. Only his.

Except she had not been his. It had been a lie. The next morning, Alessia was gone. And when he'd returned to Sicily, she'd been there.

He'd been invited to a family party but he had not realized that all branches of the Corretti family would be present. Had not realized it was an engagement party. For Alessandro and Alessia. A party to celebrate the end of a feud, the beginning of a partnership between the Battaglias and the Correttis, a change to revitalize the docklands in Palermo and strengthen their family corporation.

"How long have you and Alessia been engaged?" he asked, his eyes trained on her even as he posed the question to Alessandro.

"For a while now. But we wanted to wait to make the big announcement until all the details were finalized."

"I see," he said. *"And when is the blessed event?"*

"One month. No point in waiting."

Some of the old rage burned through the desire that had settled inside of him. She had been engaged to Alessandro when he'd taken her into his bed. She'd intended, from the beginning, to marry another man the night she'd given herself to him.

And he, he had been forced to watch her hang on his cousin's arm for the past month while his blood boiled in agony as he watched his biggest rival hold on to the one thing he wanted more than his next breath. The one thing he had always wanted, but never allowed himself to have.

He had craved violence watching the two of them together. Had longed to rip Alessandro's hands off her and show him what happened when a man touched what belonged to him.

Even now, the thought sent a rising tide of nausea through him.

What was it Alessia did to him? This wave of possessiveness, this current of passion that threatened to drown him, it was not something that was a part of him. He was a man who lived in his mind, a man who embraced logic and fact, duty and honor.

When he did not, when he gave in to emotion, the danger was far too great. He was a Corretti, cut from the same cloth as his father and grandfather, a fabric woven together with greed, violence and a passion for acquiring more money, more power, than any one man could ever need.

Even with logic, with reason, he could and had justified actions that would horrify most men. He hated to think what might happen if he were unleashed without any hold on his control.

So he shunned passion, in all areas of life.

Except one.

He pulled his car off the road and slammed on his breaks, killing the engine, his knuckles burning from the hard grip he had on the steering wheel, his breath coming in short, harsh bursts.

This was not him. He didn't know himself with Alessia, and he never had.

And nothing good could come from it. He had spent his life trying to change the man he seemed destined to be. Trying to keep control, to move his life in a different direction than the one his father would have pushed him into.

Alessia compromised that. She tested it.

He ran his fingers through his hair, trying to catch his breath.

Then he turned the key over, the engine roaring to life again. And he turned the car around, heading away from the airport, away from the city.

He punched a button on his dashboard and connected himself to his PA.

"Lucia?"

"Sì?"

"Hold my calls until further notice."

It had been three hours. No doubt the only reason her father and his men hadn't come tearing through the airport was that they would never have imagined she would do something so audacious as to run away completely.

Alessia shifted in the plastic chair and wiped her cheek again, even though her tears had dried. She had no more tears left to cry. It was all she'd done since she'd arrived.

And she'd done more since it had become clear Matteo wasn't coming.

And then she'd done more when she'd suddenly had to go into the bathroom and throw up in a public stall.

Then she'd stopped, just long enough to go into one of the airport shops and pick up the one thing she'd avoided buying for the past week.

She'd started crying again when the pregnancy test had resulted in two little pink, positive, yes-you're-having-a-baby lines.

Now she was wrung out. Sick. And completely alone.

Well, not completely alone. Not really. She was having a baby, after all.

The thought didn't comfort her so much as magnify the feeling of utter loneliness.

One thing was certain. There was no going back to Alessandro. No going back to her family. She was having the wrong man's baby. A man who clearly didn't want her.

But he did once.

That thought made her furious, defiant. Yes, he had. More than once, which was likely how the pregnancy had happened. Because there had been protection during their times in bed, but they'd also showered together in the early hours of the morning and then…then neither of them had been able to think, or spare the time.

A voice came over the loudspeaker, the last call for her flight out to New York.

She stood up, picked up her purse, the only thing she had with her, the only thing she had to her name, and handed her ticket to the man at the counter.

"Going to New York?" he asked, verifying.

She took a deep breath. "Yes."

CHAPTER TWO

HE'D NEVER EVEN opened the emails she'd been sending him. She knew, because she'd set them up so that they would send her a receipt when the addressee opened her message, but she'd never gotten one.

He didn't answer her calls, either. Not the calls to his office, not the calls to his mobile phone, not the calls to the Palazzolo Corretti, or to his personal estate outside Palermo.

Matteo Corretti was doing an exceptional job of ignoring her, and he had been for weeks now while she'd been holed up in her friend Carolina's apartment. Carolina, the friend who had talked her into a New York bachelorette party in the first place. Which, all things considered, meant she sort of owed Alessia since that bachelorette party was the source of both her problems, and her pregnancy.

No, that wasn't fair. It was her fault. Well, a lot of it was. The rest was Matteo Corretti's. Master of disguise and phone-call-avoider extraordinaire.

She wished she didn't need him but she didn't know what else to do. She was so tired. So sad, all the time. Her father wouldn't take her calls, either, her siblings, the most precious people in her life were forbidden from speaking to her. That, more than anything, was threatening to burn a hole in her soul. She felt adrift without them around her. They'd kept her going for most of her life, given her a sense of purpose, of strength and responsibility. Without them she just felt like she was floundering.

She'd had one option, of course. To terminate the pregnancy and return home. Beg her father and Alessandro for forgiveness. But she hadn't been able to face that. She'd lost so much in her life already and as confused as she was about the baby, about what it would mean for her, as terrified as she was, she couldn't face losing the tiny life inside of her.

But she would run out of money soon. Then she would be alone and penniless while Matteo Corretti spent more of his fortune on sports cars and high-rise hotels.

She wasn't going to allow it anymore. Not when she'd already decided that if he didn't want to be a part of their baby's life he would have to come tell her to her face. He would have to stand before her and denounce their child, verbally, not simply by ignoring emails and messages. He would have to make that denouncement a physical action.

Yes, she'd made the wrong decision to sleep with him without telling him about Alessandro. But it didn't give him the right to deny their child. Their child had nothing to do with her stupidity. He or she was the only innocent party in the situation.

She looked down at the screen on her phone. She had her Twitter account all set up and ready to help her contact every news outlet in the area.

She took a breath and started typing.

@theobserver @NYTnews @HBpress I'm about to make an important announcement re Matteo Corretti & the wedding scandal. Luxe Hotel on 3rd.

Then she stepped out of the back of the cab and walked up to the front steps of Matteo's world-renowned hotel, where he was rumored to be in residence, though no one would confirm it, and waited.

The sidewalks were crowded, people pushing past other people, walking with their heads down, no one sparing her a glance. Until the news crews started showing up.

First there was one, then another, and another. Some from outlets she hadn't personally included in her tweet. The small crowd drew stares, and some passersby started lingering to see what was happening.

There was no denying that she was big news. The assumption had been that she'd run off with Matteo but nothing could be further from the truth. And she was about to give the media a big dose of truth.

It didn't take long for them to catch the attention of the people inside the hotel, which had been a key part of her plan.

A sharply dressed man walked out of the front of the hotel, his expression wary. "Is there something I can help you with?"

She turned to him. "I'm just making a quick announcement. If you want to go get Matteo, that might help."

"Mr. Corretti is not in residence."

"That's like saying someone isn't At Home in a Regency novel, isn't it? He's here, but he doesn't want anyone to know it."

The reporters were watching the exchange with rapt attention, and the flash on one of the cameras started going, followed by the others.

"Mr. Corretti is not—"

She whirled around to face him again. "Fine, then if Mr. Corretti is truly not in residence you can stand out here and listen to what I have to say and relay it to your boss when you deliver dinner to the room he is not in residence in."

She turned back to the reporters, and suddenly, the official press release she'd spent hours memorizing last night seemed to shatter in her brain, making it impossible to piece back together, impossible to make sense of it.

She swallowed hard, looking at the skyline, her vision filled with concrete, glass and steel. The noise from the cars was deafening, the motion of the traffic in front of her making her head swim. "I know that the wedding has been much talked about. And that Matteo chasing me out of the church has been the headline. Well, there's more to the story."

Flashes blinded her, tape recorders shoved into her face, questions started to drown out her voice. She felt weak, shaky, and she wondered, not for the first time, if she was completely insane.

Her life in Sicily had been quiet, domestic, one surrounded by her family, one so insular that she'd been dependent upon imagination to make it bearable, a belief of something bigger looming in her future. And as a result, she had a tendency to romanticize the grand gesture in her mind. To think that somehow, no matter how bleak the situation seemed, she could fix it. That, in the end, she would make it perfect and manage to find her happy ending.

She'd done it on the night of her bachelorette party. New York was so different than the tiny village she'd been raised in. So much bigger, faster. Just being there had seemed like a dream and so when she'd been confronted with Matteo it had seemed an easy, logical thing to approach him, to follow the path their mutual attraction had led them down. It was a prime example of her putting more stock in fantasy, in the belief in happy endings, over her common sense.

This was another.

But no matter how well planned this was, she hadn't realized how she would feel, standing there with everyone watching her. She wasn't the kind of woman who was used to having all eyes on her, her aborted wedding being the exception.

"I'm pregnant, and Matteo Corretti is the father of my baby." It slipped out, bald and true, and not at all what she'd been planning to say. At least she didn't think it was.

"Mr. Corretti—" the employee was speaking into his phone now, his complexion pallid "—you need to come out here."

She released a breath she hadn't realized she'd been holding.

"When is the baby due?"

"Are you certain he's the father?"

"When did you discover you were pregnant?"

The questions were coming rapid-fire now, but she didn't need to answer them because this was never about the press. This was about getting his attention. This was about forcing a confrontation that he seemed content to avoid.

"I'll answer more questions when Matteo comes to make his statement."

"Did the two of you leave the wedding together, or are you estranged? Has he denied paternity?" one of the reporters asked.

"I…"

"What the hell is going on?"

Alessia turned and her heart caught in her throat, making it impossible to breathe. Matteo. It felt like an eternity since she'd seen him, since he'd kissed her, put his hands on her skin. An eternity.

She ached with the need to run to him, to hold on to him, use him as an anchor. In her fantasies, he had long been her knight in shining armor, a simplistic vision of a man who had saved her from a hideous fate.

But in the years since, things had changed. Become more complex, more real. He was her lover now. The father of her child. The man she had lied to. The man who had left her sitting alone in an airport, crying and clutching a positive pregnancy test.

For a moment, the longing for those simple, sun-drenched days in Sicily, when he had been nothing more than an idealized savior, was so sharp and sweet she ached.

"Mr. Corretti, is this why you broke up the wedding?"

"I didn't break up anyone's wedding," he said, his tone dark.

"No, I ran out of the wedding," she said.

"And is what why I broke up the wedding?" he asked, addressing the reporter, stormy eyes never once looking at her.

"The baby," the reporter said.

Matteo froze, his face turning to stone. "The baby." Color drained from his face, but he remained stoic, only the change in his complexion a clue as to the shock that he felt.

He didn't know. She felt the impact of that reality like a physical blow. He hadn't even listened to a single message. Hadn't opened any emails, even before she'd started tagging them to let her know when he opened them.

"Is there more than one?" This from another reporter.

"Of course not," Matteo said, his words smooth, his eyes cold like granite. "Only this one."

He came to stand beside her, his gaze still

avoiding hers. He put his arm around her waist, the sudden contact like touching an open flame, heat streaking through her veins. How did he manage to affect her this way still? After all he'd done to her? After the way he'd treated her?

"Do you have a statement?"

"Not at this point," he bit out. "But when the details for the wedding are finalized, we will be in touch."

He tightened his hold on her waist and turned them both around, away from the reporters, leading her up the steps and into the hotel. She felt very much like she was being led into the lion's den.

"What are you doing?" she asked, wishing he would move away from her, wishing he would stop touching her.

"Taking you away from the circus you created. I have no desire to discuss this with an audience."

If he wasn't so angry with her, she might think it was a good idea. But Matteo Corretti's rage was like ice-cold water in a black sea. Fathomless, with the great threat of pulling her beneath the waves.

His hold tightened with each step they took toward the hotel, and her stomach started to feel more and more unsettled until, when they passed through the revolving door and into the hotel lobby, she was afraid she might vomit on the high-gloss marble floors.

A charming photo to go with the headlines.

He released her the moment they were fully inside. "What the hell is the meaning of this?" he asked, rounding on her as his staff milled around very carefully not watching.

"Should we go somewhere more private?" she asked. Suddenly she felt like she'd rather brave his rage than put on a show. She was too tired for that. Too vulnerable. Bringing the press in was never about drawing attention to herself, it was about getting information to Matteo that he couldn't ignore. Giving the man no excuse to say he didn't know.

"Says the woman who called a bloody press conference?"

"You didn't answer my calls. Or return my messages. And I'm pretty sure now that you didn't even listen to any of them."

"I have been away," he said.

"Well, that's hardly my fault that you chose this moment to go on sabbatical. And I had no way of knowing."

He was looking at her like she'd grown an extra head. "Take me to your suite," she said.

"I'm not in the mood, Alessia."

"Neither am I!" she shot back. "I want to talk."

"It's just that last time we were in this hotel, talking was very much not on the agenda."

Her face heated, searing prickles dotting her skin. "No. That's very true. Which is how we find ourselves in this current situation."

"Communication seems to be something we don't do well with," he said. "Our lack of talking last time we were here together certainly caused some issues."

"But I want to talk now," she said, crossing her arms beneath her breasts.

He cocked his head to the side, dark eyes trained on her now with a focus he'd withheld until that moment. "You aren't afraid of me."

"No."

"A mistake, some might say, *cara mia*."

"Is that so?"

"You won't like me when I'm angry."

"You turn green and split your pants?"

"Perhaps taking this somewhere private is the best idea," he said, wrapping his fingers around her arm, just above her elbow, and directing her toward the elevator.

He pushed the up button and they both waited. She felt like she was hovering in a dream, but she dug her fingernails into her palms, and her surroundings didn't melt away. It was real. All of this.

The elevator doors slid open and they both

stepped inside. And as soon as they were closed into the lift, he rounded on her.

"You're pregnant?" His words were flat in the quiet of the elevator.

"Yes. I tried to tell you in a less public way, but it's been two months and you've been very hard to get ahold of."

"Not an accident."

"Oh, no, I know. It was far too purposeful to be accidental. You never even opened my emails."

"I blocked your address after you sent the first few."

"Uh," she said, unable to make a more eloquent sound.

"I see it offends you."

"Yes. It does offend me. Didn't it occur to you that I might have something important to tell you?"

"I didn't care," he said.

The elevator stopped at the top floor and the doors slid open. "Is there a point in me going any further, then? Or should I just go back to my friend Carolina's apartment and start a baby registry?"

"You are not leaving."

"But you just said you didn't care."

"I didn't care until I found out you were carrying my child."

She was both struck, and pleased, by his certainty that the child was his. She wouldn't have really blamed him if he'd questioned her at least once. She'd lied about her engagement to Alessandro. By omission, but still. She knew she wasn't blameless in the whole fiasco.

"What did you think I was trying to contact you for? To beg you to take me back? To beg you for more sex? Because that's what we shared that night, that's all we shared." The lie was an acid burn on her tongue. "I would hardly have burned my pride to the ground for the sake of another orgasm."

"Is that true? You would hardly be the first person to do it."

"If you mean you, I'm sure it cost you to take a Battaglia to your bed. Must have been some epic dry spell."

"And not worth the price in the end, I think." His words were designed to peel skin from bone, and they did their job. "I would say the same."

"I can see now why you ran from the wedding."

A wave of confusion hit her, and it took her a moment to realize that she hadn't told him the order in which the events had occurred. Wedding abandonment, then pregnancy test, but before she could correct him he pressed on.

"And how conveniently you've played it, too. Alessandro would, of course, know it wasn't his child as you never slept with him. I hope you're pleased with the way all of this unfolded because you have managed to ensure that you are still able to marry a Corretti, in spite of our little mistake. Good insurance for your family since, thanks to your abandonment, the deal between our family and yours has gone to hell."

"You think I planned this? You aren't even serious about marrying me, are you?"

"There is no other choice. You announced your pregnancy to the whole world."

"I had to tell you."

"And if I had chosen not to be a part of the baby's life?"

"I was going to make you tell me that to my face."

He regarded her closely. "Strange to think I ever imagined you to be soft, Alessia."

"I'm a Battaglia. I've never had the luxury of being soft."

"Clearly not." He looked at her, long and hard. "This makes sense, Alessia." His tone was all business now. Maddeningly sure and decisive. "It will put to rest rumors of bad blood, unite the families."

"You didn't seem to care about that before."

"That was before the baby. The baby changes everything."

Because he wanted to make a family? The idea, so silly and hopeful, bloomed inside of her. It was her blessing and curse that she always found the kernel of hope in any situation. It was the thing that got her through. The thing that had helped her survive the loss of her mother, the cold detachment from her father, the time spent caring for her siblings when other girls her age were out dating, having lives, fulfilling dreams.

She'd created her own. Locked them inside of her. Nurtured them.

"I… It does?" she asked, the words a whisper.

"Of course," he said, dark eyes blazing. "My child will be a Corretti. On that, there can be no compromise."

CHAPTER THREE

MATTEO'S OWN WORDS echoed in his head.

My child will be a Corretti. On that there can be no compromise.

It was true. No child of his would be raised a Battaglia. Their family feud was not simply a business matter. The Battaglias had set out to destroy his grandfather, and had they succeeded they would have wiped out the line entirely.

It was the hurt on her face that surprised him, and more than that, his response to it.

Damn Alessia Battaglia and those dark, soulful eyes. Eyes that had led him to ruin on more than one occasion.

"Because you won't allow your child to carry my name?" she asked.

"That's right."

"And what of my role in raising my child?"

"You will, of course, be present."

"And what else? Because more than mere presence is required to raise a child."

"Nannies are also required, in my experience."

"In your experience raising children, or being raised?"

"Being raised. I'm supremely responsible in my sexual encounters so I've never been in this situation before."

"Supremely responsible?" she asked, cheeks flushing a gorgeous shade of rose that reminded him of the blooms in his Sicilian palazzo. "Is that what you call having sex with your cousin's fiancée with no condom?"

Her words, so stark and angry, shocked him. Alessia had always seemed fragile to him. Sweet. But tangling with her today was forcing him to recognize that she was also a woman capable of supreme ruthlessness if the situation required it.

Something he had to reluctantly respect.

"I didn't know you were engaged to be married, as you withheld the information from me. As to the other issue, that has never happened to me before."

"So you say."

"It has not," he said.

"Well, it's not like you were overly conscious of it at the time."

Shame cracked over his insides like a whip. He had thought himself immune to shame at this point. He was wrong. "I knew. After."

"You remembered and you still didn't think to contact me?"

"I did not think it possible." The thought hadn't occurred to him because he'd been too wrapped up in simply trying to avoid her. Alessia was bad for him, a conclusion he'd come to years ago and reaffirmed the day he'd decided not to go after her.

And now he was bound to her. Bound to a woman who dug down far too deep inside of him. Who disturbed his grasp on his control. He could not afford the interruption. Could not afford to take the chance that he might lose his grip.

"Why, because only other people have the kind of sex that makes babies?"

"Do you always say what comes to your mind?"

"No. I never do. I never speak or act impulsively, I only think about it. It's just you that seems to bring it out."

"Aren't I lucky?" Her admission gripped him, held him. That there was something about him that brought about a change in her…that the thing between them didn't only shatter his well-ordered existence but hers, too, was not a comfort. Not in the least.

"Clearly, neither of us are in possession of much luck, Alessia."

"Clearly," she said.

"There is no way I will let my child be a bastard. I've seen what happens to bastards. You can ask my cousin Angelo about that." A cousin who was becoming quite the problem. It was part of why Matteo had come to New York, why he was making his way back into circulation. In his absence, Angelo had gone and bought himself a hefty amount of shares for Corretti Enterprises and at this very moment, he was sitting in Matteo's office, the new head of Corretti Hotels. He'd been about to go back and make the other man pay. Wrench the power right back from him.

Now, it seemed there was a more pressing matter.

"So, you're doing this to save face?"

"For what other reason? Do you want our child to be sneered at? Disgraced? The product of an illicit affair between two of Sicily's great warring families?"

"No."

Matteo tried not to read the emotion in her dark eyes, tried not to let them pull him in. Always, from the moment he'd seen her, he'd been fascinated. A young girl with flowers tangled in her dark hair, running around the garden of her father's home, a smile on her lips. He could remember her dancing in the grass in her bare feet, while her siblings played around her.

And he had been transfixed. Amazed by this girl who, from all he had been told, should have been visibly evil in some way. But she was a light. She held a brightness and joy like he had never seen. Watching it, being close enough to touch it, helped him pretend it was something he could feel, too.

She made him not so afraid of feeling.

She'd had a hold on him from day one. She was a sorceress. There was no other explanation. Her grip on him defied logic, defied every defense he'd built inside of himself.

And no matter how hard he tried, he could read her. Easily. She was hurt. He had hurt her.

"What is it?" he asked.

She looked away. "What do you mean?"

"Why are you hurt?"

"You've just told me how unlucky we both are that I'm pregnant—was I supposed to look happy?"

"Don't tell me you're pleased about this. Unless it was your plan."

"How could I have…planned this? That doesn't make any sense."

He pushed his fingers through his hair and turned away from her. "I know. *Che cavolo*, Alessia, I know that." He turned back to her.

"I just wanted to tell you about the baby."

He felt like he was drowning, like every breath

was suffocating him. A baby. She was having his baby. And he was just about the last man on earth who should ever be a father. He should walk away. But he couldn't.

"And this was the only way?"

Her eyes glittered with rage. "You know damn well it was!"

He did. He'd avoided her every attempt at contacting him. Had let his anger fuel the need for distance between them. Had let the very existence of the emotion serve as a reminder. And he had come back frozen again. So he'd thought. Because now Alessia was here again, pushing against that control.

"Why didn't you meet me at the airport?" she asked, her words a whisper.

"Why didn't I meet you?" he asked, his teeth gritted. "You expected me to chase after you like a dog? If you think you can bring me to heel that easily, Alessia, you are a fool."

"And if you think I'm trying to you're an idiot, Matteo Corretti. I don't want you on a leash."

"Well, you damn well have me on one!" he said, shouting for the first time, his tenuous grip on his control slipping. "What am I to do after your public display? Deny my child? Send you off to raise it on your own? Highly unlikely."

"How can we marry each other? We don't love each other. We barely like each other right now!"

"Is that so bad? You were prepared to marry Alessandro, after all. Better the devil you know. And we both know you know me much better than you knew him."

"Stop it," she said, the catch in her voice sending a hot slash of guilt through his chest. Why he was compelled to lash out at her, he wasn't sure.

Except that nothing with Alessia was ever simple. Nothing was ever straightforward. Nothing was ever neat or controlled.

It has to be.

"It's true, though, isn't it, Alessia?" he asked, his entire body tense now. He knew for a fact he was the first man to be with her, and something in him burned to know that he had been the only man. That Alessandro had never touched her as he had. "You were never with him. Not like you were with me."

The idea of his cousin's hands on her... A wave of red hazed his vision, the need for violence gripping his throat, shaking him.

He swallowed hard, battled back the rage, fought against images that were always so close to the surface when Alessia was around. A memory he had to hold on to, no matter how much he might wish for it to disappear.

Blood. Streaked up to his elbows, the skin on his knuckles broken. A beast inside of him unleashed. And Alessia's attackers on the ground, unmoving.

He blinked and banished the memory. It shouldn't linger as it did. It was but one moment of violence in a lifetime of it. And yet, it had been different. It had been an act born of passion, outside of his control, outside of rational thought.

"Tell me," he ground out.

"Do you honestly think I would sleep with Alessandro after what happened?"

"You were going to. You were prepared to marry him. To share his bed."

She nodded wordlessly. "Yes. I was."

"And then you found out about the baby."

"No," she said, her voice a whisper.

"What, then?"

"Then I saw you."

"Guilt?"

"We were in a church."

"Understandable."

"Why didn't you meet me?" she asked again, her words holding a wealth of pain.

"Because," he said, visions of blood washing through his brain again, a reminder of what happened when he let his passions have control, "I got everything I wanted from you that night. Sex. That was all I ever wanted from you, darling."

She drew back as though he'd struck her. "Is that why you've always watched me?"

"I'll admit, I had a bit of an obsession with your body, but you know you had one with mine."

"I liked you," she said, her words hard, shaky. "But you never came near me after—"

"There is no need to dredge up the past," he said, not wanting to hear her speak of that day. He didn't want to hear her side of it. How horrifying it must have been for a fourteen-year-old girl to see such violence. To see what he was capable of.

Yet, she had never looked at him with the shock, the horror, he'd deserved. There was a way she looked at him, as though she saw something in him no one else did. Something good. And he craved that feeling. It was one reason he'd taken her up on her invitation that night at the hotel bar.

Too late, he realized that he was not in control of their encounter that time, either. No, Alessia stole the control. Always.

No more, he told himself again.

Alessia swallowed back tears. This wasn't going how she'd thought it would. Now she wasn't sure what she thought. No, she knew. Part of her, this stupid, girlish, optimistic part of her, had imagined Matteo's eyes would soften, that he would smile. Touch her stomach. Take joy in the fact that they had created a life together.

And then they would live happily ever after.

She was such a fool. But Matteo had long been the knight in shining armor of her fantasies. And so in her mind he could do no wrong.

She'd always felt like she'd known him. Like she'd understood the serious, dark-eyed young man she'd caught watching her when she was in Palermo. Who had crept up to the wall around her house when he was visiting his grandmother and stood there while she'd played in the garden. Always looking like he wanted to join in, like he wanted to play, but wouldn't allow himself to.

And then…and then when she'd needed him most, he'd been there. Saved her from…she hardly even knew what horror he'd saved her from. Thank God she hadn't had to find out exactly what those two men had intended to use her for. Matteo had been there. As always. And he had protected her, shielded her.

That was why, when she'd seen him in New York, it had been easy, natural, to kiss him. To ask him to make love to her.

But after that he hadn't come to save her.

She looked at him now, at those dark eyes, hollow, his face like stone. And he seemed like a stranger. She wondered how she could have been so wrong all this time.

"I don't want to dredge up the past. But I want to know that the future won't be miserable."

"If you preferred Alessandro, you should have married him while you had him at the altar with a priest standing by. Now you belong to me, the choice has been taken. So you should make the best of it."

"Stop being such an ass!"

Now he looked shocked, which, she felt, was a bit of an accomplishment. "You want me to tell you how happy I am? You want me to lie?"

"No," she said, her stomach tightening painfully. "But stop…stop trying to hurt me."

He swore, an ugly, crude word. "I am sorry, Alessia, it is not my intent."

The apology was about the most shocking event of the afternoon. "I…I know this is unexpected. Trust me, I know."

"When did you find out?" he asked.

"At the airport. So…if you had met me, you would have found out when I did."

"And what did you do after that?"

"I waited for you," she said. "And then I got on a plane and came to New York. I have a friend here, the friend that hosted my little bachelorette party."

"Why did you come to New York?"

"Why not?" She made it sound casual, like it was almost accidental. But it wasn't. It had made her feel close to him, no matter where he might have been in the world, because it was the place she'd finally been with him the way she'd always dreamed of. "Why did you come to New York?"

"Possibly for the same reason you did," he said, his voice rough. It made her stomach twist, but she didn't want to ask him for clarification. Didn't want to hope that it had something to do with her.

She was too raw to take more of Matteo's insults. And she was even more afraid of his tenderness. That would make her crumble completely. She couldn't afford it, not now. Now she had to figure out what she was doing. What she wanted.

Could she really marry Matteo?

It was so close to her dearest fantasy. The one that had kept her awake long nights since she was a teenager. Matteo. Hers. Only hers. Such an innocent fantasy at first, and as she'd gotten older, one that had become filled with heat and passion, a longing for things she'd never experienced outside of her dreams.

"And if…" she said, hardly trusting herself to speak "…if we marry, my family will still benefit from the merger?"

"Your father will get his money. His piece of the Corretti empire, as agreed upon."

"You give it away so easily."

"Because my family still needs the docklands revitalization. And your father holds the key to that."

"And it will benefit Alessandro, too."

"Just as it would have benefitted me had he married you."

Those words, hearing that it would have benefitted him for her to marry someone else, made her feel ill. "So a win all around for the Correttis, then?"

"I suppose it is," he said.

There was a ruthless glint in his eyes now. One she had never seen directed at her before. One she'd only seen on one other occasion.

"What if I say no?" she asked, because she had to know. She wasn't sure why she was exploring her options now. Maybe because she'd already blown everything up. Her father likely hated her.... Her siblings...they must be worried sick. And she wondered if anyone was caring for them properly.

Yes, the youngest, Eva, was fourteen now and the rest of them in their late teens, but still, she was the only person who nurtured them. The only person who ever had.

The life she'd always known, the life she'd clung to for the past twenty-seven years, was changed forever. And now she felt compelled in some ways to see how far she could push it.

"You won't say no," he said.

"I won't?"

"No. Because if you do, the Battaglias are as good as bankrupt. You will be cared for, of course our child will be, too. I'm not the kind of man who would abandon his responsibility in that way. But what of your siblings? Their care will not be my problem."

"And if I marry you?"

"They'll be family. And I take care of family."

A rush of joy and terror filled her in equal parts. Because in some ways, she was getting just what she wanted. Matteo. Forever.

But this wasn't the Matteo she'd woven fantasies around. This was the real Matteo. Dark. Bitter. Emotionless in a way she'd somehow never realized before.

He'd given her passion on their night together, but for the most part, the lights had been off. She wondered now if, while his hands had moved over her body with such skill and heat, his eyes had been blank and cold. Like they were now.

She knew that what she was about to agree to wasn't the fantasy. But it was the best choice for her baby, the best choice for her family.

And more fool her, she wanted him. Still. All of those factors combined meant there was only ever one answer for her to give.

"Yes, Matteo. I'll marry you."

CHAPTER FOUR

THE HUSH IN the lobby of Matteo's plush Palermo hotel was thick, the lack of sound more pronounced and obvious than any scream could have been.

It was early in the day and employees were milling around, setting up for a wedding and mobilizing to sort out rooms and guests. As Matteo walked through, a wave of them parted, making room for him, making space. Good. He was in no mood to be confronted today. No mood for questions.

Bleached sunlight filtered through the windows, reflecting off a jewel-bright sea. A view most would find relaxing. For him, it did nothing but increase the knot of tension in his stomach. Homecoming, for him, would never be filled with a sense of comfort and belonging. For him, this setting had been the stage for violence, pain and shame that cut so deep it was a miracle he hadn't bled to death with it.

He gritted his teeth and pulled together every last ounce of control he could scrape up, cooling the anger that seemed to be on a low simmer in his blood constantly now.

He had a feeling, though, that the shock was due only in part to his presence, with a much larger part due to the woman who was trailing behind him.

He punched the up button for the elevator and the doors slid open. He looked at Alessia, who simply stood there, her hands clasped in front of her, dark eyes looking at everything but him.

"After you, *cara mia*," he said, putting his hand between the doors, keeping them from closing.

"You don't demand that a wife walk three paces behind you at all times?" she asked, her words soft, defiant.

"A woman is of very little use to me when she's behind me. Bent over in front of me is another matter, as you well know."

Her cheeks turned dark with color, and not all of it was from embarrassment. He'd made her angry, as he'd intended to do. He didn't know what it was about her that pushed him so. That made him say things like that.

That made him show anything beyond the unreadable mask he preferred to present to the world.

She was angry, but she didn't say another word. She simply stepped into the elevator, her eyes fixed to the digital readout on the wall. The doors slid closed behind them, and still she didn't look at him.

"If you brought me here to abuse me perhaps I should simply go back to my father's house and take my chances with him."

"That's what you call abuse? You didn't seem to find it so abhorrent the night you let me do it."

"But you weren't being a bastard that night. Had you approached me at the bar and used it as a pickup line I would have told you to go to hell."

"Would you have, Alessia?" he asked, anger, heat, firing in his blood. "Somehow I don't think that's true."

"No?"

"No." He turned to her, put his hand, palm flat, on the glossy marble wall behind her, drawing closer, drawing in the scent of her. *Dio.* Like lilac and sun. She was Spring standing before him, new life, new hope.

He pushed away from her, shut down the feeling.

"Shows what you know."

"I know a great deal about you."

"Stop with the you-know-me stuff. Just because we slept together—"

"You have a dimple on your right cheek. It

doesn't show every time you smile, only when you're really, really smiling. You dance by yourself in the sun, you don't like to wear shoes. You've bandaged every scraped knee your brothers and sisters ever had. And whenever you see me, you can't help yourself, you have to stare. I know you, Alessia Battaglia, don't tell me otherwise."

"You knew me, Matteo. You knew a child. I'm not the same person now."

"Then how is it you ended up in my bed the night of your bachelorette party?"

Her eyes met his for the first time all morning, for the first time since his private plane had touched down in Sicily. "Because I wanted to make a choice, Matteo. Every other choice was being made for me. I wanted to…I wanted to at least make the choice about who my first lover should be."

"Haven't you had a lot of time to make that choice?"

"When? With all of my free time? I've spent my life making sure my brothers and sisters were cared for, really cared for, not just given the bare necessities by staff. I spent my life making sure they never bore the full brunt of my father's rage. I've spent my life being the perfect daughter, the hostess for his functions, standing and smiling next to him when he got reelected for a position that he abuses."

"Why?" he asked.

"Because of my siblings. Because no matter that my father is a tyrant, he is our father. We're Battaglias. I hoped…I've always hoped I could make that mean something good. That I could make sure my brothers and sisters learned to do the right things, learned to want the right things. If I didn't make sure, they would only have my father as a guiding influence and I think we both know Antonioni Battaglia shouldn't be anyone's guiding influence."

"And what about you?"

"What about me?"

The elevator doors slid open and they stepped out into the empty hall on the top floor.

"You live your whole life for other people?"

She shook her head. "No. I live my life in the way that lets me sleep at night. Abandoning my brothers and sisters to our father would have hurt me. So it's not like I'm a martyr. I do it because I love them."

"But you ran out on the wedding."

She didn't say anything, she simply started walking down the hall, her heels clicking on the marble floor. He stood and watched her, his eyes drifting over her curves, over that gorgeous, heart-shaped backside, outlined so perfectly by her pencil skirt.

It looked like something from the Corretti clothing line. One thing he might have to thank his damn brother Luca for. But it was the only thing.

Especially since the rumor was that in his absence the other man was attempting to take Matteo's share in the Corretti family hotels. A complete mess since that bastard Angelo had his hands in it, as well.

A total mess. And one he should have anticipated. He'd dropped out of the dealings with Corretti Enterprises completely since the day of Alessia and Alessandro's aborted wedding. And the vultures had moved in. He should try to stop them, he knew that. And he could, frankly. He had his own fortune, his own power, independent of the Corretti machine, but at the moment, the most pressing issue was tied to the tall, willowy brunette who was currently sauntering in the wrong direction.

"The suite is this way," he said.

She stopped, turned sharply on her heel and started walking back toward him, past him and down the hall.

He nearly laughed at the haughty look on her face. In fact, he found he wanted to, but wasn't capable of it. It stuck in his throat, his control too tight to let it out.

He walked past her, to the door of the suite, and took a key card out of his wallet, tapping it against the reader. "My key opens all of them."

"Careful, *caro*, that sounds like a bad euphemism." She shot him a deadly look before entering the suite.

"So prickly, Alessia."

"I told you you didn't know me."

"Then help me get to know you."

"You first, Matteo."

He straightened. "I'm Matteo Corretti, oldest son of Benito Corretti. I'm sure you know all about him. My criminal father who died in a fire, locked in an endless rivalry with his brother, Carlo. You ought to know about him, too, as you were going to marry Carlo's son. I run the hotel arm of my family corporation, and I deal with my own privately owned line of boutique hotels, one of which you're standing in."

She crossed her arms and cocked her hip out to the side. "I think I read that in your online bio. And it's nothing I don't already know."

"That's all there is to know."

She didn't believe that. Not for a moment. She knew there was more to him than that. Knew it because she'd seen it. Seen his blind rage as he'd done everything in his power to protect her from a fate she didn't even like to imagine.

But he didn't speak of it. So neither did she.

"Tell me about you," he said.

"Alessia Battaglia, Pisces, oldest daughter of Antonioni. My father is a politician who does under-the-table dealings with organized-crime families. It's the thing that keeps him in power. But it doesn't make him rich. It's why he needs the Correttis." She returned his style of disclosure neatly, tartly.

"The Correttis are no longer in the organized-crime business. In that regard, my cousins, my brothers and I have done well, no matter our personal feelings for each other."

"You might not be criminals but you are rich. That's why you're so attractive. In my father's estimation at least."

"Attractive enough to trade us his daughter."

She nodded. She looked tired suddenly. Defeated. He didn't like that. He would rather have her spitting venom at him.

"You could walk away, Alessia," he said. "Even now you could. I cannot keep you here. Your father cannot hold you. You're twenty-seven. You have the freedom to do whatever you like. Hell, you could do it on my dime since I'll be supporting my child regardless of what you do."

He didn't know why he was saying it, why he was giving her the out. But part of him wished she would take it. Wished she would leave him alone, take her beauty, the temptation, the ache that seemed to lodge in his chest whenever she was around, with her. The danger she presented to the walls of protection he'd built around his life.

She didn't say anything. She didn't move. She was frozen to the spot, her lips parted slightly, her breath shallow, fast.

"Alessia, you have the freedom to walk out that door if you want. Right now."

He took a step toward her, compelled, driven by something he didn't understand. Didn't want to understand. The beast in him was roaring now and he wanted it to shut up. Wanted his control back.

He'd had a handle on it again. Had moved forward from the events of his past. Until Alessia had come back into his life, and at the moment all he wanted was for her to be gone, and for his life to go back to the way it had been.

He cupped her chin, tilted her face up so that her eyes met his. "I am not holding you here. I am not your father and I am not your jailer."

Dark eyes met his, the steel in them shocking. "No, you aren't. But you are the father of my baby. Our baby. I'm not going to walk away,

Matteo. If you want an out, you'll have to take it yourself. Don't think that I will. I'm strong enough to face this. To try to make this work."

"It would be better if you would."

"Do you really think that?"

"You think I will be a hands-on father? That I will somehow…be an influence in our child's life?" The very thought made him sick. What could he offer a child but a legacy of violence and abuse? But he couldn't walk away, either. Couldn't leave Alessia on her own. But he feared his touch would only poison a child. His baby would be born innocent, unspoiled by the world, and Matteo was supposed to hold him? With his hands? Hands that were stained with blood.

"You think you won't be?"

"How can you give what you never had?"

"I hardly remember my mother, Matteo, but I did a good job with my brothers and sisters."

"Perhaps I find that an absence of a good parent is not the same as having bad ones. What lessons shall I teach our child, *cara*? The kind my father taught me? How to find a man who owes you money? How to break his kneecaps with efficiency when he doesn't pay up? I think not."

He had thought she would look shocked by that, but she hardly flinched, her eyes never wavering from his. "Again you underestimate me, Matteo. You forget the family I come from."

"You are so soft," he said, speaking his mind, speaking his heart. "Breakable. Like a flower. You and I are not the same."

She nodded slowly. "It's easy to crush a flower. But if it's the right kind of flower, it comes back, every year, after every winter. No matter how many times you destroy the surface, it keeps on living underneath."

Her words sent a shot of pain straight to his chest, her quiet strength twisting something deep inside of him. "Don't pretend you were forced into this," he said softly. "You were given your choice."

"And you were given yours."

He nodded once and turned away from her, walked out of the room ignoring the pounding in his blood, ignoring the tightness in his chest. Trying to banish the image of his hand closing around a blossom and crushing the petals, leaving it completely destroyed.

Alessia looked around the lavish, now empty, suite that she was staying in until...until she didn't know when. Weeks of not being able to get ahold of Matteo, not knowing what she would do if she didn't, and now he was suddenly in her life like a hurricane, uprooting everything, taking control of everything.

She really shouldn't be too surprised about it.

That was one thing she did know about Matteo Corretti, beyond that stupid ream of noninformation he'd given her. He was controlled. Totally. Completely.

Twice she'd seen him lose that control. Once, on a sunny day in Sicily while he was staying at his grandparents' rural estate. The day that had cemented him in her mind as her potential salvation.

And their night in New York. There had been no control then, not for either of them.

She pictured him as he'd been then. The way he'd looked at her in the low light of the bar. She closed her eyes and she was back there. The memory still so strong, so painfully sweet.

"What brings you to New York, Alessia?"

"Bachelorette party." It was easy enough to leave out that it was for her. If he didn't know about Alessandro, then she wouldn't tell him.

"Did you order any strippers?"

Her cheeks heated. "No, gosh, why? Are you offering to fill the position?"

"How much have you had to drink?" he asked, a smile on his face. It was so rare for her to see him smile. She couldn't remember if she ever had.

"Not enough."

"I could fix that, but I think I'd like a dance

and if you're too drunk you won't be able to keep up."

"Why are you talking to me?" she asked. She'd known there was a chance he could be here. He owned the hotel, after all. Part of her had hoped she'd catch a glimpse of him. A little bit of torture, but torture that would be well worth it.

"What do you mean?"

"You haven't spoken to me since—" something flashed in his eyes, a strange unease, and she redirected her words "—in a long time."

"Too long," he said, his voice rough.

Her heart fluttered, a surge of hope moving through her. She tried to crush it, tried to stop the jittery feelings moving through her now.

"So, do you have a dance for me?" he asked. "For an old friend?"

"Yes." She couldn't deny him, couldn't deny herself.

She left her friends in the corner of the bar, at their table with all of their fruity drinks, and let Matteo lead her away from them, lead her to the darkened dance floor. A jazz quartet was playing, the music slow and sensual.

He wrapped his arms around her waist and pulled her against his body. Heat shot through her, heat and desire and lust.

His eyes locked with hers as they swayed in time to the music, and she was powerless to resist the desire to lean in and press her lips to his. His tongue touched the tip of hers, a shot of need so sharp, so strong, assaulting her she thought it would buckle her knees then and there.

She parted her lips for him, wrapping her arms around his neck, tangling her fingers in his hair. Years of fantasies added fuel to the moment.

Matteo Corretti was her ultimate fantasy. The man whose name she called out in her sleep. The man she wanted, more than anything. And this was her last chance.

Panic drove her, made her desperate. She deepened the kiss, her movements clumsy. She didn't know how to make out. She'd never really done it before. Another thing that added fuel to the fire.

She'd never lived. She'd spent all of her life at the Battaglia *castello*, taking care of her siblings, making sure her family didn't crumble. Her life existed for the comfort of others, and she needed a moment, a night, to have something different.

To have something for her.

Matteo pulled away from her, his chest rising and falling heavily with each indrawn breath. "We cannot do that here."

She shook her head. "Apparently not." The fire between them was burning too hot, too fast, threatening to rage out of control.

"I have a suite." A smile curved his lips. "I own the hotel."

She laughed, nervous, breathless. She flexed her fingers, where her engagement ring should be. The engagement ring she hadn't put on tonight as she'd gotten ready for the party.

"Please. Just one night," she said.

"Only one, *cara mia*?"

"That's all I have to give."

"I might be able to change your mind," he said, his voice rough. He leaned in and kissed her neck, his teeth scraping her delicate skin, his tongue soothing away the sting.

Yes. She wanted to shout it. *Yes, forever. Matteo,* ti amo.

Instead, she kissed him again, long and deep, pouring everything out, every emotion, every longing that had gone unanswered for so long. Every dream she knew would never be fulfilled. Because Matteo might be hers tonight, but in just a month, she would belong to another man forever.

"Take me to your room."

Alessia shook her head, brought herself back to the present. Everything had been so perfect that night. It was the morning that had broken her heart. The cold light of day spilling over her, illuminating the truth, not allowing her to hide behind fantasy any longer.

She could remember just how he'd looked, the sheets tangled around his masculine body, bright white against his dark skin. Leaving him had broken her.

She'd wanted so badly to kiss him again, but she hadn't wanted to chance waking him.

Somehow that night she'd let her fantasies become real, had let them carry her away from reality, not just in her imagination but for real. And she couldn't regret it, not then, not now.

At least, she hadn't until recently. The way Matteo looked at her now…she hated it. Hated that he saw her as a leash.

But it was too late to turn back now. The dutiful daughter had had her rebellion, and it had destroyed everything in its path.

"You don't go halfway, do you, Alessia?" she asked the empty room.

Unsurprisingly, she got no answer.

CHAPTER FIVE

"You CANNOT SIMPLY take what is mine without paying for it, Corretti."

Matteo looked at Antonioni Battaglia and fought a wave of rage. The man had no idea who he was dealing with. Matteo was a Corretti, the capability to commit hideous acts was a part of his DNA. More than that, Matteo had actually done it before. Had embraced the violence. Both with cold precision, and in the heat of rage.

The temptation to do it again was strong. Instead, he leaned forward and adjusted a glass figurine that his grandmother had had commissioned for him. A perfect model of his first hotel. Not one of the Corretti Hotels, the first hotel he'd bought with his own personal fortune.

"And what exactly is that?" Matteo asked, leaning back in his office chair.

"My daughter. You defiled her. She's much less valuable to me now, which means you'd better damn well marry her and make good on the deal I cut with your grandfather, or the Correttis won't be doing any trading out of Sicily."

"My mistake, I thought Alessia's body belonged to her, not you."

"I'm an old-fashioned man."

"Be that as it may, the law prevents you from owning anyone, which means Alessia does not belong to you." He gritted his teeth, thought of Alessia's siblings, of all she'd given up to ensure they would be cared for. "However, at my fiancée's request, I have decided to honor the agreement." He paused for a moment. "What are your other children doing at the moment?"

"I've arranged for the boys to get a job in the family business."

Matteo gritted his teeth. "Is that what they want?"

"You have to take opportunity where it exists."

"And if I created a different opportunity?" He turned the figurine again, keeping his hands busy, keeping himself from violence.

"Why should I do any more business with a Corretti than necessary?"

"Because I hold your potential fortune in the palm of my hands. Not only that, I'll be the father of your first grandchild. Mainly, though, because you'll take what I give you, and no more. So it's by my good grace that you will have anything."

Antonioni's cheeks turned red. It was clear the

old man didn't like being told what to do. "Corretti, I don't have to give your family rights to—"

"And I don't have to give you a damn thing. I know you're making deals with Angelo. And you know how I feel about Angelo, which puts you in my bad book right off. I may, however, be willing to overlook it all if you do as I ask. So I suggest you take steps to make me happy. Send your children to college. I'm paying for it."

"That's hardly necessary."

He thought of Alessia, of all she'd sacrificed for them. "Listen to me now, Battaglia, and remember what I say. Memorize it. Make a nice little plaque and hang it above your fireplace if need be: If I say it is necessary, then it is. So long as you do what I say, you'll be kept well in the lifestyle you would like to become accustomed to."

The other man nodded. "It's your dime, Corretti."

"Yes, and your life is now on my dime. Get used to that concept."

Had Alessia's father not said what he had, had he not acted as though her virginity, her body, was his bargaining tool, Matteo might not have taken such joy in letting the other man know his neck was, in effect, under his heel.

But he had. So Matteo did.

"I paid for one wedding," Battaglia said. "I'm not paying for another."

"I think I can handle that, too." Matteo picked up the tiny glass hotel, turning it in front of the light. "You're dismissed."

Battaglia liked that last order least of all, but he complied, leaving Matteo's office without another word.

Matteo tightened his hold on the small, breakable representation of his empire, curling his fingers around it, not stopping until it cracked, driving a shard deep into his palm.

He looked down, watched the blood drip down his wrist. Then he set the figurine back on his desk, examined the broken pieces. Marveled at how easy it was to destroy it with his anger.

He pulled the silk handkerchief out of the pocket of his jacket and wrapped the white fabric around his hand, pressing it hard, until a spot of crimson stained the fabric.

It was so easy to let emotion ruin things. So frighteningly easy.

He gritted his teeth, pushed the wall up around himself again. Control. He would have it, in all things. Alessia Battaglia was not allowed to steal it from him. Not anymore.

Never again.

"I've secured the marriage license, and we will have the wedding at my palazzo." His inheritance after the death of his father. A piece of his childhood he wasn't certain he wanted. But one he possessed nonetheless.

"Not at your family home?"

"I have no use for that place," he said, his tone hard. "Anyway, it has all been arranged."

Alessia stood up from the plush bed, crossing her arms beneath her breasts. "Really? And what shall I wear? How shall I fix my hair? Have you written my vows for me?"

"I don't care. Who gives a damn? And didn't someone already take care of writing vows for weddings hundreds of years ago?"

She blinked, trying to process his rapid-fire response. "I… Don't you have… I mean, don't I need to conform to some sort of image you're projecting or…something?"

"This will be a small affair. We may provide the press with a picture for proof. Or perhaps I'll just send them a photocopy of the marriage license. Anyway, you can wear what you like. I've never seen you not looking beautiful."

The compliment, careless, offhanded, sent a strange sensation through her. "Oh. Well. Thank you."

"It's the truth."

"Well, thank you again."

She wasn't sure what to do, both with him being nice and with him giving her a choice on what to wear to the wedding. Such a simple thing, but it was more than her father had given her when it came to Alessandro.

"As long as it doesn't have lace," she said.

"What?"

"The wedding dress."

"The dress for your last wedding was covered in it."

"Exactly. Hellish, awful contraption. And I didn't choose it. I didn't choose any of that."

"What would you have chosen?"

She shook her head and looked down. "Does it matter?"

"Why not? You can't walk down the aisle naked and we have to get married somewhere, so you might as well make the choice."

"I would wear something simple. Beautiful. And I would be barefoot. And it would be outside."

He lifted his hand and brushed it over his short hair. "Of course. Then we'll have it outside at the palazzo and you may forego shoes." He lowered his hand and she saw a slash of red on his palm.

She frowned and stepped forward. "What did you do?"

"What?" He turned his hand over. "Nothing. Just a cut."

"You look like you got in a fight."

His whole body tensed. "I don't get in fights."

"No, I know. I wasn't being serious." Tension held between them as they both had the same memory. She knew that was what was happening. Knew that he was thinking of the day she'd been attacked.

But she wanted to know what he remembered, how he remembered it, because it was obvious it was something he preferred to ignore. Not that she loved thinking about it except...except as horrible as it had been to have those men touching her, pawing at her, as awful as those memories were, the moment when they'd been wrenched from her, when she'd seen Matteo... the rush of relief, the feeling of absolute peace and certainty that everything would be okay, had been so real, so acute, she could still feel it.

She'd clung to him after. Clung to him and cried. And he'd stroked her cheek with his hand, wiping away her tears. Later she'd realized he'd left a streak of blood on her face, from the blood on his hands. Blood he'd shed, spilled, for her.

He'd been her hero that day, and every day since. She'd spent her whole life saving everyone else, being the stopgap for her siblings, taking her father's wrath if they'd been too noisy. Always the one to receive a slap across the face, rather than allow him near the younger children.

Matteo was the only person who'd ever stood up for her. The only one who'd ever saved her.

And so, when life got hard, when it got painful, or scary, she would imagine that he would come again. That he would pull her into impossibly strong arms and fight her demons for her.

He never did. Never again. After that day, he even stopped watching her. But having the hope of it, the fantasy, was part of what had pulled her through the bleakness of her life. Imagination had always been her escape, and he'd added a richer texture to it, given a face to her dreams for the future.

He'd asked if she always spoke her mind, and she'd told him the truth, she didn't. She kept her head down and tried to get through her life, tried to simply do the best she could. But in her mind…her imagination was her escape, and always had been. When she ran barefoot through the garden, she was somewhere else entirely.

When she went to bed at night, she read until sleep found her, so that she could have new thoughts in her head, rather than simply memories of the day.

So that she could have better dreams.

It was probably a good thing Matteo didn't know the place he occupied in her dreams. It would give him too much power. More than he already had.

"I'm not like my father," he said. "I will never strike my wife."

She looked at him and she realized that never, for one moment, had she believed he would. Her father had kept her mother "in line" with the back of his hand, and he'd done the same with her. But even having grown up with that as a normal occurrence, she'd never once imagined Matteo would do it.

"I know," she said.

"You know?"

"Yes."

"And how is it you know?"

"Because you aren't that kind of person, Matteo."

"Such confidence in me. Especially when you're one of the very few people who has actually seen what I'm capable of."

She had. She'd seen his brute strength applied to those who had dared try to harm her. It had been the most welcome sight in all of her life. "You protected me."

"I went too far."

"They would have gone further," she said.

He took a step away from her, the darkness in his eyes suddenly so deep, so pronounced, it threatened to pull her in. "I have work to do. I'll be at my downtown office. I've arranged to have a credit card issued to you." He reached into his pocket and pulled out a black card, extending his hand to her.

She took it, not ready to fight with him about it.

"If you need anything, whatever you need, it's yours." He turned away and walked out of the room, closing the door behind him.

She'd done the wrong thing again. With Matteo it seemed she could do nothing right. And she so desperately wanted to do right by him.

But it seemed impossible.

She growled, the sound releasing some of her tension. But not enough. "Matteo, why are you always so far out of my reach?"

This was Alessia's second wedding day. Weird, because she'd never technically had a boyfriend. One hot night of sex didn't really make Matteo her boyfriend. *Boyfriend* sounded too tame for a man like Matteo, anyway. Alessia finished zipping up the back of her gown. It was light, with flutter sleeves and a chiffon skirt that swirled around her ankles. It was lavender instead of white. She was a pregnant bride, after all.

There weren't many people in attendance, but she liked that better. Her father, her brothers and sisters, Matteo's grandmother, Teresa, and his mother, Simona.

She took the bouquet of lilacs she'd picked from the garden out of their vase and looked in the mirror. Nothing like what the makeup artist had managed on The Other Wedding Day, but today she at least looked like her.

She opened the guest bedroom door and tried to get a handle on her heart rate.

She was marrying Matteo Corretti today. In a sun-drenched garden. She was having his baby. She repeated that, over and over, trying to make it feel real, trying to hold on to the surge of good feelings it gave her. Because no matter how terrifying it was sometimes, it was also wonderful. A chance at something new. A chance to have a child, give that child the life that had been denied her. The life that had been denied Matteo.

The stone floor was cool beneath her bare feet, the palazzo empty, everyone outside waiting. She'd opted to forego shoes since that was how he said he knew her.

Barefoot in the garden. So, she would meet him as he remembered her. Barefoot in the garden, with her hair down. Maybe then they could start over. They were getting married today, after all, and in her mind that meant they would have to start trying to work things out. They would at least have to be civil.

She put her hands on the rail of the curved, marble staircase, still repeating her mantra. She walked through the grand foyer, decorated in traditional, ornate furniture that didn't remind her one bit of Matteo, and she opened the door, stepping out into the sun.

The music was already playing. A string quartet. She'd forgotten to say what she wanted for music but this was perfect, simple.

And in spite of what Matteo had said, there was a photographer.

But those details faded into the background when she saw Matteo, standing near the priest, his body rigid, his physique displayed to perfection by a custom-made gray suit.

There was no aisle. No loud click of marble beneath her heels, just grass beneath her feet. And the guests were standing, no chairs. Her father looked like he was ready to grab her if she decided to run. Eva, Giana, Pietro and Marco looked worried, and she didn't blame them. She had been their stability for most of their lives, their surrogate mother. And she hadn't told them she was marrying Alessandro for convenience, which meant her disappearance, subsequent reappearance with a different groom and a publicly announced pregnancy must seem a few steps beyond bizarre to them.

She gave them her best, most confident smile. This was her role. To show them it was all okay, to hold everything together.

But her eyes were drawn back to Matteo. He made her throat dry, made her heart pound.

But when she reached him, he didn't take her hand. He hardly looked at her. Instead, he looked at the priest. The words to the ceremony were traditional, words she knew by heart from attending hundreds of society weddings in her life.

There was nothing personal about them, nothing unique. And Matteo never once met her eyes.

She was afraid she was alone in her resolve to make things work. To make things happy. She swallowed hard. It was always her job to make it okay. To smooth it over. Why wasn't it working?

"You may kiss the bride."

They were the words she'd been anticipating and dreading. She let her eyes drift shut and she waited. She could feel his heat draw near to her, and then, the brush of his lips on hers, so soft, so brief, she thought she might have imagined it.

And then nothing more.

Her breath caught, her heart stopped. She opened her eyes, and Matteo was already turning to face their small audience. Then he drew her near to him, his arm tight around her waist. But there was no intimacy in the gesture. No warmth.

"Thank you for bearing witness," Matteo said, both to her father and his grandmother.

"You've done a good thing for the family, Matteo," his grandmother said, putting a hand over his. And Alessia wondered just how much trouble Matteo had been in with his family for the wedding fiasco.

She knew the media had made assumptions they'd run off together. Too bad nothing could be further from the truth.

Still, her father, his family, must think that was the truth. Because now they were back in Sicily, she was pregnant and they were married.

"Perhaps we should go inside for a drink?" her father suggested.

"A good plan, Battaglia, but we don't talk business at weddings."

Simona begged off, giving Matteo a double kiss on the cheeks and saying she had a party to get to in the city. Matteo didn't seem the least bit fazed by his mother's abandonment. He simply followed her father into the house.

She watched him walk inside, her heart feeling heavy.

Teresa offered her a smile. "I'll see that Matteo's staff finds some refreshments to serve for us. I'll only be a moment." The older woman turned and went into the house, too, leaving Alessia with her siblings.

It was Eva, fourteen and emotional, who flung herself into Alessia's arms. "Where did you go?"

"New York," Alessia said, stroking her sister's hair.

"Why?"

"I had to get away…I couldn't marry Alessandro."

"Then why did you agree to the engagement?" This from Marco, the second oldest at nineteen.

"It's complicated, Marco, as things often are with Father. You know that."

"But you wanted to marry Corretti? This Corretti, I mean," asked sixteen-year-old Pietro.

She nodded, her throat tight. "Of course." She didn't want them to be upset. Didn't want them to worry. She maybe should have thought of that before running off to New York, but she really hadn't been able to consider anyone else. For the first time, she'd been burned out on it and she'd had to take care of herself.

"They're having a baby," Giana said drily. "I assume that means she liked him at least a little bit." Then she turned back to Alessia. "I'm excited about being an aunt."

"I'm glad," she said, tugging on her sister's braid.

They spent the rest of the afternoon out in the garden, having antipasti, wine for the older children and Teresa, and lemonade for her and younger kids. Her siblings told her stories of their most recent adventures, which ended up with everyone laughing. And for the first time in months, Alessia felt at ease. This was her family, her happiness. The reason she'd agreed to marry

Alessandro. And one of the driving reasons behind her decision to marry Matteo.

Although she couldn't deny her own desire where he was concerned. Still, *happy* wasn't exactly the word that she would use to describe herself at the moment. Anxiety-ridden? Check. Sick to her stomach? That a little bit, too.

The sun was starting to sink behind the hills, gray twilight settling on the garden, the solar lights that were strung across the expanse of the grass illuminating the growing darkness.

Their father appeared on the balcony, his arms folded across his chest, his eyes settled on her siblings.

"I guess we have to go," Marco said.

"I know. Come back and stay with us anytime," she said, not even thinking to ask Matteo if it was okay. As soon as she had the thought, she banished it. If she was going to be married to the man, then she wasn't going to ask his permission to breathe in their shared home. It wasn't only his now and he would have to get used to it.

Her father was the unquestionable head of their household, but she was the heart of it. She'd kept it running, made sure the kids got their favorite meals cooked, remembered birthdays and helped with homework. Her role in their lives didn't end with her marriage, and she wasn't equipped to take on a passive role in a household, anyway.

So, on that, Matteo would just have to learn to deal.

She stopped and kissed her brothers and sisters on the head before watching them go up to where their father stood. All of them but Marco. She held him a bit longer in her embrace. "Take care of everyone," she said, a tear escaping and sliding down her cheek.

"Just like you always did," he said softly.

"And I'm still here."

"I know."

He squeezed her hand before walking up to join the rest of the family.

"And I should leave you, as well," Teresa said, standing. "It was lovely to see you again, my dear."

Teresa hadn't batted an eye at the sudden change of groom, had never seemed at all ruffled by the events.

"You care for him," she said, as if she could read Alessia's internal musings.

Alessia nodded. "I do."

"That's what these men need, Alessia. A strong woman to love them. They may fight it, but it is what they need." Teresa spoke with pain in her eyes, a pain that Alessia felt echo inside of her.

Alessia couldn't speak past the lump in her throat. She tried to avoid the *L* word. The one that was stronger than *like*. There was only so much a woman could deal with at once. So instead, she just nodded and watched Teresa walk back up toward the house.

Alessia stayed in the garden and waited. The darkness thickened, the lights burning brighter. And Matteo didn't come.

She moved into the house, walked up the stairs. The palazzo was completely quiet, the lights off. She wrapped her arms around herself, and made her way back to the bedroom Matteo had put her in to get ready.

She went in and sat on the edge of the bed and waited for her husband to come and claim his wedding night.

CHAPTER SIX

MATTEO DIDN'T GET DRUNK as a rule. Unfortunately, he had a tendency to break rules when Alessia Battaglia—or was she Alessia Corretti now?—was involved.

Damn that woman.

Even after his father's death he hadn't gotten drunk. He'd wanted to. Had wanted to incinerate the memories, destroy them as the fire had destroyed the warehouses, destroyed the man who had held so much sway over his life.

But he hadn't. Because he hadn't deserved that kind of comfort. That kind of oblivion. He'd forced himself to face it.

This…this he couldn't face.

He took another shot of whiskey and let it burn all the way down. It didn't burn as much at this point in the evening, which was something of a disappointment. He looked down at the shot glass and frowned. Then he picked it up and threw it against the wall, watching the glass burst.

Now that was satisfying.

He chuckled and lifted the bottle to his lips. *Dio*, in his current state he almost felt happy. Why the hell didn't he drink more?

"Matteo?"

He turned and saw Alessia standing in the doorway. Alessia. He wanted her. More than his next breath. He wanted those long legs wrapped around his waist, wanted to hear her husky voice whispering dirty things in his ear.

He didn't think she'd ever done that, whispered dirty things in his ear, but he could imagine it, and he wanted it. *Dio*, did he want it.

"Come here, wife," he said, pushing away from the bar, his movements unsteady.

"Are you drunk?"

"I should be. If I'm not…if I'm not there's something very wrong with this whiskey."

Her dark eyes were filled with some kind of emotion. Something strong and deep. He couldn't decipher it. He didn't want to.

"Why are you drunk?"

"Because I've been drinking. Alcohol. A lot of it."

"But why?"

"I don't know, could be because today I acquired a wife and I can't say I ever particularly wanted one."

"Thank you. I'm so glad to hear that, after the ceremony."

"You would have changed your mind? You can't. It's all over the papers, in the news all over the world. You're carrying a Corretti. You, a Battaglia. It's news, *cara*. Not since Romeo and Juliet has there been such a scandal."

"I'm not going to stab myself for you just because you've poisoned your damn self, so you can stop making those parallels anytime."

"Come to me, Alessia."

She took a step toward him, her movements unsteady, her lips turned down into a sulky frown. He wanted to kiss the expression off her face.

"You left your hair down," he said, reaching out and taking a dark lock between his thumb and forefinger, rubbing the glossy strands. "You're so beautiful. An angel. That was the first thing I thought when I saw you."

She blinked rapidly. "When?"

"When we were children. I had always been told you Battaglias were monsters. Demons. And I couldn't resist the chance to peek. And there you were, running around your father's garden. You were maybe eleven. You were dirty and your hair was tangled, but I thought you looked like heaven. You were smiling. You always smile."

He frowned, looking at her face again. "You don't smile as much now."

"I haven't had a lot of reasons to smile."

"Have you ever?"

"No. But I've made them. Because someone had to smile. Someone had to teach the children how to smile."

"And it had to be you?"

"There was no one else."

"So you carry the weight of the world, little one?"

"You should know something about that, Matteo."

He chuckled. "Perhaps a little something." He didn't feel so much like he was carrying it now.

He took her arm and tugged her forward, her dark eyes wide. "I want you," he said.

Not waiting for a response, he leaned in and kissed her. Hard. She remained immobile beneath his mouth, her lips stiff, her entire body stiff. He pulled her more firmly against him, let her feel the evidence of his arousal, let her feel all of the frustration and need that had been building inside of him for the past three months.

"Did he kiss you like this?" he asked, pressing a heated kiss to her neck, her collarbone.

She shook her head. "N-no."

"Good. I would have had to kill him."

"Stop saying things like that."

"Why?" he asked. "You and I both know that I could, Alessia. On your behalf, I could. I might not even be able to stop myself." He kissed her again, his heart pounding hard, blood pouring hot and fast through his veins.

"Matteo, stop," she said, pulling away from him.

"Why? Are you afraid of me, too, Alessia?"

She shook her head. "No, but you aren't yourself. I don't like it."

"Maybe I am myself, and in that case, you're wise not to like it."

He released his hold on her. And he realized how tight his grip had been. Regret, the kind he usually kept dammed up inside of himself, released, flooding through him. "Did I hurt you?"

She shook her head. "No."

"Don't lie."

"I wouldn't."

Suddenly, he was hit with a shot of self-realization so strong it nearly buckled his knees. He had done it again. He had let his defenses down with Alessia. Let them? He didn't allow anything, with her it was just total destruction, a sudden, real demolition that he didn't seem to be able to control at all.

"Get out," he said.

"Matteo…"

"Out!" he roared, images flashing before his eyes. Images of violence. Of bones crushing beneath his fists, of not being able to stop. Not being able to stop until he was certain they could never hurt her again.

And it melded with images of his father. His father beating men until they were unconscious. Until they didn't get back up again.

"What did they do?"

"They didn't pay."

"Is that all?"

"Is that all? Matteo, you can't let anyone disrespect you, ever. Otherwise, it gets around. You have to make them an example. Whatever you have to do to protect your power, you do it. And if people have to die to secure it, so be it. Casualties of war, figlio mio.*"*

No. He wasn't like that.

But you were, Matteo. You are.

Then in his mind, it wasn't his father doing the beating. It was him.

"Out!"

Alessia's dark eyes widened and she backed out of the room, a tear tracking down her cheek.

He sank down into a chair, his fingers curled tightly around a bottle of whiskey as the edges of his vision turned fuzzy, darkened.

Che cavolo, what was she doing to him?

Alessia slammed the bedroom door behind her and tore at the back of her wedding dress, such as it was, sobbing as she released the zipper and let it fall to the floor. She'd wanted Matteo to be the one to take it off her. She hadn't realized how much until now.

Instead, her groom was off getting drunk rather than dealing with her.

"It's more than that," she said out loud. And she knew that it was. He was getting drunk instead of dealing with a whole lot of things.

Well, it was unfair because she couldn't get drunk. She was pregnant with the man's baby, and while he numbed the pain of it all, she just had to stand around and endure it.

There was nothing new to that. She had to smile. Had to keep it all moving.

She sat down on the edge of the bed, then scooted into the middle of it, lying down, curling her knees into her chest. Tonight, there was no fantasy to save her, no way to avoid reality.

Matteo had long been her rescue from the harsh reality and pain of life. And now he was her harsh reality. And he wasn't who she'd believed he was. She'd simplified him, painted him as a savior.

She'd never realized how much he needed to be saved. The question was, was she up to the challenge? No, the real question was, did she have a choice?

There wasn't a word foul enough to help release the pain that was currently pounding through Matteo's head. So he said them all.

Matteo sat upright in the chair. He looked down at the floor, there was a mostly empty whiskey bottle lying on its side by the armchair. And there was a dark star-shaped whiskey stain on the wall, glass shards gathered beneath.

He remembered...not very much. The wedding. He was married now. He looked down at the ring on his left hand. Yes, he was married now.

He closed his eyes again, trying to lessen the pain in his head, and had a flash of lilac memory. A cloud of purple, long dark hair. He'd held her arm and pulled her against him, his lips hard on hers.

Dio, what had he done? Where had it stopped? He searched his brain desperately for an answer, tried to figure out what he'd done. What she'd done.

He stood quickly, ignoring the dizziness, the ferocious hammering in his temples. He swore again as he took his first step, he legs unsteady beneath him.

What was his problem? Where was his control? He knew better than to drink like that, knew better than to allow any lowered inhibitions.

The first time he'd gotten that drunk had been the night following Alessia's rescue. He hadn't been able to get clean. Hadn't been able to get the images out of his head. Images of what he was capable of.

The stark truth was, it hadn't been the attack that had driven him to drink. It had been what his father had said afterward.

"You are my son."

When Benito Corretti had seen his son, blood-streaked, after the confrontation with Alessia's attackers, he'd assumed that it meant Matteo was finally following in his footsteps. Had taken it as confirmation.

But Matteo hadn't. It had been six years after that night when Benito had said it to him again. And that night, Matteo had embraced the words, and proven the old man right.

He pushed the memories away, his heart pounding too hard to go there.

He knew full well that he was capable of unthinkable things, even without the loss of control. But when control was gone...when it was gone, he truly became a monster. And last night, he'd lost control around Alessia.

He had to find her.

He walked down the hall, his heart pounding a sick tempo in his skull, his entire body filled with lead.

He went down the stairs, the natural light filtering through the windows delivering a just punishment for his hideous actions.

Coffee. He would find coffee first, and then Alessia.

He stopped when he got to the dining room. It turned out he had found both at the same time.

"Good morning," Alessia said, her hands folded in front of her, her voice soft and still too loud.

"Morning," he said, refusing to call it good.

"I assume you need coffee?" she asked, indicating a French press, ready for brewing, and a cup sitting next to it.

"Yes."

"You know how that works, right?" she asked.

"Yes."

"Good."

She didn't make a move to do it for him, she simply sat in her seat, drinking a cup of tea.

He went to his spot at the expansive table, a few seats away from hers, and sat, pushing the plunger down slowly on the French press.

He poured himself a cup, left it black. He took a drink and waited a moment, letting the strong brew do its magic.

"Alessia," he said, his voice rusty, the whiskey burn seeming to linger, "last night...did I hurt you?"

"In what way?" she asked, leaning back in her chair, her dark eyes unflinching.

"Physically."

"No."

The wave of relief that washed over him was profound, strong. "I'm pleased to hear it."

"Emotionally, on the other hand, I'm not sure I faired so well."

"Why is that?"

"Well, let's see, my husband got drunk on our wedding night instead of coming to bed with me. What do you think?"

"I'm sorry if I wounded your pride," he said, "that wasn't my intention." What he'd been after was oblivion, which he should have known wasn't a safe pursuit.

"Wouldn't your pride have been wounded if I'd done the same?"

"I would have ripped the bottle out of your hand. You're pregnant."

There hadn't been a lot of time for him to really pause and think through the implications of that. It had all been about securing the marriage. Staying a step ahead of the press at all times. Making sure Alessia was legally bound to him.

"Hence the herbal tea," she said, raising her cup to him. "And the pregnancy wasn't really my point."

"Alessia…this can't be a normal marriage."

"Why not?" she asked, sitting up straighter.

"Because it simply can't be. I'm a busy man, I

travel a lot. I was never going to marry…I never would have married."

"I don't see why we can't have a normal marriage anyway. A lot of men and women travel for business, it doesn't mean they don't get married."

"I don't love you."

Alessia felt like he'd slapped her. His words were so bald, so true and unflinching. And they cut a swath of devastation through her. "I didn't ask you to," she said, because it was the only truth she could bring herself to speak.

"Perhaps not, but a wife expects it from her husband."

"I doubt my father loved my mother, and if he did, it wasn't the kind of love I would like to submit to. What about yours?"

"*Obsession,* perhaps, was a better word. My father loved Lia's mother, I'm sure of that. I'm not certain he loved mine. At least, not enough to stay away from other women. And my mother was—is, for that matter—very good at escaping unpleasant truths by way of drugs and alcohol." His headache mocked him, a reminder that he'd used alcohol for the very same reason last night.

"Perhaps it was their marriages that weren't normal. Perhaps—"

"Alessia, don't. I think you saw last night that I'm not exactly a brilliant candidate for husband or father of the year."

"So try to be. Don't just tell me you can't, Matteo, or that you don't want to. Be better. That's what I'm trying to do. I'm trying to be stronger, to do the right thing."

"Yes, because that's what you do," he said, his tone dry. "You make things better, because it makes you feel better, and as long as you feel good you assume all is right with your world. You trust your moral compass."

"Well, yes, I suppose that's true."

"I don't trust mine. I want things I shouldn't want. I have already taken what I didn't have the right to take."

"If you mean my virginity, I will throw this herbal tea in your face," she said, pregnancy hormones coming to the rescue, bringing an intense surge of anger.

"I'm not so crass, but yes. Your body, you, you aren't for me."

"For Alessandro? That's who I was for?"

"That isn't what I meant."

"The hell it's not, Matteo!" she shouted, not caring if she hurt his head. Him and his head could go to hell. "You're just like him. You think I can't make my own decisions? That I don't know my own mind? My body belongs to me, not to you, not to my father, not to Alessandro. I didn't give myself to you, I took you. I made you tremble beneath my hands, and I could do it again. Don't treat me like some fragile thing. Don't treat me like you have to protect me from myself."

He stayed calm, maddeningly so, his focus on his cup of coffee. "It's not you I'm protecting you from."

"It's you?"

A smile, void of humor, curved his lips. "I don't trust me, Alessia, why should you?"

"Well, let me put you at ease, Matteo. I don't trust anyone. Just because I jumped into bed with you doesn't mean you're the exception. I just think you're hot." She was minimizing it. Minimizing what she felt. And she hated that. But she was powerless to do anything to stop the words from coming out. She wanted to protect herself, to push him back from her vulnerable places. To keep him from hurting her.

Because the loss of Matteo in her fantasies… it was almost too much to bear. As he became her reality, she was losing her escape, and she was angry at him for taking it. For not being the ideal she had made him out to be.

"I'm flattered," he said, taking another drink of his coffee.

"How do you see this marriage going, then?"

"I don't want to hurt you."

"Assume it's too late. Where do we go from here?"

He leaned forward, his dark eyes shuttered. "When exactly are you due?"

"November 22. It was easy for them to figure out since I knew the exact date I conceived."

"I will make sure you get the best care, whatever you need. And we'll make a room for the baby."

"Well, all things considered, I suppose our child should have a room in his own house."

"I'm trying," he bit out. "I'm not made for this. I don't know how to handle it."

"Well, I do. I know exactly how much work babies are. I know exactly what it's like to raise children. I was thirteen when my mother died. Thirteen when my baby sister and the rest of my siblings became my responsibility. Babies are hard work. But you love them, so much. And at the same time, they take everything from you. I know that, I know it so well. And I'm terrified," she said, the last word breaking. It was a horrible confession, but it was true.

She'd essentially raised four children, one of them from infancy, and as much as she adored them, with every piece of herself, she also knew the cost of it. Knew just how much you poured into children. How much you gave, how much they took.

And she was doing it again. Without ever finding a place for herself in the world. Without hav-

ing the fantasies she'd craved. True love. A man
who would take care of her.

You've had some of the fantasies.

Oh, yes, she had. But one night of passion
wasn't the sum total of her life's desires.

"All of this," he said. "And still you want this
child?"

"Yes, Matteo. I do. Because babies are a lot of
work. But the love you feel for them…it's stronger than anything, than any fear. It doesn't mean
I'm not afraid, only that I know in the end the
love will win."

"Well, we can be terrified together," he said.

"You're terrified?"

"Babies are tiny. They look very easily broken."

"I'll teach you how to hold one."

Their eyes met, heat arching between them,
and this time her pregnancy hormones were
making her feel something other than anger.

She looked back down at her breakfast. "How's
your head?"

"I feel like someone put a woodpecker in my
skull."

"It's no less than you deserve."

"I will treat you better than I did last night.
That I promise you. I'm not sure what other
promises I can make, but that one…that one I
will keep."

She thought of him last night. Broken. Passionate. Needy. She wondered how much of that was the real Matteo. How much he kept hidden beneath a facade.

How much he kept from escaping. And she knew just how he felt in some ways. Knew what it was like to hide everything behind a mask. It was just that her mask was smiling, and his hardly made an expression at all.

"Will you be faithful to me?" she asked, the words catching in her throat.

Matteo looked down into his coffee for a moment, then stood, his cup in his hand. "I have some work to see to this morning, and my head is killing me. We can talk more later."

Alessia's heart squeezed tight, nausea rolling through her. "Later?"

"My head, Alessia."

My heart, you jackass. "Great. Well, perhaps we can have a meeting tonight, or something."

"We're busy tonight."

"Oh. Doing what?"

"Celebrating our marriage, quite publicly, at a charity event."

"What?" She felt far too raw to be in public.

"After what happened with Alessandro, we have to present a united front. Your not-quite wedding to him was very public, as was your announcement of your pregnancy. The entire world is very likely scratching their heads over the spectacle we've created, and now it's time to show a little bit of normal."

"But we don't have a normal marriage—I mean, so I've been told."

"As far as the media is concerned we do."

"Why? Afraid of a little scandal? You're a Corretti."

"What do you want our child to grow up and read? Because thanks to the internet, this stuff doesn't die. It's going to linger, scandal following him wherever he goes. You and I both know what that's like. To have all the other kids whisper about your parents. For our part, we aren't criminals, but we've hardly given our child a clean start."

"So we go out and look pretty and sparkly and together, and what? The press just forgets about what happened?"

"No, but perhaps they will continue on in the vein that they've started in."

"What's that?" She'd, frankly, spent a lot of energy avoiding the stories that the media had written about the wedding.

"That we were forbidden lovers, who risked it all to be together."

It wasn't far from the truth, although Matteo hadn't truly known the risk they'd been taking their night together. But she had. And she'd risked it all for the chance to be with him.

Looking at him now, dealing with all the bruises he'd inflicted on her heart, she knew she would make the same choice now. Because at least it had been her choice. Her mistake. Her very first big one. It was like a rite of passage in a way.

"Well, then, I suppose we had better get ready to put on a show. I'm not sure I have the appropriate costume, though."

"I'm sure I can come up with something."

CHAPTER SEVEN

"SOMETHING" TURNED OUT to be an evening gown from the Corretti fashion line. It was gorgeous, and it was very slinky, with silky gold fabric that molded to her curves and showed the emerging baby bump that she almost hadn't noticed until she'd put on the formfitting garment.

Of course, there was no point in hiding her pregnancy. She'd announced it on television, for heaven's sake. But even so, since she hadn't really dealt with it yet, she felt nervous about sharing it with the public like this.

She put her hand on her stomach, smoothing her palm over the small bump. She was going to be a mother. Such a frightening, amazing thing to realize. She'd been tangled up in finding Matteo, and then in the days since—had it really only been days?—she'd been dealing with having him back in her life. With marrying him. She hadn't had a chance to really think of the baby in concrete terms.

Alessia looked at herself in the mirror one more time, at her stomach, and then back at her face. Her looks had never mattered very much to her. She was comfortable with them, more or less. She was taller than almost every other woman she knew, and a good portion of the men, at an Amazonian six feet, but Matteo was taller.

He managed to make her feel small. Feminine. Beautiful.

That night they were together he'd made her feel especially beautiful. And then last night he'd made her feel especially undesirable. Funny how that worked.

She turned away from the mirror and walked out of the bedroom. Matteo was standing in the hall waiting for her, looking so handsome in his black suit she went a little weak-kneed. He was a man who had a strong effect, that was for sure.

"Don't you clean up nice," she said. "You almost look civilized."

"Appearances can be deceiving," he said.

"The devil wore Armani?"

"Something like that." He held his hand out and she hesitated for a moment before taking it and allowing him to lead her down the curved staircase and into the foyer. He opened the door for her, his actions that of a perfectly solicitous husband.

Matteo's sports car was waiting for them, the keys in the ignition.

Alessia waited until they were on the road before speaking again. "So, what's the charity?"

He shifted gears, his shoulders bunched up, muscles tense. "It's one of mine."

"You have charities?"

"Yes."

"I didn't realize."

"I thought you knew me."

"We're filled with surprises for each other, aren't we? It's a good thing we have a whole lifetime together to look forward to," she said drily.

"Yes," he said, his voice rough, unconvincing.

And she was reminded of their earlier conversation in the dining room. She'd asked him point-blank if he would be faithful, and he'd sidestepped her. She had a feeling he was doing it again.

She gritted her teeth to keep from saying anything more. To keep from asking him anything, or pressing the issue. She had some pride. She did. She was sure she did, and she was going to do everything she could to hold on to her last little bit of it.

"Well, what is your charity for, then?"

"This is an education fund. For the schools here."

"That's…great," she said. "I didn't get to do any higher education."

"Did you want to?"

"I don't know. I don't think so. I mean…I didn't really have anything I wanted to be when I grew up."

"Nothing?"

"There weren't a lot of options on the table. Though I did always think I would like to be a mother." A wife and a mother. That she would like to have someone who loved her, cherished her like the men in her much-loved books cherished their heroines. It was a small dream, one that should have been somewhat manageable.

Instead, she'd gone off and traded it in for a night of wild sex.

And darn it, she still didn't regret it. Mainly.

"Mission accomplished."

"Why, yes, Matteo, I am, as they say, living the dream."

"There's no need to be—"

"There is every need to be," she said. "Don't act like I should thank you for any of this."

"I wasn't going to," he said, his tone biting.

"You were headed there. This is not my dream." But it was close. So close that it hurt worse in some ways than not getting anywhere near it at all. Because this was proving that her dream didn't exist. That it wasn't possible.

"My apologies, *cara*, for not being your dream." His voice was rough, angry, and she wanted to know where he got off being mad after the way he'd been treating her.

"And my apologies for not being yours. I imagine if I had a room number stapled to my forehead and a bag of money in my hand I'd come a little closer."

"Now you're being absurd."

"I don't think so."

Matteo maneuvered his car through the narrow city streets, not bothering with nice things like braking before turning, and pulled up to the front of his hotel.

"It's at your hotel," she said.

"Naturally." He threw the car into Park, then got out, rounding to the passenger side and opening the door for her. "Come, my darling wife, we have a public to impress."

He extended his hand to her and she slowly reached her hand out to accept it. Lighting streaked through her, from her fingertips, spreading to every other part of her, the shock and electricity curling her toes in her pumps.

She stood, her eyes level with his thanks to her shoes. "Thank you."

A member of the hotel staff came to where they were and had a brief exchange with Matteo before getting into the car and driving it off to the parking lot. Alessia wandered to the steps of the hotel, taking two of them before pausing to wait for her husband.

Matteo turned back to her, his dark eyes glittering in the streetlamps. He moved to the stairs, and she advanced up one more, just to keep her height advantage. But Matteo wasn't having it. He got onto her stair, meeting her eyes straight on.

"There are rules tonight, Alessia, and you will play by them."

"Will I?" she asked. She wasn't sure why she was goading him. Maybe because it was the only way in all the world she could feel like she had some power. Or maybe it was because if she wasn't trying to goad him, she was longing for him. And the longing was just unacceptable.

A smile curved his lips and she couldn't help but wonder if he needed this, too. This edge of hostility, the bite of anger between them.

Although why Matteo would need anything to hold her at a distance when he'd already made his feelings quite clear was a mystery to her.

"Yes, my darling wife, you will." He put his hand on her chin, drawing close to her, his heat making her shiver deep inside. It brought her right back to that night.

To the aching, heart-rending desperation she'd felt when his lips had finally touched hers. To the moment they'd closed his hotel room door and he'd pressed her against the wall, devouring, taking, giving.

He drew his thumb across her lower lip and she snapped back to the present. "You must stop looking at me like that," he said.

"Like what?"

"Like you're frightened of me." There was an underlying note to his voice that she couldn't guess at, a frayed edge to his control that made his words gritty.

"I'm not."

"You look at me like I'm the very devil sometimes."

"You act like the very devil sometimes."

"True enough. But there are other times…"

"What other times?"

"You didn't used to look at me that way."

"How did I look at you?" she asked, her chest tightening, her stomach pulling in on itself.

"When you were a girl? With curiosity. At the hotel? Like you were hungry."

"You looked at me the same way."

"And how do you think I look at you now?"

"You don't," she whispered. "When you can help it, you don't look at me at all."

He moved his other hand up to cup her cheek, his thumb still stroking her lower lip. "I'm looking at you now."

And there was heat in his eyes. Heat like there had been their night together, the night that had started all of this. The night that had changed the course of her life.

"Because you have to," she said. "For the guests."

"Oh, yes, the guests," he said.

Suddenly, a flash pierced the dim light, interrupting their moment. They both looked in the direction of the photographer, who was still snapping pictures in spite of the fact that the moment was completely broken.

"Shall we go in?" he asked. Any evidence of frayed control was gone now, the rawness, the intensity, covered by a mask. And now her husband was replaced with a smooth, cool stranger.

She'd love to say it wasn't the man she'd married, but this was exactly the man she'd married. This guarded man with more layers of artifice than anyone she'd ever met. She had been so convinced she'd seen the man behind the fiction, that the night in the hotel she'd seen the real Matteo. That in those stolen glances they'd shared when they were young, she'd seen the truth.

That in the moment of unrestrained violence, when he'd put himself in harm's way to keep her from getting hurt, she'd seen the real man.

Now she realized what small moments those were in the entirety of Matteo's life. And for the first time, she wondered if she was simply wrong about him.

A feeling that settled sickly in her stomach, a leaden weight, as they continued up the stairs and into the entrance to the hotel's main ballroom.

There were more photographers inside, capturing photographs of the well-dressed crème de la crème of Sicilian society. And Alessia did her best to keep a smile on her face. This was her strength, being happy no matter what was going on. Keeping a smile glued to her face at whatever event she was at on behalf of her father, making sure she showed her brothers and sisters she was okay even if she'd just taken a slap to the face from their father.

But this wasn't so simple. She was having a harder time finding a place to go to inside of herself. Having a harder time finding that false feeling of hope that she'd become so good at creating for herself to help preserve her sanity.

No one could live in total hopelessness, so she'd spent her life creating hope inside of herself. She'd managed to do it through so many difficult scenarios. Why was it so hard now? So hard with Matteo?

She knew she'd already answered that question. It was too hard to retreat to a much-loved fantasy when that much-loved fantasy was standing beside you, the source of most of your angst.

Though she couldn't blame it all on Matteo. The night of her bachelorette party was the first night she'd stopped trying to find solace in herself, had stopped just trying to be happy no matter what, and had gone for what she wanted, in spite of possible consequences.

She spent the night with Matteo's arm wrapped around her waist, his touch keeping her entire body strung tight, on a slow burn. She also turned down champagne more times than she could count. Was she normally offered alcohol so much at a party? She'd never been conscious of it when she was allowed to drink it. Right now it just seemed a cruelty, since she could use the haze, but couldn't take the chance with her baby's health.

Anyway, for some reason it all smelled sour and spoiled to her now. The pregnancy was making her nose do weird things.

Although Matteo smelled just as good as he ever had. The thought made her draw a little closer to him, breathe in the scent of him, some sort of spicy cologne mingling with the scent of his skin. She was especially tuned into the scent of his skin now, the scent of his sweat.

Dio, even his sweat turned her on. Because it reminded her of his bare skin, slick from exertion, her hands roaming over his back as he thrust hard into her, his dark eyes intent on hers. And there were no walls. Not then.

She blinked and came back to the present. She really had to stop with the sexual fantasies, they did her no good.

A photographer approached them. "Smile for me?" he asked.

Matteo drew her in close to his body, and she put her hand on his chest. She knew her smile looked perfect. She had perfected her picture smile for events such as these, to put on a good front for the Battaglia family. She was an expert.

Matteo should have been, as well, but he looked like he was trying to smile around a rock in his mouth, his expression strained and unnatural.

"A dance for the new bride and groom?" the photographer asked while taking their picture, and she was sure that in that moment her smile faltered a bit.

"Of course," Matteo said, his grin widening. Was she the only one who could see the totally feral light in his eyes, who could see that none of this was real?

The photographer was smiling back, as were some of the guests standing in their immediate area, so they must not be able to tell. Must not be able to see how completely disingenuous the expression of warmth was.

"Come. Dance with me."

And so she followed him out onto the glossy marble dance floor, where other couples were holding each other close, slow dancing to a piece of piano music.

It was different from when they'd danced in New York. The ballroom was bright, crystal chandeliers hanging overhead, casting shimmering light onto caramel-colored walls and floors. The music was as bright as the lighting, nothing darkly sensual or seductive.

And yet when Matteo drew her into his hold, his arms tight, strong around her, they might as well have been the only two people in the room. Back again, shrouded in darkness in the corner of a club, stealing whatever moments together they could have before fate would force them to part forever.

Except fate had had other ideas.

She'd spent a lot of her life believing in fate, believing that the right thing would happen in the end. She questioned that now. Now she just wondered if she'd let her body lead her into an impossible situation all for the sake of assuaging rioting hormones.

"This will make a nice headline, don't you

think?" he asked, swirling her around before drawing her back in tight against him.

"I imagine it will. You're a great dancer, by the way. I don't know if I mentioned that…last time."

"You didn't, but your mouth was otherwise occupied."

Her cheeks heated. "Yes, I suppose it was."

"My mother made sure I had dance lessons starting at an early age. All a part of grooming me to take my place at the helm of Benito's empire."

"But you haven't really. Taken the helm of your father's empire, I mean."

"Not as such. We've all taken a piece of it, but in the meantime we've been working to root out the shadier elements of the business. It's one thing my brothers and I do not suffer. We're not criminals."

"A fact I appreciate. And for the record, neither is Alessandro. I would never have agreed to marry him otherwise."

"Is that so?"

"I've had enough shady dealings to last me a lifetime. My father, for all that he puts on the front of being an honorable citizen, is not. At least your fathers and your grandfather had the decency to be somewhat open about the fact that they weren't playing by the rules."

"Gentleman thugs," he said, his voice hard.

"But I'll let you in on a little secret—no matter how good you are at dancing, no matter how nicely tailored your suit is, it doesn't change the fact that when you hit a man in the legs with a metal cane, his knees shatter. And he doesn't care what you're wearing. Neither do the widows of the men you kill."

Alessia was stunned by his words, not by the content of them, not as shocked as she wished she were. People often assumed that she was some naive, cosseted flower. Her smile had that effect. They assumed she must not know how organized crime worked. But she did. She knew the reality of it. She knew her father was bound up so tightly in all of it he could hardly escape it even if he wanted to.

He was addicted to the power, and being friendly with the mob bosses was what kept him in power. He couldn't walk away easily. Not with his power, possibly not even with his life.

And yet, the Correttis had disentangled themselves from it. The Corretti men and women had walked away from it.

No, it wasn't the content of his words that had surprised her. It was the fact that he'd said them at all. Because Matteo played his cards close to his chest. Because Matteo preferred not to address the subject of his family, of that part of his past.

"You aren't like that, though."

"No?" he asked. "I'm in a suit."

"And you wouldn't do that to someone."

"Darling Alessia, you are an eternal optimist," he said, and there was something in his words she didn't like. A hard edge that made her stomach tighten. "I don't know how you manage it."

"Survival. I have to protect myself."

"I thought that was where cynics came from?"

"Perhaps a good number of them. But no matter how I feel about a situation, I've never had any control over the outcome. My mother died in childbirth, and no amount of feeling good or bad about it would have changed that. My father is a criminal, no matter the public mask he wears, who has no qualms about slapping my face to keep me in line." They swirled in a fast circle, Matteo's hold tightening on her, something dangerous flickering in his eyes. "No matter how I feel about the situation, that is the situation. If I didn't choose to be happy no matter what, I'm not sure I would have ever stopped crying, and I didn't want to live like that, either."

"And why didn't you leave?" he asked.

"Without Marco, Giana, Eva and Pietro? Never. I couldn't do it."

"With them, then."

"With no money? With my father and his men bearing down on us? If it were only myself, then

I would have left. But it was never only me. I think we were why my mother stayed, too." She swallowed hard. "And if she could do it for us, how could I do any less?"

"Your mother was good to you?"

"So good," Alessia said, remembering her beautiful, dark-haired mother, the gentle smile that had always put her at ease when her father was in the other room shouting. The sweet, soothing touch, a hand on her forehead to help her fall asleep. "I wanted to give them all what she gave to me. I was the oldest, the only one who remembered her very well. It seemed important I try to help them remember. That I give them the love I received, because I knew they would never get it from my father."

"And in New York? With me?"

"What do you mean?"

"You toed the line all of your life, Alessia. You were prepared to marry to keep your brothers and sisters safe and cared for. Why did you even chance ruining it by sleeping with me?" His hold tightened on her, his voice getting back that rough edge. That genuine quality it had been missing since they'd stepped inside the hotel.

It was a good question. It was *the* question, really.

"Tell me, *cara*," he said, and she glimpsed something in his eyes as he spoke. A desperation.

And she couldn't goad him. Couldn't lie to him. Not now.

"Did you ever want something, Matteo, with all of yourself? So much that it seemed like it was in your blood? I did. For so many years. When we were children, I wanted to cross that wall between our families' estates and take your hand, make you run with me in the grass, make you smile. And when I got older...well, I wanted something different from you, starting about the time you rescued me, and I don't want to hear about how much you regret that. It mattered to me. I dreamed of what it would be like to kiss you, and then, I dreamed of what it would be like to make love with you. So much so that by the time I saw you in New York, when you finally did kiss me, I felt like I knew the steps to the dance. And following your lead seemed the easiest thing. How could I not follow?"

"I am a man, Alessia, so I fear there is very little romance to my version of your story. From the time you started to become a woman, I dreamed of your skin against mine. Of kissing you. Of being inside you. I could not have stopped myself that night any more than you could have."

"That's good to know," she said, heat rushing through her, settling over her skin. It made her dress, so lovely and formfitting a few moments ago, feel tight. Far too tight.

"I don't understand what it is you do to me."

"I thought… I was certain that I must not be so different from all your other women."

"There weren't that many," he said. "And you are different."

It was a balm to her soul that he felt that way. That she truly hadn't been simply one in a lineup. It was easy for her, she realized, to minimize the experience on his end. It had been easy for her to justify being with him, not being honest with him, giving him a one-night stand, because she'd assumed he'd had them before. It had been easy to believe she was the only one who'd stood to be hurt or affected, because she was the virgin.

That had been unfair. And she could see now, looking into his eyes, that it wasn't true, either.

"Kiss me," he said, all of the civility gone now.

She complied, closing the short distance between them, kissing him, really kissing him, for the first time in three months. Their wedding kiss had been nothing. A pale shadow of the passion they'd shared before. A mockery of the desire that was like a living beast inside of them both.

She parted her lips for him, sucked his tongue deep inside of her mouth, not caring that it would be obvious to the people around them. Matteo was hers now, her husband. She wouldn't hide it, not from anyone. Wouldn't hide her desire.

He growled low in his throat, the sound vibrating through his body. "Careful, Alessia, or I will not be responsible for what happens."

"I don't want you to be responsible," she said, kissing his neck. Biting him lightly. There was something happening to her, something that had happened once before. A total loss of control. At the hands of Matteo Corretti.

It was like she was possessed, possessed by the desire to have him, to take him, make him hers. Make him understand what she felt. Make herself understand what she felt.

"We can't do this here," he said.

"This sounds familiar."

"It does," he said. He shifted, pulled her away from his body, twining his fingers with hers. "Come with me."

"Where?"

"Somewhere," he said.

He led her out of the ballroom, ignoring everyone who tried to talk to them. A photographer followed them and Matteo cursed, leading them a different way, down a corridor and to the elevators.

He pushed the up button and they both waited. It only took a moment for the elevator doors to slide open, and the moment they did, she was being tugged inside, tugged up against the hard wall of his chest and kissed so hard, so deep, she was afraid she would drown in it.

She heard the doors slide closed behind them, was dimly aware of the elevator starting to move. Matteo shifted their positions, put her back up against the wall, his lips hungry on hers.

"I need you," he said, his voice shaking.

"I need *you*," she said.

Her entire body had gone liquid with desire, her need for him overshadowing everything. Common sense, self-protection, everything. There was no time for thought. This was Matteo. The man she wanted with everything she had in her, the man who haunted her dreams. This was her white knight, but he was different than she'd imagined.

There was a darkness to him. An edge she'd never been able to imagine. And she found she liked it. Found she wanted a taste of it. She didn't know what that said about her, didn't know what it meant, but at the moment, she didn't care, either.

"This is a beautiful dress," he said, tracing the deep V of the neckline with his fingertip, skimming silk and skin with the movement. Her breath hitched, her entire body on edge, waiting for what he would do next. Needing it more than she needed air. "But it is not as beautiful as you. And right now, I need to see you."

He reached around, tugging on the zipper, jerking it down.

"Careful," she said, choking on the word. "You'll snag the fabric."

"I'll tear it if I have to," he said.

The top fell around her waist, revealing her breasts, covered only by a whisper-thin bra that showed the outline of her nipples beneath the insubstantial fabric.

He lifted his hand and cupped her, slid his thumb over the tightened bud. "Hot for me?" he asked.

"Yes."

"Wet for me?" He put his other hand on her hip, flexed his fingers.

She couldn't speak, she just nodded. And he closed his eyes, his expression one of pained relief like she'd never seen before.

She put her hand between her breasts, flicked the front clasp on her bra, letting it fall to the elevator floor. He looked at her, lowering his head, sucking her deep into his mouth. An arrow of pleasure shot from there down to her core. She tightened her fingers in his hair, then suddenly became conscious of the continued movement of the elevator.

"Hit the stop button," she said, her voice breathless.

"What?" he asked, lifting his head, his cheeks

flushed, his hair in disarray. Her heart nearly stopped. Matteo Corretti undone was the most amazing thing she'd ever seen.

"The elevator," she said.

He cursed and turned around, hitting the red button on the wall, the elevator coming to a halt. He cursed again and reached into his pocket, taking out his cell phone. "Just a second."

"You better not be texting," she said.

He pushed a few buttons, his eyes not straying to her. "Not exactly." He turned the screen toward her and she saw him. And her. And her breasts.

"Oh."

He pushed a few more buttons. "I have disabled the security camera now. Unless you like the idea of being on film."

She had to admit, she had a certain amount of curiosity as to what it looked like when Matteo Corretti made love to her. It was a video she wouldn't mind owning, in all honesty. But she didn't want it on security footage, either.

"Not in the mood to provide security with any early-evening jollies."

"No worries, I have now deleted that little stretch of footage. There are advantages to being a control freak. Having an app on your phone that lets you see all the security at your hotels, and do as you please with the cameras, is one of them."

He discarded his suit jacket and tie then, throwing them onto the floor of the elevator, tossing his phone down on top of them.

"Have you used that trick before?" she asked, before he lowered his head to kiss her again.

"With a woman?"

"Yes."

"Jealous?"

"Hell, yes," she said, not worried if he knew it. She wanted this moment, this desperation that was beyond anything she'd known, to be as foreign to him as it was to her.

"No, I haven't." He kissed her again, his tongue sliding against hers, and she forgot her lingering concerns.

Forgot about everything but what it felt like to have Matteo kissing her. Caressing her.

"Later—" he kissed the hollow of her throat "—I will do this right—" lowered his head and traced the line of her collarbone with his tongue. "I'll taste every inch of you. Take time to savor you. Take your clothes off slowly. Look at those gorgeous curves." He kissed her neck, bit her lightly like she'd done to him earlier. "Now, though…now I just need to be inside you."

He started to gather her skirt up in his hands,

the slippery fabric sliding up her legs easily. "Take your panties off," he said.

She complied, her hands trembling as she worked her underwear down, kicking them to the side with her heels. He pushed her dress up around her hips, his hand hot on her thigh. He tugged her leg up around his, her back pinned against the wall of the elevator.

He tested her with his other hand, teasing her clitoris, sending streaks of white heat through her body with each pass his fingers made through her slick folds. "You didn't lie," he said. "You do want me."

"Yes," she said.

"Tell me," he said.

"I want you."

"My name."

"I want you, Matteo."

He abandoned her body for a moment, working at his belt, shoving his slacks and underwear down, just enough to free his erection so that he could sink into her. It was a shock, all those weeks without him, and she'd forgotten just how big he was. Just how much he filled her. She let her head fall back against the wall of the elevator, pleasure building deep inside her, her internal muscles tightening around his length.

And then there was no more talking. There was nothing but their ragged breathing, Matteo

moving hard and fast inside her, blunt fingertips digging into her hips as he held her steady,
thrusting into her.

He lowered his head, capturing her nipple
in his mouth again. A raw sound of pleasure
escaped her lips and she didn't even care. She
wasn't embarrassed at all.

Because this was Matteo. The man she'd always wanted. Wanted enough to break out of
what was expected of her for the first time in her
life. The man who had saved her, the man who
made her angry and hurt her, the man who made
her feel things she'd never felt before.

Matteo scared her. He confused her. He made
her feel more than anyone else ever had.

And right now he was driving her to a point
she'd never even imagined, to the edge of a cliff
so high she couldn't see the bottom of the chasm
below.

She was afraid to fall, afraid to let the pleasure
that was building in her break, because she didn't
know what would greet her on the other side.
Didn't know what would happen. And something
would happen. Something would change. There
was no question. None at all.

And then he looked at her, those dark eyes
meeting hers, and she saw him. Not the mask,
the man. Raw need, desperation and a fear that
mirrored her own.

He lowered his head, his lips pressing against her neck, his thrusts losing their measured rhythm. And something in her broke, released. And she was falling, falling into that endless chasm. But she wasn't afraid anymore.

Release rolled through her in waves, stealing every breath, every thought, everything but the moment.

And when she finally did reach bottom, Matteo was there, his strong arms around her. He was breathing hard, too, sweat on his brow, the back of his shirt damp, his heartbeat raging, so hard that, with his body pressed so tightly against hers, she could feel it against her own chest.

He stepped away from her slowly, running his hand over his hair, erasing the evidence that she'd ever speared her fingers through it. That she'd messed with his well-ordered control.

He adjusted his pants. Bent and collected his jacket, putting his phone back into his pocket. And she just stood there, her back to the wall, her dress still pushed partway up around her hips, the top resting at her waist, her underwear on the floor by her feet.

Matteo put his tie around his neck and started straightening it, too, before he looked at her. "Get dressed," he said.

"What?"

"Get dressed," he said. "We have to go back to the party."

"W-we do?"

"It's my charity," he said. "I have a speech to make." He checked his wristwatch. "And it seems I'm not too late for it so I really should try to manage it."

"I…"

"Turn around," he ordered, his voice harsh.

She did as he asked. He put her straps back into place, zipped the dress back up.

"My bra…"

"You don't need it," he said.

"What should I do with it?"

He opened up his jacket and indicated his inner pocket. She bent and scooped up her bra and panties and handed them to him, and he put both tiny garments into his pocket.

"Solved," he said.

She looked down at her chest, cupped her breasts for a moment. "I'm sagging."

"You are not."

He hit the button on the elevator and it started moving again, the doors sliding open. Then he hit the button for the first floor and they waited for the doors to close again.

Alessia felt…used. No, not even that. She just felt sad. Angry, because he was able to do that with her and then go back to his purely unruffled self.

Maybe she'd been making more out of them, and the sex, than she should have. Maybe she was wrong. Maybe it didn't mean anything to him. Nothing more than just sex, anyway, and a man like Matteo surely had it quite a bit.

They rode in silence, and the doors opened again. The photographer was still out there, wandering the halls. Looking for a photo op, no doubt.

Matteo put his arm around her waist and led her through the hall, that false smile back on his face. They started back toward the ballroom and she had the strangest feeling of déjà vu. Like they were back at the beginning of the night. Like their interlude in the elevator hadn't happened at all. But it had. She knew it had.

The photographer snapped a picture. And Alessia didn't bother to smile.

CHAPTER EIGHT

MATTEO WASN'T SURE how he managed to get up and speak in front of the large crowd of people. Not when he could see Alessia in the audience, her face smooth, serene, her dark eyes the only window to the storm that lurked beneath.

A storm he was certain would boil over and onto him once they were alone.

He found he didn't mind. That he welcomed the chance to take her on because it was better than the overwhelming, biting need to take her back to the elevator and have her again. To let the elevator continue up to his suite where he would have her again. And again. Tasting her this time, truly savoring her.

Yes, fighting was infinitely better than that. He would rather have her yelling at him than sighing his name in his ear.

Because he didn't know what to do with her, what to do about his desire for her.

It wasn't what he was used to. Wasn't normal in any way.

Sex was simply a need to be met, like eating or breathing. Yes, he liked some food better than he liked others, but he wasn't a slave to cravings. He believed in moderation, in exercising control in all areas of life.

Alessia was the one craving he didn't seem to be able to fight, and that meant he had to learn how.

Anything else was inexcusable.

"Thank you all for coming tonight, and for your generous donations. I am happy to announce that I am personally matching all of the donations given tonight. And that thanks to your generosity, it is now possible for the Corretti Education Foundation to branch out into college grants. It is my belief that a good education can overcome any circumstance, and it is my goal that every person be given that chance. Thank you again, enjoy the rest of the evening."

He stepped down from the podium, not paying attention to the applause that was offered up for his speech. He could hardly hear anything over the roar of blood in his ears. Could hardly see anything but Alessia. Which was one reason he allowed himself to be pulled to the side by some of the guests, interrupted on his way back to where his wife was standing.

He stopped and talked to everyone who approached him, using it as a tactic to keep himself from having to face Alessia without his guard firmly back in place. Cowardly? Perhaps. But he found he didn't care. Not much, at least.

Alessia didn't make a move to approach him; instead, she made conversation with the people around her. And every so often she flicked him a glare with those beautiful eyes of hers, eyes that glittered beneath the lights of the chandeliers. Eyes that made promises of sensual heaven, the kind of heaven he could hardly risk trying to enter again.

Every time he touched Alessia, she tore down another piece of the wall, that very necessary wall of control he'd built around himself.

People started to disperse, and as they both went along the natural line of people that wanted to converse with them, the space between them started to close. Matteo's blood started to flow hotter, faster, just getting nearer to Alessia.

No matter there were still five hundred people in the room. No matter that he'd had her against a wall an hour earlier. Still she challenged him. Still she made him react like a teenage boy with no control over his baser urges.

Yes, think about that. Remember what that looks like.

Blind rage. Two young men, still and unmoving, blood everywhere. And then a calm. A cold sort of emptiness. If he felt anything at all it was a kind of distant satisfaction.

And then he'd looked at Alessia. At the terror in her eyes.

And he'd done what he'd sworn he would never do.

He'd wrapped his arms around her and pulled her into his chest, brushing away her tears. He'd made her cry. Horrified her, and he couldn't blame her for being horrified. It wasn't the kind of thing a girl of fourteen, or any age, should ever have to see.

When he pulled away, when he looked down at her face, her cheeks were streaked with blood. The blood from his hands. Not the only blood he had on his hands.

He breathed in sharply, taking himself back to the present. Away from blood-soaked memories.

Except it was still so easy to see them when he looked at Alessia's face. A face that had been marred with tears and blood. Because of him.

The gap between them continued to shrink, the crowd thinning, until they met in the middle, in the same group. And there was no excuse now for him not to pull her against his side, his arm wrapped around her waist. So he did.

Alessia's body was stiff at his side, but her expression was still relaxed, her smile easy. A lie.

Why had he never noticed before that Alessia's smile wasn't always genuine?

He'd assumed that it was. That Alessia displayed and felt emotion with ease and honesty. Now he wondered.

The last of the guests started to file out, leaving Alessia and Matteo standing in the empty ballroom.

He looked around, at the expansive room. This was his hotel, separate from his family dynasty, and often, looking at it, at the architecture, the expanse of it, filled him with a sense of pride. He had hotels all over the world, but this one, back in Sicily, a hotel that belonged to him and not to his family in any part, had always filled him with a particular amount of satisfaction.

Now it just seemed like a big empty room.

He picked up his phone and punched in a number. "Delay cleaning until further notice, I require the ballroom for personal use for a while."

Alessia looked at him, her dark eyes wide. "What do you need the ballroom for?"

He shrugged. "Anything I want." He walked over to the edge of the stage and sat, gripping the edge. "It is my hotel, after all."

"Yes, and you're a man who takes great pride in the ownership of whatever he can possess," she said.

"And why not?" he asked, loosening his tie,

trying not to think of Alessia's fingers on the knot, trying not to imagine her fingers at the buttons of his dress shirt as he undid the collar. "That's what it's always been about in my family. I go out of town—" and off the grid "—and my bastard cousin has taken over my office. My younger brother has managed to charm his way into the top seat of the fashion houses for Corretti. So you see? In my family, ownership is everything. And if you have to stab someone to get it, all the better."

"Metaphorical stabbing?" she asked, wrapping her arms around her waist, as if holding herself together. He hated that. Hated that he might cause her pain in any way.

"Or literal stabbing. I told you, my family has a colorful history."

"You said you and your brothers weren't criminals."

"We're not. Not convicted, anyway," he added, not sure why. Maybe because, in his heart, he knew he was one.

Knew he could be convicted for assault several times over if evidence was brought before a court.

"Why are you saying this?"

"What do you mean, why am I saying this? I'm telling you the truth. Was what I did that day near your father's gardens legal? Answer me," he said, his words echoing in the empty room.

"You saved me."

"Maybe."

"They would have raped me," she said.

He remembered it so clearly. And yet so differently.

Because he remembered coming upon Alessia, backed up against a tree, a stone wall behind her, two men in front of her, pressing her back to the tree, touching her, jeering at her. They had her shirt torn. They were pushing her skirt up. And he'd known what they intended to do. The evil they meant for his angel.

And then he remembered seeing red.

He pushed off from the stage, standing and pacing, trying to relieve the restless energy moving through him. Trying to ease the tightness in his chest.

He hadn't simply stopped when he'd gotten those men away from Alessia. Hadn't stopped when they quit fighting back. He hadn't stopped until Alessia had touched his back. And then he'd turned, a rock held tightly in his hand, ready to finish what he'd started. Ready to make sure they never got up again, ready to make sure they could never hurt another woman again. Any other woman, but most especially Alessia.

But then he'd looked into her eyes. Seen the fear. Seen the tears.

And he'd dropped his hand back to his side, letting the rock fall to the ground. Letting the rage drain from his body.

That was when he'd realized what he had done. What he had been about to do. And what it had done to Alessia to see it. More than that, it confirmed what he'd always known. That if he ever let himself go, if he ever allowed himself more than his emotionless existence, he would become a man he hated.

"I did more than save you," he said. "A lot more."

"You did what you had to."

"You say it as if I gave it some thought. I didn't. What I did was a reaction. Blind rage. As I was, if you were not there, I wouldn't have ended it until they were dead."

"You don't know that."

"That's the thing, Alessia, I do know that. I know exactly what my next move was going to be, and trust me, it's not something people get back up from."

"I wish you could see what I saw."

"And I wish like hell you hadn't seen any of it," he said, his voice rough.

"You were… I thought…I thought they were going to get away with it. That no one would hear me scream. No one would stop them. I thought that they would do it. And then you came and you didn't let them. Do you have any idea what that meant to me? Do you know what you stopped?"

"I know what I stopped."

"Then why do you regret it so much?"

"I don't regret it, not like you mean." He could remember his father's face still, as he'd administered punishment to men in his debt. The calm. The absolute calm. But worse, he could remember his father's face when someone had enraged him. Could remember how volatile, how beyond reason, he became in those situations.

And always, the old man had a smug sense that he had done what must be done. Full and complete justification for every action.

Just as Matteo had felt after Alessia's attack. How he had felt after the fire.

"To me you were just a hero," she said, her words soft.

They hit him hard, like a bullet, twisted inside of him, blooming outward and touching him everywhere, scraping his heart, his lungs. For a moment, he couldn't breathe.

"It's so much more complicated than that," he said.

"Not to me. Not to the girl you rescued. You were like... You were every unfulfilled dream from my entire life, showing up when I needed you most. How can you not understand that?"

"Maybe that," he said, "is our problem now. You know a dream, a fantasy, and I am not that man. I'm not the hero of the story."

She shook her head. "You were the hero of my story that day. And nothing will change that."

Coldness invaded him. "Is that what led you to my bed that night?"

She didn't look away. "Yes."

He swore, the word loud in the empty expanse of the ballroom. "So that was my thank-you?"

"No!" she said, the exclamation reverberating around them. "It's not like that at all. Don't make it into something like that it's… No."

"Then what, Alessia? Your fantasy of a knight?" Her cheeks turned pink and then she did look away. "*Dio*, is that what it is? You expected me to be your chivalrous knight in shining armor? What a disappointment this must be for you. You would have likely been better off with Alessandro."

"I didn't want Alessandro."

"Only because you lied to yourself about who I am."

"Who are you, then?" she asked. "You're my husband. I think you should tell me."

"I thought we went over this already."

"Yeah, you gave me that internet bio of a run-down on who you are. We told each other things we already knew."

"Why do we have to know each other?"

"Because it seems like we should. We're... married."

"Not really."

"You took me into an elevator and had me against the wall—what would make it more real for you?" she asked, the words exploding from her, crude and true, and nothing he could deny.

"That's sex, Alessia, and what we have is great, explosive sex. But that kind of thing isn't sustainable. It's not meant to be. It's not good for it to be."

"And you know this because you're constantly having spontaneous, explosive sex with strangers?"

"No."

"Then how do you know?"

"There's no control in it. No sense. We nearly let it get filmed, nearly let the elevator go to the next floor. Neither of us think when sex is involved."

"Maybe you think too much."

"And maybe you don't think enough. You feel, and look where all of that feeling has gotten you."

Her lip curled into a sneer. "Don't you dare blame this on me! Don't you dare act like it was me and my girlish feelings that led us here. That's far too innocent of a take on it, first of all. Yes, I might have built you up as a hero in my head, but what I wanted that night in New York had nothing to do with you being some kind of paragon and everything to do with me wanting you as a woman wants a man. I didn't want hearts and flowers, I wanted sex. And that was what I got. That wasn't led by my feelings," she said, her words cold, "that was led by my body and I was quite happy with the results."

"Too bad the price was so steep."

"Wasn't it?"

Alessia looked at Matteo and, for a moment, she almost hated him. Because he was fighting so hard, against her, against everything. Or maybe she was the one fighting. And she was just mad at him for not being who she'd thought he was.

And that wasn't fair, not really. He couldn't help it if he didn't line up with the fantasy she'd created about him in her head. It wasn't even fair to expect him to come close.

But no one in her life had ever been there for her, not since her mother. It had all been about her giving. And then he'd been there, and he'd put it all on the line for her, he'd given her all of himself in that moment. And yes, what he'd done had been violent, and terrifying in a way, but it was hard for her to feel any sadness for the men who would have stolen her last bit of innocence from her.

She'd grown up in a house with a criminal father who lied and stole on a regular basis. She knew about the ugliness of life. She'd lost her mother, spent her days walking on eggshells to try to avoid incurring any of her father's wrath.

But in all that time, at least, no one had forced themselves on her sexually, and considering the kind of company her father kept, it had always seemed kind of an amazing thing.

And then someone had tried to take that from her, too. But Matteo had stopped it.

"Do you understand how much of my life has been decided for me?" she asked.

"Yes," he said slowly, obviously unwilling to admit to not understanding something.

"I don't think you do. I spent my days mothering my siblings, and I don't regret it, because it had to be done, but that meant I didn't go away to school. It meant I stayed at home when a lot of girls my age would have been moving out, going to university. I went to events my father wanted me to go to, hosted parties in dresses he deemed appropriate. That day…that day on the road, those two men tried to take another choice from me. They tried to choose how I would learn about sex, how I would be introduced to it. With violence and pain and force. They tried to take something from me, and I don't just mean virginity, I mean the way I saw myself. The way I saw men. The way I saw people. And you stopped them. So I'm sorry if you don't want to have been my hero, but you were. You let me hold on to some of my innocence. You let me keep some parts of life a fantasy. I know about how harsh life can be. I know about reality, but I don't need to have every horrible thing happen to me. And it was going to." Her voice was rough, raw with tears she needed to shed.

She turned away from him, trying to catch her breath.

"And then my father told me that I was going to marry Alessandro. And I could see more choices being taken from me but this time I didn't see a way out. Then my friend Carolina said she would host a bachelorette party for me. And for once my father didn't deny me. I didn't know you would be there. And Carolina suggested we go to your hotel and I…well, then I hoped you'd be there. And you were. And I saw another chance to make a choice. So don't ask me to regret it."

His eyes were black, endless, unreadable. "I won't ask you to regret it, because then I would have to regret it, and I don't. When I found out I was your first…I can't tell you how that satisfied me, and I don't care if that's not the done thing, if I shouldn't care, because I did. I still care. I'm still glad it was me."

"I am, too," she said, her voice a whisper. The honesty cost them both, she knew.

His eyes met hers, so bleak, so filled with need. And she hoped she could fill it. Hoped she could begin to understand the man that he was and not just the man she'd created a fiction about in her head.

She nearly went to him then. Nearly touched him. Asked him to lie her down on the cold marble of the ballroom floor and make love to her again. But then she remembered. Remembered the question he hadn't answered. The one she'd been determined to get the answer to before she ever let him touch her again.

She'd messed up earlier. She hadn't been able to think clearly enough to have a conversation with him. But now, she would ask now. Again. And she would get her answer.

"Will you be faithful to me?" she asked.

He pushed his fingers through his hair. "Why do you keep asking me this?"

"Because it's a simple question and one I deserve the answer to. I'm not sleeping with you if you won't promise I'm the only woman in your life."

"I can't love you," he said, the words pulled

from him. Not *I don't love you*, like he'd said earlier, but *I can't*.

"I'm not asking you to love me, I'm asking you to not have sex with other women."

His jaw tightened, his hands clenching into fists at his sides. "To answer that question, I would have to know how I planned on conducting our relationship, and I do not know the answer to that yet."

"Were you planning on asking me?"

He shook his head. "I already told you we won't have a normal marriage."

"Why?" She knew she shouldn't ask, not in such a plaintive, needy tone, but she couldn't help herself, couldn't hide the hurt that was tearing through her. How was it she'd managed to get her dream, only to have it turn to ash the moment her fingers touched it?

"Because I cannot be a husband to you. I can't. I won't love you. I won't... I can't give what a husband is supposed to give. I don't know where to begin. I have an empire to run, my hotels, plus I have my bastard cousin installed in my offices at the family corporation, with his ass in my chair, sitting at my desk like he's the one who worked so hard for any of it. I don't have time to deal with you. If you took me on as a husband you would have me in your bed and nowhere else. And I'm not sure I want to put either of us through that."

"But you are my husband. Whether or not you want to be doesn't come into it at this point. You are my husband. You're the father of my baby."

"And our baby has the protection of my name, the validity of having married parents. I'm able to strike the deal for the docklands with your father thanks to this marriage and your siblings will be cared for. I'm sending them all to school, I don't think I told you."

Her throat closed, her body trembling. "I... No, you didn't."

"My point is, regardless of what happens behind closed doors, our marriage was a necessity, but what we choose to do in our own home rests squarely on us. And there are decisions to be made."

Decisions. She'd imagined that if she married Matteo her time for decision making would be over before it ever started. But he was telling her there was still a chance to make choices. That them legally being husband and wife didn't mean it was settled.

In some ways, the opportunity to make decisions was a heady rush of power she'd only experienced on a few occasions. In other ways... well, she wanted him to want to be married to her, if she was honest.

You're still chasing the fantasy when you have reality to contend with.

She had to stop that. She had to put it away now, the haze of fantasy. Had to stop trying to create a happy place where there wasn't one and simply stand up and face reality.

"So...if I say I don't want to be in a normal marriage, and if you can't commit to being faithful to me, does that mean that I have my choice of other lovers, too?"

Red streaked his cheekbones, his fists tightening further, a muscle in his jaw jerking. "Of course," he said, tight. Bitter.

"As long as there are no double standards," she said, keeping her words smooth and calm.

"If I release my hold on you, then I release it. We'll have to be discreet in public, naturally, but what happens behind closed doors is no one's business but our own."

"Ours and the elevator security cameras," she said.

"That will not happen again."

"It won't?"

"An unforgivable loss of control on my part."

"You've had a few of those recently."

She'd meant to spark an angry reply, to keep the fight going, because as long as they were fighting, she didn't ache for him. Wasn't so conscious of the tender emotions he made her feel.

And she wasn't so overwhelmed by the need to be skin to skin to him when they were fighting. But she didn't get anger. Instead, she got a bleak kind of pain that echoed in her soul, a hopelessness in his dark eyes that shocked her.

"Yes," he said. "I have. Always with you."

"I don't know how you are in other areas of your life. I only know how you are with me," she said.

His eyes grew darker. "A pity for you. I'm much more pleasant than this, usually."

"I make you misbehave."

He chuckled, no humor in the sound. "You could say that. We should go home."

She nodded. "Yes, we should."

They were in an empty ballroom, and she really would have loved a romantic moment with him here. The chance to dance as the only two people in the room. To go up to his suite and make love. To share a moment with each other that was out of time, apart from reality.

But they'd had their fantasy. Reality was here now, well and truly.

She still didn't want to leave.

Matteo picked up his phone and dialed. "Yes, you can send in the crew now."

She swallowed hard, feeling like they'd missed a key moment. Feeling like she'd missed one.

"Let's go," he said. There was no press now,

no one watching to see if he would put his arm around her. So he didn't. He turned and walked ahead, and she followed behind him, her heart sinking.

Matteo didn't know what he wanted. And she didn't, either.

No, that was a lie, she knew what she wanted. But it would require her to start dealing with Matteo as he was, and at some point, it would require him to meet her in the middle, it would require him to drop his guard.

She wasn't sure if either of them could do what needed to be done. Wasn't sure if they ever had a hope of fixing the tangled mess that they'd created.

She wasn't even sure if Matteo wanted to.

CHAPTER NINE

MATTEO WAS TEMPTED to drink again. He hated the temptation. He hated the feeling of temptation full stop. Before Alessia there had been no temptation.

No, that was a lie. The first temptation had been to break the rules and see what the Battaglias were really like. And so he had looked.

And from there, every temptation, every failing, had been tied to Alessia. She was his own personal road to ruin and there were some days he wondered why he bothered to stay off it.

At least he might go up in flames in her arms. At least then heat and fire might be connected with her, instead of that night his father had died.

Yes, he should just embrace it. He should just follow to road to hell and be done with it.

And bring her with you. Bring the baby with you.

Porca miseria. The baby.

He could scarcely think of the baby. He'd hardly

had a moment. He felt a little like he was going crazy sometimes, in all honesty. There was everything that was happening with Corretti Enterprises, and he had to handle it. He should go in and try to wrench the reins back from Angelo, should kick Luca out of his position and expose whatever lie he'd told to get there because he was sure the feckless playboy hadn't gotten there on merit alone.

Instead, Matteo was tied up in knots over his wife. Bewitched by a dark-haired vixen who seemed to have him in a death grip.

She was the reason he'd left, the reason he'd gone up to a remote house he owned in Germany that no one knew about. The reason he hadn't answered calls or returned emails. The reason he hadn't known or cared he was being usurped in his position as head of his branch of the family business.

He had to get a handle on it, and he had no idea how. Not when he felt like he was breaking apart from the inside out.

The business stuff, the Corretti stuff, he could handle that. But he found he didn't care to, and that was the thing that got to him.

He didn't even want to think about the baby. But he had to. Didn't want to try to figure out what to do with Alessia, who was still sleeping in the guest bedroom in the palazzo, for heaven's sake.

Something had to be done. Action had to be taken, and for the first time in his life, he felt frozen.

He set his shot glass down on the counter and tilted it to the side before pushing the bottom back down onto the tile, the sound of glass on ceramic loud and decisive. He stalked out of the bar and into the corridor, taking a breath, trying to clear his head.

Alcohol was not the answer. A loss of control was not the answer.

He had to get a grip. On his thoughts. On his actions. He had a business to try to fix, deals to cement. And all he could think about was Alessia.

He turned and faced the window that looked out on the courtyard. Moonlight was spilling over the grass, a pale shade of gray in the darkness of night.

And then he saw a shadow step into the light. The brightness of the moon illuminated the figure's hair, wild and curling in the breeze. A diaphanous gown, so sheer the light penetrated it, showed the body beneath, swirled around her legs as she turned in a slow circle.

An angel.

And then he was walking, without even thinking, he was heading outside, out to the courtyard, out to the woman who woke something deep in his soul. Something he hadn't known existed before she'd come into his life.

Something he wished he'd never discovered.

But it was too late now.

He opened the back door and stepped out onto the terrace, walking to the balustrade and grasping the stone with his hands, leaning forward, his attention fixed on the beauty before him.

On Alessia.

She was in his system, beneath his skin. So deep he wondered if he could ever be free of her. It would be harder now, all things considered. She was his wife, the mother of his child.

He could send her to live in the *palazzolo* with his mother. Perhaps his mother would enjoy a grandchild.

He sighed and dismissed that idea almost the moment it hit. A grandchild would only make his mother feel old. And would quite possibly give her worry lines thanks to all the crying.

And you would send your child to live somewhere else?

Yes. He was considering it, in all honesty.

What did he know about children? What did he know about love? Giving it. Receiving it. The kind of nurturing, the father-son bond fostered by his father was one he would just as soon forget.

A bond forged, and ended, by fire.

He threw off the memories and started down

the steps that led to the grass. His feet were bare and in that moment he realized he never went outside without his shoes. A strange realization, but he became conscious of the fact when he felt the grass beneath his feet.

Alessia turned sharply, her dark hair cascading over her shoulder in waves. "Matteo."

"What are you doing out here?"

"I needed some air."

"You like being outdoors."

She nodded. "I always have. I hated being cooped up inside my father's house. I liked to take long walks in the sun, away from the… staleness of the estate."

"You used to walk by yourself a lot."

"I still do."

"Even after the attack?" The words escaped without his permission, but he found he couldn't be sorry he'd spoken them.

"Even then."

"How?" he asked, his voice rough. "How did you keep doing that? How did you go on as if nothing had changed?"

"Life is hard, Matteo. People you love die, I know you know about that. People who should love you don't treat you any better than they'd treat a piece of property they were trying to sell for a profit. I've just always tried to see the good parts of life, because what else could I do? I could sit and feel sorry for myself, but it wouldn't change anything. And I've made the choice to stay, so that would be silly. I made the choice to stay and be there for my brothers and sisters, and I can't regret it. That means I have to find happiness in it. And that means I can't cut out my walks just because a couple of horrible men tried to steal them from me."

"And it's that simple?"

"It's not simple at all, but I do it. Because I have to find a way to live my life. My life. It's the only one I have. And I've just learned to try to love it as it is."

"And do you?" he asked. "Do you love it?"

She shook her head. "No." Her voice was a whisper. "But I'm not unhappy all the time. And I think that's something. I mean, it has to count for something."

"What about now? With this?"

"Are you happy?"

"Happiness has never been one of my primary goals. I don't know that I've ever thought about it too closely."

"Everybody wants to be happy," she said.

Matteo put his hands into his pockets and looked over the big stone wall that partitioned his estate from the rest of the world, looked up at the moon. "I want to make something different out of my family. I want to do something more than threaten and terrorize the people in Palermo. Beyond that…does it matter?"

"It does matter. Your happiness matters."

"I haven't been unhappy," he said, and then he wondered if he was lying. "What about you, Alessia?"

"I made a decision, Matteo, and it landed me in a situation that hasn't been entirely comfortable. It was my first big mistake. My first big fallout. And no, not all of it has been happy. But I can't really regret it, either."

"I'm glad you don't regret me."

"Do you regret me?"

"I should. I should regret my loss of control more than I do—" a theme in his life, it seemed "—but I find I cannot."

"What about tonight? In the elevator? Why did you just walk away?"

"I don't know what to do with us," he said, telling the truth, the honest, raw truth.

"Why do we have to know what we're doing?"

"Because this isn't some casual affair, and it never can be." Because of how she made him feel, how she challenged him. But he wouldn't say that. His honesty had limits, and that was a truth he disliked admitting even to himself. "You're my wife. We're going to have a child."

"And if we don't try, then we're going to spend

years sniping at each other and growing more and more bitter, is that better?"

"Better than hurting you? I think so."

"You've hurt me already."

"I did?"

"You won't promise to be faithful to me, you clearly hate admitting that you want me, even though as soon as we touch…Matteo, we catch fire, and you can't deny that. You know I don't have a lot of experience with men, but I know this isn't just normal. I know people don't just feel this way."

"And that's exactly why we have to be careful."

"So we'll be careful. But we're husband and wife, and I think we should try…try for the sake of our child, for our families, to make this marriage work. And I think we owe it to each other to not be unhappy."

"Alessia…"

"Let's keep taking walks, Matteo," she said, her voice husky. She took a step toward him, her hair shimmering in the dim light.

He caught her arm and pulled her in close, his heart pounding hard and fast. "I can't love you."

"You keep saying."

"You need to understand. There is a limit to what we can share. I'll have you in my bed, but that's as far as it goes. This wasn't my choice."

"I wasn't your choice?"

Her words hit him hard, and they hurt. Because no, he hadn't chosen to marry her without being forced into it. But it wasn't for lack of wanting her. If there was no family history. If he had not been the son of one of Sicily's notorious crime bosses, if there was nothing but him and Alessia and every other woman on earth, he would choose her every time.

But he couldn't discount those things. He couldn't erase what was. He couldn't make his heart anything but cold, not just toward her, but toward anyone. And he couldn't afford to allow a change.

Alessia had no idea. Not of the real reasons why. Not the depth he was truly capable of sinking to. The man underneath the iron control was the very devil, as she had once accused him of being. There was no hero beneath his armor. Only ugliness and death. Only anger, rage, and the ability and willingness to mete out destruction and pain to those who got in his way.

If he had to choose between a life without feeling or embracing the darkness, he would take the blessed numbness every time.

"You know it wasn't."

She thrust her chin into the air. "And that's how you want to start? By reminding me you didn't choose me?"

"It isn't to hurt you, or even to say that I don't want you. But I would never have tied you to me if it wasn't a necessity, and that is not a commentary on you, but on me, and what I'm able to give. There are reasons I never intended to take a wife. I know who I am, but you don't."

"Show me," she said. And he could tell she meant it, with utter conviction. But she didn't know what she was asking. She had no way of knowing. He had given her a window into his soul, a glimpse of the monster that lurked beneath his skin, but she didn't know the half of it.

Didn't know what he was truly capable of. What his father had trained him for.

And what it had all led to seven years ago during the fire that had taken Benito's and Carlo's lives.

That was when he discovered that he truly was the man his father had set out to make him. That was when he'd discovered just how deep the chill went.

He was cold all the way down. And it was only control that held it all in check.

There was only one place he had heat. Only one way he could get warm. But it was a fine line, because he needed the cold. Needed his control, even with it…even with it he was capable of things most men would never entertain thoughts of. But without it he knew the monster would truly be unleashed. That it would consume him.

"I know what I'd like to show you," he said, taking a step toward her, putting his hand on her cheek. She warmed his palm. The heat, the life, that came from her, pouring into him. She shivered beneath his hand, as though his touch had frozen her, and he found it oddly appropriate.

If he kissed her, if he moved nearer to her now, he was making the choice to drag her into the darkness with him. To take what he wanted and use her to his own selfish ends.

He could walk away from her now and he could do the right thing. Protect her, protect their child. Give them both his name and a home, his money. Everything they would need.

She didn't need him in his bed, taking his pleasure in her body, using her to feel warm.

To court the fire and passion that could burn down every last shred of his control. It would be a tightrope walk. Trying to keep the lusts of his body from turning into a desire that overwhelmed his heart.

If he wanted Alessia, there was no other choice.

It was easy with her, to focus on his body. What he wanted from her. Because she called to him, reached him, made him burn in a way no other woman ever had.

With her, though, there was always something else. Something more.

He shut it down. Severed the link. Focused on his body. The burn in his chest, his gut. Everywhere. He was so hard it hurt. Hard with the need for her. To be in her. To taste her.

He could embrace that, and that only. And consign her to a life with a man who would never give her what she deserved.

In this case, he would embrace the coldness in him. Only an utter bastard would do this to her. So it was a good thing that was what he was.

He bent his head and pressed his lips to hers. It wasn't a deep kiss, it was a test. A test for him. To see if he could touch her without losing his mind.

She was soft. So soft. So alive. A taste of pure beauty in a world so filled with ugliness and filth. She reached into him and shone a light on him. On the darkest places in him.

No. He could not allow that. This was only about sex. Only about lust.

"Only me," she said when they parted.

"What?"

"You either have only me, or every other woman you might want, but before you kiss me again, Matteo, you have to make that decision."

His lips still tasted of her skin. "You." It was an easy answer, he found.

She put her hands on his face and drew up on her tiptoes. Her kiss was deep. Filled with the need and passion that echoed inside of his body. He wrapped his arm around her waist and relished every lush detail of holding her. Her soft curves, those generous breasts pressed against his chest. He slipped his hand over her bottom, squeezed her tightly. She was everything a woman should be. Total perfection.

She kissed his jaw, her lips light on his skin, hot and so very tempting. She made him want more, stripped him of his patience. He had always been a patient lover, the kind of lover who worked to ensure his partner's pleasure before taking his own. Because he could. Because even if he took pleasure with his body, his actions were dictated by his mind.

But she challenged that. Made him want so badly to lose himself. To think of nothing but her. Alessia. He was hungry for her in a way he had never hungered for anyone or anything.

He slid his hands over the bodice of her nightgown, cupped her breasts through the thin fabric and found she had nothing on underneath. He could feel her nipples, hard and scarcely veiled by the gauzy material.

He lowered his head and circled one of the tightened buds with his tongue, drew it deep into his mouth. It wasn't enough. He needed to taste her.

Her name pounded through his head in time with the beat of his heart. His need a living, breathing thing.

He gripped the straps of her gown and tugged hard, the top giving way. It fell around her waist, exposing her to him. He smoothed his hand over her bare skin, then lowered his head again, tasting her, filling himself with her.

He dropped to his knees and took the fabric in his hands, tugging it down the rest of the way, ignoring the sound of tearing fabric.

"I liked that nightgown," she said.

"It was beautiful." He kissed her stomach. "But it was not as beautiful as you are."

"You could have asked me to take it off."

"No time," he said, tracing a line from her belly button down to the edge of her panties. "I needed to taste you."

Her response was a strangled "Oh."

"Everywhere." He tugged at the sides of her underwear and drew them down her legs, tossing them to the side. He kissed her hip bone and she shuddered. "I think you should lay down for me, *cara*."

"Why is that?"

"All the better to taste you, *cara mia*."

"Can't you do it from where you are?"

"Not the way I want to."

She complied, her movements slow, shaky. It was a sharp reminder of how innocent she still was.

You let me hold on to some of my innocence.

Her words echoed in his mind as she sank to the ground in front of him, lying back, resting on her elbows, her legs bent at the knees.

No, he would not allow himself to be painted as some kind of hero. He might have saved her innocence then, but he had spent the past months ensuring that what remained was stripped from her. And tonight, he would continue it.

Keeping her bound to him would continue it.

It was too late to turn back now. Too late to stop. He put his hand on her thigh and parted her legs gently, sliding his fingers over the slickness at the entrance of her body. "Yes," he said, unable to hold the word back, a tremor of need racking his body.

He lowered his head to take in her sweetness, to try to satiate the need he felt for her. A need that seemed to flow through his veins along with his blood, until he couldn't tell which one was sustaining him. Until he was sure he needed both to continue breathing.

He was lost in Alessia. Her flavor, her scent.

He pushed one finger deep inside her while he continued to lavish attention on her with his lips and tongue. She arched up against him, a raw cry escaping her lips. And he took it as her approval, making his strokes with mouth and hands firmer, more insistent.

She drove her fingers deep into his hair, tugging hard, the pain giving him the slight distraction he needed to continue. Helping him hold back his own need.

He slipped a second finger inside of her and her muscles pulsed around him, her body getting stiff beneath him, her sound of completion loud, desperate. Satisfying to him on a level so deep he didn't want to examine it too closely.

He didn't have time to examine it because now he needed her. Needed his own release, a ferocity that had him shaking. He rose up, pausing to kiss her breasts again, before taking possession of her mouth.

He sat up and tugged his shirt over his head, shrugging his slacks down as quickly as possible, freeing his aching erection.

"Are you ready?" he asked. He needed the answer to be yes.

"Yes."

He looked at her face, at Alessia, and as he did, he pushed inside the tight heat of her body. He nearly lost it then, a cold sweat breaking out over his skin, his muscles tense, pain coursing through him, everything in him trying to hold back. To make this last.

"Matteo."

It was her voice that broke him. Her name on his lips. He started to thrust hard into her, and no matter how he told himself to take it slow, take it gentle, he couldn't. He was a slave to her, to his need.

Finesse was lost. Control was lost.

She arched against him every time he slid home, a small sigh of pleasure on her lips. He lowered his head, buried his face in her neck, breathing her in. Lilacs and skin. And the one woman he would always know. The one woman who mattered.

Sharp nails dug into the flesh on his shoulder, but this time, the pain didn't bring him back. He lost himself, let his orgasm take him over, a rush of completion that took him under completely. He was lost in a wave, and burning. Burning hot and bright, nothing coming to put him out. To give him any relief. All he could do was hang on and weather it. Try to survive a pleasure so intense it bordered on destructive.

And when it was over, she was there, soft arms wrapped around him, her scent surrounding him.

"Will it always be like this?" Alessia's voice was broken with sharp, hard breaths.

He didn't have an answer for her. He couldn't speak. Couldn't think. And he hoped to God it wouldn't always be like this because there was no way his control could withstand it. And at the same time he knew he couldn't live with her and deny himself her body.

He would keep it under control. He would keep his heart separate from his body. He'd done it with women all his life. He'd done it when his father had asked him to learn the family business. The night his father had forced him to dole out punishment to a man in debt to the Corretti family.

He had locked his heart in ice and kept himself from feeling. His actions unconnected to anything but his mind.

He could do it again. He would.

"We should go inside," he said, sitting up, his breathing still ragged.

"Yeah. I'm pretty sure I have grass stains in… places."

He turned to her, a shocked laugh bursting from him. A real laugh. He couldn't remember the last time he'd laughed and meant it. "Well, you should be glad I made quick work of your gown, then."

"You tore it," she said, moving into a standing position and picking up her shredded garment.

"You liked it."

He could see her smile, even in the dim light. "A little."

There was a strange lightness in his chest now,

a feeling that was completely foreign to him. As though a rock had been taken off his shoulders.

"I'm hungry," she said.

She started walking back toward the house, and he kept his eyes trained on her bare backside, on the twin dimples low on her back. She was so sexy he was hard again already.

He bent and picked his underwear up from the ground, tugging the black boxer briefs on quickly and following her inside. "Do you want to eat?" he asked.

"Yes, I do." She wandered through the maze of rooms, still naked, and he followed.

"And what would you like?"

"Pasta. Have you got an apron?"

"Have I got an apron?"

"You have a cook, yes?"

"Yes."

"Does he have an apron?"

"She." He opened the pantry door and pulled a short red apron off a hook.

Alessia smiled and slipped the apron over her head, tying it tight. She was a lot taller than the little round woman he'd hired to cook his meals. The apron came down just to the tops of her thighs and it tied in the back, exposing her body to him from that angle.

"Dinner and a show," he said.

She tossed him a playful glare, then started

riffling through the cabinets. "What kind of pasta have you got?"

"Fresh in the fridge," he said.

She opened up the stainless-steel fridge and bent down, searching for a few moments before popping up with a container that held pappardelle pasta and another that had marinara sauce.

She put a pan of water on the stove, then put the sauce in another pan to reheat, and leaned back against the counter, her arms crossed beneath her breasts.

"Didn't you ever hear that a watched pot never boils?"

"No. Who says that?"

"People do," he said.

"Did your mom say it to you?"

"No. A cook we had, I think."

"Oh. It's the kind of thing my mother probably would have said to me someday. If she had lived."

"You miss her still."

"I always will. But you lost your father."

Guilt, ugly, strangling guilt, tightened in his chest. "Yes."

"So you understand."

He shook his head slowly. "I'm not sure I do."

"You don't miss him?"

"Never."

"I know your father was hard to deal with. I

know he was…I know he was shady like my father but surely you must—"

"No," he said.

"Oh."

"Will you miss your father?"

"I think so. He's not a wonderful man, but he's the only father I have."

"I would have been better off without one than the one that I had."

Alessia moved to put the pasta into the pan. "You say that with a lot of certainty."

"Trust me on this, Alessia."

They stood in silence until the pasta was done. Matteo got bowls out of the cupboard and set them on the counter and Alessia dished them both a bowl of noodles and sauce.

"Nothing like a little post…you know, snack," she said, lifting her bowl to her lips, her eyes glued to his chest. "You're barely dressed."

"You should talk," he said.

She looked down. "I'm dressed."

"Turn around." She complied, flashing her bare butt to him. "That's not dressed, my darling wife."

"Are you issuing a formal complaint?"

"Not in the least. I prefer you this way."

"Well, the apron is practical. Don't go tearing it off me if you get all impatient." She took a bit of pasta and smiled, her grin slightly impish. It made it hard to breathe.

There was something so normal about this. But it wasn't a kind of normal he knew. Not the kind he'd ever known. He wasn't the sort of man who walked barefoot in the grass and then ate pasta at midnight in his underwear.

He'd never had a chance to be that man. He wondered again at what it would be like if all the things of the world could simply fall away.

"Matteo?"

"Yes?"

"I lost you for a second. Where were you?"

"Just thinking."

"Mmm." She nodded. "I'm tempted to ask you what about but I sort of doubt you'd want to tell me."

"About my father," he said, before he could stop himself.

"You really don't miss him?"

"No." A wall of flame filled his mind. An image of the warehouse, burning. "Never."

"My father has mainly ignored my existence. The only time he's ever really acknowledged me is if he needs something, or if he's angry."

Rage churned in Matteo's stomach. "Did he hit you?"

"Yes. Not beatings or anything, but if I said

something that displeased him, he would slap my face."

"He should feel very fortunate he never did so in front of me."

Alessia was surprised at the sudden change in Matteo's demeanor. At the ice in his tone. For a moment, they'd actually been getting along. For a moment, they'd been connecting with clothes on, and that was a rarity for the two of them.

He was willing to try. He'd told her that. And he would be faithful. Those were the only two promises she required from him. Beyond that, she was willing to take her chances.

Willing to try to know the man she'd married. Past her fantasy of him as a hero, as her white knight, and as the man he truly was. No matter what that might mean.

"I handled it," she said.

"It was wrong of him."

She nodded. "I know. But I was able to keep him from ever hitting one of the other kids and that just reinforced why I was there. Yes, I bore the brunt of a lot of it. I had to plan parties and play hostess, I had to take the wrath. But I've been given praise, too."

"I was given praise by my father sometimes, too," Matteo said. There was a flatness to his tone, a darkness in his words that made her feel cold. "He spent some time, when I was a bit older, teaching me how to do business like a Corretti. Not the business we presented to the world. The clean, smooth front. Hotels, fashion houses. All of that was a cover then. A successful cover in its own right, but it wasn't the main source of industry for our family."

"I think…I mean, I think everyone knows that."

"Yes, I'm sure they do. But do you have any idea how far-reaching it was? How much power my father possessed? How he chose to exercise it?"

She shook her head, a sick weight settling in her stomach. "What did he do, Matteo? What did he do to you?"

"To me? Nothing. In the sense that he never physically harmed me."

"There are other kinds of harm."

"Remember I told you I wasn't a criminal? That's on a technicality. It's only because I was never convicted of my crimes."

"What did he do to you, Matteo?" Her stomach felt sick now, and she pushed her bowl of food across the counter, making her way to where Matteo was standing.

"When I was fifteen he started showing me the ropes. The way things worked. He took me on collection calls. We went to visit people who owed him money. Now, my father was only ever involved on the calls where people owed him a lot of money. People who were in serious trouble with him. Otherwise, his men, his hired thugs, paid the visits."

"And he took you on these…visits?"

Matteo nodded, his arms crossed over his bare chest. There was a blankness in his eyes that hurt, a total detachment that froze her inside.

"For the first few weeks I just got to watch. One quick hit to the legs. A warning. A bone-breaking warning, but much better than the kind of thing he and his thugs were willing to do."

"*Dio.* You should never have… He should never have let you see…" She stopped talking then, because she knew there was more. And that it was worse. She could feel the anxiety coming off him in waves.

She took a step toward him, put her hand on his forearm. It was damp with sweat, his muscles shaking beneath her touch.

"One night he asked me to do it," he said.

His words were heavy in the room, heavy on her. They settled over her skin, coating her, making her feel what he felt. Dirty. Ashamed. She didn't know how she was so certain that was what he felt, but she was.

"What happened?" She tried to keep her voice steady, tried to sound ready to hear it. Tried to be ready to hear it. Because he needed to say it without fear of recrimination from her. Without fear of being told there was something wrong with him.

She knew that as deeply, as innately, as she knew his other feelings.

"I did it," he said. "My father asked me to break a man's legs because he owed the family money. And I did."

CHAPTER TEN

MATTEO WAITED FOR the horror of his admission to sink in. Waited for Alessia to turn from him, to run away in utter terror and disgust. She should. He wouldn't blame her.

He also desperately wanted her to stay.

"Matteo…"

"These hands," he said, holding them out, palms up, "that have touched you, have been used in ways that a man should never use his hands."

"But you aren't like that."

He shook his head. "Clearly I am."

"But you didn't enjoy it."

"No. I didn't enjoy it." He could remember very vividly how it had felt, how the sweat had broken out on his skin. How he had vomited after. His father's men had found that terribly amusing. "But I did it."

"What would your father have done to you if you hadn't?"

He shook his head. "It doesn't matter."

"Yes, it does, Matteo, you were a boy."

"I was a boy, but I was old enough to know that what my father did, what he was, was wrong."

"And you were trapped in it."

"Maybe. And maybe that would be an acceptable excuse for some people, but it's not for me."

"Why not? You were a boy and he abused you. Tell me, and be honest, what did he say he would do to you if you didn't do it?"

Matteo was afraid for one moment that his stomach might rebel against him. "He told me if I couldn't do it to a grown man, there were some children in the village I might practice on."

Alessia's face contorted with utter horror. "Would he have done that?"

"I don't know. But I wasn't going to find out, either."

"He made you do it."

"He manipulated me into doing it, but I did it."

"How?" she asked, her voice a whisper.

"It's easy to do things, anything, when you can shut the emotion down inside yourself. I learned to do that. I learned that there was a place inside of myself as cold as any part of my father's soul. If I went there, it wasn't so hard to do." It was only after that he had broken. In the end, it was both the brokenness, and the cold, that had saved him.

His father had decided he wasn't ready. Didn't want his oldest son, the one poised to take over his empire, undermining his position by showing such weakness.

And after, the way he'd dealt with the knowledge that he'd lived with a monster, the way he'd dealt with knowing that he was capable of the very same atrocities, was to freeze out every emotion. He would not allow himself to want, to crave power or money in the way his father did. Passion, need, greed, were the enemy.

Then he'd seen Alessia. And he had allowed her a place inside him, a place that was warm and bright, one that he could retreat to. He saw happiness through her eyes when he watched her. His attraction to her not physical, but emotional. He let a part of himself live through her.

And that day when he'd seen those men attacking her, the monster inside him had met up against passion that had still existed in the depths of him, and had combined to create a violence that was beyond his control. One that frightened him much more than that moment of controlled violence in his father's presence had.

More even than that final act, the one that had removed his father from his life forever.

Because it had been a choice he'd made. It had been fueled by his emotion, by his rage, and no matter how deserving those men had been...it was what it said about himself that made him even more certain that it must never happen again. That he must never be allowed to feel like that.

"Do you see?" he asked. "Do you see what kind of man I am?"

She nodded slowly. "Yes. You're a good man, with a tragic past. And the things that happened weren't your fault."

"When I went back home the day of your attack, there was still blood all over me. I walked in, and my father was there. He looked at me, saw the evidence of what had happened. Then he smiled, and he laughed," Matteo spat. "And he said to me, 'Looks like you're ready now. I always knew you were my son.'"

That moment was burned into his brain, etched into his chest. Standing there, shell-shocked by what had happened, by what he had done. By what had nearly happened to Alessia. And having his father act as though he'd made some sort of grand passage into manhood. Having him be proud.

"He was wrong, Matteo, you aren't like him. You were protecting me, you weren't trying to extort money out of those men. It's not the same thing."

"But it's the evidence of what I'm capable of. My father had absolute conviction in what he did. He could justify it. He believed he was right, Alessia, do you understand that? He believed with conviction that he had a right to this money, that he had the right to harm those who didn't pay what he felt he was owed. All it takes is a twist of a man's convictions."

"But yours wouldn't be..."

"They wouldn't be?" He almost told her then, but he couldn't. The words he could never say out loud. The memory he barely allowed himself to have. "You honestly believe that? Everyone is corruptible, *cara*. The only way around it is to use your head, to learn what is right, and to never ever let your desire change wrong to right in your mind. Because that's what desire does. My father's desire for money, your father's desire for power, made them men who will do whatever it takes to have those things. Regardless of who they hurt. And I will never be that man."

"You aren't that man. You acted to save me, and you did it without thought to your own safety. Can't you see how good that is? How important?"

"I don't regret what I did," he said, choosing his words carefully. "I had a good reason to do it. But how many more good reasons could I find? If it suited me, if I was so immersed in my own needs, in my own desires, what else might I consider a good reason? So easily, Alessia, I could be like Benito was."

"No, that isn't true."

"Why do you think that?"

"Because you're...good."

He laughed. "You are so certain?"

"Yes. Yes, Matteo, I'm certain you're good. Do you know what I remember from that day? The way you held me after. Do you know how long it had been since someone had tried to comfort me? Since someone had wiped away my tears? Not since my mother. Before that, I had done all of the comforting, and then when I needed someone? You were there. And you told me it would be okay. More than that, you made it okay. So don't tell me you aren't good. You are."

He didn't believe her, because she didn't know the whole truth. But he wanted to hold her words tightly inside of him, wanted to cling to her vision of him, didn't want her to see him any other way.

"I got blood on your face," he said, his voice rough. "That day when I wiped your tears."

She looked at him with those dark, beautiful eyes. "It was worth it." She took a step toward him, taking his hand in hers. "Come on. Let's go to bed."

And he was powerless to do anything but follow her.

* * *

Alessia woke the next morning with a bone-deep feeling of contentment. She noticed because she'd never felt anything like it before. Had never felt like things were simply right in the world. That there wasn't anything big left to accomplish. That she just wanted to stay and live in the moment. A moment made sweeter by the fact that there was nothing pressing or horrible looming in the future.

Then she became conscious of a solid, warm weight at her back, a hand resting on her bare hip. And she was naked, which was unusual because she normally slept in a nightgown.

A nightgown that was torn.

A smile stretched across her face and she rolled over to face Matteo. Her lover. Her husband. He was still sleeping, the lines on his forehead smoothed, his expression much more relaxed than it ever was when he was awake.

She leaned over and kissed his cheek, the edge of his mouth. She wanted him again. It didn't matter how many times he'd turned to her in the middle of the night, she wanted him again. It didn't matter if they had sex, or if he just touched her, but she wanted him. His presence, his kiss, him breathing near her.

This moment was one she'd dreamed of for

half of her life. This moment with Matteo Corretti. Not with any other man.

She'd woken up next to him once before, but she hadn't been able to savor it. Her wedding had been looming in the not-too-distant future and guilt and fear had had her running out the door before Matteo had woken up.

But not this morning. This morning, she would stay with him until he woke. And maybe she would share his bed again tonight. And every night after that. He was her husband, after all, and it only seemed right that they sleep together.

They were going to try to make a real marriage out of a legal one.

He'll never love you.

She ignored the chill that spread through her veins when that thought invaded her mind. It didn't matter. She wouldn't dwell on it. Right now, she had a hope at a future she could be happy with. Matteo in her bed. In her life.

And she was having his baby. At some point, that would sink in and not just be a vague, sort of frightening, sort of wonderful thought.

But right now, she was simply lingering in the moment. Not wondering if Matteo's feelings would ever change, not worrying about changing diapers.

He shifted then, his eyes fluttering open.

"Good morning," he said. So much different than his greeting the morning after their wedding.

"Good morning, handsome."

"Handsome?"

"You are. And I've always wanted to say that." *To you.*

"Alessia…you are something."

"I know, right?" Matteo rolled over onto his back and she followed him, resting her breasts on his chest, her chin propped up on her hands. "Last night was wonderful."

He looked slightly uncomfortable. Well, she imagined she wasn't playing the part of blasé sophisticate very well, but in her defense…she wasn't one. She was a women with very little sexual experience having the time of her life with a man who'd spent years as the star attraction in her fantasies. It was sort of hard to be cool in those circumstances.

He kissed her, cupping her chin with his thumb and forefinger. She closed her eyes and hummed low in her throat. "You're so good at that," she said when they parted. "I feel like I have a post-orgasm buzz. Is that a thing?"

He rolled onto his side again and moved into a sitting position, not bothering to cover himself with the blankets.

"I don't know," he said. "I can't say I've ever experienced it."

"Oh." That hurt more than it should have. Not because she wanted him to have experienced post-orgasm buzz with anyone else, but because she wished he'd experienced it with her.

"What is it, *cara*?"

"Nothing." She put her palm flat on his chest and leaned in, her lips a whisper from his. Then his phone started vibrating on the nightstand.

"I have to take that," he said, moving away from her. He turned away from her and picked it up. "Corretti." Every muscle in his back went rigid. "What the hell do you want, Alessandro?"

Alessia's stomach rolled. Alessandro. She would rather not think about him right at the moment. She felt bad for the way things had ended. He'd been nice enough to her, distant, and there had been no attraction, but he'd been decent. And she'd sort of waited until the last minute to change her mind.

She got out of bed and started hunting for some clothes. There was nothing. Only a discarded red apron that she knew from last night didn't cover a whole lot.

"I'm busy, you can't just call a meeting and expect me to drop everything and come to you like a lapdog. Maybe you're used to your family treating you that way, but you don't get that deference from me."

Alessia picked the apron up and put it on. It was better than nothing.

Matteo stood from the bed, completely naked, pacing the room. She stood for a moment and just watched. The play of his muscles beneath sleek, olive skin was about the sexiest thing she'd ever seen.

"Angelo?" The name came out like a curse. "What are you doing meeting with that bastard?" A pause. "It was a commentary on his character, not his birth. Fine. Noon. Salvatore's."

He pushed the end-call button and tossed the phone down on the bed, continuing to prowl the room. "That was Alessandro."

"I got that."

"He wants me to come to a meeting at our grandfather's. With Angelo, of all people."

"He is your cousin. He's family, and so is Alessandro."

"I have enough family that I don't like. Why would I add any more?"

"You don't even like your brothers?"

"No."

"Why don't you like your brothers?"

"Because if I ever do seem to be in danger of being sucked into the Corretti mind-set it's when we start playing stupid business games."

"But they're your family."

"My family is a joke. We're nothing but criminals and selfish assholes who would sell each other out for the right price. And we've all done it."

"So maybe someone needs to stop," she said, her voice soft.

"I don't know if we can."

"Maybe you should be the first one?"

"Alessia…"

"Look, I know I'm not a business mind, and I know I don't understand the dynamics of your family, but if you hate this part of it so much, then end it."

"I need to get dressed."

"I'll go make breakfast," she said. "I'm dressed for it."

"You might give my staff a shock."

"Oh—" her cheeks heated "—right, on second thought I might go back to my room."

"That's fine. And after that, you can ask Giancarlo if he would have your things moved into the master suite."

"You want me to move in?"

"Yes. You tramping back to your room in an apron is going to get inconvenient quickly, don't you think?"

Alessia felt her little glow of hope grow. "Yeah. Definitely it would be a little bit inconvenient. I would love to move into your room."

"Good." He leaned in and dropped a kiss on her lips. "Now, I have to get ready."

When Salvatore had been alive, Matteo had avoided going to his grandparents' home as often as he could. The old man was a manipulator and Matteo was rarely in the mood for his kind of mind games.

Still, whenever his grandmother had needed him, he had been there. They all had. This had long been neutral ground for that very reason. For Teresa. Which made it a fitting setting for what they were doing today.

Matteo walked over the threshold and was ushered back toward the study. He didn't see his grandmother, or any of the staff. Only a hostile-looking Alessandro, and Angelo sitting in a chair, a drink in hand.

"What was so important that you needed to speak to me?"

"Sorry to interrupt the blissful honeymoon stage with your new bride. I assume she actually went through with your wedding," Alessandro said.

"She did," he said.

Angelo leaned back in one of the high-backed chairs, scanning the room. "So this is what old Corretti money buys. I think I prefer my homes."

"We all prefer not to be here," Matteo said. "Which begs the question again, why are we?"

"You married Alessia, I can only assume that means you've cut a deal with her father?"

"Trade in and out of Sicily is secured for the Correttis and the docklands are ours. The revitalization project is set to move forward."

"Handy," Angelo said, leaning forward, "because I secured a deal with Battaglia, as well." Angelo explained the details of the housing development he was working on, eased by Battaglia's connections.

"And what does that have to do with us?"

"Well," Angelo continued, "it can have a lot to do with you. Assuming you want to take steps to unify the company."

"We need to unify," Alessandro said, his tone uncompromising. "Otherwise, we'll just spend the next forty years tearing everything apart. Like our fathers did."

Matteo laughed, a black, humorless sound. "You are my cousin, Alessandro, but I have no desire to die in a warehouse fire with you."

"That's why this has to end," Alessandro said. "I have a proposal to make. One that will see everyone in the family with an equal share of power. It will put us in the position to make the company, the family, strong again. Without stooping to criminal activity to accomplish it."

Alessandro outlined his plan. It would involve everyone, including their sisters, giving everyone equal share in the company and unifying both sides for the first time.

"This will work as long as this jackass is willing to put some of the extra shares he's acquired back into the pot," Alessandro said, indicating Angelo.

"I said I would," Angelo responded, his acquiescence surprising. Equally surprising was the lack of venom and anger coming from the other man. Or maybe not. Matteo had to wonder if Angelo had met a woman. He knew just the kind of change a woman could effect on a man.

"There you are," Alessandro said. "Are you with us?"

Matteo thought of the fire. Of the last time he'd seen his father. Of all that greed had cost. This was his chance to put an end to that. To start fresh. The past could never be erased, it would always be there. But the future could be new. For him. For Alessia. For their child.

He had too many other things in his life, good things, to waste any effort holding on to hatred he didn't even have the energy to feel.

He extended his hand and Alessandro took it, shaking it firmly. Then Matteo extended his hand to Angelo and, for the first time, shook his hand. "I guess that means you're one of us now," he said to Angelo. "I don't know if you should be happy about that or not."

"I'll let you know," Angelo said. "But so far, it doesn't seem so bad."

"All right, where do I sign?"

CHAPTER ELEVEN

MATTEO WAS EXHAUSTED by the time he got around to driving back to his palazzo. Dealing with Alessandro, going to his grandfather's house, had been draining in a way he had not anticipated. And yet, in some ways, there was a weight lifted. The promise of a future that held peace instead of violence. The first time his future had ever looked that way.

And he had Alessia to go home to. That thought sent a kick of adrenaline through him, made him feel like there was warmth in his chest. Made him feel like he wasn't so cold.

He left the car parked in front of his house with the keys in the ignition. One of his staff would park it for him later. And if not, he didn't mind it being there in the morning. But he couldn't put off seeing Alessia, not for another moment. He needed to see her for some reason, needed affirmation of who he was. To see her face light

up. To have someone look at him like they didn't
know who and what he was.

Alessandro and Angelo didn't know about his
past, but they knew enough about the family to
have an idea. Alessandro certainly hadn't escaped a childhood with Carlo without gaining a
few scars of his own.

But Alessia looked at him like none of that
mattered. Like she didn't know or believe any
of it.

That isn't fair. She should know.

No, he didn't want her to know. He wanted to
keep being her knight. To have one person look
and see the man he might have been if it weren't
for Benito Corretti.

He would change what it meant to be a Corretti for his child. He would never let them see
the darkness. Never.

A fierce protectiveness surged through him,
for the first time a true understanding of what it
meant for Alessia to be pregnant.

A child. His child.

He prowled through the halls of the palazzo
and found Alessia in a sitting room, a book in
her hands, her knees drawn up to her chest. She
was wearing a simple sundress that had slid high
up her thighs. He wanted nothing more than to
push it up the rest of the way, but he also found

he didn't want to disturb her. He simply wanted to look.

She raised her focus then, and her entire countenance changed, her face catching the sunlight filtering through the window. Her dark eyes glittered, her smile bright. Had anyone else ever looked at him like that?

He didn't think they had.

"How did the meeting go?"

"We called each other names. Insulted each other's honor and then shook hands. So about as expected."

She laughed. "Good, I guess."

"Yes. We've come up with a way to divide Corretti Enterprises up evenly. A way for everyone to get their share. It's in everyone's best interests, really. Especially the generation that comes after us. Which I now have a vested interest in."

She smiled, the dimple on her left cheek deepening. "I suppose you do. And...I'm glad you do."

He moved to sit on the couch, at her feet, then he leaned in. "Can you feel the baby move yet?"

She shook her head. "No. The doctor said it will feel like a flutter, though."

"May I?" he asked, stretching his hand out, just over the small, rounded swell of her stomach.

"Of course."

He swallowed hard and placed his palm flat on her belly. It was the smallest little bump, but it was different than it had been. Evidence of the life that was growing inside her. A life they'd created.

She was going to be the mother of his child. She deserved to know. To really understand him. Not to simply look at him and see an illusion. He'd given her a taste of it earlier, but his need for that look, that one she reserved just for him, that look he only got from her, had prevented him from being honest. Had made him hold back the most essential piece of just why he was not the man to be her husband.

The depth to which he was capable of stooping.

Because no matter how bright the future had become, the past was still filled with shadows. And until they were brought into the sunlight, their power would remain.

"There is something else," he said, taking his hand from her stomach, curling it into a fist. His skin burned.

"About the meeting?"

"No," he said. "Not about the meeting."

"What about?"

"About me. About why…about why it might not be the best idea for you to try to make a marriage with me. About the limit of what I can give."

"Matteo, I already told you how I feel about what happened with your father."

"By that you mean when he took me on errands?"

"Well…yes."

"So, you don't mean what happened the night of the warehouse fire that killed him and Carlo."

"No. No one knows what happened that night."

"That isn't true," he said, the words scraping his throat raw. "Someone knows."

"Who?" she asked, but he could tell she already knew.

"I know."

"How?"

"Because, *cara mia*. I was there."

"You were there?"

He nodded slowly. Visions of fire filled his mind. Fire and brimstone, such an appropriate vision. "Yes. I was there to try to convince my father to turn over the holdings of Corretti to me entirely. I wanted to change things. To end the extortion and scams. All of it. But he wouldn't hear it. You see, at the time, he was still running criminal schemes, using the hotels, which I was managing, to help launder money. To help get counterfeit bills into circulation, into the right hands. Or wrong hands as the case may have been. I didn't want any part of it, but as long as my father was involved in the running of the corporation, that was never going to end. I wanted out."

"Oh," Alessia said, the word a whisper, as if she knew what was coming next. He didn't want her to guess at it, because he wanted, perversely, for her to believe it impossible. For her to cling to the white-knight image and turn away from the truth he was about to show her.

"I don't know how the fire started. But the warehouse was filled with counterfeiting plates, and their printing presses. That's one way to make money, right? Print your own."

He looked down at his hands, his heart pounding hard, his stomach so tight he could hardly breathe. "The fire spread quickly. I don't know where Carlo was when it broke out. But I was outside arguing with my father. And he turned and…and he looked at the blaze and he started to walk toward it."

Matteo closed his eyes, the impression of flames burning bright behind his eyelids. "I told him if he went back into that damned warehouse to rescue those plates, I would leave him to it. I told him to let it burn. To let us start over. I told him that if he went back, I would be happy to let him burn with it all, and then let him continue to burn in hell."

"Matteo...no." She shook her head, those dark eyes glistening with tears. She looked horrified. Utterly. Completely. The light was gone. His light.

"Yes," he said, his voice rough. "Can you guess what he did?"

"What?" The word was scarcely a whisper.

"He laughed. And he said, 'Just as I thought, you are my son.' He told me that no matter how I dressed it up, no matter how I pretended I had morals, I was just as bloodthirsty as he was. Just as hungry for vengeance and to have what I thought should be mine, in the fashion I saw fit. And then he walked back into the warehouse."

"What did you do?"

Matteo remembered the moment vividly. Remembered waiting for a minute, watching, letting his father's words sink in. Recognizing the truth of them. And embracing them fully. He was his father's son. And if he, or anyone else, stood a chance of ever breaking free, it had to end.

The front end of the warehouse had collapsed and Matteo had stood back, looking on, his hand curled around his phone. He could have called emergency services. He could have tried to save Benito.

But he hadn't. Instead, he'd turned his back, the heat blistering behind him, a spark falling onto his neck, singeing his flesh. And then he'd walked away. And he hadn't looked back, not once. And in that moment he was the full embodiment of everything his father had trained him to be.

He'd found out about Carlo's and Benito's deaths over the phone the next day. And there had been no more denial, no more hiding. No more believing that somewhere deep down he was good. That he had a hope of redemption.

He had let it burn in the warehouse.

"I let him die," he said. "I watched him go in, watched as the front end of the building collapsed. I could have called someone, and I didn't. I made the choice to be the man he always wanted me to be. The man I always was. I turned and I walked away. I did just as I promised I would do. I let him burn, with all of his damned money. And I can't regret the choice. He made his, I made mine. And everyone is free of him now. Of both of them."

Alessia was waxen, her skin pale, her lips tinged blue. "I don't know what to say."

"Do you see, Alessia? This is what I was trying to tell you. What you need to understand." He leaned forward, extending his hand to her, and she jerked back. Her withdrawal felt like a stab to the chest, but it was no less than he deserved. "I'm not the hero of the story. I am nothing less than the villain."

She understood now, he could see it, along with a dawning horror in her eyes that he wanted to turn away from. She was afraid. Afraid of him. He wasn't her knight anymore.

"I think maybe I should wait a few days to have my things moved into your room," she said after a long moment of silence.

He nodded. "That might be wise." Pain assaulted him and he tried to ignore it, tried to grit his teeth and sit with a neutral expression.

"I'll talk to you later?"

"Of course." He sat back on the couch and watched her leave. Then he closed his eyes and tried to picture her smile again. Tried to recapture the way she'd looked at him just a few moments before. But instead of her light, all he could see was a haunted expression, one he had put there.

Alessia was gasping for breath by the time she got to her bedroom. She closed the door behind her and put her hand on her chest, felt her heart hammering beneath her palm.

Matteo had let Benito and Carlo die.

She sucked in a shuddering breath and started pacing back and forth, fighting the tears that were threatening to spill down her cheeks.

She replayed what he had said again in her mind. He hadn't forced Benito or Carlo back into the burning building. Hadn't caused them harm with his own hands.

He had walked away. He had washed his hands and walked away, accepting in that moment whatever the consequences might be.

Alessia walked over to her bed and sat on the edge of it. And she tried to reconcile the man downstairs with the man she'd always believed him to be.

The man beneath the armor wasn't perfect. He was wounded, damaged beyond reason. Hurting. And for the first time she really understood what that meant. Understood how shut down he was. How much it would take to reach him.

And she wasn't sure if she could do it. Wasn't sure she had the strength to do it.

It had been so much easier when he was simply the fantasy. When he was the man she'd made him be in her mind. When he was an ideal, a man sent to ride to her rescue.

She'd put him in that position. From the moment she'd first seen him. Then after he had rescued her, she'd assigned him that place even more so.

The night of her bachelorette party…

"Damn you, Alessia," she said to herself.

Because she'd done it then, too. She'd used Matteo as part of her fantasy, as part of the little world she'd built up in her mind to keep herself from crumbling. She had taken him on her own terms, used him to fill a void, and never once had she truly looked into his. Never once had she truly tried to fill it.

Being there for Matteo, knowing him, meant knowing this. Meant knowing that he had faced down a terrible decision, and that he had made a terrible choice.

The wrong choice, at least in traditional terms of right and wrong.

Very few people would hold it against him that he hadn't raced into the burning building after his father, but to know that he had also not called for help. That he had meant what he'd said to his father. That he would let him, and all of it, burn. In flame. In greed. And he had.

Her lover, her Matteo, had a core of ice and steel. Getting through it, finding his heart, might be impossible. She faced that, truly faced it, for the first time.

Matteo might never love. The ending might not really be happy. The truth was, she lived her life in denial. The pursuit of contentment at least, at all costs, and if that required denial, then she employed it, and she'd always done it quite effectively.

Walking down the aisle toward Alessandro had been the first time she'd truly realized that if she didn't do something, if she didn't stop it, it wouldn't stop itself.

She wrapped her arms around herself, cold driving through her. She had another choice to make. A choice about Matteo. And she wouldn't make it lightly.

There was no sugarcoating this. No putting on blinders. It was what the wives of these Corretti men, of the Battaglia men, had always done. Looked the other way while their husbands sank into destruction and depravity, but she wouldn't do that.

If she was going to be Matteo's wife, in every sense, then she would face it all head-on.

It was empty to make a commitment to someone if you were pretending they were someone they weren't. It was empty to say you loved someone if you only loved a mirage.

Love. She had been afraid of that word in connection to Matteo for so long, and yet, she knew that was what it was. What it had always been. At least, she'd loved what she'd known about him.

Now she knew more. Now she was going to have to figure out whether she loved the idea, or the man.

Matteo lay in bed. It was past midnight. Hours since he'd last seen Alessia. Hours since they'd spoken.

His body ached, a bleeding wound in his chest where his heart should be. The absence of the heart was nothing new, but the pain was. He had lived in numbness for so long, and Alessia had come back into his life.

Then things had started to change. He'd started to want again. Started to feel again. And now he felt like he was torn open, like the healed, scarred-over, nerveless pieces of himself had been scrubbed raw again. Like he was starting over, starting back at the boy he'd been. The one who had been taken into his father's hands and molded, hard and cruel, into the image the older man had wanted to see.

He felt weak. Vulnerable in a way he could never recall feeling at any point in his life.

Alessia had walked away from him, and he couldn't blame her. In a way, it comforted him. Because at least she hadn't simply blithely walked on in her illusion of who she wanted him to be. She had heard his words. And she'd believed them.

He should be completely grateful for that. Should be happy that she knew. That she wasn't committed to a man who didn't truly exist.

But he couldn't be happy. Selfishly, he wanted her back. Wanted the light and heat and smiles. Wanted one person to look at him and see hope.

"Matteo?"

He looked up and saw Alessia standing in the doorway, her dark hair loose around her shoulders.

"Yes?" He pushed into a sitting position.

"I felt like I owed it to you to really think about what you said."

"And you owed it to you."

She nodded. "I suppose I did."

"And what conclusion have you come to?"

"You aren't the man I thought you were."

The words hit him with the force of a moving truck. "No. I'm sure in all of your fantasies about me you never once dreamed that I was a killer."

She shook her head. "I didn't. I still don't think you're that. I don't think you're perfect, either, but I don't think it was ever terribly fair of me to try to make you perfect. You had your own life apart from me. Your own experiences. My mistake was believing that everything began and ended during the times our eyes met over the garden wall. In my mind, when you held me after the attack, you went somewhere hazy, somewhere I couldn't picture. I didn't think about what you did after, not really. I didn't think of the reality of you returning home, covered in blood. I didn't think about what your father might have said to you. I knew Benito Corretti was a bad man, but for some reason I never imagined how it might have touched you. I only ever pictured you in the context of my world, my dreams and where you fit into them. It was my mistake, not yours."

"But I wouldn't have blamed you if you never imagined that. No one did. Not even my family, I'm certain of that."

"Still, I wasn't looking at you like you were a real person. And you were right to make me see."

"Alessia, if you want—"

"Let me finish. I see now. I see you, Matteo, not just the fantasy I created. And I don't want to walk away. I want to stay with you. I want to make a family with you."

"You trust me to help raise your child after you found out what I'm capable of?"

"That night of your life can't live in isolation. It's connected to the rest of your life, to all of it. To who your father was, the history of what he'd done to other people, to what he'd done to you."

"He never did anything to me, he just—"

"He forced you to do things you would never have done. He made you violate your conscience, over and over again until it was scarred. He would have turned you into a monster."

"He did, Alessia. That's the point. He did."

She shook her head. "You put a stop to it."

"I had to," he said, his voice rough. "I had to because you don't just walk away from the Correttis. It's not possible. My father would not have released his hold."

"I know. I understand."

"And you absolve me?"

"You don't need my absolution."

"But do I have it?" he asked, desperate for it, craving it more than his next breath.

She nodded. "If I have yours."

"For what?"

"For what I did. For not telling you about Alessandro. For agreeing to marry him in the first place. For trapping you in this marriage."

"You didn't trap me."

"You said—"

"Alessia, I have been manipulated into doing things far worse than marrying you, and I have done it with much greater coercion. A little news piece on what a jerk I am for not making your child legitimate was hardly going to force my hand."

"Then why did you do it?"

"To cement the deal. To give our child my name. All things I could have walked away from."

"Then forgive me, at least, for lying to you. For leaving you in the hotel room."

"I do. I was angry about it, but only because it felt so wrong to watch you walking toward him. To know that he would have you and not me. If I had known that there was a deal on the table that could be secured by marriage to you I would have been the one volunteering for the job."

A ghost of a smile touched her lips. "When my father first told me about the deal with the Correttis, that it would be sealed by marriage, I said yes immediately. I was so sure it would be you. And when it was Alessandro who showed up at the door to talk terms the next day I thought…I thought I would die."

"Waiting for your knight to rescue you?"

"Yes. I was. But I've stopped doing that now. I need to learn to rescue myself. To make my own decisions."

"You've certainly been doing that over the past couple of months."

"I have. And some of them have been bad, ill-timed decisions, but they've been mine. And I want you to know that I've made another decision."

"What is that?"

"You're my husband. And I'll take you as you are. Knowing your past, knowing the kind of man you can be. I want you to understand that I'm not sugarcoating it, or glossing over the truth. I understand what you did. I understand that… that you don't feel emotion the same way that I do. The same way most people do."

"Do you really understand that? I keep it on

a leash for a reason, Alessia, a very important reason, and I won't compromise it."

She nodded. "I know."

"And still you want to try? You want to be my wife? To let me have a hand in raising our child?"

"Yes. No matter what, you're the father of my child, Matteo, and there is no revelation that can change that. I don't want to change that."

"How can you say that with such confidence?"

"Because no matter what you might have done, you aren't cruel."

She leaned in and he took a strand of her hair between his thumb and forefinger. Soft like silk. He wanted to feel it brushing over his skin. Wanted to drown out this moment, drown out his pain, with physical pleasure.

"Am I not?" he asked.

"No."

"You're wrong there," he said. "So very wrong. I am selfish, a man who thinks of his own pleasure, his own comfort, above all else. No matter how I pretend otherwise."

"That isn't true."

"Yes, it is. Even now, all I can think about is what your bare skin will feel like beneath my hands. All I want is to lose myself in you."

"Then do it."

His every muscle locked up, so tight it was painful. "Alessia, don't."

"What?"

"Don't sacrifice yourself for me!" he roared. "Don't do this because you feel sorry for me."

"I'm not." She took a step toward him. "I want this because I want to be close to you. To know you. To be your wife in every way." A smile tugged at the corners of her lips. "I'm also not opposed to the orgasms you're so good at giving me. This is by no means unselfish on my part, trust me."

His skin felt like it was burning. Or perhaps that was the blood beneath his skin. Either way he felt like he would be consumed by his need. His desire. Passion he swore he would never allow himself to feel.

Emotion he swore he would never feel.

But in this moment with Alessia, her eyes so bright and intense, so honest, he could hold back nothing. Deny her nothing. Least of all this.

She knew the truth, and still she wanted him. Not as a perfect figure, a knight in shining armor, but as the man he was. It was a gift he didn't deserve, a gift he should turn away, because he had no right to it.

But he had spoken the truth. He was selfish. Far too selfish to do anything but take what was on offer.

"Show me you want me." His words were rough, forced through his tightened throat.

"Show me you still want me." Those words echoed through his soul, tearing through him, leaving him raw and bleeding inside.

Alessia wrapped one arm around his neck, her fingers laced in his hair, and put the other on his cheek. She pressed a kiss to his lips, soft, gentle. Purposeful. "Always."

There was no hope of him being noble, not now, not tonight. But then, that shouldn't be a surprise. He didn't do noble. He didn't do selfless. And it wouldn't start now.

He kissed her, deep and hard, his body throbbing, his heart raging. He wrapped his arms around her and pulled her in close, reveling in the feel of her. Touching Alessia was a thrill that he didn't think would ever become commonplace. He had hungered for her touch, for her closeness, for so many years, and he knew his desire for it would never fade.

If anything, it only grew.

He slid his hands down her waist, over her hips, her thighs, and gripped her hard, tugging her up into his arms, those long, lean legs wrapping around his waist as he walked them both to the bed.

Alessia started working on the knot on his tie, her movements shaky and clumsy and all the sexier for it. He sat on the bed, and Alessia remained on top of him, now resting on her knees. She tugged hard on the tie and managed to get it off, then started working at the buttons on his shirt.

He continued to kiss her, deep and desperate, pushing her dress up, past her hips, her waist, her breasts, and over her head. Her lips were swollen from kissing, her face flushed, her hair disheveled from where he'd run his fingers through it.

She looked wild, free, the most beautiful thing he'd ever seen. But then, Alessia had been, from the moment he'd seen her, the most beautiful sight he'd ever beheld. And then, when his vision of her had been one of innocence, protectiveness, it had been all about that glow that was inside of her.

He could see it, along with the outer beauty that drove him to madness. Now that their lives, their feelings, had no more innocence left, he could still see it. Still feel it deep inside of him, an ache that wouldn't ease.

She pushed his shirt off his shoulders, the buttoned cuffs snagging on his hands. A little growl escaped her lips. He wrapped one hand around her waist to hold her steady and lay back on the bed, leaving her perched over him, then he undid the buttons as quickly as possible and tossed the shirt to the side.

Alessia moved away from him, standing in front of the bed, in front of him. She met his eyes, and put her hands behind her back, her movement quick. Her bra loosened, then fell, baring her breasts to him. His stomach tightened, he could barely breathe.

She smiled, then hooked her fingers into the sides of her panties and tugged them off.

He wanted to say something. To tell her how beautiful she was, how perfect. But he couldn't speak. He could only watch, held completely under her spell.

She approached the bed, her fingers deft on his belt buckle, making quick work of his pants and underwear, and leaving him as naked as she was.

"You're so much more…just so much more than I ever imagined," she said. "I made fantasies about you, but they were a girl's fantasies. I'm not a girl, though, I'm a woman. And I'm glad you're not only that one-dimensional imagining I had of you. I'm glad you're you."

She leaned in, running the tip of her finger along the length of his rock-hard erection. Every thought ran from his head like water, his heart thundering in his ears.

Lush lips curved into a wicked smile and she leaned in, flicking her tongue over the head of his shaft. "I've never done this before. So you have to tell me if I do it wrong."

"You couldn't possibly do it wrong," he said,

not sure how he managed to speak at all. It shouldn't be possible when he couldn't breathe.

And she proved him right. Her mouth on him hot, sweet torture that streaked through his veins like flame. But where other flames destroyed, this fire cleansed. He sifted his fingers through her hair, needing an anchor. Needing to touch her, to be a part of this. Not simply on the receiving end of the pleasure she was giving him.

He needed more. Needed to taste her, too.

"Get on the bed," he growled.

She complied, not abandoning her task as she got up onto the bed, onto her knees. He sat up and she raised her head, her expression confused. Then he grasped her hips and maneuvered her around so that she was over him, so that he could taste her like she was tasting him.

She gasped when his tongue touched her.

"Don't stop," he said, the command rough, firmer than he'd intended it to be, but she didn't seem to mind.

He slipped a finger inside of her while he pleasured her with his tongue, and she gasped again, freezing for a moment before taking him fully into her mouth. His head fell back, a harsh groan on his lips.

"I can't last much longer," he said.

"Neither can I," she panted, moving away from him, returning a moment later, her thighs on either side of his. She bent down and pressed a kiss to his lips. "Ready?" she asked.

"More than."

She positioned her body so that the head of his erection met with her slick entrance, then she lowered herself down onto him, so slowly he thought he would be consumed utterly by the white heat moving through him.

She moved over him, her eyes locked with his. He grasped her hips, meeting each of her thrusts, watching her face, watching her pleasure.

He moved his hand, pressed his palm flat over her stomach, then slid it upward to cup one of her breasts. He liked the view. Liked being able to see all of her as she brought them both to the brink.

She leaned forward, kissing his lips, her breath getting harsher, faster, her movements more erratic. He lowered his hand back to her hip and strengthened his own movements, pushing them farther, faster.

They both reached the edge at the same time, and when he tipped over into the abyss, all he could do was hold on to her as release rushed through him like a wave, leaving no part of him untouched. No part of him hidden.

When the storm passed, Alessia was with him. She rested her head on his chest, her breath hot on his skin. He wrapped his arms tight around her, held her to him.

He would keep her with him, no matter what.

Yes, he was a selfish bastard.

But in this moment, he couldn't regret it. If it meant keeping Alessia, he never would.

CHAPTER TWELVE

ALESSIA WOKE UP a few hours later, feeling cold. She wasn't sure why. It was a warm evening, and she had blankets, and Matteo, to keep her warm.

Matteo.

He made her heart feel like it was cracking apart. She wanted to reach him. Wanted to touch him. Really touch him, not just with her hands on his skin, but to touch his heart.

This was so close to what she wanted. A baby. The man she loved. *Dio*, she loved him so much. It made her hurt. Not just for her, but for him. For what she knew they could have that he seemed determined to wall himself off from.

A tear slipped down her cheek and she sat up, getting out of bed and crossing to the window. Now she was crying. She wasn't really sure why she was crying, either.

But she was. Really crying. From somewhere deep inside of herself. From a bottomless well that seemed to have opened up in her.

Why did she never get what she wanted? Why was it always out of reach?

Her mother's love had been there, so briefly, long enough for her to have tasted it, to know what it was. Just so she could feel the ache keenly when it was gone? And then there was Matteo. The man she'd wanted all her life. Her hero. Her heart's desire.

And when her father said she would marry a Corretti, of course it was Matteo who had come to mind. But she'd been given to Alessandro instead. And then, one more chance, Matteo at the hotel. And she'd managed to mess that up.

In the end, she'd gotten Matteo, but in the clumsiest, most dishonest way imaginable. Not telling him she was engaged, announcing to the world she was pregnant, forcing him to marry her, in a sense.

And now there was this…this heat between them that didn't go deeper than skin on his side. This love that was burning a hole through her soul, that he would never, ever be able to return.

"Alessia?" She turned and saw Matteo sitting up, his voice filled with concern. "Are you okay? Did I hurt you?"

"No." She shook her head. And he hadn't. She'd hurt herself. "I was just…thinking." There was no point in hiding the tears. Her voice was wobbly, watery. Too late to bother with the fiction that she was fine.

"About what?"

She bit her lip. Then opted for some form of honesty. "I've been pretending."

"What do you mean?"

"My whole life. I thought if I pretended to be happy, if I made the best of what I had, that I would be okay not having it all. That if I smiled enough I would get past my mother being gone. That my father's most recent slap to my face hadn't hurt me deeper than I wanted to admit. I had to, because someone had to show my brothers and sisters that you made a choice about how you handled life. We only had what we had, and I didn't want them...I didn't want them to be sad, or to see me sad. So I protected them from what I could. I made sure they didn't know how hard it was. How bad it was. I've been carrying around the burden of everyone's happiness and just trying to make what I had work. But I'm not happy." It burst from her, truer than any words she'd ever spoken. "I don't want to smile about my childhood. It was horrible. My father was horrible. And I had to care for my siblings and it was so hard." She wiped at a tear on her cheek, tried to stop her hands from shaking. But she couldn't.

She couldn't stop shaking.

"I love them, so much, so I hate to even admit

this but…I was willing to give everything for them. And no one…no one has ever given even the smallest thing for me. And I'm sorry if that makes me a bad person but I want someone to care. I want someone to care about me."

"Alessia…"

"I'm sorry," she said, wiping at more tears. "This is…probably hormones talking."

"Is it?"

She nodded, biting her lip to keep a sob from escaping. "I'm feeling sorry for myself a little too late."

"Tell me what you want, Alessia."

It was a command, and since he was the first person to ever ask, she felt compelled to answer.

"I wish someone loved me."

"Your brothers and sisters do."

She nodded. "I know they do."

Matteo watched Alessia, her body bent in despair, her expression desolate, and felt like someone was stabbing him.

Her admission was so stark, so painful. He realized then that he had put her in a position, as his angel, his light, and he had never once sought out whether or not she needed something.

He was taking from her instead. Draining her light. Using it to illuminate the dark and void places in himself. Using her to warm his soul, and he was costing her. Just another person intent on taking from her for his own selfish needs.

"It's not the same as what you mean, though, is it?" he asked slowly.

"It's just...I can't really be myself around them," she said. "I can't show them my pain. I can't...I can't let my guard drop for a moment because then they might know, and they'll feel like they're a burden, and I just...don't want them to carry that. It's not fair."

"But what about you?"

"What about me?"

Matteo felt like someone had placed a rock in his stomach. Only hours ago, he had been content to hold Alessia tight against him. Content to keep her because she had accepted who he was, hadn't she?

But he saw now. He saw that Alessia accepted far less than she should. That she gave at the expense of herself. That she would keep doing it until the light in her had been used up. And he would be the worst offender. Because he was too closed off, too dark, to offer anything in return.

Sex wouldn't substitute, no matter how much he wanted to pretend it might. That as long as he could keep her sleepy, and naked and satisfied, he was giving.

But they were having a baby, a child. She was his wife. And life, the need for support, for touch, for caring, went well outside the bedroom. He knew that, as keenly as he knew he couldn't give it.

"I have to go," he said, his words leaden.

"What?"

"I have to go down to my offices for a few hours."

"It's four in the morning."

"I know, but this cannot wait."

"Okay," she said.

Damn her for accepting it. Damn him for making her.

He bent down and started collecting his clothes, running his fingers over his silk tie, remembering how she'd undone it only hours before with shaking fingers. How she'd kissed him. How she'd given to him.

He dressed quickly, Alessia still standing by the window, frozen, watching him.

He did the buttons on his shirt cuffs and opened his closet, retrieving his suit jacket. Then he took a breath, and turned his back on Alessia.

"I should be back later today. Feel free to go back to bed."

"In here?"

"Perhaps it would be best if you went back to your room. You haven't had your things moved, after all."

"But I made my decision."

"Perhaps I haven't made mine."

"You said you had earlier."

"Yes, I did, and then you decided you needed more time to think about it. Now I would like an extension, as well. That seems fair, doesn't it?"

He took his phone off the nightstand and curled his fingers around it. A flashback assaulted him. Of how it had been when he'd turned his back on the burning warehouse, leaving the people inside of it to deal with the consequences of their actions without his help.

But this was different. He was walking away for different reasons. It wasn't about freeing himself. This was about freeing her.

And when he returned home later in the day, perhaps he would have the strength to do it. To do what needed to be done.

Alessia didn't go back to sleep. Instead, she wandered around the palazzo like a zombie, trying to figure out why she'd exploded all over Matteo like that. And why he'd responded like he had.

It was this love business. It sucked, in her opinion.

Suddenly she'd felt like she was being torn open, like she was too full to hold everything in. Like she'd glossed over everything with that layer of contentment she'd become so good at cultivating.

She wanted more than that, and she wasn't sure why. Wasn't sure why she couldn't just keep making the best of things. She had Matteo. That should be enough.

But it wasn't.

Because you don't really have him.

She didn't. She had his name. She was married to him. She was having his baby, sharing his bed and his body, but she didn't really have him. Because the core of him remained off-limits to her. Not just her, but to everyone.

She wanted it all. Whether she should or not. Whether it made sense or not. But that was love. Which brought her back around to love sucking. Because if she could just put on a smile and deal with it, if she could just take what he was giving and not ask for any more, she was sure there could be some kind of happiness there.

But there wouldn't be joy. There wouldn't be anything deep and lasting. And she was tired of taking less than what she wanted to keep from making waves. She was so tired of it she thought she might break beneath the strain of it.

"Buongiorno."

Alessia turned and saw Matteo standing in the doorway, his hair a mess, as though he'd run his fingers through it a few too many times, his tie undone, his shirt unbuttoned at the collar. His jacket had been discarded somewhere else.

"Hello, Matteo. Did you have a good day at work?"

"I didn't go to work," he said.

His admission hit her hard. "You didn't?"

"No. I was running again. Like I did the day of your first wedding. That was what I did, you know. You asked me to go to the airport, and I nearly went. But in the end I was too angry at you. For lying. For being ready to marry him. So I went to my house in Germany, mainly because no one knows about it. And I did my best to be impossible to reach, because I didn't want to deal with any accusations. I didn't want to hear from my family. And I didn't want to hear from you, because I knew you would be too much of a temptation for me to resist. That if I read your emails or listened to your messages, I would want you back. That I would come back to you."

"So you hid instead?"

"It was easier. And today I thought I might do the same thing. Because I don't like to see you cry. I don't like seeing you sad, knowing that it's my fault."

"It's not your fault."

"Mainly I just drove," he said, as if she hadn't spoken. "A little too fast, but that's what a Ferrari is for."

"I suppose so."

"I've come to a decision."

"Wait, before you say anything, I want to say something."

"Why is it your turn?"

"Because you left this morning before I could finish. All right, not really, I didn't know what I was going to say then. But I do now."

"And what are you going to say?"

"I love you, Matteo. I think, in some ways, I always have. But more over the past months, more still when you told me your story. I am in love with you, and I want you to love me back. I'm tired of not having everything, and I think you and I could have everything. But you have to let us."

"Alessia...I can't."

"You can, you just have to....you have to..."

"What? I have to forget a lifetime of conditioning? I have to ignore the fact that my losing control, that my embracing emotion, might have horrible, devastating consequences, not just for you, but for our child? I have to ignore what I know to be true about myself, about my blood, and just...let it all go? Do you want me to just forget that I'm the sort of man who walked away and left his father to die in a burning warehouse? To just take that off like old clothes and put on something new? It wouldn't work. Even if it did it would be dangerous. I can't forget. I have to keep control."

"I don't believe you," she said.

"You don't believe me? Did you not listen to what I told you? Did you not understand? All of that, breaking that man's legs, leaving my father, that was what I am capable of when I have the most rigid control of myself. What I did to those men who attacked you? That blind rage? I didn't know what I was doing. I had no control, and if you hadn't stopped me…I would have killed them. I would have killed them and never felt an ounce of guilt for it."

"So you would have killed rapists, am I supposed to believe that makes you a bad, horrible, irredeemable person? That you would have done what you had to do to save a young girl?"

"That isn't the point," he said. "As long as I control it…as long as I don't feel, I won't do something I regret. I won't do something beyond myself. Even with control, do you see what I can do? What I have done? I can never afford to let it go. I can't afford—"

"I don't believe it. That isn't it. You're running scared, Matteo. You aren't afraid of losing control, you're afraid that if you feel you're going to have to face the guilt. The grief. You're hiding from the consequences of your actions. Hiding behind this blessed wall of cold and ice, but you can't live there forever."

"Yes, I can."

"No, you can't. Because at least for the sake of our child, our baby, Matteo, you have to break out of it."

"Has it ever once occurred to you that I don't want to?" he roared. "I don't want to feel, Alessia, I damn well don't. I don't want to face what I've done. To feel the full impact of my life. Of what was done to me. I don't want it. I don't need it. And I don't want you."

She stepped back, her body going numb suddenly. Shock. It must be that. Her body's defense because if it allowed her to feel the pain, she would collapse at his feet.

"You don't want me?" she asked.

"No. I never did. Not outside the bedroom. I told you that if you didn't expect love we would be fine. It was the one thing I told you could never be. I said no love. I promised faithfulness, a place in my home, my bed, what more did you want? I offered everything!"

"You offered me nothing," she said, her voice quivering, a slow ache starting to break through the numbness, shards of pain pushing through. "None of that means anything if you're withholding the only thing I really want."

"My love is so important? When has love ever given you anything but pain, Alessia?"

"I don't know because I've never had it for long enough to see."

"Then why make it so important?"

"Because I deserve it!" She broke then, tears spilling down her cheeks. "Don't I deserve it, Matteo?"

Matteo's face paled, and he took a step back. "Yes."

She didn't take it as a sign that she had gotten what she wanted. No, Matteo looked like someone had died.

She didn't say anything. She just waited.

"You deserve that," he said finally. "And you won't get it from me."

"Can't you just try?"

He shook his head. "I can't."

"Stop being so bloody noble. Stop being so repressed. Fight for us. Fight for this."

"No. I won't hold you to me. I won't hold you to this. That is one thing I will do for you, one thing I'll do right."

"You really think removing yourself is the only way to fix something? Keeping yourself distant?" It broke her heart. More than his rejection, it was his view of himself that left her crippled with pain.

"It's a kindness, Alessia. The best thing I've ever done. Trust me."

He turned and walked out of the room, left her standing there in the massive sitting area by herself. She couldn't cry. Couldn't bring herself to make the sound of pain that was building inside her. Endless. Bereft.

She wanted to collapse. But she couldn't. Because she had to stand strong for her child. Matteo might have walked away, but it didn't change the fact that they were having a baby. Didn't change the fact that she would be a mother in under six months.

It didn't change the fact that, no matter what, she loved Matteo Corretti with everything she had in her.

But she would never go back and demand less. Would never undo what she'd said to him. Because she had a right to ask for more. Had a right to expect more. She was willing to give to Matteo. To love him no matter who he was. No matter what he had done.

But she needed his love in return. Because she wasn't playing at love, it was real. And she refused to play at happiness, to feign joy.

She sank into one of the plush love seats, the pain from her chest spreading to the rest of her body.

She had a feeling there would be no happiness, fake or genuine, for a very long time.

CHAPTER THIRTEEN

MATTEO DIDN'T BOTHER with alcohol this time. He didn't deserve to have any of the reality of the past few hours blunted for his own comfort. He deserved for it to cut him open.

He shifted into Fifth and pushed harder on the gas pedal. Driving always helped him sort through things. And it helped him get farther away from his problems while he did it. But Alessia didn't feel any farther away.

She was with him. In him. Beneath his skin and, he feared, past his defenses.

Those defenses he had just given all to protect.

You aren't afraid of losing control, you're afraid that if you feel you're going to have to face the guilt.

That was just what he was. Afraid. To his very core.

He was scared that if he reached a hand out and asked for redemption it would truly be beyond his reach. He was afraid that if he let the door open on his emotions there would be nothing but pain, and grief, and the unending lash of guilt for all he had done, both under his father's influence, and the night of the fire.

He was afraid that he would expose himself, let himself feel it all, and he would still fall short for Alessia. That he wouldn't know how to be a real husband, or a real father.

He was afraid to want it. Afraid to try it.

She wanted him to fight for them. Nothing good came from him fighting.

Except the time you saved her.

Yes, there was that. He had always held that moment up as a banner displaying what happened when he lost control. A reminder that, as dangerous as he was in general, it was when he felt passion that he truly became a monster.

He pulled his car over to the side of the road, heart pounding, and he closed his eyes, let himself picture that day fully.

The fear in Alessia's eyes. The way those men had touched her. The rage that had poured through him.

And he knew one thing for certain in that moment. That no matter how blinded he was by anger, he would never hurt Alessia. He would never hurt his child. No, his emotions, not his mind, told him emphatically that he would die before he let any harm come to them.

That he would give everything to keep them safe.

He had been so certain, all this time, that his mind would protect him, but it had been his heart that had demanded he do whatever it took to save Alessia Battaglia from harm. It had been his heart that had demanded he spend that night in New York with her.

And it was his heart that was crumbling into pieces now. There was no protecting his defenses, because Alessia had slipped in beneath them years ago, before they had fully formed, and she was destroying them now from the inside out.

Matteo put his head on the steering wheel, his body shaking as pain worked its way through him, spreading through his veins like poison.

Something in him cracked open, every feeling, every desire, every deep need, suddenly acute and sharp. It was too much. Because it was everything all at once. Grief for the boy he'd been, for the man his father had become and what the end had done to both of them. Justification because he'd done what he had for his whole family. To free everyone. To free himself. Guilt, anguish, because in some ways he would always regret it.

And a desperate longing for redemption. A desperate wish he could go back to the beginning, to the start of it all, and take the path that would form him into Alessia's white knight. So that he could truly be the man she'd seen.

Alessia. He thought of her face. Her bright smile. Her tears.

Of meeting her eyes in the mirror at a bar, and feeling a sense of certainty, so deep, so true, he hadn't even tried to fight it.

And he felt something else. A light, flooding through his soul, touching everything. Only this time, it wasn't brief. Wasn't temporary. It stayed. It shone on everything, the ugly, the unfinished and the good. It showed him for what he was, what he could be.

Love. He loved Alessia. He had loved her all of his life.

And he wasn't the man that she should have. He wasn't the man he could have been if things had gone differently.

But with love came hope. A hope that he could try. A hope for redemption. A hope for the future.

For every dirty, broken feeling that he'd unleashed inside of him, he had let loose the good to combat it.

He had never imagined that. Had never believed that there was so much lightness in him.

It was Alessia. His love for her. His hope for their future.

He might not be the man she'd once imagined.

He might not be the man he might have been in different circumstances. But that man was the one that Alessia deserved and no less.

So he would become that man. Because he loved Alessia too much to offer her less.

Matteo picked up his phone, and dialed a number he rarely used if he could help it. But this was the start. The start of changing. He was too tired to keep fighting, anyway. Too tired to continue a rivalry he simply didn't want to be involved in. A rivalry created by his father, by Alessandro's father. They both hated those bastards so what was the point of honoring a hatred created and fostered by them?

No more. It had to end.

"Corretti."

"It's Matteo."

"Ah, Matteo." Alessandro didn't sound totally thrilled to hear from him.

"How is everything going? In terms of unifying the business?"

"Fine."

"Great. That's not exactly why I called."

"Why did you call, then? I'm a little busy."

"I called because I want to make sure that as we unify the company, we unify the family, as well. I...I don't want to keep any of this rivalry alive. I've been holding on to some things for far too long that I need to let go. This is one of them."

"Accepting my superiority?"

"If that's what it takes."

Alessandro paused for a moment. "You aren't dying, are you?"

"It feels like it. But I think it will pass." It had to. "I don't want to carry things on like Carlo and Benito did, and I don't just mean the criminal activity. If we have a problem, I say we just punch each other in the face and get it over with, rather than creating a multigenerational feud."

"That works for me."

"Good. See you at the next meeting." He hung up. It wasn't like he needed to hug it out with his cousin or anything, but he was ready to start putting things behind him. To stop shielding himself from the past and embrace the future.

A future that would include Alessia.

Alessia looked up when the Ferrari roared back onto the grounds. She was standing in the garden, doing her best to at least enjoy the waning sunlight. It was better than the whole dissolving-into-never-ending-tears bit.

Matteo left the car in the middle of the drive and strode into the yard, his eyes fixed on hers. When he reached her, he pulled her into his arms, his expression fierce. Then he lowered his head and kissed her. Long. Deep. Intense.

She wrapped her arms around his neck and kissed him back, her face wet, tasting salt from tears. She didn't know whose. She didn't care.

She didn't want to ask questions now, she just wanted to live in this moment. When they parted, Matteo buried his face in her neck and held her tight. And she held him, too. Neither of them moved, neither of them spoke.

Emotion swelled in her chest, so big she wasn't sure she could stand it. Wasn't sure she could breathe around it.

"I love you," he said. "I have never said it before, Alessia. Not to anyone. Not to a woman, not to family. So when I say it, I mean it. With everything I have, such as it is. I love you."

A sob broke through her lips and she tightened her hold on him. "I love you, too."

"Still?"

"Always."

"You were right. I was afraid. I'm still afraid. But I can't hide anymore. You made it impossible. I want to be the man worthy of that look you used to give me. I want to be everything for you, I don't just want to take from you. I was content to just take that light you carry around in you, Alessia. To let it warm me. But you deserve more than that. So I'll be more than that.

I'm not everything I should be. I'm broken. I've done things that were wrong. I've seen things no man should have to see. But I will give you everything that I have to give, and then I'll reach deep and find more, because you're right, you deserve it all. And I want you, so that means I have to figure out a way to be it all."

"Matteo, no, you don't. You just have to meet me in the middle. And love will cover our shortcomings."

"Just meet you in the middle?"

"Mainly, I just need you to love me."

"That I can do, Alessia Corretti. I've been doing it for most of my life."

"You might not believe this, Matteo, but as you are, you're my knight in shining armor. You are flawed. You've been through unimaginable things, and you love anyway. You're so strong, so brave, so utterly perfect. Well, not perfect, but perfect for me. You're the only man I've ever wanted, the only man I've ever loved. And that will never change."

"How is it that you see me, all of me, and love me, anyway?"

"That's what love is. And you know what? It's not hard to love you. You're brave, honorable. You were willing to cut off any chance at having your own happiness to try to protect the people around you. To try to do right. You're the most incredible man I've ever known."

"Quite the compliment coming from the most amazing woman. Your bravery, your willingness to love, in spite of all you've been through, that's what pulled me out of the darkness. Your light won. Your love won."

"I'm so glad it did."

He put his hand on Alessia's stomach. "This is what I want. You, me, our baby. I was too afraid before to admit how much I wanted it. Too afraid I didn't deserve it, that I would lose it. I'm still afraid I don't deserve it, but I want it so much." He leaned in and kissed her lips. "I'm not cold anymore."

"Never again," she said.

He wrapped his arms tight around her and spun them both in a circle. She laughed, and so did he. Genuine. Happy. Joy bloomed inside of her. Joy like she'd never felt before. Real, true. And for her. Not to keep those around her smiling.

"We agreed on one night. This is turning into a lot longer than one night," he said when they stopped spinning.

"It is," she said. "All things considered, I was thinking we might want to make it forever."

"Forever sounds about right."

EPILOGUE

THE CORRETTIS WERE all together. But unlike at the funerals that had been the most common reason for them to come together in the past, unlike Alessia and Alessandro's wedding-that-wasn't, there was no veiled animosity here at the celebration of Teresa's birthday. And not just Teresa's birthday, but the regeneration of the docklands. The culmination of a joint family effort. Of them coming together.

After the big ceremony down at the docklands, they'd returned to the family estate.

They had all sat down to dinner together. They had all talked, business and personal, and not a single punch had been thrown. And it wasn't only Correttis. Some of the Battaglias, Alessia's siblings, were there, as well.

Matteo considered it a resounding success.

After dinner, they all sat in the garden, lights strung overhead, a warm breeze filtering through. And Matteo felt peace.

"Hey there." Alessia walked away from where she'd been talking to his sister Lia and came to stand beside him, their daughter, Luciana Battaglia-Corretti, on her hip.

"The most beautiful women here have graced me with their presence. I am content," he said, brushing his knuckles over Alessia's cheek and dropping a kiss onto Luciana's soft head.

Matteo looked at his wife and daughter, at his family, all of them, surrounding him. That word meant something new now. The Correttis were no longer at war.

He bent down and extracted Luciana from her mother's arms, pulling his daughter close, the warm weight of her, her absolute trust in him, something he would never take for granted.

Alessia smiled at him, her eyes shining, her face glowing. "The way you look at me," he said. "Like I'm your knight in shining armor."

"You are," she said. "You saved me, after all."

Matteo looked around one more time, at all of the people in his life. People that he loved. "No, Alessia. You saved me."

* * * * *

Read on for an exclusive interview with Maisey Yates!

BEHIND THE SCENES OF SICILY'S CORRETTI DYNASTY

It's such a huge world to create—an entir Sicilian dynasty. Did you discuss parts of i with the other writers?

Yes, we had a loop set up for discussion, an there were a *lot* of details to work out. And ever so often messages would come in with the fun niest subject lines I've ever seen.

How does being part of a continuity differ from when you are writing your own stories?

I think it takes a little bit to attach to characters you didn't create from scratch, but in the end for me, I work so hard to find that attachmen that I think continuity characters end up being my favorite.

What was the biggest challenge? And what did you most enjoy about it?

I think getting to the heart of my hero. Just be cause you've been given an outline with char acters doesn't mean you've been given all the answers. In Matteo's case he was hiding some thing very dark and it was up to me to dig it out of him. I love a tortured hero, so this was right up my alley.

As you wrote your hero and heroine was there anything about them that surprised you?

Hee, hee… This goes with the above. Yes, Matteo surprised me with the depth of the darkness in him. I think Alessia surprised me with her strength. Every time she opened her mouth she had something sassy to say.

What was your favorite part of creating the world of Sicily's most famous dynasty?

I loved the family villas, the idea of old-world history and beauty. I love a country setting.

If you could have given your heroine one piece of advice before the opening pages of the book, what would it be?

It's never too late to try to claim your own independence…but next time maybe do it before you're walking down the aisle.

What was your hero's biggest secret?

Oh, now, see, I can't tell you that. I'd have to kill you. He's a very good dancer, though.

What does your hero love most about your heroine?

Her strength, her ability to love and feel in spite of everything she'd been through. He feels like he's on the outside, looking in at all that light and beauty, unable to touch it.

What does your heroine love most about your hero?

The man beneath the cold exterior. The man who has braved so much pain and come out the other side standing strong. The man who gave so much to free his family from their father.

Which of the Correttis would you most like to meet and why?

Matteo. Because he's a sexy beast. I can't lie.

**M**odern man, alienated from nature, from his gods, and from society, in an increasingly mechanized, atomized and depersonalized world, too often is unable to achieve an identity and a relatedness to others. What are the circumstances that have led to this predicament and what are the chances for alleviating it? MAN ALONE forthrightly poses the problem and offers guidance for its resolution.

Dr. Josephson, with a doctorate in sociology from Columbia, has taught at Dickinson College, Princeton and Columbia Universities. His articles and translations have appeared in THE NATION, SOCIAL FORCES and other publications. Mary Redmer Josephson is a translator and writer-editor. MAN ALONE marks the first published collaboration of this husband and wife team.

MAN ALONE:

ALIENATION IN MODERN SOCIETY

Edited, with an introduction, by
ERIC *and* MARY JOSEPHSON

A LAUREL EDITION

Published by

DELL PUBLISHING CO., INC.

750 Third Avenue, New York 17, N.Y.

© *Copyright, 1962, by Dell Publishing Co., Inc.*

Laurel ® TM 674623, Dell Publishing Co., Inc.

DEDICATION: *In Memory of Wilton*

First printing—September, 1962

Printed in U.S.A.

ACKNOWLEDGMENTS: *The following selections in this volume are reproduced by permission of the authors, their publishers, or their agents:*

from THE SANE SOCIETY by Erich Fromm. Copyright © 1955 by Erich Fromm. Reprinted by permission of Holt, Rinehart and Winston, Inc.

"On Alienated Concepts of Identity" by Ernest G. Schachtel, *The American Journal of Psychoanalysis,* November 1961. Copyright 1961 by Ernest G. Schachtel.

from "The Sovereignty of the Family" by Peter Laslett, *The Listener,* April 7, 1960. Reprinted by permission of the author. Copyright 1960 by Peter Laslett.

from A RADICAL'S AMERICA by Harvey Swados. Copyright © 1957 by Harvey Swados. Reprinted by permission of Little, Brown & Company.

from TECHNICS AND CIVILIZATION by Lewis Mumford, copyright, 1934, by Harcourt, Brace and World, Inc. and reprinted with their permission.

from SOCIAL STRUCTURE AND SOCIAL THEORY by Robert K. Merton. Copyright, 1957, by The Free Press of Glencoe, Inc. and reprinted with their permission.

from LIFE IN THE CRYSTAL PALACE by Alan Harrington. Reprinted by permission of Alfred A. Knopf, Inc. Copyright 1958, 1959 by Alan Harrington.

from THE PURSUIT OF HAPPINESS by Robert M. MacIver. Reprinted by permission of Simon & Schuster, Inc. Copyright © 1955 by Robert M. MacIver.

from THE SOCIOLOGY OF GEORG SIMMEL by Georg Simmel. Copyright, 1950, by The Free Press of Glencoe, Inc. and reprinted with their permission.

from MORE IN ANGER by Marya Mannes. Copyright © 1958 by Marya Mannes. Published by J. B. Lippincott Company.

from IRRATIONAL MAN: A STUDY IN EXISTENTIAL PHILOSOPHY by William Barrett. Copyright © 1958 by William Barrett. Reprinted by permission of Doubleday and Company, Inc.

from SOLITUDE AND PRIVACY by Paul Halmos. Copyright 1952 by Paul Halmos. Reprinted by permission of Philosophical Library and Routledge and Kegan Paul Ltd.

"Of Happiness and Despair We Have No Measure" by Ernest van den Haag, from MASS CULTURE, edited by Bernard Rosenberg and David White. Copyright, 1957, by The Free Press of Glencoe, Inc. and reprinted with their permission.

from THE POWER ELITE by C. Wright Mills. Copyright © 1956 by Oxford University Press, Inc. and reprinted by permission.

from THE ALIENATED VOTER by Murray B. Levin, New York, 1960. By permission of the publishers, Holt, Rinehart and Winston, Inc.

from THE DEMOCRATIC AND THE AUTHORITARIAN STATE by Franz Neumann. Copyright 1957 by The Free Press of Glencoe, Inc. and reprinted with their permission.

from the essay by Ignazio Silone in THE GOD THAT FAILED edited by Richard Crossman. Copyright 1949 by Ignazio Silone. Reprinted by permission of Harper & Brothers and Hamish Hamilton Ltd.

from THE COMMON SENSE OF SCIENCE by J. Bronowski. Copyright, 1953, by Harvard University Press. Reprinted by permission of the publishers.

"Reflections on the H Bomb" by Gunther Anders, *Dissent,* Spring, 1956. Copyright 1956 by Gunther Anders.

from ELMTOWN'S YOUTH: THE IMPACT OF SOCIAL CLASSES ON ADOLESCENTS by August B. Hollingshead. Copyright 1949 by John Wiley and Sons, Inc. Reprinted with permission of author and publisher.

from FAMILY AND KINSHIP IN EAST LONDON by Michael Young and Peter Willmott. Copyright 1957 by Routledge and Kegan Paul Ltd. Reprinted by permission of The Free Press of Glencoe, Inc. and Routledge and Kegan Paul Ltd.

from THE FAMILY LIFE OF OLD PEOPLE by Peter Townsend. Copyright 1957 by Routledge and Kegan Paul Ltd. Reprinted by permission of The Free Press of Glencoe, Inc. and Routledge and Kegan Paul Ltd.

from THE SOULS OF BLACK FOLK by W. E. B. DuBois, by permission of Fawcett World Library; all rights reserved.

CONTENTS

INTRODUCTION

Ours is a self-conscious age. Perhaps never before in history has man been so much a problem to himself. Rocketing through space and on the point of conquering the heavens, he is fast losing touch with his own world. Growing numbers of writers describe him in various ways as "alienated." What forces have made him so?

The past few hundred years have seen major scientific and technological revolutions in half the world, while the other half still plows the earth with dull sticks. Unparalleled economic growth has occurred side by side with the profoundest human misery; and struggles for freedom and enlightenment side by side with continuing social injustice. Our own age produced the Nazi concentration camps, two catastrophic world wars, and a dream of one world; a nuclear arms race that may put an end to civilization as we know it, and the promise of "atoms for peace."

Confronted with such mighty opposites—with apocalyptic visions of mass annihilation on the one hand, and on the other with dreams of progress and a vastly better life for increasing numbers of people—no wonder Western man feels deeply troubled as he faces the immense gulf between his finest achievements of hand and brain, and his own sorry ineptitude at coping with them; between his truly awe-inspiring accomplishments and the utter failure of his imagination to encompass them and give them meaning. Powerless in the face of modern mechanical and social forces, we have reached a point in history where knowledge and tools intended originally to serve man now threaten to destroy him.

What kind of society is it that loses control over its own tools and creations? Is it one in which the sense of community has become seriously, if not fatally, weakened? The development of nuclear weapons required the splitting of the atom. Is the society that uses such weapons itself split

and its members atomized? If so, this splitting process did
not take place suddenly, and not just a series of wars and
upheavals have brought on the crisis. Indeed, ever since
the great technological and political revolutions of the late
eighteenth century, with their shattering impact on a rigid
social order and their promise of individual freedom, one of
the most disturbing phenomena of Western culture has been
man's sense of estrangement from the world he himself has
made or inherited—in a word, man's alienation from himself and from others.

Our present age of pessimism, despair and uncertainty
succeeds a quite different earlier period of optimism, hope
and certainty—a period when man believed in himself and
the work of his hands, had faith in the powers of reason
and science, trusted his gods, and conceived his own capacity for growth as endless and his widening horizons
limitless. Bold in his desires for freedom, equality, social
justice and brotherhood, he imagined that ignorance alone
stood in the way of these desires. But tumult and violence
have unseated these traditional beliefs and values. Knowledge has spread, but it has not abolished war, or fear; nor
has it made all men brothers. Instead, men find themselves
more isolated, anxious and uneasy than ever.

Confused as to his place in the scheme of a world growing each day closer yet more impersonal, more densely
populated yet in face-to-face relations more dehumanized;
a world appealing ever more widely for his concern and
sympathy with unknown masses of men, yet fundamentally
alienating him even from his next neighbor, today Western
man has become mechanized, routinized, made comfortable
as an object; but in the profound sense displaced and
thrown off balance as a subjective creator and power.

This theme of the alienation of modern man runs
through the literature and drama of two continents; it can
be traced in the content as well as the form of modern art;
it preoccupies theologians and philosophers, and to many
psychologists and sociologists, it is the central problem of
our time. In various ways they tell us that ties have snapped
that formerly bound Western man to himself and to the
world about him. In diverse language they say that man in
modern industrial societies is rapidly becoming detached
from nature, from his old gods, from the technology that
has transformed his environment and now threatens to destroy it; from his work and its products, and from his

leisure; from the complex social institutions that presumably serve but are more likely to manipulate him; from the community in which he lives; and above all from himself—from his body and his sex, from his feelings of love and tenderness, and from his art—his creative and productive potential.

The alienated man is everyman and no man, drifting in a world that has little meaning for him and over which he exercises no power, a stranger to himself and to others. As Erich Fromm writes, "Alienation as we find it in modern society is almost total; it pervades the relationship of man to his work, to the things he consumes, to his fellows, and to himself." Or as Charles Taylor expresses it, in a mechanical and depersonalized world man has "an indefinable sense of loss; a sense that life . . . has become impoverished, that men are somehow 'deracinate and disinherited,' that society and human nature alike have been atomized, and hence mutilated, above all that men have been separated from whatever might give meaning to their work and their lives."

Such sweeping statements not only need qualification but translation into recognizable and verifiable terms. Who are the alienated? Is the phenomenon of alienation new in history, or is it age-old? If age-old, are its present-day manifestations more widespread? And if so, how can we measure the differences? Should we mention alienation par excellence and point to the prevalence of suicide today? Old Testament princes and Roman soldiers, defeated or disgraced, ran upon their spears or hanged themselves from trees. Shall we cite modern rates of homicide? The cave man too could be homicidal. Shall we refer to the numbers of insane, unknown as well as institutionalized? But men have always been mad.

So it is not to gross statistics that we look, but to the untold "lives of quiet desperation" that mark our age—the multitudes of factory and white-collar workers who find their jobs monotonous and degrading; the voters and nonvoters who feel hopeless or "don't care"; the juveniles who commit "senseless" acts of violence; the growing army of idle and lonely old people; the Negroes who "want to be treated like men"; the stupefied audiences of mass media; the people who reject the prevailing values of our culture but cannot—or may not—find any alternatives, the escapists, the retreatists, the nihilists, and the desperate citizens

who would "solve" all major political problems by moving
our society underground and blowing up the planet. There
are few statistics to tell us about them, especially as many
continue to function with the appearance of normality.
Yet even with indirect evidence it seems safe to assume
that there is something in common between them, something that touches the very roots of our social order.

The aim of this book is therefore to describe particular
conditions in modern industrial society (especially under
capitalism) that have led to man's estrangement and to show
some of the ways—both creative and destructive—in which
men and women have responded to that estrangement. What
is it in our technological and social environment that leads
to alienation? How can we so order society and integrate
people that they do not merely exchange their unbearable
sense of powerlessness and isolation for spurious "togetherness" or for new forms of coercion? These are some of the
questions with which we shall be dealing both here and in
the work of writers who make up the bulk of this volume.
Before turning to them, however, it will be necessary to define our terms and consider some of the historical forces
which have alienated man from the world about him and
from himself.

To begin with, what does alienation mean? The word
has an ancient history, being used in common discourse to
identify feelings of estrangement, or of detachment from
self and from others; and in law to describe the act of transferring property or ownership to another. An illustration
of the second usage is the "alienation" of church property
which, after the Reformation, meant a transfer from religious to secular ownership. The two meanings converge
in cases of law, now rare, when one sues some third party
for "alienating the affections" of one's spouse, the affectionate feelings being regarded as property which has been
diverted to the third person's use. In another common usage, alienation has long meant insanity; and in Europe to
this day an "alienist" is one who treats persons suffering
from mental disorders.

In modern terms, however, "alienation" has been used
by philosophers, psychologists and sociologists to refer to
an extraordinary variety of psycho-social disorders, including loss of self, anxiety states, anomie, despair, depersonalization, rootlessness, apathy, social disorganization, lone-

liness, atomization, powerlessness, meaninglessness, isolation, pessimism, and the loss of beliefs or values. Among
the social groups who have been described as alienated in
varying degree—some of whom we have already mentioned
—are women, industrial workers, white-collar workers,
migrant workers, artists, suicides, the mentally disturbed,
addicts, the aged, the young generation as a whole, juvenile
delinquents in particular, voters, non-voters, consumers,
the audiences of mass media, sex deviants, victims of prejudice and discrimination, the prejudiced, bureaucrats, political radicals, the physically handicapped, immigrants, exiles, vagabonds and recluses. This is by no means a complete
listing, yet even allowing for duplication it includes a siz-
able majority of persons living in any advanced industrial
society such as ours. Obviously we are dealing with a word
that lends itself to many different meanings. To deal with
all of them we would truly need an encyclopedia of the
social sciences.

It seems necessary therefore to distinguish between alienating conditions on the one hand and estranged states on
the other, although the distinction may be difficult, there
being no question here of a simple stimulus-response situation. It also seems appropriate to limit the term alienation
to mean an individual feeling or state of dissociation from
self, from others, and from the world at large. Such states,
although functions of the conditions that produce them,
should not be confused with the conditions themselves. The
philosopher, F. H. Heinemann, has suggested a similar
distinction. He writes: "The facts to which the term 'alienation' refers are, objectively, different kinds of dissociation,
break or rupture between human beings and their objects,
whether the latter be other persons, or the natural world,
or their own creations in art, science and society; and subjectively, the corresponding states of disequilibrium, disturbance, strangeness and anxiety."

To clarify our approach let us briefly consider a number
of concepts frequently linked with alienation. One of them
is the idea of *anomie,* developed first by Emile Durkheim
to describe conditions of normlessness, the collapse of rules
of conduct. The notion of anomie, like that of alienation
itself, has been used to refer to a wide array of social and
personal disorders. Although a number of writers have
dealt with anomie chiefly in psychological terms, Robert K.
Merton argues plausibly that it be defined as a condition

of "breakdown in the cultural structure, occurring particularly when there is an acute disjunction between the cultural norms and goals and the ... capacities of members of the group to act in accord with them." Merton thus places stress on the breakdown of values as distinguished from individual or group responses to that breakdown. As he shows, men respond to this conflict between ends and means in various deviant ways; and of those individual adaptations one in particular—"retreat" from the struggle to get ahead (as in the case of tramps and addicts)—is worth mentioning here. If we accept Merton's definition of anomie as a social condition rather than a psychological state, we can identify it as an important cause of alienation, particularly when the response takes the form of retreat; but we should not confuse it with alienation as a state of mind.

Similar considerations apply to other concepts which are often confused with alienation. For example, social isolation may lead to a state of estrangement, but not all isolates are alienated. Indeed, alienation may result from the social pressures of group, crowd or mass, as David Riesman suggests in *The Lonely Crowd*. By the same token alienation should not be confused with "social disorganization," since, as we shall see, estrangement may also result in highly organized bureaucracies. Alienation is often associated with loneliness; but again, not all lonely people are estranged, as Clark E. Moustakas points out. Moustakas helps us here by distinguishing between loneliness as a creative part of human experience and the loneliness of self-rejection which is not really loneliness but anxiety; he suggests that people who try to overcome or escape loneliness will end only by becoming self-alienated.

What we have here are important conditions or correlates of alienation. Any one of these conditions may have different effects on men and women of varying personalities in different social situations, predisposing some more and others less to alienated states. Thus one man retreats from life, another rebels; and each of these in turn exhibits many different modes of behavior.

Whatever the approach, central to the definition of alienation is the idea that man has lost his identity or "selfhood." Many writers who deal with the problem of self-alienation assume, implicitly or explicitly, that in each of us there is a "genuine," "real" or "spontaneous" self which we are prevented from knowing or achieving. But how does one achieve selfhood? The most satisfactory answer has been provided by social psychologists, notably Charles H. Cooley and George H. Mead, who argued that one acquires a self or identity through interaction with others. Cooley called this a process of acquiring a "looking-glass self" and Mead termed it "taking the role of the other." But if one acquires a self by communicating with others, especially through language, then anxiety about or loss of selfhood is a social as well as an individual problem. What this means is that the person who experiences self-alienation is not only cut off from the springs of his own creativity, but is thereby also cut off from groups of which he would otherwise be a part; and he who fails to achieve a meaningful relationship with others is deprived of some part of himself.

Among the first to concern themselves with self-alienation as a general condition were Kierkegaard and Nietzsche in their respectively despairing and angry tracts about the "nothingness" (or selflessness) that yawned before men in a technological, secular and materialistic society. Thus Kierkegaard, who felt that the self could only be preserved by identification with God, spoke of godless man's essential dread at "being dominated by an alien power which threatens our dissolution" —by which he meant the anxiety that loss of self can produce. Despair about loss of self he called a "sickness unto death." Nietzsche, however, triumphantly proclaimed the death of the gods but asked, "Do we not now wander through an endless Nothingness?" More recently, Karl Jaspers has written: "What, in all the millenniums of human history and pre-history, no god has been able to do for man, man has done for himself. It is natural enough that in these achievements of his he should discern the true inwardness of being—until he shrinks back in alarm from the void he has made for himself." The problem which Jaspers raises is whether man can preserve his selfhood or identity in a world dominated by a giant technological and bureaucratic "apparatus" of his own creation, yet alien to him. The price we pay for "progress," he suggests, is anxiety, "a dread of life perhaps unparalleled in its intensity" and increasing "to such a pitch that the sufferer may feel himself to be nothing more than a lost point in empty space, inasmuch as all human relationships appear to have no more than a temporary validity."

Posed thus the problem of selfhood has metaphysical, or more properly, ontological ramifications. In more prosaic terms alienation defined as loss of identity is better illustrated by men and women troubled over the simple yet complex question, "Who am I?" In the United States today the literature of psychoanalysis is rich in its descriptions of such cases. Thus Karen Horney describes alienation as "the remoteness of the neurotic from his own feelings, wishes, beliefs, and energies. It is the loss of the feeling of being an active, determining force in his own life. It is the loss of feeling himself as an organic whole." Or, as Fromm puts it, the alienated man is one who "does not experience himself as the center of his world, as the creator of his own acts—but his acts and their consequences have become his masters, whom he obeys, or whom he may even worship. The alienated person is out of touch with himself as he is out of touch with any other person."

Implicit in most approaches to alienation is the ideal of an "integrated" man and of a cohesive society in which he will find meaning and satisfaction in his own productivity and in his relations with others. As Emile Durkheim expressed it, man in a "solidaristic" society "will no longer find the only aim of his conduct in himself and, understanding that he is the instrument of a purpose greater than himself, he will see that he is not without significance." We may well ask, was there ever such a society? Romantic notions about our own past or about primitive cultures do not help us here.

In its panorama of disorder and change, history offers plentiful evidence that men in times past also felt no small uncertainty about themselves and their identities, suffered no little anguish of gloom, despair and feelings of detachment from each other. Karl Jaspers quotes an Egyptian chronicler of four thousand years ago: "Robbers abound. . . . No one ploughs the land. People are saying: 'We do not know what will happen from day to day.' . . . Dirt prevails everywhere, and no longer does any one wear clean raiment. . . . The country is spinning round and round like a potter's wheel. . . . Slave-women are wearing necklaces of gold and lapis lazuli. . . . No more do we hear any one laugh. . . . Great men and small agree in saying: 'Would that I had never been born.' . . . No public office stands open where it should, and the masses are like timid sheep without a shepherd. . . . Artists have ceased to ply their art. . . . The few slay the many. . . . One who yesterday was indigent is now wealthy, and the sometime rich overwhelm him with adulation. . . . Impudence is rife. . . . Oh that man could cease to be, that women should no longer conceive and give birth. Then, at length, the world would find peace."

Thucydides describes a similar moral collapse in Greece during the Peloponnesian war. As for medieval Europe, Huizinga reminds us that the Middle Ages were essentially violent in character: wars, class struggles, hysterical crowd behavior, vice and crime (on an unparalleled scale, particularly in university towns), plagues, scarcity, superstition, the conviction that the world was coming to an end—such was the "black" background of medieval life. A late medieval (fifteenth-century) French poet, Eustache Deschamps, cried:

> Why are the times so dark
> Men know each other not at all,
> But governments quite clearly change
> From bad to worse?
> Days dead and gone were more worth while,
> Now what holds sway? Deep gloom and boredom,
> Justice and law nowhere to be found.
> I know no more where I belong.

I know no more where I belong. Is this not the alienated lament of all ages?

Although medieval Europe was less harmonious than many moderns would believe, its unity, provided largely by the church and a rigid caste system, was no myth. All the more reason for Deschamps' pessimism. For as Lewis Mumford writes, "The unattached person during the Middle Ages was one either condemned to exile or doomed to death: if alive, he immediately sought to attach himself, at least to a band of robbers. To exist, one had to belong to an association: a household, a manor, a monastery, a guild; there was no security except in association, and no freedom that did not recognize the obligations of a corporate life. One lived and died in the style of one's class and corporation." Moreover, as Herbert Muller notes, "Men had known a kind of psychological security; they took for granted all the actual insecurity of life in a vale of tears."

But if the pre-industrial world was in many ways no less insecure than our own, at least work and community life were ordered on a human scale. First of all, most men lived in small, tightly knit communities in which the family was the productive unit. Second, the tools that men used, the pace of work, the distribution of things that were made—all of these were controlled by human capacities and needs. Perhaps most important, instead of being separated from what we now call "leisure" activities, work itself—ordinarily some craft—was closely integrated in the total life of individuals and communities. Peter Laslett calls this "the world we have lost." It was by no means an idyllic world, but as Laslett says, "Time was, and it was all time up to 200 years ago when the whole of life went forward in the family, in a circle of loved, familiar faces, known and fondled objects, all to human size. That time has gone forever. It makes us very different from our ancestors." Different chiefly because of the technological revolution, with its transformation of working conditions, the communities in which men live, and the whole complex social order that governs our lives. What happened, however, was not just a revolution in techniques and controls but an accompanying change in human personality or character; and it is this "characterological" revolution which must be understood if we are to determine whether alienation today differs in form and degree from the miseries of which earlier men complained. But like the scientific and political upheavals which it accompanied, this characterological change had no sudden beginning or point in time at which spontaneously "modern" man replaced "feudal" man. History here is inadequate, and our evidence largely intuitive, or derived from literary works with their descriptions of social types, or from language itself.

One of the first to suggest a fundamental change in personality was Jacob Burckhardt in his study of the Italian Renaissance. According to Burckhardt, medieval man "was conscious of himself only as a member of a race, people, party, family, or corporation—only through some general category." With the Renaissance emerges the individual as we know him. If his entrance upon the scene was gradual rather than dramatic, it is indicated nonetheless clearly by important changes in language. As Raymond

Williams points out in *The Long Revolution*, in the Middle Ages the word "individual" meant "inseparable"; and it was used chiefly in theological arguments about the Holy Trinity or to indicate a member of some group, kind or species. Williams writes: "The complexity of the term is at once apparent in this history, for it is the unit that is being defined, yet defined in terms of its membership of a class. The separable entity is being defined by a word that has meant 'inseparable.' ... The crucial history of the modern description is a change in emphasis which enabled us to think of 'the individual' as a kind of absolute, without immediate reference ... to the group of which he is a member." Williams suggests that this change took place in the late sixteenth and early seventeenth centuries; and since then we have come to speak of the " 'individual in his own right,' whereas previously to describe an individual was to give an example of the group of which he was a member, and so to offer a particular description of that group and of the relationships within it." This semantic change reflected profound changes in the social order after the medieval period, particularly the breakup of the feudal caste system. When men found that they could change their status and social mobility increased, the idea grew of being an individual apart from one's social role. Also important, as we shall see, was man's new detachment from and power over nature: when man (as subject) divorced himself from nature (as object) in order to understand and control it, individualism was given further impetus.

It is the historical emergence of the individual as we now know him, of man alone, that makes alienation so crucially a modern problem. In the past, as we saw, men felt anxiety or despair particularly when they lost the status that identified them and offered them some security. But when the medieval system collapsed, the likelihood of alienation increased appreciably. Indeed, only with the release of the individual from medieval bonds could alienation become a widespread social problem. In his *Literature and the Image of Man,* Leo Lowenthal has summed up this historical process: "The breakdown of the feudal order forced man to fall back upon himself; he had to learn how to cope with countless problems and decisions that were once taken care of by worldly and spiritual hierarchies. But together with the anxieties generated by this new autonomy he sensed a great promise, for in the period of the formation of the national state and the development of a mercantile economy his own future seemed to have infinite possibilities. At the end of the curve, in our own century, he begins to feel threatened by the encroachment of powerful social forces emanating not only from his own corner of the earth but from every part of a contracting world."

If men today fear freedom or wish to "escape" from it, this was not always so—certainly not for the optimists of the political and scientific enlightenment. But then alienation is not only an accompaniment of individualism. Perhaps above all, as we have suggested, it is a response to fearful new powers that man himself has created and that threaten his hard-won freedom. Foremost among them are the machine and the social structures which administer it. We turn now to consider these factors in more detail.

The tremendous growth of mechanical power since the eighteenth century—first steam, then electricity, and now atomic power—made possible a great increase, albeit not necessarily an equitable distribution, of social wealth. While the early stages of the industrial revolution actually impoverished millions, by almost any material standard we are today better off than were our ancestors. New mechanical power produced new wealth; but it also imposed rigid controls over human behavior. Thorstein Veblen was one of the first sociologists to interpret the broad cultural implications of mechanization: "Within the range of . . . machine-guided work, and within the range of modern life so far as it is guided by the machine process, the course of things is given mechanically, impersonally, and the resultant discipline is a discipline in the handling of impersonal facts for mechanical effect." Most directly affected are men who work with machines. As Hannah Arendt writes, "Unlike the tools of workmanship, which at every given moment in the work process remain the servants of the hand, the machines demand that the laborer serve them, that he adjust the natural rhythm of his body to their mechanical movement." But this discipline extends far beyond the work place, affecting not only factory workers but the whole of society. Indeed, as Lewis Mumford suggests, the clock rather than the steam engine became the foundation of the modern industrial system, for once machines were regulated by mechanical, or non-human, time, an impersonal new discipline was imposed on men. Today our lives are increasingly regulated by machines which set standards of performance and product, telling us when to start working, when to stop, what to do and how to do it; and the measure of our submission to mechanical controls is that we are largely unconscious of their influence. But of their influence there can be no doubt.

Historically, one of the first major results of mechanization was to transform labor: what had formerly been an integral part of human life became a means to an end. To feed and operate the machines of the new civilization required not just raw materials but "free" labor. Since industrialism was pioneered by capitalists this meant a special kind of freedom. Karl Polanyi has described the working principle of the early capitalist market economy: "Production is interaction of man and nature; if this process is to be organized through a self-regulating mechanism of barter and exchange, then man and nature must be brought into its orbit; they must be subject to supply and demand, that is, be dealt with as commodities, as goods produced for sale." But for man to be treated as a commodity, a brutal operation was required: the "freeing" of labor from traditional bonds of craft, family and community. Thus one of the many tragic ironies of the early capitalist market economy: expected automatically to produce general welfare, it split the community in ways which survive to this day. As Polanyi notes, "To separate labor from other activities of life and to subject it to the laws of the market was to annihilate all organic forms of existence and to replace them by a different type of organization, an atomistic and individualistic one."

When labor became a mechanically regulated commodity, man lost part of himself. This returns us to our major theme of alienation; for as Karl Marx saw it, the worker, having lost control over both the conditions of his labor and the fruit of his labor, become alienated from himself. The idea of alienation, however, Marx had borrowed from Hegel, who conceived it chiefly in metaphysical terms and who described it as a general human condition. In *The Philosophy of History* Hegel wrote of "spirit" (or the human mind) as "at war with itself"; in consequence, it "has to overcome itself as its [own] most formidable obstacle. That development which in the sphere of Nature is a peaceful growth, is [for the] spirit, a severe, a mighty conflict with itself. What spirit really strives for is the realization of its

Ideal being; but in doing so, it hides that goal from its own vision, and is proud and well satisfied in this alienation." For Hegel, therefore, man's own intellectual creations become independent of their creator and hence alien to him. Human achievement is a dialectical process in which man can advance to higher forms only by overcoming or mastering himself and the cultural forces that he creates. Therefore the history of man is a history of his alienation or frustration, and of his self-realization through the conquest of these frustrations.

While Hegel saw alienation as a metaphysical problem, Marx gave it a sociological frame of reference. In his essay of 1844 he wrote that under the system of private property the worker was alienated from the product of his labor and also from the means of production—both of which had become things "not belonging to him." The worker thus separated from his product is alienated from himself, since his labor is no longer his own but the property of another. Finally, he is alienated from other men, since his chief link with them now is the commodities they exchange or produce.

Marx was the first to describe this process of "reification" (or converting an abstraction into something real) by which capitalist society transforms all personal relations between men into objective relations between things or money —the substitute for commodities. Later, in *Capital*, he referred to this process as the "fetishism of commodities" and wrote: "The labor of the individual asserts itself as part of the labor of society, only by means of the relations which the act of exchange establishes directly between the products, and indirectly, through them, between the producers. To the latter, therefore, the relations connecting the labor of one individual with that of the rest appear, not as direct social relations between individuals at work, but as what they really are, material relations between persons and social relations between things." According to Marx, the disintegrative or "negative" character of capitalist society lay chiefly in its alienation of human labor and in its denial of opportunities for men to fulfill themselves in meaningful work.

The industrial revolution and its subsequent transformation of human labor into a commodity are among the major alienating forces in the capitalist world. But our picture of that world is not complete. To administer their complex technology and labor markets men developed elaborate social structures or bureaucracies which are no less impersonal in their effects than machines. Indeed, that is their aim; and the attempt further to "rationalize" the conduct of human affairs by subjecting it to rules, regularity and a hierarchy of command—the distinguishing characteristics of bureaucracy as described by Max Weber—has enormously increased the power of alien forces over men. Marx's analysis of the new conditions of labor under capitalism was complemented half a century later by Weber's studies of bureaucracy. As Weber wrote, bureaucracy became particularly appropriate for capitalism because "the more bureaucracy 'depersonalizes' itself, the more completely it succeeds in achieving the exclusion of love, hatred, and every purely personal, especially irrational and incalculable, feeling from the execution of official tasks. In the place of the old-type ruler who is moved by sympathy, favor, grace and gratitude, modern culture requires for its sustaining external apparatus the emotionally detached, and hence rigorously 'professional' expert."

Bureaucracies typify not only government—as many believe—but also industry, armies and navies, education, philanthropy, banking, communications media, and all other activities that require organized effort. For the increasing numbers who work in bureaucratic settings, the consequences are much the same as for persons directly involved in the machine process. Thus Weber extended the concept of alienated labor to all organized or institutionalized work situations and he described a universal bureaucratic trend in which soldiers, scientists, civil servants—all were "separated" or alienated from their respective means of production or administration "in the same way as capitalist enterprise has separated the workers from theirs."

But bureaucracy is not just significant because of its impersonal character or because it transforms a means—efficiency—into an end. Precisely because it represents a concentration of power, its effect, as C. Wright Mills observes, is to coerce, to manipulate. "Organized irresponsibility, in this impersonal sense, is a leading characteristic of modern industrial societies everywhere. On every hand the individual is confronted with seemingly remote organizations; he feels dwarfed and helpless before the managerial cadres and their manipulated and manipulating minions."

How industrial and bureaucratic machines alienate men

can be seen most clearly in modern conditions of work. Although there has been considerable amelioration of the harsh conditions of early capitalism, thanks to the drive for a shorter working day and the abolition of child labor, the alienation of men from the means and ends of work as described by Marx and Weber characterizes most modern industrial societies. Increasing division of labor, greater mechanization, the growth of giant industrial and financial enterprises—these are the agents of our economic power and also of individual powerlessness. For evidence we need only look at men on the job. They must work, but how and for what? Few of them have known the pursuit of individual crafts. But millions of men and women labor in large-scale enterprises where work is monotonous and repetitious and where the decreasing need for skilled workers and an increasing division of labor place both the processes and the products of work far beyond their control.

To illustrate, in a recent survey of industrial workers' attitudes Robert Dubin shows that for most of them work is *not* a central life interest. Nor do many of them value the informal associations with fellow workers that jobs offer. Dubin writes: "Not only is the workplace relatively unimportant as a place of preferred primary human relationships, but it cannot even evoke significant sentiments and emotions in its occupants." Other observers of factory life have made it abundantly clear that most workers are not happy in their jobs, that they feel trapped and degraded by their working conditions, that they have a powerful desire to escape from the factory, and that what drives them on is the incessant demands of our consumption economy. But far from escaping, growing numbers of industrial workers and their families are forced to take on additional jobs in order to keep up with the rising cost of living.

The result has been a serious fall in morale. It is a measure of the boring conditions of work in modern industry that management now gives so much attention to "human relations." For many years it was believed that if men could not obtain satisfaction in their jobs, then their "informal" associations with fellow workers would make up for the loss. The famous Hawthorne experiments at Western Electric seemed to show that increases or decreases in output were related not to physical conditions but rather to the strength of informal associations or cliques among factory workers. To raise morale and increase efficiency (the real goal) desperate and sometimes ludicrous measures were taken by management. Thus in one American factory a picture of the finished product was installed on the assembly line so that workers performing their restricted tasks might better "identify" themselves with it! But despite the great stress placed by management on "human relations," evidence of workers' continued dissatisfaction multiplies. It is reflected in restriction of output, wildcat strikes, outright sabotage and, perhaps most common, in feelings of detachment from the entire work process.

As we have suggested, it is not just industrial workers who find themselves alienated from work. A growing army of salaried or white-collar workers faces conditions which if more pleasant physically are no less disruptive psychologically. The powerlessness of factory employees is matched by the powerlessness of white collars. But bureaucracy must not be seen as alienating only when it is huge, or because it aims at ever greater efficiency. A cruel work situation is bound to evoke anger or rage, however repressed. But even under "ideal" conditions of bureaucratic order—where there are neither great creative incentives nor disruptive tensions—the result is an isolated, remote world of conformists, or what Mills calls the "cheerful robots." Like industrial management, bureaucracy does not simply turn men and women into automatons; it also wants them to like the process and to co-operate in it.

Since many giant bureaucracies are chiefly selling and marketing institutions, it is not just brain work that is being consumed but personalities as well. Here in the "personality market" as Mills describes it, bureaucracy goes "mere" industry one better in making a commodity of man. "The personality market, the most decisive effect and symptom of the great salesroom, underlies the all-pervasive distrust and self-alienation so characteristic of metropolitan people. Without common values and mutual trust, the cash nexus that links one man to another in transient contact has been made subtle in a dozen ways and made to bite deeper into all areas of life and relations. People are required by the salesman ethic and convention to pretend interest in others in order to manipulate them. . . . Men are estranged from one another as each secretly tries to make an instrument of the other, and in time a full circle is made: one makes an instrument of himself, and is estranged from it also."

In short, modern conditions of work under capitalism are alienating largely because the individual worker has lost—or is unable to gain—control over "his" technical and social machines. But there is more to it. Men who experience disorder in their careers must inevitably find disorder in their community life. Harold L. Wilensky writes, "Most men . . . never experience the joys of a life plan because most work situations do not afford the necessary stable progression over the worklife. There is a good deal of chaos in modern labor markets, chaos intrinsic to urban-industrial society. Rapid technological change dilutes old skills, makes others obsolete and creates demand for new ones; a related decentralization of industry displaces millions, creating the paradox of depressed areas in prosperous economies; metropolitan deconcentration shifts the clientele of service establishments, sometimes smashing or restructuring careers; recurrent crises such as wars, depressions, recessions, coupled with the acceleration of fad and fashion in consumption, add a note of unpredictability to the whole." The result, as Wilensky shows, is retreat from both work and community.

But what of those who are entering the labor market? What they face is not just the prospect of disorderly work careers, but also of work for no significant reason beyond consumption. Most men no longer produce useful things; they do make wasted and wasteful commodities and services. (In the United States today there are actually more people employed in providing services than in the production of goods.) The impact of these conditions on rising generations has been vividly described by Paul Goodman in his *Growing Up Absurd.* As he writes, "Economically and vocationally, a very large proportion of the young people are in a more drastic plight than anything so far mentioned. In our society as it is, there are not enough worthy jobs. But if our society, being as it is, were run more efficiently and soberly, for a majority there would soon not be any jobs at all. There is at present nearly full employment and there may be for some years, yet a vast number of young people are rationally unemployable, useless." Useless because as crafts and craftsmanship have declined, the job opportunities open to them have increasingly become variations on the theme of "boondoggling"—whether they become "organization men" or, more likely, semi-skilled factory operatives. In any case, the work available to them is unlikely to ennoble them or their society. Writes Goodman: "It's hard to grow up when there isn't enough man's work."

Will it be any easier to grow up in the future? As the age of automation approaches, promising untold wealth and leisure, the forces separating men from the means and ends of work will inevitably grow stronger. Indeed, as far as conditions of work are concerned, the submission of workers to machines will be complete. Today, as Daniel Bell observes, a man can still stop a machine or wreck it: he has the remnants of power over it. But with automation that power will be lost for good, except perhaps for a small elite of engineers who will be busy designing and tending the machines of the future. As Lewis Mumford writes in *The Transformations of Man*, "modern man has already depersonalized himself so effectively that he is no longer man enough to stand up to his machines." Looking ahead, Mumford warns: "By the perfection of the automaton man will become completely alienated from his world and reduced to nullity—the kingdom and the power and the glory now belong to the machine."

Fantasy? Already the uncanny power of machines has entered into the delusions that mark psychotic disturbances. In times past, Bruno Bettelheim observes, delusions took either human or superhuman forms; but today "what is so new in the hopes and fears of the machine age are that savior and destroyer are no longer clothed in the image of man; no longer are the figures that we imagine can save and destroy us direct projections of our human experience. What we now hope will save us, and what in our delusions we fear will destroy us, is something that no longer has human qualities." That device or projection is the machine, and not surprisingly psychoanalysts refer to a characteristic delusion, the "influencing machine," a device which some insane persons believe exerts an extraordinary and evil power over them against their will. As Bettelheim puts it, "The psychotic person ends up feeling controlled by mechanical devices that no longer resemble anything human or even animal-like. Thus modern man, when he is haunted, whether sane or profoundly disturbed, is no longer haunted by other men or by grandiose projections of man, but by machines.

This, while at the same time relying for his protection or salvation on machines."

If we have placed such great stress on our machine age and on the conditions and purposes of work, it is not because we "accept the metaphysical view that man's self is most crucially expressed in work-activity." Rather, it is because of a fundamental break in our society between work and other activities. This break has had enormous consequences. Men are dehumanized not only by the work situation but also by the ends for which our society uses work, chiefly consumption for its own sake.

As capitalism began to accumulate greater surpluses of wealth (especially for those on top) the unproductive acquisition and accumulation of goods became the primary means of achieving social status in the community. Veblen has given us the classical description of this process. He wrote: "Ownership began and grew into a human institution on grounds unrelated to the subsistence minimum. The dominant incentive was from the outset the invidious distinction attaching to wealth, and, save temporarily and by exception, no other motive has usurped the primacy at any later stage of the development." He goes on to observe that "under the regime of individual ownership the most available means of visibly achieving a purpose is that afforded by the acquisition and accumulation of goods; and as the self-regarding antithesis between man and man reaches fuller consciousness, the propensity for achievement—the instinct of workmanship—tends more and more to shape itself into a straining to excel others in pecuniary achievement." If consumption then became "conspicuous" it was because in an increasingly heterogeneous and differentiated society there was no other ready means of achieving status except by spending money and acquiring goods. But as Veblen stressed, such consumption was essentially wasteful and in conflict with what he considered a universal trait in man, the instinct of workmanship. Or, as Arendt puts it, "The industrial revolution . . . replaced all workmanship with labor, and the result has been that the things of the modern world have become labor products whose natural fate is to be consumed, instead of work products which are there to be used."

The process of consumption, reaching its highest form in the United States, is alienating in still another way. Fromm suggests, "We are surrounded by things of whose nature and origin we know nothing. . . . We consume, as we produce, without any concrete relatedness to the objects with which we deal." Moreover, the volume of consumption is determined to a large extent by the artificial stimulants of a giant advertising industry; and if consumers learn to manipulate things, they in turn are manipulated by the propagandists of commerce. The strategy of planned obsolescence—by which things are made to wear out quickly and then be replaced—may stimulate the economy, but it can hardly be said to serve human needs. In short, working chiefly to consume, consuming to achieve status, accumulating things that have no meaning, wasting on a gigantic scale—these are the conditions in which we live. The result is a wasteland of junk and of human aspirations.

Closely related to, indeed part of, the consumption process is the way modern man uses his leisure time, if he has any. The qualification is overlooked by many writers commenting on contemporary leisure behavior who assume that there have been gains in leisure for all working people. The fact is, as Harold L. Wilensky demonstrates, that we have an extremely uneven distribution of leisure. He reports: "The average man's gain in leisure with economic growth has been exaggerated. Estimates of annual and life-time leisure suggest that the skilled urban worker may have gained the position of his thirteenth century counterpart. Upper strata have, in fact, lost out. Even though their worklives are shorter and vacations longer, these men work many steady hours week after week—sometimes reaching a truly startling total." Many who do have leisure, on the other hand, are forced into it because they are marginal to the economy; and they would give up their leisure for work if they could. The shorter work-week, instead of increasing opportunities for leisure, has simply encouraged growing numbers of men and women to take on second jobs, as we noted earlier. Most critical evaluations of leisure and its uses apply more to a beckoning future (when, presumably, all of us will have joined the leisure class) than to the present.

Nevertheless, work has declined as a central activity, even if most men still work hard; and as Mills observes, a "big split" has taken place between work and leisure. Instead of being closely integrated with work, as in the past, the pursuit of leisure has become a desperate escape from work which is increasingly meaningless. Small wonder that the "idols of leisure" have replaced the "idols of work" for so many. But leisure itself has become meaningless, a packaged mass activity, its values provided by the entertainment industry. And although men are trained for work, they are not trained to spend leisure creatively. If some achieve freedom for an hour or a day, many of them, Robert MacIver points out, find only a "great emptiness." Escaping from work, they escape also from themselves.

The alienating influences of industrialism extend far beyond the individual worker; they touch with equal force upon his family and his community. Of the many effects of industrialism on the family, perhaps most important is the breakdown of the extended kinship group which, as we saw, had been the primary productive and social unit in the pre-industrial age. As the old crafts declined, and labor became increasingly divided and specialized, the economic and social base of the large family was destroyed. Lost were the customs and skills that had been passed on from one generation to another. Gone were the close bonds between young and old, and especially the respect that youth had previously given to age. Into the new industrial cities poured millions who had been cut off from their traditional family roots. These are the most visible consequences for the family of the industrial revolution.

However, considerably less is known about the more subtle psychological effects of industrialism. As Richard Titmuss observes, there are many long-range and hidden influences which may not appear until many generations later. He writes: "It must . . . be remembered that most of the long-industrialized countries of the West are still heavily burdened by the as yet uncompensated disservices of the earlier stages of their economic growth. Viewed in terms of the long-drawn cycle of family life, the violent industrial upheavals of the nineteenth century, the poverty, the unemployment, the social indiscipline, the authoritarianism of men and the cruelties to children, are by no means as remote today in their consequences as some economists and historians would have us believe." Thus the cult of "human relations" in industry and office to which we referred earlier ignores the fact that morale is not just a function of working conditions; but also of life outside the workplace. Yet what society expects of men and women outside the factory or office is considerably different from what is demanded inside. For example, while "stability" is heavily valued in family life, industrial conditions in the Western world have been marked by unemployment, the displacement of old skills, the increasing mechanization and rationalization of work and especially by changes—often loss—of status and self-respect. As Titmuss points out, there is fundamental conflict between the values or norms of expected behavior in the workplace and those norms which prevail in the wider society and which are expected to influence the worker or employee in his role as a husband and father. "In these roles, society tends increasingly to expect him not to submit to 'life as it happens' but to consciously control his affairs, to think about his children's tomorrow, to rationally and not blindly influence their behavior, and to accord to his wife a greater measure of tolerance, respect, and understanding than many husbands gave to their wives in the nineteenth century." But if workers cannot achieve stability or self-respect on the job, or have little conception of their place in the scheme of things, how can they perform satisfactorily as husbands and fathers? The answer is that many cannot.

With changes in family function, especially the decline of the large kinship group as an operating unit, have come significant changes in structure. Perhaps most important, work is now increasingly separated from family life: fathers disappear during the day, leaving children to grow up chiefly with their mothers—unless the mothers themselves are at work, as growing numbers of them are. Related to this break is the enormous suburban trend, distinguished by what sociologists call the "nuclear" family, that is, the small core unit of two parents and their children. High divorce rates in countries such as the United States are only the most dramatic evidence of the many serious strains to which the new family is exposed.

Most affected by the breakdown of the extended family or kinship group, however, are the aged. That breakdown has been accompanied by a tremendous increase in life expectancy (from 40.5 years at birth for white women in the United States in 1850 to 73.5 years in 1957) and also by earlier retirement from work. In North America and Western Europe a growing army of the aged finds itself increasingly cut off from family life and from meaningful pursuits. A recent American survey shows that the overwhelming majority of our citizens oppose the idea of having older persons live with their children. As these trends continue

—the prolongation of life, early retirement, breakdown of
the extended family—the aged become outcasts in a society
like ours that places such emphasis on youth and its energies.
Separate housing, even separate cities—this is the lot of our
elderly citizens. In their twilight world there is only fleeting
contact with the community.

If the aged are increasingly isolated from community
life, theirs is a fate which many groups share in an urban
civilization. Not only does the city weaken the traditional
kinship group; it also tends to atomize the individual by
freeing him from old bonds. The anonymity and hence the
alienation of the city dweller have never been more graph-
ically described than by Engels speaking of London in
1844:

> The restless and noisy activity of the crowded streets
> is highly distasteful, and it is surely abhorrent to human
> nature itself. Hundreds of thousands of men and women
> drawn from all classes and ranks of society pack the
> streets of London. Are they not all human beings with the
> same innate characteristics and potentialities? And do
> they not all aim at happiness by following similar meth-
> ods? Yet they rush past each other as if they had nothing
> in common. They are tacitly agreed on one thing only—
> that everyone should keep to the right of the pavement
> so as not to collide with the stream of people moving in
> the opposite direction. No one even thinks of sparing a
> glance for his neighbors in the streets. The more that
> Londoners are packed into a tiny space, the more repul-
> sive and disgraceful becomes the brutal indifference with
> which they ignore their neighbors and selfishly concen-
> trate upon their private affairs. We know well enough
> that this isolation of the individual—this narrow-
> minded egotism—is everywhere the fundamental princi-
> ple of modern society. But nowhere is this selfish egotism
> so blatantly evident as in the frantic bustle of the great
> city. The disintegration of society into individuals, each
> guided by his private principles and each pursuing his
> own aims has been pushed to its furthest limits in Lon-
> don. Here indeed human society has been split into its
> component atoms.

Thus London in 1844. But is this not also London—and
New York—more than a century later?
What Engels had described was one of the first modern

metropolises. Although some of its features have softened, it is basically the same: mechanical, atomistic, impersonal, predatory. Half a century after Engels, the German sociologist Georg Simmel observed that "the deepest problems of modern life derive from the claim of the individual to preserve the autonomy and individuality of his existence in the face of overwhelming social forces," notably life in the great city where he had become a mere cog in a machine. Today in an increasingly citified world, these pressures have mounted and men find it difficult to preserve their identity.

With the rise of the great industrial city came another historical development in the breakdown of traditional community bonds: the antagonism of social classes. As Polanyi notes, the industrial revolution caused "a social dislocation of stupendous proportions, and the problem of poverty was merely the economic aspect of this event." Those at the bottom were not the only ones affected, although in the early industrial period "huge masses of the laboring population resembled more the specters that might haunt a nightmare than human beings. But if the workers were physically dehumanized, the owning classes were morally degraded. The traditional unity of a Christian society was giving place to a denial of responsibility on the part of the well-to-do for the conditions of their fellows. The Two Nations were taking shape. To the bewilderment of thinking minds, unheard-of wealth turned out to be inseparable from unheard-of poverty. Scholars proclaimed in unison that a science had been discovered which put the laws governing man's world beyond any doubt. It was at the behest of these laws that compassion was removed from the hearts, and a stoic determination to renounce human solidarity in the name of the greatest happiness of the greatest number gained the dignity of secular religion."

The class struggles that have raged in Europe and North America may then be regarded, at least from the point of view of those at the bottom, as not just an effort to secure a larger slice of the economic pie but also as a desperate attempt to restore a lost community. If this struggle is less violent today than in the past and if the workers of Europe and America have made considerable material progress, it would be naïve to assume that they have found that community. The "two nations" described by Polanyi may not be as far apart as in the nineteenth century, but the gap between them still exists. Richard Hoggart, in his study of working class culture in Britain, shows the sharp division between "them" (those on top: bosses, policemen, judges, teachers, civil servants) and "us" in the working class. As Hoggart writes, " 'They' are 'the people at the top,' the 'higher-ups,' the people who give you your dole, call you up, tell you to go to war, fine you, made you split the family in the 'thirties to avoid a reduction in the Means Test allowance, 'get yer in the end,' 'aren't really to be trusted,' 'talk posh,' 'are all twisters really,' 'never tell yer owt' (e.g. about a relative in hospital), 'clap yer in clink,' 'will do y' down if they can,' 'summons yer,' 'are all in a click (clique) together,' 'treat y' like muck.' " Toward "them" the basic attitude is one of distrust.

Hoggart is writing chiefly of workers old enough to remember the great depression, when working class solidarity was intensified by severe distress. But if working people then had a keen sense of "them" and "us" they also had strong commitments as members of a group with common interests and needs. That is, if alienated from the larger society, at least they felt they belonged to their own class, which was not necessarily a matter of class consciousness in Marxist terms but rather a sense of sharing problems with kin and neighbors whose work and living arrangements were similar. The class conscious political parties and labor movements that grew up in nineteenth-century Europe were the products, not the cause, of these common experiences.

Has that solidarity declined? Recent developments in the United States and in Europe suggest that with greater prosperity the militancy of working class movements has fallen sharply. If not true of the older generation, still loyal to the slogans of yesteryear, it seems to be particularly true of working class youth, as Karl Bednarik shows. The young European (and even more, the young American) worker of today, he claims, is a "new type": apolitical, hedonistic, individualistic; in short, a far cry from the militant radicals of his father's generation. But the decay of working class culture, which was itself a defense against alienation, has not necessarily led to greater integration. Along with their middle class contemporaries, young workers face a world without values.

But it is not only material possessions which divide men. In a heterogeneous society like ours there are numerous and sometimes overlapping minorities or "out-groups." Because ours is a multi-racial and multi-ethnic population, we are most likely to think of such groups in terms of color and religious affiliation since these distinctions are among the most powerful of all social barriers. But it seems legitimate to broaden the concept of minority to include other groups who, because of some distinguishing characteristic, are rejected by the community. Among these groups are the young, the aged, the physically handicapped, and the sexually deviant. We do not mean to suggest that all of them face equally serious patterns of prejudice and discrimination. Majority attitudes may range from ill-concealed hate and violence at one extreme to pity at the other; and barriers to solidarity and integration differ. Negroes, for example, are segregated in enormous ghettos; while homosexuals inhabit half-worlds with no visible physical boundaries. Nevertheless, all such out-groups face a certain degree of isolation from society: they are in the community but not of it. As a result, they tend to form more or less distinct "subcultures" of their own. Although these subcultures offer some security and protection, common to most of them is a striving for integration with the majority groups on top. Furthermore, it is only natural for minority members to acquire some of the prevailing attitudes toward them. When this becomes self-hatred for sharing the despised or feared characteristic, we have perhaps the most extreme form which this pattern of alienation takes: alienated from others, they become alienated from themselves.

We began by saying that men today are estranged from others as well as from themselves. But "others" means not only the social communities in which they live; it also refers to the natural and supernatural world beyond. Thus, if we speak of man's alienation from nature, we do not mean nature in any metaphysical sense—although fairly serious metaphysical problems are involved; all we mean is that men and women today are not as close to land, air, sea, wind and mountain as their ancestors or their contemporaries who have yet to be blessed with an industrial and urban civilization. Wordsworth summed it up beautifully in his famous sonnet: "The world is too much with us; late and soon,/ Getting and spending, we lay waste our powers:/ Little we see in Nature that is ours."

Although conceptions of the external world vary widely, many primitive societies and those areas still influenced by

Oriental mysticism, feel themselves in fairly close unity with nature. In the pre-scientific Western world also man and nature were considered related parts of a more or less harmonious whole. Whether nature was considered hostile or friendly, man felt close to it. For leading thinkers in the West, however, this intimate relationship began to end with the seventeenth-century revolution in science and philosophy, and, for ordinary citizens, with the industrial revolution that followed. To understand and control nature—the goals of modern science and technology—men first had to separate or alienate themselves from it. As Whitehead puts it, "Nature, in scientific thought . . . had its laws formulated without any reference to dependence on individual observers." It is Descartes who is credited with this radical separation of man (as subject or observer) from nature (as object or external world). If, as many now charge, there is both arrogance and ontological error in the naked egoism and "selfishness" of his famous *Cogito, ergo sum,* with its extraordinary emphasis on the individual self as against the external world, we must remember that Descartes was a creature of his time—and his time was the dawn of modern scientific discovery.

What were the consequences of this division between nature and man? First of all, it led to what we now call the scientific attitude, with its spirit of detachment, a spirit which has become the keynote of our age. For as science developed, it became more abstract and increasingly remote from common life to the point where, as W. Macneile Dixon wrote, "Science is the view of life where everything human is excluded from the prospect. It is of intention inhuman, supposing, strange as it may seem, that the further we travel from ourselves the nearer we approach the truth, the further from our deepest sympathies, from all we care for, the nearer we are to reality, the stony heart of the scientific universe."

The flowering of science and technology gave man enormous power to control nature and thereby transform society. Note the word "control"; for the language we use offers a clue to the new relationship between man and nature. Thus when we speak of our power "over" nature we reveal a certain antagonism between man and the external world, with nature regarded as something to be conquered —or even destroyed. The greater that power, the more we are alienated from nature and from ourselves.

Estrangement from nature is now the common experience. Industrialism created the first cities in which nature played little or no part. Barbara and J. L. Hammond have given us a vivid description of England during the early nineteenth century: "There towns . . . were now losing their last glimpse of nature. Formerly the men and women who lived in the English town . . . were never far from the open country: their town life was fringed with orchards and gardens. But as the Industrial Revolution advanced, a Manchester was growing up in which the workmen would find it harder and harder to escape out of the wide web of smoke and squalor that enveloped their daily lives. . . . Civilization . . . was rapidly painting the green spaces black on the industrial map. Manchester still had her Angel Meadows, but they were no longer meadows, and the only angel that came near them was the Angel of Death. . . . Life in such a town brought no alleviation of the tyranny of the industrial system; it only made it more real and sombre to the mind. There was no change of scene or colour, no delight of form or design to break its brooding atmosphere. Town, tree, building, sky, all had become part of the same unrelieved picture. The men and women who left the mill and passed along the streets to their homes did not become less but more conscious of that system as a universal burden, for the town was so constructed and so governed as to enforce rather than modify, to reiterate rather than soften the impressions of an alien and unaccommodating power." He who would call this ancient history need only explore the spreading blight of modern American cities to see that the damage done to nature has been long-lasting, perhaps permanent.

That the damage was not intentional is beside the point. Ironically, contemporary scientists and philosophers today, particularly those of the existentialist school, reject the Cartesian dualism between man as subject and nature as object. But for ordinary citizens, many of them living in grim prisons of concrete and steel, the damage has already been done: the technology that classical science produced has erected almost insurmountable barriers between them and the natural world. As Susanne Langer writes in her *Philosophy in a New Key,* "We have put many stages of artifice and device, of manufacture and alteration, between ourselves and the rest of nature. The ordinary city-dweller knows nothing of the earth's productivity; he does not know the sunrise and rarely notices when the sun sets; ask him in what phase the moon is, or when the tide in the harbor is high, or even how high the average tide runs, and likely as not he cannot answer you. Seed-time and harvest are nothing to him. If he has never witnessed an earthquake, a great flood, or a hurricane, he probably does not feel the power of nature as a reality surrounding his life at all. . . . Nature, as man has always known it, he knows no more." In the Western world most of us are the city dwellers that Dr. Langer describes; and one need not be a mystic to recognize that something is missing from our lives. Are we not poorer for it?

Isolation from nature is not just a matter of living in cities; even more important it involves a momentous change in man's outlook on the world. Men do not simply coexist with nature; they search for meaning in it. For this they long depended on myth and religion. Anthropologists teach us that while there is extreme variation in man's religious experiences, primitive myths and the great ethical religions of East and West are alike in their integrative functions; that is, they explain and in their rituals support a basic solidarity of man and man, and of man and nature. It matters not whether the religionist's view of nature and society is sympathetic or unsympathetic, comforting or frightening, or whether his faith is emotional or rational. All religious beliefs known to man help create and sustain bonds between him and the external world of other men and of nature. But if faith weakens or is destroyed in the onslaught of science and secularism, man is truly alone. As Joseph Campbell writes in his *The Hero With a Thousand Faces*, "The problem of mankind today is . . . the opposite to that of men in the comparatively stable periods of those great co-ordinating mythologies which now are known as lies. Then all meaning was in the group, in the great anonymous forms, none in the self-expressive individual; today no meaning is in the group—none in the world: all is in the individual. But . . . one does not know toward what one moves. One does not know by what one is propelled. . . . Not the animal world, not the plant world, not the miracle of the spheres, but man himself is now the crucial mystery. Man is that alien presence with whom the forces of egoism must come to terms, through whom the ego is to be crucified and resurrected, and in whose image society is to be reformed."

But if the decline of what Campbell calls the "mytho-
logically instructed community" has furthered the alienation of modern man, a liberating process has also taken
place; and spiritual isolation is part of the price paid for
new-found knowledge and power. The loss of religion may
mean less psychological security but it has also meant—
since it accompanied—a great social and economic revolution. Thus Protestantism, in its attack against the power,
dogma, and the ritual of the universal church, helped to
free man for worldly activities; and, as Max Weber showed,
provided moral support for rising capitalism. Great works
resulted. But since Protestantism made man face God alone,
without the community of the medieval church, and stressed
the fundamental evil and powerlessness of man, a great
price was paid for that freedom. That price, as Erich Fromm
has so brilliantly described it in *Escape From Freedom*,
was a new and terrible isolation which was accentuated by
capitalism. For what Protestantism had started to do in
freeing man spiritually, capitalism continued to do in other
spheres. But at the same time it made the individual even
more alone and isolated and intensified his feelings of in-
significance and powerlessness.

Today we live in an increasingly secularized society and
religious faith is less than ever before a motivating force
and an explanation of the world around us. As Fromm
writes, "Our culture is perhaps the first completely secularized culture in human history. We have shoved away
awareness of and concern with the fundamental problems of
human existence. We are not concerned with the meaning of
life." What then of claims, particularly in the United States,
that we are witnessing a revival of religious faith? Is this at
best a spurious revival, in which churches of all denomina-
tions resemble social clubs, and religion itself is secularized?
Will Herberg in his study of the three major denomina-
tions in the United States says, "It is only too evident that
the religiousness characteristic of America today is very
often a religiousness without religion, a religiousness with
almost any kind of content or none, a way of sociability
or 'belonging' rather than a way of reorienting life to God.
It is thus frequently a religiousness without serious commitment, without real inner conviction, without genuine existential decision. What should reach down to the core of
existence, shattering and renewing, merely skims the surface of life, and yet succeeds in generating the sincere feel-

ing of being religious. Religion thus becomes a kind of protection the self throws up against the radical demand of faith." If so, is the weakening of traditional faith and the apparent search for a social rather than a spiritual community in the church simply another measure of alienation?

We now have a view of man divorced from nature, bereft of his religion, isolated in his community, chained to monotonous work. It is appropriate at this point to consider our evolving mass society, its culture, and its politics. One view of alienation that has gained wide currency in our time, particularly among critics of popular democracy, is a picture of man crushed by mass society. First voiced more than a hundred years ago by such gloomy prophets of democracy's "leveling effect" as Kierkegaard and Tocqueville, both of whom saw serious threats to individualism in the "tyranny of the multitude," it now finds expression in the conservative Ortega y Gasset's statement that the masses have gained "complete social power" and that "the mass crushes beneath it everything that is different, everything that is excellent, individual, qualified and select." Similarly, Jaspers has written of the individual's fate in the mass: "Man as a member of a mass is no longer his isolated self. The individual is merged in the mass, to become something other than he is when he stands alone. On the other hand in the mass the individual becomes an isolated atom whose individual craving to exist has been sacrificed, since the fiction of a general equality prevails."

At the outset, it is important to distinguish between mass society and mass culture: while closely related, they should not be confused. A mass society is one in which great numbers of people are recruited and organized for political purposes, or, particularly in the United States, for common exposure to far-reaching techniques of communication and for artificially stimulated patterns of consumption. The mass culture is the communications system that has developed during the past century (another technological revolution) for transmitting orders, messages, appeals, entertainment, information from the leaders to the led. When we talk about mass society, therefore, we do not simply mean the communications media, although they have played a vital part in the rise of that society. The media may not be neutral instruments, but what is alienating about them is the functions they perform.

Historically, the mass society resulted from the rapid increase in the size of the electorate in Western Europe and America after the turn of the century. Extension of suffrage to the working class who had fought for it, led in turn to the rise of mass political parties (chiefly in Europe) and also to new techniques of communication: mass circulation newspapers, film, radio, and television. With the first two of these media at hand, mass propaganda became a powerful weapon by the end of World War I. Since then dictatorships and advertisers have developed mass persuasion into an art. It is no coincidence that the Nazis acknowledged their debt to American advertising techniques, for in the United States the various media have been exploited chiefly by advertisers (on an unprecedented scale) and by commercial entertainment interests. It is these interests which have built the "mass culture" as we know it; and it is they who have provided that culture with its core values; it is they who administer what Veblen called "laughing gas" to an unsuspecting audience.

The results of these developments are well known. In politics, the sheer numbers of people involved tend to engulf the individual, whether he dissents from majority opinion and taste, or whether he merely conforms helplessly with the overwhelming majority. It was the weight of numbers crushing the individual that disturbed early critics of mass democracy, such as Tocqueville and Bryce. But the "fatalism of the multitude" or mass apathy stems not just from numbers; it comes also from the individual citizen's feeling of powerlessness in an increasingly complex world. As Ernst Kris and Nathan Leites have observed, "Individuals in the mass societies of the twentieth century are to an ever increasing extent involved in public affairs; it becomes increasingly difficult to ignore them. But 'ordinary' individuals have ever less the feeling that they can *understand* or *influence* the very events upon which their life and happiness [are] known to depend." Many public issues are highly complex; to exercise citizenship intelligently, men and women must have an inkling of where their interests lie. If they find politics incomprehensible, they will be encouraged to depend on experts and leaders to interpret and decide for them.

Although mass society is a political as well as a cultural phenomenon, many of its critics, among them Ortega y Gasset and T. S. Eliot, have concentrated their attack chiefly against what they regard as its vulgar values, its sameness, its threat to "high" culture. While one may share their concern about the danger of standardized tastes, or about the threat which mass behavior in politics or in culture poses for individual expression, there is far more to the problem than this—indeed, far more than many aristocratically inclined critics of mass society (and of democracy) want to see. For it is not only men of sensibility who feel crushed by the sheer weight of mass society and its values.

In short, what is alienating in mass society is not merely the corruption of art, or the power of the multitudes—a power often exaggerated—but more importantly, the atomization of individuals who make up the mass. In that society, as William Kornhauser has suggested, there is a tendency for "the aggregates of individuals [to be] related to one another only by way of their relation to a common authority, especially the state. That is, individuals are not directly related to one another in a variety of independent groups. A population in this condition is not insulated in any way from the ruling group, nor yet from elements within itself." In time the many secondary groups, associations and publics which men had formed in an earlier age tend to lose their role as intermediaries between state (or media) and individual. This tendency was particularly notable in Nazi Germany, which set out to build an elaborate system of mass control through terror and bureaucracy; but it is also apparent in our own society, despite our reputation for being a nation of joiners (the fact is that most of our citizens are not joiners).

Mass society weakens or destroys traditional human groupings, thus leaving the individual at the mercy of impersonal "communication," such as newspaper and radio. In addition, the process of communication itself, presumably a two-way system, tends to become a one-way street, with individuals more on the receiving or taking end than on the giving end. How does one talk back to a TV screen? As a result, the formation of opinion is facilitated for those who control the channels of communication—whether they be propagandists in a military dictatorship or the advertising industry in our own society; the stage is set for manipulation of tastes and opinions as obstacles to mass persuasion are removed. A manipulated mass is alienated to the extent that it is powerless to withstand these pressures. Here we can see why it is not the "masses," those dumb beasts who threaten individual excellence, but a powerful elite which monopolizes the means of communication, thereby weakening primary human relations and creating obedient multitudes.

Robert Merton writes: "On every side, they [the media audiences] feel themselves the object of manipulation. They see themselves as the target for ingenious methods of control, through advertising which cajoles, promises, terrorizes; through propaganda that, utilizing available techniques, guides the unwitting audience into opinions which may or may not coincide with the best interests of themselves or their affiliates; through cumulatively subtle methods of salesmanship which may simulate values common to both salesman and client for private and self-interested motives. In place of a sense of *Gemeinschaft*—genuine community of values—there intrudes *pseudo-Gemeinschaft* —the feigning of personal concern with the other fellow in order to manipulate him the better." No wonder that in this most alienated of societies the slogan "togetherness" was first promoted by an advertiser.

If many are persuaded to accept the spurious values handed down to them, a dissenting few can always be depended on to reject them. In this rejection can be seen still another major form of alienation, reflected at one extreme in the revolt of artists and intellectuals against what they consider the uncongenial and materialistic standards of bourgeois society. Personifying this revolt in their art, as well as in their lives, are writers like Baudelaire (an "internal emigrant" who longed to escape "anywhere out of this world"); Rimbaud (who *did* escape and whose self-imposed exile became a model for many artistic rebels following him) and Dostoyevsky (who regarded the freedom of the atheistic individual, his loneliness and isolation as the greatest of evils; and in whose works the twin themes of the atomization of society and self-alienation receive their supreme expression). We are dealing with more than mere disenchantment. Thus Charles Peguy: "The modern world debases. It debases the state; it debases man. It debases love; it debases woman. It debases the race; it debases the child. It debases the nation; it debases the family. It even . . . has succeeded in debasing what is perhaps most difficult in the world to debase—because this is something which has in itself, as in its texture, a particular

kind of dignity, like a singular incapacity for degradation
—it debases death."

The estrangement of many late-nineteenth-century
artists from prevailing cultural values established a model
of rejection; and since their time the alienated hero—if he
can be called a hero—has occupied a major place in the
world of art and literature. As Arnold Hauser notes, for
more than a century the European literary "outlook has one
constant, always predominant and ever more profoundly
rooted characteristic: the consciousness of estrangement and
loneliness." This mood colors the poetry of Yeats, Rilke,
Pound, Eliot; it figures in the works of Gide, Kafka, Thomas
Mann, Hemingway, Thomas Wolfe, Alberto Moravia, and
Sartre—to name just a few. To the alienated man as seen
by these authors, life is essentially meaningless or absurd
—the idea of absurdity being another contribution by
Kierkegaard to the lexicon of alienation. Albert Camus
writes: "A world that can be explained by reasoning, however faulty, is a familiar world. But in a universe that is suddenly deprived of illusions and of light, man feels a stranger.
His is an irremediable exile, because he is deprived of memories of a lost homeland as much he lacks the hope of a
promised land to come. This divorce between man and his
life, the actor and his setting, truly constitutes the feeling
of absurdity."

Camus' own novel, *The Stranger,* is perhaps the most
notable modern attempt to describe a man unrelated to anything or anyone at all, a man for whom everything is meaningless, a man who murders and feels nothing, a man who
ends his tale of "nothingness" and absurdity by saying, "For
all to be accomplished, for me to feel less lonely, all that
remained to hope was that on the day of my execution there
should be a huge crowd of spectators and that they should
greet me with howls of execration." In the modern theater
too, as Martin Esslin suggests, the idea that the human condition is essentially one of alienation now plays an important
part, particularly in the works of Beckett, Ionesco, and
Genet; and it is summed up in Brecht's play, *In the Jungle
of Cities,* where one character says, "If you crammed a ship
full of human bodies till it burst, the loneliness inside it
would be so great, that they would turn to ice . . . so great is
our isolation that even conflict is impossible."

But literature and drama are not the only arts which reflect man's alienation. No less striking is the transformation

of substance and form in graphic art. Here the artist's revolt is directed not only toward the atomized world of men and its values, but toward art itself which (especially in the case of surrealism) becomes deliberately nihilistic, meaningless, even anti-art and "ugly." Arnold Hauser writes of modern painting, "The new century is full of such deep antagonisms, the unity of its outlook on life is so profoundly menaced, that the combination of the farthest extremes, the unification of the greatest contradictions, becomes the main theme, often the only theme, of its art." Picasso, the leading painter of the century, immediately comes to mind. But many other artists might also be mentioned here—for example, the sculptor Giacometti with his elongated and emaciated human figures; or the British painter, Francis Bacon, with his portraits of "humanity caught at a moment of inhumanity, caught at a time of discontinuity, of appalling, invidious, silent horror."

While the alienation felt or expressed by artists is most sensational, not only artists find themselves revolted by the prevailing values of their society. Others too rebel, although more quietly. Kenneth Keniston, in a recent study of the decline of utopian thinking in the young generation in the United States, describes alienation as an "unwillingness to accept what the culture offers." He writes: "Alienation, once seen as the consequence of a cruel (but changeable) economic order, has become for many the central fact of human existence, characterizing man's 'throwness' into a world in which he has no inherent place. Formerly imposed *upon* men by the world around them, estrangement increasingly is chosen *by* them as their dominant reaction to the world." Indifference is their chief response.

Looming over the alienated mass society and its culture is the power of the modern state. Remote from human needs, implacable in its thrust for power, bureaucratic government completes the process of alienation which we have been sketching. Once again, we are witnessing not the beginning but the culmination of a long development. Ernst Cassirer traces the rise of the secular state to Machiavelli and writes: "With Machiavelli we stand at the gateway of the modern world. The desired end is attained; the state has won its full autonomy. Yet this result has had to be bought dearly. The state is entirely independent; but at the same time it is completely isolated. The sharp knife of Machiavelli's thought has cut off all the threads by which in former generations the state was fastened to the organic whole of human existence. The political world has lost its connection not only with religion or metaphysics but also with all the other forms of man's ethical and cultural life. It stands alone —in an empty space."

Of the many consequences of this rupture between state and man, most spectacular is what Cassirer calls the irrational "myth" of the state—the setting for modern dictatorship. But dictatorships represent only the most extreme form of the alienation of the state. In democratic societies also government, like so many other social institutions originally designed to serve man, threatens to become his master. "Behind the growing sense of isolation in society," says Robert Nisbet, "behind the whole quest for community which infuses so many theoretical and practical areas of contemporary life and thought, lies the growing realization that the traditional primary relationships of men have become functionally irrelevant to our State and economy and meaningless to the moral aspirations of individuals." The state has power to do great good as well as evil; and we are not joining those true reactionaries who dream of dismantling it. What we are suggesting is that the state even when providing necessary "services" is detached from individual needs. How to redress this imbalance between state and man has become a burning issue for all men, right and left, who would reorder our society.

Meanwhile, armed with ever greater police powers and increasingly effective means of persuasion, the modern state is now in a position to exploit the most terrible anxieties of men for its own purposes. A striking example of this power was provided recently when the United States Government announced that it was conducting experiments of a "death ray" or neutron bomb. This exquisitely refined weapon would operate selectively, snuffing out human and animal life among the "enemy," but leaving *things*—houses, shops, factories, furnishings, machines—untouched. "A soldier in a tank or an office staff in a building would die, but the tank and the building would remain intact. There would be no lingering radioactivity, so that the attackers could take over and occupy the tank and the building without fear of contamination." *(New York Herald Tribune,* November 2, 1961.)

Who would say that the alienation of modern man is not now complete?

In the preceding pages we have sketched some—by no means all—of the conditions and influences alienating man in modern society. Can these conditions be altered and alienation overcome? Answers to this question demand the best thinking and planning of which our civilization is capable; they require thinking from the heart as well as the head; they demand co-operation among many diverse groups and among nations. The task will be difficult, for the very tools of our analysis and planning tend to be alien forces, compelling us to deal with separate aspects of an interrelated set of problems.

Before we examine some efforts to deal with alienation, we must answer a few of the criticisms of the view advanced by Marx and by modern thinkers such as Fromm, Jaspers, Kahler and Pappenheim that alienation in modern society is almost total and that drastic change is called for. Chief among the arguments against this thesis, of course, is a simple denial that the problem is new. Man's inhumanity to man is age-old, such critics say: the oppressed poor have always been with us; work has always been drudgery (the fall of man made it so); cruelty and torment are ever the common lot. As to the danger of nuclear war and mass extermination, the human beast has always lived dangerously, invented new and more terrible weapons, and in short "loves hanging & drawing & quartering every bit as well as war & slaughtering." But, the argument runs, though this strange rather likable human animal may be foolish and destructive, yet somehow he is crafty enough to survive, both as an individual and as a species. Acceptance of things as they are and have always been is the essence of this view. Its proponents consider alienation an inescapable part of the human condition with which man must learn to live—alone. According to this approach, no amount or kind of social planning will succeed in alleviating the situation, and on the contrary may make it worse. In short, alienation is relative. Anthropology teaches that simpler, more solidaristic communities are not spared the personal disorders which we associate with complex industrial societies. And if citizens of the affluent society feel sorry for themselves, let them remember that most men on earth have never tasted any of the fruits of freedom.

Our view, however, has been that alienation in modern society represents not a change of degree but of kind. Here we borrow the words of Erich Kahler who emphasizes that "What we are concerned with . . . is . . . not *inhumanity*, which has existed all through history and constitutes part of the human form, but *a-humanity*, a phenomenon of rather recent date." This a-humanity, this breakdown of distinctively human qualities and values, culminates in such horrors as the A-bomb or the concentration camp, "the sudden slump of an overwrought civilization into that strange, systematized bestiality." As Kahler points out, "the horrors of the Nazi regime, its use of the most up-to-date techniques for atrocities of the lowest, sub-human, indeed sub-bestial kind, are in some way related to the subtlest intellectual experiences manifesting themselves in the arts and sciences." To Kahler, overcivilization and concomitant dehumanization are the most crucial problems of our age.

Another contemporary writer, Fritz Pappenheim, differentiates our present malady from those of bygone days in terms of the void between hopes and reality: "In the course of history alienation has undergone significant qualitative changes [so] that its meaning today is quite different from what it was in previous eras. In the present stage of history man has means of self-realization at his command which were unknown to him in former periods. The immense advance of science and technology has helped him to understand the forces of nature to such a degree that he is not any longer at their mercy: he has become their master and has succeeded in subjecting them to *his* ends. With this tremendous progress toward the realization of the Promethean dream, a new image has arisen of man who shapes his life and is master of his destiny. Once this concept of the individual's sovereignty has been awakened in the minds of men, a new climate is prepared. The consciousness that man's yearning for self-realization is thwarted becomes a crushing experience which could not have existed in previous stages. In such a situation the alienation of man is not any longer accepted as an inevitable fate; more than ever before in history it is felt as a threat and at the same time a challenge."

How should man face this challenge? While some say that nothing can or should be done, others urge moderate action of various kinds, from inner characterological or personality changes to minor reforms which would leave

intact the basic social and economic structure. The pallia-
tives suggested by such commentators vary widely. Thus,
more faith is called for, or more humor; more housing,
more food, more material comforts, more education to improve man's lot, but if that fails, more philosophy to endure
and somehow find fragmentary enjoyment in pleasures
more keen because they are fleeting. Among this group are
those who call for a return to religion, some with profoundly
sincere conviction, others with sharp awareness of the possibly utilitarian value of prayer or a belief in the "power
of positive thinking" to win both friends and a larger share
of worldly goods.

Still others believing in moderate action urge a revival
of small community groups with neighborhood co-operation to combat such disorders as juvenile delinquency, drug
addiction, vandalism, and other crimes. Then there are
those who despair of making work more creative and fall
back on the hope that people can somehow be trained more
"efficiently" for the use of leisure. Their assumption is that
even if work is meaningless, leisure pursuits may be enriching. But when work and leisure are divorced, is it realistic to
expect that leisure can ever be more than escape from the
dreariness of work? And escape can hardly be creative.
Similar considerations apply to the effort to plan residential neighborhoods for greater social cohesion. But again
how can this be achieved if in other areas of life—work
and leisure—men remain alienated? How plan for better
neighborhoods if men and women have little to share except
their social status?

The fact that some of these efforts turn out to be no
more than halfway measures in no way reflects on the sincerity of their advocates. Men will do many strange things
to escape their sense of isolation. They may accept illusions as reality: religiousness without religion, "para-social"
relations with mass media personalities, "human relations"
between managers and their subordinates—in place of genuine integration. But an integrated community is one in
which there is an intimate sharing of beliefs and practices.
As Durkheim taught, the more numerous and strong these
beliefs and practices, the greater the integration of the
group or community.

To achieve this goal some perfectly sober critics have
urged far-reaching change in the social order. Thus Marx,
who saw alienation chiefly in terms of work, felt that only

when the working man regained control over the means of production could he escape his estrangement. But it is worth noting that Marx envisaged more than transfer of ownership from private to public control. He was one of the first to observe that what men craved—and rarely found—was variety and meaning in work. To Marx the unalienated man was the creative man, one who could do and be many things. What Marx could not foresee was the equally important need to reduce the size of industrial and bureaucratic enterprises and give individual workers a greater voice in the management of these enterprises. Today these goals seem harder than ever to achieve. Modern industrial society, with its demand for specialists at one extreme and its destruction of skills at the other, permits little variety in the work career—except perhaps the variety of insecurity. Moreover, the production of goods and services is organized on a huge scale and the management of them is concentrated in the hands of a few; it is not shared. As we have seen, efforts to "personalize" and "humanize" large-scale and essentially impersonal industry and bureaucracy have failed. Neither big socialism (as practiced in the Soviet Union) nor big capitalism (as in the United States) has yet come to grips with these problems.

Rejecting the "total solutions" offered on the one hand by Soviet communism and on the other by American monopoly capitalism, a number of social critics on both sides of the Atlantic (for example, Erich Fromm) urge a democratic socialism which would secure a more equitable distribution of wealth and, by decentralizing and reducing the size of industrial units, offer individuals a greater opportunity for self-achievement. As models for this effort they point to frankly utopian work-communities, such as the *Ejido* or rural co-operative movement in Mexico, the "communitarian" work movement in France, and the *kibbutz* in Israel. Although varying widely in details of organization and control, these movements are self-governing and intimate in scale. Their real importance lies in restoring the connection between work and other aspects of community life. Hence they offer not only variety and participation in the processes of work, but a close sharing of the many other interests and activities that make up community life. While there is no doubt that such co-operative movements restore a sense of community and give individual members a greater sense of belongingness and relatedness, it remains to be seen whether they offer a real solution for societies like ours with their established and massive structures of production and distribution. The fact is that they have never been tried.

Men achieve solidarity not only because they plan for it. This is the important lesson of human behavior in the face of natural disasters, or in times of severe economic or military crisis. Studies of how people respond to such challenges reveal both a measurable drop in the personal disorders that we associate with alienated states and more positive feelings of individual participation and significance. Thus in Britain during the 1940 blitz many men and women, keenly aware of a common danger, felt for the first time in their lives that they counted for something and that they were part of a larger whole.

To achieve this state is the goal of all who would re-order our society and overcome alienation. The question is how it can be done, how such solidarity can be created and sustained in normal times. Radical mass movements and authoritarian regimes on right and left have perhaps come closest to achieving this goal. At any rate this has been the experience of "belief" parties, of radical youth movements, of agricultural and industrial "collectives" throughout the world. What they succeed in doing is to imbue their members with some sense of higher purpose. Our greatest error would be to assume that such solidarity is merely coerced, although the power to coerce is usually present.

That there are dangers here is all too apparent. But the greatest danger may not be coercion. Perhaps more important, "togetherness" may acquire a pathological character. Men will no longer feel alienated, but will they have exchanged their earlier state of isolation for what William H. Whyte calls an "imprisonment in brotherhood"? Authoritarian regimes are not alone in posing this problem. The social life of our organization men is not without its compulsive group forms. Fromm has argued that men will sacrifice a meaningless freedom and accept the most terrible discipline in order to feel part of something greater than themselves. But the cure may be fatal, if group pressures for conformity become irresistible. Although they are not to be equated, neither in Chinese Communist communes nor in American suburbia is there much opportunity for privacy. When he is too much a member of a group, man must lose part of himself—and thus find himself exposed to another, perhaps more terrible, form of alienation. The ultimate problem, therefore, as yet *nowhere* solved, is how to restore and preserve group solidarity without destroying the last remnants of individual autonomy.

When then are the prospects? There is the possibility that in an increasingly bipolarized world the forces of alienation on both sides will gain power, becoming so intolerant and desperate that eventually there will be no choice but mutual destruction. Even if we escape nuclear annihilation there is the grim prospect of a worldwide population explosion and the consequent need for social and economic controls on an unprecedented scale. The alternatives are not pleasant. On the one hand, a war which may end all life on earth. On the other, increasing controls to ensure survival of the species. In the not too distant future, as man multiplies at a rapid rate, "togetherness" will very likely become more than a figure of speech. Possessed of extraordinary powers for good and evil, compelled to make room for new hordes of humanity—in short, caught between the machine and the mass—can man learn to live with himself and his brothers?

If there are grounds for optimism, they are based on the judgment that many of the problems we have discussed are transitional, that is, part of the very heavy price which recent generations have had to pay for their scientific and technological progress. According to this view, man's remarkable accomplishments in science and technology can and must be matched in his social and economic arrangements. But the intelligence that has flourished in the former as yet finds no counterpart in the latter. To close this gap and help man to live with his machines and with himself— these become the highest goals for every modern society.

These questions are not academic, for if they are not answered how is the Western world to meet the direct challenge of a solidaristic Communism and its "new men"? This is not the place to draw a blueprint for change. Ours is a soft and wasteful society. If it ever needed a sense of "national purpose" now is the time. But that purpose cannot be achieved or imposed by appointing committees to select goals for us—although this reflects, at least dimly, an awareness that collective purpose is missing from our lives. Can we arrive at that sense of purpose and retain the freedom we value so highly and use so poorly? Or will we drift into a garrison state that will give us our marching orders?

Which shall we choose? The rest of the world may not wait long for us to decide. Indeed, underdeveloped countries—at the outer edge of the explosion of population and expectations—may learn from our experiences and, if they are wise, skip the difficult and painful periods of technological adjustment which we experienced. Perhaps they will reject a system like ours in which men take from one another more than they share and thereby lose an irretrievable part of themselves. The integration of modern society is no simple task and at best it is imperfectly achieved, or at great cost. But that society which fails to make the effort is not likely to survive.

I. ALIENATION AND IDENTITY

The alienated man, unable to achieve himself or reach others, uneasily asks, "Who am I?" What this means in a society like ours is suggested by the two selections that follow. The first comes from Erich Fromm's *The Sane Society*. A pioneer in psychoanalytical sociology, Fromm has long been concerned with the obstacles to self-achievement in modern society. In *Escape From Freedom,* a book whose title has already become part of our language, he showed how men will sometimes surrender part of themselves and even embrace tyranny when freedom becomes meaningless. In *The Sane Society* Fromm analyzes the conditions under democratic capitalism which deprive man of freedom or encourage him to escape from it. Central to the theme of the book is man's alienation, which Fromm considers one of the major psychological effects of capitalism: "Man does not experience himself as the active bearer of his own powers and richness, but as an impoverished 'thing,' dependent on powers outside of himself, unto whom he has projected his living substance." In the passages we have chosen Fromm shows that under capitalism alienation is the fate not only of workers but of managers (or bureaucrats) and owners or capitalists themselves.

Perhaps most striking in these pages, however, is what Fromm has to say about the process of consumption. With money, an abstraction, men acquire things to consume; but such is our dehumanized state that it is we who are consumed. Alienated from the things we consume, we are similarly alienated from each other. According to Fromm, the relationship of man to his fellows is "one between two abstractions, two living machines, who use each other." Ultimately, therefore, man is alienated from himself since his aim is to sell himself. But "things have no self and men who have become things can have no self." The idea of man's making a "thing" of himself Fromm has elsewhere described as the "marketing orientation." Closely related to it is David Riesman's picture of other-directed personalities, with their sacrifice of all that is distinctive about them to win approval of the group.

If Fromm's indictment of capitalist society seems exaggerated or oversimplified, we shall have an opportunity later on to test it as we examine in more detail the mechanisms of work and consumption. Perhaps more fundamental is Fromm's assumption that in man there is some spontaneous self which he is prevented from achieving. Helpful here is the selection by the psychoanalyst Ernest G. Schachtel, "On Alienated Concepts of Identity." In more clinical fashion Schachtel shows how neurotics, unable to achieve a sense of self, accept a "paper" identity or "personality" as a substitute. But this substitute offers little comfort.

ALIENATION UNDER CAPITALISM
/Erich Fromm

The central issue of the effects of capitalism on personality [is] the phenomenon of alienation.

By alienation is meant a mode of experience in which the person experiences himself as an alien. He has become, one might say, estranged from himself. He does not experience himself as the center of his world, as the creator of his own acts—but his acts and their consequences have become his masters, whom he obeys, or whom he may even worship. The alienated person is out of touch with himself as he is out of touch with any other person. He, like the others, is experienced as things are experienced; with the senses and with common sense, but at the same time without being related to himself and to the world outside productively.

The older meaning in which "alienation" was used was to denote an insane person; *aliéné* in French, *alienado* in Spanish are older words for the psychotic, the thoroughly and absolutely alienated person. ("Alienist," in English, is still used for the doctor who cares for the insane.)

In the last century the word "alienation" was used by Hegel and Marx, referring not to a state of insanity, but to a less drastic form of self-estrangement, which permits the person to act reasonably in practical matters, yet which constitutes one of the most severe socially patterned defects. In Marx's system alienation is called that condition of man where his "own act becomes to him an alien power, standing over and against him, instead of being ruled by him."

But while the use of the word "alienation" in this general sense is a recent one, the concept is a much older one; it is the same to which the prophets of the Old Testament referred as *idolatry*. It will help us to a better understanding of "alienation" if we begin by considering the meaning of "idolatry."

The prophets of monotheism did not denounce heathen religions as idolatrous primarily because they worshiped several gods instead of one. The essential difference between monotheism and polytheism is not one of the *number* of gods, but lies in the fact of self-alienation. Man spends his energy, his artistic capacities on building an idol, and then he worships this idol, which is nothing but the result of his own human effort. His life forces have flown into a "thing," and this thing, having become an idol, is not experienced as a result of his own productive effort, but as something apart from himself, over and against him, which he worships and to which he submits. As the prophet Hosea says (XIV, 8): "Assur shall not save us; we will not ride upon horses; *neither will we say any more to the work of our hands, you are our gods;* for in thee the fatherless finds love." Idolatrous man bows down to the work of his own hands. *The idol represents his own life-forces in an alienated form.*

The principle of monotheism, in contrast, is that man is infinite, that there is no partial quality in him which can be hypostatized to the whole. God, in the monotheistic concept, is unrecognizable and indefinable; God is not a "thing." If man is created in the likeness of God, he is created as the bearer of infinite qualities. In idolatry man bows down and submits to the projection of one partial quality in himself. He does not experience himself as the center from which living acts of love and reason radiate. He becomes a thing, his neighbor becomes a thing, just as his gods are things. "The idols of the heathen are silver and gold, the work of men's hands. They have mouths but they speak not; eyes have they, but they see not; they have ears but they hear not; neither is there any breath in their mouths.

They that make them are like them; so is everyone that trusts in them." (Psalm 135).

Monotheistic religions themselves have, to a large extent, regressed into idolatry. Man projects his power of love and of reason unto God; he does not feel them any more as his own powers, and then he prays to God to give him back some of what he, man, has projected unto God. In early Protestantism and Calvinism, the required religious attitude is that man *should* feel himself empty and impoverished, and put his trust in the grace of God, that is, into the hope that God may return to him part of his own qualities, which he has put into God.

Every act of submissive worship is an act of alienation and idolatry in this sense. What is frequently called "love" is often nothing but this idolatrous phenomenon of alienation; only that not God or an idol, but another person is worshiped in this way. The "loving" person in this type of submissive relationship, projects all his or her love, strength, thought, into the other person, and experiences the loved person as a superior being, finding satisfaction in complete submission and worship. This does not only mean that he fails to experience the loved person as a human being in his or her reality, but that he does not experience *himself* in his full reality, as the bearer of productive human powers. Just as in the case of religious idolatry, he has projected all his richness into the other person, and experiences this richness not any more as something which is his, but as something alien from himself, deposited in somebody else, with which he can get in touch only by submission to, or submergence in, the other person. The same phenomenon exists in the worshiping submission to a political leader, or to the state. The leader and the state actually are what they are by the consent of the governed. But they become idols when the individual projects all his powers into them and worships them, hoping to regain some of his powers by submission and worship.

In Rousseau's theory of the state, as in contemporary totalitarianism, the individual is supposed to abdicate his own rights and to project them unto the state as the only arbiter. In fascism and Stalinism the absolutely alienated individual worships at the altar of an idol, and it makes little difference by what names this idol is known: state, class, collective, or what else.

We can speak of idolatry or alienation not only in relationship to other people, but also in relationship to oneself, when the person is subject to irrational passions. The person who is mainly motivated by his lust for power, does not experience himself any more in the richness and limitlessness of a human being, but he becomes a slave to one partial striving in him, which is projected into external aims, by which he is "possessed." The person who is given to the exclusive pursuit of his passion for money is possessed by his striving for it; money is the idol which he worships as the projection of one isolated power in himself, his greed for it. In this sense, the neurotic person is an alienated person. His actions are not his own; while he is under the illusion of doing what *he* wants, he is driven by forces which are separated from his self, which work behind his back; he is a stranger to himself, just as his fellow man is a stranger to him. He experiences the other and himself not as what they really are, but distorted by the unconscious forces which operate in them. The insane person is the *absolutely alienated* person; he has completely lost himself as the center of his own experience; he has lost the sense of self.

What is common to all these phenomena—the worship of idols, the idolatrous worship of God, the idolatrous love for a person, the worship of a political leader or the state, and the idolatrous worship of the externalizations of irrational passions—is the process of alienation. It is the fact that *man does not experience himself as the active bearer of his own powers and richness, but as an impoverished "thing," dependent on powers outside of himself, unto whom he has projected his living substance.*

As the reference to idolatry indicates, alienation is by no means a modern phenomenon. Suffice it to say that it seems alienation differs from culture to culture, both in the specific spheres which are alienated, and in the thoroughness and completeness of the process.

Alienation as we find it in modern society is almost total; it pervades the relationship of man to his work, to the things he consumes, to the state, to his fellow man, and to himself. Man has created a world of man-made things as it never existed before. He has constructed a complicated social machine to administer the technical machine he built. Yet this whole creation of his stands over and above him. He does not feel himself as a creator and center, but as the servant of a Golem, which his hands have built. The more powerful and gigantic the forces are which he unleashes, the more powerless he feels himself as a human being. He confronts himself with his own forces embodied in things he has created, alienated from himself. He is owned by his own creation, and has lost ownership of himself. He has built a golden calf, and says "these are your gods who have brought you out of Egypt."

What happens to the *worker*? To put it in the words of a thoughtful and thorough observer of the industrial scene: "In industry the person becomes an economic atom that dances to the tune of atomistic management. Your place is just here, you will sit in this fashion, your arms will move *x* inches in a course of *y* radius and the time of movement will be .000 minutes.

"Work is becoming more repetitive and thoughtless as the planners, the micromotionists, and the scientific managers further strip the worker of his right to think and move freely. Life is being denied; need to control, creativeness, curiosity, and independent thought are being baulked, and the result, the inevitable result, is flight or fight on the part of the worker, apathy or destructiveness, psychic regression." [J. J. Gillespie.]

The role of the *manager* is also one of alienation. It is true, he manages the whole and not a part, but he too is alienated from his product as something concrete and useful. His aim is to employ profitably the capital invested by others, although in comparison with the older type of owner-manager, modern management is much less interested in the amount of profit to be paid out as dividend to the stockholder than it is in the efficient operation and expansion of the enterprise. Characteristically, within management those in charge of labor relations and of sales—that is, of human manipulation—gain, relatively speaking, an increasing importance in comparison with those in charge of the technical aspects of production.

The manager, like the worker, like everybody, deals with impersonal giants: with the giant competitive enterprise; with the giant national and world market; with the giant consumer, who has to be coaxed and manipulated; with the giant unions, and the giant government. All these giants have their own lives, as it were. They determine the activity of the manager and they direct the activity of the worker and clerk.

The problem of the manager opens up one of the most significant phenomena in an alienated culture, that of *bureaucratization*. Both big business and government administrations are conducted by a bureaucracy. Bureaucrats are specialists in the administration of things *and of men*. Due to the bigness of the apparatus to be administered, and the resulting abstractification, the bureaucrats' relationship to the people is one of complete alienation. They, the people to be administered, are objects whom the bureaucrats consider neither with love nor with hate, but completely impersonally; the manager-bureaucrat must not feel, as far as his professional activity is concerned; he must manipulate people as though they were figures, or things. Since the vastness of the organization and the extreme division of labor prevents any single individual from seeing the whole, since there is no organic, spontaneous cooperation between the various individuals or groups within the industry, the managing bureaucrats are necessary; without them the enterprise would collapse in a short time, since nobody would know the secret which makes it function. Bureaucrats are as indispensable as the tons of paper consumed under their leadership. Just because everybody senses, with a feeling of powerlessness, the vital role of the bureaucrats, they are given an almost godlike respect. If it were not for the bureaucrats, people feel, everything would go to pieces, and we would starve. Whereas, in the medieval world, the leaders were considered representatives of a god-intended order, in modern capitalism the role of the bureaucrat is hardly less sacred—since he is necessary for the survival of the whole.

Marx gave a profound definition of the bureaucrat saying: "The bureaucrat relates himself to the world as a *mere object* of his activity." It is interesting to note that the spirit of bureaucracy has entered not only business and government administration, but also trade unions and the great democratic socialist parties in England, Germany and France. In Russia, too, the bureaucratic managers and their alienated spirit have conquered the country. Russia could perhaps exist without terror—if certain conditions were given—but it could not exist without the system of total bureaucratization—that is, alienation.

What is the attitude of the *owner* of the enterprise, the capitalist? The small businessman seems to be in the same position as his predecessor a hundred years ago. He owns and directs his small enterprise, he is in touch with the whole commercial or industrial activity, and in personal contact with his employees and workers. But living in an alienated world in all other economic and social aspects, and furthermore being more under the constant pressure of bigger competitors, he is by no means as free as his grandfather was in the same business.

But what matters more and more in contemporary economy is big business, the large corporation. And the attitude of the "owner" of the big corporation to "his" property is one of almost complete alienation. His ownership consists in a piece of paper, representing a certain fluctuating amount of money; he has no responsibility for the enterprise and no concrete relationship to it in any way.

The process of *consumption* is as alienated as the process of production. In the first place, we acquire things with money; we are accustomed to this and take it for granted. But actually, this is a most peculiar way of acquiring things. Money represents labor and effort in an abstract form; not necessarily *my* labor and *my* effort, since I can have acquired it by inheritance, by fraud, by luck, or any number of ways. But even if I have acquired it by *my* effort (forgetting for the moment that *my* effort might not have brought me the money were it not for the fact that I employed men), I have acquired it in a specific way, by a specific kind of effort, corresponding to my skills and capacities, while, in spending, the money is transformed into an abstract form of labor and can be exchanged against anything else. Provided I am in the possession of money, no effort or interest of mine is necessary to acquire something. If I have the money, I can acquire an exquisite painting, even though I may not have any appreciation for art; I can buy the best phonograph, even though I have no musical taste; I can buy a library, although I use it only for the purpose of ostentation. I can buy an education, even though I have no use for it except as an additional social asset. I can even destroy the painting or the books I bought, and aside from a loss of money, I suffer no damage. Mere possession of money gives me the right to acquire and to do with my acquisition whatever I like. The *human* way of acquiring would be to make an effort qualitatively commensurate with what I acquire. The acquisition of bread and clothing would depend on no other premise than that of being alive; the acquisition of books and paintings, on my effort to understand them and my ability to use them. How this principle could be applied practically is not the point to be discussed here. What matters is that the way we acquire things is separated from the way in which we use them.

The alienating function of money in the process of acquisition and consumption has been beautifully described by Marx in the following words: "Money ... transforms the real human and natural powers into merely abstract ideas, and hence imperfections, and on the other hand it transforms the real imperfections and imaginings, the powers which only exist in the imagination of the individual into real powers. ... It transforms loyalty into vice, vice into virtue, the slave into the master, the master into the slave, ignorance into reason, and reason into ignorance. ... He who can buy valour is valiant although he be cowardly. ... Assume *man* as *man*, and his relation to the world as a human one, and you can exchange love only for love, confidence for confidence, etc. If you wish to enjoy art, you must be an artistically trained person; if you wish to have influence on other people, you must be a person who has a really stimulating and furthering influence on other people. Every one of your relationships to man and to nature must be a definite expression of your *real*, *individual* life corresponding to the object of your will. If you love without calling forth love, that is, if your love as such does not produce love, if by means of an *expression of life* as a loving person you do not make of yourself a *loved person*, then your love is impotent, a misfortune."

But beyond the method of acquisition, how do we use things, once we have acquired them? With regard to many things, there is not even the pretense of use. We acquire them to *have* them. We are satisfied with useless possession. The expensive dining set or crystal vase which we never use for fear they might break, the mansion with many unused rooms, the unnecessary cars and servants, like the ugly bric-à-brac of the lower-middle-class family, are so many examples of pleasure in possession instead of in use. However, this satisfaction in possessing per se was more prominent in the nineteenth century; today most of the satisfaction is derived from possession of things-to-be-used rather than of things-to-be-kept. This does not alter the fact, however, that even in the pleasure of things-to-be-used the satisfaction of prestige is a paramount factor. The car, the refrigerator, the television set are for real, but also for conspicuous use. They confer status on the owner.

How do we use the things we acquire? Let us begin with food and drink. We eat a bread which is tasteless and not nourishing because it appeals to our fantasy of wealth and distinction—being so white and "fresh." Actually, we "eat" a fantasy and have lost contact with the real thing we eat. Our palate, our body, are excluded from an act of consumption which primarily concerns them. We drink labels. With a bottle of Coca-Cola we drink the picture of the pretty boy and girl who drink it in the advertisement, we drink the slogan of "the pause that refreshes," we drink the great American habit; least of all do we drink with our palate. All this is even worse when it comes to the consumption of things whose whole reality is mainly the fiction the advertising campaign has created, like the "healthy" soap or dental paste.

I could go on giving examples ad infinitum. But it is unnecessary to belabor the point, since everybody can think of as many illustrations as I could give. I only want to stress the principle involved: the act of consumption should be a concrete human act, in which our senses, bodily needs, our aesthetic taste—that is to say, in which *we* as concrete, sensing, feeling, judging human beings—are involved; the act of consumption should be a meaningful, human, productive experience. In our culture, there is little of that. Consuming is essentially the satisfaction of artificially stimulated fantasies, a fantasy performance alienated from our concrete, real selves.

There is another aspect of alienation from the things we consume which needs to be mentioned. We are surrounded by things of whose nature and origin we know nothing. The telephone, radio, phonograph, and all other complicated machines are almost as mysterious to us as they would be to a man from a primitive culture; we know how to use them, that is, we know which button to turn, but we do not know on what principle they function, except in the vaguest terms of something we once learned at school. And things which do not rest upon difficult scientific principles are almost equally alien to us. We do not know how bread is made, how cloth is woven, how a table is manufactured, how glass is made. We consume, as we produce, without any concrete relatedness to the objects with which we deal; we live in a world of things, and our only connection with them is that we know how to manipulate or to consume them.

Our way of consumption necessarily results in the fact that we are never satisfied, since it is not our real concrete person which consumes a real and concrete thing. We thus develop an ever-increasing need for more things, for more consumption. It is true that as long as the living standard of the population is below a dignified level of subsistence, there is a natural need for more consumption. It is also true that there is a legitimate need for more consumption as man develops culturally and has more refined needs for better food, objects of artistic pleasure, books, etc. But our craving for consumption has lost all connection with the real needs of man. Originally, the idea of consuming more and better things was meant to give man a happier, more satisfied life. Consumption was a means to an end, that of happiness. It now has become an aim in itself. The constant increase of needs forces us to an ever-increasing effort, it makes us dependent on these needs and on the people and institutions by whose help we attain them. "Each person speculates to create a new need in the other person, in order to force him into a new dependency, to a new form of pleasure, hence to his economic ruin. . . . With a multitude of commodities grows the realm of alien things which enslave man." [Marx.]

Man today is fascinated by the possibility of buying more, better, and especially, new things. He is consumption-hungry. The act of buying and consuming has become a compulsive, irrational aim, because it is an end in itself, with little relation to the use of, or pleasure in the things bought and consumed. To buy the latest gadget, the latest model of anything that is on the market, is the dream of everybody, in comparison to which the real pleasure in use is quite secondary. Modern man, if he dared to be articulate about his concept of heaven, would describe a vision which would look like the biggest department store in the world, showing new things and gadgets, and himself having plenty of money with which to buy them. He would wander around open-mouthed in this heaven of gadgets and commodities, provided only that there were ever more and newer things to buy, and perhaps that his neighbors were just a little less privileged than he.

Significantly enough, one of the older traits of middle-class society, the attachment to possessions and property, has undergone a profound change. In the older attitude, a certain sense of loving possession existed between a man and his property. It grew on him. He was proud of it. He took good care of it, and it was painful when eventually he had to part from it because it could not be used any more. There is very little left of this sense of property today. One loves the newness of the thing bought, and is ready to betray it when something newer has appeared.

Expressing the same change in characterological terms, I can refer to what has been stated above with regard to the *hoarding* orientation as dominant in the picture of the nineteenth century. In the middle of the twentieth century the hoarding orientation has given way to the *receptive* orientation, in which the aim is to receive, to "drink in," to have something new all the time, to live with a continuously open mouth, as it were. This receptive orientation is blended with the marketing orientation, while in the nineteenth century the hoarding was blended with the exploitative orientation.

The alienated attitude toward consumption not only exists in our acquisition and consumption of commodities, but it determines far beyond this the employment of leisure time. What are we to expect? If a man works without genuine relatedness to what he is doing, if he buys and consumes commodities in an abstractified and alienated way, how can he make use of his leisure time in an active and meaningful way? He always remains the passive and alienated consumer. He "consumes" ball games, moving pictures, newspapers and magazines, books, lectures, natural scenery, social gatherings, in the same alienated and abstractified way in which he consumes the commodities he has bought. He does not participate actively, he wants to "take in" all there is to be had, and to have as much as possible of pleasure, culture and what not. Actually, he is not free to enjoy "his" leisure; his leisure-time consumption is determined by industry, as are the commodities he buys; his taste is manipulated, he wants to see and to hear what he is conditioned to want to see and to hear; entertainment is an industry like any other, the customer is made to buy fun as he is made to buy dresses and shoes. The value of the fun is determined by its success on the market, not by anything which could be measured in human terms.

In any productive and spontaneous activity, something

happens within myself while I am reading, looking at scenery, talking to friends, etcetera. I am not the same after the experience as I was before. In the alienated form of pleasure nothing happens within me; I have consumed this or that; nothing is changed within myself, and all that is left are memories of what I have done.

Man is not only alienated from the work he does, and the things and pleasures he consumes, but also from the *social forces* which determine our society and the life of everybody living in it.

Our actual helplessness before the forces which govern us appears more drastically in those social catastrophes which, even though they are denounced as regrettable accidents each time, so far have never failed to happen: economic depressions and wars. These social phenomena appear as if they were natural catastrophes, rather than what they really are, occurrences made by man, but without intention and awareness.

This anonymity of the social forces is inherent in the structure of the capitalist mode of production.

In contrast to most other societies in which social laws are explicit and fixed on the basis of political power or tradition—capitalism does not have such explicit laws. It is based on the principle that if only everybody strives for himself on the market, the common good will come of it; order and not anarchy will be the result. There are, of course, economic laws which govern the market, but these laws operate behind the back of the acting individual, who is concerned only with his private interests. You try to guess these laws of the market as a Calvinist in Geneva tried to guess whether God had predestined him for salvation or not. But the laws of the market, like God's will, are beyond the reach of your will and influence.

To a large extent the development of capitalism has proven that this principle works; and it is indeed a miracle that the antagonistic co-operation of self-contained economic entities should result in a blossoming and ever-expanding society. It is true that the capitalistic mode of production is conducive to political freedom, while any centrally planned social order is in danger of leading to political regimentation and eventually to dictatorship. While this is not the place to discuss the question of whether there are other alternatives than the choice between "free enterprise" and political regimentation, it needs to be said in this context that the very fact that we are governed by laws which we do not control, and do not even want to control, is one of the most outstanding manifestations of alienation. *We* are the producers of our economic and social arrangements, and at the same time we decline responsibility, intentionally and enthusiastically, and await hopefully or anxiously—as the case may be—what "the future" will bring. Our own actions are embodied in the laws which govern us, but these laws are above us, and we are their slaves. The giant state and economic system are not any more controlled by man. They run wild, and their leaders are like a person on a runaway horse, who is proud of managing to keep in the saddle, even though he is powerless to direct the horse.

What is modern man's *relationship to his fellow man?* It is one between two abstractions, two living machines, who use each other. The employer uses the ones whom he employs; the salesman uses his customers. Everybody is to everybody else a commodity, always to be treated with certain friendliness, because even if he is not of use now, he may be later. There is not much love or hate to be found in human relations of our day. There is, rather, a superficial friendliness, and a more than superficial fairness, but behind that surface is distance and indifference. There is also a good deal of subtle distrust. When one man says to another, "You speak to John Smith; he is all right," it is an expression of reassurance against a general distrust. Even love and the relationship between sexes have assumed this character. The great sexual emancipation, as it occurred after the First World War, was a desperate attempt to substitute mutual sexual pleasure for a deeper feeling of love. When this turned out to be a disappointment the erotic polarity between the sexes was reduced to a minimum and replaced by a friendly partnership, a small combine which has amalgamated its forces to hold out better in the daily battle of life, and to relieve the feeling of isolation and aloneness which everybody has.

The alienation between man and man results in the loss of those general and social bonds which characterize medieval as well as most other precapitalist societies. Modern society consists of "atoms" (if we use the Greek equivalent of "individual"), little particles estranged from each other but held together by selfish interests and by the necessity to make use of each other. Yet man is a social being with a deep need to share, to help, to feel as a member of a group. What has happened to these social strivings in man? They manifest themselves in the special sphere of the *public* realm, which is strictly separated from the private realm. Our private dealings with our fellow men are governed by the principle of egotism, "each for himself, God for us all," in flagrant contradiction to Christian teaching. The individual is motivated by egotistical interest, and not by solidarity with and love for his fellow man. The latter feelings may assert themselves secondarily as private acts of philanthropy or kindness, but they are not part of the basic structure of our social relations. Separated from our private life as individuals is the realm of our social life as "citizens." In this realm the state is the embodiment of our social existence; as citizens we are supposed to, and in fact usually do, exhibit a sense of social obligation and duty. We pay taxes, we vote, we respect the laws, and in the case of war we are willing to sacrifice our lives. What clearer example could there be of the separation between private and public existence than the fact that the same man who would not think of spending one hundred dollars to relieve the need of a stranger does not hesitate to risk his life to save this same stranger when in war they both happen to be soldiers in uniform? The uniform is the embodiment of our social nature—civilian garb, of our egotistic nature.

The division between the community and the political state has led to the projection of all social feelings into the state, which thus becomes an idol, a power standing over and above man. Man submits to the state as to the embodiment of his own social feelings, which he worships as powers alienated from himself; in his private life as an individual he suffers from the isolation and aloneness which are the necessary result of this separation. The worship of the state can only disappear if man takes back the social powers into himself, and builds a community in which his social feelings are not something *added* to his private existence, but in which his private and social existence are one and the same.

What is the relationship of *man toward himself?* I have described elsewhere this relationship as "marketing orientation." In this orientation, man experiences himself as a thing to be employed successfully on the market. He does not experience himself as an active agent, as the bearer of human powers. He is alienated from these powers. His aim

is to sell himself successfully on the market. His sense of
self does not stem from his activity as a loving and thinking individual, but from his socio-economic role. If things
could speak, a typewriter would answer the question "Who
are you?" by saying "I am a typewriter," and an automobile, by saying "I am an automobile," or more specifically
by saying, "I am a Ford," or "a Buick," or "a Cadillac." If
you ask a man "Who are you?", he answers "I am a manufacturer," "I am a clerk," "I am a doctor"—or "I am a married man," "I am the father of two kids," and his answer
has pretty much the same meaning as that of the speaking
thing would have. That is the way he experiences himself,
not as a man, with love, fear, convictions, doubts, but as
that abstraction, alienated from his real nature, which fulfills a certain function in the social system. His sense of
value depends on his success: on whether he can sell himself favorably, whether he can make more of himself than
he started out with, whether he is a success. His body, his
mind and his soul are his capital, and his task in life is to
invest it favorably, to make a profit of himself. Human
qualities like friendliness, courtesy, kindness, are transformed into commodities, into assets of the "personality
package," conducive to a higher price on the personality
market. If the individual fails in a profitable investment of
himself, he feels that *he* is a failure; if he succeeds, *he* is
a success. Clearly, his sense of his own value always depends on factors extraneous to himself, on the fickle judgment of the market, which decides about his value as it
decides about the value of commodities. He, like all commodities that cannot be sold profitably on the market, is
worthless as far as his exchange value is concerned, even
though his use value may be considerable.

The alienated personality who is for sale must lose a
good deal of the sense of dignity which is so characteristic
of man even in most primitive cultures. He must lose almost all sense of self, of himself as a unique and induplicable
entity. The sense of self stems from the experience of myself as the subject of *my* experiences, *my* thought, *my* feeling, *my* decision, *my* judgment, *my* action. It presupposes
that my experience is my own, and not an alienated one.
Things have no self and men who have become things can
have no self.

One cannot fully appreciate the nature of alienation
without considering one specific aspect of modern life: its

routinization, and the *repression of the awareness of the basic problems of human existence.* We touch here upon a universal problem of life. Man has to earn his daily bread, and this is always a more or less absorbing task. He has to take care of the many time- and energy-consuming tasks of daily life, and he is enmeshed in a certain routine necessary for the fulfillment of these tasks. He builds a social order, conventions, habits and ideas, which help him to perform what is necessary, and to live with his fellow man with a minimum of friction. It is characteristic of all culture that it builds a man-made, artificial world, superimposed on the natural world in which man lives. But man can fulfill himself only if he remains in touch with the fundamental facts of his existence, if he can experience the exaltation of love and solidarity, as well as the tragic fact of his aloneness and of the fragmentary character of his existence. If he is completely enmeshed in the routine and in the artifacts of life, if he cannot see anything but the man-made, common-sense appearance of the world, he loses his touch with and the grasp of himself and the world. We find in every culture the conflict between routine and the attempt to get back to the fundamental realities of existence. To help in this attempt has been one of the functions of art and of religion, even though religion itself has eventually become a new form of routine.

Even the most primitive history of man shows us an attempt to get in touch with the essence of reality by artistic creation. Primitive man is not satisfied with the practical function of his tools and weapons, but strives to adorn and beautify them, transcending their utilitarian function. Aside from art, the most significant way of breaking through the surface of routine and of getting in touch with the ultimate realities of life is to be found in what may be called by the general term of "ritual." I am referring here to ritual in the broad sense of the word, as we find it in the performance of a Greek drama, for instance, and not only to rituals in the narrower religious sense. What was the function of the Greek drama? Fundamental problems of human existence were presented in an artistic and dramatic form, and participating in the dramatic performance, the spectator—though not as a spectator in our modern sense of the consumer—was carried away from the sphere of daily routine and brought in touch with himself as a human being, with the roots of his existence. He touched the ground with his feet, and in this process gained strength by which he was brought back to himself. Whether we think of the Greek drama, the medieval passion play, or an Indian dance, whether we think of Hindu, Jewish or Christian religious rituals, we are dealing with various forms of dramatization of the fundamental problems of human existence, with an *acting out* of the very same problems which are *thought out* in philosophy and theology.

What is left of such dramatization of life in modern culture? Almost nothing. Man hardly ever gets out of the realm of man-made conventions and things, and hardly ever breaks through the surface of his routine, aside from grotesque attempts to satisfy the need for a ritual as we see it practiced in lodges and fraternities. The only phenomenon approaching the meaning of a ritual, is the participation of the spectator in competitive sports; here at least, one fundamental problem of human existence is dealt with: the fight between men and the vicarious experience of victory and defeat. But what a primitive and restricted aspect of human existence, reducing the richness of human life to one partial aspect!

If there is a fire, or a car collision in a big city, scores of people will gather and watch. Millions of people are fascinated daily by reportings of crimes and by detective stories. They religiously go to movies in which crime and passion are the two central themes. All this interest and fascination is not simply an expression of bad taste and sensationalism, but of a deep longing for a dramatization of ultimate phenomena of human existence, life and death, crime and punishment, the battle between man and nature. But while Greek drama dealt with these problems on a high artistic and metaphysical level, our modern "drama" and "ritual" are crude and do not produce any cathartic effect. All this fascination with competitive sports, crime and passion, shows the need for breaking through the routine surface, but the way of its satisfaction shows the extreme poverty of our solution.

The marketing orientation is closely related to the fact that the *need to exchange* has become a paramount drive in modern man. It is, of course, true that even in a primitive economy based on a rudimentary form of division of labor, men exchange goods with each other within the tribe or among neighboring tribes. The man who produces cloth exchanges it for grain which his neighbor may have produced, or for sickles or knives made by the blacksmith. With increasing division of labor, there is increasing exchange of goods, but normally the exchange of goods is nothing but a means to an economic end. In capitalistic society *exchanging has become an end in itself*.

ON ALIENATED CONCEPTS OF IDENTITY
/Ernest G. Schachtel

In daily life the question of identity arises when we want to claim something from the post office, or when we want to pay by check in a store where we are not known, or in crossing a border. On such occasions we are asked: "Who are you, so that I can know for sure it is you and nobody else?" And we establish our identity by showing a driver's license or a passport or some similar document which tells our name, our address, the date of our birth, and perhaps some physical characteristics. Together, these will tell us apart from anybody else and will also establish that we are the same person that was born on such and such a date. We have *papers* to establish our identity, and this paper-identity is something fixed and definite. This is also the meaning of the word "identity," as applied to people, for the average person.

Such paper-identity seems far removed, at first glance, from the current concern of psychoanalysts, philosophers, and other students of the contemporary scene, with man's search for and doubt in his identity. But actually it is quite central to it. It is a telling symbol of alienated identity. It is a kind of identity which is the product of bureaucratic needs of commerce or administration. Its most gruesome and tragic manifestations occurred in our time when men's identities were reduced to numbers in concentration and extermination camps, and when countless people fleeing from the terror of the totalitarian states were shunted from country to country because they did not have the right paper-identities.

In the case of paper-identities, the person who demands and examines one's papers is the one who, in his role as an official, is alienated from the other person as a human being.

Similarly, the guards in the concentration camps were alienated from their victims. However, many of these victims,
systematically robbed of any meaningful purpose and dignity in their lives, succumbed to their tormentors and lost
their sense of identity long before they lost their lives.

In our own and many other societies the loss of identity
takes place without the terror of the concentration camps,
in more insidious ways. I have described elsewhere how
many people in our time tend to think of their lives as
though they were answering the kind of questionnaire that
one has to fill out when, for example, applying for a passport. They tend to accept the paper-identity as their real
identity. It is tempting to do so because it is something
fixed and definite and does not require that the person be
really in touch with himself. The paper-identity corresponds
to the logical propositions concerning identity: $A = A$,
and A is not non-A.

But man is not a logical proposition, and the paper-identity does not answer the question who this person, identified
by some scrap of paper, is as a person. This question is not
simple to answer. It has haunted many people increasingly
in the last hundred years. They no longer feel certain who
they are because in modern industrial society, as Hegel and
Marx first showed, they are alienated from nature, alienated
from their fellow men, alienated from the work of their
hands and minds, and alienated from themselves. I can
only state here my belief that self-alienation, the doubt
about and search for identity, always goes together with
alienation from others and from the world around us.

The problem of identity and alienation from the self came
to the attention of psychoanalysts in the last thirty years
when they observed its role in an increasing number of
patients. Karen Horney formulated it as the problem of the
real self, as distinguished from the idealized self-image;
Fromm as the problem of the original, real self as distinguished from the conventional or pseudo-self; Erikson, who
has made the most detailed study in the development of the
sense of identity, as the problem of ego-identity.

Many patients who come to us suffer in one form or another from the lack of a sense of identity. This may take the
form of feeling like impostors—in their work, or in relation to their background, their past, or to some part of themselves that they repress or consciously want to hide because
they feel ashamed or guilty. Or else they feel that they

ought to *have* something they lack or imagine they lack, such as material possessions, prestige, or certain personal qualities or traits; or they feel that a different husband or wife, or friends different from those they have, would give them the status they want and thereby, miraculously, transform them into full-blown persons. When the lack of a sense of identity becomes conscious, it is often experienced —probably always—as a feeling that compared with others one is not fully a person.

Among adults one can observe two frequent reactions to the conscious or unconscious feeling of not being fully a person, of not having found an identity acceptable to oneself. One is an anxious retreat or depressive resignation, or a mixture of these. The other is a more or less conscious effort at disguise, at playing a role, at presenting an artificial façade to the world. These reactions are not mutually exclusive. They usually occur together, one of them being more emphasized or closer to consciousness than the other. The fear of exposure is present in both, but especially strong in people who rely on a façade. They tend to feel that they travel with a forged passport, under an assumed identity. When their disguise and the reasons for it have been analyzed, the sense of a lack of identity often comes to the fore as strongly as in those who, to begin with, have been aware of and suffered from the feeling of not really or fully being a person with a meaningful place in life. Both tend to feel that they do not really know who they are, what they want, or how they feel about other people.

When these people consult an analyst, they often expect, implicitly or explicitly, that he will tell them who they are or who they should be. Their wish and search is for a *definite, fixed identity*. They want to be a *personality*. Often these are people who suffer from over-adaptation to whatever situation they are in, and to whomever they are dealing with at the moment. They have been described pointedly in several plays and stories by Pirandello. They long for a definite, fixed, circumscribed personality. "Having" such a personality, as one has a possession, they hope will solve their dilemma. Having such a personality, they feel, is good; not having it, bad. Their wish to "possess" a definite identity does not and cannot solve the problem of their alienation from themselves, because it actually is the continuation of alienation. They want to substitute a fixed, reified personality for the on-going process of living, feeling, acting, and thinking in which alone they could find themselves. They search for a definite, stable shell called "personality" to which they want to cling. Their quest is self-defeating, because what they search for is an alienated concept of a thing, rather than a living, developing person. Their wish is a symptom, not a cure. In this symptom, however, both the malady of alienation and the longing for a more meaningful life find expression, even though in a way which perpetuates the ill from which they seek to escape. The self-conscious preoccupation with this wished-for magic object called "personality" interferes with the actual experience of living.

In calling the object of these people's search an alienated "concept" of identity, I do not mean a scientific or even an explicit concept. I am describing an implicit concept, which becomes apparent only in the analysis of the underlying, often not conscious, assumptions that direct this kind of search. This applies equally to the following examples of alienated concepts of identity.

There is one psychoanalytic term that has gained wide popularity and in popular use has changed its meaning. Such popular use always indicates a significant fact about a society and therefore deserves our attention. I refer to the term "ego." People say that something is good or bad for their "ego." They mean by this that their self-feeling—in the sense of the status which they accord to themselves—rises when something is good and falls when something is bad for their ego. In this usage ego is only part of the person. My "ego" is not identical with "I" or "self." It is not identical with the I who is well or ill, who sees and hears and touches and tastes and smells, who acts, walks, sits, stands, lies, who is moved by others, by what is seen and experienced. Moreover, what is "good" or "bad" for my ego is not at all necessarily good or bad for me, although I may be inclined to think so. The popular "ego" gains from success, winning in competition, status, being admired, flattered, loved; it does not gain from facing the truth, from loving somebody else, from humility. It behaves like a stock or a piece of merchandise endowed with self-awareness: if it is much in demand it rises, is blown up, feels important; if not, it falls, shrinks, feels it is nothing. Thus, it is an *alienated* part of the self.

But while it is only part of the self, it has the tendency to become the *focal point* of the feeling of identity and to dominate the whole life of the people who are involved with their "ego" to a significant degree. Their mood fluctuates with their "ego." They are haunted by their "ego" and preoccupied with its enhancement or its downfall. They no longer seem to feel that they have a life apart from their "ego," but they stand or fall with it. The "ego" has become their identity and at the same time the main object of their worry, ambition, and preoccupation, crowding out any real concern with themselves and with others. The popular ego can serve as the most important model of an alienated concept of identity, even though it may be surpassed in rigidity and fixedness by some other examples of such concepts, to which I shall turn now.

In her thoughtful book, *On Shame and the Search for Identity,* Helen Lynd quotes Dostoyevsky's Mitya Karamazov who, on trial for the murder of his father, suffers his worst misery when the prosecutor asks him to take off his socks. "They were very dirty . . . and now everyone could see it. All his life he had thought both his big toes hideous. He particularly loathed the coarse, flat, crooked nail on the right one and now they would all see it. Feeling intolerably ashamed. . . ." The accidental, unchangeable appearance of his feet, of the nail of his right big toe, here becomes the focal point of his identity. It is on this that he feels the peasants who stand around him and look at him will judge him and that he judges himself. Very often real or imagined physical attributes, parts of the body image or the entire body image, become focal points of identity. Many people build around such a negative identity the feeling that this particular feature unalterably determines the course of their lives, and that they are thereby doomed to unhappiness. Usually, in these cases, qualities such as attractiveness and beauty are no longer felt to be based on the alive expression and flux of human feelings, but have become fixed and dead features, or a series of poses, as in so many Hollywood stars or fashion models. These features are cut off from the center of the person and worn like a mask. Unattractiveness is experienced as not possessing this mask.

In the same way, other real or imagined attributes, or the lack of them, become focal points for a reified, alienated, negative identity. For example: feeling not sufficiently masculine or feminine, being born on the wrong side of the tracks, being a member of a minority group against which racial or religious prejudices are directed, and, in the most general form, feeling intrinsically inadequate or "bad." I do not imply, of course, that in our society the accidental circumstance of being born as the member of one social, national, or religious group or class rather than another does not result in very real, objective difficulties, disadvantages or privileges. I am concerned here only with the *attitude* which the person takes toward such handicaps or advantages, which is important for his ability to deal with them. In this attitude the structure of the sense of identity and the way in which such factors as the social background and innate advantages or handicaps are incorporated in the sense of identity play a decisive role.

What are the dynamics of such alienated concepts of identity? Sometimes they crystallize around repeated parental remarks which, rather than referring to a particular act of the child, say or imply that the child *is* or *lacks*, by its very nature, such and such; that Tom is a lazy good-for-nothing or that he is "just like Uncle Harry," who happens to be the black sheep in the family. Frequently they develop from an ego-ideal that is alien to the child's own personality, but about which he has come to feel that, unless he is such and such, he is nothing. Whatever their genetic origin, I shall consider here mainly the phenomenological structure of alienated identity concepts and the dynamics of this structure which tend to perpetuate self-alienation.

By making some quality or circumstance, real or exaggerated or imagined, the focal point of a reified identity, I look upon myself as though I were a thing (res) and the quality or circumstance a fixed attribute of this thing or object. But the "I" that feels that I am this or that, in doing so, distances itself from the very same reified object attribute which it experiences as determining its identity and very often as a bane on its life. In feeling that I am such and such, I distinguish between the unfortunate I and the presumably unalterable quality or lack which, for all time, condemns me to have this negative identity. I do not feel that *I* am *doing* this or that or failing to do it, but that there *is* a something in me or about me, or that I lack something and that this, once and for all, *makes* me this or that, fixes my identity.

The person who has this attitude toward himself usually is unaware of its being a particular attitude with concrete and far-reaching implications. He takes his attitude for granted as a natural, inevitable one and is aware only of the painful self-consciousness and self-preoccupation it involves. He cannot imagine how anyone with his "fate" could have any other attitude.

The two most significant implications of this attitude to oneself are 1) the severance from the living I of the reified attribute which is experienced as a fixed, unchangeable quality, and 2) the severance of this reified attribute from its dynamic and structural connection with other qualities, needs, acts, and experiences of the person. In other words, the reified attribute is cut off from the living, developing, fluctuating I in *time*, since it is experienced as immutable. But it is also cut off from being experienced as an *integral* part of the living personality, connected with the totality of the person's strivings, attitudes, perceptions, feelings, with his acting and failing to act.

In reality, of course, we can observe that certain actions, moods, and experiences cause changes in the role of the negative identity in the conscious feelings and thoughts of the person. However, he usually does not experience the reified attribute which forms the core of his negative self-feeling as something connected with, and due to, his own actions and attitudes, but as something fixed on which he has no influence. Furthermore, just as the person's feeling about himself may fluctuate with the ups and downs of his "ego," so it also varies with the intensity of the negative self-feeling based on some reified attribute which, at times, may disappear altogether from the conscious thoughts of the person. However, when it reappears it is "recognized" as the same unfortunate quality that throughout the past has tainted—and will forever taint—the person's life. Thus, in spite of such fluctuations, the alienated attribute is experienced as a "something" that basically does not and cannot change.

To be saddled with a reified, negative identity seems, on the face of it, nothing but a painful burden. Yet one often can see people cling to such negative self-images with a great deal of stubbornness and in the face of contradictory evidence. In psychoanalytic therapy, it is often seen that the patient who comes for help tries to convince the therapist that nothing can be done for him, since he is born with such and such a handicap or without such and such an advantage. On closer scrutiny, one may find that such insistence by the patient on the hopelessness of the situation has a way of occurring at a point when the patient is afraid to face an issue, or when he wants to be pitied rather than helped. Thus, the reified identity concept often provides a protection against an anxiety-arousing challenge, a way out of a feared situation, and thereby a certain relief.

This relief is dynamically similar to the relief observable in certain hypochondriacal and paranoid patients. It sounds paradoxical to speak of relief in the case of patients who are so obviously beset by worry, suffering, and fear as the hypochondriac and the paranoid. However, as Sullivan has pointed out, the hypochondriacal patient who is preoccupied with imagined, anticipated, or real ailments sees himself as the "customarily handicapped" one and thereby avoids the anxiety-provoking prospect of facing and dealing with his real problems. His hypochondriacal preoccupation gets the patient, in Sullivan's words, "off the spot with himself"—namely, off the spot where he would have to deal with his realistic personality problems.

The person living with an alienated and reified, negative identity concept of himself closely resembles the hypochondriacal patient, except that his unhappy preoccupation concerns not a physical ailment but a reified physical or psychic quality that has become the focal point of his self-image. The relief he gains from his burdensome preoccupation is due to the fact that the reified "bad" quality no longer is viewed as part of the on-going process of living and of goal-directed thought and action. It has been severed from the "I" that acts with foresight and responsibility and is looked upon as an inherent, unalterable, unfortunate something, an ossified part of oneself that no longer participates in the flux, growth, and development of life. It is experienced as an unchangeable fate whose bearer is doomed to live and die with it. The relief this brings is that the person no longer feels *responsible* for the supposed consequences of this fixed attribute; he is not *doing* anything for which he can be blamed, even though he may feel ashamed and unacceptable for *being* such and such. The preoccupation with the reified identity directs attention away from what he *does* to what he supposedly *is*. Furthermore, he now no longer has to do anything about it because, obviously, he can't do anything about it. Thus, the anxiety, fear, and effort that would be connected with facing and acting upon the real problem is avoided by putting up with the negative, fixed identity which, in addition, may be used to indulge self-pity and to enlist the sympathy of others.

The similarity in the dynamics of hypochondria and paranoia, on the one hand, and the alienated, reified self-concept, on the the other, lies in this *shift of responsibility and of focus* from my own actions and conduct of life to something else over which I have no control. In the alienated self-concept this something else is a reified quality, or the lack of such a quality; in hypochondria an ailment, real or imagined; in paranoia the delusional persecutors. The difference between paranoia and the alienated self-concept lies in the fact that in paranoia the shift in responsibility is brought about by delusions distorting reality, while in the alienated, negative identity concept it is brought about by an attitude which excludes part of oneself from the process of living and freezes it into a cancer-like, uncontrollable, and unalterable thing. This "thing" very often also becomes the focus, in the paranoid neuroses, of the imagined judgments, observation, and talk of other people about the patient. He believes that, just as his own thoughts tend to revolve around some reified and alienated quality, other people will be similarly preoccupied with this quality in him.

So far I have discussed mainly negative self-images. However, alienated identity concepts may be positive as well as negative. Alienated identity of the positive variety occurs in vanity, conceit and—in its more pathological form—in delusions of grandeur, just as in its negative counterpart the "I" of the vain person is severed from a fixed attribute on which the vanity is based. The person feels that he *possesses* this quality. It becomes the focal point of his identity and serves as its prop. Beauty, masculinity or femininity, being born on the right side of the tracks, success, money, prestige, or "being good" may serve as such a prop. While in the negative identity feeling a reified attribute haunts the person, such an attribute serves the positive self-image as a support. Yet it is equally alienated from the living person. This is expressed nicely in the phrase "a stuffed shirt." It is not the person in the shirt but some dead matter, some stuffing that is used to bolster and aggrandize the self-feeling. It often becomes apparent in the behavior of the person that he *leans* on this real or imagined attribute, just as it often is apparent that a person feels pulled down by the weight of some alienated negative attribute.

The reliance on an identity, on a self-image based on the

prop of some reified attribute remains precarious even where it seems to work, after a fashion, as it does in the self-satisfaction of the vain. This precariousness is inevitable, since the positive self-evaluation of such a person does not rest on a feeling of wholeness and meaningfulness in life, in thought, feeling, and deed. He is always threatened with the danger of losing this "thing," this possession, on which his self-esteem is based. This is the theme of Oscar Wilde's novel, *The Picture of Dorian Gray*. Dorian Gray exchanges his identity with the portrait of his youthful charm. He becomes the picture of himself as the beautiful youth, alienated from his actual life, which affects the portrait he has hidden in the attic, marking it over the years with his cruelty, selfishness, and greed, and with his advancing age. The portrait is the skeleton in the closet, the secret threat that hangs over the unchanging mask. Today, especially in this country where youth has become a public fetish, many thousands try to preserve its alienated mask while terrified by the prospect of suddenly growing old, when the mask can no longer be worn or will become grotesque.

I believe that in every case of alienated identity concepts there is a secret counterimage. In Dorian Gray, this is the actual, living person, transplanted to the portrait. Very often such a hidden self announces itself merely in a vague background feeling that the person would be lost, would be nothing if it were not for the alienated, reified quality on which the feeling of being something, somebody, or the feeling of vanity, is based. In this feeling both a truth and an irrational anxiety find expression. The truth is that no man who looks upon himself as a thing and bases his existence on the support of some reified attribute of this thing has found himself and his place in life. The irrational anxiety is the feeling that without the prop of such an attribute he could not live.

Similarly, in the negative alienated identity concepts there usually is a positive counterimage. It may take a generalized, vague form: If it were not for such and such (the reified attribute forming the focus of the negative identity), I would be all right, successful, wonderful, etc. Or it may take the more concrete form of some grandiose, exaggerated fantasy about one's positive qualities. These positive counterimages, too, express both an irrational hope and a truth. The irrational hope is that one may have some magical quality which will transport him into a state of security, or even superiority, because then he will possess that attribute which, instead of haunting him, will save him. But actually it is nothing but the equally reified counterpart of what at present drags him down. The truth is that man has potentialities for overcoming his alienation from himself and for living without the burden and the artificial props of alienated, reified identity concepts.

Goethe, in an interpretation of the Delphic word, "Know thyself," distinguishes between helpful self-awareness and futile and self-tormenting rumination. He opposes the "ascetic" interpretation he finds among "our modern hypochondrists" and those who turn their vengeance against themselves. Instead, he sees the real meaning of self-knowledge in taking notice of oneself and becoming aware of one's relation to other people and to the world. The pseudo-self-knowledge against which he speaks foreshadows the widespread present-day self-preoccupation which is concerned, fruitlessly, with an alienated, negative sense of identity. In contrast to this, Goethe counsels a productive self-knowledge: to pay attention to what one is actually doing in his relation to others, to the world and—we might add—to himself.

II. WORK AND LEISURE

In our society most men and women spend the major portion of their waking hours at work, a fact which should not be taken to mean that man finds or expresses himself only in his work. Yet far beyond the workplace and the time spent in it, the work we do and the way we do it shape our lives—our image of ourselves and our relations with others. In the selections that follow Peter Laslett writes with historical perspective of "The World We Have Lost," a world based on the patriarchal productive unit of pre-industrial times. As Laslett shows, this was an intimate world in which work was inseparable from other family activities. Let it be noted, however—especially for those who would turn the clock back—that this was an authoritarian world, ruled by a father or father-figure who was absolute boss. But along with the power and control exercised by this figure went duties and responsibilities toward those whose work he supervised. He ruled his flock, but he also tended it.

With large-scale industrialism this type of family industry as the basic productive unit came to an end, never to be restored. In the rise of industrial capitalism, handicrafts were replaced by machine-tool production. What this transformation meant for the ordinary worker, torn from the roots of his medieval past, was first described by Marx in his essay, "Alienated Labor." Written in his youth, in 1844, this essay remained largely unknown until much later, and only recently has it become available in translation. Showing the philosophical and literary influence of Hegel, it depicts man as alienated from a world in which nature, others, and he himself had become objects. Under capitalism, Marx wrote, "The object produced by man's labor—its product—now confronts him in the shape of an *alien thing*, a *power independent* of the producer. The product of labor is labor given embodiment in a material form;

this product is the *objectification* of labor." Furthermore, the worker is estranged from the very process of production, which is controlled not by him, but by an alien being, the capitalist. Having lost control of his work, man is alienated from others—and from himself as well. It is now fashionable among critics of Marx to correct his anti-capitalist "bias" and to show that it is not only workers under capitalism who are alienated. But as Marx made clear, both labor and "the possessing class" represent the same self-estrangement. Alienated labor is not the result, but the cause of private property. Marx's goal was to see the emancipation of all men as creative and self-expressive, free from the alien power of things.

That we are still far from this goal and that an alienated working class is still very much with us is suggested clearly in "The Myth of the Happy Worker" by Harvey Swados, a writer who has himself worked in modern American factories.

The selection by Lewis Mumford, "The Mechanical Routine" (taken from his *Technics and Civilization*) provides another picture of the world of work. Today, more than ever before, we are confronted with what Mumford calls the "ambivalent" machine—an instrument of liberation and of repression.

We are also confronted by a formidable counterpart of the machine—bureaucracy. Robert K. Merton's essay, "Bureaucratic Structure and Personality," shows that while bureaucracy aims at the "rationalization" of human behavior, it rarely achieves this goal. Blind adherence to the rules may be "dysfunctional," that is, it will prevent the bureaucracy from performing its intended function. But whether bureaucracy is efficient or inefficient, it is inherently impersonal. This impersonal character makes bureaucracy a hated and feared institution. Hence, as Merton shows, there is danger for bureaucracy when personal feelings and needs are permitted to intrude into its deliberations. Merton's picture of bureaucracy fits the institution with which most of us associate it—government. But bureaucracy is not only an alien governing power; it is for increasing numbers of professional and white-collar workers a workplace.

All the more striking, therefore, is Alan Harrington's description of "Life in the Crystal Palace." What he experienced was not a government bureau or dreary counting-house but what many would consider the ideal corporate environment—physically luxurious and at least superficially warm and friendly in its human relationships. And yet, as Harrington shows all too plainly, the Crystal Palace is no less alienating than the assembly line. Both turn out robots. Whether cheerful or cheerless, they are victims of impersonal and remote power.

Bored at work, men hope to find themselves in their leisure hours, if they have any. In "The Great Emptiness" Robert MacIver tells us that most persons have no training for leisure. And so, like the work from which it provides escape, leisure becomes a great void. Unable to achieve self-realization on the job, men at leisure are men at a loss. If MacIver's essay needs qualification, it is that leisure still remains elusive for most of our citizens who have won it in name only.

THE WORLD WE HAVE LOST
/Peter Laslett

In the year 1619 the bakers of London applied to increase the price of bread. They sent in support a complete description of a bakery and of its weekly costs. Thirteen people there were in such an establishment: the baker and his wife, four paid employees who were called journeymen, two maid-servants, two apprentices, and the baker's three children. Food cost more than anything else, more than raw materials, and nearly four times as much as wages. Clothing was charged up, too, not only for man, wife, and children but for the apprentices as well. Even school fees were included in the cost of baking bread for sale.

A London bakery was undoubtedly what we should call a commercial or an industrial undertaking, turning out loaves by the thousand. Yet it was carried on in the house of the baker himself, an ordinary house with a few extra sheds. All these people, moreover, took their meals in the house, every meal of the day. They even slept there at night; indeed they were obliged to do so, except for the journeymen. In short, universal custom and the law of the land obliged these thirteen people to live together as a family.

The only word ever used at that time to describe such a group of people was the word "family." The man at the head of the group, the man we should call the entrepreneur, or the employer or the manager, was then known as the master, or head of the family. He was father in fact to some of its members, in place of father to the rest. There was no distinction between his domestic and his economic functions. His wife was both his partner and his subordinate, a partner because she ran the family, took charge of the food and managed the women servants, a subordinate because she was woman and wife, mother and in place of mother to the rest.

The paid servants had their specified and familiar position in the family, as much part of it as the children, but not quite in the position of children. The apprentices were even more obviously extra sons, clothed and educated as well as fed, obliged to obedience and forbidden to marry, unpaid and absolutely dependent until the age of twenty-one. And if apprentices were workers who were also children, the children themselves, the sons and daughters of the master and mistress, were workers too. At the end of the century John Locke laid it down that the children of the poor must begin work for some part of the day when they reached the age of three.

We may see at once, therefore, that the world we have lost, as I have called it, was no paradise, no golden age of equality, tolerance, and loving-kindness. It is so important that I should not be misunderstood on this point that I will say at once that in my view the coming of industry cannot be shown to have brought economic oppression and exploitation with it. It was there already. The patriarchal arrangements which I have begun to describe were not new in the England of Shakespeare and of Elizabeth. These arrangements were as old as the Greeks, as old as European history, and they abused and enslaved people quite as remorselessly as the economic arrangements which had replaced them in the England of Blake and Victoria.

But there were differences in the manner of oppressing and exploiting. The ancient order of society which gave way before the coming of industry was felt by those who supported, enjoyed, and endured it to be eternal and unchangeable. There was no expectation of reform. How could there be when economic relationships were domestic relationships, and domestic relationships were rigidly regulated by the social system, by the content of Christianity itself? This is in sharp contrast with social expectations in Victorian England, and in all industrial society since. Since the coming of industry, societies have been far less stable than their predecessors. They lack the extraordinary influence for cohesiveness which familiar relationships carry with them, that power of reconciling the frustrated and the discontented by emotional means.

You have noticed that the roles we have allotted to all the members of the extended family of the master baker of London in 1619 are all, emotionally, highly symbolic and highly satisfactory. In a whole society organized like this, everyone belongs, everyone has his circle of affection, every relationship can be seen as a love relationship. It may indeed well be a love relationship. Not so with us. Who could love the name of a limited company as an apprentice could love his superbly satisfactory father-figure master, even if he were a bully and a beater, a usurer and a hypocrite? But if a family is a circle of affection, it can also be the scene of hatred. The true tyrants among men, the villains and the murderers, are jealous husbands and resentful wives, tyrannical fathers, deprived children.

In the traditional patriarchal society of Europe, which I am trying to describe, where everyone lived his whole life in a family, often in the same family, such tension must have been incessant and unrelieved, incapable of release except in crisis. Men, women, and children have to be very close together and for a very long time indeed to generate the emotional power which can give rise to a tragedy of Sophocles, or Shakespeare, or Racine. Conflict then was between individual people, on the personal scale. Clashes between whole groups, such as those which go to make our own twentieth-century society the scene of perpetual revolution as we call it, could arise far less often then.

This can only have been so if the little knot of thirteen people making bread was indeed the typical social unit of the old world, typical in size, in scale, in composition. In fact we can take the bakery to be the limiting case for the family which was sovereign in the society of our ancestors, the society of the days before the industrial revolution. We shall see in a moment what form the family took over the great expanse of society which lived on the land. But our chosen example has other things to tell us.

We may notice, for one thing, that our folk-memory of

the world we have lost is in much these terms, rather than in rural terms. We still talk to children about apprentices who marry their master's daughters, of bakers who really bake, in their houses, in their homes, of spinsters who really sit by the fire and spin. Nursery rhymes and fairy tales preserve the language pretty well unaltered. In fact a reliable guide to the subject in hand is Grimm's *Fairy Tales,* even Walt Disney. Which means that it is already half known to the historian before he starts, known by rote and not by understanding. Therefore he has neglected it, and neglecting it has failed to set up the correct contrast with the social order which has now succeeded. Without contrast there cannot be understanding, and I submit that we are unable to comprehend our industrial society because the historian whose job it is has not told us what society was like without industry. He has not told us because he thought it was too obvious.

The working family of the London baker vividly illustrates the scale of life under the old social order: no group of persons larger than a family, fifteen or twenty at most; no object larger than London Bridge or St. Paul's Cathedral; no workaday building larger than an ordinary house. Everything physical was on the human scale. Everything temporal was, also. The death of the head of a family in the world of commerce and industry which we have been describing was almost certainly the end to its existence. The hope was that a son would succeed, or, if there was no son, an apprentice instead, which was why it was important that he should marry the master's own kin. Often, surprisingly often, the widow would herself carry on, though it could not be for long.

This, then, was not simply a world without factories; it was a world without firms, a world without economic continuity. Since every activity was limited by what could be organized within a family, and within the lifetime of a family, there was an unending struggle to manufacture continuity, to provide an expectation for the future. "One hundred and twenty family uprising and downlying, whereof you may take out six or seven, and all the rest were servants and retainers": this was the household of the Herberts, Earls of Pembroke in the years before the Civil War, and it illustrates the symbolic function of the aristocratic family —to defy the limitation on size, to build big, to raise up a line which should remain for ever.

We may pause here to point out that our argument is not complete. There was an organization in the social structure of Europe before the coming of industry which transcended the family in size and in endurance. This was the Christian church. It is true to say that the ordinary Englishman went to a gathering larger than could take place in an ordinary house only when he went to church. Looked at simply from the point of view of scale we can see now that the function of the church in such a society was of an entirely different order from its function today, its function in any industrial society.

There were also, we must add, companies of master craftsmen in the towns, guilds which did something to mediate between independent households. But these were not companies as we understand them today, not amalgamations of scores or hundreds of people into production units. The number of companies in our sense was so small that their importance in the social structure was negligible. They were mainly confined to foreign trading and, though pregnant of the future, the historian has grossly exaggerated their importance.

The last thing we must remark upon in our chosen example is the fact that in this baking household the sexes and ages were mingled together. Children might sometimes go out to school, but few adults went out to work, and there was absolutely nothing to correspond to the hundreds of young men at the assembly line, the hundreds of young women in the offices, the lonely lives of housekeeping wives which we now know only too well. Old people did not live alone or in institutions: they were at home, in the families of their sons and daughters. There were no hotels, no young men or young women living on their own. The family group which dominated society was what we should undoubtedly call a "balanced unit," and call it "healthy" too.

When we turn from the hand-made city of London to the hand-moulded immensity of rural England, we may carry similar sentimental prejudice along with us. To every farm there was a family, and each rural family spread over its fields like the family of the master-craftsman over his manufactory. When a farm was small, a man tilled it with the help of his wife and children. No single man, we must remember, would take charge of the land. He had to be a householder, just as the butchers, bakers, and candle-stick makers had to be householders before they could set up on their own. Marriage in this society was the entry to full membership.

When more labor was needed, the farming householder would extend his working family by taking on young men and women to live in his family and work with them. The servants in husbandry, as they were called, stayed there until it was time for them to marry, when, the sons of landless men and landless themselves, they became cottagers or laborers. The families of these laborers were the poorest of all. Work was done by the day, and the farmer who employed a man either fed him at the family table or gave him money instead: all wage rates, which were fixed by the local bench of justices, were in two forms, either with or without meat and drink. The day laborer visiting a farm was made a member of the family by breaking bread with the rest of them. It was almost a sacramental matter.

Inside the cottages the women were spinning the yarn which the clothiers had brought them, clothiers who were the capitalists organizing the great English woolen industry. For industry at this time was carried on not only in one household alone, as in the bakery we have talked about, but by what is called the putting-out system, in which several households were set on work by one middleman: not employed, it must be noted, though that word was used in its then different sense, not exclusively occupied, for apart from his farmwork the laborer might have a piece of land of his own, but supplemented with industrial earnings.

Such was the idyllic patriarchalism which Marx and Engels had in mind in 1848 when they talked, in the *Communist Manifesto,* of the capitalists and their drive towards naked exploitation. I have hinted that the historians, beginning perhaps with the great Marx himself, have misunderstood the process which gave birth to the modern world because they have not properly appreciated the familial structure of the society which existed before the modern world began. One or two points of criticism have been touched already; but I should like to set out some heads of proposals, as they would have said in seventeenth-century England.

I suggest, in the first place, that unless we have a fairly exact idea of what the final unit of a society is, we are hopelessly vague about what the whole society is like. Historians talk all the time about "England," the "nation," the "country": what it did and what it thought. They have to.

But what do these words mean? Who was England in, say, the year 1650? Not every single person living then within our boundaries: no one with a historical sense would claim that. But only a recognition that people came not in individuals but in clots, in families of the sort I have described, only that recognition makes clear that England in its first definition meant only those grown males who were heads of households, who were literate and who had some degree of individuality. This at once excludes all women, all those under the age of nearly thirty, for all these persons were caught up, so to speak—"subsumed" is the ugly word I shall use—in the personalities of the heads of the families to which they belonged. England, in fact, meant a far, far smaller number of persons even than this would imply.

Historians have not, it seems to me, tended to talk about "England" with any sign that they recognized these very important qualifications as to the use of the word. But they seem, of recent years anyway, to be fairly confident that they know what it was that transformed this patriarchal world into the world we live in now. Capitalism did a great deal of it, they say, and it is capitalism which we must contrast with the patriarchal society: capitalism, with its new "spirit," whatever that dangerous word may be doing in the historian's vocabulary, was the great disruptive force which broke up the world we have lost and dethroned the family from its sovereignty in society.

But by the seventeenth century capitalism was at least 300 years old, and perhaps much older. We have seen, in the example of the way in which the putting-out system of industry came to the rescue of the laborer on the land, that capitalism was perfectly compatible with family economic arrangements. Capitalism, we shall conclude, is an incomplete description: it simply cannot do the historian's work which has been thrust upon it.

The historical distortions which have risen from the word capitalism are a result, I believe, in some degree to a faulty sense of proportion, which we can only now begin to correct. With the "capitalism-changed-the-world" way of thinking goes a division of history into the ancient, feudal, and bourgeois eras or stages. I think that the contrast which we have been trying to draw here between the world we have lost and the world we now inhabit makes all other divisions into subdivisions. European society is of the patriarchal type, and with some variations, of which perhaps the feudal variation went furthest, it was patriarchal in its institutions right up to the coming of the factories, the offices, and the rest. It is now patriarchal no longer, except in a vestigial way, and in its emotional predisposition. It is now time that we divided history up again in accordance with what is really important.

The word alienation is part of the cant of the mid-twentieth century, and it began as an attempt to describe the separation of the worker from a world of work. We need not accept all that this expression has come to convey in order to recognize that it does point us the way to realizing something of the first importance to us all in relation to our past. Time was, and it was all time up to 200 years ago, when the whole of life went forward in the family, in a circle of loved, familiar faces, known and fondled objects, all to human size. That time has gone forever. It makes us very different from our ancestors.

ALIENATED LABOR
/Karl Marx

We began with the premises of political economy. Accepting its terminology and its laws, we presupposed private property, the separation of labor, capital, and land; and of wages, profit and rent; the division of labor, competition, the concept of exchange-value. From political economy itself and in its own terms, we showed how the worker sinks to the level of a commodity, and indeed the most wretched of all commodities, since the harder he labors and the more he produces, the more miserable he becomes. We saw also that competition inevitably results in the accumulation of capital in a few hands, and hence the restoration of monopoly in a more terrible form; and finally, that the distinction between capitalist and landlord—like the difference between farm laborer and factory worker—melts away; and the whole of society divides basically into two classes: property owners and propertyless workers.

Political economy begins with the fact of private property without in any way accounting for that fact. Instead,

Translated by Eric and Mary Redmer Josephson

it takes the material processes of private property as they actually occur, presents these processes in general, abstract formulas, and then offers these formulas as laws. It does not comprehend these laws, that is, it fails to show how they arise out of the nature of private property. Political economy tells us nothing about the source of the distinction of labor from capital, or of capital from land. When, for example, economists define the relationship of wages to profit, they take the interests of capitalists as the basis; in other words, they take for granted what they should explain. Similarly, competition is accounted for by external circumstances. Political economy never tells us whether these external and seemingly accidental circumstances are perhaps a necessary development. To economists, exchange itself seems an accidental fact. The only moving forces that political economy recognizes are human greed and the war among the greedy—competition.

Precisely because political economy fails to grasp the interconnections within the system, it was possible to counterpose the doctrine of competition to the doctrine of monopoly, the doctrine of freedom of crafts to that of the guilds, the doctrine of the division of landed property to that of the great estates; because competition, freedom of crafts and the division of landed property were seen merely as chance developments brought about by contrivance and force, rather than as the necessary, inevitable and natural consequences of monopoly, the guild system, and feudal property.

Thus we now have to understand the essential connection between private property, greed, the separation of labor, capital and land, exchange and competition, value and the devaluation of men, monopoly and competition—between this whole system of alienation and the money system.

Let us begin our explanation not as the economist does, with some legendary primordial situation, which clarifies nothing, but merely removes the question to a gray and nebulous distance. The economist takes for granted what remains to be demonstrated, namely, the necessary relationship between two things—between, for example, division of labor and exchange. In the same way theology explains the origin of evil by the fall of man, that is, it takes as a premise what it should explain.

We shall begin with a contemporary economic fact. The worker becomes all the poorer the more wealth he produces, the more his production increases in power and volume. The worker becomes an ever cheaper commodity the more commodities he creates. As the world of things increases in value, the human world becomes devalued. For labor not only produces commodities; it makes a commodity of the work process itself, as well as of the worker —and indeed at the same rate as it produces goods.

This means simply that the object produced by man's labor—its product—now confronts him in the shape of an alien thing, a power independent of the producer. The product of labor is labor given embodiment in a material form; this product is the objectification of labor. The performance of work is thus at the same time its objectification. In the sphere of political economy, the performance of work appears as a material loss, a departure from reality for the worker; objectification appears both as deprivation of the object and enslavement to it; and appropriation of the product by others as alienation.

The reduction of labor to a mere commodity—in short, the dehumanization of work—goes so far that the worker is reduced to the point of starving to death. So remote from life has work become that the worker is robbed of the real things essential not only for his existence but for his work. Indeed, work itself becomes something which he can obtain only with the greatest difficulty and at intervals. And so much does appropriation of his product by others appear as alienation that the more things the worker produces, the fewer can he possess and the more he falls under the domination of the wealth he produces but cannot enjoy—capital.

All these consequences flow from the fact that the worker is related to the product of his labor as to an alien thing. From this premise it is clear that the more the worker exerts himself, the more powerful becomes the world of things which he creates and which confront him as alien objects; hence the poorer he becomes in his inner life, and the less belongs to him as his own. It is the same with religion. The more man puts into God, the less he retains in himself. The worker puts his life into the things he makes; and his life then belongs to him no more, but to the product of his labor. The greater the worker's activity, therefore, the more pointless his life becomes. Whatever the product of his labor, it is no longer his own. Therefore, the greater this product, the more he is diminished. The alienation of the worker from his product means not only that his labor becomes an impersonal object and takes on its own existence, but that it exists outside himself, independently, and alien to him, and that it opposes itself to him as an autonomous power. The life which he has conferred on the object confronts him in the end as a hostile and alien force.

Let us now look more closely at the phenomenon of objectification and its result for the worker: alienation and, in effect, divorce from the product of his labor. To understand this, we must realize that the worker can create nothing without nature, without the sensuous, external world which provides the raw material for his labor. But just as nature provides labor with means of existence in the sense of furnishing raw material which labor processes, so also does it provide means for the worker's physical subsistence. Thus the more the worker by his labor appropriates the external, sensuous world of nature, the more he deprives himself of the means of life in two respects: first, that the sensuous external world becomes progressively detached from him as the medium necessary to his labor; and secondly, that nature becomes increasingly remote from him as the medium through which he gains his physical subsistence.

In both respects, therefore, the worker becomes a slave of things; first, in that labor itself is something he obtains— that is, he gets work; and secondly, in that he obtains thereby the physical means of subsistence. Thus, things enable him to exist, first as a worker, and secondly, as one in bondage to physical objects. The culmination of this process of enslavement is that only as a worker can he maintain himself in his bondage and only as a bondsman to things can he find work.

In the laws of political economy, the alienation of the worker from his product is expressed as follows: the more the worker produces, the less he has to consume; the more value he creates, the more valueless, the more unworthy he becomes; the better formed is his product, the more deformed becomes the worker; the more civilized his product, the more brutalized becomes the worker; the mightier the work, the more powerless the worker; the more ingenious the work, the duller becomes the worker and the more he becomes nature's bondsman.

Political economy conceals the alienation inherent in labor by avoiding any mention of the evil effects of work on those who work. Thus, whereas labor produces miracles for the rich, for the worker it produces destitution. Labor produces palaces, but for the worker, hovels. It produces beauty, but it cripples the worker. It replaces labor by machines, but how does it treat the worker? By throwing some workers back into a barbarous kind of work, and by turning the rest into machines. It produces intelligence, but for the worker, stupidity and cretinism.

Fundamentally, the relationship of labor to the product of labor is the relationship of the worker to the object of his production. The relationship of property owners to the objects of production and to production itself is only a consequence of this primary relationship, and simply confirms it. We shall consider this other aspect later. When we ask, then, what is the essential relationship of labor, we are concerned with the relationship of the worker to production.

Thus far we have considered only one aspect of the alienation of the worker, namely, his relationship to the product of his labor. But his estrangement is manifest not only in the result, but throughout the work process—within productive activity itself. How could the worker stand in an alien relationship to the product of his activity if he were not alienated in the very act of production? The product after all is but the résumé of his activity, of production. Hence if the product of labor is alienation, production itself must be active alienation—the alienation of activity, the activity of alienation. The alienation of the product of labor merely sums up the alienation in the work process itself.

What then do we mean by the alienation of labor? First, that the work he performs is extraneous to the worker, that is, it is not personal to him, is not part of his nature; therefore he does not fulfill himself in work, but actually denies himself; feels miserable rather than content, cannot freely develop his physical and mental powers, but instead becomes physically exhausted and mentally debased. Only while not working can the worker be himself; for while at work he experiences himself as a stranger. Therefore only during leisure hours does he feel at home, while at work he feels homeless. His labor is not voluntary, but coerced, forced labor. It satisfies no spontaneous creative urge, but is only a means for the satisfaction of wants which have nothing to do with work. Its alien character therefore is revealed by the fact that when no physical or other compulsion exists, work is avoided like the plague. Extraneous labor, labor in which man alienates himself, is a labor of self-sacrifice, of mortification. Finally, the alienated character of work for the worker is shown by the fact that the work he does is not his own, but another's, and that at work he belongs not to himself, but to another. Just as in religion the spontaneous activity of human imagination, of the human brain and heart, is seen as a force from outside the individual reacting upon him as the alien activity of gods or devils, so the worker's labor is no more his own spontaneous activity; but is something impersonal, inhuman and belonging to another. Through his work the laborer loses his identity.

As a result, man—the worker—feels freely active only in his animal functions—eating, drinking, procreating, or at most in his dwelling and personal adornment—while in his human and social functions he is reduced to an animal. The animal becomes human, and the human becomes animal. Certainly eating, drinking and procreating are also genuinely human functions; but abstractly considered, apart from all other human activities and regarded as ultimate ends in themselves, they are merely animal functions.

We have considered the alienation of practical human activity or labor from two aspects. First, the relationship of the worker to the product of labor as an alien object which dominates him. This relationship implies at the same time a relationship to the sensuous external world of nature as an alien and hostile world. Second, the relationship of labor to the act of production within the work process. This is the relationship of the worker to his own activity as something alien, and not belonging to him, it is activity as misery, strength as weakness, creation as emasculation; it is the worker's own physical and mental energy, his personal life (for what is life but activity?) as an activity which is turned against himself, which neither depends on nor belongs to him. Here we have self-alienation as opposed to alienation from things.

And now we see that yet a third aspect of alienated labor can be deduced from the two already considered. For man is a creature of his species [*Gattungswesen*] not only because in practice and in theory he adopts mankind as the object of his creation—indeed his field is the whole of nature—but also because within himself he, one man, represents the whole of mankind and therefore he is a universal and a free being.

The life of the species, for man as for animals, has its

physical basis in the fact that man, like the animals, lives on nature; and since man is more universal than animals, so too the realm of nature on which he lives is more universal. Just as plants, animals, stones, the air, light, etc. theoretically form a part of human consciousness, as subjects for natural science and art, providing man with intellectual and spiritual nourishment from the non-human world—nourishment which he must first prepare and transform before he can enjoy and absorb it—so too this non-human world is a practical part of human life and activity, since man also subsists physically on nature's products in the form of food, heat, clothing, shelter, etc. The universality of man in practice is seen in the universality which makes the whole of nature conceivable as man's inorganic body, since nature is first, his direct means of existence, and second, the raw material, the field, the instrument of his vital activity. Nature is man's inorganic body, that is, nature apart from the human body itself. To say that man lives on nature means that nature is his body with which he must remain in constant and vital contact in order not to die. And to say that man's physical and spiritual life is linked to nature is simply an expression of the interdependence of all natural forces, for man himself is part of nature.

Just as alienated labor separates man from nature and from himself—his own active functions and life activity—so too it alienates him from the species, from other men. It degrades all the life of the species and makes some cold and abstract notion of individual life and toil into the goal of the entire species, whose common life also then becomes abstract and alienated.

What happens in the end is that man regards his labor—his life-activity, his productive life—merely as a means of satisfying his drive for physical existence. Yet productive life is the real life of the species. We live in order to create more living things. The whole character of a species is evident in its particular type of life-activity; and free, conscious activity is the generic character of human beings. But alienated labor reduces this area of productive life to a mere means of existence.

Among animals there is no question of regarding one part of life as cut off from the rest; the animal is one with its life-activity. Man, on the other hand, makes his life-activity the object of his conscious will; and this is what distinguishes him from animals. It is because of this free, conscious activity that he is a creature of his species. Or perhaps it is because he is a creature of his species that he is a conscious being, that he is able to direct his life-activity; and that he treats his own life as subject matter and as an object of his own determination. Alienated labor reverses this relationship: man, the self-conscious being, turns his chief activity—labor, which should express his profound essence—into a mere means of physical existence.

In manipulating inorganic nature and creating an objective world by his practical activity, man confirms himself as a conscious creature of his species, that is, as a member of his whole species, a being who regards the whole of mankind as involved in himself, and himself as part of mankind. Admittedly animals also produce, building, as do bees, ants or beavers, their nests or dens. But animals produce only for their own immediate needs or for those of their young. Animal production is limited, while man's production is universal. The animal produces only under compulsion of direct physical need, while man produces even when free from physical need, and only truly produces or creates when truly free from such need. Animals produce or reproduce only themselves, while man reproduces the whole of nature. Whatever animals produce—nests or food—is only for their own bodies; but man's creations supply the needs of many species. And whereas animals construct only in accordance with the standards and needs of their kind, man designs and produces in accordance with the standards of all known species and can apply the standards appropriate to the subject. Man therefore designs in accordance with the laws of beauty.

Thus it is precisely in shaping the objective world that man really proves himself as a creature of his species; for in this handiwork resides his active species-life. By means of man's productivity, nature appears to him as his work and his reality. The true object of man's labor therefore is the objectification of man's species-life—his profound essence; for in his labor man duplicates himself not merely intellectually, in consciousness, but also actively, in reality; and in the world that he has made man contemplates his own image. When, therefore, alienated labor tears away from man the object of his production, it snatches from him his species-life—the essence of his being—and transforms his advantage over animals into a disadvantage, insofar as his inorganic body, nature, is withdrawn from him.

Hence, in degrading labor—which should be man's free, spontaneous activity—to a mere means of physical subsistence, alienated labor degrades man's essential life to a mere means to an end. The awareness which man should have of his relationship to the rest of mankind is reduced to a state of detachment in which he and his fellows become simply unfeeling objects. Thus alienated labor turns man's essential humanity into a non-human property. It estranges man from his own human body, and estranges him from nature and from his own spiritual essence—his human being.

An immediate consequence of man's estrangement from the product of his labor is man's estrangement from man. When man confronts himself, he confronts other men. What characterizes his relationship to his work, to the product of his labor, and to himself also characterizes his relationship to other men, their work, and the products of their labor.

In general, the statement that man is alienated from the larger life of his species means that men are alienated from each other and from human nature. Man's self-estrangement—and indeed all his attitudes to himself—first finds expression in his relationship to other men. Thus in the relationship of alienated labor each man's view of his fellows is determined by the narrow standards and activities of the work place.

We started with an economic fact, the separation of the worker from the means of production. From this fact flows our concept of alienated or estranged labor; and in analyzing this concept, we merely analyzed a fact of political economy.

Let us now see how alienated labor appears in real life. If the product of my labor is alien to me, if it confronts me as an alien power, to whom then does it belong? If my own activity belongs not to me, but is an alien, forced activity, to whom does it then belong? It must belong to a being other than me. Who then is this being?

Is it the gods? In ancient times the major productive effort was evidently in the service of the gods—for example, temple building in Egypt, India, Mexico; and the product of that effort belonged to the gods. But the gods were never the lords of labor. Neither was nature ever man's taskmaster. What a contradiction it would be if man—as he more and more subjugated nature by his labor, rendering divine miracles superfluous by the wonders of industry—if man were then to renounce his pleasure in producing and his enjoyment of the product merely in order to continue serving the gods.

Hence, the alien being to whom labor and the product of labor belong, in whose service labor is performed and for whose enjoyment the product of labor serves—this being can only be man himself. So, if the product of labor does not belong to the worker, if it confronts him as an alien power, this must mean that it belongs to a man other than the worker. If the worker's activity is a torment to him, it must be a source of enjoyment and pleasure to another man. Neither the gods nor nature but only man himself can be this alien power over men.

Let us consider our earlier statement that man's relation to himself first becomes objectified, embodied and real through his relation to other men. Therefore, if he is related to the product of his objectified labor as to an alien, hostile, powerful and independent object, then he is related in such a way that someone else is master of this object—someone who is alien, hostile, powerful and independent of him. If his own activity is not free, then he is related to it as an activity in the service, and under the domination, coercion and yoke, of another man.

The alienation of man from himself and from nature appears in his relationships with other men. Thus religious self-alienation necessarily appears in the relationship between laymen and priest—or—since we are here dealing with the spiritual world—between laymen and intercessor. In the everyday, practical world, however, self-alienation manifests itself only through real, practical relationships between men. The medium through which alienation occurs is itself a practical one. As alienated laborer, man not only establishes a certain relationship to the object and process of production as to alien and hostile powers; he also fixes the relationship of other men to his production and to his product; and the relationship between himself and other men. Just as he turns his own production into a real loss, a punishment, and his own product into something not belonging to him; so he brings about the domination of the non-producer over production and its product. In becoming alienated from his own activity, he surrenders power over that activity to a stranger.

So far we have considered this alienated relationship only

from the worker's standpoint. Later we shall also consider it from the standpoint of the non-worker, since through the process of alienating his labor the worker brings forth another man who stands outside the work process. The relationship of the worker to work also determines the relationship of the capitalist—or whatever one chooses to call the master of labor—to work. Private property thus is essentially the result, the necessary consequence of alienated labor and of the extraneous relationship of the worker to nature and to himself. Hence private property results from the phenomenon of alienated labor—that is, alienated labor, alienated life and alienated man.

We took the concept of alienated labor and alienated life from political economy and from an analysis of the movement of private property. But analysis of this movement shows that although private property appears to be the source and cause of labor's alienation, it is really the consequence—just as the gods are originally not the cause but the effect of man's intellectual confusion. Later on, however, this relationship becomes reciprocal.

Only at the final stage of the development of private property is its secret revealed, namely, that on the one hand it is the product of alienated labor, and on the other hand it is the means by which labor becomes estranged, and by which the estrangement is perpetuated.

This development illuminates several unresolved conflicts. Political economy starts with labor as the real soul of production, yet attributes nothing to labor and everything to private property. Faced with this contradiction, Proudhon decided in favor of labor and against private property. We suggest, however, that this apparent contradiction is really a contradiction within alienated labor itself, and that political economy has merely formulated the laws of alienated labor.

We also suggest that wages and private property are identical: when the product or object of labor pays for labor itself, wages are only a necessary consequence of labor's alienation. In the wage system labor does not appear as an end in itself but as the servant of wages. We shall develop this point later on. Meanwhile, what are the consequences?

An enforced rise in wages—disregarding all other difficulties, especially the fact that such an anomaly could only be maintained by force—would therefore be nothing but a better payment of slaves and would not restore, either for the worker or for work, human significance and dignity. Indeed, even the equality of wages demanded by Proudhon would only transform the relationship of the present-day worker to his labor into the relationship of all men to labor. Society then would be conceived as an abstract capitalist. Wages are an immediate consequence of the alienation of labor, and alienated labor is the immediate cause of private property. The downfall of one means the downfall of the other.

From the relationship of alienated labor to private property it also follows that the emancipation of society from private property and hence from servitude takes the political form of the emancipation of the workers. This is not because the emancipation of workers alone is at stake, but because their liberation means the emancipation of all humanity. All human servitude is involved in the relationship of the worker to production, and all forms of servitude are only modifications and consequences of this relationship.

Just as we have derived the concept of private property from our analysis of alienated labor, so every category of political economy can be developed with the help of these two factors; and in each of these categories—trade, competition, capital, money—we find only a particular expression of these basic factors.

Before considering this framework, however, let us try to solve two problems. First, we wish to ascertain the general nature of private property as it has resulted from alienated labor and as it relates to truly human, social property. Second, we have taken as a fact and analyzed the alienation of labor. We now ask, how does man come to alienate his labor? How is this estrangement rooted in the nature of human development? We moved toward solving this problem when we transformed our question about the origin of private property into a question about the relation of alienated labor to the course of human development. For in speaking of private property one may think he is dealing with something external to man. But in speaking of labor, one is directly concerned with man himself. This new formulation of the question contains its own solution.

As to the first problem—the general nature of private property and its relation to truly human property—we have divided estranged labor into two elements which condition each other, or rather constitute different expressions of the same relationship. Appropriation appears as alienation, or as estrangement; and estrangement appears to be appropriation, the adoption of one's product by someone else for his own use exclusively.

We have considered one aspect—alienated labor in relation to the worker himself, that is, estranged labor as it affects the working man. And we found that the necessary consequence of this relation was the property relation of the non-worker to the worker and to work. Private property as the concrete, condensed expression of estranged labor includes both relations—the relationship of the worker to work, to his product, and to the non-worker; and the relationship of the non-worker to the worker and to the worker's product.

We saw that to the worker who appropriates nature by his labor, this appropriation appears as alienation, his own spontaneous activity belongs to another man, vitality becomes a sacrifice of life, and production of the object becomes loss of the object to an alien power or person. Let us now consider the relation of this alien man to the worker, to labor, and to the object of labor.

First, it must be noted that everything which for the worker becomes an alienated activity, for the non-worker becomes an alienated state of mind. Second, what for the worker is a highly practical attitude toward production and the product of labor becomes for the non-worker a mere theoretical attitude. Third, the non-worker does everything against the worker which the latter does against himself, but the non-worker does not do against himself what he does against the worker.

Let us examine these three relationships more closely.*

* [Here the manuscript breaks off unfinished—*Tr. Note*.]

THE MYTH OF THE HAPPY WORKER
/Harvey Swados

> "From where we sit in the company," says one of the best personnel men in the country, "we have to look at only the aspects of work that cut across all sorts of jobs —administration and human relations. Now these are aspects of work, abstractions, but it's easy for personnel people to get so hipped on their importance that they look on the specific tasks of making things and selling them as secondary . . ."
> —*The Organization Man,* by William H. Whyte Jr.

The personnel man who made this remark to Mr. Whyte differed from his brothers only in that he had a moment of insight. Actually, "the specific tasks of making things" are now not only regarded by his white-collar fellows as "secondary," but as irrelevant to the vaguer but more "challenging" tasks of the man at the desk. This is true not just of the personnel man, who places workers, replaces them, displaces them—in brief, manipulates them. The union leader also, who represents workers and sometimes manipulates them, seems increasingly to regard what his workers do as merely subsidiary to the job he himself is doing in the larger community. This job may be building the Red Cross or the Community Chest, or it may sometimes be—as the Senate hearings suggest—participating in such communal endeavors as gambling, prostitution and improving the breed. In any case, the impression is left that the problems of the workers in the background (or underground) have been stabilized, if not permanently solved.

With the personnel man and the union leader, both of whom presumably see the worker from day to day, growing so far away from him, it is hardly to be wondered at that the middle class in general, and articulate middle-class intellectuals in particular, see the worker vaguely, as through a cloud. One gets the impression that when they do consider him, they operate from one of two unspoken assumptions: (1) The worker has died out like the passenger pigeon, or is dying out, or becoming accultured, like the Navajo; (2) If he *is* still around, he is just like the rest of us—fat, satisfied, smug, a little restless, but hardly distinguishable from his fellow TV-viewers of the middle class.

Lest it be thought that (1) is somewhat exaggerated, I hasten to quote from a recently-published article apparently dedicated to the laudable task of urging slothful middle-class intellectuals to wake up and live: "The old-style sweat-shop crippled mainly the working people. Now there are no workers left in America; we are almost all middle class as to income and expectations." I do not believe the writer meant to state—although he comes perilously close to it —that nobody works any more. If I understand him correctly, he is referring to the fact that the worker's rise in real income over the last decade, plus the diffusion of middle-class tastes and values throughout a large part of the underlying population, have made it increasingly difficult to tell blue-collar from white-collar worker without a program. In short, if the worker earns like the middle class, votes like the middle class, dresses like the middle class, dreams like the middle class, then he ceases to exist as a worker.

But there is one thing that the worker doesn't do like the middle class: he works like a worker. The steel-mill puddler does not yet sort memos, the coal miner does not yet sit in conferences, the cotton millhand does not yet sip martinis from his lunchbox. The worker's attitude toward his work is generally compounded of hatred, shame and resignation.

Before I spell out what I think this means, I should like first to examine some of the implications of the widely-held belief that "we are almost all middle class as to income and expectations." I am neither economist, sociologist nor politician, and I hold in my hand no doctored statistics to be haggled over. I am by profession a writer who has had occasion to work in factories at various times during the thirties, forties and fifties. The following observations are simply impressions based on my last period of factory servitude, in 1956.

The average automobile worker gets a little better than two dollars an hour. As such he is one of the best-paid factory workers in the country. After twenty years of militant struggle led by the union that I believe to be still the finest and most democratic labor organization in the United States, he is earning less than the starting salaries offered to inexperienced and often semi-literate college graduates without dependents. After compulsory deductions for taxes, social security, old-age insurance and union dues, and optional deductions for hospitalization and assorted charities, his pay check for forty hours of work is going to be closer to seventy than to eighty dollars a week. Does this make him middle class as to income? Does it rate with the weekly take of a dentist, an accountant, a salesman, a draftsman, a journalist? Surely it would be more to the point to ask how a family man can get by in the fifties on that kind of income. I know how he does it, and I should think the answers would be a little disconcerting to those who wax glib on the satisfactory status of the "formerly" underprivileged.

For one thing, he works a lot longer than forty hours a week—when he can. Since no automobile company is as yet in a position to guarantee its workers anything like fifty weeks of steady forty-hour paychecks, the auto worker knows he has to make it while he can. During peak production periods he therefore puts in nine, ten, eleven and often twelve hours a day on the assembly line for weeks on end. And that's not all. If he has dependents, as like as not he also holds down a "spare-time" job. I have worked on the line with men who doubled as mechanics, repairmen, salesmen, contractors, builders, farmers, cab-drivers, lumberyard workers, countermen. I would guess that there are many more of these than show up in the official statistics: often a man will work for less if he can be paid under the counter with tax-free dollars.

Nor is that all. The factory worker with dependents cannot carry the debt load he now shoulders—the middle-class debt load, if you like, of nagging payments on car, washer, dryer, TV, clothing, house itself—without family help. Even if he puts in fifty, sixty or seventy hours a week at one or two jobs, he has to count on his wife's paycheck, or his son's, his daughter's, his brother-in-law's; or on his mother's social security, or his father's veteran's pension. The working-class family today is not typically held together by the male wage-earner, but by multiple wage-earners often of several generations who club together to get the things they want and need—or are pressured into believing they must have. It is at best a precarious arrangement; as for its toll on the physical organism and the psyche, that is a question perhaps worthy of further investigation by those who currently pronounce themselves bored with Utopia Unlimited in the Fat Fifties.

But what of the worker's middle-class expectations? I had been under the impression that this was the rock on which Socialist agitation had foundered for generations: it proved useless to tell the proletarian that he had a world to win when he was reasonably certain that with a few breaks he could have his own gas station. If these expectations have changed at all in recent years, they would seem to have narrowed rather than expanded, leaving a psychological increment of resignation rather than of unbounded optimism (except among the very young—and even among them the optimism focuses more often on better-paying opportunities elsewhere in the labor market than on illusory hopes of swift status advancement). The worker's expectations are for better pay, more humane working conditions, more job security. As long as he feels that he is going to achieve them through an extension of existing conditions, for that long he is going to continue to be a middle-class conservative in temper. But only for that long.

I suspect that what middle-class writers mean by the worker's middle-class expectations are his cravings for commodities—his determination to have not only fin-tailed cars and single-unit washer-dryers, but butterfly chairs in the rumpus room, African masks on the wall and power boats in the garage. Before the middle-class intellectuals condemn these expectations too harshly, let them consider, first, who has been utilizing every known technique of suasion and propaganda to convert luxuries into necessities, and second, at what cost these new necessities are acquired by the American working-class family.

Now I should like to return to the second image of the American worker: satisfied, doped by TV, essentially middle class in outlook. This is an image bred not of communication with workers (except as mediated by hired interviewers sent "into the field" like anthropologists or entomologists), but of contempt for people, based perhaps on self-contempt and on a feeling among intellectuals that the worker has let them down. In order to see this clearly, we have to place it against the intellectual's changing attitudes toward the worker since the thirties.

At the time of the organization of the CIO, the middle-class intellectual saw the proletarian as society's figure of virtue—heroic, magnanimous, bearing in his loins the seeds of a better future; he would have found ludicrous the suggestion that a sit-down striker might harbor anti-Semitic feelings. After Pearl Harbor, the glamorization of the worker was taken over as a function of government. Then, however, he was no longer the builder of the future good society; instead he was second only to the fighting man as the vital winner of the war. Many intellectuals, as government employees, found themselves helping to create this new portrait of the worker as patriot.

But in the decade following the war intellectuals have discovered that workers are no longer either building socialism or forging the tools of victory. All they are doing is making the things that other people buy. That, and participating in the great commodity scramble. The disillusionment, it would seem, is almost too terrible to bear. Word has gotten around among the highbrows that the worker is not heroic or idealistic; public-opinion polls prove that he wants barbecue pits more than foreign aid and air-conditioning more than desegregation, that he doesn't particularly want to go on strike, that he is reluctant to form a Labor Party, that he votes for Stevenson and often even for Eisenhower and Nixon—that he is, in short, animated by the same aspirations as drive the middle class onward and upward in suburbia.

There is of course a certain admixture of self-delusion in the middle-class attitude that workers are now the same as everybody else. For me it was expressed most precisely last year in the dismay and sympathy with which middle-class friends greeted the news that I had gone back to work in a factory. If workers are now full-fledged members of the middle class, why the dismay? What difference whether one sits in an office or stands in a shop? The answer is so obvious that one feels shame at laboring the point. But I have news for my friends among the intellectuals. The answer is obvious to workers, too.

They know that there is a difference between working with your back and working with your behind (I do not make the distinction between hand-work and brain-work, since we are all learning that white-collar work is becoming less and less brain-work). They know that they work harder than the middle class for less money. Nor is it simply a question of status, that magic word so dear to the hearts of the sociologues, the new anatomizers of the American corpus. It is not simply status-hunger that makes a man hate work which pays *less* than other work he knows about, if *more* than any other work he has been trained for (the

only reason my fellow-workers stayed on the assembly line,
they told me again and again). It is not simply status-hunger
that makes a man hate work that is mindless, endless, stupe-
fying, sweaty, filthy, noisy, exhausting, insecure in its prospects and practically without hope of advancement.

The plain truth is that factory work is degrading. It is degrading to any man who ever dreams of doing something
worthwhile with his life; and it is about time we faced the
fact. The more a man is exposed to middle-class values, the
more sophisticated he becomes and the more production-
line work is degrading to him. The immigrant who slaved in
the poorly-lighted, foul, vermin-ridden sweatshop found his
work less degrading than the native-born high school graduate who reads Judge Parker, Rex Morgan, M.D., and Judd
Saxon, Business Executive, in the funnies, and works in a
fluorescent factory with ticker-tape production-control machines. For the immigrant laborer, even the one who did not
dream of socialism, his long hours were going to buy him
freedom. For the factory worker of the fifties, his long hours
are going to buy him commodities . . . and maybe reduce a
few of his debts.

Almost without exception, the men with whom I worked
on the assembly line last year felt like trapped animals. Depending on their age and personal circumstances, they
were either resigned to their fate, furiously angry at *themselves* for what they were doing, or desperately hunting
other work that would pay as well and in addition offer
some variety, some prospect of change and betterment. They
were sick of being pushed around by harried foremen
(themselves more pitied than hated), sick of working like
blinkered donkeys, sick of being dependent for their livelihood on a maniacal production-merchandising setup, sick
of working in a place where there was no spot to relax during the twelve-minute rest period. (Some day—let us
hope—we will marvel that production was still so wor-
shipped in the fifties that new factories could be built with
every splendid facility for the storage and movement of essential parts, but with no place for a resting worker to sit
down for a moment but on a fire plug, the edge of a packing
case, or the sputum- and oil-stained stairway of a toilet.)

The older men stay put and wait for their vacations. But
since the assembly line demands young blood (you have
a hard time getting hired if you are over thirty-five), the
factory in which I worked was aswarm with new faces

every day; labor turnover was so fantastic and absenteeism so rampant, with the young men knocking off a day or two every week to hunt up other jobs, that the company was forced to over-hire in order to have sufficient workers on hand at the starting siren.

To those who will object—fortified by their readings in C. Wright Mills and A. C. Spectorsky—that the white-collar commuter, too, dislikes his work, accepts it only because it buys his family commodities, and is constantly on the prowl for other work, I can only reply that for me at any rate this is proof not of the disappearance of the working-class but of the proletarianization of the middle class. Perhaps it is not taking place quite in the way that Marx envisaged it, but the alienation of the white-collar man (like that of the laborer) from both his tools and whatever he produces, the slavery that chains the exurbanite to the commuting timetable (as the worker is still chained to the time-clock), the anxiety that sends the white-collar man home with his briefcase for an evening's work (as it degrades the workingman into pleading for long hours of overtime), the displacement of the white-collar slum from the wrong side of the tracks to the suburbs (just as the working-class slum is moved from old-law tenements to skyscraper barracks)—all these mean to me that the white-collar man is entering (though his arms may be loaded with commodities) the gray world of the working man.

Three quotations from men with whom I worked may help to bring my view into focus:

Before starting work: "Come on, suckers, they say the Foundation wants to give away *more* than half a billion this year. Let's do and die for the old Foundation."

During rest period: "Ever stop to think how we crawl here bumper to bumper, and crawl home bumper to bumper, and we've got to turn out more every minute to keep our jobs, when there isn't even any room for them on the highways?"

At quitting time (this from older foremen, whose job is not only to keep things moving, but by extension to serve as company spokesmen): "You're smart to get out of here. . . . I curse the day I ever started, now I'm stuck: any man with brains that stays here ought to have his head examined. This is no place for an intelligent human being."

Such is the attitude towards the work. And towards the product? On the one hand it is admired and desired as a symbol of freedom, almost a substitute for freedom, not because the worker participated in making it, but because our whole culture is dedicated to the proposition that the automobile is both necessary and beautiful. On the other hand it is hated and despised—so much that if your new car smells bad it may be due to a banana peel crammed down its gullet and sealed up thereafter, so much so that if your dealer can't locate the rattle in your new car you might ask him to open the welds on one of those tail fins and vacuum out the nuts and bolts thrown in by workers sabotaging their own product.

Sooner or later, if we want a decent society—by which I do not mean a society glutted with commodities or one maintained in precarious equilibrium by over-buying and forced premature obsolescence—we are going to have to come face to face with the problem of work. Apparently the Russians have committed themselves to the replenishment of their labor force through automatic recruitment of those intellectually incapable of keeping up with severe scholastic requirements in the public educational system. Apparently we, too, are heading in the same direction: although our economy is not directed, and although college education is as yet far from free, we seem to be operating in this capitalist economy on the totalitarian assumption that we can funnel the underprivileged, undereducated, or just plain underequipped, into the factory, where we can proceed to forget about them once we have posted the minimum fair labor standards on the factory wall.

If this is what we want, let's be honest enough to say so. If we conclude that there is nothing noble about repetitive work, but that it is nevertheless good enough for the lower orders, let's say that, too, so we will at least know where we stand. But if we cling to the belief that other men are our brothers, not just Egyptians, or Israelis, or Hungarians, but *all* men, including millions of Americans who grind their lives away on an insane treadmill, then we will have to start thinking about how their work and their lives can be made meaningful. That is what I assume the Hungarians, both workers and intellectuals, have been thinking about. Since no one has been ordering us what to think, since no one has been forbidding our intellectuals to fraternize with our workers, shouldn't it be a little easier for us to admit, first, that our problems exist, then to state them, and then to see if we can resolve them?

THE MECHANICAL ROUTINE
/Lewis Mumford

Let the reader examine for himself the part played by
mechanical routine and mechanical apparatus in his day,
from the alarm-clock that wakes him to the radio program
that puts him to sleep. Instead of adding to his burden by
recapitulating it, I purpose to summarize the results of his
investigations, and analyze the consequences.

The first characteristic of modern machine civilization is
its temporal regularity. From the moment of waking, the
rhythm of the day is punctuated by the clock. Irrespective
of strain or fatigue, despite reluctance or apathy, the household rises close to its set hour. Tardiness in rising is penal-
ized by extra haste in eating breakfast or in walking to catch
the train: in the long run, it may even mean the loss of a
job or of advancement in business. Breakfast, lunch, dinner, occur at regular hours and are of definitely limited
duration: a million people perform these functions within
a very narrow band of time, and only minor provisions
are made for those who would have food outside this regular schedule. As the scale of industrial organization grows,
the punctuality and regularity of the mechanical régime
tend to increase with it: the time-clock enters automatically to regulate the entrance and exit of the worker, while
an irregular worker—tempted by the trout in spring streams
or ducks on salt meadows—finds that these impulses are as
unfavorably treated as habitual drunkenness: if he would
retain them, he must remain attached to the less routinized
provinces of agriculture. "The refractory tempers of work-
people accustomed to irregular paroxysms of diligence,"
of which Ure wrote a century ago with such pious horror,
have indeed been tamed.

Under capitalism time-keeping is not merely a means of
co-ordinating and interrelating complicated functions; it
is also like money an independent commodity with a value
of its own. The schoolteacher, the lawyer, even the doctor
with his schedule of operations conform their functions to
a timetable almost as rigorous as that of the locomotive

engineer. In the case of childbirth, patience rather than instrumentation is one of the chief requirements for a successful normal delivery and one of the major safeguards against infection in a difficult one. Here the mechanical interference of the obstetrician, eager to resume his rounds, has apparently been largely responsible for the current discreditable record of American physicians, utilizing the most sanitary hospital equipment, in comparison with midwives who do not attempt brusquely to hasten the processes of nature. While regularity in certain physical functions, like eating and eliminating, may in fact assist in maintaining health, in other matters, like play, sexual intercourse, and other forms of recreation the strength of the impulse itself is pulsating rather than evenly recurrent: here habits fostered by the clock or the calendar may lead to dullness and decay.

Hence the existence of a machine civilization, completely timed and scheduled and regulated, does not necessarily guarantee maximum efficiency in any sense. Time-keeping establishes a useful point of reference, and is invaluable for co-ordinating diverse groups and functions which lack any other common frame of activity. In the practice of an individual's vocation such regularity may greatly assist concentration and economize effort. But to make it arbitrarily rule over human functions is to reduce existence itself to mere time-serving and to spread the shades of the prison house over too large an area of human conduct. The regularity that produces apathy and atrophy—that *acedia* which was the bane of monastic existence, as it is likewise of the army—is as wasteful as the irregularity that produces disorder and confusion. To utilize the accidental, the unpredictable, the fitful is as necessary, even in terms of economy, as to utilize the regular: activities which exclude the operations of chance impulses forfeit some of the advantages of regularity.

In short: mechanical time is not an absolute. And a population trained to keep to a mechanical time routine at whatever sacrifice to health, convenience, and organic felicity may well suffer from the strain of that discipline and find life impossible without the most strenuous compensations. The fact that sexual intercourse in a modern city is limited, for workers in all grades and departments, to the fatigued hours of the day may add to the efficiency of the working life only by a too-heavy sacrifice in personal and organic relations. Not the least of the blessings promised by the shortening of working hours is the opportunity to carry into bodily play the vigor that has hitherto been exhausted in the service of machines.

Next to mechanical regularity, one notes the fact that a good part of the mechanical elements in the day are attempts to counteract the effects of lengthening time and space distances. The refrigeration of eggs, for example, is an effort to space their distribution more uniformly than the hen herself is capable of doing: the pasteurization of milk is an attempt to counteract the effect of the time consumed in completing the chain between the cow and the remote consumer. The accompanying pieces of mechanical apparatus do nothing to improve the product itself: refrigeration merely halts the process of decomposition, while pasteurization actually robs the milk of some of its value as nutriment. Where it is possible to distribute the population closer to the rural centers where milk and butter and green vegetables are grown, the elaborate mechanical apparatus for counteracting time and space distances may to a large degree be diminished.

One might multiply such examples from many departments; they point to a fact about the machine that has not been generally recognized by those quaint apologists for machine-capitalism who look upon every extra expenditure of horsepower and every fresh piece of mechanical apparatus as an automatic net gain in efficiency. In *The Instinct of Workmanship* Veblen has indeed wondered whether the typewriter, the telephone, and the automobile, though creditable technological achievements "have not wasted more effort and substance than they have saved," whether they are not to be credited with an appreciable economic loss, because they have increased the pace and the volume of correspondence and communication and travel out of all proportion to the real need. And Mr. Bertrand Russell has noted that each improvement in locomotion has increased the area over which people are compelled to move: so that a person who would have had to spend half an hour to walk to work a century ago must still spend half an hour to reach his destination, because the contrivance that would have enabled him to save time had he remained in his original situation now—by driving him to a more distant residential area—effectually cancels out the gain.

One further effect of our closer time co-ordination and our instantaneous communication must be noted here: broken time and broken attention. The difficulties of transport and communication before 1850 automatically acted as a selective screen, which permitted no more stimuli to reach a person than he could handle: a certain urgency was necessary before one received a call from a long distance or was compelled to make a journey oneself: this condition of slow physical locomotion kept intercourse down to a human scale, and under definite control. Nowadays this screen has vanished: the remote is as close as the near; the ephemeral is as emphatic as the durable. While the tempo of the day has been quickened by instantaneous communication the rhythm of the day has been broken: the radio, the telephone, the daily newspaper clamor for attention, and amid the host of stimuli to which people are subjected, it becomes more and more difficult to absorb and cope with any one part of the environment, to say nothing of dealing with it as a whole. The common man is as subject to these interruptions as the scholar or the man of affairs, and even the weekly period of cessation from familiar tasks and contemplative reverie, which was one of the great contributions of Western religion to the discipline of the personal life, has become an ever remoter possibility. These mechanical aids to efficiency and cooperation and intelligence have been mercilessly exploited, through commercial and political pressure: but so far— since unregulated and undisciplined—they have been obstacles to the very ends they affect to further. We have multiplied the mechanical demands without multiplying in any degree our human capacities for registering and reacting intelligently to them. With the successive demands of the outside world so frequent and so imperative, without any respect to their real importance, the inner world becomes progressively meager and formless: instead of active selection there is passive absorption ending in the state happily described by Victor Branford as "addled subjectivity."

One of the by-products of the development of mechanical devices and mechanical standards has been the nullification of skill. What has taken place here within the factory has also taken place in the final utilization of its products. The safety razor, for example, has changed the operation of shaving from a hazardous one, best left to a trained barber, to a rapid commonplace of the day which even the most inept males can perform. The automobile has transformed engine-driving from the specialized task of the locomotive engineer to the occupation of millions of amateurs. The camera has in part transformed the artful reproductions of the wood engraver to a relatively simple photo-chemical process in which anyone can acquire at least the rudiments. As in manufacture the human function first becomes specialized, then mechanized, and finally automatic or at least semi-automatic.

When the last stage is reached, the function again takes on some of its original non-specialized character: photography helps recultivate the eye, the telephone the voice, the radio the ear, just as the motor car has restored some of the manual and operative skills that the machine was banishing from other departments of existence at the same time that it has given to the driver a sense of power and autonomous direction—a feeling of firm command in the midst of potentially constant danger—that had been taken away from him in other departments of life by the machine. So, too, mechanization, by lessening the need for domestic service, has increased the amount of personal autonomy and personal participation in the household. In short, mechanization creates new occasions for human effort; and on the whole the effects are more educative than were the semi-automatic services of slaves and menials in the older civilizations. For the mechanical nullification of skill can take place only up to a certain point. It is only when one has completely lost the power of discrimination that a standardized canned soup can, without further preparation, take the place of a home-cooked one, or when one has lost prudence completely that a four-wheel brake can serve instead of a good driver. Inventions like these increase the province and multiply the interests of the amateur. When automatism becomes general and the benefits of mechanization are socialized, men will be back once more in the Edenlike state in which they have existed in regions of natural increment, like the South Seas: the ritual of leisure will replace the ritual of work, and work itself will become a kind of game. That is, in fact, the ideal goal of a completely mechanized and automatized system of power production: the elimination of work: the universal achievement of leisure. In his discussion of slavery Aristotle said that when the shuttle wove by itself and the plectrum played by itself chief workmen would not need helpers nor masters slaves. At the time he wrote, he believed that he was establishing the eternal validity of slavery; but for us today he was in reality justifying the existence of the machine. Work, it is true, is the constant form of man's interaction with his environment, if by work one means the sum total of exertions necessary to maintain life; and lack of work usually means an impairment of function and a breakdown in organic relationship that leads to substitute forms of work, such as invalidism and neurosis. But work in the form of unwilling drudgery or of that sedentary routine which, as Mr. Alfred Zimmern reminds us, the Athenians so properly despised—work in these degrading forms is the true province of machines. Instead of reducing human beings to work-mechanisms, we can now transfer the main part of burden to automatic machines. This potentiality, still so far from effective achievement for mankind at large, is perhaps the largest justification of the mechanical developments of the last thousand years.

From the social standpoint, one final characterization of the machine, perhaps the most important of all, must be noted: the machine imposes the necessity for collective effort and widens its range. To the extent that men have escaped the control of nature they must submit to the control of society. As in a serial operation every part must function smoothly and be geared to the right speed in order to ensure the effective working of the process as a whole, so in society at large there must be a close articulation between all its elements. Individual self-sufficiency is another way of saying technological crudeness: as our technics becomes more refined it becomes impossible to work the machine without large-scale collective cooperation, and in the long run a high technics is possible only on a basis of worldwide trade and intellectual intercourse. The machine has broken down the relative isolation—never complete even in the most primitive societies—of the handicraft period: it has intensified the need for collective effort and collective order. The efforts to achieve collective participation have been fumbling and empirical: so for the most part, people are conscious of the necessity in the form of limitations upon personal freedom and initiative—limitations like the automatic traffic signals of a congested center, or like the red-tape in a large commercial organization. The collective nature of the machine process demands a special enlargement of the imagination and a special education in order to keep the collective demand itself from becoming an act of external regimentation. To the extent that the collective discipline becomes effective and the various groups in society are worked into a nicely interlocking organization, special provisions must be made for isolated and anarchic elements that are not included in such a wide-reaching collectivism—elements that cannot without danger be ignored or repressed. But to abandon the social collectivism imposed by modern technics means to return to nature and be at the mercy of natural forces.

The regularization of time, the increase in mechanical power, the multiplication of goods, the contraction of time and space, the standardization of performance and product, the transfer of skill to automata, and the increase of collective interdependence—these, then, are the chief characteristics of our machine civilization. They are the basis of the particular forms of life and modes of expression that distinguish Western Civilization, at least in degree, from the various earlier civilizations that preceded it.

In the translation of technical improvements into social processes, however, the machine has undergone a perversion: instead of being utilized as an instrument of life, it has tended to become an absolute. Power and social control, once exercised chiefly by military groups who had conquered and seized the land, have gone since the seventeenth century to those who have organized and controlled and owned the machine. The machine has been valued because —it increased the employment of machines. And such employment was the source of profits, power, and wealth to the new ruling classes, benefits which had hitherto gone to traders or to those who monopolized the land. Jungles and tropical islands were invaded during the nineteenth century for the purpose of making new converts to the machine: explorers like Stanley endured incredible tortures and hardships in order to bring the benefits of the machine to inaccessible regions tapped by the Congo: insulated countries like Japan were entered forcibly at the point of the gun in order to make way for the trader: natives in Africa and the Americas were saddled with false debts or malicious taxes in order to give them an incentive to work and to consume in the machine fashion—and thus to supply an outlet for the goods of America and Europe, or to ensure the regular gathering of rubber and lac.

The injunction to use machines was so imperative, from the standpoint of those who owned them and whose means and place in society depended upon them, that it placed upon the worker a special burden, the duty to consume machine-products, while it placed upon the manufacturer and the engineer the duty of inventing products weak enough and shoddy enough—like the safety razor blade or the common run of American woolens—to lend themselves to rapid replacement. The great heresy to the machine was to believe in an institution or a habit of action or a system of ideas that would lessen this service to the machines: for under capitalist direction the aim of mechanism is not to save labor but to eliminate all labor except that which can be channeled at a profit through the factory.

At the beginning, the machine was an attempt to substitute quantity for value in the calculus of life. Between the conception of the machine and its utilization, as Krannhals points out, a necessary psychological and social process was skipped: the stage of evaluation. Thus a steam turbine may contribute thousands of horsepower, and a speedboat may achieve speed: but these facts, which perhaps satisfy the engineer, do not necessarily integrate them in society. Railroads may be quicker than canalboats, and a gas lamp may be brighter than a candle: but it is only in terms of human purpose and in relation to a human and social scheme of values that speed or brightness have any meaning. If one wishes to absorb the scenery, the slow motion of a canalboat may be preferable to the fast motion of a motor car; and if one wishes to appreciate the mysterious darkness and the strange forms of a natural cave, it is better to penetrate it with uncertain steps, with the aid of a torch or a lantern, than to descend into it by means of an elevator, as in the famous caves of Virginia, and to have the mystery entirely erased by a grand display of electric lights—a commercialized perversion that puts the whole spectacle upon the low dramatic level of a cockney amusement park.

Because the process of social evaluation was largely absent among the people who developed the machine in the eighteenth and nineteenth centuries the machine raced like an engine without a governor, tending to overheat its own bearings and lower its efficiency without any compensatory gain. This left the process of evaluation to groups who remained outside the machine milieu, and who un-

fortunately often lacked the knowledge and the understanding that would have made their criticisms more pertinent.

The important thing to bear in mind is that the failure to
evaluate the machine and to integrate it in society as a
whole was not due simply to defects in distributing income,
to errors of management, to the greed and narrow-minded-
ness of the industrial leaders: it was also due to a weakness
of the entire philosophy upon which the new techniques
and inventions were grounded. The leaders and enterprisers
of the period believed that they had avoided the necessity
for introducing values, except those which were automatically recorded in profits and prices. They believed that
the problem of justly distributing goods could be side-
tracked by creating an abundance of them: that the problem of applying one's energies wisely could be cancelled
out simply by multiplying them: in short, that most of the
difficulties that had hitherto vexed mankind had a mathematical or mechanical—that is a quantitative—solution.
The belief that values could be dispensed with constituted
the new system of values. Values, divorced from the current processes of life, remained the concern of those who
reacted against the machine. Meanwhile, the current processes justified themselves solely in terms of quantity production and cash results. When the machine as a whole
overspeeded and purchasing power failed to keep pace with
dishonest overcapitalization and exorbitant profits—then
the whole machine went suddenly into reverse, stripped its
gears, and came to a standstill: a humiliating failure, a dire
social loss.

One is confronted, then, by the fact that the machine is
ambivalent. It is both an instrument of liberation and one
of repression. It has economized human energy and it has
misdirected it. It has created a wide framework of order
and it has produced muddle and chaos. It has nobly served
human purposes and it has distorted and denied them.

BUREAUCRATIC STRUCTURE AND PERSONALITY
/Robert K. Merton

A formal, rationally organized social structure involves clearly defined patterns of activity in which, ideally, every series of actions is functionally related to the purposes of the organization. In such an organization there is integrated a series of offices, of hierarchized statuses, in which inhere a number of obligations and privileges closely defined by limited and specific rules. Each of these offices contains an area of imputed competence and responsibility. Authority, the power of control which derives from an acknowledged status, inheres in the office and not in the particular person who performs the official role. Official action ordinarily occurs within the framework of pre-existing rules of the organization. The system of prescribed relations between the various offices involves a considerable degree of formality and clearly defined social distance between the occupants of these positions. Formality is manifested by means of a more or less complicated social ritual which symbolizes and supports the pecking order of the various offices. Such formality, which is integrated with the distribution of authority within the system, serves to minimize friction by largely restricting (official) contact to modes which are previously defined by the rules of the organization. Ready calculability of others' behavior and a stable set of mutual expectations is thus built up. Moreover, formality facilitates the interaction of the occupants of offices despite their (possibly hostile) private attitudes toward one another. In this way, the subordinate is protected from the arbitrary action of his superior, since the actions of both are constrained by a mutually recognized set of rules. Specific procedural devices foster objectivity and restrain the "quick passage of impulse into action."

The ideal type of such formal organization is bureaucracy and in many respects, the classical analysis of bureaucracy is that by Max Weber. As Weber indicates, bureaucracy involves a clear-cut division of integrated activities which are regarded as duties inherent in the office. A system of differentiated controls and sanctions is stated in the regulations. The assignment of roles occurs on the basis of technical qualifications which are ascertained through formalized, impersonal procedures (*e.g.*, examinations). Within the structure of hierarchically arranged authority, the activities of "trained and salaried experts" are governed by general, abstract, and clearly defined rules which preclude the necessity for the issuance of specific instructions for each specific case. The generality of the rules requires the constant use of *categorization*, whereby individual problems and cases are classified on the basis of designated criteria and are treated accordingly. The pure type of bureaucratic official is appointed, either by a superior or through the exercise of impersonal competition; he is not elected. A measure of flexibility in the bureaucracy is attained by electing higher functionaries who presumably express the will of the electorate (*e.g.*, a body of citizens or a board of directors). The election of higher officials is designed to affect the purposes of the organization, but the technical procedures for attaining these ends are carried out by continuing bureaucratic personnel.

Most bureaucratic offices involve the expectation of lifelong tenure, in the absence of disturbing factors which may decrease the size of the organization. Bureaucracy maximizes vocational security. The function of security of tenure, pensions, incremental salaries and regularized procedures for promotion is to ensure the devoted performance of official duties, without regard for extraneous pressures. The chief merit of bureaucracy is its technical efficiency, with a premium placed on precision, speed, expert control, continuity, discretion, and optimal returns on input. The structure is one which approaches the complete elimination of personalized relationships and nonrational considerations (hostility, anxiety, affectual involvements, etc.).

With increasing bureaucratization, it becomes plain to all who would see that man is to a very important degree controlled by his social relations to the instruments of production. This can no longer seem only a tenet of Marxism, but a stubborn fact to be acknowledged by all, quite apart from their ideological persuasion. Bureaucratization makes readily visible what was previously dim and obscure. More and more people discover that to work, they must be employed. For to work, one must have tools and equipment. And the tools and equipment are increasingly available only in bureaucracies, private or public. Consequently, one must be employed by the bureaucracies in order to have access to tools in order to work in order to live. It is in this sense that bureaucratization entails separation of individuals from the instruments of production, as in modern capitalistic enterprise or in state communistic enterprise (of the midcentury variety), just as in the post-feudal army, bureaucratization entailed complete separation from the instruments of destruction. Typically, the worker no longer owns his tools, nor the soldier his weapons. And in this special sense, more and more people become workers, either blue collar or white collar or stiff shirt. So develops, for example, the new type of scientific worker, as the scientist is "separated" from his technical equipment—after all, the physicist does not ordinarily own his cyclotron. To work at his research, he must be employed by a bureaucracy with laboratory resources.

Bureaucracy is administration which almost completely avoids public discussion of its techniques, although there may occur public discussion of its policies. This secrecy is confined neither to public nor to private bureaucracies. It is held to be necessary to keep valuable information from private economic competitors or from foreign and potentially hostile political groups. And though it is not often so called, espionage among competitors is perhaps as common, if not as intricately organized, in systems of private economic enterprise as in systems of national states. Cost figures, lists of clients, new technical processes, plans for production—all these are typically regarded as essential secrets of private economic bureaucracies which might be revealed if the bases of all decisions and policies had to be publicly defended.

In these bold outlines, the positive attainments and functions of bureaucratic organization are emphasized and the internal stresses and strains of such structures are almost wholly neglected. The community at large, however, evidently emphasizes the imperfections of bureaucracy, as is suggested by the fact that the "horrid hybrid," bureaucrat, has become an epithet, a *Schimpfwort*.

The transition to a study of the negative aspects of bureaucracy is afforded by the application of Veblen's concept of "trained incapacity," Dewey's notion of "occupational psychosis" or Warnotte's view of "professional deformation." Trained incapacity refers to that state of affairs in which one's abilities function as inadequacies or blind spots. Actions based upon training and skills which have been successfully applied in the past may result in inappropriate responses *under changed conditions*. An inadequate flexibility in the application of skills, will, in a changing milieu, result in more or less serious maladjustments. Thus, to adopt a barnyard illustration used in this connection by [Kenneth] Burke, chickens may be readily conditioned to interpret the sound of a bell as a signal for food. The same bell may now be used to summon the trained chickens to their doom as they are assembled to suffer decapitation. In general, one adopts measures in keeping with one's past training and, under new conditions which are not recognized as *significantly* different, the very soundness of this training may lead to the adoption of the wrong procedures. Again, in Burke's almost echolalic phrase, "people may be unfitted by being fit in an unfit fitness"; their training may become an incapacity.

Dewey's concept of occupational psychosis rests upon much the same observations. As a result of their day to day routines, people develop special preferences, antipathies, discriminations and emphases. (The term psychosis is used by Dewey to denote a "pronounced character of the mind.") These psychoses develop through demands put upon the individual by the particular organization of his occupational role.

The concepts of both Veblen and Dewey refer to a fundamental ambivalence. Any action can be considered in terms of what it attains or what it fails to attain. "A way of seeing is also a way of not seeing—a focus upon object *A* involves a neglect of object *B*." In his discussion, Weber is almost exclusively concerned with what the bureaucratic structure attains: precision, reliability, efficiency. This same structure may be examined from another perspective provided by the ambivalence. What are the limitations of the organizations designed to attain these goals?

For reasons which we have already noted, the bureaucratic structure exerts a constant pressure upon the official to be "methodical, prudent, disciplined." If the bureaucracy is to operate successfully, it must attain a high degree of reliability of behavior, an unusual degree of conformity with prescribed patterns of action. Hence, the fundamental importance of discipline which may be as highly developed in a religious or economic bureaucracy as in the army.

Discipline can be effective only if the ideal patterns are buttressed by strong sentiments which entail devotion to one's duties, a keen sense of the limitation of one's authority and competence, and methodical performance of routine activities. The efficacy of social structure depends ultimately upon infusing group participants with appropriate attitudes and sentiments. As we shall see, there are definite arrangements in the bureaucracy for inculcating and reinforcing these sentiments.

At the moment, it suffices to observe that in order to ensure discipline (the necessary reliability of response), these sentiments are often more intense than is technically necessary. There is a margin of safety, so to speak, in the pressure exerted by these sentiments upon the bureaucrat to conform to his patterned obligations, in much the same sense that added allowances (precautionary overestimations) are made by the engineer in designing the supports for a bridge. But this very emphasis leads to a transference of the sentiments from the *aims* of the organization onto the particular details of behavior required by the rules. Adherence to the rules, originally conceived as a means, becomes transformed into an end-in-itself; there occurs the familiar process of *displacement of goals* whereby "an instrumental value becomes a terminal value." Discipline, readily interpreted as conformance with regulations, whatever the situation, is seen not as a measure designed for specific purposes but becomes an immediate value in the life-organization of the bureaucrat. This emphasis, resulting from the displacement of the original goals, develops into rigidities and an inability to adjust readily. Formalism, even ritualism, ensues with an unchallenged insistence upon punctilious adherence to formalized procedures. This may be exaggerated to the point where primary concern with conformity to the rules interferes with the achievement of the purposes of the organization, in which case we have the familiar phenomenon of the technicism or red tape of the official. An extreme product of this process of displacement of goals is the bureaucratic virtuoso, who never forgets a single rule binding his action and hence is unable to assist many of his clients. A case in point, where strict recognition of the limits of authority and literal adherence to rules produced this result, is the pathetic plight of Bernt Balchen, Admiral Byrd's pilot in the flight over the South Pole.

According to a ruling of the department of labor Bernt Balchen . . . cannot receive his citizenship papers. Balchen, a native of Norway, declared his intention in 1927. It is held that he has failed to meet the condition of five years' continuous residence in the United States. The Byrd antarctic voyage took him out of the country, although he was on a ship carrying the American flag, was an invaluable member of the American expedition, and in a region to which there is an American claim because of the exploration and occupation of it by Americans, this region being Little America.

The bureau of naturalization explains that it cannot proceed on the assumption that Little America is American soil. That would be *trespass on international questions* where it has no sanction. So far as the bureau is concerned, Balchen was out of the country and *technically* has not complied with the law of naturalization. [*Chicago Tribune*, June 24, 1931.]

Such inadequacies in orientation which involve trained incapacity clearly derive from structural sources. The process may be briefly recapitulated. (1) An effective bureaucracy demands reliability of response and strict devotion to regulations. (2) Such devotion to the rules leads to their transformation into absolutes; they are no longer conceived as relative to a set of purposes. (3) This interferes with ready adaptation under special conditions not clearly envisaged by those who drew up the general rules. (4) Thus, the very elements which conduce toward efficiency in general produce inefficiency in specific instances. Full realization of the inadequacy is seldom attained by members of the group who have not divorced themselves from the meanings which the rules have for them. These rules in time become symbolic in cast, rather than strictly utilitarian.

Thus far, we have treated the ingrained sentiments making for rigorous discipline simply as data, as given. However, definite features of the bureaucratic structure may be seen to conduce to these sentiments. The bureaucrat's official life is planned for him in terms of a graded career, through the organizational devices of promotion by seniority, pensions, incremental salaries, *etc.*, all of which are designed to provide incentives for disciplined action and conformity to the official regulations. The official is tacitly expected to and largely does adapt his thoughts, feelings and actions to the prospect of this career. But *these very devices* which increase the probability of conformance also lead to an over-concern with strict adherence to regulations which induces timidity, conservatism, and technicism. Displacement of sentiments from goals onto means is fostered by the tremendous symbolic significance of the means (rules).

Another feature of the bureaucratic structure tends to produce much the same result. Functionaries have the sense of a common destiny for all those who work together. They share the same interests, especially since there is relatively little competition insofar as promotion is in terms of seniority. In-group aggression is thus minimized and this arrangement is therefore conceived to be positively functional for the bureaucracy. However, the *esprit de corps* and informal social organization which typically develops in such situations often leads the personnel to defend their entrenched interests rather than to assist their clientele and elected higher officials. As [A. Lawrence] Lowell reports, if the bureaucrats believe that their status is not adequately recognized by an incoming elected official, detailed information will be withheld from him, leading him to errors for which he is held responsible. Or, if he seeks to dominate fully, and thus violates the sentiment of self-integrity of the bureaucrats, he may have documents brought to him in such numbers that he cannot manage to sign them all, let alone read them. This illustrates the defensive informal organization which tends to arise whenever there is an apparent threat to the integrity of the group.

It would be much too facile and partly erroneous to attribute such resistance by bureaucrats simply to vested interests. Vested interests oppose any new order which either eliminates or at least makes uncertain their differential advantage deriving from the current arrangements. This is undoubtedly involved in part in bureaucratic resistance to change but another process is perhaps more significant. As we have seen, bureaucratic officials affectively identify themselves with their way of life. They have a pride of craft which leads them to resist change in established routines; at least, those changes which are felt to be imposed by others. This nonlogical pride of craft is a familiar pattern found even—to judge from Sutherland's *Professional Thief*—among pickpockets who, despite the risk, delight in mastering the prestige-bearing feat of "beating a left breech" (picking the left front trousers pocket).

In a stimulating paper, [Everett] Hughes has applied the concepts of "secular" and "sacred" to various types of division of labor; "the sacredness" of caste and *Stände* prerogatives contrasts sharply with the increasing secularism of occupational differentiation in our society. However, as our discussion suggests, there may ensue, in particular vocations and in particular types of organization, the *process of sanctification* (viewed as the counterpart of the process of secularization). This is to say that through sentiment-formation, emotional dependence upon bureaucratic symbols and status, and affective involvement in spheres of competence and authority, there develop prerogatives involving attitudes of moral legitimacy which are established as values in their own right, and are no longer viewed as merely technical means for expediting administration. One may note a tendency for certain bureaucratic norms, originally introduced for technical reasons, to become rigidified and sacred, although, as Durkheim would say, they are *laïque en apparence*. Durkheim has touched on this general process in his description of the attitudes and values which persist in the organic solidarity of a highly differentiated society.

Another feature of the bureaucratic structure, the stress on depersonalization of relationships, also plays its part in the bureaucrat's trained incapacity. The personality pattern of the bureaucrat is nucleated about this norm of impersonality. Both this and the categorizing tendency, which develops from the dominant role of general, abstract rules, tend to produce conflict in the bureaucrat's contacts with the public or clientele. Since functionaries minimize personal relations and resort to categorization, the peculiarities of individual cases are often ignored. But the client who, quite understandably, is convinced of the special features of *his* own problem often objects to such categorical treatment. Stereotyped behavior is not adapted to the exigencies of individual problems. The impersonal treatment of affairs which are at times of great personal significance to the client gives rise to the charge of "arrogance" and "haughtiness" of the bureaucrat. Thus, at the Greenwich Employment Exchange, the unemployed worker who is securing his insurance payment resents what he deems to be "the impersonality and, at times, the apparent abruptness and even harshness of his treatment by the clerks. . . . Some men complain of the superior attitude which the clerks have." [E. W. Bakke.]

Still another source of conflict with the public derives from the bureaucratic structure. The bureaucrat, in part irrespective of his position within the hierarchy, acts as a representative of the power and prestige of the entire structure. In his official role he is vested with definite authority. This often leads to an actually or apparently domineering attitude, which may only be exaggerated by a discrepancy between his position within the hierarchy and his position with reference to the public. Protest and recourse to other officials on the part of the client are often ineffective or largely precluded by the previously mentioned *esprit de corps* which joins the officials into a more or less solidary in-group. This source of conflict *may* be minimized in private enterprise since the client can register an effective protest by transferring his trade to another organization within the competitive system. But with the monopolistic nature of the public organization, no such alternative is possible. Moreover, in this case, tension is increased because of a discrepancy between ideology and fact: the governmental personnel are held to be "servants of the people," but in fact they are often superordinate, and release of tension can seldom be afforded by turning to other agencies for the necessary service. This tension is in part attributable to the confusion of the status of bureaucrat and client; the client may consider himself socially superior to the official who is at the moment dominant.

Thus, with respect to the relations between officials and clientele, one structural source of conflict is the pressure for formal and impersonal treatment when individual, personalized consideration is desired by the client. The conflict may be viewed, then, as deriving from the introduction of inappropriate attitudes and relationships. Conflict with*in* the bureaucratic structure arises from the converse situation, namely, when personalized relationships are substituted for the structurally required impersonal relationships. This type of conflict may be characterized as follows.

The bureaucracy, as we have seen, is organized as a secondary, formal group. The normal responses involved in this organized network of social expectations are supported by affective attitudes of members of the group. Since the group is oriented toward secondary norms of impersonality, any failure to conform to these norms will arouse antagonism from those who have identified themselves with the legitimacy of these rules. Hence, the substitution of personal for impersonal treatment within the structure is met with widespread disapproval and is characterized by such epithets as graft, favoritism, nepotism, apple-polishing, etc. These epithets are clearly manifestations of injured sentiments. The function of such virtually automatic resentment can be clearly seen in terms of the requirements of bureaucratic structure.

Bureaucracy is a secondary group structure designed to carry on certain activities which cannot be satisfactorily performed on the basis of primary group criteria. Hence behavior which runs counter to these formalized norms becomes the object of emotionalized disapproval. This constitutes a functionally significant defense set up against tendencies which jeopardize the performance of socially necessary activities. To be sure, these reactions are not rationally determined practices explicitly designed for the fulfillment of this function. Rather, viewed in terms of the individual's interpretation of the situation, such resentment is simply an immediate response opposing the "dishonesty" of those who violate the rules of the game. However, this subjective frame of reference notwithstanding, these reactions serve the latent function of maintaining the essential structural elements of bureaucracy by reaffirming the necessity for formalized, secondary relations and by helping to prevent the disintegration of the bureaucratic structure which would occur should these be supplanted by personalized relations. This type of conflict may be generically described as the intrusion of primary group attitudes when secondary group attitudes are institutionally demanded, just as the bureaucrat-client conflict often derives from interaction on impersonal terms when personal treatment is individually demanded.

LIFE IN THE CRYSTAL PALACE
/Alan Harrington

Happy families are all alike, said Tolstoy. Whether this is true of great corporations I don't know, because I have belonged to only one. The company I have been with for more than three years is one of the world's largest, having some thirty-four thousand employees in the United States and overseas. There are more than five hundred of us here at headquarters—and we are a happy family. I say this without irony, not for the reason that I am in the public-relations department, but because it is the truth. We give every appearance of happiness. We are also in many respects pretty much alike, at least on the surface.

It is not that our company makes us behave in a certain way. That kind of thing is out of date. Most of our people tend to live and talk alike, and think along the same general lines, for the simple reason that the company treats us so well. Life is good, life is gentle. Barring a deep depression or war, we need never worry about money again. We will never have to go job-hunting again. We may get ahead at different speeds, and some will climb a bit higher than others, but whatever happens the future is as secure as it can be. And the test is not arduous. Unless for some obscure reason we choose to escape back into your anxious world (where the competition is so hard and pitiless and your ego is constantly under attack) we will each enjoy a comfortable journey to what our house organ calls "green pastures," which is, of course, retirement.

"Is this sort of existence worth living?" you ask. I think that depends on who you are and also on the person you could become. There are two ways of looking at it: (1) If you are not going to set the world on fire anyway, it is better to spend your life in nice surroundings; (2) looking back, you *might* have had a more adventuresome time and struggled harder to make your mark in the world if the big company hadn't made things soft for you.

But it is all too easy to be glib in disapproving of the kindly corporation. We are then in the position of scorning the earthly paradise, and that cannot be done lightly. To be honest, we should put aside the convenient clichés— that big business firms, for example, are by their very nature heartless, exploitive, enforcers of conformity, etc. It is commonly assumed that a big, apparently impersonal authority is made up of bad fellows. How much more bewildering and exasperating to discover that they are good fellows!

I went into my job at the corporation with a poor spirit. I was suspicious of large companies, and swore that nobody was going to turn me into a robot. My situation was untenable anyway. I had just sold my first novel, a satire about a man who, under the pressure of business, had turned himself into a Nothing. In a year the grenade would go off, and of course the writer would be fired.

Particularly disconcerting in the early days was the gentleness of my new associates. Most public-relations offices are filled with edgy, hustling people. Here there was such courtesy and regard for your comfort . . . it was unfair. When I arrived, everyone turned and smiled, and they all came over to say how glad they were that I was with them. The boss took my arm and had me in for a long talk. "We want you to be happy here," he said earnestly. "Is there anything we can do? Please let us know." When you discover that the members of the company team really care about you it is a shock to the nervous system. The skeptical newcomer stands there, shifting his feet, not knowing what to do with his preconceived resentment.

I went through the orientation course, and completed all the forms and saw that I was protected against everything. I had a momentary fearful sensation of being enfolded in the wings of the corporation and borne aloft. "How's everything going?" inquired one of the orientation men, and I grunted at his civil question.

Now I was one of the group, hunched gloomily over a typewriter amid smiling faces. With the exception of the department head and assistant manager, our public-relations staff worked in one large room. We did our jobs in leisurely fashion with a carpet of non-glare fluorescent lighting above and a thick wall-to-wall carpet below. The usual office noises were hushed. Typewriters made a faint clack. Our mild jokes were lost in the air. It seemed to me a strange pressure chamber in which there was no pressure. This was a temporary arrangement. Next year the company was moving to a new office building in the suburbs, and it would be a fabulous place—a great office-palace on a hilltop surrounded by fields and woodlands. Everybody talked about the palace and what a marvelous headquarters it would be. The enthusiasm bored me, and I thought: "Well, I'll never see it."

That was a long time ago. Today I continue to live in the city but commute in reverse to the suburbs, and every weekday I sit down to work in the country palace. Here, after three years, are some general impressions of our corporate life:

The corporation is decent. Most of our men have deep, comfortable voices. You have stood beside them in slow elevators, and heard these vibrant tones of people whose throats are utterly relaxed. And why shouldn't they be relaxed? Once you join our company, so far as the job is concerned, you will have to create your own anxieties. The company won't provide any for you.

There is no getting around it—our working conditions are sensational. The lower and middle echelons arrive at nine and, except in very rare instances, go home at quarter-to-five. Many of the higher executives work longer and harder, according to their inclinations, but seldom in response to an emergency. Rather it is a pleasure for them.

This is a company whose products move easily in great packages across the continent. Demand is constant and growing, since our products are good for people and contribute to the nation's health and well-being. The supply is adjusted from time to time in order to keep prices at a reasonable level. There is no reason for anyone to kill himself through overwork.

The savage, messianic executive of the type described in Rod Serling's *Patterns* would find himself out of place here. In fact, he would be embarrassing. In the unlikely event of his coming with us, the moment he started shouting at anybody he would be taken aside and admonished in a nice way. (We do have one high-ranking officer a bit like that, but he is old and close to retirement. He is very much the exception.)

A full recital of our employee benefits would—and does, in the indoctrination period—take all day, but here are just a few of them. We have a fine pension fund, a fantastically inexpensive medical program for you and your family, and a low-premium life-insurance policy for double your salary. The company will invest five per cent of your pay in blue-chip stocks and contribute on your behalf another three per cent. The company picks up half of your luncheon check. When we moved to the suburbs, the company paid its employees' moving expenses and helped them settle in their new homes. For those who didn't wish to move ... a bus waits at the railroad station for commuters from the city and drives them to the hilltop office building.

The only unsatisfactory working condition, I think, is that you must be content with a two-week vacation until you have been with the company for ten years. In other words, the experience you may have gained elsewhere, precisely the experience the company has *bought,* counts for nothing in terms of vacation time. But this policy is fairly standard practice. It certainly inhibits a man's desire (say, after nine years) to change companies for a better job. Thus, it is at least a minor pressure against free-spirited enterprise. All the benefits exert pressure, too. There is nothing sinister about them, since admittedly they are for your own material comfort—and isn't that supposed to be one of the goals of mankind? What happens is that, as the years go by, the temptation to strike out on your own or take another job becomes less and less. Gradually you become accustomed to the Utopian drift. Soon another inhibition may make you even more amenable. If you have been in easy circumstances for a number of years, you feel that you are out of shape. Even in younger men the hard muscle of ambition tends to go slack, and you hesitate to take a chance in the jungle again.

On top of all this, it is practically impossible to be fired. Unless you drink to alcoholism or someone finds your hand in the cash box, the company can afford to keep you around indefinitely. Occasionally under great provocation—such as a scandal that reaches the tabloids—there may be a transfer. Once in a while a prematurely crusty old-timer is retired. Otherwise the ax will not fall.

Every so often I hear my seniors at the corporation inveigh against socialism, and it seems strange. I think that our company resembles nothing so much as a private socialist system. We are taken care of from our children's cradles to our own graves. We move with carefully graduated rank, station, and salary through the decades. By what marvelous process of self-deception do we consider our individual enterprise to be private? The truth is that we work communally. In our daily work most of us have not made an important decision in years, except in consultation with others.

Good people work here. Since joining the company I have not heard one person raise his voice to another in anger, and rarely even in irritation. Apparently when you remove fear from a man's life you also remove his stinger. Since there is no severe competition within our shop, we are serene. We do compete mildly perhaps, by trying to achieve good marks in the hope that our department head will recommend a promotion or an increase to the Salary Committee. Cutting out the other fellow and using tricks to make him look bad is hardly ever done. At higher levels, now and then, executive empires will bump into each other and there will be skirmishes along the border. But these are for the most part carried on without bullying and table-pounding, and the worst that can happen to the loser is that he will be moved sideways into a smaller empire.

It would be wrong to say that our employees are not lively. They smoke and drink and love, and go on camping trips, go skiing, and operate power boats, and read things and go to the movies, and ride motorcycles like anybody else. In the office they know what to do (usually after consultation) in almost any circumstance. What a great many of them have lost, it seems to me, is temperament, in the sense of mettle. We speak of a mettlesome horse. Well, these are not mettlesome people. They lack, perhaps, the capacity to be mean and ornery when the ego is threatened—because at our company we do not threaten people's egos. Rather the ego tends to atrophy through disuse.

Another curious thing is our talent for being extremely friendly without saying anything to each other. I remember a conversation that went something like this:

"Jim! Where did you come from? I haven't seen you in— I guess it's been about a year and a half."

"Just about that, Bill. A year and a half at least."

"What are you up to, for goodness' sake?"

"I've been in Washington, and now I'm going back overseas."

"Always on the move!"

"Well, I guess I am. I just thought I'd come down and have a chat with you before leaving."

"It's great that you did. How's your family?"

"Fine, Bill, how is yours?"

"They're fine, too."

"The years go by, don't they?"

"They sure do."

"Well. . . ."

"Well. . . ."

"Well, I guess I'd better be moving along."

"It's been wonderful talking to you, Jim. Look, before you get on the plane, why don't you come down for another talk?"

"I will, boy. You can count on it."

Also common among our employees is a genuine and lively interest in the careers of upper-level executives whom they may never have laid eyes on. As the gentlemen move from one station to another, their progress is followed with exclamations and inside comments. "Hmm, Jackson has moved to Purchasing! I thought so." "Look at Welsh—he's taken over the top spot in Patagonia. Anybody can tell that they're setting him up for a vice-presidency." Who *cared* about Jackson and Welsh? At one point, I did. I had to prepare a press release about them, and update—add two more lines to—their official biographies.

The role of the corporation's top directors in our cosmos is an interesting one. In our company, members of the board are not remote figures from outside who drop in to attend meetings now and then. They are on the job every day. They recognize us, nod, and often say hello. I have found these august gentlemen to be amiable and even shy in the presence of their inferiors, but their appearance on the scene is the occasion of total respect, body and soul, such as I have never witnessed outside the army. They are not feared either. They conduct themselves in a friendly, most democratic manner. It is not awe they inspire but, so far as I can see, pure admiration. I was once talking to a young man in the employee-relations department when his eyes, gazing over my shoulder, suddenly lit up with joy. I turned, expecting to see our pretty receptionist, but it was a director passing by and giving us a wave of his hand.

Team play is the thing. Team play means that you alone can't get too far out ahead of the troops. You can't, because in our company it is necessary to consult and check over everything. Someone will ask whether this doesn't lead to a certain amount of mediocrity. It does. We have a substantial number of mediocre people in the company—that is, men and women of ordinary ability who would probably never originate anything under any circumstances.

But where organizing an effort is concerned it is sometimes better to have mediocre talent than a bunch of creative individuals who disturb the situation by questioning everything. In terms of performance, if you have a slow but sure operation, mediocre personnel, including your nephews, can carry it out beautifully. In *planning,* mediocrity has and still does hurt the company.

Our method is to get together and talk it out, each one of us contributing his mite. Why have one man make a decision when thirty-three can do it better? The consequence of this policy is that our executives commit few errors—although sometimes they arrive at the right decision three years too late. But the sure markets for the company's products bring in so much money that the mistake is buried under mountains of dollar bills. Our interminable round of conferences may also be counted on to produce by default serious errors of omission. These don't hurt noticeably either, for the reason cited above.

I got over my impatience at the slow pace of things, but I felt it once at a lecture given to senior and junior executives on the new central filing system that would go into effect when we reached the palace. A fierce little girl, a vestal of the files, told us how it was going to be. We sat, without anyone suggesting it, according to rank, and I could work out the possible course of my company career, if I stayed with it, just by looking at the assemblage of heads in front of me—bald and white in the front rows, then pepper-and-salt, and gradually back where I was, the black, brown, and blond heads of hair. I thought of my own head, slowly changing through the years as I moved up a row or two, with never a chance by a brilliant coup of jumping while still brown-headed—or even pepper-and-salt—over several rows and landing among the white thatches. How could I make such a leap when anything I accomplish I do as a member of a group?

A little more tension would be welcome. This may be based on fragmentary evidence, but I suspect that when people are not placed under at least a minimum of tension they seek it out in their dreams. One day I overheard our press-relations man conferring with our public-relations manager, Mac Tyler, who said: "Maybe next time, Walt, you had better try it the other way." The press man came out of the office and saw me. "Boy!" he said, "I sure got a bawling out on that!"

Another man of some rank joined his local Democratic Party, and worked hard at it during the presidential campaign. But he felt guilty about what he had done. Finally he rushed upstairs and confessed to the president of the corporation. "Gosh," he told me afterward in a disappointed tone, "he didn't mind at all. He just put his hand on my shoulder and said: 'Don't worry, Fred, I'm a Jeffersonian Republican myself!' "

We conform by choice. Critics of big business are constantly on the watch for the kind of over-cooperation that a company explicitly demands of its members. Our company doesn't demand anything. Oh, there is tactful pressure on us to join the annuity and insurance program, and a rather strong insistence on Red Cross and Community Chest contributions, but nothing serious.

What you have to watch out for is the amount of compliance you fall into by yourself, without realizing it. Something like this almost happened to me when my book was published. Far from resenting the satire, most of our employees who read it enjoyed the book. I was asked to autograph dozens of copies, and several were bought and prominently displayed in the company lending library. I had thought of myself as a writer in temporary captivity. Now that was no longer possible. A captive of what? Good Will?

I began to feel what I now recognize was a gradually deepening contentment. If you are on the watch for the symptoms, here are a few: (1) You find that you are planning your life defensively, in terms of savings plans and pensions, rather than thinking speculatively of moving up fast—faster than the others. (2) You become much less impatient over inefficiency, shrug your shoulders and accept it as the way things are. (3) Your critical faculties become dull; you accept second-best; it seems unsporting to complain. (4) Nothing makes you nervous. (5) You find that you are content to talk to people without saying anything. (6) You mention something like (improvising now) "our Human Development Department" to outsiders and learn with surprise that they think you have made a joke.

During this period of contentment, which lasted quite a few months, I did not concern myself with anything beyond the requirements of my job. I became easy-going and promiscuously nice, and had a harmless word for everybody. Finally, I was reminded that this sort of thing was the mark of a fat soul. A succession of incidents helped indicate what was wrong.

We are remote from the lives of others. Shortly before we moved to the country the press-relations man and I were looking out of our eleventh-floor window in the direction of the waterfront. We saw a half-circle of men gathered on a far-off pier. "Isn't that what they call a shape-up?" he asked with faint curiosity. It was easy to tell that he barely imagined that these men existed and that their quaint customs were real.

Some weeks before, I had looked down on a gentleman in a homburg and cutaway, running among the crowds in the financial district. He carried a bouquet of red roses wrapped in green paper. You don't associate this street with flowers, and it was exciting to see him running, holding his green wrapping like a torch of something beautiful in this place. And then he died on his feet, twisting over and slumping to the pavement. His head rested against the wall of a building. He rested with the flowers flung across his knees and his fine hat askew, and the absurd and living gallantry that produced this death *could* only be nothing to us or to anyone in the crowds that simply swerved around him and kept going, because of the way we are concentrated and oriented away from things like that.

How remote we were too from the crazy musicians who arrived on a blustery fall day with the idea that, since this was a financial center, there would be a rain of coins from the tall buildings in response to their trumpet, guitar, and bass fiddle. The wind swirled their jazz among the canyons. I saw that no one was paying them the slightest attention. Feeling guilty, I threw them a quarter, but they didn't see it. They danced and made jazz in the cold, while upstairs we went on with our work, and they didn't exist, and it was nobody's fault.

It isn't that we should have been expected to know about longshoremen, or care particularly about the man in the homburg, or throw coins to the brave musicians, but we have simply, systematically, avoided letting these aspects of life into our field of vision. We came in from the suburbs and plundered the city, and left each night without having the least idea of what was going on there. Even our daily experience in the rapid transit was spent behind a newspaper; taxis shielded us from the bad sections of town. We never heard guitars strumming on the dirty doorsteps, nor comprehended the possible excitement of disorderly feelings that make other people so much more alive than we are.

And when the corporation moved to the country our isolation from all that became completely splendid. Now most of us could anticipate fifteen- and thirty-minute rides in car pools from our suburban homes to a suburban office. You could almost hear an official sigh of contentment on the day that we moved.

This way to the palace. Point your car along a winding drive-way up the green hillside shaded with great elm trees. Enter the wide and friendly doorway and look at the murals in our lobby. They will tell you the story of our industry. As you go through the offices, you will probably marvel as we did at all the comforts and services we have. Imagine a sea of blond desks with tan chairs, outdoor lighting pouring in everywhere, roomy offices with individually-controlled air-conditioning and area-controlled Music by Muzak coming out of the walls. We need few private secretaries. All we have to do is pick up a phoning device and dictate our message to a disc that whirls in a sunny room in another part of the building. Here a pool of stenographers type all day long with buttons in their ears. We don't see them and they don't see us, but they know our voices.

A high-speed pneumatic tube system winds through the entire building. We send material from one office to another not by messenger but by torpedo containers traveling twenty-five feet a second. Simply have the attendant put your paper, magazine, or memo in the plastic carrier. He inserts the container in the tube, dials the appropriate number, and, whoosh, it is shot across the building. There is a complete sound system throughout headquarters. If, for example, a bad storm is forecast, there will be an "Attention Please," and you may go home early. At noon, enjoy movies in an auditorium the size of a small theater, visit the library, watch the World Series on color TV, or play darts and table tennis in the game room. The finest catering service and a staff of friendly waitresses bring you luncheon. Then go to the company store, pitch horseshoes, or take a brief stroll under the elms.

What happens to an office force when it is offered facilities like these? At first there were a few small complaints. The main difficulty is that we find it all but impossible to get off the campus. You can speed several miles to town for a quick lunch. Otherwise you stay on the grounds until closing. City employees everywhere have the chance to renew, at least slightly, their connection with the world during lunch hour. When we first came many of us rambled in the woods and picked flowers, but we seldom do that anymore.

As for our work-efficiency, I think it has diminished a bit as a result of what one of my friends calls "our incestuous situation." When you are isolated in the country it is not easy to feel that sense of urgency that distinguishes most businessmen.

I sometimes have a feeling of being in limbo. More than ever one feels—ungratefully—over-protected. While on the job, I actually can't feel hot or cold. I can't even get sick. This will sound ridiculous, but when the company obtained a supply of influenza shots, I found myself in the absurd position of refusing one. For some reason I wanted a chance to resist the flu in my own way.

What is the moral of all this? I am not quite sure, but some time ago Dostoyevsky put it in *Notes from Underground:*

> Does not man, perhaps, love something besides well-being? Perhaps he is just as fond of suffering? Perhaps suffering is just as great a benefit to him as well-being?

> ... In the 'Crystal Palace' (suffering) is unthinkable. ... You believe, do you not, in a crystal palace which shall be forever unbreakable—in an edifice, that is to say, at which no one shall be able to put out his tongue, or in any other way to mock? Now, for the very reason that it must be made of crystal, and forever unbreakable, and one whereat no one shall put out his tongue, I should fight shy of such a building.

THE GREAT EMPTINESS
/Robert MacIver

"In the sweat of thy face shalt thou eat bread." From this primal decree millions of human beings are now liberated. More and more men have more and more leisure. The working day grows shorter, the week end longer. More and more women are released at an earlier age from the heavier tasks of the rearing of children, in the small family of today, when kindergarten and school and clinic and restaurant come to their aid. More and more people are freed for other things, released from the exhaustion of their energies in the mere satisfaction of elementary wants. No longer is the pattern so simple as that of Longfellow's blacksmith, who "something attempted, something done, has earned a night's repose."

Released from what? When necessity no longer drives, when people own long hours in which to do what they want, what do they want to do? Where necessity is heavy upon men, they yearn for the joys of leisure. Now many have enough leisure. What are the joys they find?

The shorter working day is also a different working day. Nearly all men work for others, not for themselves—not the way a man works who has his own little plot of earth and must give himself up to its cultivation. For many, work has become a routine—not too onerous, not too rewarding, and by no means engrossing—a daily routine until the bell rings and sets them free again. For what?

It is a marvelous liberation for those who learn to use it; and there are many ways. It is the great emptiness for those who don't.

People of a placid disposition do not know the great emptiness. When the day's work is done, they betake themselves to their quiet interests, their hobbies, their gardens or their amateur workbenches or their stamp collecting or their games or their social affairs or their church activities or whatever it be. When they need more sting in life, they have a mild "fling," taking a little "moral holiday." Some find indulgence enough in the vicarious pleasure of snidely malicious gossip. Their habits are early formed and they keep a modicum of contentment.

But the number of the placid is growing less. The conditions of our civilization do not encourage that mood. For one thing, the old-time acceptance of authority, as God-given or nature-based, is much less common. Religion is for very many an ancient tale, "a tale of little meaning, though the words are strong," reduced to ritual or the moral precepts of the Sunday pulpit. There is little allegiance to the doctrine that every man has his allotted place. How could there be when competition has become a law of life? There is incessant movement and disturbance and upheaval. And with the new leisure there come new excitations, new stimuli to unrest.

So the new leisure has brought its seeming opposite, restlessness. And because these cannot be reconciled the great emptiness comes.

Faced with the great emptiness, unprepared to meet it, most people resort to one or another way of escape, according to their kind. Those who are less conscious of their need succeed in concealing it from themselves. They find their satisfaction in the great new world of means without ends. Those who are more conscious of it cannot conceal it; they only distract themselves from the thought of it. Their common recourse is excitation, and they seek it in diverse ways.

The first kind are go-getters. When they are efficient or unscrupulous or both, they rise in the world. They amass things. They make some money. They win some place and power. Not *for* anything, not to do anything with it. Their values are relative, which means they are no values at all. They make money to make more money. They win some power that enables them to seek more power. They are practical men. They keep right on being practical, until their unlived lives are at an end. If they stopped being practical, the great emptiness would engulf them. They are like planes that must keep on flying because they have no landing gear. The engines go fast and faster, but they are going nowhere. They make good progress to nothingness.

They take pride in their progress. They are outdistancing other men. They are always calculating the distance they have gained. It shows what can be done when you have the know-how. They feel superior and that sustains them. They stay assured in the world of means. What matters is the winning.

> "But what good came of it at last?"
> Quoth little Peterkin.
> "Why that I cannot tell," said he,
> "But 'twas a famous victory."

Victory for the sake of the winning, means for the sake of the acquiring, that is success. So the circle spins forever, means without end, world without end. Amen.

The second kind have it worse. They are the more sensitive kind, often the more gifted. They want their lives to have some meaning, some fulfilment. They want the feel of living for some worthwhile end. But often there is something wrong with the seeking. They too suffer from the intrusive ego. Their seeking lacks adequate sincerity. The need of success is greater for them than the need of the thing that is sought. If, for example, they pursue some art, the art itself counts less than the renown of the artist. They would be great artists, great writers, opera singers, pathfinders. They aim high, but the mark is higher than their reach. When they miss it they grow disillusioned. They are thrust back on their unsatisfied egos, and the great emptiness lies before them.

They try to escape, but they run from themselves. They try to forget, but their only recourse is an excitation of the senses. This stimulant needs to be incessantly repeated. The little spell of liberation, the false glow, the hour of oblivion, leaves them the more desolate and adds new tensions to the returning emptiness. Then there is leisure no more, no relaxedness, no return to the things they once loved, no lingering ease of quiet discourse with friends, no natural savor of living, no perception of the unfolding wonder of things. But instead they pass from excitation to a hollow release, from release to tension, from tension to new excitation. Nothing is itself any more. And no more at the end of the day do they sink peacefully into the marvelous process of slowly gathering sleep.

Once they were so eager to make life feel real; now they shun its reality and are driven to pursue phantoms, the will-o'-the-wisp of sense-spurred distraction, the unseeing ghosts of once clear-eyed joys, the phantom Aphrodite.

But it is not only the more cultivated, the more sophisticated, and the well-to-do with their more ample opportunities, who feel the great emptiness. In other ways it besets large numbers who, finding little satisfaction in their daily work, seek compensation in the leisure they now possess. There are many besides, people who win early pensions or otherwise can get along without toil through legacies or rents or other sources of unearned income, women who have no family cares—the new, unopulent leisure class.

They have no training for leisure. They have, most of them, no strong interests or devotions. The habits of their work time convey no meaning to the time of liberation. Most of them live in cities, in drab and narrow confines within which they revolve in casual little circles. They see nothing ahead but the coming of old age. They want to regain the feel of life. Time is theirs, but they cannot redeem it.

So they too betake themselves, in their various ways, to some form of excitation. Having no recourse in themselves, they must get out of themselves. They take the easy ways out because they see no alternative. They have never learned to climb the paths leading to the pleasures that wait in the realm of ideas, in the growing revelation of the nature of things, in the treasuries of the arts, and in the rich lore of the libraries. They must seek instead the quick transport, the dream, the adventure, in the tavern or where the gamblers meet.

They would cover the emptiness they cannot fill. They make a goal of what is a diversion. The healthy being craves an occasional wildness, a jolt from normality, a sharpening of the edge of appetite, his own little festival of the Saturnalia, a brief excursion from his way of life. But for these others the diversion becomes the way of life and diverts no more. For them the filled glass is not the cheerful accompaniment of pleasant reunions but a deceitful medicine for the ennui of living. For them the gambling venture is no mere holiday flutter but a never-satisfied urge that forever defeats itself.

In 1946, in straitened England, the then equivalent of half a billion dollars was placed in bets on the horses and the dogs. Besides which, vast sums changed hands on the results of football games. For hundreds of thousands of people the major news in the daily papers, day after day and month after month, was the lists of the winners and the betting odds. England was not, is not, alone in this respect. It is only that the figures happen to be more accessible.

A former addict explained in the London *Spectator* why men do it. The gambler, he said, "gambles because it provides an emotional tension which his mind demands. He is suffering from a deficiency disease, and the only antidote he knows is gambling." He is trying to escape the great emptiness. An English worker of the semi-skilled category once said to me: "A fellow has to do something, and what is there? Maybe I have a shilling or two in my pocket. Maybe I could buy an extra shirt. It's no go. So I put them on the dogs."

By these resorts people do not escape the great emptiness. What they get is a sequence of brief delusions of escape. In time the only thing they can escape to is what they themselves know for a delusion. The resort is only a drug to make them forget the disease. As with all such drugs, the dose must be continually renewed, and it becomes harder and harder to return to the pre-addict stage. They come to look on the great emptiness as something inherent in the very nature of things. That is all life is. Now they know the drug is a delusion, but they do not know that it has bred a deeper delusion.

There are other avenues of escape that, while they may still be delusive, have the merit of not being recognized as such. Which means that the escape is actually made. In every large city, and notably in those areas where people go to spend their retirement, where the climate is mild and sunny, all kinds of special cults flourish and new ones are frequently born. To these places repair the hucksters of the supernatural and find a ready market for their wares. There are to be found the prophets of mystical union, robed and turbaned preachers of the Light of Asia, interpreters of the Rosy Cross, exponents of the heavenly trance, new healers of the soul, tuners-in of the Infinite, operators in spiritual magics. Considerable numbers flock to them, some to seek a new sensation and then pass on, but some to stay and become disciples or devotees.

These last are the credulous ones, the unsophisticate, the suggestible. They search no more. The emptiness is filled. They have undergone a kind of hypnosis. They live in the nebula of their mystical dream. They meet reality no more. But at least, in a manner, they have found their peace.

Back in the days when unremitting toil was the lot of all but the very few and leisure still a hopeless yearning, hard and painful as life was, it still felt real. People were in *rapport* with the small bit of reality allotted to them, the sense of the earth, the tang of the changing seasons, the consciousness of the eternal on-going of birth and death. Now, when so many have leisure, they become detached from themselves, not merely from the earth. From all the widened horizons of our greater world a thousand voices call us to come near, to understand, and to enjoy, but our ears are not trained to hear them. The leisure is ours but not the skill to use it. So leisure becomes a void, and from the ensuing restlessness men take refuge in delusive excitations or fictitious visions, returning to their own earth no more.

III. MASS CULTURE

As we have just seen, men are alienated because of the conditions in which they work and play. In this section we shall examine the cultural values which industrial societies produce. What are those values? What effect do they have on men's striving for self-achievement? Our opening selection is a work by the German sociologist, Georg Simmel, "The Metropolis and Mental Life," written over half a century ago. The urban culture Simmel describes is a money culture, that is, money stamps its character. As he writes, monetary interests lend urban society its essentially impersonal character and make man a mere cog in a giant machine. To survive as an individual in this calculating world, man must use his head more than his heart. The result, as Simmel shows, is a blasé attitude in which nerves and feelings are blunted. If the individual does survive, it is only at the most terrible cost. Most, however, are overwhelmed by the splendor and pressures of the metropolis.

When the system of private property produces a surplus of wealth, the possession of wealth becomes the primary means of achieving social status. In time "mere" wealth becomes an end in itself. Or, as Veblen described it, it becomes "conspicuous" waste. Conspicuous because men's wealth, if it is to secure them the "esteem" of their peers, must be seen; wasteful, because material but not human ends are served. Marya Mannes' "Wasteland" provides a short but vivid description of the wreckage that such a system leaves in its wake.

As material values have gained pre-eminence, spiritual values have declined in direct proportion. The significance of this development is suggested by the philosopher, William Barrett, in a section from his study of existentialism. To Barrett "the central fact of modern history . . . is unquestionably the decline of religion" as a ruling force in men's lives. While one may argue with this claim, there can be no disputing the decline. As Barrett writes, "In losing religion, man lost the concrete connection with a transcendent realm of being; he was set free to deal with this world in all its brute objectivity. But he was bound to feel homeless in such a world, which no longer answered the needs of his spirit." Just how homeless is shown in Durkheim's *Suicide* in which he relates anomie to the decline of religion and the stimulation of material desires. As Durkheim showed, when faith is no longer a sustaining power and anarchy rules in the economy, any serious breakdown in that economy will have dire results for its victims. Lacking moral stability, they may take their own lives.

The decline of religion is only one aspect of the breakdown of an earlier solidarity. In his study of the decline of the choral dance, Paul Halmos shows how this form of collective behavior, religious in origin, was an important means of establishing and sustaining group cohesion. But it could not survive the downfall of medieval culture. After the industrial revolution men and women continued to dance, but rarely in cohesive groups. (In our latest dance craze, the "twist," bodies never touch.) To Halmos the decline of group dancing is a paradigm of what he calls "desocialization" or decay. He concludes: "The perpetuation and further growth of a desocializing culture involves the inevitability of its own eventual destruction."

Is this pessimistic outlook justified? In place of earlier and cohering beliefs and activities, we now have mass culture. As Ernest van den Haag makes clear in "Of Happiness and of Despair We Have No Measure," that culture adds to man's estrangement: "All mass media in the end alienate people from personal experience and, though appearing to offset it, intensify their moral isolation from each other, from reality and from themselves."

THE METROPOLIS AND MENTAL LIFE
/Georg Simmel

The deepest problems of modern life derive from the claim of the individual to preserve the autonomy and individuality of his existence in the face of overwhelming social forces, of historical heritage, of external culture, and of the technique of life. The fight with nature which prim-

Translated by H. H. Gerth and C. Wright Mills.

itive man has to wage for his *bodily* existence attains in this modern form its latest transformation. The eighteenth century called upon man to free himself of all the historical bonds in the state and in religion, in morals and in economics. Man's nature, originally good and common to all, should develop unhampered. In addition to more liberty, the nineteenth century demanded the functional specialization of man and his work; this specialization makes one individual incomparable to another, and each of them indispensable to the highest possible extent. However, this specialization makes each man the more directly dependent upon the supplementary activities of all others. Nietzsche sees the full development of the individual conditioned by the most ruthless struggle of individuals; socialism believes in the suppression of all competition for the same reason. Be that as it may, in all these positions the same basic motive is at work: the person resists being leveled down and worn out by a social-technological mechanism. An inquiry into the inner meaning of specifically modern life and its products, into the soul of the cultural body, so to speak, must seek to solve the equation which structures like the metropolis set up between the individual and the superindividual contents of life. Such an inquiry must answer the question of how the personality accommodates itself in the adjustments to external forces.

The psychological basis of the metropolitan type of individuality consists in the *intensification of nervous stimulation* which results from the swift and uninterrupted change of outer and inner stimuli. Man is a differentiating creature. His mind is stimulated by the difference between a momentary impression and the one which preceded it. Lasting impressions, impressions which differ only slightly from one another, impressions which take a regular and habitual course and show regular and habitual contrasts—all these use up, so to speak, less consciousness than does the rapid crowding of changing images, the sharp discontinuity in the grasp of a single glance, and the unexpectedness of onrushing impressions. These are the psychological conditions which the metropolis creates. With each crossing of the street, with the tempo and multiplicity of economic, occupational and social life, the city sets up a deep contrast with small town and rural life with reference to the sensory foundations of psychic life. The metropolis exacts from man as a discriminating creature a different amount of consciousness than does rural life. Here the rhythm of life and sensory mental imagery flows more slowly, more habitually, and more evenly. Precisely in this connection the sophisticated character of metropolitan psychic life becomes understandable—as over against small town life which rests more upon deeply felt and emotional relationships. These latter are rooted in the more unconscious layers of the psyche and grow most readily in the steady rhythm of uninterrupted habituations. The intellect, however, has its locus in the transparent, conscious, higher layers of the psyche; it is the most adaptable of our inner forces. In order to accommodate to change and to the contrast of phenomena, the intellect does not require any shocks and inner upheavals; it is only through such upheavals that the more conservative mind could accommodate to the metropolitan rhythm of events. Thus the metropolitan type of man—which, of course, exists in a thousand individual variants—develops an organ protecting him against the threatening currents and discrepancies of his external environment which would uproot him. He reacts with his head instead of his heart. In this an increased awareness assumes the psychic prerogative. Metropolitan life, thus, underlies a heightened awareness and a predominance of intelligence in metropolitan man. The reaction to metropolitan phenomena is shifted to that organ which is least sensitive and quite remote from the depth of the personality. Intellectuality is thus seen to preserve subjective life against the overwhelming power of metropolitan life, and intellectuality branches out in many directions and is integrated with numerous discrete phenomena.

The metropolis has always been the seat of the money economy. Here the multiplicity and concentration of economic exchange gives an importance to the means of exchange which the scantiness of rural commerce would not have allowed. Money economy and the dominance of the intellect are intrinsically connected. They share a matter-of-fact attitude in dealing with men and with things; and, in this attitude, a formal justice is often coupled with an inconsiderate hardness. The intellectually sophisticated person is indifferent to all genuine individuality, because relationships and reactions result from it which cannot be exhausted with logical operations. In the same manner, the individuality of phenomena is not commensurate with the pecuniary principle. Money is concerned only with what is common to all: it asks for the exchange value, it reduces all quality and individuality to the question: How much? All intimate emotional relations between persons are founded in their individuality, whereas in rational relations man is reckoned with like a number, like an element which is in itself indifferent. Only the objective measurable achievement is of interest. Thus metropolitan man reckons with his merchants and customers, his domestic servants and often even with persons with whom he is obliged to have social intercourse. These features of intellectuality contrast with the nature of the small circle in which the inevitable knowledge of individuality as inevitably produces a warmer tone of behavior, a behavior which is beyond a mere objective balancing of service and return. In the sphere of the economic psychology of the small group it is of importance that under primitive conditions production serves the customer who orders the goods, so that the producer and the consumer are acquainted. The modern metropolis, however, is supplied almost entirely by production for the market, that is, for entirely unknown purchasers who never personally enter the producer's actual field of vision. Through this anonymity the interests of each party acquire an unmerciful matter-of-factness; and the intellectually calculating economic egoism of both parties need not fear any deflection because of the imponderables of personal relationships. The money economy dominates the metropolis; it has displaced the last survivals of domestic production and the direct barter of goods; it minimizes, from day to day, the amount of work ordered by customers. The matter-of-fact attitude is obviously so intimately interrelated with the money economy, which is dominant in the metropolis, that nobody can say whether the intellectualistic mentality first promoted the money economy or whether the latter determined the former. The metropolitan way of life is certainly the most fertile soil for this reciprocity, a point which I shall document merely by citing the dictum of the most eminent English constitutional historian: throughout the whole course of English history, London has never acted as England's heart but often as England's intellect and always as her moneybag!

In certain seemingly insignificant traits, which lie upon the surface of life, the same psychic currents characteristically unite. Modern mind has become more and more calculating. The calculative exactness of practical life which the money economy had brought about corresponds to the ideal of natural science: to transform the world into an arithmetic problem, to fix every part of the world by mathematical formulas. Only money economy has filled the days of so many people with weighing, calculating, with numerical determinations, with a reduction of qualitative values to quantitative ones. Through the calculative nature of money a new precision, a certainty in the definition of identities and differences, an unambiguousness in agreements and arrangements has been brought about in the relations of life-elements—just as externally this precision has been effected by the universal diffusion of pocket watches. However, the conditions of metropolitan life are at once cause and effect of this trait. The relationships and affairs of the typical metropolitan usually are so varied and complex that without the strictest punctuality in promises and services the whole structure would break down into an inextricable chaos. Above all, this necessity is brought about by the aggregation of so many people with such differentiated interests, who must integrate their relations and activities into a highly complex organism. If all clocks and watches in Berlin would suddenly go wrong in different ways, even if only by one hour, all economic life and communication of the city would be disrupted for a long time. In addition an apparently mere external factor—long distances—would make all waiting and broken appointments result in an ill-afforded waste of time. Thus, the technique of metropolitan life is unimaginable without the most punctual integration of all activities and mutual relations into a stable and impersonal time schedule. Here again the general conclusions of this entire task of reflection become obvious, namely, that from each point on the surface of existence—however closely attached to the surface alone —one may drop a sounding into the depth of the psyche so that all the most banal externalities of life finally are connected with the ultimate decisions concerning the meaning and style of life. Punctuality, calculability, exactness are forced upon life by the complexity and extension of metropolitan existence and are not only most intimately connected with its money economy and intellectualistic character. These traits must also color the contents of life and favor the exclusion of those irrational, instinctive, sovereign traits and impulses which aim at determining the mode of life from within, instead of receiving the general and precisely schematized form of life from without. Even though sovereign types of personality, characterized by irrational impulses, are by no means impossible in the city, they are, nevertheless, opposed to typical city life. The passionate hatred of men like Ruskin and Nietzsche for the metropolis is understandable in these terms. Their natures discovered the value of life alone in the unschematized existence which cannot be defined with precision for all alike. From the same source of this hatred of the metropolis surged their hatred of money economy and of the intellectualism of modern existence.

The same factors which have thus coalesced into the exactness and minute precision of the form of life have coalesced into a structure of the highest impersonality; on the other hand, they have promoted a highly personal subjectivity. There is perhaps no psychic phenomenon which has been so unconditionally reserved to the metropolis as has the blasé attitude. The blasé attitude results first from the rapidly changing and closely compressed contrasting stimulations of the nerves. From this, the enhancement of metropolitan intellectuality, also, seems originally to stem. Therefore, stupid people who are not intellectually alive in the first place usually are not exactly blasé. A life in boundless pursuit of pleasure makes one blasé because it agitates the nerves to their strongest reactivity for such a long time that they finally cease to react at all. In the same way, through the rapidity and contradictoriness of their changes, more harmless impressions force such violent responses, tearing the nerves so brutally hither and thither that their last reserves of strength are spent; and if one remains in the same milieu they have no time to gather new strength. An incapacity thus emerges to react to new sensations with the appropriate energy. This constitutes that blasé attitude which, in fact, every metropolitan child shows when compared with children of quieter and less changeable milieus.

This physiological source of the metropolitan blasé attitude is joined by another source which flows from the money economy. The essence of the blasé attitude consists in the blunting of discrimination. This does not mean that the objects are not perceived, as is the case with the half-wit, but rather that the meaning and differing values of things, and thereby the things themselves, are experienced as insubstantial. They appear to the blasé person in an evenly flat and gray tone; no one object deserves preference over any other. This mood is the faithful subjective reflection of the completely internalized money economy. By being the equivalent to all the manifold things in one and the same way, money becomes the most frightful leveler. For money expresses all qualitative differences of things in terms of "how much?" Money, with all its colorlessness and indifference, becomes the common denominator of all values; irreparably it hollows out the core of things, their individuality, their specific value, and their incomparability. All things float with equal specific gravity in the constantly moving stream of money. All things lie on the same level and differ from one another only in the size of the area which they cover. In the individual case this coloration, or rather discoloration, of things through their money equivalence may be unnoticeably minute. However, through the relations of the rich to the objects to be had for money, perhaps even through the total character which the mentality of the contemporary public everywhere imparts to these objects, the exclusively pecuniary evaluation of objects has become quite considerable. The large cities, the main seats of the money exchange, bring the purchasability of things to the fore much more impressively than do smaller localities. That is why cities are also the genuine locale of the blasé attitude. In the blasé attitude the concentration of men and things stimulates the nervous system of the individual to its highest achievement so that it attains its peak. Through the mere quantitative intensification of the same conditioning factors this achievement is transformed into its opposite and appears in the peculiar adjustment of the blasé attitude. In this phenomenon the nerves find in the refusal to react to their stimulation the last possibility of accommodating to the contents and forms of metropolitan life. The self-preservation of certain personalities is bought at the price of devaluating the whole objective world, a devaluation which in the end unavoidably drags one's own personality down into a feeling of the same worthlessness.

Whereas the subject of this form of existence has to come to terms with it entirely for himself, his self-preservation in the face of the large city demands from him a no less negative behavior of a social nature. This mental attitude of metropolitans toward one another we may designate, from a formal point of view, as reserve. If so many inner reactions were responses to the continuous external contacts with innumerable people as are those in the small town, where one knows almost everybody one meets and where one has a positive relation to almost everyone, one would be completely atomized internally and come to an unimaginable psychic state. Partly this psychological fact, partly the right to distrust which men have in the face of the touch-and-go elements of metropolitan life, necessitates our reserve. As a result of this reserve we frequently do not even know by sight those who have been our neighbors for years. And it is this reserve which in the eyes of the small-town people makes us appear to be cold and heartless. Indeed, if I do not deceive myself, the inner aspect of this outer reserve is not only indifference but, more often than we are aware, it is a slight aversion, a mutual strangeness and repulsion, which will break into hatred and fight at the moment of a closer contact, however caused. The whole inner organization of such an extensive communicative life rests upon an extremely varied hierarchy of sympathies, indifferences, and aversions of the briefest as well as of the most permanent nature. The sphere of indifference in this hierarchy is not as large as might appear on the surface. Our psychic activity still responds to almost every impression of somebody else with a somewhat distinct feeling. The unconscious, fluid and changing character of this impression seems to result in a state of indifference. Actually this indifference would be just as unnatural as the diffusion of indiscriminate mutual suggestion would be unbearable. From both these typical dangers of the metropolis, indifference and indiscriminate suggestibility, antipathy protects us. A latent antipathy and the preparatory stage of practical antagonism effect the distances and aversions without which this mode of life could not at all be led. The extent and the mixture of this style of life, the rhythm of its emergence and disappearance, the forms in which it is satisfied—all these, with the unifying motives in the narrower sense, form the inseparable whole of the metropolitan style of life. What appears in the metropolitan style of life directly as dissociation is in reality only one of its elemental forms of socialization.

This reserve with its overtone of hidden aversion appears in turn as the form or the cloak of a more general mental phenomenon of the metropolis: it grants to the individual a kind and an amount of personal freedom which has no analogy whatsoever under other conditions. The metropolis goes back to one of the large developmental tendencies of social life as such, to one of the few tendencies for which an approximately universal formula can be discovered. The earliest phase of social formations found in historical as well as in contemporary social structures is this: a relatively small circle firmly closed against neighboring, strange, or in some way antagonistic circles. However, this circle is closely coherent and allows its individual members only a narrow field for the development of unique qualities and free, self-responsible movements. Political and kinship groups, parties and religious associations begin in this way. The self-preservation of very young associations requires the establishment of strict boundaries and a centripetal unity. Therefore they cannot allow the individual freedom and unique inner and outer development. From this stage social development proceeds at once in two different, yet corresponding, directions. To the extent to which the group grows—numerically, spatially, in significance and in content of life—to the same degree the group's direct, inner unity loosens, and the rigidity of the original demarcation against others is softened through mutual relations and connections. At the same time, the individual gains freedom of movement, far beyond the first jealous delimitation. The individual also gains a specific individuality to which the division of labor in the enlarged group gives both occasion and necessity. The state and Christianity, guilds and political parties, and innumerable other groups have developed according to this formula, however much, of course, the special conditions and forces of the respective groups have modified the general scheme. This scheme seems to me distinctly recognizable also in the evolution of individuality within urban life. The small-town life in Antiquity and in the Middle Ages set barriers against movement and relations of the individual toward the outside, and it set up barriers against individual independence and differentiation within the individual self. These barriers were such that under them modern man could not have breathed. Even today a metropolitan man who is placed in a small town feels a restriction similar, at least, in kind. The smaller the circle which forms our milieu is, and the more restricted those relations to others are which dissolve the boundaries of the individual, the more anxiously the circle guards the achievements, the conduct of life, and the outlook of the individual, and the more readily a quantitative and qualitative specialization would break up the framework of the whole little circle.

The ancient *polis* in this respect seems to have had the very character of a small town. The constant threat to its existence at the hands of enemies from near and afar effected strict coherence in political and military respects, a supervision of the citizen by the citizen, a jealousy of the whole against the individual whose particular life was suppressed to such a degree that he could compensate only by acting as a despot in his own household. The tremendous agitation and excitement, the unique colorfulness of Athenian life, can perhaps be understood in terms of the fact that a people of incomparably individualized personalities struggled against the constant inner and outer pressure of a deindividualizing small town. This produced a tense atmosphere in which the weaker individuals were suppressed and those of stronger natures were incited to prove themselves in the most passionate manner. This is precisely why it was that there blossomed in Athens what must be called, without defining it exactly, "the general human character" in the intellectual development of our species. For we maintain factual as well as historical validity for the following connection: the most extensive and the most general contents and forms of life are most intimately connected with the most individual ones. They have a preparatory stage in common, that is, they find their enemy in narrow formations and groupings the maintenance of which places both of them into a state of defense against expanse and generality lying without and the freely moving individuality within. Just as in the feudal age, the "free" man was the one who stood under the law of the land, that is, under the law of the largest social orbit, and the unfree man was the one who derived his right merely from the narrow circle of a feudal association and was excluded from the larger social orbit—so today metropolitan man is "free" in a spiritualized and refined sense, in contrast to the pettiness and prejudices which hem in the small-town man. For the reciprocal reserve and indifference and the intellectual life conditions of large circles are never felt more strongly by the individual in their impact upon his independence than in the thickest crowd of the big city. This is because the bodily proximity and narrowness of space makes the mental distance only the more visible. It is obviously only the obverse of this freedom if, under certain circumstances, one nowhere feels as lonely and lost as in the metropolitan crowd. For here as elsewhere it is by no means necessary that the freedom of man be reflected in his emotional life as comfort.

It is not only the immediate size of the area and the number of persons which, because of the universal historical correlation between the enlargement of the circle and the personal inner and outer freedom, has made the metropolis the locale of freedom. It is rather in transcending this visible expanse that any given city becomes the seat of cosmopolitanism. The horizon of the city expands in a manner comparable to the way in which wealth develops; a certain amount of property increases in a quasi-automatical way in ever more rapid progression. As soon as a certain limit has been passed, the economic, personal, and intellectual relations of the citizenry, the sphere of intellectual predominance of the city over its hinterland, grow as in geometrical progression. Every gain in dynamic extension becomes a step, not for an equal, but for a new and larger extension. From every thread spinning out of the city, ever new threads grow as if by themselves, just as within the city the unearned increment of ground rent, through the mere increase in communication, brings the owner automatically increasing profits. At this point, the quantitative aspect of life is transformed directly into qualitative traits of character. The sphere of life of the small town is, in the main, self-contained and autarchic. For it is the decisive nature of the metropolis that its inner life overflows by waves into a far-flung national or international area. Weimar is not an example to the contrary, since its significance was hinged upon individual personalities and died with them; whereas the metropolis is indeed characterized by its essential independence even from the most eminent individual personalities. This is the counterpart to the independence, and it is the price the individual pays for the independence, which he enjoys in the metropolis. The most significant characteristic of the metropolis is this functional extension beyond its physical boundaries. And this efficacy reacts in turn and gives weight, importance, and responsibility to metropolitan life. Man does not end with the limits of his body or the area comprising his immediate activity. Rather is the range of the person constituted by the sum of effects emanating from him temporally and spatially. In the same way, a city consists of its total effects which extend beyond its immediate confines. Only this range is the city's actual extent in which its existence is expressed. This fact makes it obvious that individual freedom, the logical and historical complement of such extension, is not to be understood only in the negative sense of mere freedom of mobility and elimination of prejudices and petty philistinism. The essential point is that the particularity and incomparability, which ultimately every human being possesses, be somehow expressed in the working-out of a way of life. That we follow the laws of our own nature—and this after all is freedom—becomes obvious and convincing to ourselves and to others only if the expressions of this nature differ from the expressions of others. Only our unmistakability proves that our way of life has not been superimposed by others.

Cities are, first of all, seats of the highest economic division of labor. They produce thereby such extreme phenomena as in Paris the remunerative occupation of the *quatorzième*. They are persons who identify themselves by signs on their residences and who are ready at the dinner hour in correct attire, so that they can be quickly called upon if a dinner party should consist of thirteen persons. In the measure of its expansion, the city offers more and more the decisive conditions of the division of labor. It offers a circle which through its size can absorb a highly diverse variety of services. At the same time, the concentration of individuals and their struggle for customers compel the individual to specialize in a function from which he cannot be readily displaced by another. It is decisive that city life has transformed the struggle with nature for livelihood into an inter-human struggle for gain, which here is not granted by nature but by other men. For specialization does not flow only from the competition for gain but also from the underlying fact that the seller must always seek to call forth new and differentiated needs of the lured customer. In order to find a source of income which is not yet exhausted, and to find a function which cannot readily be displaced, it is necessary to specialize in one's services. This process promotes differentiation, refinement, and the enrichment of the public's needs, which obviously must lead to growing personal differences within this public.

All this forms the transition to the individualization of mental and psychic traits which the city occasions in proportion to its size. There is a whole series of obvious causes underlying this process. First, one must meet the difficulty of asserting his own personality within the dimensions of metropolitan life. Where the quantitative increase in importance and the expense of energy reach their limits, one seizes upon qualitative differentiation in order somehow to attract the attention of the social circle by playing upon its sensitivity for differences. Finally, man is tempted to adopt the most tendentious peculiarities, that is, the specifically metropolitan extravagances of mannerism, caprice, and preciousness. Now, the meaning of these extravagances does not at all lie in the contents of such behavior, but rather in its form of "being different," of standing out in a striking manner and thereby attracting attention. For many character types, ultimately the only means of saving for themselves some modicum of self-esteem and the sense of filling a position is indirect, through the awareness of others. In the same sense a seemingly insignificant factor is operating, the cumulative effects of which are, however, still noticeable. I refer to the brevity and scarcity of the inter-human contacts granted to the metropolitan man, as compared with social intercourse in the small town. The temptation to appear "to the point," to appear concentrated and strikingly characteristic, lies much closer to the individual in brief metropolitan contacts than in an atmosphere in which frequent and prolonged association assures the personality of an unambiguous image of himself in the eyes of the other.

The most profound reason, however, why the metropolis conduces to the urge for the most individual personal existence—no matter whether justified and successful—appears to me to be the following: the development of modern culture is characterized by the preponderance of what one may call the "objective spirit" over the "subjective spirit." This is to say, in language as well as in law, in the technique of production as well as in art, in science as well as in the objects of the domestic environment, there is embodied a sum of spirit. The individual in his intellectual development follows the growth of this spirit very imperfectly and at an ever increasing distance. If, for instance, we view the immense culture which for the last hundred years has been embodied in things and in knowledge, in institutions and in comforts, and if we compare all this with the cultural progress of the individual during the same period—at least in high status groups—a frightful disproportion in growth between the two becomes evident. Indeed, at some points we notice a retrogression in the culture of the individual with reference to spirituality, delicacy, and idealism. This discrepancy results essentially from the growing division of labor. For the division of labor demands from the individual an ever more one-sided accomplishment, and the greatest advance in a one-sided pursuit only too frequently means dearth to the personality of the individual. In any case, he can cope less and less with the overgrowth of objective culture. The individual is reduced to a negligible quantity, perhaps less in his consciousness than in his practice and in the totality of his obscure emotional states that are derived from this practice. The individual has become a mere cog in an enormous organization of things and powers which tear from his hands all progress, spirituality, and value in order to transform them from their subjective form into the form of a purely objective life. It needs merely to be pointed out that the metropolis is the genuine arena of this culture which outgrows all personal life. Here in buildings and educational institutions, in the wonders and comforts of space-conquering technology, in the formations of community life, and in the visible institutions of the state, is offered such an overwhelming fullness of crystallized and impersonalized spirit that the personality, so to speak, cannot maintain itself under its impact. On the one hand, life is made infinitely easy for the personality in that stimulations, interests, uses of time and consciousness are offered to it from all sides. They carry the person as if in a stream, and one needs hardly to swim for oneself. On the other hand, however, life is composed more and more of these impersonal contents and offerings which tend to displace the genuine personal colorations and incomparabilities. This results in the individual's summoning the utmost in uniqueness and particularization, in order to preserve his most personal core. He has to exaggerate this personal element in order to remain audible even to himself. The atrophy of individual culture through the hypertrophy of objective culture is one reason for the bitter hatred which the preachers of the most extreme individualism, above all Nietzsche, harbor against the metropolis. But it is, indeed, also a reason why these preachers are so passionately loved in the metropolis and why they appear to the metropolitan man as the prophets and saviors of his most unsatisfied yearnings.

If one asks for the historical position of these two forms

of individualism which are nourished by the quantitative relation of the metropolis, namely, individual independence and the elaboration of individuality itself, then the metropolis assumes an entirely new rank order in the world history of the spirit. The eighteenth century found the individual in oppressive bonds which had become meaningless —bonds of a political, agrarian, guild, and religious character. They were restraints which, so to speak, forced upon man an unnatural form and outmoded, unjust inequalities. In this situation the cry for liberty and equality arose, the belief in the individual's full freedom of movement in all social and intellectual relationships. Freedom would at once permit the noble substance common to all to come to the fore, a substance which nature had deposited in every man and which society and history had only deformed. Besides this eighteenth-century ideal of liberalism, in the nineteenth century, through Goethe and Romanticism, on the one hand, and through the economic division of labor, on the other hand, another ideal arose: individuals liberated from historical bonds now wished to distinguish themselves from one another. The carrier of man's values is no longer the "general human being" in every individual, but rather man's qualitative uniqueness and irreplaceability. The external and internal history of our time takes its course within the struggle and in the changing entanglements of these two ways of defining the individual's role in the whole of society. It is the function of the metropolis to provide the arena for this struggle and its reconciliation. For the metropolis presents the peculiar conditions which are revealed to us as the opportunities and the stimuli for the development of both these ways of allocating roles to men. Therewith these conditions gain a unique place, pregnant with inestimable meanings for the development of psychic existence. The metropolis reveals itself as one of those great historical formations in which opposing streams which enclose life unfold, as well as join one another with equal right. However, in this process the currents of life, whether their individual phenomena touch us sympathetically or antipathetically, entirely transcend the sphere for which the judge's attitude is appropriate. Since such forces of life have grown into the roots and into the crown of the whole of the historical life in which we, in our fleeting existence, as a cell, belong only as a part, it is not our task either to accuse or to pardon, but only to understand.

WASTELAND
/Marya Mannes

Cans. Beer cans. Glinting on the verges of a million miles of roadways, lying in scrub, grass, dirt, leaves, sand, mud, but never hidden. Piel's, Rheingold, Ballantine, Schaefer, Schlitz, shining in the sun or picked by moon or the beams of headlights at night; washed by rain or flattened by wheels, but never dulled, never buried, never destroyed. Here is the mark of savages, the testament of wasters, the stain of prosperity.

Who are these men who defile the grassy borders of our roads and lanes, who pollute our ponds, who spoil the purity of our ocean beaches with the empty vessels of their thirst? Who are the men who make these vessels in millions and then say, "Drink—and discard"? What society is this that can afford to cast away a million tons of metal and to make of wild and fruitful land a garbage heap?

What manner of men and women need thirty feet of steel and two hundred horsepower to take them, singly, to their small destinations? Who demand that what they eat is wrapped so that forests are cut down to make the paper that is thrown away, and what they smoke and chew is sealed so that the sealers can be tossed in gutters and caught in twigs and grass?

What kind of men can afford to make the streets of their towns and cities hideous with neon at night, and their roadways hideous with signs by day, wasting beauty; who leave the carcasses of cars to rot in heaps; who spill their trash into ravines and make smoking mountains of refuse for the town's rats? What manner of men choke off the life in rivers, streams and lakes with the waste of their produce, making poison of water?

Who is as rich as that? Slowly the wasters and despoilers are impoverishing our land, our nature, and our beauty, so that there will not be one beach, one hill, one lane, one meadow, one forest free from the debris of man and the stigma of his improvidence.

Who is so rich that he can squander forever the wealth of earth and water for the trivial needs of vanity or the compulsive demands of greed; or so prosperous in land that he can sacrifice nature for unnatural desires? The earth we abuse and the living things we kill will, in the end, take their revenge; for in exploiting their presence we are diminishing our future.

And what will we leave behind us when we are long dead? Temples? Amphora? Sunken treasure?

Or mountains of twisted, rusted steel, canyons of plastic containers, and a million miles of shores garlanded, not with the lovely wrack of the sea, but with the cans and bottles and light-bulbs and boxes of a people who conserved their convenience at the expense of their heritage, and whose ephemeral prosperity was built on waste.

THE DECLINE OF RELIGION
/William Barrett

The central fact of modern history in the West—by which we mean the long period from the end of the Middle Ages to the present—is unquestionably the decline of religion. No doubt, the churches are still very powerful organizations; there are millions of churchgoers all over the world; and even the purely intellectual possibilities of religious belief look better to churchmen now than in the bleak days of self-confident nineteenth-century materialism. A few years ago there was even considerable talk about a "religious revival," and some popular and patriotic periodicals such as *Life* magazine gave a great deal of space to it; but the talk has by now pretty much died down, the movement, if any, subsided, and the American public buys more automobiles and television sets than ever before. When *Life* magazine promotes a revival of religion, one is only too painfully aware from the nature of this publication that religion is considered as being in the national interest; one could scarcely have a clearer indication of the broader historical fact that in the modern world the nation-state, a thoroughly secular institution, outranks any church.

The decline of religion in modern times means simply that religion is no longer the uncontested center and ruler of man's life, and that the church is no longer the final and unquestioned home and asylum of his being. The deepest significance of this change does not even appear principally at the purely intellectual level, in loss of belief, though this loss due to the critical inroads of science has been a major historical cause of the decline. The waning of religion is a much more concrete and complex fact than a mere change in conscious outlook; it penetrates the deepest strata of man's total psychic life. It is indeed one of the major stages in man's psychic evolution—as Nietzsche, almost alone among nineteenth-century philosophers, was to see. Religion to medieval man was not so much a theological system as a solid psychological matrix surrounding the individual's life from birth to death, sanctifying and enclosing all its ordinary and extraordinary occasions in sacrament and ritual. The loss of the church was the loss of a whole system of symbols, images, dogmas, and rites which had the psychological validity of immediate experience, and within which hitherto the whole psychic life of Western man had been safely contained. In losing religion, man lost the concrete connection with a transcendent realm of being; he was set free to deal with this world in all its brute objectivity. But he was bound to feel homeless in such a world, which no longer answered the needs of his spirit. A home is the accepted framework which habitually contains our life. To lose one's psychic container is to be cast adrift, to become a wanderer upon the face of the earth. Henceforth, in seeking his own human completeness man would have to do for himself what he once had done for him, unconsciously, by the church, through the medium of its sacramental life. Naturally enough, man's feeling of homelessness did not make itself felt for some time; the Renaissance man was still enthralled by a new and powerful vision of mastery over the whole earth.

No believer, no matter how sincere, could possibly write the *Divine Comedy* today, even if he possessed a talent equal to Dante's. Visions and symbols do not have the immediate and overwhelming reality for us that they had for the medieval poet. In the *Divine Comedy* the whole of nature is merely a canvas upon which the religious symbol and image are painted. Western man has spent more than five hundred years—half a millennium—in stripping nature of these projections and turning it into a realm of neutral objects which his science may control. Thus it could hardly be expected that the religious image would have the same force for us as it did for Dante. This is simply a psychic fact within human history; psychic facts have just as much historical validity as the facts that we now, unlike the man of Dante's time, travel in airplanes and work in factories regulated by computing machines. A great work of art can never be repeated—the history of art shows us time and again that literal imitation leads to pastiche—because it springs from the human soul, which evolves like everything else in nature. This point must be insisted upon, contrary to the view of some of our more enthusiastic medievalists who picture the psychic containment of medieval man as a situation of human completeness to which we must return. History has never allowed man to return to the past in any total sense. And our psychological problems cannot be solved by a regression to a past state in which they had not yet been brought into being. On the other hand, enlightened and progressive thinkers are equally blind when they fail to recognize that every major step forward by mankind entails some loss, the sacrifice of an older security and the creation and heightening of new tensions. (We should bear this in mind against some of the criticisms of Existentialism as a philosophy that has unbearably heightened human tensions: it did not create those tensions, which were already at work in the soul of modern man, but simply sought to give them philosophic expression, rather than evading them by pretending they were not there.)

It is far from true that the passage from the Middle Ages to modern times is the substitution of a rational for a religious outlook; on the contrary, the whole of medieval philosophy—as Whitehead has very aptly remarked—is one of "unbounded rationalism" in comparison with modern thought. Certainly, the difference between a St. Thomas Aquinas in the thirteenth century and a Kant at the end of the eighteenth century is conclusive on this point: For Aquinas the whole natural world, and particularly this natural world as it opens toward God as First Cause, was transparently accessible to human reason; while to Kant, writing at the bitter end of the century of Enlightenment, the limits of human reason had very radically shrunk. (Indeed, as we shall see later, the very meaning of human reason became altered in Kant.) But this "unbounded rationalism" of the medieval philosopher is altogether different from the untrammeled use later thinkers made of human reason, applying it like an acid solvent to all things human or divine. The rationalism of the medieval philosophers was contained by the mysteries of faith and dogma, which were altogether beyond the grasp of human reason, but were nevertheless powerfully real and meaningful to man as symbols that kept the vital circuit open between reason and emotion, between the rational and non-rational in the human psyche. Hence, this rationalism of the medieval philosophers does not end with the attenuated, bleak, or grim picture of man we find in the modern rationalists. Here, once again, the condition under which the philosopher creates his philosophy, like that under which the poet creates his poetry, has to do with deeper levels of his being —deeper than the merely conscious level of having or not having a rational point of view. We could not expect to produce a St. Thomas Aquinas, any more than a Dante, today. The total psychic condition of man—of which after all thinking is one of the manifestations—has evolved too radically. Which may be why present-day Thomists have on the whole remained singularly unconvincing to their contemporaries.

At the gateway that leads from the Middle Ages into the modern world stand Science (which later became the spirit of the Enlightenment), Protestantism, and Capitalism. At first glance, the spirit of Protestantism would seem to have very little to do with that of the New Science, since in matters religious Protestantism placed all the weight of its emphasis upon the irrational datum of faith, as against the imposing rational structures of medieval theology, and there is Luther's famous curse upon "the whore, Reason." In secular matters, however—and particularly in its relation toward nature—Protestantism fitted in very well with the New Science. By stripping away the wealth of images and symbols from medieval Christianity, Protestantism unveiled nature as a realm of objects hostile to the spirit and to be conquered by puritan zeal and industry. Thus Protestantism, like science, helped carry forward that immense project of modern man: the despiritualization of nature, the emptying of it of all the symbolic images projected upon it by the human psyche. With Protestantism begins that long modern struggle, which reaches its culmination in the twentieth century, to strip man naked. To be sure, in all of this the aim was progress, and Protestantism did succeed in raising the religious consciousness to a higher level of individual sincerity, soul-searching, and strenuous inwardness. Man was impoverished in order to come face to face with his God and the severe and inexplicable demands of his faith; but in the process he was stripped of all the mediating rites and dogmas that could make this confrontation less dangerous to his psychic balance. Protestantism achieved a heightening of the religious consciousness, but at the same time severed this consciousness from the deep unconscious life of our total human nature. In this respect, its historical thrust runs parallel to that of the New Science and capitalism, since science was making the mythical and symbolic picture of nature disappear before the success of its own rational explanations, and capitalism was opening up the whole world as a field of operations for rationally planned enterprise.

Faith, for Protestantism, is nevertheless the irrational and numinous center of religion; Luther was saturated with the feeling of St. Paul that man of himself can do nothing and only God working in us can bring salvation. Here the inflation of human consciousness is radically denied, and the conscious mind is recognized as the mere instrument and plaything of a much greater unconscious force. Faith is an abyss that engulfs the rational nature of man. The Protestant doctrine of original sin is in all its severity a kind of compensatory recognition of those depths below the level of consciousness where the earnest soul demands to interrogate itself—except that those depths are cast into the outer darkness of depravity. So long as faith retained its intensity, however, the irrational elements of human nature were accorded recognition and a central place in the total human economy. But as the modern world moves onward, it becomes more and more secularized in every department of life; faith consequently becomes attenuated, and Protestant man begins to look more and more like a gaunt skeleton, a sculpture by Giacometti. A secular civilization leaves him more starkly naked than the iconoclasm of the Reformation had ever dreamed. The more severely he struggles to hold on to the primal face-to-face relation with God, the more tenuous this becomes, until in the end the relation to God Himself threatens to become a relation to Nothing-

ness. In this sense Kierkegaard, in the middle of the nineteenth century, was the reckoning point of the whole Protestant Reformation that began three centuries earlier: He sees
faith for the uncompromising and desperate wager it is, if
one takes it in all its Protestant strictness; and he cannot say,
like his Catholic counterpart Pascal, "Stupefy yourself, take
holy water, receive the sacraments, and in the end all shall
be well"—for Protestant man has forsworn the sacraments
and natural symbols of the soul as the snares and pomp of
the devil. Some of Kierkegaard's books, such as *The Sickness Unto Death* and *The Concept of Dread,* are still frightening to our contemporaries and so are excused or merely
passed over as the personal outpourings of a very melancholy temperament; yet they are the truthful record of
what the Protestant soul must experience on the brink of
the great Void. Protestant man is the beginning of the
West's fateful encounter with Nothingness—an encounter
that was long overdue and is perhaps only now in the
twentieth century reaching its culmination.

THE DECLINE OF THE CHORAL DANCE
/Paul Halmos

> "One may judge of a King by the state
> of dancing during his reign."
> *Ancient Chinese maxim.*

Artistic expression, even when dilettante, is one of the
most satisfactory forms of objectifying and thus projecting
inner tensions. The dance is undoubtedly the most ancient
form of artistic expression; its unique position among the
arts is guaranteed by more than mere seniority: as we have
seen, the dance is essentially a cooperative art, an art of the
group and not of the solitary individual. Though there are
isolated examples of solo and couple dances among primitive peoples, they are not truly solo or couple performances;
they presuppose the presence of singing and rhythmically
tapping audiences who open the dance or who join in it
later. In pre-cultural human society dance must have been
a universal form of expressing strong emotions collectively.

Admittedly, there have been reports of some danceless peoples, yet so long as we accept testimonies from observers on animal-dances—e.g. Köhler's reports that his apes had danced too—we cannot be far wrong in concluding that the dance was a universal play-form in pre-cultural communities.

Primitive peoples dance for every occasion—birth, initiation, marriage, death, war and so on. Sometimes the motive-force appears to be an overflow of vitality and joy, at other times it seems to issue from a craving for the dissolution of the self, or it may be linked with magical practices, e.g. rain-making dances, hunting dances or war dances.

Oesterley believed that "all dancing was originally religious and was performed for religious purposes." He insisted that the dance was sacred in origin and that every other type of dance was derived from this original religious dance. Oesterley sensed that in the dance the individual exerted himself to reach beyond his limited selfhood and merge with a reality larger than himself. From the biological point of view this larger reality is the totality of the species, and not much can be gained by saying that a communion with the community is merely a symbolization of a more significant and higher union, a union with God or with the essential principle of the universe. A social communion is complete and there is nothing in it which transcends the species. It is, of course, true that a religious symbolization and dramatization of phylic communion can substantially aid the latter when the communal principle of the ritual is stressed, but this does not alter the biosocial character of the experience. This is what Trigant Burrow meant when he wrote: "Psychologically, the normal mind is synonymous with the mystical mind." And his comment on the Oesterley type of religious interpretation was: "In our unconsciousness we deny the collateral immediacy of our social inclusiveness and for this reason we project the lineal image of indefinite extension composing man's dream of a personal life eternal. *Denying our organic unity of compass, we compensate in a fanciful unity of duration.*" (Italics mine.)

Whether the ostensible purpose of these primitive dances is animistic-religious or magical-material, one constant feature in them is that they are group performances and not solo or couple acts. The main crises of human life are dramatized, couched in movement and shared by all who participate in the dance, thus alleviating the inflictions which inevitably follow from human existence, and enriching and ornamenting the joys which are incidental to life.

The choral dance is the physical manifestation of groupward drives. Whatever vital experience the primitive group has to face, its sharing by every member is made possible by the translation of that experience into rhythmic muscular movements simultaneously executed by all. The speechless eloquence of posture and gesture supplemented the primitive vocabulary of prehistoric humanity and became a powerful medium of social intercourse.

The choral dance was not merely instrumental in securing group unity for ulterior purposes like a good harvest or the propitiation of evil demons. The groupward drives, the yearning for a tangible, physically manifested unity exist on their own account and suffuse the dance ritual whatever its ostensible purpose. In the choral dance an inarticulate consensus and an absolute fraternity are reaffirmed from time to time, thus tightening up group cohesion and conserving solidarity. In it the individual member finds a reassurance that he is not alone.

In some early civilizations this potential of the choral dance was recognized, e.g. the training of the Greek soldier included the performance of martial dances. The dance "was a means of giving soldiers carriage, agility and health, and cultivating *esprit de corps*." [Troy and Margaret Kinney.] John Martin interprets the meaning of primitive war dances in a similar way: "War dances not only constitute a popular form of entertainment but serve at the same time to crystallize group solidarity. . . ." Max von Boehm writes in very much the same vein on this subject: "Das gibt ihm (dem Tanz) seinen hohen sozialen Wert, er ist als ein Element der Ordnung anzusprechen, das bei den Beteiligten *ein einheitliches Empfinden und ein Gefühl der Gemeinsamkeit hervorruft*." And later on: "Der Tanz erfüllt die Masse mit den gemeinsamen Empfindungen und regt sie zu den gemeinsamen Gefühlsäusserungen an, *die jedem Volke Lebensbedürfnis sind* und die im Stadium einer fortgeschrittenen Kultur durch andere Hebel, als da sind Konfession, Partei, u.a., ausgelost werden." (Italics mine.) It is very significant that a German writer should look upon political parties as media of biosocial participation. The latter may be served incidentally and surreptitiously in the larger framework of political-mystical allegiances, but a centralist party can hardly be described as a biosocial group.

While Oesterley contended that the dance was originally nothing but a vehicle of religious mysticism, to us it appears that it was a medium of a paradigmatic experience which at its core was strictly social or communal.

The experience of a union, however, is not merely a gratification of social hunger, of the instinct of gregariousness, that is, of biosocial need. The satisfaction of this propensity is often accompanied by an auto-intoxication comparable only to sexual ecstasy which results in a temporary draining of the will from stubborn self-regard and in the gathering of reckless sacrificial emotions. Under these conditions individual separateness disappears and phylic unity is complete; and it is under these conditions that the group's reality is supreme and exclusive. Through the choral dance primitive man successfully achieved two objectives:

(a) the effective sharing of the burdens of his conflicts and tensions, a sharing which reaffirmed and deepened the bonds of fellow-feeling;

(b) a catharsis through the rhythmic communal rapture which renewed and strengthened the individual.

The choral dance, therefore, was not only a socio-political vehicle of group solidarity but also a primitive method of group psychotherapy.

This second function is effectively portrayed by Curt Sachs: "Repressed powers are loosed and seek expression; an innate sense of rhythm orders them into lively harmony. Harmony deadens and dissipates the will, the dancer gives himself over to the supreme delights of play prescribed by custom, gives himself over to the exhilaration which carries him away from the monotony of everyday life, from palpable reality, from the sober facts of experience. . . . In the ecstasy of the dancer, man bridges the chasm between this and the other world. . . . Captivated and entranced he bursts his earthly chain and trembling feels himself in tune with all the world."

The "chasm" here referred to is that which exists between one solitary individual and another. The transcending of solitariness has always appeared to mystics, poets and philosophers as a communion with the Godhead, a "surrender to the essential beauty of nature" or an "acceptance of the universe." Whilst all that they experienced was a spiritualized, symbolical expression of their biosocial life.

Over and above the satisfaction of these biosocial needs and the individual therapeutic benefits there were other reasons, concessions by the *Principium Individuationis*, which made man seek for and submit to absolute collective loyalties. Individual survival as much as group survival dictated close cohesion: the small groups of men were surrounded by a hostile nature and by an often hostile rivalry of neighboring groups. When the tribes had been welded into states and empires and the preservation of security was no longer a daily anxiety, collective loyalties took on a more diffuse, anemic character or thickened only occasionally in emergencies. Consequently a ritual of communal solidarity was no longer a routine practice. At the lower level of local groups it lingered on for a while as a rare festivity to be held on a few specified occasions. It is for this reason that the choral dance reached its final form in the prehistoric era and has not changed its basic patterns ever since. "Strange as it may sound—since the Stone Age, the dance has taken on as little in the way of new forms as of new content. The history of the creative dance takes place in prehistory." [Curt Sachs.]

The choral dance as the cultural form of a pre-cultural, biosocial practice survived for a long time. We find choral dances widely practiced as late as the sixteenth and seventeenth centuries. These are, however, no longer the comprehensive experiences their pre-cultural predecessors used to be. Even so they continued to fulfill an integrative function in rural communities which were isolated and enslaved by feudal bondage. If there were real peasant communities under feudal lordship these were made possible by integrative practices issuing from the community itself and not by the strictures imposed on the community by feudal rule. The latter could have created only compounds of serfs and not village communities.

Towards the end of the feudal era the choral dance began to decline. For some time after the sixteenth century choral dances and couple dances persisted together. At the beginning of the nineteenth century the spread of the waltz, the polka, the Boston finally ended the popularity of the choral dances. During the intervening centuries there were numerous pointers suggesting the presence of some kind of a transition in this process. The group is "broken up" into independent couples: the minuet, allemand, passepied, bourrée, gigue are mixed dances with a strong choral framework; the cotillion-quadrille type of so-called "square dances" represents the link between the choral and couple dances.

This later transition is already a historical and not a phylogenetic process; it is not our task to sketch the history of an art form but to examine whether it continues to answer the requirements of a biosocial need. It may be of some advantage, perhaps for the sake of bringing a contrast into high relief, to analyze the contemporary function of the dance. This contrast is presented to show the biosocial impoverishment of our species and complete our outline of the phylogenetic process.

Today the dance is hardly ever the function of the group as a whole. Going to a dance very often means "going out," that is outside the group, preferably in twos. In the age of the tango (1900), the shimmy (1920) or the jitterbug (at the time of writing), the dance has been reduced to the role of being a medium of courtship, of sexual titillation, and of motor frenzy. The modern dance may serve sexual and matrimonial purposes well, but these purposes can hardly be described as communal. The couple arrive *en deux* and rarely join others among the dancers. The big city dance halls, and the dance floors of restaurants, night clubs and so on are removed from the community, are outside the community, and it is perhaps this character of such places which makes them eminently suitable for the purposes of present-day dancing.

Apart from the popular couple dances, we have spectacular stage dancing, ballet, etc.; but these belong to the split world of performers and audiences, and with these we are not concerned here. After all, the hypertrophy of audiences is just another symptom of desocialization, a symptom which calls for specific study.

Today the commercialization of dance activities has largely stabilized the hegemony of the isolate couple dance. The dance has ceased to be an opportunity when participation inertia can be overcome and when an ease in intimate contact can be developed. It is no longer an important formalizer of social skill, of manners, and it has become arid, businesslike or downright erotic, and non-social.

Twenty-four years ago LeRoy E. Bowman and Maria Ward Lambkin, writing of the dance halls of New York, said:

"The dance palaces hug the central portion of the city

where recreational business concentrates and neighborhood relations are almost absent ... there is little or no pretence of social control or of intent to regard personal or group relations: there is merely a recognition of a want for a dance place with or without food and drink, and a commercial answer for that want."

The picture presented here has not altered since these lines were written. The dance today is a degenerated survival of an ancient group language, a language which was meant to be a medium of solidarity, of self-expression and release. In our times it is an empty form at best, when it does not serve other ulterior ends. The two investigators quote the observation of another writer: " 'One feels little doubt that the regular patron of the dance hall is bored. Large numbers admit without hesitation that they are bored, but say that as nothing else in the way of amusement is to be found easily, they come to the dance hall.' "

The "taxi dance hall" represents a logical and therefore not unexpected stage in the history of the dance. Here commercialization is complete and the beginnings of prostitution are apparent. P. G. Cressey made a thorough study of the taxi dance hall, and it appears from his account that the form of dance practiced in these places is a mechanical, overtly sexual pastime for thousands of solitary rejected men and a spurious source of income for hundreds of women, many of whom combine this work with prostitution. Cressey writes: "It is significant to note ... that the more regular patron is seldom a member of a gang ... the institution serves chiefly the distraught, the individualized and the egocentric." And: "There is little conversation. The patron may sit for hours beside others of his sex without conversing with them. The girls, likewise, when not dancing stand for long periods beside each other without talking." Cressey comes to the conclusion that, "In the last analysis the problem of the taxi dance hall can be regarded as the problem of the modern city," in which the criteria of life are "mobility, impersonality and anonymity."

There is no reliable material available on modern dancing habits in the home or in semi-public, exclusive places. Whatever the merits of these recreations may be they are, as a rule, delimited from the community by class and are, at any rate, occasions for couple dancing. At best these are harmless play-forms of the parlor game type or they are ceremonious, socialite shows in both of which the dance is merely an optional activity of individuals and not a communal ritual of all those present. Furthermore, on these occasions, the competitive features of social life dominate over the cooperative communal ones: physical attractiveness, wealth and rank, achievements of many kinds and so on are assessed, compared and approval or rejection registered often through the very media of dance etiquette.

The history of the choral dance shows a continuous decline which runs parallel with the long-drawn-out process of desocialization. The choral dance is not merely a symptom of group integration but also a uniquely ancient sustainer of biosocial group life. "The decline of the choral dance is a cause and an indication of social development. The choral dance, communal dances, demand a compact social order: they require an association in the dance which is something more than the current execution of a series of figures and movements." [Sachs.] The breaking up of rural communities by the Industrial Revolution and the rise of individualism stopped the choral dances and surrendered the floor, or the village green, to the couple dances. Huizinga went as far as to describe the suppression of the choral dance as a symptom of declining culture. This view implies that the process we labelled "desocialization" and defined as the cultural limitation of man's biosocial participation is in itself a manifestation of declining culture. But if desocialization runs through the whole of cultural history, how can we describe it as a manifestation of declining culture? It is wiser to leave out of our account terms like "declining culture" which are heavily laden with value judgments. On the other hand we should stress that the perpetuation and further growth of a desocializing culture involves the inevitability of its own eventual destruction. Desocialization is decay which affects the entire social-cultural life of human communities; this decay has been speeded up during the last few centuries and contemporary culture is pregnant with catastrophe.

The thesis here expounded comprises a claim that this process of desocialization is simultaneous with the process of cultural development; in other words, it seems to be suggested that whilst there is culture there will always be frustrations imposed on man's biosocial needs. Hence it should be reaffirmed that this prognosis was suggested only if the cultures of chance and of misrepresentation continue. It is necessary to state that culture is not incompatible with a

biosocially balanced life provided it comprises an awareness of biological sociality and the institutions through
which this awareness can be expressed.

Taking the whole era of cultures as a phase of man's
phylogenetic history we may say, in the light of the fore-
going, that desocialization is, in the first place, a phylogenetic process. We selected the choral dance for the
purpose of illustrating this phylogenetic development. Naturally, the choral dance was by no means the only medium of
biosocial contact in pre-cultural human society. Yet it was
chosen because it is the only known non-economic social
form which, having existed preculturally, continued
throughout the historically charted centuries. Even if its evidence is not decisive, it is at least the most suggestive indi-
cator of phylogenetic changes in the realm of the social.

SUMMARY

On the pre-cultural level the relatedness of the individual
to his fellows was intimate and absolute. With the emergence
of cultural forms a certain measure of rigidity appears which
grows at the expense of spontaneous and unreserved participation. The decline of the choral dances is a decline of
biosocial life. First, it becomes formalized by culture; and
second, it is eliminated by a later culture which has become
incompatible with it; the disappearance of the choral dances
coincides with a historical event, a profound social-cultural
change, i.e. the Industrial Revolution. It seems, therefore,
that desocialization has been inflicted on human communities by their culture in two stages: (a) on their elevation
from a pre-cultural state at the beginning of a historical career, (b) at the end of a series of unplanned, fortuitous cultures, since the Industrial Revolution, until, and in our
time.

OF HAPPINESS AND OF DESPAIR WE HAVE NO MEASURE
/Ernest van den Haag

> "non ridere non lugere, neque
> destestari; sed intelligere."   —*Spinoza*

How is the mass market formed on which popular culture is sold and perpetuated? In the first place, individual
taste has become uneconomic for the purchaser and for the

seller, and this effectively stunts its growth. People are prepared accordingly throughout the educational process. Group acceptance, shared taste, takes the place of authority and of individual moral and aesthetic judgment and standards. But people often move from group to group. Any taste therefore that cannot be sloughed off—an individual taste, not easily divided from the person in whom it dwells—becomes an obstacle to adaptation. Success is hindered by a discriminating personal taste which expresses or continues an individual personality, and success is fostered by an unselective appetite.

Numerous precautions are taken, beginning in nursery school (itself hardly an individualizing institution) to avoid elaboration of personal discernment and to instill fear of separation from the group. Group acceptance is stressed through formal and informal popularity contests, teamwork, and polling. Education altogether stresses group instruction. For instance, the size of his classes and the class average, not the qualities of individual pupils, are often considered the measure of the teacher. The student himself is so much treated as part of a group that, except in higher education (which is only partly immune), he may be automatically promoted with his group regardless of individual achievement or variation. Finally, the surviving individual talent is instructed not to cultivate, but to share, itself. The writer gives a writing course, the scholar lectures and writes popularizations, the beauty models or appears on TV, and the singer deserts the concert hall for the juke box.

The aggregate effect of advertising is to bring about wide sharing of tastes. The actual social function of advertising is *not* to mold taste in any particular way, nor to debase it. This goes for manufacturers, publishers and movie-makers too. They are quite content to produce and advertise what people want—be it T. S. Eliot or Edgar Guest, Kierkegaard or Norman Vincent Peale, "September Morn" or mobiles. It does not matter what people want to buy as long as they want to buy enough of the same thing to make mass production possible. Advertising helps to unify taste, to de-individualize it and thus to make mass production possible.

There is no evidence to support conspiracy theories which hold that wicked capitalists, through advertising and mass media, deliberately (or stupidly) debauch the originally good, natural taste of the masses. Mass production— capitalist or socialist—demands unified taste; efficiency (or profitableness) is dependent only on its being shared by sizeable groups.

Can one say anything about mass tastes beyond saying that they are widely shared? Are they homogenized on the "lowest common denominator"? There seems to be no good reason to assume that the lowest tastes are most widespread. One may say something of the sort about some crowds united temporarily by crude common appetites at the expense of reason, restraint and refinement. But why consider consumers a crowd? Even the fare offered by the entertainment media is usually consumed by people separately or in very small groups. (Except for movies, but moviegoers are isolated from each other though they are together.)

Producers have no interest in lowering taste or in catering to low rather than high taste. They seek to provide for a *modal* average of tastes which through advertising they try to make as congruent with the *mean* average as possible. Neither average can be identical with the "lowest common denominator."

Yet in one sense consumers are treated as a crowd: their individual tastes are not catered to. The mass-produced article need not aim low, but it must aim at an average of tastes. In satisfying all (or at least many) individual tastes in some respects, it violates each in other respects. For there are—so far—no average persons having average tastes. Averages are but statistical composites. A mass-produced article, while reflecting nearly everybody's taste to some extent, is unlikely to embody anybody's taste fully. This is one source of the sense of violation which is rationalized vaguely in theories about deliberate debasement of taste.

The sense of violation springs from the same thwarting of individuality that makes prostitution (or promiscuity) psychologically offensive. The cost of cheap and easy availability, of mass production, is wide appeal; and the cost of wide appeal is de-individualization of the relationship between those who cater and those who are catered to; and of the relationship of both to the object of the transaction. By using each other indiscriminately as impersonal instruments (the seller for profit, the buyer for sensation—or, in promiscuity, both parties for sensation and relief of anxiety) the prostitute and her client sacrifice to seemingly more urgent demands the self which, in order to grow, needs continuity, discrimination and completeness in relationships. Though profit and sensation can be achieved by depersonalization, the satisfaction ultimately sought cannot be, for the very part of personality in which it is felt—the individual self—is stunted and atrophied, at least if de-individualization continues long enough and is comprehensive. Ultimately, the sense of violation too is numbed.

Now, the depersonalizing effects of the mass production of some things—say, electric clocks—may be minor as far as consumers are concerned and more than offset by the advantages of cheapness. The same cannot be said for mass entertainment or education. And though some individuals may, society cannot have one without the other. The effects of mass production on people as producers and consumers are likely to be cumulative. Besides, even goods that seem purely utilitarian include elements of non-utilitarian, of aesthetic and psychic (e.g., prestige) appeal. Indeed, less than half of consumer expenditure goes for the satisfaction of simple biological needs. (More, perhaps, in the lowest income groups, and much less still in the higher ones.) Distinctions of this kind are necessarily hazy, but if cigarettes, newspapers, television, drinks, shaving lotion or lipstick, the prestige location of one's apartment, the fashionableness of one's clothing, etc., are taken to satisfy nonbiological needs—and we can do without them biologically—then we are motivated by psychic needs in spending most of our money. This, of course, is not in itself objectionable—except that the processes by which many of these needs now arise and are stilled bring to mind the processes by which bread is now mass produced.

In milling and baking, bread is deprived of any taste whatever and of all vitamins. Some of the vitamins are then added again (taste is provided by advertising). Quite similarly with all mass-produced articles. They can no more express the individual taste of producers than that of consumers. They become impersonal objects, however pseudo-personalized. Producers and consumers go through the mass production mill to come out homogenized and de-characterized—only it does not seem possible to reinject the individualities which have been ground out, the way the vitamins are added to enrich bread. The "human relations" industry tries to do just that and it doubtlessly supplies a de-

mand and can be helpful, just as chemical sedatives or stimulants can be. But it seems unlikely that any assembly line
—including one manned by human relations counselors—
can give more than the illusion of individuality.

To produce more, people work under de-individualizing
conditions and are rewarded by high income and leisure.
Thus they can and do consume more. But as consumers,
they must once more rid themselves of individual tastes.
The benefits of mass production are reaped only by matching de-individualizing work with equally de-individualizing
consumption. The more discontinuous income earning and
spending become physically, the more continuous they seem
to become psychologically. Failure to repress individual
personality in or after working hours is costly; in the end
the production of standardized things by persons demands
also the production of standardized persons.

In a material sense, this assembly-line shaping, packaging
and distributing of persons, of life, occurs already. Most
people perch unsteadily in mass-produced, impermanent
dwellings throughout their lives. They are born in hospitals,
fed in cafeterias, married in hotels. After terminal care,
they die in hospitals, are shelved briefly in funeral homes,
and are finally incinerated. On each of these occasions—and
how many others?—efficiency and economy are obtained
and individuality and continuity stripped off. If one lives
and dies discontinuously and promiscuously in anonymous
surroundings, it becomes hard to identify with anything,
even the self, and uneconomic to be attached to anything,
even one's own individuality. The rhythm of individual life
loses autonomy, spontaneity, and distinction when it is tied
into a stream of traffic and carried along according to the
speed of the road, as we are, in going to work, or play,
or in doing anything. Traffic lights signal when to stop and
go, and much as we seem to be driving we are driven. To
stop spontaneously, to exclaim, *Verweile doch Du bist so
schoen* (Stay, for you are beautiful), may not lose the modern Faust his soul—but it will cause a traffic jam.

One motive for delinquency—a way of getting out of line
—is, possibly, a preference for occasional prison terms to
imprisonment by routine. Crime, by its ultimate irrationality, may protest against the subordination of individual
spontaneity to social efficiency. Three further reactions to
anonymity may be noted:

(1) The prestige of histrionics has risen. We long to impersonate, to get a name—better a pseudonym than to remain nameless; better a borrowed character than none; better to impersonate than never to feel like a person. The wish to be oneself does not occur, for the only self known is empty and must be filled from the outside.

(2) The attempt to become "interesting" (no doubt unconsciously to become interested) by buying a ready-made individuality, through "sending for," "enrolling in," or "reading up on" something, or "going places."

(3) Impersonal and abstract things and utilitarian relationships are cozily "personalized" as though to offset the depersonalization of individual life.

De-individualization, however, should not be viewed as a grim, deliberate, or coercive process. It is induced gradually by economic rewards and not experienced as de-individualization at all, though the symptoms are demonstrable. Most of the people who are nourished with homogenized pap never had solid food on which to cut their teeth. They feel vaguely restless and dissatisfied, but do not know what they are pining for and could not masticate or digest it if they had it. The cooks are kept busy ransacking all the recipes the world has ever known to prepare new dishes. But the texture is always the same, always mushy, for the materials are always strained, blended, beaten, heated, and cooled until it is.

Let us briefly tour the institutional kitchens where "recreation" is cooked up—movies, radio, television.

Mass media cannot afford to step on anyone's toes, and this implies a number of restrictions which, though less significant than the positive prescriptions, are not negligible. We can forebear rehearsing tiresome minutiae—forbidden words, topics, situations, actions; but the countless dangerous associations mass media must avoid deserve some scrutiny.

No religious, racial, occupational, national, economic, political, etc., group can be offended. Hence: Can an evil man be Jewish? Left-handed? Pipesmoking? Can he perish in an airplane accident? Can a villain have any qualities shared with non-villains and a hero have disapproved traits? In short, can either be human? The playwright or script writer may not mean to say that Jews are evil or all evil men left-handed, or all pipesmokers; he may not intend to advocate bigamy or to suggest that airplanes are dangerous or

that we ought to be atheists. Joseph Conrad did not intend
The Nigger of the Narcissus as an anti-Negro tract, any
more than Shakespeare intended *Othello* as a tract against
handkerchiefs (in favor of Kleenex?). No matter. There
is a danger that the play will be so understood. In Shylock
and Fagin, Shakespeare and Dickens created individuals,
experiences, and ideas and, unlike copywriters or propagandists, did not intend them as instructions on how to act
and think. Yet the groups that press restrictions on mass
media are not wrong. For the audience tends to react as
though such instruction had been received.

The audience of mass media always expects to be sold
goods, stereotypes, and recipes for living—a new vitamin
for that tired, listless feeling, or a new line for romance.
And the audience is usually right: the same actress who just
implored a soap-opera husband not to leave her and the
kids turns and implores one and all in identically sincere
and personal tones to buy insurance or perfume. The small
boy's heroes admonish him to get mommy to buy this or
that (and even if the heroes didn't, someone will sell Davy
Crockett caps to the small boy). In many breakfast and
news shows, advertising recommendations are deliberately
mixed in with "actual" expressions of opinion. Even non-
professionals—society leaders, well-known novelists, successful and "average" common men—ringingly declare
their profound personal convictions on brands of soap, or
beer, or God: "This I believe." The line dividing views
and characters presented as fiction and as "real" becomes
hazy and the audience necessarily muddled about separating
advertisements, pleas, and recipes from art. In such a context, the audience cannot receive art as individual experience and perspective on experience. Art becomes irrelevant. It is not perceived in its own terms, but first reduced
to, then accepted or rejected as, a series of rules and
opinions on what to expect or do.

The idea that something must be sold is held by the media
managers as fervently as it is held by the audience. It
transcends the commercial motives which begot it. Thus
public or educational stations, which do not accept com-
merical advertising, spend nearly as much time on (non-
commercial) attempts to sell something as do commercial
ones. They sell themselves or their program, or next week's
offering—anything at all, as long as something is sold:
"please listen again tomorrow," "please send for our book-

let," "please do this or don't do that"—the listener must always be hectored, sold on or wheedled into something.

How, then, could the audience see that a character such as Shylock simply is? A character in the audience's experience always exists for a purpose; a character is invented to sell something, a point of view, or a product, or himself. It is never an end in itself. Hence the audience always asks, Should we buy his line?, and it is nearly impossible to present something without suggesting by implication that it be bought. Art, like love, can be experienced only as a personal, continuous, cumulative relationship. Else art becomes entertainment—dull entertainment often—just as love is reduced to sex or prestige. Not that art should not be entertaining; but it is no more deliberately aimed at entertainment than love is. Art (and love) must be felt; they cannot be manufactured by someone to suit the taste of someone else. Yet mass-media fare is prepared for consumers devoted to amusement, not, as art (and love) must be, devoted to the work (or person) itself.

The circumstances which permit the experience of art are rare in our society anyway and they cannot be expected in the audience of mass media. That audience is dispersed and heterogeneous, and though it listens often, it does so incidentally and intermittently and poised to leave if not immediately enthralled and kept amused. Such an audience is captured by loud, broad, and easy charms, by advertising posters, by copywriter's prose. And the conditions and conditioning of the audience demand a mad mixture of important and trivial matters, atom bombs, hit tunes, symphonies, B.O., sob stories, hotcha girls, round tables and jokes. It jells into one thing: diversion. Hence what art is presented is received as entertainment or propaganda. Shylock would be understood as an anti-Semitic stereotype. The mass media may as well fit their offerings to the audience which they address and, knowing the limitations of that audience, they would be irresponsible to disregard the kind of understanding and misunderstanding their offerings will meet. They must omit, therefore, all human experience likely to be misunderstood—all experience and expression, the meaning of which is not obvious and approved. Which is to say that the mass media cannot touch the experiences that art, philosophy and literature deal with: relevant and significant human experience presented in relevant and significant form. For if it is such, it is new, doubtful, difficult, perhaps offensive, at any rate easily mis-understood. Art is not concerned with making the obvious and approved more obvious and approved; it is precisely after this point that art begins and the mass media stop.

When attempting to be serious, the mass media must rig up pseudo-problems and solve them by cliché. They can-not touch real problems or real solutions. Plots are packed with actions which obscure the vagueness and irrelevance of meanings and solutions. Similarly, to replace actual indi-viduality, each character and situation is tricked up with numerous identifying details and mannerisms. The more realistic the characteristics, the less real the character usually, or the situation, and the less revealing. Literal realism cannot replace relevance. Mass media inveigh against sin and against all evils accepted as such. But they cannot question things not acknowledged as evil or appear to support things felt as evil. Even *Rigoletto*, were it a modern work, could not be broadcast since crime and im-morality pay and the ending is unhappy for everybody but the villain.

Combating legal censorship, organized group pressures, and advertising agencies is gallantly romantic—and as quixotic as man's rage against his own mirrored image. These agencies are interested only in presenting what is wanted and in preventing what might offend people. They are nuisances perhaps, but things could not be very differ-ent without them. Policemen do not create the law, though becoming the target of the few who would defy it.

The very nature of mass media excludes art, and re-quires surrogation by popular culture. Though the Hays production code applies only to movies, its basic rule states a principle which all mass media must follow: "Cor-rect standards of life, subject only to the requirements of drama and entertainment" must be upheld. Doubtless "correct standards" are those standards most of the audi-ence is likely to believe correct. They authorize whatever does not upset or offend the audience, and nothing else. "Correct standards of life" must exclude art (except oc-casional classics). For art is bound to differ from the ac-cepted, that is, the customary moral and aesthetic view, at least as it takes shape in the audience's mind. Art is always a fresh vision of the world, a new experience or creation of life. If it does not break, or develop, or renew in significant aspects the traditional, customary, accepted aesthetic and moral standards, if it merely repeats without creating, it is not art. If it does, it is incompatible with the "correct standards of life" which must control mass media.

Mass media thus never can question man's fate where it is questionable; they cannot sow doubt about an accepted style of life, or an approved major principle. To be sure, mass media often feature challenges to this and that, and clashes of opinion. These are part of our accepted style of life, as long as challenges do not defy anything but sin and evil in the accepted places and manner. The mass media must hold up "correct standards of life" whereas art must create, not uphold views. When filmed or broadcast, the visions of the playwright or novelist cannot deviate from the accepted "correct standards" and they must be entertaining. They must conform to the taste of the audience; they cannot form it. Virtue must triumph entertainingly—virtue as the audience sees it.

The poets, Shelley thought, are "the unacknowledged legislators of the world." Shelley's poets wrote for a few who would take the trouble to understand them. They addressed an audience that knew and shared the common traditions they were developing. High culture was cultivated in special institutions—courts, monasteries, churches, universities—by people who devoted their lives to the development of its traditions, and were neither isolated nor surrounded by masses wishing to be entertained. (Besides, there were no means of addressing a mass.) There was no need and no temptation for the artist to do anything but to create in his own terms. Poets, painters, or philosophers lived in and were of the group for whom they produced, as did most people, were they peasants, artisans or artists. The relations between producers of culture and consumers were so personal (as were the relations between producers and consumers generally) that one can hardly speak of an impersonal market in which one sold, the other bought.

In both high and folk culture, each bounded and autonomous universe—court or village—relied on the particular cultivators and inventors of its arts and sciences no less than the latter relied on their patrons. Each region or court depended on its musicians as it depended on its craftsmen, and vice versa. The mutual personal dependence had disadvantages and advantages, as has any close relationship. Michelangelo or Beethoven depended on irksome individual patrons more than they would today. On the other hand, whatever the patrons' tastes or demands, they were individual and not average tastes or demands. Folk culture grew without professional help. High culture was cultivated like an orchard or garden. But both folk and high cultures grew from within the groups they distinguished and remained within them.

High culture was entirely dominated by people with more than average prestige, power and income—by the elite as a group, who also dominated politics and society in general. This group determined what was to be produced, culturally and otherwise; and they took their toll often by oppression and spoliation of the mass of people whom they ruled.

With the development of industry, the elite as a group lost its power. The great mass of consumers now determines what is to be produced. Elite status, leadership in any form, is achieved and kept today by catering to the masses, not by plundering or oppressing them. The nobleman may have become rich by robbing (taking from) his peasants. But the industrialist becomes a millionaire by selling to (exchanging with) farmers. And his business is helped by giving his customers, via television, the entertainers they want. These in turn reach elite status by appealing to the masses. So do politicians.

The elite no longer determines what is produced, any more than it dominates society in other respects. Rather, the elite becomes the elite by producing the goods that sell, the goods that cater to an average of tastes. With respect to culture, the elite neither imposes any taste nor cultivates one of its own. It markets and helps homogenize and distribute popular culture—that which appeals to an average of tastes—through the mass media. The changes in income distribution, mobility and communication, the economics of mass production already discussed, have caused the power of individual consumers to wane. But the power of consumers as a group has risen and that of producers as a group has dwindled.

With the invention of mass media, a mass market for culture became possible. The economies yielded by the mass production of automobiles became available in the mass production of entertainment. Producers of popular culture supply this new mass market. Popular culture does not *grow* within a group. It is manufactured by one group —in Hollywood or in New York—for sale to an anonymous mass market. The product must meet an average of tastes and it loses in spontaneity and individuality what it gains in accessibility and cheapness. The creators of popular culture are not a sovereign group of "unacknowledged legislators." They work for Hooper ratings to give people what they want. Above all, they are salesmen; they sell entertainment and produce with sales in mind. The creators of high culture are no longer insulated from the demands of the mass market by an educated elite, as they still were during the nineteenth century (and there are no stable, isolated communities in which folk culture could grow). They do not create for or have personal relationships with patrons whom they can lead as a man may lead in a conversation. A personal tutor is much more dependent on a few persons than a television lecturer. But his influence on his pupil is also much greater than the influence of any one television lecturer on any one pupil.

Today's movie producer, singer, or writer is less dependent on the taste of an individual customer, or village, or court, than was the artist of yore; but he does depend far more on the average of tastes, and he can influence it far less. He need not cater to any individual taste—not even his own. He caters to an impersonal market. He is not involved in a conversation. He is like a speaker addressing a mass meeting and attempting to curry its favor.

All mass media in the end alienate people from personal experience and, though appearing to offset it, intensify their moral isolation from each other, from reality and from themselves. One may turn to the mass media when lonely or bored. But mass media, once they become a habit, impair the capacity for meaningful experience. Though more diffuse and not as gripping, the habit feeds on itself, establishing a vicious circle as addictions do.

The mass media do not physically replace individual activities and contacts—excursions, travel, parties, etc. But they impinge on all. The portable radio is taken everywhere—from seashore to mountaintop—and everywhere it isolates the bearer from his surroundings, from other people, and from himself. Most people escape being by themselves at any time by voluntarily tuning in on something or somebody. Anyway, it is nearly beyond the power of individuals to escape broadcasts. Music and public announcements are piped into restaurants, bars, shops, cafes, and lobbies, into public means of transportation, and even taxis. You can turn off your radio but not your neighbor's, nor can you silence his portable or the set at the restaurant. Fortunately, most persons do not seem to miss privacy, the cost of which is even more beyond the average income than the cost of individuality.

People are never quite in one place or group without at the same time, singly or collectively, gravitating somewhere else, abstracted, if not transported by the mass media. The incessant announcements, arpeggios, croonings, sobs, bellows, brayings and jingles draw to some faraway world at large and by weakening community with immediate surroundings make people lonely even when in a crowd and crowded even when alone.

We have already stressed that mass media must offer homogenized fare to meet an average of tastes. Further, whatever the quality of the offerings, the very fact that one after the other is absorbed continuously, indiscriminately and casually, trivializes all. Even the most profound of experiences, articulated too often on the same level, is reduced to a cliché. The impact of each of the offerings of mass media is thus weakened by the next one. But the impact of the stream of all mass-media offerings is cumulative and strong. It lessens people's capacity to experience life itself.

Sometimes it is argued that the audience confuses actuality with mass-media fiction and reacts to the characters and situations that appear in soap operas or comic strips as though they were real. For instance, wedding presents are sent to fictional couples. It seems more likely, however, that the audience prefers to invest fiction with reality—as a person might prefer to dream—without actually confusing it with reality. After all, even the kids know that Hopalong Cassidy is an actor and the adults know that "I Love Lucy" is fiction. Both, however, may attempt to live the fiction because they prefer it to their own lives. The significant effect is not the (quite limited) investment of fiction with reality, but the de-realization of life lived in largely fictitious terms. Art can deepen the perception of reality. But popular culture veils it, diverts from it, and becomes an obstacle to experiencing it. It is not so much an escape from life but an invasion of life first, and ultimately evasion altogether.

Parents, well knowing that mass media can absorb energy, often lighten the strain that the attempts of their children to reach for activity and direct experience would impose; they allow some energy to be absorbed by the vicarious experience of the television screen. Before television, the cradle was rocked, or poppy juice given, to inhibit the initiative and motility of small children. Television, unlike these physical sedatives, tranquillizes by means of substitute gratifications. Manufactured activities and plots are offered to still the child's hunger for experiencing life. They effectively neutralize initiative and channel imagination. But the early introduction of de-individualized characters and situations and early homogenization of taste on a diet of meaningless activity hardly foster development. Perhaps poppy juice, offering no models in which to cast the imagination, was better.

The homogenizing effect of comic books or television, the fact that they neither express nor appeal to individuality, seems far more injurious to the child's mind and character than the violence they feature, though it is the latter that is often blamed for juvenile delinquency. The blame is misplaced. Violence is not new to life or fiction. It waxed large in ancient fables, fairy tales, and in tragedies from Sophocles to Shakespeare.

Mom always knew that "her boy could not have thought of it," that the other boys must have seduced him. The belief that viewing or reading about violence persuades children to engage in it is Mom's ancient conviction disguised as psychiatry. Children are quite spontaneously bloodthirsty and need both direct and fantasy outlets for violence. What is wrong with the violence of the mass media is not that it is violence, but that it is not art—that it is meaningless violence which thrills but does not gratify. The violence of the desire for life and meaning is displaced and appears as a desire for meaningless violence. But the violence which is ceaselessly supplied cannot ultimately gratify it because it does not meet the repressed desire.

We have hinted that the gratifications offered by popular culture are spurious and unsatisfactory. Let us summarize these hints now, and then try to make explicit the psychological effects we implied before.

While immensely augmenting our comforts, our conveniences and our leisure, and disproportionately raising the real income of the poor, industry has also impoverished life. Mass production and consumption, mobility, the homogenization of taste and finally of society were among the costs of higher productivity. They de-individualized life and drained each of our ends of meaning as we achieved it. Pursuit thus became boundless. The increased leisure time would hang heavy on our hands, were it not for the mass media which help us kill it. They inexorably exclude art and anything of significance when it cannot be reduced to mass entertainment, but they divert us from the passage of the time they keep us from filling. They also tend to draw into the mass market talents and works that might otherwise produce new visions and they abstract much of the capacity to experience art or life directly and deeply. What they do, however, is what people demand.

We scrutinized the causes, the effects and the general characteristics of popular culture and found them unavoidable in a mass-production economy. But we have hardly touched on the contents of popular culture. Some work on this subject has been done and much remains. Limitations of scope also restricted us from stressing the many material advantages of industrialism. We do not intend to deny them. Finally, prophecy too is beyond our means. True, extrapolation of present trends makes a dismal picture. But there is comfort in the fact that no extrapolation has ever predicted the future correctly. Elements can be forecast, but only prophets can do more (and they are unreliable, or hard to interpret). History has always had surprises up its sleeves—it would be most surprising if it changed its ways. Our ignorance here leaves the rosy as well as the grim possibilities open for the future. But this does not allow us to avert our gaze from the present and from the outlook it affords. Neither is cheerful.

The gist of any culture is an ethos which gives meaning to the lives of those who dwell in it. If this be the purport of popular culture, it is foiled. We have suggested how it comes to grief in various aspects. What makes popular culture as a whole so disconcerting is best set forth now by exploring the relationship among diversion, art and boredom.

Freud thought of art as a diversion, "an illusion in contrast to reality," a "substitute gratification" like a dream. In this he fully shared what was and still is the popular view of art. It is a correct view—of popular "art," of pseudo-art produced to meet the demand for diversion. But it is a mistaken, reductive definition of art.

Freud finds the "dreamwork" attempting to hide or disguise the dreamer's true wishes and fears so that they may not alarm his consciousness. The "substitute gratification" produced by the dreamwork, mainly by displacements, helps the dreamer continue sleeping. However, one major function of art is precisely to undo this dreamwork, to see through disguises, to reveal to our consciousness the true nature of our wishes and fears. The dreamwork covers, to protect sleep. Art discovers and attempts to awaken the sleeper. Whereas the dreamwork tries to aid repression, the work of art intensifies and deepens perception and experience of the world and of the self. It attempts to pluck the heart of the mystery, to show where "the action lies in its true nature."

Though dreams and art both may disregard literal reality, they do so to answer opposite needs. The dream may ignore reality to keep the sleeper's eyes closed. Art transcends immediate reality to encompass wider views, penetrate into deeper experience and lead to a fuller confrontation of man's predicament. The dreamwork even tries to cover upsetting basic impulses with harmless immediate reality. Art, in contrast, ignores the immediate only to uncover the essential. Artistic revelation need not be concerned with outer or with social reality. It may be purely aesthetic. But it can never be an illusion if it is art. Far from distracting from reality, art is a form of reality which strips life of the fortuitous to lay bare its essentials and permit us to experience them.

In popular culture, however, "art" is all that Freud said art is, and no more. Like the dreamwork, popular culture distorts human experience to draw "substitute gratifications" or reassurances from it. Like the dreamwork, it presents "an illusion in contrast to reality." For this reason, popular "art" falls short of satisfaction. And all of popular culture leaves one vaguely discontented because, like popular art, it is only a "substitute gratification"; like a dream, it distracts from life and from real gratification.

Substitute gratifications are uneconomic, as Freud often stressed. They do not in the end gratify as much, and they cost more psychologically than the real gratifications which they shut out. This is why sublimation and realistic control are to be preferred to substitution and repression. That is why reality is to be preferred to illusion, full experience to symptomatic displacements and defense mechanisms. Yet substitute gratifications, habitually resorted to, incapacitate the individual for real ones. In part they cause or strengthen internalized hindrances to real and gratifying experience; in part they are longed for because internal barriers have already blocked real gratification of the original impulses.

Though the specific role it plays varies with the influence of other formative factors in the life of each individual, popular culture must be counted among the baffling variety of causes and effects of defense mechanisms and repressions. It may do much damage, or do none at all, or be the only relief possible, however deficient. But whenever popular culture plays a major role in life significant repressions have taken (or are taking) place. Popular culture supplants those gratifications, which are no longer sought because of the repression of the original impulses. But it is a substitute and spurious. It founders and cannot succeed because neither desire nor gratification are true. "Nought's had, all's spent/ where desire is got without content."

It may seem paradoxical to describe popular culture in terms of repression. Far from repressed, it strikes one as uninhibited. Yet the seeming paradox disappears if we assume that the uproarious din, the raucous noise and the shouting are attempts to drown the shriek of unused capacities, of repressed individuality, as it is bent into futility.

Repression bars impulses from awareness without satisfying them. This damming up always generates a feeling of futility and apathy or, in defense against it, an agitated need for action. The former may be called listless, the latter restless boredom. They may alternate and they may enter consciousness only through anxiety and a sense of meaninglessness, fatigue and nonfulfillment. Sometimes there is such a general numbing of the eagerness too often turned aside that only a dull feeling of dreariness and emptiness remains. More often, there is an insatiable longing for things to happen. The external world is to supply these events to fill the emptiness. Yet the bored person cannot designate what would satisfy a craving as ceaseless as it is vague. It is not satisfied by any event supplied.

The yearning for diversion to which popular culture caters cannot be sated by diversion "whereof a little more than a little is by much too much," because no displaced craving can be satisfied by catering to it in its displaced form. Only when it becomes possible to experience the desire in its true form and to dispense with the internalized processes that balked and displaced it does actual gratification become possible. Diversion at most, through weariness and fatigue, can numb and distract anxiety.

For instance, in many popular movies the tear ducts are massaged and thrills are produced by mechanized assaults on the centers of sensation. We are diverted temporarily and in the end perhaps drained—but not gratified. Direct manipulation of sensations can produce increases and discharges of tension, as does masturbation, but it is a substitute. It does not involve the whole individual as an individual, it does not involve reality but counterfeits it. Sensations directly stimulated and discharged without being intensified and completed through feelings sifted and acknowledged by the intellect are debasing because they do not involve the whole individual in his relation to reality. When one becomes inured to bypassing reality and individuality in favor of meaningless excitement, ultimate gratification becomes impossible.

Once fundamental impulses are thwarted beyond retrieving, once they are so deeply repressed that no awareness is left of their aims, once the desire for a meaningful life has been lost as well as the capacity to create it, only a void remains. Life fades into tedium when the barrier between impulses and aims is so high that neither penetrates into consciousness and no sublimation whatever takes place. Diversion, however frantic, can overwhelm temporarily but not ultimately relieve the boredom which oozes from nonfulfillment.

Though the bored person hungers for things to happen to him, the disheartening fact is that when they do he empties them of the very meaning he unconsciously yearns for by using them as distractions. In popular culture even the second coming would become just another barren "thrill" to be watched on television till Milton Berle comes on. No distraction can cure boredom, just as the company so unceasingly pursued cannot stave off loneliness. The bored person is lonely for himself, not, as he thinks, for others. He misses the individuality, the capacity for experience from which he is debarred. No distraction can restore it. Hence he goes unrelieved and insatiable.

The popular demand for "inside" stories, for vicarious sharing of the private lives of "personalities" rests on the craving for private life—even someone else's—of those who are dimly aware of having none whatever, or at least no life that holds their interest. The attempts to allay boredom are as assiduous as they are unavailing. Countless books pretend to teach by general rules and devices what cannot be learned by devices and rules. Individual personalities cannot be mass produced (with happiness thrown in or your money back). Nevertheless, the message of much popular culture is "you, too, can be happy" if you only buy this car or that hair tonic; you will be thrilled, you will have adventure, romance, popularity—you will no longer be lonely and left out if you follow this formula. And success, happiness or at least freedom from anxiety is also the burden of popular religion, as unchristian in these its aims as it is in its means. From Dale Carnegie to Norman Vincent Peale to Harry and Bonaro Overstreet only the vocabulary changes. The principle remains the same. The formula is well illustrated in the following.

Warm Smile Is an Attribute of Charm

For this, train the upper lip by this method:

1. Stretch the upper lip down over the teeth. Say "Mo-o-o-o."
2. Hold the lip between the teeth and smile.
3. Purse the lips, pull them downward and grin.
4. Let the lower jaw fall and try to touch your nose with your upper lip.

Months of daily practice are necessary to eliminate strain from the new way of smiling, but it, too, can become as natural as all beguiling smiles must be.

[*Indianapolis News*.]

Whatever the formula, nothing can be more tiresome than the tireless, cheerless pursuit of pleasure. Days go slowly when they are empty; one cannot tell one from the other. And yet the years go fast. When time is endlessly killed, one lives in an endless present until time ends without ever having passed, leaving a person who never lived to exclaim, "I wasted time and now doth time waste me."

To the Christian, despair is a sin not because there is anything to be hoped for in this life, but because to despair is to lack faith in redemption from it—in the life everlasting. As for the pleasures of this life, they are not worth pursuing. Lancelot Andrewes described them: ". . . though they fade not of themselves yet to us they fade. We are hungry and we eat. Eat we not till that fades and we are as weary of our fulness as we were of our fast-ing? We are weary and we rest. Rest we not till that fades and we are as weary of our rest as ever we were of our weariness?" Our bodies and minds themselves fade as do their pleasures. The insults of time are spared to none of us. Such is the human predicament.

In *Civilization and Its Discontents,* Freud pointed to the additional burdens that civilization imposes on human beings. They, too, are inevitable, for civilization, despite its cost, eases the total burden we bear.

A little more than a hundred years ago, Henry David Thoreau wrote in *Walden*: "The mass of men lead lives of quiet desperation. . . . A stereotyped but unconscious despair is concealed even under what are called the games and amusements of mankind." Despair, we find, is no longer quiet. Popular culture tries to exorcise it with much clanging and banging. Perhaps it takes more noise to drone it out. Perhaps we are less willing to face it. But whether wrapped in popular culture, we are less happy than our quieter ancestors, or the natives of Bali, must remain an open question despite all romanticizing. (Nor do we have a feasible alternative to popular culture. Besides, a proposal for "the mass of men" would be unlikely to affect the substance of popular culture. And counsel to individuals must be individual.)

There have been periods happier and others more desperate than ours. But we don't know which. And even an assertion as reasonable as this is a conjecture like any comparison of today's bliss with yesterday's. The happiness felt in disparate groups, in disparate periods and places cannot be measured and compared. Our contention is simply that by distracting from the human predicament and blocking individuation and experience, popular culture impoverishes life without leading to contentment. But whether "the mass of men" felt better or worse without the mass-production techniques of which popular culture is an ineluctable part, we shall never know. Of happiness and of despair, we have no measure.

IV. POLITICS

In the preceding section we dealt with cultural aspects of the mass society. To the politics of that society C. Wright Mills provides a useful introduction. His chapter on "The Mass Society" (here reprinted from *The Power Elite*) traces the transformation of the small and more intimate "public" of early democratic experience into mass society as we now know it, with far fewer people expressing opinions than receiving them, and with far fewer opportunities for meaningful activity.

Mills shows how the elites who control the media of communication are increasingly able to manipulate tastes and opinions, since those at the receiving end cannot answer back. At the top, therefore, according to Mills, power is ever more concentrated, while at the bottom, in the mass, the individual is powerless to influence events and institutions.

Is this an exaggerated picture? Our second selection, "Political Alienation" by Murray B. Levin, suggests not. After a survey of voters in Boston, Levin reports that "a large proportion of the electorate feels politically powerless because it believes that the community is controlled by a small group of powerful and selfish individuals who use public office for personal gain." Men respond to this situation in various ways, often with feelings of apathy about politics, which in turn leads to withdrawal from political activity. Other citizens, equally alienated, express their anxieties by identifying themselves with a "charismatic" leader who they expect will save them.

In his remarkable essay, "Anxiety and Politics," Franz Neumann shows the motives and mechanisms of this process. What he calls "caesaristic identification"—that is, powerful psychological attachment of masses to a leader—arises in time of crisis when "the situation of masses is objectively endangered, when the masses are incapable of understanding the historical process, and when the anxiety activated by the danger becomes neurotic persecutory (aggressive) anxiety through manipulation." Such movements often seize upon some "conspiratorial" theory of history. As Neumann writes, "Just as the masses hope for their deliverance from distress through absolute oneness with a person, so they ascribe their distress to certain persons, who have brought this distress into the world through the conspiracy." Violent hatred is then directed against the "devilish" conspirators. Numerous examples are presented, notably the theory of Communist conspiracy, now such a potent force in American politics, or not long ago among the Nazis the idea of a Jewish plot. As Neumann shows, the result is not merely a break with the "rules of the game" (i.e., a dictatorship replacing a democracy) but, if the mass movement is to retain power, a perpetuation or "institutionalization" of the anxieties which helped to create it. Again, the "cure" is still another form of alienation.

But not only anxiety or fear motivates people to accept radical solutions and break with the past. As our last selection we have chosen Ignazio Silone's account of how he became a Communist. If Silone was alienated and rebellious, it was in his hatred for social injustice in pre-Fascist Italy. But as he himself says, hatred and love were combined: hatred for the conditions in which the people of his district lived; love for those who suffered. When Silone cut his ties to become a member of the Communist Party he found joy and solidarity in his new fellowship. Although Silone later became disillusioned and broke with the Communist Party, he never lost the sense of social justice that had induced him to join the Party in the first place.

THE MASS SOCIETY
/C. Wright Mills

In the standard image of power and decision, no force is held to be as important as The Great American Public. More than merely another check and balance, this public is thought to be the seat of all legitimate power. In official life as in popular folklore, it is held to be the very balance wheel of democratic power. In the end, all liberal theorists rest their notions of the power system upon the political role of this public; all official decisions, as well as private decisions of consequence, are justified as in the public's welfare; all formal proclamations are in its name.

Let us therefore consider the classic public of democratic theory in the generous spirit in which Rousseau once cried, "Opinion, Queen of the World, is not subject to the power of kings; they are themselves its first slaves."

The most important feature of the public of opinion, which the rise of the democratic middle class initiates, is the free ebb and flow of discussion. The possibilities of answering back, of organizing autonomous organs of public opinion, of realizing opinion in action, are held to be established by democratic institutions. The opinion that results from public discussion is understood to be a resolution that is then carried out by public action; it is, in one version, the "general will" of the people, which the legislative organ enacts into law, thus lending to it legal force. Congress, or Parliament, as an institution, crowns all the scattered publics; it is the archetype for each of the little circles of face-to-face citizens discussing their public business.

This eighteenth-century idea of the public of public opinion parallels the economic idea of the market of the free economy. Here is the market composed of freely competing entrepreneurs; there is the public composed of discussion circles of opinion peers. As price is the result of anonymous, equally weighted, bargaining individuals, so public opinion is the result of each man's having thought things out for himself and contributing his voice to the great chorus. To be sure, some might have more influence on the state of opinion than others, but no one group monopolizes the discussion, or by itself determines the opinions that prevail.

Innumerable discussion circles are knit together by mobile people who carry opinions from one to another, and struggle for the power of larger command. The public is thus organized into associations and parties, each representing a set of viewpoints, each trying to acquire a place in the Congress, where the discussion continues. Out of the little circles of people talking with one another, the larger forces of social movements and political parties develop; and the discussion of opinion is the important phase in a total act by which public affairs are conducted.

The autonomy of these discussions is an important element in the idea of public opinion as a democratic legitimation. The opinions formed are actively realized within the prevailing institutions of power; all authoritative agents are made or broken by the prevailing opinions of these publics. And, in so far as the public is frustrated in realizing its demands, its members may go beyond criticism of specific policies; they may question the very legitimations of legal authority. That is one meaning of Jefferson's comment on the need for an occasional "revolution."

The public, so conceived, is the loom of classic, eighteenth-century democracy; discussion is at once the threads and the shuttle tying the discussion circles together. It lies at the root of the conception of authority by discussion, and it is based upon the hope that truth and justice will somehow come out of society as a great apparatus of free discussion. The people are presented with problems. They discuss them. They decide on them. They formulate viewpoints. These viewpoints are organized, and they compete. One viewpoint "wins out." Then the people act out this view, or their representatives are instructed to act it out, and this they promptly do.

Such are the images of the public of classic democracy which are still used as the working justifications of power in American society. But now we must recognize this description as a set of images out of a fairy tale: they are not adequate even as an approximate model of how the American system of power works. The issues that now shape man's fate are neither raised nor decided by the public at large. The idea of the community of publics is not a description of fact, but an assertion of an ideal, an assertion of a legitimation masquerading—as legitimations are now apt to do —as fact. For now the public of public opinion is recognized by all those who have considered it carefully as something less than it once was.

These doubts are asserted positively in the statement that the classic community of publics is being transformed into a society of masses. This transformation, in fact, is one of the keys to the social and psychological meaning of modern life in America.

I. In the democratic society of publics it was assumed, with John Locke, that the individual conscience was the ultimate seat of judgment and hence the final court of appeal. But this principle was challenged—as E. H. Carr has put it—when Rousseau "for the first time thought in terms of the sovereignty of the whole people, and faced the issue of mass democracy."

II. In the democratic society of publics it was assumed that among the individuals who composed it there was a natural and peaceful harmony of interests. But this essentially conservative doctrine gave way to the Utilitarian doctrine that such a harmony of interests had first to be created by reform before it could work, and later to the Marxian doctrine of class struggle, which surely was then, and certainly is now, closer to reality than any assumed harmony of interests.

III. In the democratic society of publics it was assumed that before public action would be taken, there would be rational discussion between individuals which would determine the action, and that, accordingly, the public opinion that resulted would be the infallible voice of reason. But this has been challenged not only (1) by the assumed need for experts to decide delicate and intricate issues, but (2) by the discovery—as by Freud—of the irrationality of the man in the street, and (3) by the discovery—as by Marx—of the socially conditioned nature of what was once assumed to be autonomous reason.

IV. In the democratic society of publics it was assumed that after determining what is true and right and just, the public would act accordingly or see that its representatives did so. In the long run, public opinion will not only be right, but public opinion will prevail. This assumption has been upset by the great gap now existing between the underlying population and those who make decisions in its name, decisions of enormous consequence which the public often does not even know are being made until well after the fact.

Given these assumptions, it is not difficult to understand the articulate optimism of many nineteenth-century thinkers, for the theory of the public is, in many ways, a projection upon the community at large of the intellectual's ideal of the supremacy of intellect. The "evolution of the intellect," Comte asserted, "determines the main course of social evolution." If looking about them, nineteenth-century thinkers still saw irrationality and ignorance and apathy, all that was merely an intellectual lag, to which the spread of education would soon put an end.

How much the cogency of the classic view of the public

rested upon a restriction of this public to the carefully educated is revealed by the fact that by 1859 even John Stuart
Mill was writing of "the tyranny of the majority," and both
Tocqueville and Burckhardt anticipated the view popular-
ized in the recent past by such political moralists as Ortega
y Gasset. In a word, the transformation of public into mass
—and all that this implies—has been at once one of the
major trends of modern societies and one of the major factors in the collapse of that liberal optimism which determined so much of the intellectual mood of the nineteenth
century.

By the middle of that century: individualism had begun
to be replaced by collective forms of economic and political
life; harmony of interests by inharmonious struggle of
classes and organized pressures; rational discussions undermined by expert decisions on complicated issues, by recognition of the interested bias of argument by vested position;
and by the discovery of the effectiveness of irrational appeal to the citizen. Moreover, certain structural changes
of modern society, which we shall presently consider, had
begun to cut off the public from the power of active decision.

The transformation of public into mass is of particular
concern to us, for it provides an important clue to the meaning of the power elite. If that elite is truly responsible to,
or even exists in connection with, a community of publics,
it carries a very different meaning than if such a public is
being transformed into a society of masses.

The United States today is not altogether a mass society, and it has never been altogether a community of
publics. These phrases are names for extreme types; they
point to certain features of reality, but they are themselves
constructions; social reality is always some sort of mixture
of the two. Yet we cannot readily understand just how
much of which is mixed into our situation if we do not first
understand, in terms of explicit dimensions, the clear-cut
and extreme types:

At least four dimensions must be attended to if we are
to grasp the differences between public and mass.

1. There is first, the ratio of the givers of opinion to
the receivers, which is the simplest way to state the social
meaning of the formal media of mass communication. More
than anything else, it is the shift in this ratio which is
central to the problems of the public and of public opinion

in latter-day phases of democracy. At one extreme on the scale of communication, two people talk personally with each other; at the opposite extreme, one spokesman talks impersonally through a network of communications to millions of listeners and viewers. In between these extremes there are assemblages and political rallies, parliamentary sessions, law-court debates, small discussion circles dominated by one man, open discussion circles with talk moving freely back and forth among fifty people, and so on.

II. The second dimension to which we must pay attention is the possibility of answering back an opinion without internal or external reprisals being taken. Technical conditions of the means of communication, in imposing a lower ratio of speakers to listeners, may obviate the possibility of freely answering back. Informal rules, resting upon conventional sanction and upon the informal structure of opinion leadership, may govern who can speak, when, and for how long. Such rules may or may not be in congruence with formal rules and with institutional sanctions which govern the process of communication. In the extreme case, we may conceive of an absolute monopoly of communication to pacified media groups whose members cannot answer back even "in private." At the opposite extreme, the conditions may allow and the rules may uphold the wide and symmetrical formation of opinion.

III. We must also consider the relation of the formation of opinion to its realization in social action, the ease with which opinion is effective in the shaping of decisions of powerful consequence. This opportunity for people to act out their opinions collectively is of course limited by their position in the structure of power. This structure may be such as to limit decisively this capacity, or it may allow or even invite such action. It may confine social action to local areas or it may enlarge the area of opportunity; it may make action intermittent or more or less continuous.

IV. There is, finally, the degree to which institutional authority, with its sanctions and controls, penetrates the public. Here the problem is the degree to which the public has genuine autonomy from instituted authority. At one extreme, no agent of formal authority moves among the autonomous public. At the opposite extreme, the public is terrorized into uniformity by the infiltration of informers and the universalization of suspicion. One thinks of the late Nazi street-and-block system, the eighteenth-century Japanese kumi, the Soviet cell structure. In the extreme, the formal structure of power coincides, as it were, with the informal ebb and flow of influence by discussion, which is thus killed off.

By combining these several points, we can construct little models or diagrams of several types of societies. Since "the problem of public opinion" as we know it is set by the eclipse of the classic bourgeois public, we are here concerned with only two types: public and mass.

In a *public*, as we may understand the term, (1) virtually as many people express opinions as receive them. (2) Public communications are so organized that there is a chance immediately and effectively to answer back any opinion expressed in public. Opinion formed by such discussion (3) readily finds an outlet in effective action, even against—if necessary—the prevailing system of authority. And (4) authoritative institutions do not penetrate the public, which is thus more or less autonomous in its operations. When these conditions prevail, we have the working model of a community of publics, and this model fits closely the several assumptions of classic democratic theory.

At the opposite extreme, in a *mass*, (1) far fewer people express opinions than receive them; for the community of publics becomes an abstract collection of individuals who receive impressions from the mass media. (2) The communications that prevail are so organized that it is difficult or impossible for the individual to answer back immediately or with any effect. (3) The realization of opinion in action is controlled by authorities who organize and control the channels of such action. (4) The mass has no autonomy from institutions; on the contrary, agents of authorized institutions penetrate this mass, reducing any autonomy it may have in the formation of opinion by discussion.

The public and the mass may be most readily distinguished by their dominant modes of communication: in a community of publics, discussion is the ascendant means of communication, and the mass media, if they exist, simply enlarge and animate discussion, linking one *primary public* with the discussions of another. In a mass society, the dominant type of communication is the formal media, and the publics become mere *media markets:* all those exposed to the contents of given mass media.

From almost any angle of vision that we might assume, when we look upon the public, we realize that we have moved a considerable distance along the road to the mass society. At the end of that road there is totalitarianism, as in Nazi Germany or in Communist Russia. We are not yet at that end. In the United States today, media markets are not entirely ascendant over primary publics. But surely we can see that many aspects of the public life of our times are more the features of a mass society than of a community of publics.

What is happening might again be stated in terms of the historical parallel between the economic market and the public of public opinion. In brief, there is a movement from widely scattered little powers to concentrated powers and the attempt at monopoly control from powerful centers, which, being partially hidden, are centers of manipulation as well as of authority. The small shop serving the neighborhood is replaced by the anonymity of the national corporation: mass advertisement replaces the personal influence of opinion between merchant and customer. The political leader hooks up his speech to a national network and speaks, with appropriate personal touches, to a million people he never saw and never will see. Entire brackets of professions and industries are in the "opinion business," impersonally manipulating the public for hire.

In the primary public the competition of opinions goes on between people holding views in the service of their interests and their reasoning. But in the mass society of media markets, competition, if any, goes on between the manipulators with their mass media on the one hand, and the people receiving their propaganda on the other.

Under such conditions, it is not surprising that there should arise a conception of public opinion as a mere reaction—we cannot say "response"—to the content of the mass media. In this view, the public is merely the collectivity of individuals each rather passively exposed to the mass media and rather helplessly opened up to the suggestions and manipulations that flow from these media. The fact of manipulation from centralized points of control constitutes, as it were, an expropriation of the old multitude of little opinion producers and consumers operating in a free and balanced market.

In official circles, the very term itself, "the public"—as Walter Lippmann noted thirty years ago—has come to have a phantom meaning, which dramatically reveals its eclipse. From the standpoint of the deciding elite, some of those who clamor publicly can be identified as Labor, others as Business, still others as Farmer. Those who can *not* readily be so identified make up The Public. In this usage, the public is composed of the unidentified and the non-partisan in a world of defined and partisan interests. It is socially composed of well-educated salaried professionals, especially college professors; of non-unionized employees, especially white-collar people, along with self-employed professionals and small businessmen.

In this faint echo of the classic notion, the public consists of those remnants of the middle classes, old and new, whose interests are not explicitly defined, organized, or clamorous. In a curious adaptation, "the public" often becomes, in fact, "the unattached expert," who, although well informed, has never taken a clear-cut, public stand on controversial issues which are brought to a focus by organized interests. These are the "public" members of the board, the commission, the committee. What the public stands for, accordingly, is often a vagueness of policy (called open-mindedness), a lack of involvement in public affairs (known as reasonableness), and a professional disinterest (known as tolerance).

Some such official members of the public, as in the field of labor-management mediation, start out very young and make a career out of being careful to be informed but never taking a strong position; and there are many others, quite unofficial, who take such professionals as a sort of model. The only trouble is that they are acting as if they were disinterested judges but they do not have the power of judges; hence their reasonableness, their tolerance, and their open-mindedness do not often count for much in the shaping of human affairs.

All those trends that make for the decline of the politician and of his balancing society bear decisively upon the transformation of public into mass. One of the most important of the structural transformations involved is the decline of the voluntary association as a genuine instrument of the public. As we have already seen, the executive ascendancy in economic, military, and political institutions has lowered the effective use of all those voluntary associations which operate between the state and the economy on the one hand, and the family and the individual in the primary group on the other. It is not only that institutions of power have become large-scale and inaccessibly centralized; they have at the same time become less political and more administrative, and it is within this great change of framework that the organized public has waned.

In terms of *scale,* the transformation of public into mass has been underpinned by the shift from a political public decisively restricted in size (by property and education, as well as by sex and age) to a greatly enlarged mass having only the qualifications of citizenship and age.

In terms of *organization,* the transformation has been underpinned by the shift from the individual and his primary community to the voluntary association and the mass party as the major units of organized power.

Voluntary associations have become larger to the extent that they have become effective; and to just that extent they have become inaccessible to the individual who would shape by discussion the policies of the organization to which he belongs. Accordingly, along with older institutions, these voluntary associations have lost their grip on the individual. As more people are drawn into the political arena, these associations become mass in scale; and as the power of the individual becomes more dependent upon such mass associations, they are less accessible to the individual's influence.

Mass democracy means the struggle of powerful and large-scale interest groups and associations, which stand between the big decisions that are made by state, corporation, army, and the will of the individual citizen as a member of the public. Since these middle-level associations are the citizen's major link with decision, his relation to them is of decisive importance. For it is only through them that he exercises such power as he may have.

The gap between the members and the leaders of the mass association is becoming increasingly wider. As soon as a man gets to be a leader of an association large enough to count he readily becomes lost as an instrument of that association. He does so (1) in the interests of maintaining his leading position in, or rather over, his mass association, and he does so (2) because he comes to see himself not as a mere delegate, instructed or not, of the mass association he represents, but as a member of "an elite" composed of such men as himself. These facts, in turn, lead to (3) the big gap between the terms in which issues are debated and resolved among members of this elite, and the terms in which they are presented to the members of the various mass associations. For the decisions that are made must *take into account* those who are important—other elites—but they must be *sold* to the mass memberships.

The gap between speaker and listener, between power and public, leads less to any iron law of oligarchy than to the law of spokesmanship: as the pressure group expands, its leaders come to organize the opinions they "represent." So elections, as we have seen, become contests between two giant and unwieldy parties, neither of which the individual can truly feel that he influences, and neither of which is capable of winning psychologically impressive or politically decisive majorities. And, in all this, the parties are of the same general form as other mass associations.

When we say that man in the mass is without any sense of political belonging, we have in mind a political fact rather than merely a style of feeling. We have in mind (I.) a certain way of belonging (II.) to a certain kind of organization.

I. The way of belonging here implied rests upon a belief in the purposes and in the leaders of an organization, and thus enables men and women freely to be at home within it. To belong in this way is to make the human association a psychological center of one's self, to take into our conscience, deliberately and freely, its rules of conduct and its purposes, which we thus shape and which in turn shape us. We do not have this kind of belonging to any political organization.

II. The kind of organization we have in mind is a voluntary association which has three decisive characteristics: first, it is a context in which reasonable opinions may be formulated; second, it is an agency by which reasonable activities may be undertaken; and third, it is a powerful enough unit, in comparison with other organizations of power, to make a difference.

It is because they do not find available associations at once psychologically meaningful and historically effective that men often feel uneasy in their political and economic loyalties. The effective units of power are now the huge corporation, the inaccessible government, the grim military establishment. Between these, on the one hand, and the family and the small community on the other, we find no intermediate associations in which men feel secure and with which they feel powerful. There is little live political struggle. Instead, there is administration from above, and the political vacuum below. The primary publics are now either so small as to be swamped, and hence give up; or so large as to be merely another feature of the generally distant structure of power, and hence inaccessible.

Public opinion exists when people who are not in the government of a country claim the right to express political opinions freely and publicly, and the right that these opinions should influence or determine the policies, personnel, and actions of their government. In this formal sense there has been and there is a definite public opinion in the United States. And yet, with modern developments this formal right—when it does still exist as a right—does not mean what it once did. The older world of voluntary organization was as different from the world of the mass organization, as was Tom Paine's world of pamphleteering from the world of the mass media.

Since the French Revolution, conservative thinkers have Viewed With Alarm the rise of the public, which they called the masses, or something to that effect. "The populace is sovereign, and the tide of barbarism mounts," wrote Gustave Le Bon. "The divine right of the masses is about to replace the divine right of kings," and already "the destinies of nations are elaborated at present in the heart of the masses, and no longer in the councils of princes." During the twentieth century, liberal and even socialist thinkers have followed suit, with more explicit reference to what we have called the society of masses. From Le Bon to Emil Lederer and Ortega y Gasset, they have held that the influence of the mass is unfortunately increasing.

But surely those who have supposed the masses to be all powerful, or at least well on their way to triumph, are wrong. In our time, as Chakhotin knew, the influence of autonomous collectivities within political life is in fact diminishing. Furthermore, such influence as they do have is guided; they must now be seen not as publics acting autonomously, but as masses manipulated at focal points into crowds of demonstrators. For as publics become masses, masses sometimes become crowds; and, in crowds, the psychical rape by the mass media is supplemented up-close by the harsh and sudden harangue. Then the people in the crowd disperse again—as atomized and submissive masses.

In all modern societies, the autonomous associations standing between the various classes and the state tend to lose their effectiveness as vehicles of reasoned opinion and instruments for the rational exertion of political will. Such associations can be deliberately broken up and thus turned into passive instruments of rule, or they can more slowly wither away from lack of use in the face of centralized means of power. But whether they are destroyed in a week, or wither in a generation, such associations are replaced in virtually every sphere of life by centralized organizations, and it is such organizations with all their new means of power that take charge of the terrorized or—as the case may be—merely intimidated, society of masses.

The institutional trends that make for a society of masses are to a considerable extent a matter of impersonal drift, but the remnants of the public are also exposed to more "personal" and intentional forces. With the broadening of the base of politics within the context of a folk-lore of democratic decision-making, and with the increased means of mass persuasion that are available, the public of public opinion has become the object of intensive efforts to control, manage, manipulate, and increasingly intimidate.

In political, military, economic realms, power becomes, in varying degrees, uneasy before the suspected opinions of masses, and, accordingly, opinion-making becomes an accepted technique of power-holding and power-getting. The minority electorate of the propertied and the educated is replaced by the total suffrage—and intensive campaigns for the vote. The small eighteenth-century professional army is replaced by the mass army of conscripts—and by the problems of nationalist morale. The small shop is replaced by the mass-production industry—and the national advertisement.

As the scale of institutions has become larger and more centralized, so has the range and intensity of the opinion-makers' efforts. The means of opinion-making, in fact, have paralleled in range and efficiency the other institutions of greater scale that cradle the modern society of masses. Accordingly, in addition to their enlarged and centralized means of administration, exploitation, and violence, the modern elite have had placed within their grasp historically unique instruments of psychic management and manipulation, which include universal compulsory education as well as the media of mass communication.

Early observers believed that the increase in the range and volume of the formal means of communication would enlarge and animate the primary public. In such optimistic views—written before radio and television and movies—the formal media are understood as simply multiplying the scope and pace of personal discussion. Modern conditions, Charles Cooley wrote, "enlarge indefinitely the competition of ideas, and whatever has owed its persistence merely to lack of comparison is likely to go, for that which is really congenial to the choosing mind will be all the more cherished and increased." Still excited by the break-up of the conventional consensus of the local community, he saw the new means of communication as furthering the conversational dynamic of classic democracy, and with it the growth of rational and free individuality.

No one really knows all the functions of the mass media, for in their entirety these functions are probably so pervasive and so subtle that they cannot be caught by the means of social research now available. But we do now have reason to believe that these media have helped less to enlarge and animate the discussions of primary publics than to transform them into a set of media markets in mass-like society. I do not refer merely to the higher ratio of deliverers of opinion to receivers and to the decreased chance to answer back; nor do I refer merely to the violent banalization and stereotyping of our very sense organs in terms of which these media now compete for "attention." I have in mind a sort of psychological illiteracy that is facilitated by the media, and that is expressed in several ways:

I. Very little of what we think we know of the social realities of the world have we found out first-hand. Most of "the pictures in our heads" we have gained from these media—even to the point where we often do not really believe what we see before us until we read about it in the paper or hear about it on the radio. The media not only give us information; they guide our very experiences. Our standards of credulity, our standards of reality, tend to be set by these media rather than by our own fragmentary experience.

Accordingly, even if the individual has direct, personal experience of events, it is not really direct and primary: it is organized in stereotypes. It takes long and skillful training to so uproot such stereotypes that an individual sees things freshly, in an unstereotyped manner. One might suppose, for example, that if all the people went through a depression they would all "experience it," and in terms of this experience, that they would all debunk or reject or at least refract what the media say about it. But experience of such a *structural* shift has to be organized and interpreted if it is to count in the making of opinion.

The kind of experience, in short, that might serve as a basis for resistance to mass media is not an experience of raw events, but the experience of meanings. The fleck of interpretation must be there in the experience if we are to use the word experience seriously. And the capacity for such experience is socially implanted. The individual does not trust his own experience, as I have said, until it is confirmed by others or by the media. Usually such direct exposure is not accepted if it disturbs loyalties and beliefs that the individual already holds. To be accepted, it must relieve or justify the feelings that often lie in the back of his mind as key features of his ideological loyalties.

Stereotypes of loyalty underlie beliefs and feelings about given symbols and emblems; they are the very ways in which men see the social world and in terms of which men make up their specific opinions and views of events. They are the results of previous experience, which affect present and future experience. It goes without saying that men are often unaware of these loyalties, that often they could not formulate them explicitly. Yet such general stereotypes make for the acceptance or the rejection of specific opinions not so much by the force of logical consistency as by their emotional affinity and by the way in which they relieve anxieties. To accept opinions in their terms is to gain the good solid feeling of being correct without having to think. When ideological stereotypes and specific opinions are linked in this way, there is a lowering of the kind of anxiety which arises when loyalty and belief are not in accord. Such ideologies lead to a willingness to accept a given line of belief; then there is no need, emotionally or rationally, to overcome resistance to given items in that line; cumulative selections of specific opinions and feelings become the pre-organized attitudes and emotions that shape the opinion-life of the person.

These deeper beliefs and feelings are a sort of lens through which men experience their worlds, they strongly condition acceptance or rejection of specific opinions, and they set men's orientation toward prevailing authorities. Three decades ago, Walter Lippmann saw such prior convictions as biases: they kept men from defining reality in an adequate way. They are still biases. But today they can often be seen as "good biases"; inadequate and misleading as they often are, they are less so than the crackpot realism of the higher authorities and opinion-makers. They are the lower common sense and as such a factor of resistance. But we must recognize, especially when the pace of change is so deep and fast, that common sense is more often common than sense. And, above all, we must recognize that "the common sense" of our children is going to be less the result of any firm social tradition than of the stereotypes carried by the mass media to which they are now so fully exposed. They are the first generation to be so exposed.

II. So long as the media are not entirely monopolized, the individual can play one medium off against another; he can compare them, and hence resist what any one of them puts out. The more genuine competition there is among the media, the more resistance the individual might be able to command. But how much is this now the case? *Do* people compare reports on public events or policies, playing one medium's content off against another's?

The answer is: generally no, very few do: (1) We know that people tend strongly to select those media which carry contents with which they already agree. There is a kind of selection of new opinions on the basis of prior opinions. No one seems to search out such counter-statements as may be found in alternative media offerings. Given radio programs and magazines and newspapers often get a rather consistent public, and thus reinforce their messages in the minds of that public. (2) This idea of playing one medium off against another assumes that the media really have varying contents. It assumes genuine competition, which is not widely true. The media display an apparent variety and competition, but on closer view they seem to compete more in terms of variations on a few standardized themes than of clashing issues. The freedom to raise issues effectively seems more and more to be confined to those few interests that have ready and continual access to these media.

III. The media have not only filtered into our experience of external realities, they have also entered into our very experience of our own selves. They have provided us with new identities and new aspirations of what we should like to be, and what we should like to appear to be. They have provided in the models of conduct they hold out to us a new and larger and more flexible set of appraisals of our very selves. In terms of the modern theory of the self, we may say that the media bring the reader, listener, viewer into the sight of larger, higher reference groups—groups, real or imagined, up-close or vicarious, personally known or distractedly glimpsed—which are looking glasses for his self-image. They have multiplied the groups to which we look for confirmation of our self-image.

More than that: (1) the media tell the man in the mass who he is—they give him identity; (2) they tell him what he wants to be—they give him aspirations; (3) they tell him how to get that way—they give him technique; and (4) they tell him how to feel that he is that way even when he is not—they give him escape. The gaps between the identity and aspiration lead to technique and/or to escape. That is probably the basic psychological formula of the mass media today. But, as a formula, it is not attuned to the development of the human being. It is the formula of a pseudo-world which the media invent and sustain.

IV. As they now generally prevail, the mass media, especially television, often encroach upon the small-scale discussion, and destroy the chance for the reasonable and leisurely and human interchange of opinion. They are an important cause of the destruction of privacy in its full human meaning. That is an important reason why they not only fail as an educational force, but are a malign force: they do not articulate for the viewer or listener the broader sources of his private tensions and anxieties, his inarticulate resentments and half-formed hopes. They neither enable the individual to transcend his narrow milieu nor clarify its private meaning.

The media provide much information and news about what is happening in the world, but they do not often enable the listener or the viewer truly to connect his daily life with these larger realities. They do not connect the information they provide on public issues with the troubles felt by the individual. They do not increase rational in-

sight into tensions, either those in the individual or those
of the society which are reflected in the individual. On the
contrary, they distract him and obscure his chance to understand himself or his world, by fastening his attention
upon artificial frenzies that are resolved within the program framework, usually by violent action or by what is
called humor. In short, for the viewer they are not really
resolved at all. The chief distracting tension of the media
is between the wanting and the not having of commodities
or of women held to be good looking. There is almost always the general tone of animated distraction, of suspended
agitation, but it is going nowhere and it has nowhere to go.

But the media, as now organized and operated, are even
more than a major cause of the transformation of America
into a mass society. They are also among the most important of those increased means of power now at the disposal
of elites of wealth and power; moreover, some of the higher
agents of these media are themselves either among the elites
or very important among their servants.

Alongside or just below the elite, there is the propagandist, the publicity expert, the public-relations man, who
would control the very formation of public opinion in order
to be able to include it as one more pacified item in calcu-
lations of effective power, increased prestige, more secure
wealth. Over the last quarter of a century, the attitudes of
these manipulators toward their task have gone through a
sort of dialectic:

In the beginning, there is great faith in what the mass
media can do. Words win wars or sell soap; they move
people, they restrain people. "Only cost," the advertising
man of the twenties proclaims, "limits the delivery of public opinion in any direction on any topic." The opinion-
maker's belief in the media as mass persuaders almost
amounts to magic—but he can believe mass communications omnipotent only so long as the public is trustful. It
does not remain trustful. The mass media say so very
many and such competitively exaggerated things; they
banalize their message and they cancel one another out.
The "propaganda phobia," in reaction to wartime lies and
postwar disenchantment, does not help matters, even though
memory is both short and subject to official distortion. This
distrust of the magic of media is translated into a slogan

among the opinion managers. Across their banners they write: "Mass Persuasion Is Not Enough."

Frustrated, they reason; and reasoning, they come to accept the principle of social context. To change opinion and activity, they say to one another, we must pay close attention to the full context and lives of the people to be managed. Along with mass persuasion, we must somehow use personal influence; we must reach people in their life context and *through* other people, their daily associates, those whom they trust: we must get at them by some kind of "personal" persuasion. We must not show our hand directly; rather than merely advise or command, we must manipulate.

Now this live and immediate social context in which people live and which exerts a steady expectation upon them is of course what we have called the primary public. Anyone who has seen the inside of an advertising agency or public-relations office knows that the primary public is still the great unsolved problem of the opinion-makers. Negatively, their recognition of the influence of social context upon opinion and public activity implies that the articulate public resists and refracts the communications of the mass media. Positively, this recognition implies that the public is not composed of isolated individuals, but rather of persons who not only have prior opinions that must be reckoned with, but who continually influence each other in complex and intimate, in direct and continual ways.

In their attempts to neutralize or to turn to their own use the articulate public, the opinion-makers try to make it a relay network for their views. If the opinion-makers have so much power that they can act directly and openly upon the primary publics, they may become authoritative; but, if they do not have such power and hence have to operate indirectly and without visibility, they will assume the stance of manipulators.

Authority is power that is explicit and more or less "voluntarily" obeyed; manipulation is the "secret" exercise of power, unknown to those who are influenced. In the model of the classic democratic society, manipulation is not a problem, because formal authority resides in the public itself and in its representatives who are made or broken by the public. In the completely authoritarian society, manipulation is not a problem, because authority is openly identified with the ruling institutions and their agents, who may use authority explicitly and nakedly. They do not, in the extreme case, have to gain or retain power by hiding its exercise.

Manipulation becomes a problem wherever men have power that is concentrated and willful but do not have authority, or when, for any reason, they do not wish to use their power openly. Then the powerful seek to rule without showing their powerfulness. They want to rule, as it were, secretly, without publicized legitimation. It is in this mixed case—as in the intermediate reality of the American today—that manipulation is a prime way of exercising power. Small circles of men are making decisions which they need to have at least authorized by indifferent or recalcitrant people over whom they do not exercise explicit authority. So the small circle tries to manipulate these people into willing acceptance or cheerful support of their decisions or opinions—or at least to the rejection of possible counter-opinions.

Authority *formally* resides "in the people," but the power of initiation is in fact held by small circles of men. That is why the standard strategy of manipulation is to make it appear that the people, or at least, a large group of them, "really made the decision." That is why even when the authority is available, men with access to it may still prefer the secret, quieter ways of manipulation.

But are not the people now more educated? Why not emphasize the spread of education rather than the increased effects of the mass media? The answer, in brief, is that mass education, in many respects, has become— another mass medium.

The prime task of public education, as it came widely to be understood in this country, was political: to make the citizen more knowledgeable and thus better able to think and to judge of public affairs. In time, the function of education shifted from the political to the economic: to train people for better-paying jobs and thus to get ahead. This is especially true of the high-school movement, which has met the business demands for white-collar skills at the public's expense. In large part education has become merely vocational; in so far as its political task is concerned, in many schools, that has been reduced to a routine training of nationalist loyalties.

The training of skills that are of more or less direct use

in the vocational life is an important task to perform, but ought not to be mistaken for liberal education: job advancement, no matter on what levels, is not the same as self-development, although the two are now systematically confused. Among "skills," some are more and some are less relevant to the aims of liberal—that is to say, liberating—education. Skills and values cannot be so easily separated as the academic search for supposedly neutral skills causes us to assume. And especially not when we speak seriously of liberal education. Of course, there is a scale, with skills at one end and values at the other, but it is the middle range of this scale, which one might call sensibilities, that are of most relevance to the classic public.

To train someone to operate a lathe or to read and write is pretty much education of skill; to evoke from people an understanding of what they really want out of their lives or to debate with them stoic, Christian and humanist ways of living, is pretty much a clear-cut education of values. But to assist in the birth among a group of people of those cultural and political and technical sensibilities which would make them genuine members of a genuinely liberal public, this is at once a training in skills and an education of values. It includes a sort of therapy in the ancient sense of clarifying one's knowledge of one's self; it includes the imparting of all those skills of controversy with one's self, which we call thinking; and with others, which we call debate. And the end product of such liberal education of sensibilities is simply the self-educating, self-cultivating man or woman.

The knowledgeable man in the genuine public is able to turn his personal troubles into social issues, to see their relevance for his community and his community's relevance for them. He understands that what he thinks and feels as personal troubles are very often not only that but problems shared by others and indeed not subject to solution by any one individual but only by modifications of the structure of the groups in which he lives and sometimes the structure of the entire society.

Men in masses are gripped by personal troubles, but they are not aware of their true meaning and source. Men in public confront issues, and they are aware of their terms. It is the task of the liberal institution, as of the liberally educated man, continually to translate troubles into issues and issues into the terms of their human meaning for the individual. In the absence of deep and wide political debate, schools for adults and adolescents could perhaps become hospitable frameworks for just such debate. In a community of publics the task of liberal education would be: to keep the public from being overwhelmed; to help produce the disciplined and informed mind that cannot be overwhelmed; to help develop the bold and sensible individual that cannot be sunk by the burdens of mass life. But educational practice has not made knowledge directly relevant to the human need of the troubled person of the twentieth century or to the social practices of the citizens. This citizen cannot now see the roots of his own biases and frustrations, nor think clearly about himself, nor for that matter about anything else. He does not see the frustration of idea, of intellect, by the present organization of society, and he is not able to meet the tasks now confronting "the intelligent citizen."

Educational institutions have not done these things and, except in rare instances, they are not doing them. They have become mere elevators of occupational and social ascent, and, on all levels, they have become politically timid. Moreover, in the hands of "professional educators," many schools have come to operate on an ideology of "life adjustment" that encourages happy acceptance of mass ways of life rather than the struggle for individual and public transcendence.

There is not much doubt that modern regressive educators have adapted their notions of educational content and practice to the idea of the mass. They do not effectively proclaim standards of cultural level and intellectual rigor; rather they often deal in the trivia of vocational tricks and "adjustment to life"—meaning the slack life of masses. "Democratic schools" often mean the furtherance of intellectual mediocrity, vocational training, nationalistic loyalties, and little else.

The structural trends of modern society and the manipulative character of its communication technique come to a point of coincidence in the mass society, which is largely a metropolitan society. The growth of the metropolis, segregating men and women into narrowed routines and environments, causes them to lose any firm sense of their integrity as a public. The members of publics in smaller communities know each other more or less fully, because they meet in the several aspects of the total life routine. The members of masses in a metropolitan society know one another only as fractions in specialized milieux: the man who fixes the car, the girl who serves your lunch, the sales-lady, the women who take care of your child at school during the day. Prejudgment and stereotype flourish when people meet in such ways. The human reality of others does not, cannot, come through.

People, we know, tend to select those formal media which confirm what they already believe and enjoy. In a parallel way, they tend in the metropolitan segregation to come into live touch with those whose opinions are similar to theirs. Others they tend to treat unseriously. In the metropolitan society they develop, in their defense, a blasé manner that reaches deeper than a manner. They do not, accordingly, experience genuine clashes of viewpoint, genuine issues. And when they do, they tend to consider it mere rudeness.

Sunk in their routines, they do not transcend, even by discussion, much less by action, their more or less narrow lives. They do not gain a view of the structure of their society and of their role as a public within it. The city is a structure composed of such little environments, and the people in them tend to be detached from one another. The "stimulating variety" of the city does not stimulate the men and women of "the bedroom belt," the one-class sub-urbs, who can go through life knowing only their own kind. If they do reach for one another, they do so only through stereotypes and prejudiced images of the creatures of other milieux. Each is trapped by his confining circle; each is cut off from easily identifiable groups. It is for people in such narrow milieux that the mass media can create a pseudo-world beyond, and a pseudo-world within themselves as well.

Publics live in milieux but they can transcend them—individually by intellectual effort; socially by public ac-tion. By reflection and debate and by organized action, a community of publics comes to feel itself and comes in fact to be active at points of structural relevance.

But members of a mass exist in milieux and cannot get out of them, either by mind or by activity, except—in the extreme case—under "the organized spontaneity" of the bureaucrat on a motorcycle. We have not yet reached the extreme case, but observing metropolitan man in the Amer-ican mass we can surely see the psychological preparations for it.

We may think of it in this way: When a handful of men do not have jobs, and do not seek work, we look for the causes in their immediate situation and character. But when twelve million men are unemployed, then we cannot believe that all of them suddenly "got lazy" and turned out to be "no good." Economists call this "structural unemployment"—meaning, for one thing, that the men involved cannot themselves control their job chances. Structural unemployment does not originate in one factory or in one town, nor is it due to anything that one factory or one town does or fails to do. Moreover, there is little or nothing that one ordinary man in one factory in one town can do about it when it sweeps over his personal milieu.

Now, this distinction, between social structure and personal milieu, is one of the most important available in the sociological studies. It offers us a ready understanding of the position of "the public" in America today. In every major area of life, the loss of a sense of structure and the submergence into powerless milieux is the cardinal fact. In the military it is most obvious, for here the roles men play are strictly confining; only the command posts at the top afford a view of the structure of the whole, and moreover, this view is a closely guarded official secret. In the division of labor too, the jobs men enact in the economic hierarchies are also more or less narrow milieux and the positions from which a view of the production process as a whole can be had are centralized, as men are alienated not only from the product and the tools of their labor, but from any understanding of the structure and the processes of production. In the political order, in the fragmentation of the lower and in the distracting proliferation of the middle-level organization, men cannot see the whole, cannot see the top, and cannot state the issues that will in fact determine the whole structure in which they live and their place within it.

This loss of any structural view or position is the decisive meaning of the lament over the loss of community. In the great city, the division of milieux and of segregating routines reaches the point of closest contact with the individual and the family, for, although the city is not the unit of prime decision, even the city cannot be seen as a total structure by most of its citizens.

On the one hand, there is the increased scale and centralization of the structure of decision; and, on the other, the increasingly narrow sorting out of men into milieux. From both sides, there is the increased dependence upon the formal media of communication, including those of education itself. But the man in the mass does not gain a transcending view from these media; instead he gets his experience stereotyped, and then he gets sunk further by that experience. He cannot detach himself in order to observe, much less to evaluate, what he is experiencing, much less what he is not experiencing. Rather than that internal discussion we call reflection, he is accompanied through his life-experience with a sort of unconscious, echoing monologue. He has no projects of his own: he fulfills the routines that exist. He does not transcend whatever he is at any moment, because he does not, he cannot, transcend his daily milieux. He is not truly aware of his own daily experience and of its actual standards: he drifts, he fulfills habits, his behavior a result of a planless mixture of the confused standards and the uncriticized expectations that he has taken over from others whom he no longer really knows or trusts, if indeed he ever really did.

He takes things for granted, he makes the best of them, he tries to look ahead—a year or two perhaps, or even longer if he has children or a mortgage—but he does not seriously ask, What do I want? How can I get it? A vague optimism suffuses and sustains him, broken occasionally by little miseries and disappointments that are soon buried. He is smug, from the standpoint of those who think something might be the matter with the mass style of life in the metropolitan frenzy where self-making is an externally busy branch of industry. By what standards does he judge himself and his efforts? What is really important to him? Where are the models of excellence for this man?

He loses his independence, and more importantly, he loses the desire to be independent: in fact, he does not have hold of the idea of being an independent individual with his own mind and his own worked-out way of life. It is not that he likes or does not like this life; it is that the question does not come up sharp and clear so he is not bitter and he is not sweet about conditions and events. He thinks he wants merely to get his share of what is around with as little trouble as he can and with as much fun as possible.

Such order and movement as his life possesses are in conformity with external routines; otherwise his day-to-day experience is a vague chaos—although he often does not know it because, strictly speaking, he does not truly possess or observe his own experience. He does not formulate his desires; they are insinuated into him. And, in the mass, he loses the self-confidence of the human being—if indeed he has ever had it. For life in a society of masses implants insecurity and furthers impotence; it makes men uneasy and vaguely anxious; it isolates the individual from the solid group; it destroys firm group standards. Acting without goals, the man in the mass just feels pointless.

The idea of a mass society suggests the idea of an elite of power. The idea of the public, in contrast, suggests the liberal tradition of a society without any power elite, or at any rate with shifting elites of no sovereign consequence. For, if a genuine public is sovereign, it needs no master; but the masses, in their full development, are sovereign only in some plebiscitarian moment of adulation to an elite as authoritative celebrity. The political structure of a democratic state requires the public; and, the democratic man, in his rhetoric, must assert that this public is the very seat of sovereignty.

But now, given all those forces that have enlarged and centralized the political order and made modern societies less political and more administrative; given the transformation of the old middle classes into something which perhaps should not even be called middle class; given all the mass communications that do not truly communicate; given all the metropolitan segregation that is not community; given the absence of voluntary associations that really connect the public at large with the centers of power—what is happening is the decline of a set of publics that is sovereign only in the most formal and rhetorical sense. Moreover, in many countries the remnants of such publics as remain are now being frightened out of existence. They lose their will for rationally considered decision and action because they do not possess the instruments for such decision and action; they lose their sense of political belonging because they do not belong; they lose their political will because they see no way to realize it.

The top of modern American society is increasingly unified, and often seems willfully co-ordinated: at the top there has emerged an elite of power. The middle levels are a drifting set of stalemated, balancing forces: the middle does not link the bottom with the top. The bottom of this society is politically fragmented, and even as a passive fact, increasingly powerless: at the bottom there is emerging a mass society.

POLITICAL ALIENATION
/Murray Levin

Our analysis of this post-election survey has shown that a large proportion of the electorate feels politically powerless because it believes that the community is controlled by a small group of powerful and selfish individuals who use public office for personal gain. Many voters assume that this power elite is irresponsible and unaffected by the outcome of elections. Those who embrace this view feel that voting is meaningless because they see the candidates as undesirable and the electoral process as a sham. We suggest the term "political alienation" to refer to these attitudes. Since sufficient information is available from other American cities to indicate that feelings of political alienation are widespread, we feel justified in theorizing about the forms of political alienation, the mechanisms by which it is handled, and its implications for democratic politics.

Hegel first used the term alienation to denote man's detachment from nature and himself arising out of man's self-consciousness. Other observers have seen alienation within man, between man and his institutions, and between man and man. They have attributed the origin of feelings of alienation to machinery, mass communications, the size of modern communities, the transition from *gemeinschaft* to *gesellschaft,* original sin, mass society, lack of religion, and capitalist commodity production. Some view alienation as unique to modern society while others see it as a permanent condition.

Feelings of alienation are labeled "good" or "bad" according to whether they arise from causes or lead to results which the critic approves or disapproves. The essential characteristic of the alienated man is his belief that he is not able to fulfill what he believes is his rightful role in society. The alienated man is acutely aware of the discrepancy between who he is and what he believes he should be.

Alienation must be distinguished from two related but not identical concepts: anomie and personal disorganization. Alienation refers to a psychological state of an individual characterized by feelings of estrangement, while anomie refers to a relative normlessness of a social system. Personal disorganization refers to disordered behavior arising from internal conflict within the individual. These states may correlate with one another but they are not identical.

Here we shall examine political alienation as typified in the Boston mayoralty election of 1959. From the Powers-Collins controversy and its outcome we shall delineate four types of political alienation, examine the causes for them, and specify several mechanisms for the handling of feelings of political alienation.

The data collected in this post-election survey indicate that voting was based on distrust and negativism rather than on positive conviction. "Collins is the lesser of two evils. He is not much better than Powers." "Neither candidate appealed to me." "Felt neither one would make a good mayor." "Voting wouldn't do any good." ". . . both no good." "I don't like the caliber of the candidates." "I think they're all the same. It doesn't matter who you vote for." "Felt they were all no good." These negative feelings reflect a widespread belief that politicians are somewhat dishonest. "I guess they're all a little crooked." "A typical Boston politician is a crook." "They tie-up with racketeers— All of them do it." "I don't think he will have too many crooks around." "He probably would not steal as much." "I don't believe he has too much integrity." "I knew they were crooks, but I don't like to see it right on TV." "He gave a lot of double talk." "Talks too much, does very little."

The view that the candidates were primarily interested in furthering their selfish ends rather than the general welfare was expressed by several voters. "He is an opportunist—out for himself with the interest of Boston secondary." "He was against everything that might have helped Boston, was all for himself." "Collins is for Collins."

Some respondents believe that the candidates were obligated to and dominated by a small group of self-interested contributors. "Powers was being sponsored by too many business interests. I mean those people not concerned with the social welfare of the voting public." "Too much of a politician, commitments to groups." "I thought he might be looking out for those racketeers." "Tied up with racketeers." "His affiliation with other big politicians and use of the machine." "Too many prior commitments—too many political entanglements." "You can't tell me Collins didn't have one thousand people on his back." "Collins is a political appointee . . . he must have tie-ins like everybody."

The candidates and their backers were seen as a power elite which controls the city in its own interest. "He is tied up with professionals—type with cigars, part of the South Boston crowd who have the city in their pocket, and take care of themselves." "I don't like the idea that since all the big guys are for him, the little people, like us, should be for him too." "He has too many prior commitments although I don't think he is a racketeer." "Too many apron strings, hard to hold office without doing favors." "His connection with big business. He wasn't doing his own talking."

Campaign contributors are stereotyped as buyers purchasing future political favors. The extravagance of the campaign is interpreted by many as a measure of the degree to which the candidate is under obligation to pay back a profitable return. "He spent too much money campaigning. I thought of where all those funds came from." "Powers was spending so much money and had so much political backing I began to wonder what everybody was expecting to gain from his election." "I felt he made deals with backers of the campaign." "In the Charlestown paper there was so much about Powers I got sick of him. Everyone was supporting him, it seems as though there was a fear of him." "His high-pressure tactics—too much money—too powerful."

Many voters complained that the candidates did not present a serious and meaningful discussion of issues. "He didn't have any program at all and I didn't know what to make of him other than he's done a good job to bring his family up." "He seemed to be more against Powers as an individual rather than on the issues." "In his campaign all he did was attack Powers and hardly ever talked about the issues." "Powers' failure to present a campaign—he didn't have much confidence in the intelligence of the public." "No concrete platform; too evasive." "He didn't say anything and I heard him speak for 45 minutes." "Both men were talking in circles about Boston's needs and how to meet them." "He had a lot of phony talk."

These feelings of the electorate go beyond resentment

toward the particular candidate in this election; they indicate a widespread disgust and disillusionment with the political process and politicians in general: "Voting wouldn't do any good—both no good." This negativism fosters a belief that reform is impossible and highly unlikely, and that it makes little difference which candidate wins the election. Of those who voted for Powers 43 percent thought he would be no better when in office than Collins, while 57 percent of those who voted for Collins thought he would be no better than his opponent. Under these conditions, politics, as it is characterized in American political folklore, tends to lose its meaning. The average voter believes that he is not part of the political structure and that he has no influence upon it.

The attitudes described above are not universally held in Boston. There are voters who believed that their candidate is honest, has integrity, and will fight for the best interest of the community. Some individuals who voted for Collins saw him as "courageous," "honest," "a crusader," and "sincere"; others who voted for Powers pictured him as "intelligent," "experienced," and "honest." However, these views are not shared by a large segment of the electorate who disliked the candidates, distrusted politicians in general, and believed that voting makes no difference. It is this group which feels alienated.

Since feelings of political alienation were so significant in determining the outcome of this election, an analysis of the forms of political alienation is indicated. We believe that this election is sufficiently typical of American municipal elections to warrant putting these conclusions in general terms.

Political alienation is the feeling of an individual that he is not a part of the political process. The politically alienated believe that their vote makes no difference. This belief arises from the feeling that political decisions are made by a group of political insiders who are not responsive to the average citizens—the political outsiders. Political alienation may be expressed in feelings of political powerlessness, meaninglessness, estrangement from political activity, and normlessness.

Political powerlessness is the feeling of an individual that his political action has no influence in determining the course of political events. Those who feel politically powerless do not believe that their vote, or for that matter any action they might perform, can determine the broader outcome they desire. This feeling of powerlessness arises from and contributes to the belief that the community is not controlled by the voters, but rather by a small number of powerful and influential persons who remain in control regardless of the outcome of elections. This theory of social conflict between the powerful and powerless is not identical to the Marxian theory of social conflict between capitalists and proletarians. The powerful are not necessarily capitalists, they may be professional politicians, labor leaders, underworld figures, or businessmen.

Many voters believe that the powerful, who are most often identified as politicians, businessmen, and the underworld, continuously exploit the public. The politician needs campaign contributions, the businessman needs licenses, tax abatements, and city contracts, and the underworld needs police immunity. This provides the setting for the mutually satisfactory relationships among the powerful, from which the average voter is excluded. The feelings of powerlessness among the electorate are sharpened by the view that regardless of the outcome of the election, the powerful remain in control by realigning themselves with the newly elected. These voters view the political process as a secret conspiracy, the object of which is to plunder them.

Political alienation may also be experienced in the form of meaninglessness. An individual may experience feelings of meaninglessness in two ways. He may believe that the election is without meaning because there are no real differences between the candidates, or he may feel that an intelligent and rational decision is impossible because the information upon which, he thinks, such a decision must be made is lacking. The degree of meaninglessness will vary with the disparity between the amount of information considered necessary and that available. If the candidates and platforms are very similar or identical, it will be difficult to find "meaningful" information on which to base a voting decision.

In municipal politics another source of meaninglessness is likely to be present in the nature of city government. In theory, and to a large extent in practice, there are no issues in a controversial sense. Indeed, in the usual textbook version, a city government is a "bundle of services." In practice the political choices available to the administrators of a city government are severely circumscribed by economic re-

alities and by state law. There exist only a small number
of ways in which revenue can be raised and these are generally exploited to their fullest. At the same time the services which the city must maintain pre-empt almost all of
the city's budget. The police force, the fire department, and
the school system must maintain the standards of a going
social system. Therefore the minimal facilities which a city
must provide to maintain its viability tend to be not much
less than the maximal facilities it can achieve with available funds. The municipal public official necessarily operates within a narrow range of alternate programs.

Municipal elections therefore tend to center around the
inefficiency or dishonesty of the administration, not its
program. Consequently, the "honesty" of the candidate is
often the variable about which most information is demanded by voters who wish to make a "meaningful" decision. However, information concerning the honesty of the
candidate is difficult to secure because corrupt and dishonest
activities are carefully hidden from the public. It is precisely the absence of information on this problem which
brings about feelings of meaninglessness.

Under these circumstances an individual who feels alienated in the "meaningless" sense will tend either not to vote,
to believe his vote makes no difference, or to make his decision in terms of what he believes are inadequate standards.
Since relevant factors are absent, many voting decisions
are based on "gut reactions"—intuitive emotional responses
to the candidate's physical appearance, voice, and personality. "Don't like his looks," "tough," "ugly looking," "smug
—looks crooked," "something about his eyes."

Feelings of political meaninglessness give rise to a low
sense of confidence among many voters that their voting
decision was correct: that their candidate would be a better
mayor. When relevant facts are not available, voters cannot
predict the future course of political action with any sense
of certainty. This also contributes to feelings of powerlessness.

Feelings of political alienation may also be experienced in
the sense of the lowering of an individual's political ethics.
This occurs when standards of political behavior are violated in order to achieve some goal. This is likely to occur
when the political structure prevents the attainment of political objectives through institutionally prescribed means.
An example of this would be an individual who believes that

paying off a public official is illegitimate, yet does so. The fact that the individual may be reluctant to bribe a public official does not alter the fact that he is lowering his standards of political ethics.

When individuals believe that corrupt practices are the only ways to achieve political goals and when they feel that corruption is widespread, there will be a greater tendency to resort to it. If the corruption becomes the generally accepted method of dealing with public officials, the stigma attached to it tends to disappear and the political community becomes normless, *i.e.*, anomic.

Political estrangement refers to the inability of an individual to find direct satisfactions in political activity itself, that is, gratification from fulfilling his obligations as a responsible citizen. Both politically active and politically inactive individuals may be politically estranged. Political activists are estranged if their activity is motivated by goals of personal monetary gain rather than a sense of their obligation as citizens. Individuals who do have a sense of community responsibility are likely to find other community activities, such as support of a symphony orchestra, charities, or clubs, a more rewarding way of fulfilling this obligation than being politically active. This is political estrangement.

Four aspects of political alienation—powerlessness, meaninglessness, the lowering of norms, and estrangement —have been distinguished. The extent to which a particular individual is affected by any one of these forms can be related to such variables as social class, age, and religion.

Separation of a population according to income tends to include separation according to education and occupation as well. Data on income were obtained in this survey and will be used as a gross measure of social-class difference. The majority of the Boston electorate, who are elementary or high-school graduates, employed in blue-collar or white-collar jobs, and in the lower-income group, might be expected to feel alienated primarily in the sense of powerlessness. It is this group which is in fact furthest removed from the seats of political power. They have relatively little contact with the city as compared to home owners and businessmen, and when they do have contact, they lack the economic means to participate in the "business" of politics. Collins' major campaign appeal was directed to those who feel powerless. His campaign slogan was "Stop Power Politics," and he presented himself as leading a battle against the politicians. Powers' prolific use of political endorsements did not hinder the image Collins was creating. The data collected in our survey shows that the lower-income groups switched from Powers to Collins in larger proportions than did the middle- or upper-income groups. This implies that feelings of powerlessness were greater in the lower-income groups.

In contrast to the lower-income groups, the upper-income groups, who have more economic power, might be expected to experience political alienation in the forms of meaninglessness, lowering of norms, and estrangement more than in the form of powerlessness. Upper-income groups have more education, which tends to develop more rigorous standards of clarity of information on which to base decisions. The data show that this group had greater interest in political programs and expressed fewer "gut reactions" than did lower-income groups. With higher standards of clarity there are likely to be stronger feelings of political meaninglessness.

The upper-income groups include businessmen and property owners who necessarily have more contact with the city because they may require licenses of various kinds, tax abatements, and building inspection certificates. Since they have economic power, they are in a position to purchase special political consideration. Those who do this will experience political alienation in the form of lowering of political norms.

Upper-income groups include some individuals with a sense of community responsibility. Because of the disjunction of their political values and the political structure, they are likely to be active in nonpolitical civic activities such as charities or service organizations.

Age is another variable related to political alienation. Older persons, who have lived in Boston for many years and have observed the political structure over a long time, might be expected to show greater feelings of alienation. This age group had the largest proportion of individuals who thought that the man they supported would be no better than his opponent. Having observed more elections, they seem to feel more strongly that the effect of their vote makes little difference in the long run.

Religion is another sociocultural variable to be considered. Since Boston is a strongly Catholic city, it might be expected that Protestants and Jews, having less political power, would have stronger feelings of political alienation. In support of this are the facts that a smaller percentage of Protestants and Jews voted than did Catholics and that a greater proportion voted for Collins, whose campaign was largely an appeal to the politically alienated.

Feelings of political alienation may be expressed through rational activism, withdrawal, projection, or identification with a charismatic leader. These are conscious or unconscious mechanisms by which an individual may handle the uncomfortable feelings of political alienation. Some forms of alienation lead to specific mechanisms, for example, feelings of estrangement inevitably lead to withdrawal because gratification is found only in nonpolitical activity. Other forms may result in one or more of several mechanisms, for example, feelings of powerlessness may lead to political activism or to projection and identification with a charismatic leader.

Rational activism is political action based on a realistic evaluation of the political situation, the object of which is to promote a political structure consonant with political values. The frustration arising from political alienation can be a spur to rational activism; feelings of powerlessness can lead to increased political activity. Feelings of meaninglessness can lead to demands for more information rather than withdrawal or "blind" voting. And guilt, resulting from normlessness, can result in activity directed toward raising political standards. Mature individuals, who are those able to tolerate frustration and to act on their beliefs, are those most likely to handle their feelings of political alienation through rational activism. This activity may occur within existing political institutions or it may be directed toward the creation of a new set of political institutions. Rational activism is more likely to be the response to feelings of political alienation when individuals believe that their activity has a reasonable chance of bringing about a change.

Political withdrawal is the removal of an individual's interest and activity from politics. This may occur as a result of a conscious rational decision based on a realistic estimate of the political situation or as an affective, unconscious response. In the latter case the anger and resentment of political alienation may be internalized within the individual rather than expressed outwardly. This mechanism is more likely to occur when the individual feels that any political effort on his part has little chance of producing an effect.

Although an individual may have withdrawn from political interests, he is not likely to escape entirely from politics. Municipal problems of education, traffic, and taxes may affect him personally, or he may note the recurrent exposure of corruption in newspapers. Consequently, additional mechanisms of expression of political alienation are likely to be used. There may be projection, identification with a charismatic leader, or rational activism.

Feelings of anger and resentment which arise from political alienation may be projected on to some other individual or group. This group is seen as participating in a hostile conspiracy. Political leaders may use this mechanism because it establishes a sense of identity between them and the voters to whom they are appealing.

The conspiratorial theory is particularly appealing to individuals who have feelings of powerlessness and normlessness because it accounts for the absence of power and the lowering of values in a simple and easily understood fashion. The individual who projects sees himself as powerless because sinister forces have successfully conspired to destroy the traditional political rules in such a way that he is excluded from exercising his rights. Hofstadter has observed that:

> this kind of thinking frequently occurs when political and social antagonisms are sharp. Certain audiences are especially susceptible to it—particularly, those who have obtained a low level of education, whose access to information is poor, and who are so completely shut out from access to the centers of power that they feel deprived of self-defense and subjected to unlimited manipulation by those who wield power.

Another mechanism for dealing with feelings of political alienation is identification with a charismatic leader. This is the attempt of an individual to feel powerful by incorporating within himself the attitudes, beliefs, and actions held by a leader whom he perceives as powerful. "Charismatic" refers to an extraordinary quality of a person regardless of whether this quality is actual, alleged, or presumed. In taking over the attributes of a charismatic leader, the individual may enter into activity he would otherwise abhor. German *bourgeoisie* who identified with Hitler approved of and took part in behavior their consciences would otherwise not allow them to do.

Rational activism is behavior based on logical reasoning and an undistorted perception of political realities. Withdrawal may be a rational response in some situations and an irrational, affective response in other circumstances. The mechanisms of projection resulting in conspiratorial thinking and identification with a charismatic leader are irrational, affective responses. They are also regressive, in that they are more characteristic of a child's than of an adult's handling of a problem.

When feelings of political alienation are widespread, individuals will adopt one or more of the mechanisms we have described to handle the frustration and anxiety associated with them. The political behavior of each individual will be affected by the particular mechanism or mechanisms he selects.

We have described the forms of political alienation and the mechanisms by which they may be expressed. When political alienation is widespread, it may be a major factor in determining the outcome of an election. The astute politician is aware of this; consequently his strategy takes these factors into account.

The election we have analyzed took place in a community where feelings of political alienation, frustration, and disillusionment with the political process are widespread. When this situation exists, the voting behavior of the electorate is less predictable than otherwise, since a decision is likely to arise from negative rather than from positive convictions and may change on the basis of minor issues, fleeting incidents, or "gut reactions."

The analysis of the statements of the individuals we interviewed shows that they hold an image of the political structure which is similar to that developed by modern political science. They perceive the hierarchical arrangements of power and influence, and they relate various power groupings to each other. They are aware of the uses and abuses of political office; and they know that their role is not one that the grammar-school version of democratic theory taught them. They have, however, greatly exaggerated their lack of power and, perhaps, the extent of corruption. The election, after all, resulted in the downfall of the group associated with one candidate and the elevation to power of another group which probably did not believe it had a serious chance of winning. All the money that was given to the group which lost the election and all the promises that may have been made to the contributors have been to no avail, for the personnel now in power are different. The antagonisms built up during the campaign may mean that the "outs" are really out of City Hall in the near future.

The election upset was to a large extent a response to feelings of political alienation. Senator Powers followed the time-honored rules of campaigning. He spent large amounts of money on advertising which portrayed him as a devoted public servant and friend of the people, shook as many hands as possible, attended numerous house parties, recounted his experience, contributed to charities of all faiths, was photographed with prominent religious leaders, attacked his opponent, and emphasized the support of municipal, state, and national politicians; but although he had 54 percent more votes than Collins in the primary, he failed to win. This has shaken politicians' faith in the traditional vote-getting techniques.

Although there are many reasons why Powers lost, it is clear that one of the most important was the fact that he presented himself as a powerful professional politician—a serious mistake in a community where a considerable amount of political alienation exists. The alienated are not positively disposed toward those whom they identify as powerful. Under these circumstances, the candidate must reevaluate old methods, reformulate his strategy, and experiment with new techniques. A number of countervailing strategies are available to him.

The candidate may create a strong sense of identity with the electorate by presenting himself as the underdog in a struggle against a power elite. Whether he does this or not, he certainly should not emphasize a background of power or the massive support of other political figures who may also be associated with "the powerful." Since an elaborate campaign is viewed as collusion with "the powerful," the candidate must avoid the appearance of an opulent campaign.

Of course, a candidate may appeal to regressive mechanisms of projection and identification with a charismatic leader. Collins successfully appealed to those who tend to think in conspiratorial terms (a form of projection) via his slogan, "Stop power politics, elect a hands-free mayor," and such techniques as his essay contest on a definition of "power politics." The electorate, however, did not view him as a charismatic leader.

The professional politicians may court popular esteem by throwing the support of "the organization" behind a "clean" amateur; that is, some well-known citizen who has not had contact with the politicians and therefore does not share their stigma. The stigma which is attached to "the politician" by the alienated is not likely to rub off on such an individual, at least during the beginning of the campaign. The difficulty with this procedure, from the point of view of "the organization," is that such a candidate may be unreliable.

ANXIETY AND POLITICS
/Franz Neumann

In his Letters "Ueber die aesthetische Erziehung des Menschen," Schiller has magnificently described man in modern society. "Man portrays himself," he writes, "and what a form is presented in the drama of the modern age! Barrenness here, license there; the two extremes of human decay, and both united in a single period." As Rousseau did before him, Schiller indicts civilization itself: "It was culture itself which inflicted this wound on modern humanity." And this wound was inflicted on man by the division of labor: "Gratification is separated from labor, means from ends, effort from reward. Eternally *fettered* only to a single little fragment of the whole, man fashions himself only as a fragment. . . ." His indictment of modern society reaches its climax in the characterization of love: "So jealous is the state for the sole possession of its servants that it would sooner agree (and who could blame it?) to share them with a Venus Cytherea than with a Venus Urania." Schiller has, of course, taken the two forms of the goddess of love from Plato's Symposium and thus identifies Venus Cytherea with venal but Urania with genuine love.

What Schiller describes so impressively is what Hegel and Marx were to characterize as alienation. Schiller contrasts the "polypus nature" of the Greek states, "where each

Translated by Peter Gay.

individual enjoyed an independent existence and, if necessary, could become a whole," with modern society which is one of hierarchical division of labor. Modern society produces a fragmentation not only of social functions but of man himself who, as it were, keeps his different faculties in different pigeonholes—love, labor, leisure, culture—that are somehow held together by an externally operating mechanism that is neither comprehended nor comprehensible. One may—as I do—consider Schiller's (as also Hegel's) analysis of the Greek state as strongly unrealistic and one may, perhaps, even see certain dangers in the glorification of Greece; nevertheless, his analysis of modern man, pointing far beyond his age, remains valid and it is perhaps only today that we have become fully conscious of how true Schiller's Letters are.

In his *Theologische Jugendschriften,* Hegel developed for the first time the concept of alienation. In his draft, entitled "Love," he defined love as the "whole," as "a feeling, but not a single feeling." "In it, life finds itself, as a duplication of its self, and as its unity." But this love is frequently shattered by the resistance of the outside world, the social world of property, a world indeed which man has created through his own labor and knowledge but which has become an alien, a dead world through property. Man is alienated from himself. Since we are here not concerned with the Hegelian concept of alienation, we may pass over the development of his concept.

It is equally unnecessary for us here to develop fully Marx's concept of alienation. For Marx it is the commodity that determines human activity, that is, the objects which are supposed to serve man become the tyrant of man. For according to Marx, who thus fully agrees with Schiller, Hegel, and Feuerbach, man is a universal being. Man is free if he "recognizes himself in a world he has himself made." But that does not happen. Since "alienating labor (1) alienates man from nature, (2) alienates him from himself, his own active function, his life's activity, it alienates man from his species." The separation of labor from the object is thus for him a threefold one: man is alienated from external nature, from himself, and from his fellowmen. The relations of men to one another are reified: personal relations appear as objective relations between things (commodities).

Man, (not only the worker, since the process of alienation

affects society as a whole) is thus for Marx as for Schiller, Feuerbach, and Hegel, a multilated man.

But these theories of alienation are not adequate. While the principles developed by Hegel and Marx must not be given up, these theories need supplementation and deepening. Their inadequacy consists in this, that they oppose universal or nearly universal man (of ancient Greece in Schiller and Hegel) to the mutilated man of the modern world. But there is no historical form of society in which men have ever existed as universal beings; for slavery is not compatible with universality. My meaning may, perhaps, become clearer, if I distinguish three strata of alienation: the stratum of psychology; that of society; and that of politics.

We can get at the problem of alienation, and thus of anxiety in politics, only if we start with a clean separation of the three strata and concepts, in order to bring them together again. Neither alienation nor anxiety is to be found only in modern society and only in modern man, although the different structures of society and of the state modify the forms of expression which alienation and anxiety take. The modifications are hard to determine, and I shall not attempt here to undertake a systematic analysis. But I shall try to point up the problem and to make the theory somewhat more concrete by means of (more or less arbitrary) examples.

Freud's thesis in his *Civilization and its Discontents* is this: "The goal toward which the pleasure-principle impels us—of becoming happy—is not attainable"; because for Freud suffering springs from three sources: external nature, which we can never dominate completely, the susceptibility to illness and the mortality of the body, and social institutions.

However, the statement that society prevents happiness, and consequently that every socio-political institution is repressive, does not lead to hostility toward civilization. For the limitation, which is imposed upon the libidinal as well as the destructive instincts, creates conflicts, inescapable conflicts, which are the very motors of progress in history. But conflicts deepen with the progress of civilization, for Freud states that increasing technical progress, which in itself ought to make possible a greater measure of instinct gratification, fails to do so. There arises here a psychological lag that grows ever wider—a formulation that I should like to borrow from the "cultural lag" of American sociology.

Thus, every society is built upon the renunciation of instinctual gratifications. Freud finds that it is "not easy to understand how it can become possible to withold satisfaction from an instinct. Nor is it by any means without risk to do so; if the deprivation is not made good economically, one can be certain of producing serious disorders."

To be sure, according to Freud it is conceivable "that a civilized community could consist of pairs of individuals (who love each other) libidinally satisfied in each other, and linked to all the others by work and common interests. If this were so, culture would not need to levy energy from sexuality." But the opposite is true and has always been true. For at bottom Freud does not believe in this "conceivable ideal." The differences between the different forms of society—which are decisive for us—do not play a decisive role for him. The renunciation of instinctual gratification and the cultural tendency toward the limitation of love operate at all levels of society. It is these renunciations and limitations which we characterize as psychological alienation of man, or perhaps even better as alienation of the ego from the dynamics of instinct.

Still another preparatory step is necessary: we have to establish the logical connection between alienation and anxiety. This is extremely difficult because the discussion of the problem of anxiety has by no means reached the clarity which would make it possible for an outsider—like myself—to adopt an unambiguous position toward the various opinions. Nevertheless it seems to me that the differences in the conception of the origin of anxiety do not have a decisive significance for my analysis, although they are, of course, highly relevant in other contexts. Freud himself had originally derived anxiety from the repression of libidinous impulses, and thus had seen it as an automatic transformation of instinctual energy. This view he later modified. Others claim, on the other hand, that there is a single inborn faculty for being afraid. Rank, in his famous work, derives anxiety from the trauma of birth. And a number of analysts have tried, more or less successfully, to combine the various theories in many ways.

The following propositions seem to me more or less acceptable.

One must distinguish between true anxiety (*Realangst*) and neurotic anxiety. The difference is of considerable consequence especially for the understanding of the political importance of anxiety. The first—true anxiety—thus appears as a reaction to concrete danger situations; the second —neurotic anxiety—is produced by the ego, in order to avoid in advance even the remotest threat of danger. True anxiety is thus produced through the threat of an external object; neurotic anxiety, which may have a real basis, on the other hand is produced from within, through the ego.

Since anxiety is produced by the ego, the seat of anxiety is in the ego, not in the id—the structure of instincts. But from the analysis of the problem of psychological alienation it follows necessarily that anxiety, feelings of guilt, and the need for self-punishment are responses to internal threats to basic instinctual demands so that anxiety exists as a permanent condition. The external dangers which threaten a man meet the inner anxiety and are thus frequently experienced as even more dangerous than they really are. At the same time, these same external dangers intensify the inner anxiety. The painful tension which is evoked by the combination of inner anxiety and external danger can express itself in either of two forms: in depressive or in persecutory anxiety. The differentiation is important because it helps us to evaluate the political function of anxiety more correctly.

In the history of the individual there are certain typical dangers which produce anxiety. For the child, the withdrawal of love is of decisive importance. On this point there seems to be no doubt among psychologists. From the numerous phobias we may learn a great deal about the relation between anxiety and the renunciation of instinctual gratification. For inhibitions are a functional restraint of the ego; the ego renounces many activities in order to avoid a conflict with the id and the conscience. We know that the phobic symptoms are a substitute for gratifications of the instincts that have been denied or are unattainable. In other words, the ego creates anxiety through repression.

If I have correctly reproduced the most important results of analytical theory concerning the origin of anxiety, several important consequences for the analysis of political behavior seem to follow immediately. Anxiety can play very different roles in the life of men; that is, the activation of a state of anxiety through a danger can have a beneficial as well as destructive effect. We may perhaps distinguish three different consequences:

a) Anxiety can play a warning role, a kind of mentor role, for man. Affective anxiety may allow a presentiment of external dangers. Thus, anxiety also contains a protective function for it permits man to take precautions in order to ward off the danger.

b) Anxiety can have a destructive effect, especially when the neurotic element is strongly present; that is, it can make man incapable of collecting himself either to escape the danger or to fight against it; it can paralyze man and degenerate into a panicky anxiety.

c) Finally, anxiety can have a cathartic effect; man can be strengthened inwardly when he has successfully avoided a danger or when he has prevailed against it. One may perhaps even say (although I cannot prove this) that the man who has conquered anxiety in coming to terms with a danger, may be more capable of making decisions in freedom than the one who never had to seriously wrestle with a danger. This may be an important qualification of the proposition that anxiety can make free decision impossible.

Our analysis of the relation of alienation to anxiety does not yet permit us to understand the political significance of these phenomena, because it is still in the realm of individual psychology. How does it happen that masses sell their souls to leaders and follow them blindly? On what does the power of attraction of leaders over masses rest? What are the historical situations in which this identification of leader and masses is successful, and what view of history do the men have who accept leaders?

Thus the question concerning the essence of identification of masses and a leader stands in the center of group-psychological analysis. Without it the problem of the integration or collectivization of the individual in a mass cannot be understood. I assume that the history of the theories of group psychology is familiar. The extraordinary difficulty in the comprehension of group-psychological phenomena lies first of all in our own prejudices; for the experiences of the last decades have instilled in us all more or less strong prejudices against the masses, and we associate with "masses" the epithet "mob," a group of men who are capable of every atrocity. In fact the science of group psychology began with this aristocratic prejudice in the work of the Italian, Scipio Sighèle; and Le Bon's famous book is completely in this tradition. His theses are familiar. Man in the mass descends; he is, as it were, hypnotized by the leader *(operateur)* and in this condition is capable of committing acts which he would never commit as an individual. As the slave of unconscious—i.e., for Le Bon, regressive —sentiments, man in the mass is degraded into a barbarian: "Isolated, he may be a cultivated individual; in a crowd, he is a barbarian—that is, a creature acting by instinct. He possesses the spontaneity, the violence, the ferocity, and also the enthusiasm and heroism of primitive beings." Critics of Le Bon, among them Freud, have pointed out that his theory, which rests on Sighele and Tarde, is inadequate in two aspects: the answer to the question, What holds the masses together? is inadequate, for the existence of a "racial soul" is unproved. In addition, in Le Bon the decisive problem—the role of the leader-hypnotist—remains unclarified. As is frequently true in social-psychological studies, the descriptions of psychological states are adequate, the theoretical analyses, the answers to "Why?," are inadequate.

From the outset, Freud sees the problem in the way in which we have put it, namely, as that of the identification of masses with a leader—an identification which becomes of decisive significance particularly in an anxiety situation. And he sees in the libido the cement which holds leader and masses together, whereby, as is known, the concept of libido is to be taken in a very broad sense, to include the instinctual activities which "in relations between the sexes ... force their way toward sexual union," as well as those which "in other circumstances ... are diverted from this aim or are prevented from reaching it, though always preserving enough of their original nature to keep their identity recognizable (as in such features as the longings for proximity, and self-sacrifice)."

The cement which holds the mass together and ties them to the leader is thus a sum of instincts that are inhibited in their aims. In this manner, I believe, the logical connection between alienation and mass behavior has been established.

Since the identification of masses with the leader is an alienation of the individual member, identification always constitutes a regression, and a twofold one. On the one hand, the history of man is the history of his emergence from the primal horde and of his progressive individualization; thus the identification with a leader in a mass is a kind of *historical* regression. This identification is also a "substitute for a libidinal object tie," thus a *psychological* regression, a damaging of the ego, perhaps even the loss of the ego.

But this judgment is valid only for the libido-charged, i.e., affective, identification of an individual in a mass with a leader; and not as a matter of course (and perhaps not at all) for that of lovers and of small groups. Non-affective identification too, cannot be simply considered as regressive. For identification with organizations (church, army) is not always libidinally charged. MacDougall's emphasis on the significance of organization must therefore be taken seriously.

It is thus necessary to make distinctions. There are non-affective identifications, in which coercion or common material interests play an essential role, either in bureaucratic-hierarchic, or in cooperative form. It seems to me to be incorrect, above all for recent history, to see in the identification of the soldier with the army, i.e., in the loyalty to an organization, an actual identification of the soldier with the commander-in-chief. Surely there are examples of this: Alexander, Hannibal, Caesar, Wallenstein, Napoleon. But the commander-in-chief of the twentieth century is much more the technician of war than the leader of men, and the libidinal tie of the soldier is, if I may coin the phrase, essentially cooperative, namely, with the smallest group of comrades with whom he shares dangers.

Thus I would like to establish two fundamental types of identification: a libido-charged (affective) and a libido-free (non-affective); and maintain generally (as it follows from MacDougall's psychology) that the non-affective identification with an organization is less regressive than the affective identification with a leader. Non-affective loyalty is transferable; personal loyalty, on the other hand, is not. The former always contains strong rationalist elements, elements of calculability between organization and individual, and thus prevents the total extinction of the ego.

But I believe that one must also distinguish two types within affective identification. One may call them cooperative and caesaristic. It is conceivable (and it has probably happened in short periods in history) that many equals identify themselves cooperatively with one another in such a manner that their egos are merged in the collective ego. But this cooperative form is rare, limited to short periods or in any case operative only for small groups. The decisive affective identification is that of masses with leaders. It is —as I have said—the most regressive form, for it is built upon a nearly total ego-shrinkage. It is the form which is of decisive significance for us. We call it caesaristic identification.

Caesaristic identifications may play a role in history when the situation of masses is objectively endangered, when the masses are incapable of understanding the historical process, and when the anxiety activated by the danger becomes neurotic persecutory (aggressive) anxiety through manipulation.

From this follows, first of all, that not every situation dangerous to masses must lead to a caesaristic movement; it follows, further, that not every mass movement is based on anxiety, and thus not every mass movement need be caesaristic.

Thus it is a question of determining the historical conditions in which a regressive movement under a Caesar tries to win political power.

However, before we describe these historical situations, I may perhaps point to a clue which will frequently permit us an early diagnosis of the regressive character of such a mass movement. This clue is the view of history which the masses and the leaders employ. It may be called the conspiracy theory of history, a theory of history characterized by a false concreteness. The connection between caesarism and this view of history is quite evident. Just as the masses hope for their deliverance from distress through absolute oneness with a person, so they ascribe their distress to certain persons, who have brought this distress into the world through a conspiracy. The historical process is personified in this manner. Hatred, resentment, dread created by great upheavals, are concentrated on certain persons who are denounced as devilish conspirators. Nothing would be more incorrect than to characterize the enemies as scapegoats (as often happens in the literature), for they appear as genuine enemies whom one must extirpate and not as substitutes whom one only needs to send into the wilderness. It is a false concreteness and therefore an especially dangerous view of history. Indeed, the danger consists in the fact that this view of history is never completely false, but always contains a kernel of truth and, indeed, must contain it, if it is to have a convincing effect. The truer it is, one might say, the less regressive the movement; the falser, the more regressive.

It is my thesis that wherever affective (i.e., caesaristic) leader-identifications occur in politics, masses and leader have this view of history: that the distress which has befallen the masses has been brought about exclusively by a conspiracy of certain persons or groups against the people.

With this view of history, true anxiety, which had been produced by war, want, hunger, anarchy, is to be transformed into neurotic anxiety and is to be overcome by means of identification with the leader-demagogue through total ego-renunciation, to the advantage of the leader and his clique, whose true interests do not necessarily have to correspond to those of the masses.

Of course, I cannot provide conclusive proof, but I believe that by pointing to certain historical events I can make clear the connection between this view of history and caesarism.

An interesting affective identification of leader and masses is the relation of Cola di Rienzo to the Roman people. I assume that his story is familiar—the rise of the hack lawyer, son of a Roman innkeeper and a washerwoman, to Tribune of the Roman people and dictator of Rome, his expulsion and return with the aid of the Church, and his assassination by the Colonna family in the year 1354. The view of history of Cola and of the Roman people was quite simple: Rome has been ruined by feudal lords; their destruction will permit Rome to rise again to its ancient greatness. This is how Petrarca formulates it in his famous letter of congratulation to Cola: "These barons in whose defense you (the Romans) have so often shed your blood, whom you have nourished with your own substance . . . these barons have judged you unworthy of liberty. They have gathered the mangled remnants of the state in the caverns and abominable retreats of bandits. . . . They have been restrained neither by pity for their unhappy country, nor by love for it. . . . Do not suffer any of the rapacious wolves whom you have driven from the fold to rush again into your midst. Even now they are prowling restlessly around, endeavoring through fraud and deceit . . . to regain an entrance to the city whence they were violently expelled." It cannot be denied that the feudal lords, above all the Colonna and Orsini, had pursued a criminal policy. Without this element of truth Cola's propaganda and policy would never have been successful. But fundamentally this was a false concreteness—for even if he had succeeded in liquidating the barons, what would have been decisively improved in Rome? The historical facts—the residence of the Papal Court in Avignon; the economic decay of Rome; the regrouping of class relations through the rise of the bourgeois *cavalerotti*—all that Cola could not change. It can hardly be doubted that anxiety, even purely physical fear of the arbitrariness of the barons, drove the people to Cola. Cola succeeded in strengthening this anxiety by extremely skillful propaganda and achieved victory. But the leader himself must feel no anxiety or at least must not show it. He must stand above the masses. But in this Cola was deficient. In all other matters his relation corresponded exactly to that of the libido-charged identification leader-masses, and it is regrettable that time does not permit me to describe and analyze his propaganda themes, his ceremonial, and his ritual. It was Cola's fundamental mistake that he was not enough of a Caesar. To be sure, he publicly humiliated the barons, but he did not liquidate them—whether out of cowardice, decency, or tactical considerations. But the masses of Rome expected that he would act in accordance with their view of history. He did not do this. Thus he had to fall.

I have mentioned Cola di Rienzo because it is a marginal case in which it is doubtful whether we are dealing with a regressive or progressive movement, that is, a movement which really has the realization of the freedom of man as its goal.

The eight French religious wars of the sixteenth century furnish excellent material for the illumination of the character of caesaristic as well as organizational identifications. All three parties—Huguenots, Catholics, and *Politiques* —were faced with grave problems: the disintegration of the old society through silver inflation, loss of wealth on the one hand, enrichment on the other, the beginnings of radical changes in class relations and the dissolution of the absolute monarchy after the death of Francis I. It is against this background that the religious wars must be understood. Their course is doubtless familiar to you.

Catholics and Protestants alike saw the problem of France only as a religious problem, and therefore ascribed the distress of France exclusively to their religious opponents, conjectured (partly justifiably) that these opponents represented a great and sinister conspiracy, developed or employed theories of caesaristic identification, and consistently proceeded to extirpate the opponent wherever opportunity offered.

The Huguenot pamphleteer Francois Hotman in his *Tiger* saw in the Cardinal Guise "a detestable monster," whose aim it was to ruin France, to assassinate the King, and to conspire with the aid of the women near the King and the High Constable of France against "the crown of France, the goods of widows and orphans, the blood of the poor and innocent." Calvin's theory of the secular redeemer sent by God to overthrow tyrants—in the seventeenth century the basis of Cromwell's leadership—became the Protestant theory of caesarism. The Catholics—with a longer tradition of tyrannicide—developed a pseudo-democratic theory of identification, above all in the writings of the Leaguist preachers and Jesuits. In these inflammatory pamphlets whose demagogy even surpasses that of the Huguenots, the theory of democracy is fitted out with theocratic traits, the masses of the people are integrated through the social contract, in order to be identified with Henry of Guise with the aid of the theocratic element. Whoever takes the trouble to study the eighth religious war (the War of the 3 Henrys) and the Parisian uprising, will find there all the elements which I consider decisive: appeal to anxiety, personification of evils, first with Henry III, then with Henry of Navarre, identification of the masses with Henry of Guise.

Both positions, the Catholic and the Huguenot, are similarly regressive, while that of the *Politiques,* which Henry IV was later to convert into action, is incomparably more progressive. Indeed, the great merit of the chief representative of the party of the *Politiques,* Jean Bodin, consists in this: he saw the economic problems of France clearly; he understood the false concreteness of the view of history of both parties. If he championed absolute monarchy—that is, the identification of the people with the monarch—he did so because he was to place himself above the religions that were fighting each other and to ally himself with the households of the third estate in order to save France. Despite the absolute submission to the prince which is demanded of the people, this identification contains the two rational elements which I mentioned before: loyalty becomes transferable, i.e., the office is separated from the officeholder; and the relation between citizen and state becomes rational. Thus Bodin has a certain justification in calling his theory a theory of the constitutional state (*droit gouvernement*) despite his absolutism. I believe that the French religious wars of the sixteenth century make my thesis a little clearer: that the non-affective identification with an institution (state) is less regressive than identification with a leader.

Naturally I cannot here discuss all similar situations. The religious struggles of the sixteenth and seventeenth centuries are full of such historical constructions.

One need only read, for example, the terrible Calvinist fanatic John Knox in his famous *First Blast of the Trumpet against the Monstrous Regiment of Women* and we will find there: "We se our countrie set furthe for a pray to foreine nations, we heare the blood of our brethren, the membres of Christ Iesus most cruelly to be shed, and the monstruous empire of a cruell woman . . . we knowe to be the onlie occasion of all these miseries." The rule of the Catholic Catherine de Medici, of Marie of Lorraine (the predecessor of Mary Stuart), and of Mary Tudor appears here not only as a violation of divine commandment (because God has subjected women to men) but as a genuine conspiracy against the true religion. Unfortunately, John Knox had the ill luck of seeing Protestantism restored in England by a woman, and he apologized to Elizabeth in a *Second Blast* for his first attack.

Instead of continuing with this survey, it may perhaps be more useful to discuss five fundamental models of conspiracy theories, all of which show this sequence: intensification of anxiety through manipulation, identification, false concreteness. They are:

    a) the Jesuit conspiracy
    b) the Freemason conspiracy
    c) the Communist conspiracy
    d) the Capitalist conspiracy
    e) the Jewish conspiracy.

The *Jesuit order* is indeed defined by many as a conspiracy, and the Monita Secreta of 1614, composed by a Polish ex-Jesuit, fulfills the need for a secret plan of operations with the help of which one can hold the order responsible for every crime and every misfortune and can stir up the masses. This has always been relatively simple in times of crisis. St. Bartholomew's Night, the assassination of Henry III by Jacques Clément, the attempt on the life of Henry IV by Barrière and Chastel as well as his assassination by Ravaignac, the English Gunpowder plot of 1605, the outbreak of the Thirty Years' War, to say nothing of innumerable less important crimes and misfortunes, were ascribed to the Jesuits. That these tales should have been believed, is naturally connected with the significance of false concreteness in politics. There is some truth in many of these accusations. It is precisely in this element of truth that the danger of these views of history lies.

The denunciation of the *freemasons* is a similar matter. Thus, the English believed the Jacobite conspiracies to be the work of freemasons; the French Revolution was ascribed to a mysterious group of Bavarian Illuminati, and this view of history again is closely connected with the anti-Jesuit one, since the Bavarian Illuminati had been founded by Adam Weishaupt in 1776 in order to combat the influence of the Jesuits. Again these assertions have some truth in them. Most of the Encyclopedists were freemasons and more than half of the members of the Estates General belonged to freemasonic lodges. But surely no detailed discussion is needed to show that the conspiracy theory represents a blurring of history.

The theory of the *Communist conspiracy* follows the same model and serves the same purposes. Thus the Russian October Revolution is explained solely as a Blanquist conspiracy, embodied in Trotsky's military revolutionary committee; the German Revolution of 1918 is laid to the charge of the devilish Lenin; the seizure of power by the Bolsheviks in the satellite states is traced back to sinister conspiracies in the Kremlin, and generally the relation of Bolshevism to the world is equated with that of a conspiracy of a small group against the welfare of humanity. Again, this is partly true. The October Revolution was a conspiracy —but in a definite historical situation and with an ideology. The Bolsheviks would gladly have manipulated the German Revolution of 1918—but they had neither the means nor the intelligence to do it, nor could they, even if cleverer, have prevailed in the concrete situation. The Communists in the satellite states naturally conspired—but they could come to power only because the Red Army stood behind them and because the objective situation favored them. No conspiracy, no matter how clever, would have been of any use and was of any use in Western Europe. Nevertheless, the conspiracy theory is believed not only by the masses, but even by serious writers who, strongly under the influence of Pareto's simplistic antithesis between elite and masses, generally tend to see in politics nothing but the manipulation of the masses by elites, and for whom psychology and political science are nothing but techniques of manipulation.

The purpose of the theory is clear: potential anxiety—whose concrete significance still needs to be clarified—is actualized by reference to the devilish conspirators: family, property, morality, religion are threatened by the conspiracy. Anxiety easily becomes neurotic persecutory anxiety, which in turn can, under certain circumstances, lead to a totalitarian mass movement.

We could cite a great many more cases in which history was viewed with false concreteness. Especially American history is full of examples of such movements. There is, for instance, the Know-Nothing Party of 1854-55 with its hatred of the Irish Catholics and the German immigrants. It originated in the secret "Order of the Star-Spangled-Banner" which was founded by native-born Protestants; they mistreated Catholics and when asked about the Order they would answer, "I know nothing."

The Ku Klux Klan is better known. Fear of status loss on the part of the whites, especially of the poor whites, vis-à-vis the Negroes and fear of the Pope and the Catholics were the basic factors which made this secret society into a terroristic organization, from its foundation in 1867 to the present day.

The Populist Party (1892), on the other hand, was born out of an agrarian depression, as a protest against the rule of the railway, industrial, and credit monopolies, and against the gold standard. One of its leaders developed a genuine theory of conspiracy: "According to my views of the subject the conspiracy which seems to have been formed here and in Europe to destroy . . . from three-sevenths to one-half of the metallic money of the world, is the most gigantic crime of this or any other age." (Quoted in S. E. Morrison and H. S. Commager, *The Growth of the American Republic,* Vol. II [1940], p. 245.)

In similar fashion, Bolshevism operates with the *theory of capitalist encirclement,* in which the capitalists as a rule are personified by Wall Street. Now again there can be no doubt that there was a policy of encirclement against Bolshevist Russia at the beginning of the revolution; but it would be fatal to believe that the terror was the consequence of the policy of intervention and of the cold war. Possibly the policy of encirclement strengthened the terror, just as the wars of intervention during the French Revolution gave Robespierre's Terror a new impetus. But the terror as a normal method of politics against the class opponent is contained in the Leninist definition of the dictatorship of the proletariat; it was then extended to the party and finally to the supposedly classless society, without a visible connection with the intensity of the capitalist policy of encirclement. But the Bolshevist view of history, steadily activating anxiety, made possible identification with the leader Stalin and thus underpinned his caesarist dictatorship.

The most important type—if only because of its immense political influence—is the theory of the *conspiracy of the Jews* according to the *Protocols of the Elders of Zion*. These contain the secret plans of Jewish leaders, supposedly formulated in the year 1897, for achieving Jewish world domination by force, terror, corruption, the disintegrating influence of liberalism, freemasonry, etc. This world domination was to be a mock-democracy, through which the Jewish leaders were to operate. That the *Protocols* are a forgery, prepared by Czarist Russians, was definitely established by the Bern trial of 1934-35. It is equally beyond question that they are essentially a plagiarism of the work by Maurice Joly directed against Napoleon III, *Dialogue aux Enfers entre Machiavel et Montesquieu*.

But if the *Protocols* represent a forgery, and if the plans for a Jewish world conspiracy belong in the realm of mythology, where then does that kernel of truth lie which according to my view is necessary to make possible the influence which anti-Semitism and the *Protocols* have had? I shall confine my analysis to Germany, but the German situation can be understood only when one becomes aware of the fact that in Germany before 1933 spontaneous anti-Semitism was extremely weak. As early as 1942, I wrote, in opposition to an almost unanimous opinion: "The writer's personal conviction, paradoxical as it may seem, is that the German people are the least anti-Semitic of all." I still hold to this view today; for it is precisely the weakness of spontaneous anti-Semitism in Germany which explains the concentration of National Socialism on it as the decisive political weapon.

The element of truth (if one may call it that) is first of all a religious one: the catechistic representation of the crucifixion and with it the blood guilt of the Jews. But this is a thoroughly ambivalent element: for it is precisely the crucifixion of Christ which makes possible the salvation of Christians (and all men); and the spiritually Semitic origin of Christianity is acknowledged by the Church. While thus the historical-religious defamation of the Jews forms the basis without which anti-Semitism could hardly be activated, the catechistic representation of the crucifixion is not sufficient by itself. The existence of a total anti-Semitism can perhaps be better understood if we start from the policy of National Socialism and seek to understand the role of anti-Semitism within the political system. I can sketch the problem only in its broadest outlines. Germany of 1930-33 was the land of alienation and anxiety. The facts are familiar: defeat, a tame, unfinished revolution, inflation, depression, non-identification with the existing political parties, non-functioning of the political system—all these are symptoms of moral, social, and political homelessness. The inability to understand why man should be so hard-pressed stimulated anxiety which was made into nearly neurotic anxiety by the National Socialist policy of terror and its propaganda of anti-Semitism. The goal of National Socialism was clear: the welding together of the people with the charismatic leader, for the purpose of the conquest of Europe and perhaps of the world, and the creation of a racial hegemony of the Germans over all other peoples.

But how was the people to be integrated, despite all cleavages of class, party, religion? Only through hatred of an enemy. But how could one settle on the enemy? It could not be Bolshevism, because it was too strong; the Catholic Church could not be so designated because it was needed politically and loyalties to it were anchored too securely. The Jews remained. They appeared in the public consciousness as powerful, but were in reality weak. They were relative strangers, and at the same time the concrete symbols of a so-called parasitical capitalism, through their position in commerce and finance; they incarnated a supposedly decadent morality through their *avant garde* position in art and literature; they seemed to be the successful competitors sexually and professionally. With all this, the thesis of the Jewish conspiracy had the element of truth necessary to permit this view of history to become a frightful weapon. It would be mistaken to want to construe a connection between the socio-economic status of a person and his anti-Semitism; that is, to claim that the academically educated person is more immune than the uneducated, or the poorly paid more immune than the better paid. What is correct, however, is that there exists a connection between loss of social status and anti-Semitism. The fear of social degradation thus creates for itself "a target for the discharge of the resentments arising from damaged self-esteem." [Harold D. Lasswell.]

This leads us to the analysis of the historical situations in which anxiety grips the masses.

We have distinguished three strata of alienation. The psychological stratum remains no matter what social institutions man lives in. It creates potential anxiety which man in the mass attempts to overcome through ego-surrender. This affective identification with a leader is facilitated by the notion of false concreteness, the theory of conspiracy.

But so far we have not yet said when such regressive mass movements are activated; that is, when potential anxiety can be activated in such a manner that it can become a cruel weapon in the hands of irresponsible leaders.

In order to get at this problem we must take into account the two other strata of alienation: the social and political.

Alienation of labor: it is the separation of labor from the product of labor through hierarchical division of labor which characterizes modern industrial society. Probably no one doubts that the division of labor as well as the hierarchical organization of labor have shown a steady rise since the industrial revolution of the eighteenth century. German romantic psychology of labor calls this the "despiritualization of labor" (*Entseelung der Arbeit*). This concept as well as the various remedies are dangerous— for they cover up the inevitability of this process of alienation which must be admitted, understood, and accepted. If this does not happen, if one refuses to take account of the inevitability of the division of labor and of the hierarchical ordering of the process of labor, and attempts to "spiritualize" labor instead of restricting it to a minimum, then social anxiety is deepened. The attitude of the so-called "new middle class" (salaried employees) can be understood from this process.

While the so-called new middle class does labor which—to remain with the language of German psychology of labor—is "more de-spiritualized" than that of the industrial worker, and although his average income probably lies below that of the industrial worker, he yet holds fast to his middle class ideology and customs. Thus he refuses to take account of the inevitability of the process and—as in Germany before 1933—becomes the social stratum most susceptible to caesarism.

In a society which is constituted by competition, the competitor is supposed to be rewarded for his effort when he is competent; that is, when he exerts himself, is intelligent, and accepts risks. There is little doubt that the principle of competition dominates not only the economy but all social relations. Karen Horney, a representative of Freudian revisionism, claims that the destructive character of competition creates great anxiety in neurotic persons. Now this is not convincing when genuine competition really prevails, that is, competition in which relatively equally strong persons fight with fair methods; that is, the kind of competition which Adam Smith defines in his *Theory of Moral Sentiments* as follows: "One individual must never prefer himself so much even to any other individual as to hurt or injure that other in order to benefit himself, though the benefit of the one should be much greater than the hurt or injury to the other." And again, "In the race for wealth and honours and preferments, each may run as hard as he can and strain every nerve and every muscle in order to outstrip all his competitors. But if he jostle or throw down any of them, the indulgence of the spectator is entirely at an end. It is in violation of fair play, which they cannot admit of." I cannot here undertake a social analysis to show that this ethically circumscribed competition does not exist and perhaps never has existed, that in reality a monopolist struggle hides behind it, that, in other words, the efforts of the individual, his intelligence, his vision, his readiness to take risks, are easily shattered by the constellations of power.

Behind the mask of competition, which must not necessarily have destructive effects if it rationally organizes a society, there hide in fact relations of dependence. To be successful in present-day society, it is much more important to stand in well with the powerful than to preserve oneself through one's own strength. Modern man knows this. It is precisely the impotence of the individual who has to accommodate himself to the technological apparatus which is destructive and anxiety-creating.

But even where genuine competition is effective, no effort will help if crises ruin the merchant. The inability to understand the process of crises, and the frequent need to ascribe blame for them to sinister powers, is an additional factor in the destruction of ego. This psychological process operated in the so-called "old middle class" of Germany before 1933. But—to repeat—it is hard to see why fair competition must have destructive functions.

In every society that is composed of antagonistic groups there is an ascent and descent of groups. It is my contention that persecutory anxiety—but one that, as we said above, has a real basis—is produced when a group is threatened in its prestige, income, or even its existence; i.e., when it declines and does not understand the historical process or is prevented from understanding it. The examples are too numerous to be possibly mentioned here. German National Socialism and Italian Fascism are classical examples.

But not only social classes resist their degradation by means of such mass movements; religious and racial conflicts, too, frequently produce similar phenomena. The conflict between Negroes and whites in the southern states of the United States, the contemporary struggle of the South African government against the natives, take place in accord with the following scheme: the anxiety of a dominant white minority that it will be degraded through the economic and political rise of Negroes is used in propagandist fashion for the creation of affective mass movements, which frequently take on a fascist character.

Social alienation, i.e., the fear of social degradation, is not adequate by itself. The elements of political alienation must be added. Since I devote a separate essay to this phenomenon, I shall only point out briefly what I have in mind. As a rule one is satisfied (above all, in the American literature) with defining abstention from voting at elections as political apathy. But I have pointed out elsewhere that the word "apathy" describes three different political reactions: first, the lack of interest in politics, say, the opinion that politics is not the business of the citizen because it is, after all, only a struggle between small cliques and that therefore fundamentally nothing ever changes; then, the Epicurean attitude toward politics, the view that politics and state only have to supply the element of order within which man devotes himself to his perfection, so that forms of state and of government appear as secondary matters; and finally, as the third reaction, the conscious rejection of the whole political system which expresses itself as apathy because the individual sees no possibility of changing anything in the system through his efforts. Political life can, for example, be exhausted in the competition of political parties which are purely machines without mass participation, but which monopolize politics to such an extent that a new party cannot make its way within the valid rules of the game. This third form of apathy forms the core of what I characterize as political alienation. Usually this apathy, if it operates within social alienation, leads to the partial paralysis of the state and opens the way to a caesarist movement which, scorning the rules of the game, utilizes the inability of the citizen to make individual decisions and compensates for the loss of ego with identification with a Caesar.

The caesaristic movement is compelled not only to activate but to institutionalize anxiety. The institutionalization of anxiety is necessary because the caesaristic movement can never endure a long wait for power. This is precisely what follows from its affective basis. While the non-affective mass organization, such as a normal political party, can exist for a long time without disintegrating, the caesarist movement must hurry precisely because of the instability of the cement that holds it together: the libido-charged affectivity. After it has come to power it faces the need of institutionalizing anxiety as a means of preventing the extinction of its affective base by its bureaucratic structure.

The techniques are familiar: propaganda and terror, i.e., the incalculability of sanctions. I do not need to discuss this here. Montesquieu, building on Aristotle and Machiavelli, distinguished between one tyrannical and three constitutional governmental and social systems. According to him, monarchy rests on the honor of the monarch; aristocracy, on the moderation of the aristocrats; democracy, on virtue (i.e., with him, patriotism); but tyranny, on fear. It must, however, not be overlooked—and our introductory remarks about alienation and anxiety had no other meaning—that every political system is based on anxiety. But there is more than a quantitative difference between the anxiety which is institutionalized in a totally repressive system and that which is the basis of a halfway liberal one. These are qualitatively different states of affairs. One may perhaps say that the totally repressive system institutionalizes depressive and persecutory anxiety, the halfway liberal system, true anxiety.

Once the connection between anxiety and guilt is seen, it will at once become obvious that these are different states of affairs.

In his *Peloponnesian War*, Thucydides reports the following about Sparta: "Indeed fear of their [the Helots'] numbers and obstinacy even persuaded the Lacedaemonians to the action which I shall now relate. . . . The Helots were invited by a proclamation to pick out those of their number who claimed to have most distinguished themselves against the enemy, in order that they might receive their freedom; the object being to test them, as it was thought that the first to claim their freedom would be the most high-spirited and the most apt to rebel. As many as two thousand were selected accordingly, who crowned themselves and went round the temples, rejoicing in their new freedom. The Spartans, however, soon afterwards did away with them, and no one ever knew how each of them perished."

With his customary psychological penetration this greatest of all historians saw clearly the connection of anxiety and collective guilt. And then we read Plutarch's description of the terrible Cryptia, the Spartan secret police: "By this ordinance, the magistrates [i.e., the Ephors] dispatched privately some of the ablest of the young men into the country, from time to time, armed only with their daggers, and taking a little necessary provision with them; in the daytime, they hid themselves in out-of-the-way places, and there lay close, but in the night issued out into the highways and killed all the helots they could light upon." Here is a striking example of what we have in mind.

Who does not here think of Dostoyevsky's *The Possessed*, when Stavrogin gives the following piece of advice: "All that business of titles and sentimentalism is a very good cement, but there is something better; persuade four members of the circle to do for a fifth on the pretence that he is a traitor, and you'll tie them all together with the blood they've shed as though it were a knot. They'll be your slaves, they won't dare to rebel or call you to account.

Ha ha ha!" This famous passage in Dostoyevsky is important not only because it verifies our psychological theory, but also because it shows at the same time that the leader activates anxiety through guilt for his own advantage, not for the sake of the led.

I do not wish here to discuss the psychological theory concerning the relation of anxiety and guilt. According to Freud, man's feeling of guilt stems from the Oedipus complex. It is this aggression that the child represses and thus effects an unconscious feeling of guilt. The feeling of guilt is the superego, man's conscience. But that is precisely why the intensification of the unconscious feeling of guilt permits man to become a criminal.

If one examines the Spartan example, Stavrogin's advice, the Fehme-murders, and the collective crimes of the SS, one may perhaps undertake the following psychological analysis:

There are anxiety and an unconscious feeling of guilt. It is the task of the leader, by creating neurotic anxiety, to tie the led so closely to the leader that they would perish without identification with him. Then the leader orders the commission of crimes; but these are, in accord with the morality that prevails in the group—with the Lacedaemonians, the Nihilists, the SS—no crimes, but fundamentally moral acts. But the conscience—the superego—protests against the morality of the crimes, for the old moral convictions cannot simply be extirpated. The feeling of guilt is thus repressed and makes anxiety a nearly panicky one, which can be overcome only through unconditional surrender to the leader and compels the commission of new crimes.

This is how I see the connection between anxiety and guilt in a totally repressive society. Hence this anxiety is qualitatively different from the anxiety that is the basis of every political system.

You will ask me, "What can be done to prevent anxiety—which cannot be eliminated—from becoming neurotic-destructive? Can the state accomplish this?" Schiller—and with this we return to our point of departure—denies this in his Seventh Letter. He asks and replies: "Should we expect this effect from the state? That is impossible, since the state, as at present constituted, has caused the evil, and the ideal state of reason cannot be the foundation of this improved humanity but must itself be founded thereon."

As educators we may thus perhaps say that education deserves the first rank. But Schiller replies to this in the Ninth Letter with the question, "But are we not proceeding in a circle? Theoretical culture is supposed to induce the practical, and yet the latter is to be the condition of the former? All political improvements should result from education of character—but how can the character ennoble itself under the influence of a barbarous civil polity?"

Surely there are also other individual solutions—such as love. But it is, after all, accidental whether or not one experiences it, and the risk can be enormous with loss of object.

Hence there remains for us as citizens of the university and of the state the dual offensive on anxiety and for liberty: that of education and that of politics.

Politics, again, should be a dual thing for us: the penetration of the subject matter of our academic discipline with the problems of politics—naturally not day-to-day politics—and the taking of positions on political questions. If we are serious about the humanization of politics; if we wish to prevent a demagogue from using anxiety and apathy, then we—as teachers and students—must not be silent. We must suppress our arrogance, inertia, and our revulsion from the alleged dirt of day-to-day politics. We must speak and write. Idealism, as it is expressed so nobly in Schiller's Letters, must not be for us only a beautiful façade, it must not once more become that notorious form of idealism which in the past disguised the most reactionary and antilibertarian aims.

Only through our own responsible educational and political activity can the words of idealism become history.

THE MAKING OF A COMMUNIST
/Ignazio Silone

At the age of seventeen, and in time of war, one does not join a revolutionary movement which is persecuted by the government, unless one's motives are serious.

I grew up in a mountainous district of southern Italy. The phenomenon which most impressed me, when I arrived at the age of reason, was the violent contrast, the incomprehensible, absurd, monstrous contrast between family and private life—in the main decent, honest, and well-conducted—and social relations, which were very often crude and full of hatred and deceit. Many terrifying stories are known of the misery and desperation of the southern provinces (I have told some myself), but I do not intend to refer now to events that caused a stir, so much as to the little occurrences of daily life. It was these commonplace minor events that showed up the strange double existence of the people among whom I grew up, the observation of which was one of the agonizing secrets of my adolescence.

I was a child just five years old when, one Sunday, while crossing the little square of my native village with my mother leading me by the hand, I witnessed the cruel, stupid spectacle of one of the local gentry setting his great dog at a poor woman, a seamstress, who was just coming out of church. The wretched woman was flung to the ground, badly mauled, and her dress was torn to ribbons. Indignation in the village was general, but silent. I have never understood how the poor woman ever got the unhappy idea of taking proceedings against the squire; but the only result was to add a mockery of justice to the harm already done. Although, I must repeat, everybody pitied her and many people helped her secretly, the unfortunate woman could not find a single witness prepared to give evidence before the magistrate, nor a lawyer to conduct the prosecution. On the other hand, the squire's supposedly left-wing lawyer turned up punctually, and so did a number of bribed witnesses who perjured themselves by giving a grotesque version of what had happened, and accusing the woman of having provoked the dog. The magistrate—a most worthy, honest person in private life—acquitted the squire and condemned the poor woman to pay the costs.

"It went very much against the grain with me," he excused himself a few days later at our house. "On my word of honor, I do assure you, I was very sorry about it. But even if I had been present at the disgusting incident as a private citizen and couldn't have avoided blaming him, still as a judge I had to go by the evidence of the case, and unfortunately it was in favor of the dog." "A real judge," he used to love to say, sententiously, "must be able to conceal his own egoistic feelings, and be impartial." "Really, you know," my mother used to comment, "it's a horrible profession. Better to keep ourselves to ourselves at home. My son," she used to say to me, "when you're grown up, be whatever you like, but not a judge."

I can remember other typical little incidents like that of the squire, the dog, and the seamstress. But I should not like to suggest, by quoting such episodes, that we were ignorant of the sacred concepts of Justice and Truth or that we held them in contempt. On the contrary; at school, in church, and at public celebrations they were often discussed with eloquence and veneration, but in rather abstract terms. To define our curious situation more exactly, I should add that it was based on a deception of which all of us, even the children, were aware; and yet it still persisted, being built on something quite apart from the ignorance and stupidity of individuals.

I remember a lively discussion one day in my catechism class between the boys who were being prepared for confirmation and the parish priest. The subject was a marionette show at which we boys had been present with the priest the day before. It was about the dramatic adventures of a child who was persecuted by the devil. At one point the child-marionette had appeared on the stage trembling with fear and, to escape the devil who was searching for him, had hidden under a bed in a corner of the stage; shortly afterward the devil-marionette arrived and looked for him in vain. "But he *must* be here," said the devil-marionette. "I can smell him. Now I'll ask these good people in the audience." And he turned to us and asked: "My dear children, have you by any chance seen that naughty child I'm looking for, hiding anywhere?" "No, no, no," we all chorused at once, as energetically as possible. "Where is he then? I can't see him," the devil insisted. "He's left, he's gone away," we all shouted. "He's gone to Lisbon." (In our part of Italy, Lisbon is still the furthermost point of the globe, even today.) I should add that none of us, when we went to the theater, had expected to be questioned by a devil-marionette; our behavior was therefore entirely instinctive and spontaneous. And I imagine that children in any other part of the world would have reacted in the same way. But our parish priest, a most worthy, cultured and pious person, was not altogether pleased. We had told a lie, he warned us with a worried look. We had told it for good ends, of course, but still it remained a lie. One must never tell lies. "Not even to the devil?" we asked in surprise. "A lie is always a sin," the priest replied. "Even to the magistrate?" asked one of the boys. The priest rebuked him severely. "I'm here to teach you Christian doctrine and not to talk nonsense. What happens outside the church is no concern of mine." And he began to explain the doctrine about truth and lies in general in the most eloquent language. But that day the question of lies *in general* was of no interest to us children; we wanted to know, "Ought we to have told the devil where the child was hiding, yes or no?" "That's not the point," the poor priest kept repeating to us rather uneasily. "A lie is always a lie. It might be a big sin, a medium sin, an average sort of sin, or a little tiny sin, but it's always a sin. Truth must be honored."

"The truth is," we said, "that there was the devil on one side and the child on the other. We wanted to help the child, that's the real truth." "But you've told a lie," the parish priest kept on repeating. "For good ends, I know, but still a lie." To end it, I put forward an objection of unheard-of perfidy, and, considering my age, considerable precocity: "If it'd been a priest instead of a child," I asked, "what ought we to have replied to the devil?" The parish priest blushed, avoided a reply, and, as a punishment for my impertinence, made me spend the rest of the lesson on my knees beside him, "Are you sorry?" he asked me at the end of the lesson. "Of course," I replied. "If the devil asks me for your address, I'll give it to him at once."

It was certainly unusual for a discussion in such terms to take place in a catechism class, although free discussion was quite frequent in our family circle and among our friends. But this intellectual liveliness did not even create a stir in the humiliating and primitive stagnation of our social life.

Some time earlier the so-called democratic system had, however, introduced a new technical detail into the relations between citizen and State. This was the secret vote, which though not in itself enough to change things radically, sometimes produced results which were surprising, and, as far as public order was concerned, scandalous. Though these incidents were isolated and had no immediate sequel, they were none the less disturbing.

I was seven years old when the first election campaign, which I can remember, took place in my district. At that time we still had no political parties, so the announcement of this campaign was received with very little interest. But popular feeling ran high when it was disclosed that one of the candidates was "the Prince." There was no need to add Christian and surname to realize which Prince was meant. He was the owner of the great estate formed by the arbitrary occupation of the vast tracts of land reclaimed in the previous century from the Lake of Fucino. About eight thousand families (that is, the majority of the local population) are still employed today in cultivating the estate's fourteen thousand hectares. The Prince was deigning to solicit "his" families for their vote so that he could become their deputy in parliament. The agents of the estate, who were working for the Prince, talked in impeccably liberal phrases: "Naturally," said they, "naturally, no one will be forced to vote for the Prince, that's understood; in the same way that no one, naturally, can force the Prince to allow people who don't vote for him to work on his land. This is the period of real liberty for everybody; you're free, and so is the Prince." The announcement of these "liberal" principles produced general and understandable consternation among the peasants. For, as may easily be guessed, the Prince was the most hated person in our part of the country. As long as he remained in the invisible Olympus of the great feudal proprietor (none of the eight thousand tenants had seen him, up to then, even from afar) public hatred for him was allowed, and belonged to the same category as curses against hostile deities; such curses, though useless, are satisfying. But now the clouds were being rent, and the Prince was coming down within reach of mortal men. From now on, consequently, they would have to keep their expressions of hatred within the narrow circle of private life and get ready to welcome him with due honors in the village streets.

My father seemed reluctant to accept this kind of logic. He was the youngest of several brothers, all of them peasant proprietors; the youngest, the most restless, and the only one with any inclinations toward insubordination. One evening his older brothers came and urged him, in the common interest, to be prudent and careful. For me (to whom no one paid any attention, for grown-ups think that children don't understand such things) it was a most instructive evening. "The Prince being a candidate is a real farce," the eldest brother admitted. "Political candidatures should be reserved for lawyers and other such windbags. But as the Prince is a candidate, all we can do is support him." "If the

Prince's candidature is a farce," replied my father, "I don't understand why we should support him." "Because we're his dependents, as you know perfectly well." "Not in politics," said my father. "In politics we're free." "We don't cultivate politics, we cultivate the land," they answered him. "As cultivators of the land we depend on the Prince." "There's no mention of politics in our contracts for the land, only of potatoes and beetroots. As voters we're free." "The Prince's bailiff will also be free not to renew our contracts," they answered him. "That's why we're forced to be on his side." "I can't vote for someone merely because I'm forced to," said my father. "I'd feel humiliated." "No one will know how you vote," they answered him. "In the secrecy of the polling booth you can vote as you like, freely. But during the electioneering campaign we must be on the Prince's side, all of us together." "I'd be pleased to do it if I wasn't ashamed to," said my father, "but, do believe me, I'd be too much ashamed." To settle it, my uncles and my father reached this compromise: he would not come out either on the Prince's side or against him.

The Prince's election tour was prepared by the civil authorities, the police, the carabineers, and the agents of the estate. One Sunday, the Prince deigned to pass through the principal villages in the constituency, without stopping and without making any speeches. This tour of his was remembered for a long time in our district, mainly because he made it in a motorcar, and it was the first time we had seen one. The word "motorcar" itself had not yet found a place in our everyday language, and the peasants called it a "horseless carriage." Strange legends were current among the people about the invisible motive force which took the place of the horses, about the diabolical speed which the new vehicle could reach, and about the ruinous effect, particularly on the vines, of the stink it left behind it. That Sunday the entire population of the village had gone to meet the Prince on the road by which he was due to arrive. There were numerous visible signs of the collective admiration and affection for the Prince. The crowds were dressed up in their best, and were in a perfectly understandable state of excitement. The "horseless carriage" arrived late, and roared through the crowd and the village, without stopping and without even slowing down, leaving a thick white dust cloud behind it. The Prince's agents then explained, to anyone who cared to listen, that the "horseless carriage" went by "petrol vapor" and could only stop when the petrol had finished. "It isn't like horses," they explained, "where all one need do is to pull on the reins. There aren't any reins at all. Did you notice any reins?"

Two days later a strange little old man arrived from Rome; he wore glasses, and had a black stick and a small suitcase. Nobody knew him. He said he was an oculist and had put himself up as candidate against the Prince. A few people gathered round him out of curiosity, mainly children and women, who had not the right to vote. I was among the children, in my short trousers and with my schoolbooks under my arm. We begged the old man to make a speech. He said to us: "Remind your parents that the vote is secret. Nothing else." Then he said, "I am poor; I live by being an oculist; but if any of you have anything wrong with your eyes I'm willing to treat them for nothing." So we brought him an old woman who sold vegetables. She had bad eyes, and he cleaned them up and gave her a little phial with drops in it and explained how to use it. Then he said to us (we were only a group of children): "Remind your parents that the vote is secret," and he went away. But the Prince's election was so certain, to judge by the festive throngs which had welcomed him during his electioneering tour, that the authorities and the agents of the estate had announced in advance a whole program for the celebration of the inevitable victory. My father, according to the agreement with his brothers, did not side with either candidate, but managed to get himself included among the scrutineers of the ballot-papers. Great was everybody's surprise when it became known that in the secrecy of the polling booths an enormous majority had voted against the Prince and for the unknown oculist. It was a great scandal; the authorities called it sheer treachery. But the treachery was of such proportions that the agents of the estate could not take any reprisals against anyone.

After this, social life went back to normal. Nobody asked himself: Why can the will of the people only express itself sporadically? Why can it not become a permanent and stable basis for the reorganization of public life? And yet, it would be incorrect to conclude, from a false interpretation of the episode I have just recorded, that the major obstacle was fear. Our people have never been cowardly or spineless or weak. On the contrary the rigors of the climate, the heaviness of the work, the harsh conditions of the struggle for existence, have made them into one of the toughest, hardest, and most enduring peoples in the whole of Italy. So much so, that there are fewer references in our local annals to political surprises resulting from the secret vote than there are to revolts, localized and short-lived, but violent, destructive and almost savage. These humiliated and downtrodden people could endure the worst abuses without complaint, but then they would break out on unforeseen occasions.

My native village, at the period to which I am now refer-ring, had some five thousand inhabitants, and public order was in the keeping of about twenty carabineers, commanded by a lieutenant. This excessive number of police is in itself revealing. There was not much sympathy between the sol-diers and the carabineers during the First World War, be-cause the latter were on duty in the rear areas, and some of them, it was said, took too much interest in the wives and fiancées of the men at the front. In small places, rumors of this kind are immediately given a very exact personal application. So it happened one evening that three soldiers, home from the front on short leave, had a quarrel with some carabineers and were arrested by them. This action was ridiculous and ungallant to begin with, but it became absolutely monstrous when the commanding officer of the carabineers canceled the three soldiers' leave and sent them back to the front. I was a close friend of one of them (he was killed in the war afterward), and his old mother came sobbing to me to tell me about the affair. I begged the mayor, the magistrate and the parish priest to intervene, but they all declared it was outside their province. "If that's the way things are," I said, "there's nothing for it but *rev-olution!*" We have always used this fateful historical term, in our dialect, in order to describe a mere violent demon-stration. In those wartime years, for example, two "revolu-tions" had already taken place in my native village, the first against the town council because of bread rationing, the second against the church because the seat of the bish-opric had been transferred to another township. The third, which I am about to describe, went down in history as "the revolution of the three soldiers." The men were to be es-corted to the train at five o'clock; so the revolution was arranged for half an hour earlier, in front of the barracks. Unfortunately it took a more serious turn than had been intended. It began as a joke, which three of us boys were bold enough to start. One of us, at the agreed moment, went up the bell-tower and began hammering away at the great bell, the signal in our part of the country denoting a serious fire or other public danger. The other two went off to meet the peasants to explain what was happening. Alarmed by the ringing of the tocsin, they had at once stopped working in the fields, and were hurrying anxiously toward the village.

In a few minutes a threatening and tumultuous crowd had collected in front of the barracks. They began by shouting abuse, then they threw stones, and finally shots were fired. The siege of the barracks lasted until late at night. Rage had made my fellow-villagers unrecognizable. In the end, the windows and gates of the barracks were broken open; the carabineers fled across the orchards and fields under cover of darkness; and the three soldiers, whom everyone had forgotten, went back to their homes unobserved. So we boys found ourselves absolute masters of the place for an entire night. "Now what are we going to do?" the other boys asked me. (My authority came, mainly, from the fact that I knew Latin.) "Tomorrow morning," I said, "the village is sure to be reoccupied by hundreds and hundreds of armed men, carabineers and police, who'll arrive from Avezzano, Sulmona, Aquila, and perhaps even from Rome." "But what are we going to do tonight, before they arrive?" the other boys insisted. "Obviously one night is not enough to create a new order of things," I said, thinking I had guessed what they were after. "Couldn't we take advantage of the fact that the whole village is asleep, to make Socialism?"

That was what the other boys wanted me to suggest. Perhaps they were still overexcited from their riotous evening; perhaps they really believed that anything was possible now. "I don't think," I said, "I honestly don't think that, even if the whole village is asleep, one can make Socialism in a single night." I must mention in my own justification that at that time the theory of Socialism overnight had not yet been propounded. "One night, though, might be enough to sleep in one's own bed before going to prison," one of the others finally suggested. And as we were tired, we all found this advice both sensible and acceptable.

Such episodes of violence—with their inevitable sequel of mass arrests, trials, legal expenses, and prison sentences—reinforced distrust, diffidence, and skepticism in the peasants' minds. For them, the State became the irremediable creation of the devil. A good Christian, if he wanted to save his soul, should avoid, as far as possible, all contact with the State. The State always stands for swindling, intrigue and privilege, and could not stand for anything else. Neither law nor force can change it. If retribution occasionally catches up with it, this can only be by the dispensation of God.

In 1915 an earthquake of exceptional violence destroyed a large part of our province and killed, in thirty seconds, about fifty thousand people. I was surprised to see how much my fellow-villagers took this appalling catastrophe as a matter of course. The geologists' complicated explanations, reported in the newspapers, aroused their contempt. In a district like ours, where so many injustices go unpunished, people regarded the recurrent earthquakes as a phenomenon requiring no further explanation. In fact, it was astonishing that earthquakes were not more frequent. An earthquake buries rich and poor, learned and illiterate, authorities and subjects alike beneath its ruined houses. Here lies, moreover, the real explanation of the Italians' well-known powers of endurance when faced with the cataclysms of nature. An earthquake achieves what the law promises but does not in practice maintain—the equality of all men. A neighbor of ours, a woman who kept a bakery, lay buried, but not hurt, for several days after the earthquake, when her house was completely destroyed. Not realizing that the disaster was general, and imagining that it was only her own house which had fallen down, either because of some defect in its construction or because someone had put a curse on it, the poor woman was greatly distressed; so much so that when a rescue party wanted to drag her out of the ruins she absolutely refused. She calmed down, however, and quickly regained her strength and her wish to live and to rebuild her house, the moment she was told there had been an earthquake and that an enormous number of other houses had collapsed as well.

What seemed to the poor people of our part of the world a much more serious calamity than any natural cataclysm was what happened *after* the earthquake. The State reconstruction program was carried out to the accompaniment of innumerable intrigues, frauds, thefts, swindles, embezzlements, and dishonesty of every kind. An acquaintance of mine, who had been sacked by one of the government departments concerned, gave me some information of this sort about certain criminal acts which were being committed by the head engineers of the department. Impressed rather than surprised, I hastened to pass on the facts to some persons in authority, whom I knew to be upright and honest, so that they could denounce the criminals. Far from denying the truth of what I told them, my honorable friends were in a position to confirm it. But, even then, they advised me not to get mixed up in it or to get worked up, in my simplicity, about things of that kind. "You're young," they said to me affectionately, "you must finish your studies, you've got your career to think of, you shouldn't compromise yourself with things that don't concern you." "Of course," I said, "it would be better for the denunciation to come from grown-up people like yourselves, people with authority, rather than from a boy of seventeen."

They were horrified. "We are not madmen," they answered. "We shall mind our own business and nobody else's."

I then talked the matter over with some reverend priests, and then with some of my more courageous relations. All of them, while admitting that they were already aware of the shameful things that were happening, begged me not to get mixed up in that hornets' nest, but to think of my studies, of my career, and of my future. "With pleasure," I replied, "but isn't one of you ready to denounce the thieves?" "We are not madmen," they replied, scandalized, "these things have nothing to do with us."

I then began to wonder seriously whether it mightn't be a good thing to organize, together with some other boys, a new "revolution" that would end up with a good bonfire of the corrupt engineers' offices; but I was dissuaded by the acquaintance who had given me the proof of their crooked dealings: a bonfire, he pointed out, would destroy the proofs of the crimes. He was older and more experienced than myself; he suggested I should get the denunciation printed in some newspaper. But which newspaper? "There's only one," he explained, "which could have any interest in publishing your denunciation, and that's the Socialist paper." So I set to work and wrote three articles, the first of my life, giving a detailed exposure of the corrupt behavior of State engineers in my part of the country, and sent them off to *Avanti*. The first two were printed at once and aroused much comment among the readers of the paper,

but none at all among the authorities. The third article did
not appear, because, as I learned later, a leading Socialist
intervened with the editorial staff. This showed me that the
system of deception and fraud oppressing us was much
vaster than at first appeared, and that its invisible ramifications extended even into Socialism. However, the partial
denunciation which had appeared unexpectedly in the press
contained enough material for a number of law-suits, or at
least for a board of enquiry; but nothing happened. The engineers, whom I had denounced as thieves and bandits and
against whom quite specific charges had been leveled, did
not even attempt to justify themselves or to issue a general
denial. There was a short period of expectancy, and then
everyone went back to his own affairs.

The student who had dared to throw down the challenge was considered, by the most charitably-minded, an
impulsive and strange boy. One must remember that the
economic poverty of the southern provinces offers small
scope for a career to the youths leaving school by the thousand every year. Our only important industry is State employment. This does not require exceptional intelligence,
merely a docile disposition and a readiness to toe the line
in politics. The young men of the South, who have grown
up in the atmosphere I have briefly described, tend naturally, if they have a minimum of sensitiveness in human
relationships, toward anarchy and rebellion. For those still
on the threshold of youth, to become a civil servant means
renunciation, capitulation, and the mortification of their
souls. That is why people say: anarchists at twenty, con-
servatives at thirty. Nor is the education imparted in the
schools, whether public or private, designed to strengthen
character. Most of the later years of my school-life I spent
in private Catholic institutions. Latin and Greek were ex-
cellently taught there; the education in private or personal
habits was simple and clean; but civic instruction and training were deplorable. Our history teachers were openly critical of the official views; the mythology of the Risorgimento
and its heroes (Mazzini, Garibaldi, Victor Emmanuel II,
Cavour) were the objects of derision and disparagement; the
literature prevalent at the time (Carducci, D'Annunzio)
was despised.

Insofar as this method of teaching developed the pupils'
critical spirit, it had its advantages. But the same priestly
schoolmasters, since they had to prepare us for the State

school examinations—and the fame and prosperity of their academies depended on the results we achieved—also taught us, and recommended us to uphold in our examinations, the points of view completely opposed to their own convictions. Meanwhile, the State examiners, who knew we came from confessional schools, enjoyed questioning us on the most controversial subjects, and then praising us ironically for the liberal and unprejudiced way in which we had been taught. The falseness, hypocrisy, and double-facedness of all this were so blatant that they could not but perturb anyone with the slightest inborn respect for culture. But it was equally inevitable that the average unfortunate student ended by considering diplomas, and his future job in a government office, as the supreme realities of life.

"People who are born in this district are really out of luck," Dr. F. J., a doctor in a village near mine, used to say. "There's no halfway house here; you've got either to rebel or become an accomplice." He rebelled. He declared himself an anarchist. He made Tolstoyan speeches to the poor. He was the scandal of the entire neighborhood, loathed by the rich, despised by the poor, and secretly pitied by a few. His post as panel-doctor was finally taken away from him, and he literally died of hunger.

I realize that the progress which I have been tracing in these pages is too summary to seem anything but strained. And if I touch on this objection now, it is not to refute it or to swear to the absolute truth of my explanations; I can guarantee their sincerity, not their objectivity. I am myself sometimes astonished to find, when I go back over that remote, almost prehistoric, period of our lives with my contemporaries, how they cannot remember at all, or only very vaguely, incidents which had a decisive influence on me; whereas on the contrary, they can clearly recall other circumstances which to me were pointless and insignificant. Are they, these contemporaries of mine, all "unconscious accomplices"? And by what destiny or virtue does one, at a certain age, make the important choice, and become "accomplice" or "rebel"? From what source do some people derive their spontaneous intolerance of injustice, even though the injustice affects only others? And that sudden feeling of guilt at sitting down to a well-laden table, when others are having to go hungry? And that pride which makes poverty and prison preferable to contempt?

I don't know. Perhaps no one knows. At a certain point,

even the fullest and deepest confession becomes a mere statement of fact and not an answer. Anyone who has reflected seriously about himself or others knows how profoundly secret are certain decisions, how mysterious and unaccountable certain vocations.

There was a point in my rebellion where hatred and love coincided; both the facts which justified my indignation and the moral motives which demanded it stemmed directly from the district where I was born. This explains, too, why everything I have happened to write up to now, and probably everything I shall ever write, although I have traveled and lived abroad, is concerned solely with this same district, or more precisely with the part of it which can be seen from the house where I was born—not more than thirty or forty kilometers on one side or the other. It is a district, like the rest of the Abruzzi, poor in secular history, and almost entirely Christian and medieval in its formation. The only buildings worthy of note are churches and monasteries. Its only illustrious sons for many centuries have been saints and stone-carvers. The conditions of human existence have always been particularly difficult there; pain has always been accepted there as first among the laws of nature, and the Cross welcomed and honored because of it. Franciscanism and anarchy have always been the two most accessible forms of rebellion for lively spirits in our part of the world. The ashes of skepticism have never suffocated, in the hearts of those who suffered most, the ancient hope of the Kingdom of God on earth, the old expectation of charity taking the place of law, the old dream of Gioacchino da Fiore, of the "Spirituali," of the Celestimisto.* And this is a fact of enormous, fundamental importance; in a disappointed, arid, exhausted, weary country such as ours, it constitutes real riches, it is a miraculous reserve. The politicians are unaware of its existence, the clergy are afraid of it; only the saints, perhaps, know where to find it. What for us has always been much more difficult, if not impossible, has been to discern the ways and means to a political revolution, *hic et nunc,* to the creation of a free and ordered society.

I thought I had reached this discovery, when I moved to the town and made my first contact with the workers' movement. It was a kind of flight, a safety exit from un-

---

* Followers of Pope Celestine V, an Abruzzi hermit who, elected Pope in August, 1294, abdicated three and a half months later. He was canonized in 1313.

bearable solitude, the sighting of *terra firma,* the discovery of a new continent. But it was not easy to reconcile a spirit in moral mutiny against an unacceptable long-established social reality with the "scientific" demands of a minutely codified political doctrine.

For me to join the Party of Proletarian Revolution was not just a simple matter of signing up with a political organization; it meant a conversion, a complete dedication. Those were still the days when to declare oneself a Socialist or a Communist was equivalent to throwing oneself to the winds, and meant breaking with one's parents and not finding a job. If the material consequences were harsh and hard, the difficulties of spiritual adaptation were no less painful. My own internal world, the "Middle Ages," which I had inherited and which were rooted in my soul, and from which, in the last analysis, I had derived my initial aspiration to revolt, were shaken to their foundations, as though by an earthquake. Everything was thrown into the melting-pot, everything became a problem. Life, death, love, good, evil, truth, all changed their meaning or lost it altogether. It is easy enough to court danger when one is no longer alone; but who can describe the dismay of once and for all renouncing one's faith in the individual immortality of the soul? It was too serious for me to be able to discuss it with anyone; my Party comrades would have found it a subject for mockery, and I no longer had any other friends. So, unknown to anyone, the whole world took on a different aspect. How men are to be pitied!

The conditions of life imposed on the Communists by the Fascist conquest of the State were very hard. But they also served to confirm some of the Communists' political theses, and provided an opportunity to create a type of organization which was in no way incompatible with the Communist mentality. So I too had to adapt myself, for a number of years, to living like a foreigner in my own country. One had to change one's name, abandon every former link with family and friends, and live a false life to remove any suspicion of conspiratorial activity. The Party became family, school, church, barracks; the world that lay beyond it was to be destroyed and built anew. The psychological mechanism whereby each single militant becomes progressively identified with the collective organization is the same as that used in certain religious orders and military colleges, with almost identical results. Every sacrifice was welcomed as a personal contribution to the "price of collective redemption"; and it should be emphasized that the links which bound us to the Party grew steadily firmer, not in spite of the dangers and sacrifices involved, but because of them. This explains the attraction exercised by Communism on certain categories of young men and of women, on intellectuals, and on the highly sensitive and generous people who suffer most from the wastefulness of bourgeois society. Anyone who thinks he can wean the best and most serious-minded young people away from Communism by enticing them into a well-warmed hall to play billiards, starts from an extremely limited and unintelligent conception of mankind.

V. SCIENCE AND WAR

As worker and consumer man is increasingly alienated by the power of machines which regulate his daily life, even determining his values. The technology which produces machines, however, is but the offspring of a science which, as it developed the means to transform our planet or destroy it, has become ever more remote from the lives of ordinary citizens and perhaps the ultimate factor in their alienation. To such citizens science appears magical and mysterious in its capacity for and neutrality toward good or evil. Is this entirely due to faults in education which, as C. P. Snow suggests, separate men of humanistic learning from men of science? Undoubtedly, Western education has failed to help rising generations of non-scientists to understand science. But the fault lies with the men of science too, as J. Bronowski, himself a scientist, observes. In "Science, the Destroyer or Creator" (reprinted here), Bronowski writes that scientists "have enjoyed acting the mysterious stranger, the powerful voice without emotion, the expert and the god. They have failed to make themselves comfortable in the talk of people in the street; no one taught them the knack, of course, but they were not keen to learn. And now they find the distance which they enjoyed has turned to distrust, and the awe has turned to fear; and people who are by no means fools really believe that we should be better off without science." Science and society are out of step. Can their mutual alienation be overcome? Bronowski, who would certainly agree that time is short for this rapprochement, answers affirmatively but with the proviso that both sides make the necessary effort.

Against his guardedly optimistic view is the more pessimistic outlook of philosophers who see man as unable to live with and control the extraordinary knowledge and power which his fertile brain has devised. In "Reflections on the H Bomb" Gunther Anders shows that it is not merely the bomb itself which threatens our existence, but a bureaucratization of mass destruction and an incapacity for fear. The first of these factors deprives even the participants in mass destruction of any sense of responsibility for their acts. As for the second, Anders writes that "the helplessness with which contemporary mankind reacts—or rather fails to react—to the existence of the superbomb bespeaks a lack of freedom the like of which has never before existed in history." To Anders this marks "the freezing point of human freedom."

SCIENCE, THE DESTROYER OR CREATOR
/J. Bronowski

We all know the story of the sorcerer's apprentice; or *Frankenstein* which Mary Shelley wrote in competition with her husband and Byron; or some other story of the same kind out of the macabre invention of the nineteenth century. In these stories, someone who has special powers over nature conjures or creates a stick or a machine to do his work for him; and then finds that he cannot take back the life he has given it. The mindless monster overwhelms him; and what began as an invention to do the housework ends by destroying the master with the house.

These stories have become the epitome of our own fears. We have been inventing machines at a growing pace now for about three hundred years. This is a short span even in our recorded history, and it is not a thousandth part of our history as men. In that short moment of time we have found a remarkable insight into the workings of nature. We have used it to make ourselves far more flexible in our adaptation to the outside world than any other animal has ever been. We can survive in climates which even germs find difficult. We can grow our own food and meat. We can travel overland and we can tunnel and swim and fly, all in the one body. More important than any of these, we have come nearest to the dream which Lamarck had, that animals might inherit the skills which their parents learned. We have discovered the means to record our experience so that others may live it again.

The history of other animal species shows that the most successful in the struggle for survival have been those which were most adaptable to changes in their world. We have made ourselves by means of our tools beyond all measure more adaptable than any other species, living or extinct; and we continue to do so with gathering speed. Yet today we are afraid of our own shadow in the nine o'clock news; and we wonder whether we shall survive so over-specialized a creature as the Pekinese.

Everyone likes to blame his sense of defeat on someone else; and for some time scientists have been a favorite scapegoat. I want to look at their responsibility, and for that matter at everybody's, rather more closely. They do have a special responsibility; do not let us argue that out of existence; but it is a complicated one, and it is not the whole responsibility. For example, science obviously is not responsible for the readiness of people, who do not take their private quarrels beyond the stage of insult, to carry their public quarrels to the point of war. Many animals fight for their needs, and some for their mere greeds, to the point of death. Bucks fight for females, and birds fight for their territories. The fighting habits of man are odd because he displays them only in groups. But they were not supplied by scientists. On the contrary, science has helped to end several kinds of group murder, such as witch hunting and the taboos of the early nineteenth century against disinfecting hospitals.

Neither is science responsible for the existence of groups which believe themselves to be in competition: for the existence above all of nations. And the threat of war today is always a national threat. Some bone of contention and competition is identified with a national need: Fiume or the Polish corridor or the dignity of the Austrian Empire; and in the end nations are willing to organize and to invite the death of citizens on both sides in order to reach these collective aims. Science did not create the nations; on the contrary, it has helped to soften those strong national idiosyncrasies which it seems necessary to exploit if war is to be made with enthusiasm. And wars are not made by *any* traditional groups: they are made by highly organized so-

cieties, they are made by nations. Most of us have seen
Yorkshiremen invade Old Trafford, and a bloody nose or
two if the day was thirsty. But no Yorkshireman would
have grown pale if he had been told that Lancashire had the
atomic bomb.

The sense of doom in us today is not a fear of science;
it is a fear of war. And the causes of war were not created
by science; they do not differ in kind from the known
causes of the War of Jenkins' Ear or the Wars of the
Roses, which were carried on with only the most modest
scientific aids. No, science has not invented war; but it has
turned it into a very different thing. The people who distrust it are not wrong. The man in the pub who says "It'll
wipe out the world," the woman in the queue who says
"It isn't natural"—they do not express themselves very
well; but what they are trying to say does make sense.
Science has enlarged the mechanism of war, and it has distorted it. It has done this in at least two ways.

First, science has obviously multiplied the power of the
warmakers. The weapons of the moment can kill more people more secretly and more unpleasantly than those of the
past. This progress, as for want of another word I must
call it—this progress has been going on for some time; and
for some time it has been said, of each new weapon,
that it is so destructive or so horrible that it will frighten
people into their wits, and force the nations to give up war
for lack of cannon fodder. This hope has never been fulfilled, and I know no one who takes refuge in it today. The
acts of men and women are not dictated by such simple
compulsions; and they themselves do not stand in any simple
relation to the decisions of the nations which they compose.
Grapeshot and TNT and gas have not helped to outlaw war;
and I see no sign that the hydrogen bomb or a whiff of bac-
teria will be more successful in making men wise by compulsion.

Secondly, science at the same time has given the nations quite new occasions for falling out. I do not mean
such simple objectives as someone else's uranium mine, or
a Pacific Island which happens to be knee-deep in organic fertilizer. I do not even mean merely another nation's factories and her skilled population. These are all
parts of the surplus above our simple needs which they
themselves help to create and which gives our civilization

its character. And war in our world battens on this surplus. This is the object of the greed of nations, and this also gives them the leisure to train and the means to arm for war. At bottom, we have remained individually too greedy to distribute our surplus, and collectively too stupid to pile it up in any more useful form than the traditional mountains of arms. Science can claim to have created the surplus in our societies, and we know from the working day and the working diet how greatly it has increased it in the last two hundred years. Science has created the surplus. Now put this year's budget beside the budget of 1750, anywhere in the world, and you will see what we are doing with it.

I myself think there is a third dimension which science has added to modern war. It has created war nerves and the war of nerves. I am not thinking about the technical conditions for a war of nerves: the camera man and the radio and the massed display of strength. I am thinking of the climate in which this stage lightning flickers and is made to seem real. The last twenty years have given us a frightening show of these mental states. There is a division in the mind of each of us, that has become plain, between the man and the brute; and the rift can be opened, the man submerged, with a cynical simplicity, with the meanest tools of envy and frustration, which in my boyhood would have been thought inconceivable in a civilized society. I shall come back to this cleavage in our minds, for it is much more than an item in a list of war crimes. But it is an item. It helps to create the conditions for disaster. And I think that science has contributed to it. Science; the fact that science is there, mysterious, powerful; the fact that most people are impressed by it but ignorant and helpless—all this seems to me to have contributed to the division in our minds. And scientists cannot escape the responsibility for this. They have enjoyed acting the mysterious stranger, the powerful voice without emotion, the expert and the god. They have failed to make themselves comfortable in the talk of people in the street; no one taught them the knack, of course, but they were not keen to learn. And now they find the distance which they enjoyed has turned to distrust, and the awe has turned to fear; and people who are by no means fools really believe that we should be better off without science.

These are the indictments which scientists cannot escape.

Of course, they are often badly phrased, so that scientists can side-step them with generalities about the common responsibility, and who voted the credits for atomic research anyway; which are perfectly just, but not at all relevant. That is not the heart of the matter; and the people in queues and pubs are humbly groping for the heart. They are not good at saying things and they do not give model answers to interviewers. But when we say "We've forgotten what's right," when they say "We're not fit to handle such things," what is in their minds is perfectly true. Science and society are out of joint. Science has given to no one in particular a power which no one in particular knows how to use. Why do not scientists invent something sensible? Wives say it every time they stub their toe on the waste bin, and husbands say it whenever a fuse blows. Why is it the business of no one in particular to stop fitting science for death and to begin fitting it into our lives? We will agree that warlike science is no more than a by-product of a warlike society. Science has merely provided the means, for good or for bad; and society has seized it for bad. But what are we going to do about it?

The first thing to do, it seems to me, is to treat this as a scientific question: by which I mean as a practical and sensible question, which deserves a factual approach and a reasoned answer. Now that I have apologized on behalf of scientists, and this on a scale which some of them will certainly think too ample, let us cut out what usually happens to the argument at this point, the rush of recriminations. The scientists are conscious of their mistakes; and I do not want to discuss the mistakes of non-scientists—although they have made a great many—except those which we all must begin to make good.

I have said that a scientific answer must be practical as well as sensible. This really rules out at once the panaceas which also tend to run the argument into a blind alley at this stage; the panaceas which say summarily "Get rid of them." Naturally, it does not seem to me to be sensible to get rid of scientists; but in any case, it plainly is not practical. And whatever we do with our own scientists, it very plainly is not practical to get rid of the scientists of rival nations; because if there existed the conditions for agreement among nations on this far-reaching scheme, then the conditions for war would already have disappeared. If there existed the conditions for international agreement, say to suspend all scientific research, or to abandon warlike research, or in any other way to forgo science as an instrument of nationalism—if such agreements could be reached, then they would already be superfluous; because the conditions for war would already have disappeared. So, however we might sigh for Samuel Butler's panacea in *Erewhon*, simply to give up all machines, there is no point in talking about it. I believe it would be a disaster for mankind like the coming of the Dark Ages. But there is no point in arguing this. It just is not practical, nationally or internationally.

There are no panaceas at all; and we had better face that. There is nothing that we can do overnight, in a week or a month, which can straighten by a laying on of hands the ancient distortion of our society. Do not let us fancy that any one of us out of the blue will concoct that stirring letter to *The Times* which will change the black mood of history—and the instructions to diplomats. Putting scientists in the Cabinet will not do that, and women in the War Office will not, nor will bishops in the Privy Council. There are no panaceas. We are the heirs to a tradition which has left science and society out of step. The man in the street is right: we have never learned to handle such things. Nothing will do but that we learn. But learning is not done in a year. Our ultimate survival is in our own hands. Our survival while we are learning is a much chancier thing. We had better be realistic about that.

Meanwhile we had better settle down to work for our ultimate survival; and we had better start now. We have seen that the diagnosis has turned out to be not very difficult. Science and our social habits are out of step. And the cure is no deeper either. We must learn to match them. And there is no way of learning this unless we learn to understand *both*.

Of the two, of course, the one which is strange is science. I have already blamed the scientist for that. He has been the monk of our age, timid, thwarted, anxious to be asked to help; and with a secret ambition to play the Grey Eminence. Through years of childhood poverty he dreamed of this. Scientific skill was a blue door beckoning to him, which would open into the society of dignitaries of state. But the private motives of scientists are not the trend of science. The trend of science is made by the needs of society: navigation before the eighteenth century, manufacture thereafter; and in our age I believe the liberation of personality. Whatever the part which scientists like to act, or for that matter which painters like to dress, science shares the aims of our society just as art does. The difficulties of understanding either are not fundamental; they are difficulties only of language. To grow familiar with the large ideas of science calls for patience and an effort of attention; and I hope I have shown that it repays them.

For two hundred years, these ideas have been applied to technical needs; and they have made our world anew, triumphantly, from top to toe. Our shoes are tanned and stitched, our clothes are spun and dyed and woven, we are lighted and carried and doctored by means which were unknown to neat Mr. Pope at Twickenham in 1740. We may not think that is much to put against the eighty thousand dead in Hiroshima, or we may. We may not think it recompenses us for the absence of any Mr. Pope from Twickenham today; we may even hold it responsible. It is certainly not a spiritual achievement. But it has not yet tried to be. It has applied its ideas monotonously to shoe-leather and bicycle bells. And it has made a superb job of them. Compare its record in its own field with that of any other ideas of the same age: Burke's ideas of the imagination, or Bentham's on government, or Adam Smith on political economy. If any ideas have a claim to be called creative, because they have created something, then certainly it is the ideas of science.

We may think that all that science has created is comfort; and it certainly has done that—the very word "comfortable" in the modern sense dates from the Industrial Revolution. But have we always stopped to think what science has done not to our mode of living but to our life? We talk about research for death, the threat of war and the number of civilians who get killed. But have we always weighed this against the increase in our own life span? Let us do a small sum. The number of people killed in Great Britain in six years of war by German bombs, flying bombs, and V2's was sixty thousand. They were an average lot of people, which means that on an average they lost half their expectation of life. Quite an easy long division shows that the effect of this in our population of fifty million people was to shorten the average span of life by less than one tenth of one per cent. This is considerably less than a fortnight. Put this on the debt side. And on the credit side, we know that in the last hundred years the average span of life in England has increased by twenty years. That is the price of science, take it or leave it—a fortnight for twenty years of life. And these twenty years have been created by applying to daily life, to clothing and bedding, to hygiene and infection, to birth and death, the simple ideas of science—the fundamental ideas I have been talking about: order, cause, and chance. If any ideas have a claim to be called creative, because they have created life, it is the ideas of science.

We have not neglected these ideas altogether in our social organization. But, it is a point I have made several times, we have got hopelessly behind with them. The idea of order is now old enough to have reached at least our filing cabinets. The idea of cause and effect has entered our habits, until it has become the new *a priori* in the making of administrative plans. The difficulty is to dislodge it, now that it is hardening into a scholastic formula. For the idea which has given a new vigor to science in our generation is larger than the machinery of cause and effect. It stipulates no special mechanism between the present and the future. It is content to predict the future, without insisting that the computation must follow the steps of causal law. I have called this the idea of chance, because its method is statistical, and because it recognizes that every prediction carries with it its own measurable uncertainty. A good prediction is one which defines its area of uncertainty; a bad prediction ignores it. And at bottom this is no more than the return to the essentially empirical, the experimental nature of science. Science is a great many things, and I have called them a great many names; but in the end they all return to this: science is the acceptance of what works and the rejection of what does not. That needs more courage than we might think.

It needs more courage than we have ever found when we have faced our worldly problems. This is how society has lost touch with science: because it has hesitated to judge itself by the same impersonal code of what works and what does not. We have clung to Adam Smith and Burke, or we have agitated for Plato or Aquinas, through wars and famine, through rising and falling birth-rates, and through libraries of learned argument. And in the end, our eyes have always wandered from the birth-rate to the argument: from the birth-rate to what we have wanted to believe. Here is the crux of what I have been saying. Here is our ultimate hope of saving ourselves from extinction. We must learn to understand that the content of all knowledge is empirical; that its test is whether it works; and we must learn to act on that understanding in the world as well as in the laboratory.

This is the message of science: our ideas must be realistic, flexible, unbigoted—they must be human, they must create their own authority. If any ideas have a claim to be called creative, because they have liberated that creative impulse, it is the ideas of science.

This is not only a material code. On the contrary, my hope is that it may heal the spiritual cleft which two wars have uncovered. I have seen in my lifetime an abyss open in the human mind: a gulf between the endeavor to be man, and the relish in being brute. The scientist has indeed had a hand in this, and every other specialist too, with his prim detachment and his oracular airs. But of course, the large strain which has opened this fault is social. We have made men live in two halves, a Sunday half and a workday half. We have ordered them to love their neighbor and to turn the other cheek, in a society which has constantly compelled them to shoulder their neighbor aside and to turn their backs. So we have created a savage sense of failure which, as we know now to our cost, can be tapped with an ease which is frightening; and which can thrust up, with explosive force, a symbol to repeat to an unhappy people its most degrading dream.

Can science heal that neurotic flaw in us? If science cannot, then nothing can. Let us stop pretending. There is no cure in high moral precepts. We have preached them too long to men who are forced to live how they can: *that* makes the strain which they have not been able to bear. We need an ethic which is moral *and* which works. It is often said that science has destroyed our values and put nothing in their place. What has really happened of course is that science has shown in harsh relief the division between our values and our world. We have not begun to let science get into our heads; where then was it supposed to create these values? We have used it as a machine without will, the conjured spirit to do the chores. I believe that science can create values: and will create them precisely as literature does, by looking into the human personality; by discovering what divides it and what cements it. That is how great writers have explored man, and this whether they themselves as men have been driven by the anguish in *Gulliver's Travels* or the sympathy in *Moll Flanders*. The insight of science is not different from that of the arts. Science will create values, I believe, and discover virtues, when it looks into man; when it explores what makes him man and not an animal, and what makes his societies human and not animal packs.

I believe that we can reach this unity in our culture. I began this book by recalling that nations in their great ages have not been great in art or science, but in art and science. Rembrandt was the contemporary of Huygens and Spinoza. At that very time, Isaac Newton walked with Dryden and Christopher Wren. We know that ours is a remarkable age of science. It is for us to use it to broaden and to liberate our culture. These are the marks of science: that it is open for all to hear, and all are free to speak their minds in it. They are marks of the world at its best, and the human spirit at its most challenging.

REFLECTIONS ON THE H BOMB
/Gunther Anders

If there is anything that modern man regards as infinite, it is no longer God; nor is it nature, let alone morality or culture; it is his own power. *Creatio ex nihilo,* which was once the mark of omnipotence, has been supplanted by its opposite, *potestas annihilationis* or *reductio ad nihil;* and this power to destroy, to reduce to nothingness lies in our own hands. The Promethean dream of omnipotence has at long last come true, though in an unexpected form. Since we are in a position to inflict absolute destruction on each other, we have apocalyptic powers. It is we who are the infinite.

To say this is easy, but the fact is so tremendous that all historically recorded developments, including epochal

Translated by Norbert Guterman.

changes, seem trifling in comparison: all history is now reduced to prehistory. For we are not merely a new historical generation of men; indeed, we are no longer what until today men have called "men." Although we are unchanged anatomically, our completely changed relation to the cosmos and to ourselves has transformed us into a new species —beings that differ from the previous type of man no less than Nietzsche's superman differed from man. In other words—and this is not meant as a mere metaphor—we are Titans, at least as long as we are omnipotent without making *definitive* use of this omnipotence of ours.

In fact, during the short period of our supremacy the gulf separating us Titans from the men of yesterday has become so wide that the latter are beginning to seem alien to us. This is reflected, to take a salient example, in our attitude toward Faust, the hero in whom the last generations of our forefathers saw the embodiment of their deepest yearnings. Faust strives desperately to be a Titan; his torment is caused by his inability to transcend his finitude. We, who are no longer finite, cannot even share this torment in our imagination. The infinite longing for the infinite, which Faust symbolizes, and which for almost a thousand years was the source of man's greatest sufferings and greatest achievements, has become so completely a thing of the past that it is difficult for us to visualize it; at bottom we only know that it had once existed. What our parents, the last humans, regarded as the most important thing is meaningless to us, their sons, the first Titans; the very concepts by means of which they articulated their history have become obsolete.

For instance, the antithesis between the Apollonian and the Dionysiac principle: The former denoted the happy harmony of the finite; the latter, the intoxication found in exploding the boundaries of the finite. Since we are no longer finite, since we have the "explosion" behind us, the antithesis has become unreal.

The infinite longing some of us still experience is a nostalgia for finitude, the good old finitude of the past; in other words, some of us long to be rid of our Titanism, and to be men again, men like those of the golden age of yesterday. Needless to say, this longing is as romantic and utopian as was that of the Luddites; and like all longings of this kind, it weakens those who indulge in it, while it strengthens the self-assurance of those who are sufficiently unimaginative and unscrupulous to put to actual use the omnipotence they possess. But the starving workmen who early in the nineteenth century rose against the machines could hardly have suspected that a day would come when their longing for the past would assume truly mythological dimensions—when man could be appropriately described as the Titan who strives desperately to recover his humanity.

Curiously enough, omnipotence has become truly dangerous only after we have got hold of it. Before then, all manifestations of omnipotence, whether regarded as natural or supernatural (this distinction, too, has become unimportant), have been relatively benign: in each instance the threat was partial, only particular things were destroyed —"merely" people, cities, empires, or cultures—but we were always spared, if "we" denotes mankind.

No wonder that no one actually considered the possibility of a total peril, except for a few scientific philosophers who toyed with the idea of a cosmic catastrophe (such as the extinction of the sun), and for a minority of Christians who took eschatology seriously and expected the world to end at any moment.

With one stroke all this has changed. There is little hope that we, cosmic parvenus, usurpers of the apocalypse, will be as merciful as the forces responsible for former cataclysms were out of compassion or indifference, or by accident. Rather, there is no hope at all: the actual masters of the infinite are no more imaginatively or emotionally equal to this possession of theirs than their prospective victims, i.e., ourselves; and they are incapable, and indeed must remain incapable, of looking upon their contraption as anything but a means to further finite interests, including the most limited party interests. Because we are the first men with the power to unleash a world cataclysm, we are also the first to live continually under its threat. Because we are the first Titans, we are also the first dwarfs or pygmies, or whatever we may call beings such as ourselves who are mortal not only as individuals, but also as a group, and who are granted survival only until further orders.

We have just emerged from a period in which for Europeans natural death was an unnatural or at least an exceptional occurrence. A man who died of old age aroused envy: he was looked upon as one who could afford the luxury of a peaceful and individual death, as a kind of slacker who had managed to escape from the general fate of extermination, or even as a sort of secret agent in the service of cosmic foreign powers through which he had been able to obtain such a special favor. Occasionally natural death was viewed in a different light—as evidence of man's freedom and sovereignty, as a twin brother of Stoic suicide—but even then natural death was felt to be unnatural and exceptional. During the war, being killed was thus the most common form of dying: the model for our finitude was Abel, not Adam.

In the extermination camps natural death was completely eliminated. There the lethal machines operated with absolute efficiency, leaving no uneconomical residues of life. There the venerable proposition, All men are mortal, had already become an understatement. If this proposition had been inscribed on the entrance gates to the gas chambers, instead of the usual misleading, "Shower Baths," it would have aroused jeers; and in this jeering laughter the voices of the victims would have joined in an infernal unison with the voices of their guards. For the truth contained in the old proposition was now more adequately expressed in a new proposition—"All men are exterminable."

Whatever changes have taken place in the world during the ten years since the end of the war, they have not affected the validity of the new proposition: the truth it expresses is confirmed by the general threat hanging over us. Its implications have even become more sinister: for what is exterminable today is not "merely" all men, but mankind as a whole. This change inaugurates a new historical epoch, if the term "epoch" may be applied to the short time intervals in question. Accordingly, all history can be divided into three chapters, with the following captions: (1) All men are mortal, (2) All men are exterminable, and (3) Mankind as a whole is exterminable.

Under the present dispensation, human mortality has acquired an entirely new meaning—it is only today that its ultimate horror is brought home to us. To be sure, even previously no one was exempt from mortality; but everyone regarded himself as mortal within a larger whole, the human world; and while no one ever explicitly ascribed immortality to the latter, the threat of its mortality stared no one in the face either. Only because there was such a "space" within which one died, could there arise that peculiar aspiration to give the lie to one's mortality through the acquisition of fame. Admittedly the attempt has never been very successful; immortality among mortals has never been a safe metaphysical investment. The famous men were always like those ship passengers of the *Arabian Nights*, who enjoyed the highest reputation aboard, but whose reputation enjoyed no reputation, because the very existence of the ship was totally unknown on land. Still, as compared with what we have today, fame was something. For today our fear of death is extended to all of mankind; and if mankind were to perish leaving no memory in any being, engulfing all existence in darkness, no empire will have existed, no idea, no struggle, no love, no pain, no hope, no comfort, no sacrifice—everything will have been in vain, and there would be only that which had *been*, and nothing else.

Even to us, who are still living in the existing world, the past, that which merely *was*, seems dead; but the end of mankind would destroy even this death and force it, as it were, to die a second time, so that the past will not even have been the past—for how would that which merely had been differ from that which had never been? Nor would the future be spared: it would be dead even before being born. Ecclesiastes's disconsolate, "There is nothing new under the sun," would be succeeded by the even more disconsolate, "Nothing ever was," which no one would record and which for that reason would never be challenged.

Let us assume that the bomb has been exploded.

To call this "an action" is inappropriate. The chain of events leading up to the explosion is composed of so many links, the process has involved so many different agencies, so many intermediate steps and partial actions, none of which is the crucial one, that in the end no one can be regarded as the agent. Everyone has a good conscience, because no conscience was required at any point. Bad conscience has once and for all been transferred to moral machines, electronic oracles: those cybernetic contraptions, which are the quintessence of science, and hence of progress and of morality, have assumed all responsibility, while man self-righteously washes his hands. Since all these machines can do is to evaluate profits and losses, they implicitly make the loss finite, and hence justifiable, although it is precisely this evaluation that destroys us, the evaluated ones, even before we are actually destroyed. Because responsibility has been displaced on to an object, which is regarded as "objective," it has become a mere response; the Ought is merely the correct chess move, and the Ought Not, the wrong chess move. The cybernetic machines are interested only in determining the means that can be advantageously used in a situation defined by the factors $a, b, c \ldots \ldots n$. Nothing else matters: after all, the continued existence of our world cannot be regarded as one of the factors. The question of the rightness of the goal to be achieved by the mechanically calculated means is forgotten by the operators of the machine or their employers, i.e., by those who bow to its judgment the moment it begins to calculate. To mistrust the solutions provided by the machine, i.e., to question the responses that have taken the place of responsibility, would be to question the very principle of our mechanized existence. No one would venture to create such a precedent.

Even where robots are not resorted to, the monstrous undertaking is immensely facilitated by the fact that it is not carried out by individuals, but by a complex and vastly ramified organization. If the organization of an undertaking is "all right," and if the machines function smoothly, the performance too seems "all right" and smooth. Each participant, each intermediary, performs or has insight into only the job assigned to him; and certainly each works conscientiously. The specialized worker is not conscious of the fact that the conscientious efforts of a number of specialists can add up to the most monstrous lack of conscience: just as in any other industrial enterprise he has no insight into the process as a whole. In so far as *conscientia* derives from *scire*, i.e., conscience from knowledge, such a failure to become conscious certainly points to a lack of conscience. But this does not mean that any of the participants acts against his conscience, or has no conscience— such immoral possibilities are still comfortingly human, they still presuppose beings that might have a conscience. Rather, the crucial point here is that such possibilities are excluded in advance. We are here beyond both morality and immorality. To blame the participants for their lack of conscience would be as meaningless as to ascribe courage or cowardice to one's hand. Just as a mere hand cannot be cowardly, so a mere participant cannot have conscience. The division of labor prevents him so completely from having clear insight into the productive process, that the lack of conscience we must ascribe to him is no longer an individual moral deficiency.

And yet it may result in the death of all mankind.

The "action" of unleashing the bomb is not merely irresponsible in the ordinary sense of the term: irresponsibility still falls within the realm of the morally discussible, while here we are confronted with something for which no one can even be held accountable. The consequences of this "action" are so great that the agent cannot possibly grasp them before, during, or after his action. Moreover, in this case there can be no goal, no positive value that can even approximately equal the magnitude of the means used to achieve it.

This incommensurability of cause and effect or means and end is not in the least likely to prevent the action; on the contrary, it facilitates the action. To murder an individual is far more difficult than to throw a bomb that kills countless individuals; and we would be willing to shake hands with the perpetrator of the second rather than of the first crime. Offenses that transcend our imagination by virtue of their monstrosity are committed more readily, for the inhibitions normally present when the consequences of a projected action are more or less calculable are no longer operative. The Biblical "They know not what they do" here assumes a new, unexpectedly terrifying meaning: the very monstrousness of the deed makes possible a new, truly infernal innocence.

The situation is not entirely unfamiliar. The mass exterminations under Hitler could be carried out precisely because they were monstrous—because they absolutely transcended the moral imagination of the agents, and because the moral emotions that normally precede, accompany, or follow actions could not arise in this case. But can one speak here of "agents"? The men who carry out such actions are always co-agents: they are either half-active and half-passive cogs in a vast mechanism, or they serve merely to touch off an effect that has been prepared in advance to the extent of 99 per cent. The categories of "coagent" and "touching off" are unknown in traditional ethics. This is not to be interpreted as a justification of the German crimes. The concept of collective guilt was morally indispensable: something had to be done to prevent these crimes from being quickly forgotten. But the concept proved inadequate because the crime in question transcended the ordinary dimensions of an immoral act; because a situation in which all perpetrators are merely co-perpetrators, and all non-perpetrators are indirectly perpetrators, requires entirely new concepts; and above all because the number of dead was too great for any kind of reaction. Just as men can produce acoustic vibrations unperceivable by the human ear, so they can perform actions that lie outside the realm of moral apperception.

Let us sum up the main points of our arguments. Shocking as this may sound, the murder of an individual is a relatively human action—not because the effect of an individual murder is quantitatively smaller than that of a mass murder or a total extermination (for deaths cannot really be added; the very plural form of the noun "death" is absurd, for each individual death is qualitatively unique), but because the individual murderer still can react to his crime in a human way. It is possible to mourn one victim of murder, not a million victims. One can repent one murder, not a million murdered. In other words, in the case of an individual murder, man's emotional, imaginative, and moral capacity are congruent or at least commensurable with his capacity for action. And this congruence, this condition in which man is more or less equal to himself, is no doubt the basic prerequisite of that which is called "humanity." It is this congruence that is absent today. Consequently, modern unmorality does not primarily consist in man's failure to conform to a specific more-than-human image of man; perhaps not even in his failure to meet the requirements of a just society; but rather in his half-guilty and half-innocent failure to conform to himself, that is to say, in the fact that his capacity for action has outgrown his emotional, imaginative, and moral capacities.

We have good reason to think that our fear is by far too small: it should paralyze us or keep us in a continual state of alarm. It does not because we are psychically unequal to the danger confronting us, because we are incapable of producing a fear commensurate with it, let alone of constantly maintaining it in the midst of our still seemingly normal everyday life.

Just like our reason, our psyche is limited in the Kantian sense: our emotions have only a limited capacity and elasticity. We have scruples about murdering one man; we have less scruples about shooting a hundred men; and no scruples at all about bombing a city out of existence. A city full of dead people remains a mere word to us.

All this should be investigated by a Critique of Pure Feeling, not for the purpose of reaching a moral verdict, but in order to determine the boundaries of our emotional capacity. What disturbs us today is not the fact that we are not omnipotent and omniscient, but the reverse, namely, the fact that our imaginative and emotional capacities are too small as measured against our knowledge and power, that imaginatively and emotionally we are so to speak smaller than ourselves. Each of us moderns is an inverted Faust: whereas Faust had infinite anticipations and boundless feelings, and suffered because his finite knowledge and power were unequal to these feelings, we know more and produce greater things than we can imagine or feel.

As a rule, then, we are incapable of producing fear; only occasionally does it happen that we attempt to produce it, or that we are overwhelmed and stunned by a tidal wave of anguish. But what stuns or panics us at such moments is the realization not of the danger threatening us, but of the futility of our attempts to produce an adequate response to it. Having experienced this failure we usually relax and return shamefaced, irritated, or perhaps even relieved, to the human dimensions of our psychic life commensurable with our everyday surroundings. Such a return, however pleasant it may be subjectively, is of course sheer suicide from the objective point of view. For there is nothing and there can be nothing that increases the danger more than our failure to realize it intellectually and emotionally, and our resigned acceptance of this failure. In fact, the helplessness with which contemporary mankind reacts—or rather fails to react—to the existence of the superbomb bespeaks a lack of freedom the like of which has never before existed in history—and surely history cannot be said to have been poor in varieties of unfreedom.

We have indeed reached the freezing point of human freedom.

The Stoic, robbed of the autonomy of action, was certainly unfree; but how free the Stoic still was, since he could think and feel as he pleased!

Later there was the even more impoverished type of man, who could think only what others had thought for him, who indeed could not feel anything except what he was supposed to feel; but how free even this type of man was, since he still could speak, think, and feel what he was supposed to speak, think, and feel!

Truly unfree, divested of all dignity, definitively the most deprived of men are those confronted with situations and things with which they cannot cope by definition, to which they are unequal linguistically, intellectually, and emotionally—ourselves.

If all is not to be lost we must first and foremost develop our moral imagination: this is the crucial task facing us. We must strive to increase the capacity and elasticity of our intellectual and emotional faculties, to match the incalculable increase of our productive and destructive powers. Only where these two aspects of man's nature are properly balanced can there be responsibility, and moral action and counter-action.

Whether we can achieve such a balance, is an open question. Our emotional capacity may turn out to be limited a priori; perhaps it cannot be extended at will and *ad infinitum*. If this were so, and if we were to resign ourselves to such a state of affairs, we would have to give up all hope. But the moralist cannot do so in any case: even if he believed in the theoretical impossibility of transcending those limits, he would still have to demand that they be transcended in practice. Academic discussions are pointless here: the question can be decided only by an actual attempt, or, more accurately, by repeated attempts, i.e., spiritual exercises. It is immaterial whether such exercises aim at a merely quantitative extension of our ordinary imagination and emotional performance, or at a sensational, "impossible" transcending of our *proportio humana*, whose boundaries are supposedly fixed once and for all. The philosophical significance of such exercises can be worried about later. What matters at present is only that an attempt at violent self-transformation be made, and that it be successful. For we cannot continue as we are.

In our emotional responses we remain at the rudimentary stage of small artisans: we are barely able to repent an individual murder; whereas in our capacity for killing, for producing corpses, we have already entered the proud stage of industrial mass production. Indeed, the performances of our heart—our inhibitions, fears, worries, regrets—are in inverse ratio to the dimensions of our deeds, i.e., the former grow smaller as the latter increase. This gulf between our emotional capacity and our destructive powers, aside from representing a physical threat to our lives, makes us the most divided, the most disproportionate, the most inhuman beings that have ever existed. As against this modern cleavage, all older spiritual conflicts, for instance, the conflict between mind and body or duty and inclination, were relatively harmless. However violently the struggle may have raged within us, it remained human; the contending principles were attuned to each other, they were in actual contact, neither of them lost sight of the other, and each of them was essentially human. At least on the battlefield of the contending principles man preserved his existence unchallenged: man was still there.

Not so today. Even this minimum of man's identity with himself is gone. For the horror of man's present condition consists precisely in this, that the conflicting forces within him are no longer inter-related: they are so far removed from each other, each has become so completely independent, that they no longer even come to grips. They can no longer confront each other in battle, the conflict can no longer be fought out. In short, man *as* producer, and man *as* a being capable of emotions, have lost sight of each other. Reality now seems attributable only to each of the specialized fragments designated by an "as." What made us shudder ten years ago—the fact that one and the same man could be guard in an extermination camp and good father and husband, that *as* the former he could be so radically different from himself *as* the latter, and that the two parts he played or the two fragments he was did not in the least stand in each other's way because they no longer knew each other—this horrifying example of guilelessness in horror has not remained an isolated phenomenon. Each of us, like this schizophrenic in the truest sense of the term, is split into two separate beings; each of us is like a worm artificially or spontaneously divided into two halves, which are unconcerned with each other and move in different directions.

True, the split has not been entirely consummated; despite everything the two halves of our being are still connected by the thinnest of threads, and the producer half, by far the stronger, drags the emotional half behind it. The unity is not organic, it is that of two different beings meaninglessly grown together. But the existence of this minimal connection is no comfort. On the contrary, the fact that we are split in two, and that there is no internal principle integrating these halves, defines the misery and disgrace of our condition.

VI. SOCIAL ISOLATION

Work, popular culture, politics, science—all contribute to the alienation of modern man. But they tell us little about men's community life or their isolation from each other because of social status, age or race. Our first selection, by August Hollingshead, describes the extreme social isolation of the poor in "Elmtown," a small American midwestern city. Elmtown's social structure, according to Hollingshead, "is composed of five strata whose members understand with varying degrees of precision how each ranks in the hierarchical order." In the passages we have selected, Hollingshead portrays the cultural characteristics of "Class V," those at the bottom of the heap. How they live and what the rest of the community thinks of them are made vividly clear. In almost any sense of the phrase they are social outcasts and treated as such. Hollingshead conducted his study some twenty years ago. Is this then ancient history? Most decidedly not. Despite great economic growth since World War II, poverty and its social consequences persist for many citizens of our "affluent" society; and our tendency to "forget" the poor is still another measure of their alienation and ours.

Poverty is only one of many isolating factors. Improvement in social status may also lead to alienation. In "Keeping Themselves to Themselves," Michael Young and Peter Willmott deal with families transplanted to a new suburban development from the East End of London (an area corresponding sociologically to the lower East Side of Manhattan). As Young and Willmott report, these people left the intimacy and solidarity of a slum with its close ties for a chillier life in new surroundings. How keenly East Enders feel the difference is made abundantly clear. Now their lives are no longer focused on people but on their houses and possessions, on the struggle for status. Frequently there was considerable bitterness. Young and Willmott studied their East End families soon after the move to the suburbs; and it is likely that warmer relations developed among neighbors later on. But if they are united chiefly by competition for social status, can this ever take the place of family-centered community life? "Neighbors do not make up for kin."

The suburban environment has been made familiar to us in numerous American studies, such as *The Lonely Crowd, Crestwood Heights, The Exurbanites,* and *The Organization Man.* What is unique about the Young and Willmott study, however, is that it shows how the expanding metropolis loosens the ties of kin and neighborhood in the very process of building new communities.

In breaking up the traditional family-centered life, modern society deals harshly with those who are most vulnerable, particularly the aged. Peter Townsend, author of our third selection, reports on another survey of family life in the London area. Among the aged, he suggests, there is a distinction to be drawn between social isolation and loneliness. In the first state the aged person has few social contacts; in the second he feels cut off, especially if he has lost a loved one. The isolation of the aged is grim enough; but as Townsend demonstrates, when the aged are also bereaved, the result is not just loneliness but often a rapid decline of faculties and even of the will to live. To sustain the aged our society has found no substitute for the family.

The isolation of the "nuclear" family from its roots is just one of the ways in which men become separated from each other. The last two selections which follow have to do with race relations in the United States. Not ordinary sociological documents, they have much sociological significance; for they tell us in vivid terms what it is like to be a Negro in America. The first of them, by W. E. B. Du Bois, was written more than half a century ago; and if there has been gradual change in the status of Negroes since that time the problem he describes is essentially the same today: "To be a poor man is hard, but to be a poor race in a land of dollars is the very bottom of hardships." The second of them, by the brilliant contemporary writer James Baldwin, is about Harlem; and Baldwin writes his own summary: "Negroes want to be treated like men: a perfectly straightforward statement, containing only seven words. People who have mastered Kant, Hegel, Shakespeare, Marx, Freud, and the Bible find this statement utterly impenetrable."

THOSE ON THE BOTTOM
/August Hollingshead

Elmtowners in general are inconsistent in the way they talk and act with reference to the idea of classes. If they are asked bluntly, "Do you believe there are 'classes' in the community?" they are very likely to say, "No." Yet, they will tell you the Binghams are "a leading family here," or the "Sweitzers are like the Binghams, Woodsons, McDermotts, and Jennings'. These families are different from the rest of us; they are very exclusive. I guess you'd call them our aristocracy." During the course of the conversation, the same speaker will say that there are several different "types of families" in the community and, justifying his judgment by describing the "way they live," place them in different categories. The democratic tradition that there are no classes in American society is the reason for this type of behavior. Therefore, Elmtowners deny the existence of class directly but act as if classes exist. However, many Elmtowners openly say that there are three classes in the community—"upper," "middle," and "lower"—but when they are requested to name persons in, let us say, the "lower class" they generally divide the class into the "good" lower class people and the "worthless, ne'er-do-wells." The same kind of break appears in the "middle class." Separation of the "middle class" into "upper middle" and "lower middle" is quite conventional.

Even though Elmtowners are inconsistent in their designations of a particular class, the systematic analysis of selected cultural traits associated with each of the five classes, based upon data collected from the 535 families of the adolescents, supplemented by interviews and observations, reveal that the possession of a constellation of differentially evaluated social symbols—functional, pecuniary, religious, educational, reputational, power, lineage, proper associates, memberships in associations—are relied upon by Elmtowners to "hang people on the peg they belong on," to determine "their place in the community" or "their standing in life."

Class V occupies the lowest-ranking stations in the prestige structure. It is looked upon as the scum of the city by the higher classes. It is believed generally that nothing beyond charity can be done for these people, and only a minimum of that is justified since they show little or no inclination to help themselves. It is the opinion of the upper classes that:

They have no respect for the law, or themselves.

They enjoy their shacks and huts along the river or across the tracks and love their dirty, smoky, low-class dives and taverns.

Whole families—children, in-laws, mistresses, and all —live in one shack.

This is the crime class that produces the delinquency and sexual promiscuity that fills the paper.

Their interests lie in sex and its perversion. The girls are always pregnant; the families are huge; incestual relations occur frequently.

They are not inspired by education, and only a few are able to make any attainments along this line.

They are loud in their speech, vulgar in their actions, sloppy in their dress, and indifferent toward their plight. Their vocabulary develops as profanity is learned.

If they work, they work at very menial jobs.

Their life experiences are purely physical, and even these are on a low plane.

They have no interest in health and medical care.

The men are too lazy to work or do odd jobs around town.

They support the Democratic party because of the relief obtained during the depression.

This group lives for a Saturday of drinking or fighting. They are of low character and breed and have a criminal record for a pedigree.

Class V persons, passive and fatalistic, realize that they are "on the bottom" and believe that they can do nothing to improve their position. They desire money, possessions, education, and favorable prestige, but they do not know how these are achieved. When a class V person attempts to improve his position, he is discriminated against by the higher classes, and by many members of his own class who think he is trying to "put on airs." One woman with considerable insight into her class position summarized it thus:

Survival for us depends on staying on good terms with the rich people and the law. Whenever I think about myself and the kids, I am reminded what my father used to say, "We are the ones who are told what to do, when and how" around here. This town takes us for granted. Most people think the people down here [the tannery flats] are too ignorant to do anything and don't care; I guess they're right.

To generalize a little more, class V persons give the impression of being resigned to a life of frustration and defeat in a community that despises them for their disregard of morals, lack of "success" goals, and dire poverty.

Family support comes from many sources. The father is the chief breadwinner in three families out of five, but his earnings are meager. Ninety-two per cent are unskilled and semi-skilled laborers or machine operators. Not one is a farm owner, and only 8 are farm tenants; 2 are notions salesmen; and 8 operate very small businesses, such as hauling coal from local mines, ash and trash hauling, repair and sales of old cars. Fifty-five per cent of the mothers "work out" part or full time as waitresses, dishwashers, cooks, washwomen, janitresses, cleaning women, and unskilled domestic workers. Many younger women and girls work on the production line of a local manufacturer who is reputed to give them preference in his shops because they can be hired for lower wages than class IV workers.

Income from wages provides them with enough money to obtain the most meager necessities of life; however, in many cases it is inadequate even for this, and they rely upon private charity and public relief. Annual family income ranges from about $500 to a high of $1,500. The modal income fell in the $800 to $899 bracket. Income varies from year to year, depending upon work conditions and wages. Between 1937 and 1941, the private earnings of 53 per cent of these families were supplemented by township relief during at least one-fourth of each year. This figure does not take into consideration federal subsidies, such as WPA and NYA, which prevailed in that period; neither does it include private charity in the form of "outfitting the children" with clothes.

Gifts of partially worn-out clothing, linens, bedding, old furniture, dishes, and food are a regular part of the private relief and indirect wage system supported by the two highest classes and to some extent by class III. These gifts are given informally to persons who perform domestic service for the donors. Begging by class V's is frowned upon strongly; consequently, needy families do not solicit things in an overt manner, but any class V person knows how to make his wants known to an employer in a humble, discreet manner that generally brings the desired results. Semipublic charity is dispensed through sewing circles, guilds, and clubs that make clothing for infants. The ever-popular rummage sale, one of which is held almost every Saturday by some "middle-class" organization, may be viewed as another form of charity to the two lower classes. Many class V women regularly buy their family's best clothes from these sales. As one class II woman said, "This year, Mrs. Gordon Sweitzer [class I] will have a striking dress, next year you will see it on Mrs. Luke Jenkins [class IV] in the Baptist choir, and three years from now Pearl Soper [class V] will be trying to catch some loafer's eye with it."

Bank credit is non-existent, and even the small-loan broker has learned through experience to be careful with class V:

> Before I loan one of them a cent, I investigate carefully and make sure they own what they put up for security. There is not a person in that class who has not been in here one time or another for a loan. If they have a job and can give me good evidence they can pay back a loan, I will let them have from $10 to $25 at first. If they pay it back, just as they agreed to, I will let them have a little more next time. Eighty per cent of the loans I have written off were made to the class represented by the names you have there. [A group of class V's we were checking for loans.]

Exactly one-half of the class V families studied have procured small personal loans, none over $50; this is the limit the broker will loan to persons he does not believe to be "good risks." Repeated loans to the class V's are discouraged; the mean is eight loans per family for those who manage to obtain them. On the other hand, the broker encourages class IV's to borrow time after time, since he considers them "good risks."

The uncertain nature of their employment results in long periods of idleness; also illness, real or imagined, may result in a voluntary layoff for a few days that, to persons in the higher classes, appears to be laziness. Whatever the conditioning factors, these people are far more irregular in their employment than the class IV's. They will leave a job casually, often without notice, and for flimsy reasons. Employers do not like to hire them unless labor is scarce or they can be induced to work for low wages. Even then they are placed in the simplest and most menial jobs. The work history of a father or mother is generally known to employers, and he acts in the light of it when a son or daughter of one of these families asks him for employment.

All population elements are represented, but three families out of five (58 per cent) trace their ancestry to "American stock" that came to Elmtown before the Civil War. In spite of popular belief, "the Irish element" has contributed less than 9 per cent to the ranks of class V. The Poles are found here twice as frequently, and the Germans and Norwegians only one-third as frequently as we may expect if chance factors alone are operating. The concentration of "American stock" is overlooked by Elmtowners who commonly use a European ancestral background as a symbolic label. This is understandable in the case of the Poles; they were imported as strikebreakers, and they have not outlived this experience or their ethnic background. Many of these "American" families have lived in Elmtown as long as its "leading families"; however, length of residence is their only similarity to leading families, for through the generations they have achieved notorious histories. Unfortunately, the unsavory reputation of an ancestor is remembered and often used as an explanation for present delinquency. It is interesting to note that the doctrine of "blood" which explains the rise to eminence of class I is used in the same way to justify the derogation of class V. And, significantly, present behavior of class V gives the people who hold such beliefs a basis for their conviction. Sociologically, such an explanation is unwarranted, but Elmtowners are not sociologists! Often such remarks as the following are made about these families or some member of them, "Blood will out"; "You can't expect anything else from such people"; "His great-grandfather was hanged for killing a neighbor in cold blood!"

Class V families are excluded from the two leading residential areas. They are found in the others, with large concentrations north of the tracks and below the canal. Below the canal and the Mill Addition are populated mainly by "Americans." Down by the Mill is "Irish heaven," whereas the section north of the tracks is divided into the Norwegian and Polish areas. A low, flat, swamp-like sub-area within this section, Frog Hollow, is almost exclusively Polish. The higher ground north of the tracks, populated mainly by Norwegians with a slight intermingling of Irish and Germans, is known as "Ixnay." Below the canal is referred to by many names, all symbolic of its undesirability: down by the garbage dump; where the river rats live; behind the tannery; the bush apes' home; squatters' paradise; where you'll find the God-damned yellow hammers; the tannery flats; and along the tow-path.

The dilapidated, box-like homes contain crude pieces of badly abused furniture, usually acquired secondhand. A combination wood and coal stove, or kerosene burner, is used for both cooking and heating. An unpainted table and a few chairs held together with baling wire, together with an ancient sideboard—with shelves above to hold the assorted dishes, and drawers below for pots, pans, and groceries—furnish the combined kitchen and dining room. There may be some well-worn linoleum or strips of roofing on the floor. The "front room" generally serves a dual purpose, living room by day and bedroom by night. Here too the floor is often covered with linoleum or roofing strips, seldom with a woven rug. Two or three overly used chairs in various stages of disrepair share the room with a sagging sofa that leads a double life as the routine of day alternates with that of night. If an additional bed is needed, an iron one may stand in a corner or along one wall. A simple mirror that shows signs of age, perhaps abuse, shares the wall with a few cheap prints of pictures cut from magazines that show how undressed a woman may be without being nude. Now and again a colored print of a saint and a motion picture star will be pasted or nailed beside a siren. An improvised wardrobe made by driving a row of nails in the wall generally occupies one corner. A table, radio, and some means of lighting the room complete its furnishings. Old iron beds that sag in the middle, made with blankets and comforts in the absence of sheets, a chest of drawers, a chair or two, and a mirror that looks out on the stringy curtains and the bare floor complete the furnishings of the tiny bedrooms. Musical instruments, magazines, and newspapers other than *The Bugle* seldom find their way into these homes. Less than 1 per cent have telephones.

Privacy in the home is almost non-existent; parents, children, "in-laws" and their children, and parts of a broken family may live in two or three rooms. There is little differentiation in the use of rooms—kitchen, dining room, living room, and bedroom functions may be combined from necessity into a single use area. Bath and toilet facilities are found in approximately one home in seven. City water is piped near or into 77 per cent of the homes within the city limits, except those below the canal. Water for these homes is either carried from the town pump, also located in this area, or from the river. Outside the town, wells, springs, and creeks are used for a water supply. Some 4 per cent of the homes were equipped with furnace heat; the rest were heated with wood- or coal-burning stoves.

The family residence is rented in four cases out of five (81 per cent). The few that are owned have either been inherited or built along the canal and in the tannery flats by their present owners. A few Poles have bought homes in Frogtown from the English and Scotch who formerly inhabited this area. Although it is popularly believed that these people buy cars rather than homes, only 57 per cent own cars, the great majority (83 per cent) being more than 7 years old.

The family pattern is unique. The husband-wife relationship is more or less an unstable one, even though the marriage is sanctioned either by law or understandings between the partners. Disagreements leading to quarrels and vicious fights, followed by desertion by either the man or the woman, possibly divorce, are not unusual. The evidence indicates that few compulsive factors, such as neighborhood solidarity, religious teachings, or ethical considerations, operate to maintain a stable marital relationship. On the contrary, the class culture has established a family pattern where serial monogamy is the rule. Legal marriages are restricted within narrow limits to class equals. However, exploitive sex liaisons between males from the higher classes frequently occur with teen-age girls, but they rarely result in marriage. Marriage occurs in the middle teens for the girls and the late teens or early twenties for the boys. Doctors, nurses, and public officials who know these families best estimate that from one-fifth to one-fourth of all births are illegitimate. Irrespective of the degree of error in this estimate, 78 per cent of the mothers gave birth to their first child before they were 20 years of age. Another trait that marks the family complex is the large number of children. The mean is 5.6 per mother, the range, 1 to 13. There is little pre-natal or post-natal care of either mother or child. The child is generally delivered at home, usually by a local doctor, the county nurse, or a midwife, but in the late 1930's some expectant mothers entered the local hospital. Hospital deliveries, however, are a recent innovation and not widely diffused. Death, desertion, separation, or divorce has broken more than half the families (56 per cent). The burden of child care, as well as support, falls on the mother more often than on the father when the family is broken. The mother-child relation is the strongest and most enduring family tie.

Formal educational experience is limited in large part to the elementary school. Two parents out of three (67 per cent) quit school before the eighth grade was reached; the third completed it. Seven fathers and six mothers out of 230 have completed a year or more of high school; only one father and four mothers have graduated. None has attended any type of school after leaving the public school system.

Religious ties are either very tenuous or non-existent. Only 71 per cent of the families claim any religious connections; many of these are merely "in spirit." More than 9 families out of 10 have no active connection with a church, and active hostility toward churches, ministers, and pious people is encountered more frequently than real or professed church work. One woman epitomized the situation when she said bitterly, "The 'Everyone Welcome' signs in front of the churches should add 'except people like us'— we're not wanted." She was right—they are not wanted by the congregations and several of the ministers. Ministers in the high-prestige churches (Federated, Methodist, and Lutheran) indicate they have no objections to class V persons coming to service and participating in church activities, but they know that members of the congregation resent the presence of these people; so they do not encourage their attendance. Ministers in the low-ranking churches do not believe that their people resent the presence of class V's in church activities.

Three ministers related stories about unpleasant experiences they had with certain of these families before they learned that it is wise to "follow the line of least resistance" and let them alone. Four frankly stated that these people are beyond help, as far as the ministers are concerned, and they do not try to reach them in any way. Seven reported that they officiate at funerals, weddings, and baptisms if they are asked; two refuse to perform these rites on religious grounds.

The church schedules reveal that attendance at religious services and participation in auxiliary church activities are limited, with few exceptions, to the higher-ranking classes. Ninety-eight per cent of the class V fathers are either completely unknown to the ministers or do not attend church if they are known. Five attend church services rarely or irregularly; not one is categorized as a "church worker." The participation figures for the mothers are little different: 90 per cent either are unknown or do not attend church; 7 per cent attend services either rarely or irregularly; 3 per cent are reported to be church workers. These church workers are in the Pentecostal, Pilgrim Holiness, and Church of God congregations that meet in abandoned stores, lofts, and private homes. Even the Free Methodists, who are largely class IV's, apparently do not welcome too intimate contact with these women in their strivings for salvation through good work. One minister cynically said with reference to them, "You will find in the churches these women who shout the longest and loudest about sin—hours on end —while their husbands are out lying with some harlot."

Their extensive leisure time is spent in the community or in nearby ones, since they have little money to spend in travel; neither are their automobiles in good enough repair to stand the rigor of long trips. The men and boys are more mobile than the women and girls; when they leave the community, it is usually in search of work, adventure, often to avoid the sheriff. When the family goes away, it generally carries its belongings with it in a search for economic betterment. In these periodic moves, it usually encounters the same kind of conditions, so it comes back after a few months or years. Possibly as many as one-fourth of the families drift in and out of the community. These floating families have a more or less fixed routine which they follow in the course of the years. They may go to Michigan in the summer to pick and pack fruit, on to Wisconsin for the cranberry season, then back to Elmtown for the winter and early spring. The younger children may enroll in school, the older boys try to find work in the bowling alley or on barges that ply the river; the girls and women find work as maids, cleaning women, or dishwashers until the family decides to move again.

Class V persons are almost totally isolated from organized community activities. A few men claim membership in veterans' organizations, but they neither pay dues nor attend meetings. Workers in the Mill belong to the union, since this is a closed shop; the others follow lines of work not organized by the unions. Time has little value in the daily routine. Even getting to work on time and staying on the job are not too highly regarded. Employers complained bitterly about their loose work habits. They claim that these people come to work at irregular times, leave when they feel like it, and lay off on the least excuse. Since they do not participate in organized community affairs, hours off the job and during the periods of unemployment or layoff are spent the way the person chooses without too much interference from neighbors. Leisure is expended in loafing around the neighborhood, in the downtown district, along the river, and at home. Their social life consists of informal visits between neighbors, gossip, petty gambling, visits to the cheaper theaters, going to town, drinking in the home or public taverns, with now and again a fist fight. The family is so loosely organized that the members usually go their own way in search of amusement or pleasure. The cliques are severely age- and sex-graded; men associate with men and women with women, except in their ubiquitous sex play.

Organized dinners and parties where guests are invited to the home on a Saturday night are unknown. Festive gatherings take place on Sunday when many branches of the family unite for a brief spell of merrymaking. The low-ranking taverns are filled on Saturday nights with class V's of all ages who gather there for their big social night. Small children are kept up until after midnight in the hot, smoke-filled, poorly lighted, noisy "poor man's night club." Young couples wander in and out; often preliminary "passes" are made in preparation for a later seduction. Almost every Saturday night the police are called to some low-ranking tavern to break up a fight between half-drunk customers.

The police, sheriff, prosecuting attorney, and judge know these families from frequent contact through the years, whereas the ministers and school officials may be only slightly acquainted with them. Between 1934 and 1941, 8 per cent of the mothers and 46 per cent of the fathers had been convicted once or more in the local courts. Public drinking, disorderly conduct, family neglect, and sex offenses were the charges against the women; they averaged 1.5 convictions each. The men were more or less chronic offenders who were convicted of habitual public drunkenness, 49 per cent; miscellaneous offenses, 30 per cent; offenses against property, 12 per cent; sex and family neglect, 9 per cent. They averaged 4.1 convictions each in the eight years covered by reliable court records. Their misdeeds are prominently written up in *The Bugle*. If they do not reach the paper, they are known by some persons in the higher classes who delight in telling about them to their acquaintances.

KEEPING THEMSELVES TO THEMSELVES
/Michael Young and Peter Willmott

We have now described some of the effects of migration. People's relatives are no longer neighbors sharing the intimacies of daily life. Their new neighbors are strangers, drawn from every part of the East End, and they are, as we have seen, treated with reserve. In point of services, neighbors do not make up for kin.

Our informants were so eager to talk about their neighbors, and generally about their attitude to other residents on the estate, that we feel bound to report them. They frequently complained of the unfriendliness of the place, which they found all the more mysterious because it was so different from Bethnal Green. Why should Greenleigh be considered unfriendly?

The prevailing attitude is expressed by Mr. Morrow. "You can't get away from it, they're not so friendly down here. It's not 'Hello, Joe,' 'Hello, mate.' They pass you with a side-glance as though they don't know you." And by Mr. Adams. "We all come from the slums, not Park Lane, but they don't mix. In Bethnal Green you always used to have a little laugh on the doorstep. There's none of that in Greenleigh. You're English, but you feel like a foreigner here, I don't know why. Up there you'd lived for years, and you knew how to deal with the people there. People here are different." And by Mr. Prince. "The neighbors round here are very quiet. They all keep themselves to themselves. They all come from the East End but they all seem to change when they come down here."

Of the 41 couples, 23 considered that other people were unfriendly, eight were undecided one way or another and ten considered them friendly: the recorded opinions are those of the couples because in no interview did husband and wife appear to hold strongly different views. How does this majority who consider their fellow residents unfriendly feel about themselves? Do they also label themselves unfriendly? No one admits it, some indignantly deny it. If they are hostile themselves, they do not acknowledge it, but attribute the feeling to others. Yet they mostly reveal that their own behavior is the same as they resent in others; that (since *others* are unfriendly) to withdraw will avoid trouble and keep the peace; that coexistence is safer, because more realistic, than cooperation. "The policy here is don't have a lot to do with each other, then there won't be any trouble," says Mr. Chortle succinctly.

This attitude is supported by reference to the skirmishes and back-biting which have resulted from being "too friendly" in the past. "It's better if you just talk to neighbors and don't get too friendly," concludes Mr. Sandeman from his past experience. "You stop friends if you don't get to know them too well. When you get to know them you're always getting little troubles breaking out. I've had too much of that and so I'm not getting too friendly now."

Mr. Young told his wife, "When I walk into these four walls, I always tell her 'Don't make too many friends. They turn out to be enemies.'" And one experience had turned Mr. Yule into a recluse. "We don't mix very well in this part of the estate. At first I used to lend every Tom, Dick or Harry all my tools or lawn mower or anything. Then I had £20 pinched from my wallet. Now we don't want to know anyone—we keep ourselves to ourselves. There's a good old saying—the Englishman's home is his castle. It's very true."

Usually the troubles are shadowy affairs which have happened to people other than oneself. "We're friendly," says Mr. Wild in the usual style, "but we don't get too involved, because we've found that causes gossip and trouble. We've seen it happen with other people, so we don't want it to happen to us. Now we keep ourselves to ourselves." Whatever the justification, the result is the same. People do not treat others either as enemies or friends. They are wary, though polite. They pass the time of day in the road. They have an occasional word over the fence or a chat at the garden gate. They nod to each other in the shops. Neighbors even borrow and lend little things to each other, and when this accommodation is refused, it is a sign that acquaintance has turned into enmity. Mrs. Chortle has broken off trading as well as diplomatic relations with one of her neighbors. "These people are very dirty," she said, "and I've told them I don't want to borrow or lend." So has Mrs. Morrow, for the different reason that "Just because they've got a couple of ha'pence more than you they don't want to know you. In Bethnal Green it was different—neighbors were more friendly."

Even where relations have not been severed, there is little of the mateyness so characteristic of Bethnal Green. Mr. Stirling summed it up by remarking, "I don't mind saying hello to any of them, or passing the time of day with them, but if they don't want to have anything to do with me, I don't want to have anything to do with them. I'm not bothered about them. I'm only interested in my own little family. My wife and my two children—they're the people that I care about. My life down here is my home."

Women feel the lack of friends, as of kin, more keenly than their menfolk. Those who do not follow their husbands into the society of the workplace—and loneliness is one of the common reasons for doing so—have to spend their day alone, "looking at ourselves all day," as they say. In one interview the husband was congratulating himself on having a house, a garden, a bathroom and a TV— "the tellie is a bit of a friend down here"—when his wife broke in to say, "It's all right for you. What about all the time I have to spend here on my own?" This difference in their life may cause sharp contention, especially in the early years. "When we first came," said Mrs. Haddon, "I'd just had the baby and it was all a misery, not knowing anyone. I sat on the stairs and cried my eyes out. For the first two years we were swaying whether to go back. I wanted to and my husband didn't. We used to have terrible arguments about it. I used to say, "It's all right for you. I have to sit here all day. You do get a break.'"

Not that all women resent it. A few, like Mrs. Painswick, actually welcome seclusion. She had been more averse to the quarrels amongst the "rowdy, shouty" Bethnal Greeners than appreciative of the mateyness to which quarrels are the counterpart, and finds the less intense life of Greenleigh a pleasant contrast. "In London people had more squabbles. We haven't seen neighbors out here having words."

When people regard others as unfriendly, the comparisons they implicitly make are with Bethnal Green. We have already discussed the reasons why people living in the borough considered that a friendly place. They and their relatives had lived there a long time, and consequently had around them a host of long-standing friends and acquaintances. At Greenleigh they neither share long residence with their fellow tenants nor as a rule have kin to serve as bridges between the family and the wider community. These two vital interlocked conditions of friendliness are missing, and their absence goes far to explain the attitude we have illustrated.

It also accounts for the astringency of the criticism. Migrants, to the United States or to housing estates, always take part of their homeland with them, our informants like everyone else. They take with them the standards of Bethnal Green, derived from a close community of kindred and neighbors. Friends, within and without the kinship network, were the unavoidable accompaniment of the kind of life they led—too much so for devotees of quiet and privacy. They grew up with their friends, they met them at auntie's, for ten years they walked down the street with them to work. They are used to friendliness, and, their standards in this regard being so high, they are all the more censorious about the other tenants of the County Council. They are harsh in their comment, where someone arriving from a less settled district, or from another and even newer housing estate, might be accustomed to the standoffishness, and, by his canons, even impressed by the good behavior, of the same neighbors.

It would not matter quite so much people being newcomers if they had moved into an established community. The place would then already have been criss-crossed with ties of kinship and friendship, and one friend made would have been an introduction to several. But Greenleigh was built in the late 1940's on ground that had been open fields before. The nearest substantial settlement, a few miles away at Barnhurst, is the antithesis of East London, an outer suburb of privately-owned houses, mainly built between the wars for the rising middle classes of the time. The distance between the estate and its neighbor is magnified by the resentment, real and imagined, of the old residents of Barnhurst at the intrusion of rough East Enders into the rides of Essex and, what is worse, living in houses not very unlike their own put up at the expense of the taxpayer. "People at Barnhurst look down on us. They treat us like dirt. They're a different class of people. They've got money." "It's not so easy for the girls to get boys down here. If people from the estate go to the dance hall at Barnhurst they all look down on them. There's a lot of class distinction down here." These, the kind of thoughts harbored by the ex-Bethnal Greeners, do nothing to make for ease of communication between the two places. So there is no tradition into which the newcomers can enter. If Barnhurst has any influence upon Greenleigh, it is to sharpen the resentment of the estate against its environment and to stimulate the aspiration for material standards as high.

Nor would it matter quite so much if the residents of Greenleigh all had the same origin. No doubt if they all came from Bethnal Green, they would get on much better than they do: many of them would have known each other before and, anyway, at least have a background in common. As it is, they arrive from all over London, though with East Enders predominant. Such a vast common origin might be enough to bind together a group of Cockneys in the Western Desert; Western Essex is too near for that. When all are from London, no one is from London: they are from one of the many districts into which the city is divided. What is then emphasized is far more their difference than their sameness. The native of Bethnal Green feels himself different from the native of Stepney or Hackney. One of our informants, who had recently moved into Bethnal Green from Hackney, a few minutes away, told us "I honestly don't like telling people I live in Bethnal Green. I come from Hackney myself, and when I was a child living in Hackney, my parents wouldn't let me come to Bethnal Green. I thought it was something terrible." These distinctions are carried over to Greenleigh, where it is no virtue in a neighbor to have come from Stepney, rather the opposite. Mr. Abbot summed it up as follows: "You've not grown up with them. They come from different neighborhoods, they're different sorts of people and they don't mix."

We had expected that, despite these disadvantages, people would, in the course of time, settle down and make new friendships, and our surprise was that this had not happened to a greater extent. The informants who had been on the estate longest had no higher opinion than others of the friendliness of their fellows. Four of the 18 couples who had been there six or seven years judged other people to be friendly, as did six of the 23 couples with residence for five years or less. Mr. Wild was one who commented on how long it was taking for time its wonders to perform.

"They're all Londoners here but they get highbrow when they get here. They're not so friendly. Coming from a turning like the one where we lived, we knew everyone. We were bred and born amongst them, like one big family we were. We knew all their troubles and everything. Here they are all total strangers to each other and so they are all wary of each other. It's a question of time, I suppose. But we've been here four years and I don't see any change yet. It does seem to be taking a very long while to get friendly."

One reason it is taking so long is that the estate is so strung out—the number of people per acre at Greenleigh being only one-fifth what it is in Bethnal Green—and low density does not encourage sociability.

In Bethnal Green your pub, and your shop, is a "local." There people meet their neighbors. At Greenleigh they are put off by the distance. They don't go to the pub because it may take 20 minutes to walk, instead of one minute as in Bethnal Green. They don't go to the shops, which are grouped into specialized centers instead of being scattered in converted houses through the ordinary streets, more than they have to, again because of the distance. And they don't go so much to either because when they get there, the people are gathered from the corners of the estate, instead of being neighbors with whom they already have a point of contact. The pubs and shops of Bethnal Green serve so well as "neighborhood centers" because there are so many of them: they provide the same small face-to-face groups with continual opportunities to meet. Where they are few and large, as at Greenleigh, they do not serve this purpose so well.

The relatives of Bethnal Green have not, therefore, been replaced by the neighbors of Greenleigh. The newcomers are surrounded by strangers instead of kin. Their lives outside the family are no longer centered on people; their lives are centered on the house. This change from a people-centered to a house-centered existence is one of the fundamental changes resulting from the migration. It goes some way to explain the competition for status which is in itself the result of isolation from kin and the cause of estrangement from neighbors, the reason why coexistence, instead of being just a state of neutrality—a tacit agreement to live and let live—is frequently infused with so much bitterness.

When we asked what in their view had made people change since they moved from East London, time and time again our informants gave the same kind of suggestive answers—that people had become, as they put it, "toffee-nosed," "big-headed," "high and mighty," "jealous," "a cut above everybody else."

"It's like a strange land in your own country," said Mrs. Ames. "People are jealous out here. They're made to be much quieter in a high-class way, if you know what I mean. They get snobbish, and when you get snobbish you're not sociable any more."

"I'm surprised," said Mr. Tonks, "at the way people vote Conservative at Greenleigh when the L.C.C. built these houses for them. One has a little car or something and so he thinks himself superior. People seem to think only of themselves when they get here."

"The neighbor runs away with the idea that she's a cut above everybody else, but when you get down to brass tacks," which Mrs. Berry proceeded to do, "she's worse off than you'll ever be. She's one of those people, you know what I mean, she's very toffee-nosed. There are some people down here who get like that."

What about the informants themselves? Did they too think themselves superior? Just as people were less ready to label themselves "unfriendly" than they were others, so they were less ready to admit they themselves felt superior. Not many showed their mind so clearly as Mrs. Abbot who said "As soon as they get down here they get big ideas, and yet they've never been used to it. They're *nothing* really." Or as Mr. Haddon: "Some people are inclined to think they're better than some other people in the East End of London, but they're not. I've met them and mixed with them and I find that they're actually lower than the others —they haven't the ability to be sociable. That's what it is. So they put themselves a bit above others so as to give a

let-out to their feelings." Yet we formed the strong impression that most of the critics of the "big-heads" did at
least in part share the attitude they complained of.

One key to this attitude, as we have said, is the house.
When they compare it with the gloomy tenement or decaying cottage, is it any wonder that they should feel they have
moved up in the world?

> "When people moved out here it was a big change for
> them," said Mr. Adams. "In Bethnal Green the people
> were cooped up in two rooms or something like that, and
> when they get here they think they've bettered them-
> selves—and so they have bettered themselves. And they
> try to raise their standard of living."

A house is one bearer of status in any society—it most certainly is in a country where a semi-detached surburban
house with a garden has become the signal mark of the
middle classes. When the migrants compare the new with
the old, is it any wonder that they should for a time feel
"big-headed"? In their mind's eye the people with whom
they compare themselves may be less their fellow-residents
at Greenleigh with their identical houses than their old
neighbors of Bethnal Green, and, compared to them, they
are in this one way undeniably superior.

Mr. Berry, a milkman, was one of several who connected
the "snobbishness" with the possession of a new house.

> "I deliver milk all over the estate so I think I know
> practically everybody on this estate. And I can tell you
> that when they move down here—I suppose it's just that
> they've got a new house—they just think they're a cut
> above everybody else."

Mrs. Allen, although rather more tentative, was of the
same mind.

> "I don't like it, the atmosphere. People are not the
> same; I don't know if they get big-headed because
> they've got a house. Out here you just get a good morn-
> ing."

The women most appreciate their new workshop and
nursery. The man's status is the status of his job; the woman's the status of her home. Since she has moved up most
in the world, she is only being realistic to recognize it.

"When I was in London I had a four-roomed house on my own, but you get a few of them who come from, say, two rooms. Then they get a house. Well, they've worked hard—you must admit they've worked hard—they've got themselves a nice home, television and all that. So you find this type of person temporarily gets a bit to thinking that they are somebody. You do find it with some people, and I think you find it more amongst the women than amongst the men."

The house when the builders leave it is only a shell. The house when people move into it comes to life. They bestow an authority upon it, even vest it with a kind of personality: up to a point it then decrees what they shall do within its walls. The house is also a challenge, demanding that their style of life shall accord with the standard it sets. When they make a first cup of tea after the removal van has driven away and look around their mansion, they are conscious not only of all they have got which they never had before but also of all the things they need which they still lack. The furniture brought from Bethnal Green looks old and forlorn against the bright paint. They need carpets for the lounge, lino for the stairs and mats for the front door. They need curtains. They need another bed. They need a kitchen table. They need new lampshades, pots and pans, grass seed and spades, clothes lines and bath mats, Airwick and Jeyes, mops and pails—all the paraphernalia of modern life for a house two or three times larger and a hundred times grander than the one they left behind them. With the aid of their belongings, they need somehow to live the kind of life, be the kind of people, that will fit into Forest Close or Cambridge Avenue. Then they, and the house, can at last be comfortable. They have to acquire new property. They have to acquire new habits. If they are to settle at Greenleigh, they have to make a profound adjustment in their lives: that is the challenge.

The first essential is money for material possessions. When people move to Greenleigh the standard of life, measured by the quality of housing, is at once raised. They attempt to bring the level in other respects up to the same standard. Furniture and carpets have to be bought, and although, with the aid of the ever more ubiquitous hire purchase, this can be done without capital, it cannot be done without a burden on income. Moreover, the house is only the beginning. A nice house and shabby clothes, a neat garden and an old box of a pram, do not go together. "My sister gave me a beautiful Dunkley pram," said Mrs. Berry, "because I was going to such a beautiful new house." Smartness calls for smartness.

As well as appurtenances for the house, there is more need too for the sort of possessions which will improve communications with the outer world. The Bethnal Greener's society is close by. He does not need a telephone to make appointments to see his friends because they are only a few minutes away. He does not need a highly developed time-sense (as we discovered to our cost when interviewing) because it does not matter greatly whether he goes round to Mum's at 10 o'clock or 11. If Mum is not there someone will explain where she has gone. He does not have to have a car or a motor cycle because relatives and friends, even work, are at walking distance.

At Greenleigh a person has to organize his life more closely, develop a more exact sense of time and be prepared to travel to avoid being cut off from social contact altogether. In some ways the more self-contained home is less self-contained than ever. Greenleigh is part of a larger world. A person's shops are a mile off, his work six miles away and his relatives 10 or 20 miles away, some of them on the surburban circuit of housing estates—Oxhey, Debden, Harold Hill, Becontree—along which no buses ply. Distances to shops, work and relatives are not walking distances any more. They are motoring distances: a car, like a telephone, can overcome geography and organize a more scattered life into a manageable whole. With a car he can, without having to expose himself to the wintry winds which blow over the fields, get to work, to his relatives in Bethnal Green Road or to his friends who have gone over to Kent. "Now that we've got the car," said Mr. Marsh, "we can see the wife's sister at Laindon more often." She was now seen every fortnight instead of every three or four months. Cars are beginning to move from luxury to necessity. "I don't want to win £75,000. I just want to win £500—so that I can get myself a little car. I could get a nice little car for that. You really need a car down here," said Mr. Adams. One of the more fortunate, Mr. Berry, who had already achieved the two accomplishments of the complete man, discoursed on their necessity.

"There are two things that I think are essential when you live on an estate. One's a telephone, the other's a car. I don't like having to pay my telephone bill, but I think it's worth it. It means my brother can ring me up on the estate any time he wants to. And if you're in any trouble—if there's anything wrong with one of the boys say—I can ring up a doctor if I need one. You don't need a telephone in Bethnal Green, because the doctor's on the doorstep. Practically anywhere you live in Bethnal Green there's a doctor near at hand. And you need a car for traveling about. We're so far away from everywhere out here that it's actually cheaper to run a car than it is to pay fares."

Greenleigh already has many more telephones than Bethnal Green, where you can go down the street to your relatives as quickly as, and more cheaply than, you can phone them; the figures for residential subscribers being 88 per thousand at Greenleigh and only 13 in Bethnal Green.

Greenleigh, though composed mainly of manual workers like Bethnal Green, has nearly seven times more telephones per head and, if our informants are any guide, at least one motive is to keep in touch with the kin left behind. "We can't get up to see them very often," said Mrs. Adams. "That's really why we had the phone put in here. If you can only hear each other it's something. It does keep you in touch with home." But if telephones can be installed easily enough, garages cannot. They were not a necessity when the architects made the future in County Hall. A garage, now as rare in 20th-century Greenleigh as an indoor lavatory was in 19th-century Bethnal Green, could be as much a motive for migration in the future. Cars, telephones, telegrams and letters represent not so much a new and higher standard of life as a means of clinging to something of the old. Where you could walk to your enjoyment, you did not need a car. Where you cannot walk, and public transport is inconvenient or too expensive, you need a car.

This understandable urge to acquisition can easily become competitive. People struggle to raise their all-round standards to those of the home, and in the course of doing so, they look for guidance to their neighbors. To begin with, the first-comers have to make their own way. The later arrivals have their model at hand. The neighbors have put up nice curtains. Have we? They have got their garden planted with privet and new grass-seed. Have we? They have a lawn-mower and a Dunkley pram. What have we got? The new arrivals watch the first-comers, and the first-comers watch the new arrivals. All being under the same pressure for material advance, they naturally mark each other's progress. Those who make the most progress are those who have proved their claim to respectability, Greenleigh-style. The fact that people are watching their neighbors and their neighbors watching them provides the further stimulus, reinforcing the process set in motion by the new house, to conform to the norms of the estate. There is anxiety lest they do not fit.

"People are not very friendly here. It's the same on all the estates. They've nothing else to do when they've finished work except watch you. It's all jealousy. They're afraid you'll get a penny more than they have. In London people have other things to occupy their minds. Here when they've done their work they've nothing to do. They're at the window and they notice everything. They say 'Mrs. Brown's got a new hat on.' They don't miss anything. I think the trouble is they've never been used to a nice house. When they come from London they think they're high and mighty. If you've got something they'll go into debt to get it themselves."

After the house has schooled its tenants, there is still much uncertainty about the proper way to behave in this new and strange environment. What the house does not do, the neighbors finish off. By their example they indicate the code to be followed. Hence, if one person has a refrigerator, next-door thinks she should have one; if A has a car, B wants one too.

"If," says Mrs. Abbot, "you make your garden one way, they'll knock all theirs to pieces to make theirs like it. It's the same with curtains—if you put up new curtains, they have new curtains in a couple of months. And if someone buys a new rug they have to hang it on the line so you can see it."

The struggle for possessions is one in which comparisons with other people are constantly made. Some of those who have achieved a more complete respectability look down on the others; those with less money resent the more successful and keep as far away from them as they can. "The whole answer is—the whole trouble is, many men can't earn enough. They have to hide behind curtains. They've got a certain amount of pride." Resentment may also produce an aggressive spirit. "This place is all right for middle-class people, people with a bit of money. It's no good for poorer people—I think they've all got money troubles, that's why they're so spiteful to each other."

We have been arguing that, the possession of a new house having sharpened the desire for other material goods, the striving for them becomes a competitive affair. The house is a major part of the explanation. But there is more to it than that.

In Bethnal Green people, as we said earlier, commonly belong to a close network of personal relationships. They know intimately dozens of other local people living near at hand, their school-friends, their work-mates, their pub-friends, and above all their relatives. They know them well because they have known them over a long period of time. Common family residence since childhood is the matrix of friendship. In this situation, Bethnal Greeners are not, as we see it, concerned to any marked extent with what is usually thought of as "status". It is true, of course, that people have different incomes, different kinds of jobs, different kinds of houses—in this respect there is much less uniformity than at Greenleigh—even different standards of education. But these attributes are not so important in evaluating others. It is personal characteristics which matter. The first thing they think of about Bert is not that he has a "fridge" and a car. They see him as bad-tempered, or a real good sport, or the man with a way with women, or one of the best boxers of the Repton Club, or the person who got married to Ada last year. In a community of long-standing, status, in so far as it is determined by job and income and education, is more or less irrelevant to a person's worth. He is judged instead, if he is judged at all, more in the round, as a person with the usual mixture of all kinds of qualities, some good, some bad, many indefinable. He is more of a life-portrait than a figure on a scale.

People in Bethnal Green are less concerned with "getting on." Naturally they want to have more money and a better education for their children. The borough belongs to the same society as the estate, one in which standards and aspirations are moving upward together. But the urge is less compulsive. They stand well with plenty of other people whether or not they have net curtains and a fine pram. Their credit with others does not depend so much on their "success" as on the subtleties of behavior in their many face-to-face relationships. They have the security of belonging to a series of small and overlapping groups, and from their fellows they get the respect they need.

How different is Greenleigh we have already seen. Where nearly everyone is a stranger, there is no means of uncovering personality. People cannot be judged by their personal characteristics: a person can certainly see that his neighbor works in his back garden in his shirt sleeves and his wife goes down to the shops in a blue coat, with two canvas bags: but that is not much of a guide to character. Judgment must therefore rest on the trappings of the man rather than on the man himself. If people have nothing else to go by, they judge from his appearance, his house, or even his Minimotor. He is evaluated accordingly. Once the accepted standards are few, and mostly to do with wealth, they become the standards by which "status" is judged. In Bethnal Green it is not easy to give a man a single status, because he has so many; he has, in addition to the status of citizen, a low status as a scholar, high as a darts-player, low as a bargainer, and high as a story-teller. In Greenleigh, he has something much more nearly approaching one status because something much more nearly approaching one criterion is used: his possessions.

Or rather we should say that the family has one status. The small group which lives inside the same house hangs together, and where people are known as "from No. 22" or "37," their identity being traced to the house which is the fixed entity, each one of them affects the credit of the other. The children, in particular, must be well dressed so that neighbors, and even more school friends and teachers, will think well of them, and of the parents.

> "We always see that the children look smart. At these new schools, you like them to go to school respectable. We like to keep them up to the standard out here."

The status is that of the family of marriage much more sharply than it is in Bethnal Green. In Bethnal Green the number of relatives who influence a person's standing is much larger, and they also are varied in their attributes.

From a prominent local personality, a street-trader, say, a councillor, or a publican, a person can borrow prestige; but through another relative he may be associated with a less enviable reputation. One connection confers high status, another low. It is therefore all the more difficult to give a person a single rating. On the other hand, the comparative isolation of the family at Greenleigh encourages the kind of simplified judgment of which we have been speaking.

People at Greenleigh want to get on in the light of these simple standards, and they are liable to be more anxious about it just because they no longer belong to small local groups. Their relationships are window-to-window, not face-to-face. Their need for respect is just as strong as it ever was, but instead of being able to find satisfaction in actual living relationships, through the personal respect that accompanies almost any steady human interaction, they have to turn to the other kind of respect which is awarded, by some strange sort of common understanding, for the quantity and quality of possessions with which the person surrounds himself. Those are the rules of the game and they are, under strong pressure from the neighbors, almost universally observed. Indeed, one of the most striking things about Greenleigh is the great influence the neighbors have, all the greater because they are anonymous. Though people stay in their houses, they do in a sense belong to a strong and compelling group. They do not know their judge personally but her influence is continuously felt. One might even suggest, to generalize, that the less the personal respect received in small group relationships, the greater is the striving for the kind of impersonal respect embodied in a status judgment. The lonely man, fearing he is looked down on, becomes the acquisitive man; possession the balm to anxiety; anxiety the spur to unfriendliness.

We took as our starting point people's remarks —so frequent and vehement as to demand discussion —about the unfriendliness of their fellow residents. We have suggested two main explanations. Negatively, people are without the old relatives. Positively, they have a new house. In a life now house-centered instead of kinship-centered, competition for status takes the form of a struggle for material acquisition. In the absence of small groups which join one family to another, in the absence of strong personal associations which extend from one household to

another, people think that they are judged, and judge
others, by the material standards which are the outward
and visible mark of respectability.

ISOLATION, LONELINESS AND THE HOLD ON LIFE
/Peter Townsend

The questions of social isolation and loneliness in old
age will be discussed here. A distinction is made between
the two: to be socially isolated is to have few contacts
with family and community; to be lonely is to have an un-
welcome *feeling* of lack or loss of companionship. The one
is objective, the other subjective and, as we shall see, the
two do not coincide.

The poorest people, socially as well as financially, were
those most isolated from family life. Social isolation needs
to be measured by reference to objective criteria. The problem is rather like that of measuring poverty. "Poverty" is
essentially a relative rather than an absolute term, and discovering its extent in a population is usually divided into
two stages. Most people agree on the first stage, which is to
place individuals on a scale according to their income;
they often disagree about the second, which involves de-
ciding how far up the scale the poverty "line" should be
drawn. The task of measuring isolation can also be divided
in this way by placing individuals on a scale according
to their degree of isolation and by drawing a line at some
point on the scale so that those below the line would, by
common consent, be called "the isolated."

There were 20 people who were very isolated. Their ages
ranged from 64 to 83. They comprised two married women,
two widowers, eight widows, five spinsters and three bachelors. Thirteen of them lived alone; 12 had no children and
half of the rest had sons only. It is worth examining their
circumstances, taking first those with children. Four of the
eight with surviving children had daughters. One was a
widow living with her only daughter, unmarried; she had
few other relatives and all lived outside London. The second was a widow who had come with her only daughter
from Scotland after the war, leaving friends and relatives

behind. They were together until the housing authorities gave them two separate homes, several miles apart; now one of her daughter's children lived with her but she saw the rest of the family once a week or less. The third was a very infirm widow whose only daughter was married to a naval officer, obliged to live near Portsmouth; she lived in the same house as a widowed and childless sister and saw her every day but infirmity prevented other social contacts. The fourth was a widower of 80 who said his daughter and son living in Bethnal Green visited him twice a week to see he was all right but did not spend much time with him, now his wife was dead; he had a drink with a friend twice a week but infirmity precluded other activities.

The other four very isolated people with children had sons only. One was a married woman whose only son had moved into his wife's home district outside London; she and her husband had only one relative in Bethnal Green, the wife's unmarried sister, who was seen each week, and they had no friends or outside social activities, largely because the husband could not walk. Another was a widower, living with an unmarried son, who saw two married sons about once a week; he had no other surviving relatives. The two remaining people were both widows living alone. One had three sons living outside London, two of them visited her once a week; she saw a sister and two aged aunts in Bethnal Green every week but she spent much of her time on her own. The other had two illegitimate sons but no other relatives; she saw these sons occasionally.

There remain the childless and the unmarried. Most were in a worse position. The 10 most isolated people of the 203 interviewed were all unmarried or childless. The circumstances of two are summarized below.

Miss Paley, aged 67, lived in a one-room tenement flat. It was a large airless room with dismal orange-brown wallpaper peeling off in huge strips. Two or three mats, ingrained with dirt, covered the floor. There was an old iron bedstead propped up in the middle by two bits of wood and on this was a heap of gray and brown blankets. An ancient iron mangle stood in a corner and there was a gas stove, a gas mantel for lighting, three or four wooden chairs and a table with a flat-iron propping up one of its legs. Miss Paley wore a pair of stockings, extensively patched and tied around her knees, and a ram-

shackle navy-blue skirt and slip. Her skin had the white-
ness of someone who rarely went out and she was very
shy of her appearance, particularly the open sores on
her face. She said she suffered from blood poisoning,
but had not seen her doctor since the war. (This was confirmed by the doctor.) She was the only child of parents
who had been street traders and who had died when she
was young, in the 1880s. "I was with my aunt until I was
nearly 40. She was 85 when she died. I had cousins in
the street but they were my aunt's children. In the war
they got scattered. They all had families to bring up and
I haven't met them since the war. I don't know where
they are. They had to leave me behind. I don't want them
people. I do my work in my own way. They wouldn't
have the patience with me." Persistent questioning failed
to reveal a single relative with whom she had any contact. She did not go to the cinema, to a club or to church,
and had no radio. She had spent Christmas on her own
and had never had a holiday away from home. She
sometimes made conversation with her neighbors in the
street but because of her appearance did not go into their
homes or they into hers. She had only one friend, a
young woman who "used to live in the street where I
lived," and they visited one another about once a week.
Her answer to a question about membership of a club
was typical of much she said. "No, I can't be shut in.
I don't go to those clubs. They'd be too much excitement
for me." At one point she said she went to bed about
8 pm and got up between 10 and 11 the next day. I
also found she had an hour or two in bed in the after-
noons.

Mr. Fortune, aged 76, lived alone in a two-room
council flat. There were two wooden chairs, an orange-
box converted into a cupboard, a gas stove, a table covered with newspaper, a battered old pram with tins and
boxes inside, a pair of wooden steps and little else in the
sitting-room. There was no fire, although the interview
took place on a cold February morning. Mr. Fortune
had been a cripple from birth and he was partly deaf.
He was unmarried and his five siblings were dead. An
older widowed sister-in-law lived about a mile away with
an unmarried son and daughter. These three and two
married nieces living in another East London borough

were seen from once a month to a few times a year. Asked how often he saw his sister-in-law Mr. Fortune said, "Only when I go there. It's a hard job to walk down there in winter time and I haven't seen her for three or four months." Asked about an old people's club he said, "No. I'm simply as I am now. I shouldn't like to join. Walking is such a painful job for me. I can't get any amusement out of it." He spoke to one or two of the neighbors outside his flat but he had no regular contact with any of them. He had one regular friend, living a few blocks away, who came over to see him on a Sunday about once a month, "more when there's fine weather." He was not a churchgoer, never went to a cinema, rarely went to a pub because he could not afford a drink, had never had a holiday in his life and spent Christmas on his own. "My nephew came down for an hour. He gave me a little present, 2s. 6d. No, I didn't get any cards." He received a non-contributory pension and supplementary assistance through the National Assistance Board, which recently arranged for him to have a woman home-help for two hours a week. Her regular call was the main event of the week. "I sit here messing about. Last week I was making an indoor aerial. I made those steps over there. I like listening to the wireless and making all manner of things. My time's taken up, I can tell you, with that and cooking and tidying-up."

The most striking fact about the most isolated people was that they had few surviving relatives, particularly near-relatives of their own or of succeeding generations. This lent special significance to familiar references to fathers having weaker ties with children than mothers, to sons being drawn into their wives' families, and to distant relatives being lost sight of after the death of "connecting" relatives. The isolated included a comparatively high number of unmarried and childless people, of those possessing sons but not daughters and of those without siblings. Rarely did they have friends, become members of clubs or otherwise participate in outside social activities in compensation. Nearly all of them were retired and most were infirm; some were shy of revealing to others how ill or poverty-stricken they were or how they had "let themselves go." They had little or no means of regular contact with the younger generation, and for one reason or another could not be brought into club activities.

One of the most striking results of the whole inquiry was that those living in relative isolation from family and community did not always say they were lonely.

Particular importance was attached during the interviews to "loneliness." The question was not asked until most of an individual's activities had been discussed and care was taken to ensure as serious and as considered a response as possible. One difficulty had to be overcome. A few people liked to let their children think they were lonely so the latter would visit them as much as possible. This meant they were not inclined to give an honest answer if children were present. In an early interview one married woman, asked whether she ever got lonely, said, "Sometimes I do when they are all at work." But she hesitated before answering and looked at two married daughters, who were in the room. On a subsequent call, when this woman was alone, she told me she was "never lonely really, but I like my children to call." A widow, who was alone when interviewed, said she was never lonely. In fascinating contrast to this was a statement of one of her married daughters, who was interviewed independently. "She's not too badly off. The most she complains of is loneliness. She's always wanting us to go up there." Care was therefore taken to ask about loneliness so far as possible when the old person was alone and to check any answer which seemed doubtful.

Some people living at the center of a large family complained of loneliness and some who were living in extreme isolation repeated several times with vigor that they were never lonely—such as Miss Paley and Mr. Fortune, described above. Despite there being a significant association between isolation and loneliness about a half of the isolated and rather isolated said they were not lonely; over a fifth of the first group said they were.

What is the explanation? Previous investigations have pointed to the multiplicity of causes of loneliness. In his Wolverhampton study Sheldon showed that those experiencing loneliness tended to be widowed and single people, to be living alone, to be in their eighties rather than in their sixties, to be men rather than women and to be the relatively infirm. He concluded, "Loneliness cannot be regarded as the simple direct result of social circumstances, but is rather an individual response to an external situation to which other old people may react quite differently." There seemed to be no single cause of severe loneliness in old people.

In several respects the present inquiry reached similar results. Forty-six per cent of widowed people said they were very or sometimes lonely, 42 per cent of those living alone, 53 per cent of those in their late seventies and eighties and 43 per cent of those who were infirm, compared with 27 per cent in the sample as a whole. But it is possible that less emphasis should be given to personal differences and to a multiplicity of causes. The results also suggested that a single social factor may be fundamental to loneliness. This is the recent deprivation of the company of a close relative, usually a husband or wife or a child, through death, illness or migration. Examination of individual interview-reports showed that of the 56 people saying they were very or sometimes lonely, 28 had been recently bereaved and 17 separated from children. This seemed to be the chief cause of their loneliness. A further 11 had experienced other drastic changes in family circumstances. It is necessary to consider these lonely people.

All but four of the 28 who had been recently bereaved had lost a husband or wife within the previous 10 years. "No one knows what loneliness is till your partner happens to go." "You don't realize it until you know it. But loneliness is the worst thing you can suffer in life." The men in particular talked about their bereavement with very deep feeling. "I miss her. Every time I look over there—that's her seat. People kept telling me to have someone to look after me but I said to myself, there'll never be another woman who will take her place." Three of them did not talk, they wept.

Mr. Heart had lost his wife seven years earlier. He lived with an unmarried son but he had no daughter. "Sometimes I get lonely. I think of her. There's not a day passes but she's in my mind. When she died I don't know how I stood on my feet. You don't know what it is when you don't have a wife. . . . I wish I had a daughter. If you had a daughter it would put you in mind of your wife. Sometimes I think I hear her calling in the next room. She was what you call exceptional, exceptional

good. You never had to run round any public house for
her. My son still goes and puts flowers on her grave.
. . . You can't tell how you miss someone until they go.
Death's a terrible thing, to lose someone you love."

One of the major consequences of a wife's death was that
the man saw less of his children. He acknowledged it was
the mother who held the family together. "When my missus
was alive I had to come and have tea in the bedroom because there wasn't room in here. The place was crowded out
with them (married children and their families on Satur-
days and Sundays)." "My daughters used to come round
often when my wife was alive, but I don't see so much of
them now. But they like to know I'm comfortable and being
looked after." Widowers in fact saw less of their children,
particularly of their sons, than married men and married
or widowed women, as judged by average frequency of
contact. But this falling-off did not apply to all a widower's
children. A close relationship with one child was usually
maintained. Several lived with a single or married daughter,
or visited a married daughter daily, and then described
the pleasure grandchildren gave them. "My young grand-
daughter likes swinging and I pick her up and she swings
between my legs. And then she climbs up on me. Playing
with my grandchildren is my greatest pleasure." They found
some consolation here. "I'm a grandfather," said one man,
"and that's the only goodness I get out of life."

The loss of the marriage partner was not quite such a
disaster for women. They had always depended less on husbands than husbands on them, and they found it easier to
console themselves with their families. Nevertheless, many
of them were lonely, particularly if their husbands had died
recently and particularly if infirmity or shortage of relatives
prevented them from finding comfort readily in the companionship of others. One woman's husband had died eight
years previously. She had no children. "I get so lonely I
could fill up the teapot with tears."

Mrs. Pridy was very infirm and her husband had died
only a year previously, when she was 80. She lived with
a daughter and grandchildren. "I sit here for hours and
hours sometimes thinking about it. I get depressed and I
start crying. We was always together. I can remember
even his laughing. "Come on, girl," he'd say, "don't get
sitting about. Let's liven 'em up." They say what is to

be will be. I never thought he'd. . . . But we've all got to go. A good many of them don't even know he's gone (neighbors). I sit here for hours thinking about him. I can't get over it."

Almost every man and woman whose husband or wife had died within the previous five years, compared with a half between five and ten years and a quarter over that limit, felt lonely. The shorter the period since the death the more likely were people to complain of loneliness. Although practically everyone felt lonely at first after about five or six years the presence or not of an affectionate family seemed to determine how long such feelings persisted.

Four people had lost a child and not a husband recently. Three were women widowed in the 1914 war who said a son had died in the previous few years. One had lost two sons in the 1939 war and another three years previously. "I could cry my heart out sometimes when I sit here." There was also a married woman whose only son had been killed at Arnhem in 1944. "He's never out of my mind. I always see him in my mind and they're still talking about wars." In speaking of the loss of children and other relatives it was notable how long people felt grief and how indelible was the memory of these people. The "In Memoriam" column of a local East London newspaper provides many examples of the feelings of relatives for those who have died, some of them several years previously. In the following three illustrations, printed in 1955, only the names have been changed.

HOWARD—To the beautiful memory of my beloved daughter, Alice, who fell asleep June 17th, 1949.

> Time takes away the edge of grief,
> But memories turn back every leaf.
> Ever in our thoughts—Mum and all.

TALEWILL—In treasured memory of our dear Mum, who fell asleep June 7th, 1945.

> Not a day do we forget you, Mum,
> In our hearts you are ever near,
> Loved, remembered, longed for always,
> Bringing many a silent tear.
>   Sadly missed—Loving sons and daughters.

HUGGINS—In loving memory of a dear nephew who passed away June 6th, 1953.

> Sad and sudden was the call,
> To one so dearly loved by all,

This month of June comes with regret,
It brings back a tragedy we shall never forget.
> —From Aunt Caroline, Uncle Bill, Uncle Herbert, Uncle Steve and cousins Mary, Alice and children.

After bereavement, recent separation from children and grandchildren was the most important reason for loneliness, affecting 17 of the 56 people. Eleven of the 17 had no contact with a child living in the district although recently at least one child had been there. What happened was that, if the last child to get married moved out of the district or was unable to find a home in it and there were no other children living nearby, the old person greatly missed their daily companionship, particularly if widowed. A further three old persons had a son living nearby but the daughters had recently moved away. And three widows who had been living with married children now lived alone, although some of their children still lived in the same district.

Mrs. Marvel was 80 and she lived alone in a new council flat. Her husband had been dead for 30 years. None of her six surviving children lived in Bethnal Green although five of the six visited her regularly once or twice a week. A married daughter lived with her until she obtained a council house outside London five years previously. Mrs. Marvel wanted to stay in the district where she had lived nearly all her life. Speaking of her former home, which was recently demolished, she said, "We went in ten and came out one." Later she said, "I'm sometimes lonely, especially as my children are away. Still, I count my blessings. They're all good children."

Mrs. Foreman had been a widow for over 30 years. She had no daughters and until twelve months previously had been living with her married son. He had now moved to a new housing estate. Although she stayed with him every weekend she was lonely at home. "I don't like coming back here. I get the hump."

There remained 11 whose loneliness seemed to be due to other causes. All had recently experienced a marked change in their social circumstances. The husband of one and the daughter of another were in hospital, and had been there for some months. A third complained bitterly about the new council flat to which she had been moved a year previously; she was among neighbors she did not know or like and she was further from two of her relatives. Two married men were infirm and could not leave the house; both had retired within the past three years. A married woman had experienced several drastic changes in the past few years and was one of the most lonely of all those interviewed. As an extreme example, she is worth noting.

Mrs. Austin, in her late sixties, lived in a council flat with her husband. She said she missed not having her seven children around her and that she was "very lonely. I can't account for it at all. I get so depressed." Five of the seven had married within a space of three years around 1950 and had left home one after another. All but two had moved to housing estates outside London or in other East London boroughs. These two lived about a mile away. One son, to whom she was particularly attached, had been killed in an accident several years previously. Soon after the children had married Mr. and Mrs. Austin had to leave their home, because it was to be demolished. "I can't settle here. I'd been over 40 years in one house. Since it's been pulled down and we've come here I've hardly spoken to my next-door neighbors. All the old neighbors have gone. You can't go in and out like you used to." She saw much less of her children than formerly, although her two youngest visited her twice a week and three of the others once a fortnight. Her only sister had died three years ago. Because of headaches she could no longer read and because of a fall which damaged her hand she could no longer knit. Her husband had been in ill-health for several years and was on bad terms with some of the children. Mrs. Austin had made two attempts at suicide and had recently spent six months in a mental hospital.

In this example nearly all the disturbing social changes that can occur in the life of an old person had occurred. Close relatives had died, the children had migrated, the old home and neighborhood had to be given up and many activities had to be abandoned because of increasing infirmity. This was desolation with a vengeance. Now to be *desolate*, as defined earlier, is to have been deprived recently of the companionship of someone who is loved. And the main conclusion of this analysis is that people saying they were lonely were nearly all people who had been deprived recently of the companionship of someone they loved. They were *desolates* and not necessarily *isolates*. They were isolated only in the sense that they had *become* isolated, relative to their previous situation. Many were not short of company. Several widowed people, in particular, lived with children and grandchildren and had many social activities.

We have seen that desolation, or the loss of someone who is loved, is more important than social isolation in explaining the loneliness of old people. Such a change may explain much more than loneliness, for it affects a person's health and whole state of mind. The problems of the physical and mental health of old people need to be studied against their known social condition and the sudden changes in that condition. In Bethnal Green many people talked of the drastic effects of retirement on men and of bereavement on both men and women. Remarks about people who had just retired or who had been recently widowed suggested they had less will to live and deteriorated quickly. "He didn't want to live any more." "Men break up when they give up work. They soon go." "He just went to pieces when she died." "She was left all alone in the world and didn't want to go on living." "I've got nothing left to live for." "He won't be long in following her." These remarks deserve careful attention. They imply the possibility of sudden physical degeneration, after retirement, for men, and after bereavement, for men and women.

While this is a very complex matter which cannot be discussed in detail here, three separate points seem to be worth making. The first concerns widows and widowers. The difficulties of old people in adapting themselves to new situations are well known. It may be particularly difficult for them to adjust their lives to the fact of bereavement. This is strongly supported by what they say about loneliness. The suggestion is that the mortality rates for people widowed in old age are likely to be higher than the rates for single and married people, and even than for people, of the same age, widowed when young.

Precise statistical data are not available to test this supposition. What evidence there is does not distinguish between those widowed late in life and other widowed people. But it is certainly not in conflict with the supposition. Mortality rates, by age and marital status, are available. These show higher death rates among older widowed people than others. There may be a number of reasons why the death rates for older widowed people tend to be higher than those for single and married people. Some may catch the illnesses from which their husbands or wives died. On the face of it, however, the influence of recent bereavement upon the rates may be worth careful study.

The second point concerns the higher death rates for older men than for older women. The differences between men and women may not be explained entirely by biological and physiological differences. Social factors may play a significant part here too. For example, the man in Bethnal Green, on retirement, had to change virtually his whole style of living; deserted by workmates and friends and thrown back on his family, he could rarely do other than play second fiddle to his wife. On the other hand his wife, to whom the affairs of household and family had always been dominant, could usually go on to a ripe old age doing most of the things she had always done. Sheldon observed that fewer women than men were in extreme good- or ill-health and while more of them had subnormal health their hold on life was tenacious. The present limited findings, so far as they go, confirm his observation. It is possible that the effect of retirement on men and that the security of women in job and family may contribute to the woman's greater expectation of life.

The third point in this matter of the effect of social factors upon health concerns social isolation. The trials and tribulations of old age may be harder for isolated people to bear, because they are not sustained by family and friends. A crude hypothesis may be put forward. Those who are socially isolated in old age, particularly those with the fewest contacts with relatives, tend to make greater claims on hospital and other health and social services and to die earlier than others.

In old age the death rates for bachelors are higher than those for married men but lower than those for widowers. The differences between single and married women seem to be very slight, except at the oldest ages. The subject is, however, very complex because of the influence of physical selection for marriage and of diseases associated with childbearing, to say nothing of the changes in patterns of marriage. There has been a rise in marriage rates since 1939. As those who marry are likely, on average, to be in better health than the unmarried it seems that as the number of spinsters becomes progressively smaller, a higher proportion will have inferior vitality. Recent evidence has shown that death rates of single women, relatively to married women, have increased in the last 20 years. Safer childbearing has also contributed to the relative improvement in the death rates of married women. Even so, in a long analysis comparing the mortality of single and married women before the war the Registrar General stated, "It is difficult to escape the conclusion that in the present state of society the married condition *per se* for women is more favorable to vitality than the single condition at ages up to 60."

Other data concern the once-married but childless. Since 1938 information has been obtained, at the registration of deaths of women who were or had at any time been married, as to whether they had had children. The number of such children, and whether they were live or still-born, is not recorded. Infertility rates, derived from such information, are published from time to time. The infertility rates for older deceased widows are lower than those for older deceased married women. This "unexpected" relationship, as it is described in the Statistical Review, may be due to a number of factors. One is that women with children may live longer, or may more often outlive their husbands, than childless women because the company of children helps them to keep a hold on life. All the available information about death-rates is, however, rather scanty. None of it—so far as the writer is aware—allows any exact test of an association between death and social isolation or, more generally, any systematic study of the relation between longevity and social circumstances.

Some of these speculations may deserve further inquiry. Comfort has stated that senescence is a change in the behavior of an organism with age, which leads to a decreased power of survival and adjustment. Here it is suggested that the social and especially the family circumstances of individuals are a major determinant of the rate of decline in the power of self-adjustment and self-defense in later life. Broadly speaking there may be a marked association between each of three social factors, these being social isolation, social desolation, and retirement, and the expectation of life of old people. Biological, physiological and health factors aside, one would expect, on the rather limited evidence from the present study, that old women and, to a lesser extent, old men who are at the center of a secure family live longer than those who are socially isolated or desolated, particularly the latter.

OF OUR SPIRITUAL STRIVINGS
/W. E. B. DuBois

O water, voice of my heart, crying in the sand,
    All night long crying with a mournful cry,
As I lie and listen, and cannot understand
      The voice of my heart in my side or the
        voice of the sea,
O water, crying for rest, is it I, is it I?
    All night long the water is crying to me.

Unresting water, there shall never be rest
    Till the last moon droop and the last tide fail,
And the fire of the end begin to burn in the west;
      And the heart shall be weary and wonder
        and cry like the sea,
    All life long crying without avail,
      As the water all night long is crying to me.
                        Arthur Symons

Between me and the other world there is ever an unasked question: unasked by some through feelings of delicacy; by others through the difficulty of rightly framing it. All, nevertheless, flutter round it. They approach me in a half-hesitant sort of way, eye me curiously or compassionately, and then, instead of saying directly, How does it feel to be a problem? they say, I know an excellent colored man in my town; or, I fought at Mechanicsville; or, Do not these Southern outrages make your blood boil? At these I smile, or am interested, or reduce the boiling to a simmer, as the occasion may require. To the real question, How does it feel to be a problem? I answer seldom a word.

And yet, being a problem is a strange experience—peculiar even for one who has never been anything else, save perhaps in babyhood and in Europe. It is in the early days of rollicking boyhood that the revelation first bursts upon one, all in a day, as it were. I remember well when the shadow swept across me. I was a little thing, away up in the hills of New England, where the dark Housatonic winds between Hoosac and Taghkanic to the sea. In a wee wooden schoolhouse, something put it into the boys' and girls' heads to buy gorgeous visiting-cards—ten cents a package—and exchange. The exchange was merry till one girl, a tall newcomer, refused my card—refused it peremptorily, with a glance. Then it dawned upon me with a certain suddenness that I was different from the others; or like, mayhap, in heart and life and longing, but shut out from their world by a vast veil. I had thereafter no desire to tear down that veil, to creep through; I held all beyond it in common contempt, and lived above it in a region of blue sky and great wandering shadows. That sky was bluest when I could beat my mates at examination time, or beat them at a foot race, or even beat their stringy heads. Alas, with the years all this fine contempt began to fade; for the worlds I longed for, and all their dazzling opportunities, were theirs, not mine. But they should not keep these prizes, I said; some, all, I would wrest from them. Just how I would do it I could never decide: by reading law, by healing the sick, by telling the wonderful tales that swam in my head—some way. With other black boys the strife was not so fiercely sunny: their youth shrunk into tasteless sycophancy, or into silent hatred of the pale world about them and mocking distrust of everything white; or wasted itself in a bitter cry, Why did God make me an outcast and a stranger in mine own house? The shades of the prison-house closed round about us all: walls strait and stubborn to the whitest, but relentlessly narrow, tall, and unscalable to sons of night who must plod darkly on in resignation, or beat unavailing palms against the stone, or steadily, half hopelessly, watch the streak of blue above.

After the Egyptian and Indian, the Greek and Roman, the Teuton and Mongolian, the Negro is a sort of seventh son, born with a veil, and gifted with second-sight in this American world—a world which yields him no true self-consciousness, but only lets him see himself through the revelation of the other world. It is a peculiar sensation, this double-consciousness, this sense of always looking at one's self through the eyes of others, of measuring one's soul by the tape of a world that looks on in amused contempt and pity. One ever feels his twoness—an American, a Negro; two souls, two thoughts, two unreconciled strivings; two warring ideals in one dark body, whose dogged strength alone keeps it from being torn asunder.

The history of the American Negro is the history of this strife—this longing to attain self-conscious manhood, to merge his double self into a better and truer self. In this merging he wishes neither of the older selves to be lost. He would not Africanize America, for America has too much to teach the world and Africa. He would not bleach his Negro soul in a flood of white Americanism, for he knows that Negro blood has a message for the world. He simply wishes to make it possible for a man to be both a Negro and an American, without being cursed and spit upon by his fellows, without having the doors of Opportunity closed roughly in his face.

This, then, is the end of his striving: to be a co-worker in the kingdom of culture, to escape both death and isolation, to husband and use his best powers and his latent genius. These powers of body and mind have in the past been strangely wasted, dispersed, or forgotten. The shadow of a mighty Negro past flits through the tale of Ethiopia the Shadowy and of Egypt the Sphinx. Throughout history, the powers of single black men flash here and there like falling stars, and die sometimes before the world has rightly gauged their brightness. Here in America, in the few days since Emancipation, the black man's turning hither and thither in hesitant and doubtful striving has often made his very strength to lose effectiveness, to seem like absence of power, like weakness. And yet it is not weakness—it is the contradiction of double aims. The double-aimed struggle of the black artisan—on the one hand to escape white contempt for a nation of mere hewers of wood and drawers of water, and on the other hand to plough and nail and dig for a poverty-stricken horde—could only result in making him a poor craftsman, for he had but half a heart in either cause. By the poverty and ignorance of his people, the Negro minister or doctor was tempted toward quackery and demagogy; and by the criticism of the other world, toward ideals that made him ashamed of his lowly tasks. The would-be black *savant* was confronted by the paradox that the knowledge his people needed was a twice-told tale to his white neighbors, while the knowledge which would teach the white world was Greek to his own flesh and blood. The

innate love of harmony and beauty that set the ruder souls
of his people a-dancing and a-singing raised but confusion
and doubt in the soul of the black artist; for the beauty
revealed to him was the soul-beauty of a race which his
larger audience despised, and he could not articulate the
message of another people. This waste of double aims, this
seeking to satisfy two unreconciled ideals, has wrought sad
havoc with the courage and faith and deeds of ten thousand thousand people—has sent them often wooing false
gods and invoking false means of salvation, and at times
has even seemed about to make them ashamed of themselves.

Away back in the days of bondage they thought to see
in one divine event the end of all doubt and disappointment;
few men ever worshiped Freedom with half such unquestioning faith as did the American Negro for two centuries.
To him, so far as he thought and dreamed, slavery was indeed the sum of all villainies, the cause of all sorrow, the
root of all prejudice; Emancipation was the key to a promised land of sweeter beauty than ever stretched before the
eyes of wearied Israelites. In song and exhortation swelled
one refrain—Liberty; in his tears and curses the God he implored had Freedom in his right hand. At last it came—
suddenly, fearfully, like a dream. With one wild carnival
of blood and passion came the message in his own plaintive cadences:

> "Shout, O children!
> Shout, you're free!
> For God has bought your liberty!"

Years have passed away since then—ten, twenty, forty;
forty years of national life, forty years of renewal and
development, and yet the swarthy specter sits in its accustomed seat at the Nation's feast. In vain do we cry to this
our vastest social problem:

> "Take any shape but that, and my firm nerves
> Shall never tremble!"

The Nation has not yet found peace from its sins; the
freedman has not yet found in freedom his promised land.
Whatever of good may have come in these years of change,
the shadow of a deep disappointment rests upon the Negro
people—a disappointment all the more bitter because the

unattained ideal was unbounded save by the simple ignorance of a lowly people.

The first decade was merely a prolongation of the vain search for freedom, the boon that seemed ever barely to elude their grasp, like a tantalizing will-o'-the-wisp, maddening and misleading the headless host. The holocaust of war, the terrors of the Ku Klux Klan, the lies of carpetbaggers, the disorganization of industry, and the contradictory advice of friends and foes, left the bewildered serf with no new watchword beyond the old cry for freedom. As the time flew, however, he began to grasp a new idea. The ideal of liberty demanded for its attainment powerful means, and these the Fifteenth Amendment gave him. The ballot, which before he had looked upon as a visible sign of freedom, he now regarded as the chief means of gaining and perfecting the liberty with which war had partially endowed him. And why not? Had not votes made war and emancipated millions? Had not votes enfranchised the freedmen? Was anything impossible to a power that had done all this? A million black men started with renewed zeal to vote themselves into the kingdom. So the decade flew away, the revolution of 1876 came, and left the half-free serf weary, wondering, but still inspired. Slowly but steadily, in the following years, a new vision began gradually to replace the dream of political power—a powerful movement, the rise of another ideal to guide the unguided, another pillar of fire by night after a clouded day. It was the ideal of "book-learning"; the curiosity, born of compulsory ignorance, to know and test the power of the cabalistic letters of the white man, the longing to know. Here at last seemed to have been discovered the mountain path to Canaan; longer than the highway of Emancipation and law, steep and rugged, but straight, leading to heights high enough to overlook life.

Up the new path the advance guard toiled, slowly, heavily, doggedly; only those who have watched and guided the faltering feet, the misty minds, the dull understandings, of the dark pupils of these schools know how faithfully, how piteously, this people strove to learn. It was weary work. The cold statistician wrote down the inches of progress here and there, noted also where here and there a foot had slipped or some one had fallen. To the tired climbers, the horizon was ever dark, the mists were often

cold, the Canaan was always dim and far away. If, however, the vistas disclosed as yet no goal, no resting-place,
little but flattery and criticism, the journey at least gave
leisure for reflection and self-examination; it changed the
child of Emancipation to the youth with dawning self-consciousness, self-realization, self-respect. In those somber
forests of his striving his own soul rose before him, and he
saw himself, darkly as through a veil; and yet he saw in
himself some faint revelation of his power, of his mission.
He began to have a dim feeling that, to attain his place in
the world, he must be himself, and not another. For the
first time he sought to analyze the burden he bore upon
his back, that dead-weight of social degradation partially
masked behind a half-named Negro problem. He felt his
poverty; without a cent, without a home, without land,
tools, or savings, he had entered into competition with rich,
landed, skilled neighbors. To be a poor man is hard, but to
be a poor race in a land of dollars is the very bottom of
hardships. He felt the weight of his ignorance—not simply
of letters, but of life, of business, of the humanities; the
accumulated sloth and shirking and awkwardness of decades
and centuries shackled his hands and feet. Nor was his
burden all poverty and ignorance. The red stain of bastardy,
which two centuries of systematic legal defilement of Negro women had stamped upon his race, meant not only the
loss of ancient African chastity, but also the hereditary
weight of a mass of corruption from white adulterers,
threatening almost the obliteration of the Negro home.

A people thus handicapped ought not to be asked to race
with the world, but rather allowed to give all its time and
thought to its own social problems. But alas! while sociologists gleefully count his bastards and his prostitutes, the very
soul of the toiling, sweating black man is darkened by the
shadow of a vast despair. Men call the shadow prejudice,
and learnedly explain it as the natural defence of culture
against barbarism, learning against ignorance, purity against
crime, the "higher" against the "lower" races. To which
the Negro cries Amen! and swears that to so much of this
strange prejudice as is founded on just homage to civilization, culture, righteousness, and progress, he humbly bows
and meekly does obeisance. But before that nameless prejudice that leaps beyond all this he stands helpless,
dismayed, and well-nigh speechless; before that personal disrespect and mockery, the ridicule and systematic humilia-

tion, the distortion of fact and wanton license of fancy, the cynical ignoring of the better and the boisterous welcoming of the worse, the all-pervading desire to inculcate disdain for everything black, from Toussaint to the devil—before this there rises a sickening despair that would disarm and discourage any nation save that black host to whom "discouragement" is an unwritten word.

But the facing of so vast a prejudice could not but bring the inevitable self-questioning, self-disparagement, and lowering of ideals which ever accompany repression and breed in an atmosphere of contempt and hate. Whisperings and portents came borne upon the four winds: Lo! we are diseased and dying, cried the dark hosts; we cannot write, our voting is vain; what need of education, since we must always cook and serve? And the Nation echoed and enforced this self-criticism, saying: Be content to be servants, and nothing more; what need of higher culture for half-men? Away with the black man's ballot, by force or fraud—and behold the suicide of a race! Nevertheless, out of the evil came something of good—the more careful adjustment of education to real life, the clearer perception of the Negroes' social responsibilities, and the sobering realization of the meaning of progress.

So dawned the time of *Sturm und Drang:* storm and stress today rock our little boat on the mad waters of the world-sea; there is within and without the sound of conflict, the burning of body and rending of soul; inspiration strives with doubt, and faith with vain questionings. The bright ideals of the past—physical freedom, political power, the training of brains and the training of hands—all these in turn have waxed and waned, until even the last grows dim and overcast. Are they all wrong, all false? No, not that, but each alone was oversimple and incomplete—the dreams of a credulous race-childhood, or the fond imaginings of the other world which does not know and does not want to know our power. To be really true, all these ideals must be melted and welded into one. The training of the schools we need today more than ever—the training of deft hands, quick eyes and ears, and above all the broader, deeper, higher culture of gifted minds and pure hearts. The power of the ballot we need in sheer self-defence—else what shall save us from a second slavery? Freedom, too, the long-sought, we still seek—the freedom of life and limb, the freedom to work and think, the freedom to love and aspire. Work, culture, liberty—all these we need, not singly but together, not successively but together, each growing and aiding each, and all striving toward that vaster ideal that swims before the Negro people, the ideal of human brotherhood, gained through the unifying ideal of Race; the ideal of fostering and developing the traits and talents of the Negro, not in opposition to or contempt for other races, but rather in large conformity to the greater ideals of the American Republic, in order that some day on American soil two world-races may give each to each those characteristics both so sadly lack. We the darker ones come even now not altogether emptyhanded: there are today no truer exponents of the pure human spirit of the Declaration of Independence than the American Negroes; there is no true American music but the wild sweet melodies of the Negro slave; the American fairy tales and folklore are Indian and African; and, all in all, we black men seem the sole oasis of simple faith and reverence in a dusty desert of dollars and smartness. Will America be poorer if she replace her brutal dyspeptic blundering with light-hearted but determined Negro humility? or her coarse and cruel wit with loving jovial good-humor? or her vulgar music with the soul of the Sorrow Songs?

Merely a concrete test of the underlying principles of the great republic is the Negro Problem, and the spiritual striving of the freedmen's sons is the travail of souls whose burden is almost beyond the measure of their strength, but who bear it in the name of an historic race, in the name of this the land of their fathers' fathers, and in the name of human opportunity.

FIFTH AVENUE, UPTOWN
/James Baldwin

There is a housing project standing now where the house in which we grew up once stood, and one of those stunted city trees is snarling where our doorway used to be. This is on the rehabilitated side of the avenue. The other side of the avenue—for progress takes time—has not been rehabilitated yet and it looks exactly as it looked in the days when we sat with our noses pressed against the window-pane, longing to be allowed to go "across the street." The grocery store which gave us credit is still there, and there can be no doubt that it is still giving credit. The people in the project certainly need it—far more, indeed, than they ever needed the project. The last time I passed by, the Jewish proprietor was still standing among his shelves, looking sadder and heavier but scarcely any older. Further down the block stands the shoe-repair store in which our shoes were repaired until reparation became impossible and in which, then, we bought all our "new" ones. The Negro proprietor is still in the window, head down, working at the leather.

These two, I imagine, could tell a long tale if they would (perhaps they would be glad to if they could), having watched so many, for so long, struggling in the fishhooks, the barbed wire, of this avenue.

The avenue is elsewhere the renowned and elegant Fifth. The area I am describing, which, in today's gang parlance, would be called "the turf," is bounded by Lenox Avenue on the west, the Harlem River on the east, 135th Street on the north, and 130th Street on the south. We never lived beyond these boundaries; this is where we grew up. Walking along 145th Street—for example—familiar as it is, and similar, does not have the same impact because I do not know any of the people on the block. But when I turn east on 131st Street and Lenox Avenue, there is first a soda-pop joint, then a shoeshine "parlor," then a grocery store, then a dry cleaners', then the houses. All along the street there are people who watched me grow up, people who grew up with me, people I watched grow up along with my brothers and sisters; and, sometimes in my arms, sometimes underfoot, sometimes at my shoulder—or on it—their children, a riot, a forest of children, who include my nieces and nephews.

When we reach the end of this long block, we find ourselves on wide, filthy, hostile Fifth Avenue, facing that project which hangs over the avenue like a monument to the folly, and the cowardice, of good intentions. All along the block, for anyone who knows it, are immense human gaps, like craters. These gaps are not created merely by those who have moved away, inevitably into some other ghetto; or by those who have risen, almost always into a greater capacity for self-loathing and self-delusion; or yet by those who, by whatever means—War II, the Korean war, a policeman's gun or billy, a gang war, a brawl, madness, an overdose of heroin, or, simply, unnatural exhaustion—are dead. I am talking about those who are left, and I am talking principally about the young. What are they doing? Well, some, a minority, are fanatical churchgoers, members of the more extreme of the Holy Roller sects. Many, many more are "moslems," by affiliation or sympathy, that is to say that they are united by nothing more—and nothing less—than a hatred of the white world and all its works. They are present, for example, at every Buy Black street-corner meeting—meetings in which the speaker urges his hearers to cease trading with white men and establish a separate economy. Neither the speaker nor his hearers can possibly do this, of course, since Negroes do not own General Motors or RCA or the A&P, nor, indeed, do they own more than a wholly insufficient fraction of anything else in Harlem (those who *do* own anything are more interested in their profits than in their fellows). But these meetings nevertheless keep alive in the participators a certain pride of bitterness without which, however futile this bitterness may be, they could scarcely remain alive at all. Many have given up. They stay home and watch the TV screen, living on the earnings of their parents, cousins, brothers, or uncles, and only leave the house to go to the movies or to the nearest bar. "How're you making it?" one may ask, running into them along the block, or in the bar. "Oh, I'm TV-ing it"; with the saddest, sweetest, most shamefaced of smiles, and from a great distance. This distance one is compelled to respect; anyone who has traveled so far will not easily be dragged again into the world. There are further retreats, of course, than the TV screen or the bar. There are those who are simply sitting on their stoops, "stoned," animated for a moment only, and hideously, by the approach of someone who may lend them the money for a "fix." Or by the approach of someone from whom they can purchase it, one of the shrewd ones, on the way to prison or just coming out.

And the others, who have avoided all of these deaths, get up in the morning and go downtown to meet "the man." They work in the white man's world all day and come home in the evening to this fetid block. They struggle to instill in their children some private sense of honor or dignity which will help the child to survive. This means, of course, that they must struggle, stolidly, incessantly, to keep this sense alive in themselves, in spite of the insults, the indifference, and the cruelty they are certain to encounter in their working day. They patiently browbeat the landlord into fixing the heat, the plaster, the plumbing; this demands prodigious patience; nor is patience usually enough. In trying to make their hovels habitable, they are perpetually throwing good money after bad. Such frustration, so long endured, is driving many strong, admirable men and women whose only crime is color to the very gates of paranoia.

One remembers them from another time—playing handball in the playground, going to church, wondering if they were going to be promoted at school. One remembers them going off to war—gladly, to escape this block. One remembers their return. Perhaps one remembers their wedding day. And one sees where the girl is now—vainly looking for salvation from some other embittered, trussed, and struggling boy—and sees the all-but-abandoned children in the streets.

Now I am perfectly aware that there are other slums in which white men are fighting for their lives, and mainly losing. I know that blood is also flowing through those streets and that the human damage there is incalculable. People are continually pointing out to me the wretchedness of white people in order to console me for the wretchedness of blacks. But an itemized account of the American failure does not console me and it should not console anyone else. That hundreds and thousands of white people are living, in effect, no better than the "niggers" is not a fact to be regarded with complacency. The social and moral bankruptcy suggested by this fact is of the bitterest, most terrifying kind.

The people, however, who believe that this democratic anguish has some consoling value are always pointing out that So-and-So, white, and So-and-So, black, rose from the slums into the big time. The existence—the public existence—of, say, Frank Sinatra and Sammy Davis, Jr. proves to them that America is still the land of opportunity and that inequalities vanish before the determined will. It proves nothing of the sort. The determined will is rare—at the moment, in this country, it is unspeakably rare—and the inequalities suffered by the many are in no way justified by the rise of a few. A few have always risen—in every country, every era, and in the teeth of regimes which can by no stretch of the imagination be thought of as free. Not all these people, it is worth remembering, left the world better than they found it. The determined will is rare, but it is not invariably benevolent. Furthermore, the American equation of success with the big time reveals an awful disrespect for human life and human achievement. This equation has placed our cities among the most dangerous in the world and has placed our youth among the most empty and most bewildered. The situation of our youth is not mysterious. Children have never been very good at listening to their elders, but they have never failed to imitate them. They must, they have no other models. That is exactly what our children are doing. They are imitating our immorality, our disrespect for the pain of others.

All other slum dwellers, when the bank account permits it, can move out of the slum and vanish altogether from the eye of persecution. No Negro in this country has ever made that much money and it will be a long time before any Negro does. The Negroes in Harlem, who have no money, spend what they have on such gimcracks as they are sold. These include "wider" TV screens, more "faithful" hi-fi sets, more "powerful" cars, all of which, of course, are obsolete long before they are paid for. Anyone who has ever struggled with poverty knows how extremely expensive it is to be poor; and if one is a member of a captive population, economically speaking, one's feet have simply been placed on the treadmill forever. One is victimized, economically, in a thousand ways—rent, for example, or car insurance. Go shopping one day in Harlem— for anything—and compare Harlem prices and quality with those downtown.

The people who have managed to get off this block have only got as far as a more respectable ghetto. This respectable ghetto does not even have the advantages of the disreputable one, friends, neighbors, a familiar church, and friendly tradesmen; and it is not, moreover, in the nature of any ghetto to remain respectable long. Every Sunday, people who have left the block take the lonely ride back, dragging their increasingly discontented children with them. They spend the day talking, not always with words, about the trouble they've seen and the trouble—one must watch their eyes as they watch their children—they are only too likely to see. For children do not like ghettos. It takes them nearly no time to discover exactly why they are there.

The projects in Harlem are hated. They are hated almost

as much as policemen, and this is saying a great deal. And they are hated for the same reason: both reveal, unbearably, the real attitude of the white world, no matter how many liberal speeches are made, no matter how many lofty editorials are written, no matter how many civil-rights commissions are set up.

The projects are hideous, of course, there being a law, apparently respected throughout the world, that popular housing shall be as cheerless as a prison. They are lumped all over Harlem, colorless, bleak, high, and revolting. The wide windows look out on Harlem's invincible and indescribable squalor: the Park Avenue railroad tracks, around which, about forty years ago, the present dark community began; the unrehabilitated houses, bowed down, it would seem, under the great weight of frustration and bitterness they contain; the dark, the ominous schoolhouses from which the child may emerge maimed, blinded, hooked, or enraged for life; and the churches, churches, block upon block of churches, niched in the walls like cannon in the walls of a fortress. Even if the administration of the projects were not so insanely humiliating (for example: one must report raises in salary to the management, which will then eat up the profit by raising one's rent; the management has the right to know who is staying in your apartment; the management can ask you to leave, at their discretion), the projects would still be hated because they are an insult to the meanest intelligence.

Harlem got its first private project, Riverton—which is now, naturally, a slum—about twelve years ago because at that time Negroes were not allowed to live in Stuyvesant Town. Harlem watched Riverton go up, therefore, in the most violent bitterness of spirit, and hated it long before the builders arrived. They began hating it at about the time people began moving out of their condemned houses to make room for this additional proof of how thoroughly the white world despised them. And they had scarcely moved in, naturally, before they began smashing windows, defacing walls, urinating in the elevators, and fornicating in the playgrounds. Liberals, both white and black, were appalled at the spectacle. I was appalled by the liberal innocence—or cynicism, which comes out in practice as much the same thing. Other people were delighted to be able to point to proof positive that nothing could be done to better the lot of the colored people. They were, and are, right in one respect: that nothing can be done as long as they are treated like colored people. The people in Harlem know they are living there because white people do not think they are good enough to live anywhere else. No amount of "improvement" can sweeten this fact. Whatever money is now being earmarked to improve this, or any other ghetto, might as well be burnt. A ghetto can be improved in one way only: out of existence.

Similarly the only way to police a ghetto is to be oppressive. None of Commissioner Kennedy's policemen, even with the best will in the world, have any way of understanding the lives led by the people they swagger about in two's and three's controlling. Their very presence is an insult, and it would be, even if they spent their entire day feeding gumdrops to children. They represent the force of the white world; and that world's real intentions are, simply, for that world's criminal profit and ease, to keep the black man corraled up here, in his place. The badge, the gun in the holster, and the swinging club make vivid what will happen should his rebellion become overt. Rare, indeed, is the Harlem citizen, from the most circumspect church member to the most shiftless adolescent, who does not have a long tale to tell of police incompetence, injustice, or brutality. I myself have witnessed and endured it more than once. The businessmen and racketeers also have a story. And so do the prostitutes. (And this is not, perhaps, the place to discuss Harlem's very complex attitude towards black policemen, nor the reasons, according to Harlem, that they are nearly all downtown.)

It is hard, on the other hand, to blame the policeman, blank, good-natured, thoughtless, and insuperably innocent, for being such a perfect representative of the people he serves. He, too, believes in good intentions and is astounded and offended when they are not taken for the deed. He has never, himself, done anything for which to be hated—which of us has?—and yet he is facing, daily and nightly, people who would gladly see him dead, and he knows it. There is no way for him not to know it: there are few things under heaven more unnerving than the silent, accumulating contempt and hatred of a people. He moves through Harlem, therefore, like an occupying soldier in a bitterly hostile country; which is precisely what, and where, he is, and is the reason he walks in two's and three's. And he is not the only one who knows why he is always in company: the people who are watching him know why, too. Any street meeting, sacred or secular, which he and his colleagues uneasily cover has as its explicit or implicit burden the cruelty and injustice of the white domination. And these days, of course, in terms increasingly vivid and jubilant, it speaks of the end of that domination. The white policeman, standing on a Harlem street corner, finds himself at the very center of the revolution now occurring in the world. He is not prepared for it—naturally, nobody is—and, what is possibly much more to the point, he is exposed, as few white people are, to the anguish of the black people around him. Even if he is gifted with the merest mustard grain of imagination, something must seep in. He cannot avoid observing that some of the children, in spite of their color, remind him of children he has known and loved, perhaps even of his own children. He knows that he certainly does not want *his* children living this way. He can retreat from his uneasiness in only one direction: into a callousness which very shortly becomes second nature. He becomes more callous, the population becomes more hostile, the situation grows more tense, and the police force is increased. One day, to everyone's astonishment, someone drops a match in the powder keg and everything blows up. Before the dust has settled or the blood congealed, editorials, speeches, and civil-rights commissions are loud in the land, demanding to know what happened. What happened is that Negroes want to be treated like men.

Negroes want to be treated like men: a perfectly straightforward statement, containing only seven words. People who have mastered Kant, Hegel, Shakespeare, Marx, Freud, and the Bible find this statement utterly impenetrable. The idea seems to threaten profound, barely conscious assumptions. A kind of panic paralyzes their features, as though they found themselves trapped on the edge of a steep place. I once tried to describe to a very-well-known American intellectual the conditions among Negroes in the South. My recital disturbed him and made him indignant; and he asked me in perfect innocence, "Why don't all the Negroes in the South move North?" I tried to explain what *has* happened, unfailingly, whenever a significant body of Negroes move North. They do not escape jim-crow: they merely encounter another, not-less-deadly variety. They do not move to Chicago, they move to the South Side; they do not move to New York, they move to

Harlem. The pressure within the ghetto causes the ghetto walls to expand, and this expansion is always violent. White people hold the line as long as they can, and in as many ways as they can, from verbal intimidation to physical violence. But inevitably the border which has divided the ghetto from the rest of the world falls into the hands of the ghetto. The white people fall back bitterly before the black horde; the landlords make a tidy profit by raising the rent, chopping up the rooms, and all but dispensing with the upkeep; and what has once been a neighborhood turns into a "turf." This is precisely what happened when the Puerto Ricans arrived in their thousands—and the bitterness thus caused is, as I write, being fought out all up and down those streets.

Northerners indulge in an extremely dangerous luxury. They seem to feel that because they fought on the right side during the Civil War, and won, that they have earned the right merely to deplore what is going on in the South, without taking any responsibility for it; and that they can ignore what is happening in Northern cities because what is happening in Little Rock or Birmingham is worse. Well, in the first place, it is not possible for anyone who has not endured both to know which is "worse." I know Negroes who prefer the South and white Southerners, because "At least there, you haven't got to play any guessing games!" The guessing games referred to have driven more than one Negro into the narcotics ward, the madhouse, or the river. I know another Negro, a man very dear to me, who says, with conviction and with truth, "The spirit of the South is the spirit of America." He was born in the North and did his military training in the South. He did not, as far as I can gather, find the South "worse"; he found it, if anything, all too familiar. In the second place, though, even if Birmingham *is* worse, no doubt Johannesburg, South Africa, beats it by several miles, and Buchenwald was one of the worst things that ever happened in the entire history of the world. The world has never lacked for horrifying examples; but I do not believe that these examples are meant to be used as justification for our own crimes. This perpetual justification empties the heart of all human feeling. The emptier our hearts become, the greater will be our crimes. Thirdly, the South is not merely an embarrassingly backward region, but a part of this country, and what happens there concerns every one of us.

As far as the color problem is concerned, there is but one great difference between the Southern white and the Northerner: the Southerner remembers, historically, and in his own psyche, a kind of Eden in which he loved black people and they loved him. Historically, the flaming sword laid across this Eden is the Civil War. Personally, it is the Southerner's sexual coming of age, when, without any warning, unbreakable taboos are set up between himself and his past. Everything, thereafter, is permitted him except the love he remembers and has never ceased to need. The resulting, indescribable torment affects every Southern mind and is the basis of the Southern hysteria.

None of this is true for the Northerner. Negroes represent nothing to him personally, except, perhaps, the dangers of carnality. He never sees Negroes. Southerners see them all the time. Northerners never think about them whereas Southerners are never really thinking of anything else. Negroes are, therefore, ignored in the North and are under surveillance in the South, and suffer hideously in both places. Neither the Southerner nor the Northerner is able to look on the Negro simply as a man. It seems to be indispensable to the national self-esteem that the Negro be considered either as a kind of ward (in which case we are told how many Negroes, comparatively, bought Cadillacs last year and how few, comparatively, were lynched), or as a victim (in which case we are promised that he will never vote in our assemblies or go to school with our kids). They are two sides of the same coin and the South will not change—*cannot* change—until the North changes. The country will not change until it re-examines itself and discovers what it really means by freedom. In the meantime, generations keep being born, bitterness is increased by incompetence, pride, and folly, and the world shrinks around us.

It is a terrible, an inexorable, law that one cannot deny the humanity of another without diminishing one's own: in the face of one's victim, one sees oneself. Walk through the streets of Harlem and see what we, this nation, have become.

VII. REBELS, DEVIANTS AND RETREATISTS

The alienating conditions we have described so far pervade modern society and touch vast numbers of men and women —factory workers, white-collar workers, organization men, voters, audiences, the aged, Negroes. Although alienated, their responses—except in time of severe crisis—are subdued; theirs are the lives of quiet desperation. This section deals with people who do not sit and take it: they rebel, retreat, or deviate in some significant way from ordinary behavior. In grouping together artistic rebels, juvenile delinquents, addicts, sexual deviants, psychotics and suicides, we most certainly do not mean to suggest that they are similar in nature or that there is any simple explanation for them. Nor is this intended to be a catalogue of "maladjustment" or "social disorganization." Rather, it is a sampling of a number of major types of alienated behavior, each one of which deserves and often receives whole volumes of treatment. These people are alike only in that they feel cut off or have cut themselves off from the main stream of community life.

In choosing as our first selection several pages from Dostoyevsky's short novel, *Notes from Underground,* we present the quintessence of the nineteenth-century intellectual revolt against materialism. Written in 1864, this curious work focuses its attack on the "Crystal Palace," a celebrated English exhibition of science and technology, but for Dostoyevsky a symbol of all that was wrong with the world. In truly nihilistic spirit Dostoyevsky rages against the idea that by using reason alone man can progress to higher forms. This "underground man" scorns reason (or science), planning and progress; he derides or would destroy their works to preserve his freedom—even a freedom underground.

At first glance there is an unbridgeable gap between Dostoyevsky's underground man and present-day juvenile delinquents. Possibly, however, the author of *The Possessed* would have found kindred spirits among these young rebels. In his trenchant analysis of juvenile delinquency in America, Albert Cohen shows how this form of behavior is not merely a reflection of personality difficulties, slums and broken homes, but is directly related to the structure of our society and its prevailing values. Thus while delinquency is not exclusively working-class in origin, it may be interpreted in large part as the frustrated and violent response of those at the bottom to middle-class values which schools and other institutions seek to impose but which—given the obstacles to social advancement—they are unable to achieve. Isolated from the community, working-class boys can achieve status or recognition chiefly in their gangs, which offer a "solution." It is in the nature of that solution, as Cohen observes, to reject the middle-class values which society tries to impose and to sanction that rejection. Cohen concludes: "The same value system, impinging upon children differently equipped to meet it, is instrumental in generating both delinquency and respectability." That delinquency may have sinister political and racial overtones is suggested by Clancy Sigal's "Short Talk with a Fascist Beast," a vivid description of youthful participants in a London race riot.

If delinquents are clearly rebellious, no such simple statement can be made about addicts, the next group described or discussed here. Some may be rebellious and others escapist or retreatist; but all are victims of a chemical compulsion whereby alcohol or drug becomes the master. Neuroses unquestionably lie at the root of addictions, but alone cannot explain why people drown in drink or drugs. Evidence shows that physiological factors and nutritional elements are also involved. Nevertheless, addictions have serious psychological and social consequences; the addict's behavior is generally unacceptable; society is hostile; and the victim responds with feelings of guilt and remorse, and further undesirable behavior. The heavy drinker often becomes isolated from family and community as a result of his condition. It is a measure of the intricacy of the problem that while psychotherapy alone has been notoriously unsuccessful in curing alcoholics, combined with diet and drugs it has often proved helpful. Alcoholics Anonymous, a quasi-religious movement, has scored notable successes in restoring alcoholics to community life.

While alcoholism is serious enough; drug addiction is perhaps more terrible still—especially in the United States, where the non-medical use of narcotics is a criminal offense and the public is violent in disapprobation. Furthermore, while alcoholics may find solidarity in a movement such as A.A., narcotics addicts huddle together for mutual protection while under the influence. Theirs is truly a league of the damned. William Burroughs, himself a former addict, tells us, "Nothing ever happens in the junk world."

Nothingness, however, is precisely what many addicts and alcoholics seek, as Elmer Bendiner shows in his description of the "Bowery men." Here in this brotherhood of the beaten and defeated, men find a perfect hiding place from the world, find what so many citizens of the modern world seek and never find—an escape from tensions. In this respect, at least, as Bendiner observes, they have something in common with the organization man. But while he fails to achieve tranquillity, they succeed.

Bowery men are deviants in that they reject the drive for status. But what of those who deviate in that most sensitive area of human experience, sexual behavior? Are they not also alienated—either by choice or because of society's hostility? Donald Cory, an acknowledged homosexual, offers an interesting description of homosexuals as a minority group. Like other minorities seeking a place in the community which has been denied them, they wage a grim struggle against society's rejection. And as in the case of other minorities, part of their fate is to "internalize" the contempt of the majority.

Another kind of outcast is represented by the anonymous and gifted English prostitute who wrote "Streetwalker." For her there is no in-group to offer defense against a hostile world. Instead of fighting back, she welcomes her rootlessness. Her choice is homelessness: "The slight security I would be able to enjoy, by allowing myself to pretend that my personality was contained in something more than the shell of my body, would make the nights—which hold no safety and in which I must be constantly alert, constantly rootless—even more desolate."

Streetwalker has chosen alienation as a way of life (until at last she decides to make a fresh start). But others, more properly described as psychotic, have no opportunity to make a choice. For them the ties have snapped. They most certainly snapped for "Joey" as described in Bruno Bettelheim's remarkable case study of a schizophrenic child who "converted himself into a 'machine' because he did not dare be human." One must not read too much into Joey's mechanical fantasy world; after all, most of us are not schizophrenic. But our society produced him, and his delusion is only an extreme form of escape.

We conclude this section with a study of suicide in Denmark, a country with one of the highest rates in the world— twice that of the United States and England—despite its more comprehensive system of social security. Herbert Hendin explains why this is so; he links suicide to early upbringing, in which the Danish child's dependence on his mother is encouraged, aggression is strictly checked, and the arousal of guilt feelings is used as a disciplinary technique. As a result, aggressive feelings are turned inward. This alone does not explain suicide, as Hendin observes. Among the other factors involved is a fairly common belief in the idea of reunion after death with a lost loved one. Competitiveness, often associated with suicide elsewhere, "has little bearing on Danish suicide." The author remarks that Danish and American character traits are quite different. Differences in personality traits may explain why we are half as likely to kill ourselves as the Danes. May it also explain why we are ten times more likely to kill each other?

NOTES FROM UNDERGROUND
/Fyodor Dostoyevsky

But these are all golden dreams. Oh, tell me, who was it first announced, who was it first proclaimed, that man only does nasty things because he does not know his own interests; and that if he were enlightened, if his eyes were opened to his real normal interests, man would at once cease to do nasty things, would at once become good and noble because, being enlightened and understanding his real advantage, he would see his own advantage in the good and nothing else, and we all know that not one man can, consciously, act against his own interests, consequently, so to say,

Translated by Constance Garnett.

through necessity, he would begin doing good? Oh, the babe! Oh, the pure, innocent child! Why, in the first place, when in all these thousands of years has there been a time when man has acted only from his own interest? What is to be done with the millions of facts that bear witness that men, *consciously,* that is, fully understanding their real interests, have left them in the background and have rushed headlong on another path, to meet peril and danger, compelled to this course by nobody and by nothing, but, as it were, simply disliking the beaten track, and have obstinately, willfully, struck out another difficult, absurd way, seeking it almost in the darkness. So, I suppose, this obstinacy and perversity were pleasanter to them than any advantage. . . . Advantage! What is advantage?

And will you take it upon yourself to define with perfect accuracy in what the advantage of man consists? And what if it so happens that a man's advantage, *sometimes,* not only may, but even must, consist in his desiring in certain cases what is harmful to himself and not advantageous. And if so, there can be such a case, the whole principle falls into dust. What do you think—are there such cases? You laugh; laugh away, gentlemen, but only answer me: have man's advantages been reckoned up with perfect certainty? Are there not some which not only have not been included but cannot possibly be included under any classification? You see, you gentlemen have, to the best of my knowledge, taken your whole register of human advantages from the averages of statistical figures and politico-economical formulas. Your advantages are prosperity, wealth, freedom, peace—and so on, and so on. So that the man who should, for instance, go openly and knowingly in opposition to all that list would, to your thinking, and indeed mine too, of course, be an obscurantist or an absolute madman: would not he? But, you know, this is what is surprising: why does it so happen that all these statisticians, sages and lovers of humanity, when they reckon up human advantages invariably leave out one? They don't even take it into their reckoning in the form in which it should be taken and the whole reckoning depends upon that. It would be no great matter, they would simply have to take it, this advantage, and add it to the list. But the trouble is, that this strange advantage does not fall under any classification and is not in place in any list. I have a friend for instance . . . Ech!

gentlemen, but of course he is your friend, too; and indeed there is no one, no one, to whom he is not a friend!

When he prepares for any undertaking this gentleman immediately explains to you, elegantly and clearly, exactly how he must act in accordance with the laws of reason and truth. What is more, he will talk to you with excitement and passion of the true normal interests of man; with irony he will upbraid the short-sighted fools who do not understand their own interests, nor the true significance of virtue; and, within a quarter of an hour, without any sudden outside provocation, but simply through something inside him which is stronger than all his interests, he will go off on quite a different tack—that is, act in direct opposition to what he has just been saying about himself, in opposition to the laws of reason, in opposition to his own advantage— in fact, in opposition to everything. . . . I warn you that my friend is a compound personality, and therefore it is difficult to blame him as an individual. The fact is, gentlemen, it seems there must really exist something that is dearer to almost every man than his greatest advantages, or (not to be illogical) there is a most advantageous advantage (the very one omitted of which we spoke just now) which is more important and more advantageous than all other advantages, for the sake of which a man if necessary is ready to act in opposition to all laws; that is, in opposition to reason, honour, peace, prosperity—in fact, in opposition to all those excellent and useful things if only he can attain that fundamental, most advantageous advantage which is dearer to him than all. "Yes, but it's advantage all the same" you will retort. But excuse me, I'll make the point clear, and it is not a case of playing upon words. What matters is, that this advantage is remarkable from the very fact that it breaks down all our classifications, and continually shatters every system constructed by lovers of mankind for the benefit of mankind. In fact, it upsets everything. But before I mention this advantage to you, I want to compromise myself personally, and therefore I boldly declare that all these fine systems—all these theories for explaining to mankind their real normal interests, in order that inevitably striving to pursue these interests they may at once become good and noble—are, in my opinion, so far, mere logical exercises! Yes, logical exercises. Why, to maintain this theory of the regeneration of mankind by means of the pursuit of his own advantage is to my mind almost the same thing as . . . as to affirm, for instance, following Buckle, that through civilization mankind becomes softer, and consequently less bloodthirsty, and less fitted for warfare.

Logically it does seem to follow from his arguments. But man has such a predilection for systems and abstract deductions that he is ready to distort the truth intentionally, he is ready to deny the evidence of his senses only to justify his logic. I take this example because it is the most glaring instance of it. Only look about you: blood is being spilt in streams, and in the merriest way, as though it were champagne. Take the whole of the nineteenth century in which Buckle lived. Take Napoleon—the Great and also the present one. Take North America—the eternal union. Take the farce of Schleswig-Holstein. . . . And what is it that civilization softens in us? The only gain of civilization for mankind is the greater capacity for variety of sensations—and absolutely nothing more. And through the development of this many-sidedness man may come to finding enjoyment in bloodshed. In fact, this has already happened to him. Have you noticed that it is the most civilized gentlemen who have been the subtlest slaughterers, to whom the Attilas and Stenka Razins could not hold a candle, and if they are not so conspicuous as the Attilas and Stenka Razins it is simply because they are so often met with, are so ordinary and have become so familiar to us. In any case civilization has made mankind if not more bloodthirsty, at least more vilely, more loathsomely blood-thirsty. In old days he saw justice in bloodshed and with his conscience at peace exterminated those he thought proper. Now we do think bloodshed abominable and yet we engage in this abomination, and with more energy than ever. Which is worse? Decide that for yourselves.

They say that Cleopatra (excuse an instance from Roman history) was fond of sticking gold pins into her slave-girls' breasts and derived gratification from their screams and writhings. You will say that that was in the comparatively barbarous times; that these are barbarous times too, because also, comparatively speaking, pins are stuck in even now; that though man has now learned to see more clearly than in barbarous ages, he is still far from having learnt to act as reason and science would dictate. But yet you are fully convinced that he will be sure to learn when he gets rid of certain old bad habits, and when common sense and science have completely re-educated human nature and turned it in a normal direction. You are confident that then man will cease from *intentional* error and will, so to say, be compelled not to want to set his will against his normal interests. That is not all; then, you say, science itself will teach man (though to my mind it's a superfluous luxury) that he never has really had any caprice or will of his own, and that he himself is something of the nature of a piano-key or the stop of an organ, and that there are, besides, things called the laws of nature; so that everything he does is not done by his willing it, but is done of itself, by the laws of nature. Consequently we have only to discover these laws of nature, and man will no longer have to answer for his actions and life will become exceedingly easy for him. All human actions will then, of course, be tabulated according to these laws, mathematically, like tables of logarithms up to 108,000, and entered in an index; or, better still, there would be published certain edifying works of the nature of encyclopaedic lexicons, in which everything will be so clearly calculated and explained that there will be no more incidents or adventures in the world.

Then—this is all what you say—new economic relations will be established, all ready-made and worked out with mathematical exactitude, so that every possible question will vanish in the twinkling of an eye, simply because every possible answer to it will be provided. Then the "Palace of Crystal" will be built. Then . . . In fact, those will be halcyon days. Of course there is no guaranteeing (this is my comment) that it will not be, for instance, frightfully dull then (for what will one have to do when everything will be calculated and tabulated?), but on the other hand everything will be extraordinarily rational. Of course boredom may lead you to anything. It is boredom sets one sticking golden pins into people, but all that would not matter. What is bad (this is my comment again) is that I dare say people will be thankful for the gold pins then. Man is stupid, you know, phenomenally stupid; or rather he is not at all stupid, but he is so ungrateful that you could not find another like him in all creation. I, for instance, would not be in the least surprised if all of a sudden, apropos of nothing, in the midst of general prosperity a gentleman with an ignoble, or rather with a reactionary and ironical, countenance were to arise and putting his arms akimbo, say to us all: "I say, gentlemen, hadn't we better kick over the whole show and scatter rationalism to the winds, simply to send these logarithms to the devil, and to enable us to live once more at our own sweet foolish will!" That again would not matter; but what is annoying is that he would be sure to find followers—such is the nature of man. And all that for the most foolish reason, which, one would think, was hardly worth mentioning: that is, that man everywhere and at all times, whoever he may be, has preferred to act as he chose and not in the least as his reason and advantage dictated. And one may choose what is contrary to one's own interests, and sometimes one *positively ought* (that is my idea). One's own free unfettered choice, one's own caprice—however wild it may be, one's own fancy worked up at times to frenzy—is that very "most advantageous advantage" which we have overlooked, which comes under no classification and against which all systems and theories are continually being shattered to atoms. And how do these wiseacres know that man wants a normal, a virtuous choice? What has made them conceive that man must want a rationally advantageous choice? What man wants is simply *independent* choice, whatever that independence may cost and wherever it may lead. And choice, of course, the devil only knows what choice. . . .

"Ha! ha! ha! But you know there is no such thing as choice in reality, say what you like," you will interpose with a chuckle. "Science has succeeded in so far analyzing man that we know already that choice and what is called freedom of will is nothing else than—"

Stay, gentlemen, I meant to begin with that myself. I confess, I was rather frightened. I was just going to say that the devil only knows what choice depends on, and that perhaps that was a very good thing, but I remembered the teaching of science . . . and pulled myself up. And here you have begun upon it. Indeed, if there really is some day discovered a formula for all our desires and caprices—that is, an explanation of what they depend upon, by what laws they arise, how they develop, what they are aiming at in one case and in another and so on, that is, a real mathematical formula—then, most likely, man will at once cease to feel desire, indeed, he will be certain to. For who would want to choose by rule? Besides, he will at once be transformed from a human being into an organ-stop or something of the sort; for what is a man without desires, without free will and without choice, if not a stop in an organ? What do you think? Let us reckon the chances—can such a thing happen or not?

"H'm!" you decide. "Our choice is usually mistaken from a false view of our advantage. We sometimes choose absolute nonsense because in our foolishness we see in that nonsense the easiest means for attaining a supposed advantage. But when all that is explained and worked out on paper (which is perfectly possible, for it is contemptible and senseless to suppose that some laws of nature man will never understand), then certainly so-called desires will no longer exist. For if a desire should come into conflict with reason we shall then reason and not desire, because it will be impossible retaining our reason to be *senseless* in our desires, and in that way knowingly act against reason and desire to injure ourselves. And as all choice and reasoning can be really calculated—because there will some day be discovered the laws of our so-called free will—so, joking apart, there may one day be something like a table constructed of them, so that we really shall choose in accordance with it. If, for instance, some day they calculate and prove to me that I made a long nose at some one because I could not help making a long nose at him and that I had to do it in that particular way, what *freedom* is left me, especially if I am a learned man and have taken my degree somewhere? Then I should be able to calculate my whole life for thirty years beforehand. In short, if this could be arranged there would be nothing left for us to do; anyway, we should have to understand that. And, in fact, we ought unwearyingly to repeat to ourselves that at such and such a time and in such and such circumstances Nature does not ask our leave; that we have got to take her as she is and not fashion her to suit our fancy, and if we really aspire to formulas and tables of rules, and well, even . . . to the chemical retort, there's no help for it, we must accept the retort too, or else it will be accepted without our consent. . . ."

Yes, but here I come to a stop! Gentlemen, you must excuse me for being over-philosophical; it's the result of forty years underground! Allow me to indulge my fancy. You see, gentlemen, reason is an excellent thing, there's no disputing that, but reason is nothing but reason and satisfies only the rational side of man's nature, while will is a manifestation of the whole life, that is, of the whole human life including reason and all the impulses. And although our life, in this manifestation of it, is often worthless, yet it is life and not simply extracting square roots. Here I, for instance, quite naturally want to live, in order to satisfy all my capacities for life, and not simply my capacity for reasoning, that is, not simply one-twentieth of my capacity for life. What does reason know? Reason only knows what it has succeeded in learning (some things, perhaps, it will never learn; this is a poor comfort, but why not say so frankly?) and human nature acts as a whole, with everything that is in it, consciously or unconsciously, and, even if it goes wrong, it lives. I suspect, gentlemen, that you are looking at me with compassion; you tell me again that an enlightened and developed man, such, in short, as the future man will be, cannot consciously desire anything disadvantageous to himself, that that can be proved mathematically. I thoroughly agree, it can—by mathematics.

But I repeat for the hundredth time, there is one case, one only, when man may consciously, purposely, desire what is injurious to himself, what is stupid, very stupid—simply in order to have the right to desire for himself even what is very stupid and not to be bound by an obligation to desire only what is sensible. Of course, this very stupid thing, this caprice of ours, may be in reality, gentlemen, more advantageous for us than anything else on earth, especially in certain cases. And in particular it may be more advantageous than any advantage even when it does us obvious harm, and contradicts the soundest conclusions of our reason concerning our advantage—for in any circumstances it preserves for us what is most precious and most important—that is, our personality, our individuality. Some, you see, maintain that this really is the most precious thing for mankind; choice can, of course, if it chooses, be in agreement with reason; and especially if this be not abused but kept within bounds. It is profitable and sometimes even praiseworthy. But very often, and even most often, choice is utterly and stubbornly opposed to reason . . . and . . . and . . . do you know that that, too, is profitable, sometimes even praiseworthy? Gentlemen, let us suppose that man is not stupid. (Indeed one cannot refuse to suppose that, if only from the one consideration, that if man is stupid, then who is wise?) But if he is not stupid, he is monstrously ungrateful! Phenomenally ungrateful. In fact, I believe that the best definition of man is the ungrateful biped. But that is not all, that is not his worst defect; his worst defect is his perpetual moral obliquity—perpetual, from the days of the Flood to the Schleswig-Holstein period.

Moral obliquity and consequently lack of good sense; for it has long been accepted that lack of good sense is due to no other cause than moral obliquity. Put it to the test and cast your eyes upon the history of mankind. What will you see? Is it a grand spectacle? Grand, if you like. Take the Colossus of Rhodes, for instance, that's worth something. With good reason Mr. Anaevsky testifies of it that some say that it is the work of man's hands, while others maintain that it has been created by Nature herself. Is it many-colored? It may be it is many-colored, too: if one takes the dress uniforms, military and civilian, of all peoples in all ages—that alone is worth something, and if you take the undress uniforms you will never get to the end of it; no historian would be equal to the job. Is it monotonous? It may be it's monotonous too: it's fighting and fighting; they are fighting now, they fought first and they fought last—you will admit that it is almost too monotonous. In short, one may say anything about the history of the world—anything that might enter the most disordered imagination.

The only thing one can't say is that it's rational. The very word sticks in one's throat. And, indeed, this is the odd thing that is continually happening: there are continually turning up in life moral and rational persons, sages and lovers of humanity, who make it their object to live all their lives as morally and rationally as possible, to be, so to speak, a light to their neighbors simply in order to show them that it is possible to live morally and rationally in this world. And yet we all know that those very people sooner or later have been false to themselves, playing some queer trick, often a most unseemly one. Now I ask you: what can be expected of man since he is a being endowed with such strange qualities? Shower upon him every earthly blessing, drown him in a sea of happiness, so that nothing but bubbles of bliss can be seen on the surface; give him economic prosperity, such that he should have nothing else to do but sleep, eat cakes and busy himself with the continuation of his species, and even then out of sheer ingratitude, sheer spite, man would play you some nasty trick. He would even risk his cakes and would deliberately desire the most fatal rubbish, the most uneconomical absurdity, simply to introduce into all this positive good sense his fatal fantastic element. It is just his fantastic dreams, his vulgar folly, that he will desire to retain, simply in order to prove to himself—as though that were so necessary—that men still are men and not the keys of a piano, which the laws of nature threaten to control so completely that soon one will be able to desire nothing but by the calendar. And that is not all: even if man really were nothing but a piano-key, even if this were proved to him by natural science and mathematics, even then he would not become reasonable, but would purposely do something perverse out of simple ingratitude, simply to gain his point. And if he does not find means he will contrive destruction and chaos, will contrive sufferings of all sorts, only to gain his point! He will launch a curse upon the world, and as only man can curse (it is his privilege, the primary distinction between him and other animals) it may be by his curse alone he will attain his object—that is, convince himself that he is a man and not a piano-key! If you say that all this, too, can be calculated and tabulated—chaos and darkness and curses, so that the mere possibility of calculating it all beforehand would stop it all, and reason would reassert itself—then man would purposely go mad in order to be rid of reason and gain his point! I believe in it, I answer for it, for the whole work of man really seems to consist in nothing but proving to himself every minute that he is a man and not a piano-key! It may be at the cost of his skin, it may be by cannibalism! And this being so, can one help being tempted to rejoice that it has not yet come off, and that desire still depends on something we don't know?

You will scream at me (that is, if you condescend to do so) that no one is touching my free will, that all they are concerned with is that my will should of itself, of its own free will, coincide with my own normal interests, with the laws of nature and arithmetic.

Good heavens, gentlemen, what sort of free will is left when we come to tabulation and arithmetic, when it will all be a case of twice two makes four? Twice two makes four without my will. As if free will meant that!

Gentlemen, I am joking, and I know myself that my jokes are not brilliant, but you know one can't take everything as a joke. I am, perhaps, jesting against the grain. Gentlemen, I am tormented by questions; answer them for me.

You, for instance, want to cure men of their old habits and reform their will in accordance with science and good sense. But how do you know, not only that it is possible, but also that it is *desirable*, to reform man in that way? And what leads you to the conclusion that man's inclinations *need* reforming? In short, how do you know that such a reformation will be a benefit to man? And to go to the root of the matter, why are you so positively convinced that not to act against his real normal interests guaranteed by the conclusions of reason and arithmetic is certainly always advantageous for man and must always be a law for mankind? So far, you know, this is only your supposition. It may be the law of logic, but not the law of humanity. You think, gentlemen, perhaps that I am mad? Allow me to defend myself. I agree that man is pre-eminently a creative animal, predestined to strive consciously for an object and to engage in engineering—that is, incessantly and eternally to make new roads, *wherever they may lead*. But the reason why he wants sometimes to go off at a tangent may just be that he is *predestined* to make the road, and perhaps, too, that however stupid the "direct" practical man may be, the thought sometimes will occur to him that the road almost always does lead *somewhere*, and that the destination it leads to is less important than the process of making it, and that the chief thing is to save the well-conducted child from despising engineering, and so giving way to the fatal idleness, which, as we all know, is the mother of all the vices. Man likes to make roads and to create, that is a fact beyond dispute. But why has he such a passionate love for destruction and chaos also? Tell me that! But on that point I want to say a couple of words myself. May it not be that he loves chaos and destruction (there can be no disputing that he does sometimes love it) because he is instinctively afraid of attaining his object and completing the edifice he is constructing? Who knows, perhaps he only loves that edifice from a distance, and is by no means in love with it at close quarters; perhaps he only loves building it and does not want to live in it, but will leave it, when completed, for the use of *les animaux domestiques*—such as the ants, the sheep, and so on. Now the ants have quite a different taste. They have a marvelous edifice of that pattern which endures for ever—the ant-heap.

With the ant-heap the respectable race of ants began and with the ant-heap they will probably end, which does the greatest credit to their perseverance and good sense. But man is a frivolous and incongruous creature, and perhaps, like a chess-player, loves the process of the game, not the end of it. And who knows (there is no saying with certainty), perhaps the only goal on earth to which mankind is striving lies in this incessant process of attaining, in other words, in life itself, and not in the thing to be attained, which must always be expressed as a formula, as positive as twice two makes four, and such positiveness is not life, gentlemen, but is the beginning of death. Anyway, man has always been afraid of this mathematical certainty, and I am afraid of it now. Granted that man does nothing but seek that mathematical certainty, he traverses oceans, sacrifices his life in the quest, but to succeed, really to find it, he dreads, I assure you. He feels that when he has found it there will be nothing for him to look for. When workmen have finished their work they do at least receive their pay, they go to the tavern, then they are taken to the police-station—and there is occupation for a week. But where can man go? Anyway, one can observe a certain awkwardness about him when he has attained such objects. He loves the process of attaining, but does not quite like to have attained, and that, of course, is very absurd. In fact, man is a comical creature; there seems to be a kind of jest in it all. But yet mathematical certainty is, after all, something insufferable. Twice two makes four seems to me simply a piece of insolence. Twice two makes four is a pert coxcomb who stands with arms akimbo barring your path and spitting. I admit that twice two makes four is an excellent thing, but if we are to give everything its due, twice two makes five is sometimes a very charming thing too.

And why are you so firmly, so triumphantly, convinced that only the normal and the positive—in other words, only what is conducive to welfare—is for the advantage of man? Is not reason in error as regards advantage? Does not man, perhaps, love something besides well-being? Perhaps he is just as fond of suffering? Perhaps suffering is just as great a benefit to him as well-being? Man is sometimes extraordinarily, passionately, in love with suffering, and that is a fact. There is no need to appeal to universal history to prove that; only ask yourself, if you are a man and have lived at all. As far as my personal opinion is concerned, to care only for well-being seems to me positively ill-bred. Whether it's good or bad, it is sometimes very pleasant, too, to smash things. I hold no brief for suffering nor for well-being either. I am standing for . . . my caprice, and for its being guaranteed to me when necessary. Suffering would be out of place in vaudevilles, for instance; I know that. In the "Palace of Crystal" it is unthinkable; suffering means doubt, negation, and what would be the good of a "Palace of Crystal" if there could be any doubt about it? And yet I think man will never renounce real suffering, that is, destruction and chaos. Why, suffering is the sole origin of consciousness. Though I did lay it down at the beginning that consciousness is the greatest misfortune for man, yet I know man prizes it and would not give it up for any satisfaction. Consciousness, for instance, is infinitely superior to twice two makes four. Once you have mathematical certainty there is nothing left to do or to understand. There will be nothing left but to bottle up your five senses and plunge into contemplation. While if you stick to consciousness, even though the same result is attained, you can at least flog yourself at times, and that will, at any rate, liven you up. Reactionary as it is, corporal punishment is better than nothing.

You believe in a palace of crystal that can never be destroyed—a palace at which one will not be able to put out one's tongue or make a long nose on the sly. And perhaps that is just why I am afraid of this edifice that it is of crystal and can never be destroyed and that one cannot put one's tongue out at it even on the sly.

You see, if it were not a palace, but a hen-house, I might creep into it to avoid getting wet, and yet I would not call the hen-house a palace out of gratitude to it for keeping me dry. You laugh and say that in such circumstances a hen-house is as good as a mansion. Yes, I answer, if one had to live simply to keep out of the rain.

But what is to be done if I have taken it into my head that that is not the only object in life, and that if one must live one had better live in a mansion. That is my choice, my desire. You will only eradicate it when you have changed my preference. Well, do change it, allure me with something else, give me another ideal. But meanwhile I will not take a hen-house for a mansion. The palace of crystal may be an idle dream, it may be that it is inconsistent with the laws of nature and that I have invented it only through my own stupidity, through the old-fashioned irrational habits of my generation. But what does it matter to me that it is inconsistent? That makes no difference since it exists in my desires, or rather exists as long as my desires exist. Perhaps you are laughing again? Laugh away; I will put up with any mockery rather than pretend that I am satisfied when I am hungry. I know, anyway, that I will not be put off with a compromise, with a recurring zero, simply because it is consistent with the laws of nature and actually exists. I will not accept as the crown of my desires a block of buildings with tenements for the poor on a lease of a thousand years, and perhaps with a sign-board of a dentist hanging out. Destroy my desires, eradicate my ideals, show me something better, and I will follow you. You will say, perhaps, that is not worth your trouble; but in that case I can give you the same answer. We are discussing things seriously; but if you won't deign to give me your attention, I will drop your acquaintance. I can retreat into my underground hole.

But while I am alive and have desires I would rather my hand were withered off than bring one brick to such a building! Don't remind me that I have just rejected the palace of crystal for the sole reason that one cannot put out one's tongue at it. I did not say that because I am so fond of putting my tongue out. Perhaps the thing I resented was, that of all your edifices there has not been one at which one could not put out one's tongue. On the contrary, I would let my tongue be cut off out of gratitude if things could be so arranged that I should lose all desire to put it out. It is not my fault that things cannot be so arranged, and that one must be satisfied with model flats. Then why am I made with such desires? Can I have been constructed simply in order to come to the conclusion that all my construction is a cheat? Can this be my whole purpose? I do not believe it.

But do you know what: I am convinced that we underground folk ought to be kept on a curb. Though we may sit forty years underground without speaking, when we do come out into the light of day and break out we talk and talk and talk. . . .

THE BOTTOM OF THE HEAP: PROBLEMS OF THE WORKING CLASS BOY
/Albert Cohen

What is it about the structure of American society that produces delinquency in certain sectors of that society . . . ? We believe that problems of adjustment to social class play a vital role in the genesis of the delinquent subculture. First and most obviously, the working class child shares the social class status of his parents. In the status game, then, the working-class child starts out with a handicap and, to the extent that he cares what middle-class persons think of him or has internalized the dominant middle-class attitudes toward social class position, he may be expected to feel some "shame." Margaret Mead has put the point with characteristic trenchancy if somewhat dubious melodrama:

> "Shame is felt perhaps most strongly over the failures of other people, especially one's parents, who have not been successful, who have not worked hard enough to have an inside bathroom or an automobile or to send one to a private school, to live on the right street, or go to the right church. As class is an expression of economic success, then it follows that to belong as a child or an adolescent in a class below others is a statement that one's parents have failed, they did not make good. This is bad enough when they have not risen, unbearable if they have started to fall even lower. Deeper than our disapproval of any breaking of the ten commandments lies our conviction that a failure to keep moving is an unforgivable sin."

Furthermore, people of status tend to be people of power and property. They have the means to make more certain that their children will obtain respect and other rewards which have status significance even where title in terms of deserving middle-class conduct is dubious. Hollingshead, in his *Elmtown's Youth*, stresses throughout the importance of parental status in obtaining special consideration in school activities and on the job through "connections" and other means of exerting pressure. Finally, parents of good standing in the class system can usually provide their children with money, clothes, cars, homes and other material amenities which not only function as external trappings and insignia of status, but which serve also as means and avenues to activities and relationships which confer status. Like his parents, a child is unlikely to be invited to participate in activities which require a material apparatus he cannot afford; if invited, he is less likely to accept for fear of embarrassment; and if he accepts, he is less likely to be in a position to reciprocate and therefore to sustain a relationship premised on a certain amount of reciprocity. It seems reasonable to assume that out of all this there arise feelings of inferiority and perhaps resentment and hostility. It is remarkable, however, that there is relatively little research explicitly designed to test this assumption.

However, invidious status distinctions among young people are, after all, a result of individual differences in conformity to a set of conduct norms as well as simple functions of their parents' social status. Havighurst and Taba in their *Adolescent Character and Personality* have shown that variations in "character reputation" scores cannot be explained simply as a result of social class membership. The existence of "achieved" as well as "ascribed" criteria of status for children makes it possible for some working-class children to "rise above" the status to which the social class position of their parents would otherwise consign them. However, this does not make the situation psychologically any easier for those of their brethren who remain behind, or rather, below. Low achieved status is no pleasanter than low ascribed status, and very likely a good deal more unpleasant, for reasons we have indicated earlier; it reflects more directly on the *personal* inadequacy of the child and leaves him with fewer convenient rationalizations.

One of the situations in which children of all social levels come together and compete for status in terms of the same set of middle-class criteria and in which working-class children are most likely to be found wanting is in the school. American educators are enamored of the idea of "democracy" as a goal of the schools. An examination of their writings reveals that "democracy" signifies "the fullest realization of the individual's potentialities," "the development of skills to an optimal level," "the development of character and abilities which can be admired by others," "preparation for effective participation in the adult vocational world." Despite reservations such as "with due regard to individual differences," this conception of "democratic" education implies that a major function of the schools is to "promote," "encourage," "motivate," "stimulate," in brief, *reward* middle-class ambition and conformity to middle-class expectations. However sincerely one may desire to avoid odious comparisons and to avoid, thereby, injury to the self-esteem of those who do not conform to one's expectations, it is extremely difficult to reward, however subtly, successful conformity without at the same time, by implication, condemning and punishing the non-conformist. That same teacher who prides himself on his recognition and encouragement of deserving working-class children dramatizes, by that very show of pride, the superior merit of the "college-boy" working-class child to his less gifted or "[street] corner-boy" working-class classmates.

There are three good reasons why status in the school, insofar as it depends upon recognition by the teacher, should be measured by middle-class standards.

First, the teacher is *hired* to foster the development of middle-class personalities. The middle-class board of education, the middle-class parents whom they represent and, it is to be presumed, many of the working-class parents as well expect the teacher to define his job as the indoctrination of middle-class aspirations, character, skills and manners.

Second, the teacher himself is almost certain to be a middle-class person, who personally values ambition and achievement and spontaneously recognizes and rewards these virtues in others.

The third relates to the school itself as a social system with certain "structural imperatives" of its own. The teacher's textbooks in education and his own supervisors may stress "individualization" and "consideration for the needs, limitations and special problems of each student." Nonetheless, the teacher actually handles 20, 30 or 40 students at a time. Regardless of what he conceives his proper function to be, he necessarily looks with favor on the quiet, cooperative, "well-behaved" pupils who make his job easier and with disapproval and vexation on the lusty, irrepressible, boisterous youngsters who are destructive of order, routine and predictability in the classroom. Furthermore, the teacher himself is likely to be upwardly mobile or at least anxious about the security of his tenure in his present job. He is motivated, therefore, to conform to the criteria in terms of which *his* superiors evaluate *him*. Those superiors may themselves be "progressive" and in teacher meetings preach "democracy in the classroom" and "individualization" and indeed genuinely believe in those goals. However, the degree to which a teacher tries to achieve these goals or succeeds in doing so is not highly visible and readily determined. On the other hand, grades, performance on standardized examinations, the cleanliness and orderliness of the classroom and the frequency with which children are sent to the "front office" are among the most easily determined and "objective" bases for the evaluation of teacher performance. A good "rating," then, by his supervisors is possible only if the teacher sacrifices to some degree the very "individualization" and "tolerance" which those same supervisors may urge upon him.

Research on the kinds of behavior which teachers regard as the most "problematical" among their pupils gives results consistent with our expectations. The most serious problems, from the standpoint of the teacher, are those children who are restless and unruly, who fidget and squirm, who annoy and distract, who create "discipline" problems. The "good" children are the studious, the obedient, the docile. It is precisely the working-class children who are most likely to be "problems" because of their relative lack of training in order and discipline, their lack of interest in intellectual achievement and their lack of reinforcement by the home in conformity to the requirements of the school. Both in terms of "conduct" and in terms of academic achievement, the failures in the classroom are drawn disproportionately from the lower social class levels. The child has little or no choice in selecting the group within which he shall compete for status and, in the words of Troyer, he is "evaluated against the total range of the ability distribution.

"It is here that, day after day, most of the children in the lower fourth of the distribution have their sense of worth destroyed, develop feelings of insecurity, become frustrated and lose confidence in their ability to learn even that which they are capable of learning."

In settlement houses and other adult-sponsored and managed recreational agencies similar conflicts may often be seen between the middle-class values of the adults in charge and the working-class values of the children for whose benefit the institutions ostensibly exist. Such organizations smile upon neat, orderly, polite, personable, mannerly children who "want to make something of themselves." The sponsors, directors and group work leaders find it a pleasure to work with such children, whose values are so like their own, and make them feel welcome and respected. They do indeed feel a special responsibility toward the boy whose family and neighborhood culture have not equipped him with those values, the "rough" boy, the "dirty" boy, the "bum" who just "hangs around" with the gang on the corner, in the pool hall or in the candy store. But the responsibility they feel toward him is to encourage him to engage in more "worthwhile" activities, to join and to be a "responsible" member of some "wholesome" adult-supervised club or other group, to expurgate his language and, in general, to participate in the "constructive" program of the institution. Indeed, like the school, it functions to select potentially upwardly mobile working-class children and to help and encourage them in the upward climb. It is a common experience of such organizations that they "are very successful and do a lot of good but don't seem to get the children who need them most." The reason is that here, as in the school, it is almost impossible to reward one kind of behavior without at the same time, by implication or quite openly, punishing its absence or its opposite. The corner boy, as Whyte has shown vividly and in detail, quickly senses that he is under the critical or at best condescending surveillance of people who are "foreigners" to his community and who appraise him in terms of values which he does not share. He is aware that he is being invidiously compared to others; he is uncomfortable; he finds it hard to accommodate himself to the rules of the organization. To win the favor of the people in charge he must change his habits, his values, his ambitions, his speech and his associates. Even were these things possible, the game might not be worth the candle. So, having sampled what they have to offer, he returns to the street or to his "clubhouse" in a cellar where "facilities" are meager but human relations more satisfying.

Not only in terms of standards of middle-class adults but in terms of their children's standards as well, the working-class culture is likely to be a "failure." Despite the existence among middle-class children of a "youth culture" which may differ in significant ways from the culture of their parents, the standards these children apply are likely to relegate to an inferior status their working-class peers. Coyle quotes from a fieldworker's report:

"Gradually the group became more critical of prospective members. A process somewhat evident from the beginning became more obvious. In general only boys who measured up to the group's unwritten, unspoken and largely unconscious standards were ever considered. These standards, characteristics of their middle-class homes, required the suppression of impulsive disorderly behavior and put a high value on controlled cooperative attitudes. Hence even these normally healthy and boisterous boys were capable of rejecting schoolmates they considered too wild and boisterous. Coincident with this was an emphasis on intellectual capacity and achievement. They preferred "smart" as contrasted with "dumb" prospects. The boys seemed to use their club unconsciously to express and reinforce the standards learned in their homes and the community."

Havighurst and Taba point out that not only teachers but schoolmates, in evaluating the character of other children, tend to give the highest ratings to the children of the higher social levels, although the correlation between social class and character reputation is far from perfect. Positive correlations between various indices of social class status of the home and social status in the school as measured by pupils' choices have been found by Bonney and others. Hollingshead has shown how social class and the behavior and personality associated with social class membership operate to determine prestige and clique and date patterns among high school boys and girls. "This process operates in all classes, but it is especially noticeable in contacts with class V [lower-lower]. This class is so repugnant socially that adolescents in the higher classes avoid clique and dating ties with its members." Furthermore, working-class children are less likely to participate, and if they participate are less likely to achieve prominence, in extra-curricular activities, which are an important arena for the competition for status in the eyes of the students themselves. In the area of organized athletics the working-class boy is perhaps least unfitted for successful competition. Even here, however, he is likely to be at a disadvantage. Adherence to a training regimen and a schedule does not come to him as easily as to the middle-class boy and, unless he chooses to loosen his ties to his working-class friends, he is likely to find some conflict between the claims of the gang and those of his athletic career. Finally, although we must not mimimize the importance of athletic achievement as a status-ladder, it is, after all, granted to relatively few, of whatever social class background, to achieve conspicuously in this area.

In summary, it may confidently be said that the working-class boy, particularly if his training and values be those we have here defined as working-class, is more likely than his middle-class peers to find himself at the bottom of the status hierarchy whenever he moves in a middle-class world, whether it be of adults or of children. To the degree to which he values middle-class status, either because he values the good opinion of middle-class persons or because he has to some degree internalized middle-class standards himself, he faces a problem of adjustment and is in the market for a "solution."

The delinquent subculture, we suggest, is a way of dealing with the problems of adjustment we have described. These problems are chiefly status problems: certain children are denied status in the respectable society because they cannot meet the criteria of the respectable status system. The delinquent subculture deals with these problems by providing criteria of status which these children *can* meet.

We remarked earlier that our ego-involvement in a given comparison with others depends upon our "status universe." "Whom do we measure ourselves against?" is the crucial question. In some other societies virtue may consist in willing acceptance of the role of peasant, low-born commoner or member of an inferior caste and in conformity to the expectations of that role. If others are richer, more nobly-born or more able than oneself, it is by the will of an inscrutable Providence and not to be imputed to one's own moral defect. The sting of status inferiority is thereby removed or mitigated; one measures himself only against those of like social position. We have suggested, however, that an important feature of American "democracy," perhaps of the Western European tradition in general, is the tendency to measure oneself against "all comers." This means that, for children as for adults, one's sense of personal worth is at stake in status comparisons with all other persons, at least of one's own age and sex, whatever their family background or material circumstances. It means that, in the lower levels of our status hierarchies, whether adult or juvenile, there is a chronic fund of motivation, conscious or repressed, to elevate one's status position, either by striving to climb within the established status system or by redefining the criteria of status so that one's present attributes become status-giving assets.

It may be argued that the working-class boy does not *care* what middle-class people think of him, that he is ego-involved only in the opinions of his family, his friends, his working-class neighbors. A definitive answer to this argument can come only from research designed to get at the facts. This research, in our opinion, is yet to be done. There is, however, reason to believe that most children are sensitive *to some degree* about the attitudes of *any persons* with whom they are thrown into more than the most superficial kind of contact. The contempt or indifference of others, particularly of those like schoolmates and teachers, with whom we are constrained to associate for long hours every day, is difficult, we suggest, to shrug off. It poses a problem with which one may conceivably attempt to cope in a variety of ways. One may make an active effort to change himself in conformity with the expectations of others; one may attempt to justify or explain away his inferiority in terms which will exculpate him; one may tell oneself that he really doesn't care what these people think; one may react with anger and aggression. But the least probable response is simple, uncomplicated, honest indifference. If we grant the probable truth of the claim that most American working-class children are most sensitive to status sources on their own level, it does not follow that they take lightly rejection, disparagement and censure from other status sources.

Even on their "own" social level, the situation is far from simple. The "working class," we have repeatedly emphasized, is not culturally homogeneous. Not only is there much diversity in the cultural standards applied by one's own working-class neighbors and kin so that it is difficult to find a "working-class" milieu in which "middle-class" standards are not important. In addition, the "working-class" culture we have described is, after all, an ideal type; most working-class *people* are culturally ambivalent. Due to lack of capacity, of the requisite "character structure" or of "luck," they may be working-class in terms of job and income; they may have accepted this status with resignation and rationalized it to their satisfaction; and by example, by class-linked techniques of child training and by failure to support the middle-class agencies of socialization they may have produced children deficient in the attributes that make for status in middle-class terms. Nevertheless, all their lives, through all the major media of mass indoctrination—the schools, the movies, the radio, the newspapers and the magazines—the middle-class powers-that-be that manipulate these media have been trying to "sell" them on middle-class values and the middle-class standard of living. Then there is the "propaganda of the deed," the fact that they have seen with their own eyes working-class contemporaries "get ahead" and "make the grade" in a middle-class world. In consequence of all this, we suspect that few working-class parents unequivocally repudiate as intrinsically worthless middle-class objectives. There is good reason to believe that the modesty of working-class aspirations is partly a matter of trimming one's sails to the available opportunities and resources and partly a matter of unwillingness to accept the discipline which upward striving entails.

However complete and successful one's accommodation to an humble status, the vitality of middle-class goals, of the "American dream," is nonetheless likely to manifest itself in his aspirations for his children. His expectations may not be grandiose, but he will want his children to be "better off" than he. Whatever his own work history and social reputation may be, he will want his children to be "steady" and "respectable." He may exert few positive pressures to "succeed" and the experiences he provides his children may even incapacitate them for success; he may be puzzled at the way they "turn out." But whatever the measure of his own responsibility in accounting for the product, he is not likely to judge that product by unadulterated "corner-boy" standards. Even "corner-boy" parents, although they may value in their children such corner-boy virtues as generosity to friends, personal loyalty and

physical prowess, are likely also to be gratified by recognition by middle-class representatives and by the
kinds of achievement for which the college-boy way of life
is a prerequisite. Even in the working-class milieu from
which he acquired his incapacity for middle-class achievement, the working-class corner-boy may find himself at a
status disadvantage as against his more upwardly mobile
peers.

Lastly, of course, is that most ubiquitous and inescapable of status sources, oneself. Technically, we do not call
the person's attitudes towards himself "status" but rather
"self-esteem," or, when the quality of the self-attitude is
specifically moral, "conscience" or "superego." The important question for us is this: To what extent, if at all, do boys
who are typically "working-class" and "corner-boy" in their
overt behavior evaluate themselves by "middle-class," "college-boy" standards? For our overt behavior, however closely
it conforms to one set of norms, need not argue against the
existence or effectiveness of alternative and conflicting
norms. The failure of our own behavior to conform to our
own expectations is an elementary and commonplace fact
which gives rise to the tremendously important consequences of guilt, self-recrimination, anxiety and self-hatred.
The reasons for the failure of self-expectations and overt
conduct to agree are complex. One reason is that we often
internalize more than one set of norms, each of which
would dictate a different course of action in a given life-
situation; since we can only *do* one thing at a time, however, we are forced to choose between them or somehow to
compromise. In either case, we fall short of the full realization of our own expectations and must somehow cope with
the residual discrepancy between those expectations and our
overt behavior.

It is a plausible assumption, then, that the working-class
boy whose status is low in middle-class terms *cares* about
that status, that this status confronts him with a genuine
problem of adjustment. To this problem of adjustment
there are a variety of conceivable responses, of which participation in the creation and the maintenance of the delinquent subculture is one. . . . What does the delinquent
response have to offer? Let us be clear, first, about what this
response is. The hallmark of the delinquent subculture is the
explicit and wholesale repudiation of middle-class standards

and the adoption of their very antithesis. *The corner-boy culture is not specifically delinquent.* Where it leads to behavior which may be defined as delinquent, *e.g.,* truancy, it does so not because nonconformity to middle-class norms *defines* conformity to corner-boy norms but because conformity to middle-class norms *interferes with* conformity to corner-boy norms. The corner-boy plays truant because he does not like school, because he wishes to escape from a dull and unrewarding and perhaps humiliating situation. But truancy is not defined as intrinsically valuable and status-giving. The member of the delinquent subculture plays truant because "good" middle-class (and working-class) children do not play truant. Corner-boy resistance to being herded and marshaled by middle-class figures is not the same as the delinquent's flouting and jeering of those middle-class figures and active ridicule of those who submit. The corner-boy's ethic of reciprocity, his quasi-communal attitude toward the property of in-group members, is shared by the delinquent. But this ethic of reciprocity does not sanction the deliberate and "malicious" violation of the property rights of persons outside the in-group. We have observed that the differences between the corner-boy and the college-boy or middle-class culture are profound but that in many ways they are profound differences in emphasis. We have remarked that the corner-boy culture does not so much repudiate the value of many middle-class achievements as it emphasizes certain other values which make such achievements improbable. In short, the corner-boy culture temporizes with middle-class morality; the full-fledged delinquent subculture does not.

It is precisely here, we suggest, in the refusal to temporize, that the appeal of the delinquent subculture lies. Let us recall that it is characteristically American, not specifically working-class or middle-class, to measure oneself against the widest possible status universe, to seek status against "all comers," to be "as good as" or "better than" anybody—anybody, that is, within one's own age and sex category. As long as the working-class corner-boy clings to a version, however attenuated and adulterated, of the middle-class culture, he must recognize his inferiority to working-class and middle-class college-boys. The delinquent subculture, on the other hand, permits no ambiguity of the status of the delinquent relative to that of anybody else. In terms of the norms of the delinquent subculture, defined by its negative polarity to the respectable status system, the delinquent's very nonconformity to middle-class standards sets him above the most exemplary college boy.

Another important function of the delinquent subculture is the legitimation of aggression. We surmise that a certain amount of hostility is generated among working-class children against middle-class persons, with their airs of superiority, disdain or condescension and against middle-class norms, which are, in a sense, the cause of their status-frustration. To infer inclinations to aggression from the existence of frustration is hazardous; we know that aggression is not an inevitable and not the only consequence of frustration. Nevertheless, despite our imperfect knowledge of these things, we would be blind if we failed to recognize that bitterness, hostility and jealousy and all sorts of retributive fantasies are among the most common and typically human responses to public humiliation. However, for the child who temporizes with middle-class morality, overt aggression and even the conscious recognition of his own hostile impulses are inhibited, for he acknowledges the *legitimacy* of the rules in terms of which he is stigmatized. For the child who breaks clean with middle-class morality, on the other hand, there are no moral inhibitions on the free expression of aggression against the sources of his frustration. Moreover, the connection we suggest between status-frustration and the aggressiveness of the delinquent subculture seems to us more plausible than many frustration-aggression hypotheses because it involves no assumptions about obscure and dubious "displacement" of aggression against "substitute" targets. The target in this case is the manifest cause of the status problem.

It seems to us that the mechanism of "reaction-formation" should also play a part here. Its hallmark is an "exaggerated," "disproportionate," "abnormal" intensity of response, "inappropriate" to the stimulus which seems to elicit it. The unintelligibility of the response, the "overreaction," becomes intelligible when we see that it has the function of reassuring the actor against an *inner* threat to his defenses as well as the function of meeting an external situation on its own terms. Thus we have the mother who "compulsively" showers "inordinate" affection upon a child to reassure herself against her latent hostility and we have the male adolescent whose awkward and immoderate masculinity reflects a basic insecurity about his own sex-role.

In like manner, we would expect the delinquent boy who, after all, has been socialized in a society dominated by a middle-class morality and who can never quite escape the blandishments of middle-class society, to seek to maintain his safeguards against seduction. Reaction-formation, in his case, should take the form of an "irrational," "malicious," "unaccountable" hostility to the enemy within the gates as well as without: the norms of the respectable middle-class society.

If our reasoning is correct, it should throw some light upon the peculiar quality of "property delinquency" in the delinquent subculture. We have already seen how the rewardingness of a college-boy and middle-class way of life depends, to a great extent, upon general respect for property rights. In an urban society, in particular, the possession and display of property are the most ready and public badges of reputable social class status and are, for that reason, extraordinarily ego-involved. That property actually is a reward for middle-class morality is in part only a plausible fiction, but in general there is certainly a relationship between the practice of that morality and the possession of property. The middle-classes have, then, a strong interest in scrupulous regard for property rights, not only because property is "intrinsically" valuable but because the full enjoyment of their status requires that that status be readily recognizable and therefore that property adhere to those who earn it. The cavalier misappropriation or destruction of property, therefore, is not only a diversion or diminution of wealth; it is an attack on the middle-class where their egos are most vulnerable. Group stealing, institutionalized in the delinquent subculture, is not just a way of *getting* something. It is a means that is the antithesis of sober and diligent "labor in a calling." It expresses contempt for a way of life by making its opposite a criterion of status. Money and other valuables are not, as such, despised by the delinquent. For the delinquent, and the non-delinquent alike, money is a most glamorous and efficient means to a variety of ends and one cannot have too much of it. But, in the delinquent subculture, the stolen dollar has an odor of sanctity that does not attach to the dollar saved or the dollar earned.

This delinquent system of values and way of life does its job of problem-solving most effectively when it is adopted as a group solution. We have stressed in our chapter on the general theory of subcultures that the efficacy of a given change in values as a solution and therefore the motivation to such a change depends heavily upon the availability of "reference groups" within which the "deviant values" are already institutionalized, or whose members would stand to profit from such a system of deviant values if each were assured of the support and concurrence of the others. So it is with delinquency. We do not suggest that joining in the creation or perpetuation of a delinquent subculture is the only road to delinquency. We do believe, however, that for most delinquents delinquency would not be available as a response were it not socially legitimized and given a kind of respectability, albeit by a restricted community of fellow-adventurers. In this respect, the adoption of delinquency is like the adoption of the practice of appearing at the office in open-collar and shirt sleeves. Is it much more comfortable, is it more sensible than the full regalia? Is it neat? Is it dignified? The arguments in the affirmative will appear much more forceful if the practice is already established in one's milieu or if one senses that others are prepared to go along if someone makes the first tentative gestures. Indeed, to many of those who sweat and chafe in ties and jackets, the possibility of an alternative may not even occur until they discover that it has been adopted by their colleagues.

This way of looking at delinquency suggests an answer to a certain paradox. Countless mothers have protested that their "Johnny" was a good boy until he fell in with a certain bunch. But the mothers of each of Johnny's companions hold the same view with respect to their own offspring. It is conceivable and even probable that some of these mothers are naïve, that one or more of these youngsters are "rotten apples" who infected the others. We suggest, however, that all of the mothers may be right, that there is a certain chemistry in the group situation itself which engenders that which was not there before, that group interaction is a sort of catalyst which releases potentialities not otherwise visible. This is especially true when we are dealing with a problem of status-frustration. Status, by definition, is a grant of respect from others. A new system of norms, which measures status by criteria which one can meet, is of no value unless others are prepared to apply those criteria, and others are not likely to do so unless one is prepared to reciprocate.

We have referred to a lingering ambivalence in the delinquent's own value system, an ambivalence which threatens the adjustment he has achieved and which is met through the mechanism of reaction-formation. The delinquent may have to contend with another ambivalence, in the area of his status sources. The delinquent subculture offers him status *as against* other children of whatever social level, but it offers him this status *in the eyes of* his fellow delinquents only. To the extent that there remains a desire for recognition from groups whose respect has been forfeited by commitment to a new subculture, his satisfaction in his solution is imperfect and adulterated. He can perfect his solution only by rejecting as status sources those who reject him. This too may require a certain measure of reaction-formation, going beyond indifference to active hostility and contempt for all those who do not share his subculture. He becomes all the more dependent upon his delinquent gang. Outside that gang his status position is now weaker than ever. The gang itself tends toward a kind of sectarian solidarity, because the benefits of membership can only be realized in active face-to-face relationships with group members.

This interpretation of the delinquent subculture has important implications for the "sociology of social problems." People are prone to assume that those things which we define as evil and those which we define as good have their origins in separate and distinct features of our society. Evil flows from poisoned wells; good flows from pure and crystal fountains. The same source cannot feed both. Our view is different. It holds that those values which are at the core of "the American way of life," which help to motivate the behavior which we most esteem as "typically American," are among the major determinants of that which we stigmatize as "pathological." More specifically, it holds that the problems of adjustment to which the delinquent subculture is a response are determined, in part, by those very values which respectable society holds most sacred. The same value system, impinging upon children differently equipped to meet it, is instrumental in generating both delinquency and respectability.

SHORT TALK WITH A FASCIST BEAST
/Clancy Sigal

It is a normal evening at the coffee-bar where I'm in the habit of dropping by. The kids are jiving and punching each other around in the juke-box room, an amateur rock-and-roll session is in violent practice upstairs somewhere, and some of us are gathered at the counter sucking Pepsi-Cola through straws. Through the big front window we can see a few of the boys horsing around on their hire-purchased motorbikes. Fat, moonfaced Dave walks in and asks us if we want a ride on his bike and we say no, we'll hang around a while.

Len buys Ginger and Dave and me Pepsis. He's on casual work now, he says, after quitting a warehouse where he moved fridges. "Keep on casual till they nick me," he says. I tell Len that I've heard he was up at Notting Hill during the troubles. "Yeah," Len replies, "three nights all in a row." He is stating a fact, not boasting. "What were you doing up there?" I ask. "Hittin' the nigs," he says.

Dave, off his motorbike, offers that he spent only a single night "huntin' nigs." Ginger, who resembles Jimmy Dean and likes being told about it, says, "Nah, that wasn't the way—all in a mob. Coppers see you. Thing to do, three, four of us, down a side street at night, in a fast car, jump out, do a nig, jump in. That way you can do a dozen blackies a night."

Len is a lanky, shamble-shouldered bleach-haired boy, with a tall thin blond face and small blank eyes and virtually no upper eyelids. I ask Len if he enjoyed himself during the riots. He says, "Sure." I ask him what he did. "Hit nigs," he says and shrugs. Did many boys from the café go with him? No, not many. "It was the Fascists done the work up there," Len says. How is he so sure? "I drove around, first night, in a jeep with one of them. A reporter from one of the newspapers gets out of his car and asks us what the trouble is. This Fascist smashed him square in the face, 'e did. Reporter got back in his car and rolled up all the windows." Dave and Ginger say they chased a few colored men without much success.

Dave says that his high point came when he led a mob of teen-agers to St. Mark's Crescent and pointed a milk bottle at a colored house. Ginger has no individual exploits to his credit. He wears a brightly colored Palm Beach shirt and talks like an American radio comedian. He doesn't tell jokes, just maintains a patter of small, pseudo-ironical remarks. They listen while Len speaks of the Fascists. He says that, contrary to public belief, the Fascists still wear the black shirt with the silver lightning insignia. Is he a member of the Union Movement himself? With a quick dart of the long blond head he says no, not a member, only a follower. "Fascists was active before all the troubles," he says, "and now they're gettin' lots of members. Brown shirts started that way, didn't they? I mean, it don't mean just because you start out small that you some day won't be over the whole country, does it?" Dave and Ginger remain neutral in the face of ideology. What Len was doing at Notting Hill was fine with them, but not when he wants to do it in uniform.

I ask Len if it is the uniform that attracts him. He says no, not particularly, it is what the Fascists stand for. "Riddin' Britain of the nigs," he says. When I ask him what he has against the "nigs," Dave and Ginger chime in eagerly. It isn't so much the Indians and Africans they mind. It's the Jamaicans, their word for all West Indians.

Dave says, "Y'know, when I went in for my national assistance, all they'd give me was two quid after an argument. Crazy Jamaican after me comes out with seven." How did the Jamaican manage this? Dave says the Jamaican claimed a family back in the islands. Ginger says, "They come here and they use all our money, lower our standards, that's what they do." "Darkies live on two quid a week," says Ginger, "eatin' cat food. It's the truth. I seen 'em." "Live like pigs," says Dave.

Len adds, "An' the way they all walk around, they got no respect. The clothes they wear. I seen one last night, suit the color of milk, milk mind you, black shoes with a green tassel, and with a girl." Was the girl white? Len nods. He says, "Ever see the pants they wear? Big and wide up here, tiny and little at the bottom. Why do they have to dress that way? Crazy pants." His own trousers are drainpipe, of a gray tweed material I am not familiar with. Ten minutes later he is to tell me that he had to sleep at a friend's house a week ago because of a row with his old lady over his trousers.

It boils down to this: the West Indians live too high and live like pigs. When I ask them if they do not see a contradiction in this, Len with the plodding seriousness that is characteristic, says sincerely, after a little confused thought, "They live in dirt in private and like kings the rest of the time." He says he used to live in Notting Hill but that a colored man bought the house and threw them out.

"The coppers," says Len, "they was all on the side of the blackies." Dave and Ginger nod vigorously. I say that the colored people I have spoken to claim differently. "Cor," exclaims Ginger, "see what we mean? Liars all, the blacks. Can't trust any of 'em." Do they know any colored people personally? Vague replies. Len grins slyly, more animation than I usually get from him. "Yeah, I knew one," he says. "Hit him over the head with my shovel." It happened three weeks ago, at work. "See what I mean?" says Len. "I was working on this building site. Driving a dump truck. I got sick, y'know. Out two days. While I was gone this blackie tells the boss he can drive a truck too. When I comes back there he is in my cab. I tell him to get down out of my truck and he says no he won't. So me and my mates pull him down and I hit him over the head with my shovel."

Ginger says, "What are you gonna do with people who come to take your jobs? How much you willin' to work for, Len?" Len says, 12, 14 quid a week. "No," says Ginger, "I mean, how much *would* you work for?" Len says staunchly, "I'd work for eight quid." "See," says Ginger. "Guv'nor knows Len won't work for less than eight, a blackie'll come along who says 'six' and he's the one who gets the job." Len, Dave and Ginger all left school at 15. They are 18 now. Len is a casual laborer, Dave a public service worker, while Ginger is an assistant to a skilled craftsman.

Dave says, "Four years." Ginger says, "Four almighty years." Len says, "Four years is a long time." The boys are genuinely in awe. Len snaps out of it. "Four bloody years for *that?* Salmon, that Yid." When the boys talk it is with a peculiar, rushing, staccato tempo which is the trademark of their group. Dave and Ginger swear the West Indians are lazy, and that the "guv'nors" prefer them to native-born Englishmen; that they live on nothing a week, and spend all their money on offensive hedonisms, and are worse than savages. Do they resent the West Indians fighting back? "Bloody well do," says Dave. "What right they got comin' to this country, anyway? We get the worst types." All agree that the colored immigrants ought to be returned to their source, but if they are not, to serve docilely as fair game for mobs.

Len says, "On the second day I got me a few. Fell in with this crowd chasing nigs. We saw a nigger conductor on a trolley bus. We chased it. All the people in the bus ran out. But I didn't get to the nig. The mob was in there before me." I asked Len if he was disappointed. He nods sadly. "That's all right," he says. "Later on, on the corner there was this gang, and they was kicking this blackie on the ground. I ran up and got a few kicks in too." I asked him if he thought this was fair. "Yeah, it was fair," he says. Dave and Ginger leave for a ride on Dave's motorbike. Len and I watch them roar away.

"I hate the niggers," says Len complacently. I ask him if Mr. Justice Salmon's decision will affect his street activities. "Four years," Len muses, "four years is a long time. Nah, I ain't goin' to go to the neck for any nigger." He says that after the Old Bailey sentences he stopped carrying a flick knife. "I used to have a gun too," he says. "But not now. You know, those coppers at Notting Hill. They'd see us lacing a blackie and they'd stand off, just watchin' us, y'know, and then when we was through they'd come charging through and frisk us for knives, things like that. You had a weapon they'd take you away. But first they'd just stand there and watch." Even more than Mr. Justice Salmon's sentences he resented chasing after a colored man with a mob, only to be peppered with milk bottles by West Indians on a roof-top. It infuriates him to see colored men fight back.

"That's why I'm with the Fascists," he says. "They're against the blacks. That Salmon, he's a Communist. The Labour Party is Communist too. Like the unions." His mother and father, he says, are strict Labour supporters. Is he against the Labour Party? "Nah, I'm for them. They're for y'know—us. I'm for the unions too." Even though they were dominated by Communists? "Sure," he says, "I like the Communist Party. It's powerful, like." How can he be for the Communists when the Fascists hate them?

Len says, "Well, y'know, I'm for the Fascists when

they're against the nigs. But the Fascists is really for the rich people y'know, like the Tories. All for the guv'nors, people like that. But the Communists are very powerful." I told him the Communist Party of Britain was quite small.

"But," he says, "they got Russia behind them." His voice is full of marvel. "I admire Russia. Y'know, the people. They're peaceful. They're strong. When they say they'll do a thing, they do it. Not like us. Makes you think: they got a weapon over there can wipe us all out, with one wave of a general's arm. Destroy us completely and totally. Honest, those Russians. When they say they'll do a thing, they do it. Like in Hungary. I pity those people, the Hungarians. But did you see the Russians went in and stopped them. Tanks. Not like us in Cyprus. Our soldiers get shot in the back and what do we do? The Communists is for the small man."

Dave and Ginger come back in time to hear Len say, "Them Royals. I'd like to murder them." Dave and Ginger are profoundly shocked. Dave puts in, "Nah, why d'you want to say that, Len?" "Yeah," says Ginger, "the Queen's O.K." Before Len can reply, they quickly wander off to the men's room. They cannot bear to hear Len's reasons. Len puts it to me: "Would you like havin' all that royalty? Usin' up our money for polo and yachts and goin' around just doin' nothing. It's all for show. We don't need them." I ask Len if he thinks it will be quiet now at Notting Hill. "Yeah," he says, "it's all over." A moment later he says, "As long as the nigs stay there'll be trouble." Will he be one of the ones to make it? "No," he says. "Well, maybe, you never can tell. Why can't they be just like the Paddies. Just come here and work. They're good workers, those Paddies."

It's warm in the café, and Len and I stand outside the doorway. I tell Len I hear he writes plays. He smiles shyly. "Just two," he says. "Second one ain't finished. I . . ." he shrugs, "trouble is . . . I can't write. It's hard, like." He is embarrassed. I say that I would like to see one of his plays. He goes into the café and comes out bearing a manuscript. It is crudely typed and enclosed in professional folder-covers. "I paid to have that done," he says.

On the street corner, in the glow of the lamp, I read the play. It is about an English pilot who crash-lands his plane in the jungle. Aboard are a judge, a movie star, a headmaster, a company director and a policeman. It becomes necessary for them to eat one another for survival.

Only the pilot survives, a young, almost teen-age pilot.
When he gets back to England he must stand trial for manslaughter, a martyr. Most of the play is concerned with the
pilot conducting his own defense and explaining why he
found it necessary to eat parts of the judge, the movie star,
the headmaster, the company director and the policeman.

ALCOHOLISM
/Selden Bacon

Great social problems can be disregarded or responded
to ineffectively if they have been carefully hidden, as in the
case of venereal diseases, or if they are loudly and continuously talked about in distorted and misleading ways.
This last has been the development in the field of alcoholism. As a result, new attempts to meet the problems of
alcoholism are confronted with a task of uprooting old and
fallacious conceptions in addition to the task of presenting
new and more efficient responses to this age old problem.

To list some of the most common distortions: Alcohol
is the cause of alcoholism; drunkenness and alcoholism are
the same thing; alcoholism is often inherited and (completely incompatible with this and equally fallacious) alcoholism is due to lack of will power; alcohol is a stimulant;
alcohol damages nervous tissue; alcohol causes 60 or 80 or
100 per cent of crime; most alcoholics come from the lowest
social strata; "It Never Could Happen to Me"; and so on
and so on. All these ideas are fallacious, and this can be
proved by logic, by facts, and by experimentation. But to
have people accept the proofs and act accordingly is far
from easy.

To appreciate the nature and extent of alcoholism, it is
necessary to realize that there is a large body of organized
misinformation and that this and the accompanying misconceptions are a part of the casual, undefined thinking of
many, many Americans. Unless this is realized, all that follows will be useless or misused. If one believes, for example,
that alcoholism is a deviation from morality and that de-
viations from morality should be punished, then, no matter
what other knowledge or conceptions are present, one is

going to punish the alcoholic by attitude, words, imprisonment, or otherwise. Punishment, however, will not alleviate, cure, or prevent any sickness, whether mumps, mental disease, or alcoholism. To this, the answer of the man with unconsciously distorted training is almost sure. He knows that Tom, Dick, or Harry, punished after being drunk, never got drunk again or never took a drink again. He does not realize that this observation is irrelevant because drunkenness and alcoholism are quite different things. Misconceptions pile upon misconceptions. It might have been better, for any ultimate solution, if this problem had been hidden rather than have been so loudly, so continuously, and so mistakenly talked about.

What is an alcoholic? Alcoholics may be distinguished from other drinkers primarily by the purpose for which they drink. Some people drink to fulfill a religious ritual, others in order to be polite, still others for a good time, or to make friends, to experiment, show off, get warm or cool, quench thirst, or because they like a particular alcoholic beverage as a condiment, or because they want to go on a spree. None of these is the purpose of the alcoholic, although he might claim any or all to satisfy some questioner. The alcoholic drinks because he has to if he is to go on living. He drinks *compulsively;* that is, a power greater than rational planning brings him to drinking and to excessive drinking. Most alcoholics hate liquor, hate drinking, hate the taste, hate the results, hate themselves for succumbing, but they can't stop. Their drinking is as compulsive as the stealing by a kleptomaniac or the continual hand-washing of a person with a neurosis about cleanliness. It is useful to think of their drinking behavior as a symptom of some inner maladjustment which they do not understand and cannot control. The drinking may be the outward, obvious accompaniment of this more basic and hidden factor.

From this statement alone it can be seen that alcoholism and drunkenness are different phenomena. All alcoholics exhibit drunkenness, but many who get drunk are not alcoholics. For example, the college boy on a spree, or a member of a group which drinks regularly (and usually to excess) on specific occasions, such as holidays, reunions, Saturday nights, may or may not get drunk, but they are not alcoholics unless their drinking is compulsive, brought about by some inner need or unresolved conflict.

Compulsive drinking is a progressive condition. Its course may be rapid or extremely slow. Some few persons exhibit wild drinking behavior and uncontrollable need for alcohol immediately following their introduction to drinking. These individuals are probably in the category of psychotics; their alcoholism may be very obvious, but in actuality it is only a minor symptom of a major disease.

A great many alcoholics have a history of 10 or 15 years of relatively controlled drinking. Sometimes in their career they may have experienced a few "blackouts" during drunkenness; they may have started sneaking a few drinks more than their companions. After a while it began to happen that on occasions when they "only intended to have a couple" they wound up drunk. They may have developed a need to rationalize their heavy drinking. Solitary drinking, morning drinking, and benders may appear as a regular practice anywhere from 4 to 7 years after the first blackouts. By this time the stage of alcoholism has been achieved, but it may not be recognized by the individual or by more than a few intimates. Attempts at control or at changing the pattern of drinking may follow. Feelings of remorse become persistent. The individual becomes socially isolated. He may develop deep anxieties, tremors, obvious physical symptoms. It may be 7 to 10 years from the time of his first "blackout," 15 years since his first drink. By now, however, he is recognized by all, perhaps even by himself, as an alcoholic. Some may take only three years to reach the undoubted stage of alcoholism.

A clinical description of the alcoholic as he appears in the final stages may conclude this statement answering the question "What is an alcoholic?" No two alcoholics are identical. Some are sufficiently different to be labeled as different types. Nevertheless there are enough common characteristics in addition to the compulsive nature of the drinking and the progressive nature of the affliction to allow a general statement.

Physically, many alcoholics in the later stages of this condition are characterized by undernourishment, highly irregular routine, inadequate sleep, and an over-all attitude of hopelessness, plus unrelieved tension. As a result they are highly susceptible to accidents and to other diseases. It should be carefully noted that these are not directly effects of alcohol. They follow upon the behavioral consequences of continued excessive drinking. Not all alcoholics present this picture since they may be closely protected by family, friends, or independent means.

Psychologically the alcoholic in the later and last stages of this illness is characterized (1) by being in continual and awful pain, (2) by a set of responses which may be summed up as immaturity, and (3) by an over-all attitude of extreme egocentricity.

The pain is not merely or even importantly related to the physical aspects of his condition or the inconveniences occasioned by his type of life. It is centered around his inner feelings of self-depreciation, self-hate, self-pity, guilt, and all-encompassing remorse. Since he cannot explain this, he often attempts to hide it. Pain, however, is the constant comrade of the alcoholic. And a dreadful (in the real meaning of the term) comrade it is.

The immaturity of the alcoholic may be illustrated by his rapid mood swings, superficially sly rationalizations, adolescent self-consciousness, magnificent ideals which are almost inevitably linked with minuscule accomplishments, and juvenile techniques of hiding bottles, lying about drinking, and wheedling pity and free drinks.

The alcoholic generally lacks interest in anything outside of himself and his problems. Such outside interests as he may manifest are usually temporary and directly and immediately related to a desire to show off or achieve some quick benefit. His continual comparison of all things to himself, easy cynicism about anything not connected to himself, self-pity, intense feelings of guilt and increasingly solitary existence, all bear witness to his egocentricity.

Socially, the alcoholic in the final stages tends to be isolated, undersocialized. An amazing proportion of alcoholic males have never married. Of those who have, the proportion of separated and divorced is many times that in the general population. The alcoholic frequently moves from place to place, from job to job. He has few if any close friends. Typically, the alcoholic doesn't do very much; he doesn't have hobbies, go to the movies, join in any group activities.

As a result of this undersocialization or desocialization the alcoholic is susceptible to fewer stimuli than people with friends and group membership. He receives fewer satisfactions and rewards. Punishment is less and less meaningful since the strength of punishment varies with its source; if a father or wife or friend punishes, the effect is far greater than if the action comes from an impersonal source. Since the alcoholic has given up these associations, he is less stimulated, and only with difficulty is rewarded or punished effectively. He becomes his own source of stimulation, reward and punishment and thus he may vary greatly from the social norms, possess ridiculous ideals, vastly over-punish himself, and lapse into minimum activity.

Why does one become an alcoholic? Since no final answer to this question is available, since the subject is complex and the size of this paper limited, a relatively brief and dogmatically phrased description will follow. In accord with the two essentials for the development of the condition, it will be divided into two parts: one, the habitual use of alcohol; two, certain personality types or structures.* Neither of these can alone bring on alcoholism. There are many individuals with personalities similar to those found in alcoholics who never become alcoholics, who may never touch alcohol; there are tens of millions of individuals who use alcohol who never become alcoholics. The combination of the two factors is essential for the appearance of alcoholism.

Alcohol is a depressant, the direct opposite of a stimulant. Taken in sufficient quantities it produces sleep. Its depressant action is gradual, however; and as it depresses certain control functions of the brain it allows behavior and attitudes which are usually repressed. (It is this less-controlled behavior which makes people believe that it is a stimulant.) Alcohol, even in small quantities, lowers sensitivity, relieves tension, allows the forgetting of difficult and unpleasant conceptions and memories. It reduces accuracy of judgment and discrimination, especially about the self. With alcohol, then, one can temporarily escape worries and anxieties, temporarily ease tensions, feel as if one were happy, clever, witty, graceful or, at least, less unhappy, less inept, less dull, less awkward. And one can gain this temporary feeling without utilizing the effort and ability which real achievement of such feeling would demand.

Of the personality types significant for alcoholism only two will be mentioned. It should be recognized that there are psychotics and feebleminded persons who are also alcoholics, that there are persons, apparently quite normal, who under extraordinary stress may become compulsive

* [There is now much evidence of a physiological or constitutional basis for alcoholism.—EDITORS.]

drinkers. The great bulk of the alcoholics, however, fit into the two classes to be described, the primary and the secondary compulsive drinker types.

The primary type may be likened to that category of persons labeled neurotic. This over-used and little understood word in the present instance at least serves to point out that primary compulsive drinkers were definitely maladjusted *before* they began drinking. Here, for example, is the individual whose personality was warped, whose emotional development was unhealthy from infancy or childhood on. The maladjustment might be seen as an inability to compete with equals or superiors without feeling extreme anxiety or apprehension of undefined, future pain. Or it might be seen as an unusual fear of contact with those of the opposite sex, or as a general conception of the self as unworthy, inefficient, and socially awkward. These states of mind are fairly common though irregular occurrences among adolescents, but as continued attitudes in a young or middle-aged adult they are out of keeping with the demands of our society. In the early twenties and certainly by the age of thirty there is great pressure on adults to be socially and economically competitive and appropriately self-assertive, to be married, and to have attained a relatively mature independence and self-control. As individuals of poor or no adjustment along these lines grow older, the pressures upon them grow stronger and the maladjustment becomes increasingly harder to bear. No statement is presented to explain why or how these individuals come to be "neurotics." It is a matter of common observation that there are many such persons.

If such persons are, like most Americans, introduced to the custom of drinking, and if anxieties about drinking are not too great and no other way out of their dilemma is found, then they are likely candidates to start out on the road to alcholism. Alcohol allows them to compete without anxiety, to mingle without or with less fear in mixed company, perhaps even to initiate courtship behavior, to forget their own interpretation of their personal inadequacies; it allows them relief from whatever their problem may be. Small wonder that they come to lean upon this crutch with increasing dependency. This development illustrates the conception that for the type of person described alcohol is an adjustment.

However, the alcohol wears off while the neurotic characteristics remain as before. Furthermore, the memory of having acted aggressively or assertively, of having shown interest in the opposite sex because of alcohol creates new anxieties; the knowledge of having been "out-of-control" also adds guilt and remorse. However, in the long run the rewards of drinking for the incipient alcoholic are greater than these feelings. Later on he may use alcohol to get rid of the post-alcoholic guilt and anxiety. Thus a vicious circle comes into operation.

The vicious circle is stimulated further by the inevitable extension and intensification of old problems and the rise of new ones due to increasing periods of inebriety. Family and friends, employers and neighbors, customers and strangers, all will punish the person who often gets drunk. With the increase in problems the relieving, soothing, encouraging effects of alcohol become all the more desirable. So, although alcohol is an adjustment, it is a short-run, temporary adjustment and leads to further maladjustment.

Before his drinking starts the secondary compulsive type appears on the surface as a fairly well adjusted person. He or she has utilized social customs, attitudes and organizations with considerable ability. Certainly the label "neurotic" would never have been applied. Some of this type may be more extroverted than those around them, tending to be the leader in the group, the excessive practical joker, the most aggressive salesman. The implication from this is that they have to work harder than others to achieve a sense of personal adequacy, of being a significant member of their group. Whatever the case, it is noticeable that they can differ markedly from the earlier mentioned "neurotic" type, that they have utilized customs, associations and attitudes which were socially acceptable; this plays an important role in the discussion of therapy.

The prospective secondary type of compulsive drinker, when introduced to the drinking custom, appears to take to it with great satisfaction. He already belongs to a group which usually drinks a good deal or he shortly joins such a group and becomes a regular drinker, later perhaps a heavy drinker, but he is not yet an alcoholic; he is in control of the drinking, not the drinking in control of him. Many people can be so characterized, and they need not become alcoholics. For the individual in whom we are interested, however, a process sets in which has been called the pampering effect of alcohol.

Alcohol lowers sensitivity, discrimination, control and efficiency. Unless counteracting forces arise, it allows the drinker to respond to stimuli less adequately and to follow personal inclinations in the face of contrary social demands with less notice and less care. As a result the fairly constant heavy drinker may become a more careless worker, a more thoughtless father and husband, a more demanding friend, a more aggressive neighbor. Nor is this the only effect. On the negative side he may be seen as failing to exercise his social abilities and his intellectual techniques. Without practice the personality assets become dulled and more difficult to use. This process may take place by almost imperceptible steps.

The result of this process is inevitable—occupational, familial, financial, and neighborly problems are going to arise. Unfortunately, the individual has learned a simple response to avoid such problems—drinking. Again a vicious circle can be seen.

A second result of this process, a result which may confuse the therapist, is that the personality of the drinker seems to change. The change is not hard to explain. The individual finds himself losing the affection and regard of his wife, his boss, his friends; whereupon he loses affection and regard for them. He finds that he is less popular in his club, among fellow workers or in community groups; whereupon he gives up these organizations. He can hardly help but realize that his work is not as good as it was; whereupon he talks it up, idealizes what he is going to do, what he has done; while realistic accomplishment continues downhill. He becomes increasingly isolated and consequently self-centered. As he loses friends and interests, he becomes cynical, self-conscious and suspicious of others. He rationalizes his situation, and as his rationalizations are not subject to the discipline of realistic give-and-take, he becomes overly idealistic or overly optimistic or pessimistic. Gradually he takes on more and more of the characteristics of the primary type. When he has achieved the full status of an alcoholic he may seem not a whit different from the primary type. From the point of view of rehabilitation, however, he or she is a decidedly different person; the chances of recovery are far better than for those of the primary type.

These descriptions of the two largest categories of compulsive drinkers, categories based on the developmental nature of the disease, are not a full answer to the question "Why does one become an alcoholic?" They may help, however, toward a better understanding of the sorts of processes, conditions and factors involved in the development of that condition.

BOWERY MAN ON THE COUCH
/Elmer Bendiner

The search for a common denominator among Bowery Men always begins—and frequently ends—with the finding that they are all alcoholics. However, this scarcely makes a reliable distinguishing hallmark of the species, because, in the first place, most alcoholics do not become Bowery Men and, in the second place, drinking, while certainly part of life on the Bowery, is not usually an important reason for being there.

To insist that a man is on Skid Row because he drinks is like arguing that a man becomes a millionaire because he wears a top hat.

Furthermore, if you expect to find the grim, solitary, ugly drunk, downing massive doses calculated to lay him out cold in the shortest possible time, you are less likely to find him in a Bowery saloon than you are among the family men who inhabit the cocktail bars of commuters' trains.

A somewhat limited but interesting survey by Alcoholics Anonymous found that ninety-two per cent of the moneyed and family class of chronic drinkers are solitary addicts. But on the Bowery and other Skid Rows only ten per cent habitually drink alone, according to a study of *Alcohol and the Homeless Man* by sociologist Robert Strauss.

The same conclusion may be reached with less scientific certainty, perhaps, but more pleasantly by taking a walk along the Street. You can see the Bowery drunk spiking his cheap wine with raw alcohol and passing the bottle among his friends, or even among strangers. He drinks to fend off loneliness, or sometimes the lesser chill that the wind sends slashing through his rags. He aspires only to warmth and everlasting "highness," rarely to total oblivion.

On that sunny plateau the Bowery Man has the camara-
derie that is more precious to him than love or friendship
of the sort so highly valued in the dank valleys of sobriety.
He does not want friends—with their incessant demands
upon him—but he craves the illusion of friendship. He
wants good fellows about him who can help to kill the time
that weighs like an albatross about his neck.

For him alcohol makes possible a world with rounded,
smooth edges—a world of brothers, but not of brotherhood and all the dreary responsibilities which that concept
entails.

The Bowery Man is a social drinker with a sense of group
responsibility. He panhandles for liquor money to hold up
his end of the bargain so that he may contribute his mite
to the collective fund. Then, when the bottle goes around,
he takes only one gulp at a time, and that one is nicely
proportioned to his investment in the bottle.

If his particular drinking group stakes him to a drink, he
repays it with scrupulous correctness. There is an elaborate
courtesy in these circles that only a gauche newcomer from
uptown would violate. For example, when a man is pitch-
ing a line to someone who might give him the price of a
drink, he is not to be interrupted or distracted. If he fails,
another can try, but there is no uncouth struggling over a
"live one" as the prospect is respectfully dubbed.

These decorous manners may perhaps serve to distinguish
the Bowery Man from an ad agency executive, but they
do not mark him as unique.

If not alcohol, what else sets these men apart? What
makes them a community? Certainly they do not look
alike. They make no gray and faceless mass. Here are
Swedes and Irish and Poles, Midwesterners, Southerners,
New England farm boys run to seed, Negro boys, tall and
rangy, with life still in them, and old Negroes with the
beards and eyes of patriarchs.

Here are cripples and well men, sullen and simple. Some
laugh as they shoot crap on the sidewalk. Some just stand
in their several layers of rags and look with mild, vacant
eyes at the scene and at the stranger who walks among
them from the world uptown.

Sociologists have counted their noses, tabulated their
previous occupations, the first names of their grandparents,
and the color of their skins. Psychologists have distributed
Rorschach tests free to the needy. Conclusions from all these

efforts vary in many respects, but there are some hard, unassailable facts in the picture.

There are many Irishmen on the Bowery, for example, very few Italians or Jews, and almost no Chinese, although Chinatown is handy.

There are obvious reasons for some Irishmen to linger among the Home Guard. When they fled the famines they became wild geese scattering over the whole world, and many took to the sea. The sailor, until he was organized into a trade union, was the traditional foot-loose wanderer for whom no home was really possible, who cultivated a scorn for the landlubber. For seamen who were beached, the Bowery became a shelter.

Many Irishmen who did not take to the sea went into one form of transportation or another. They built the railroads and ran them. They dug the canals and skinned the mules that towed the barges from Albany to Buffalo.

Men in transport are men on the go, homeless men who in between jobs, or after the last job, find their home with the other homeless.

There is therefore an historical reason for the Irish on the Bowery, but psychologists tend to dismiss this explanation as superficial. The important factors are to be found in family life, they say. Dr. Boris Levinson, who has reported on the Bowery men for the *Psychiatric Quarterly* and other learned publications, studs his papers with charts that would bring a look of astonishment to his subjects, the quiet old bags of bones asleep in the Bowery doorways.

He finds the Irish family to be dominated as a rule by the mother. This generality seems incontrovertible—as generalities go—and even the Irish attest to it willingly enough.

The Irishman's mother tends to be a Madonna and other women—particularly those who would lower themselves to go with him—are likely, in his view, to be whores. He is likely to marry late and then set his wife upon a pedestal. In the psychologist's opinion, marriage to a saint is not conducive to a healthy sex life, but the normal Irishman can take all this in his stride and become a poet, a politician, a bus driver, a priest or anything else.

But an Irishman who has some unusual weakness in his moral fiber may refrain from marriage altogether and run away from the women he fears. He takes to drink easily because the Irish traditionally do not look upon alcohol as repulsive.

Alcoholism, in itself, says Dr. Levinson, quoting Freud, implies tendencies to homosexuality. In fact, though, homosexuality is present but not rife on the Bowery. When the brothels on the street closed, it was for lack of customers, not because the girls had competition.

It seems that there is a flight from *all* sexuality on the Bowery. There is, in part, the atmosphere of a monastery—a silent withdrawal from all the joys of the world save the passport to Nirvana contained in a little alcohol.

Psychologist Marvin K. Opler drew this comparison between Irish and Italian families:

"The Irish family tends to be dominated by the mother; the father is often a weak and shadowy figure. ... In the Irish home active expression of emotion is frowned upon; sexual feelings are clouded with conceptions of sin. All this is reflected in the personality of the male offspring. The Irish male is apt to be quiet, repressed, shy or fearful of women and as his literature attests, given to fantasy as an outlet for his emotions."

Opler's Italian family looked quite different:

"The dominant figure is the father. He rules the family with a sometimes benevolent, sometimes rough hand. Emotions and passions are allowed free expression. Little or no sin or guilt is attached to sex. As a result the Italian male is proverbially excitable, given to acting out his emotions and sometimes hostile to his father and older brothers (to whom the father may delegate authority over him)."

This is not to say that the freewheeling, uninhibited Latin may not end up in worse places than the Bowery, but apparently he does not usually seek out this secular, creedless monastery. He has no talent for self-obliteration.

The Negro is yet another story. As we have seen, he was on the Bowery when the Dutch of New Amsterdam set him free so that he could take the brunt of an Indian attack. Later he was moved down to the squalid tenements of the Five Points near Mulberry Bend. After that he did not reappear in the city's history until mobs made a victim of him during the draft riots.

But the depression brought a new wave of Negroes to the Bowery. They were a younger group of men than the whites who were tossed up by the storm and beached on the Bowery. Nose-counters and interviewers discovered that the average Negro on the Bowery in those days had done more traveling on the road than his white counterpart, but that he was also more likely to have been married, and more likely to be free of the neuroses and psychoses that marked his white brothers on the breadlines.

Were the Negroes' wives displaced, lost, stolen? Why did the storm uproot more stable, wholesome, settled Negroes than whites?

The answers seem to lie more with the economist than the psychologist. Perhaps the economic soil in which Negro families grew was so thin, the roots so close to the surface, that even the strongest could not resist. In depression times the steadiest Negro family lived in marginal soil close to the hunger line, and the wind that might make a white family man shut the blinds was enough to rip the Negro up by the roots and set him adrift.

Perhaps, too, economic troubles were less traumatic to the Negro than to his white brother. He was more used to them.

In any case, the Negro came to the Bowery and the sociologists found him in good shape when he got there, regardless of how he felt about it. When the defense boom came many of the Negroes left but some stayed on, seeing in life on the Bowery what the Irish and the Swedes and Poles saw, seeing in it what the seaman and the hobo and the bum saw—an end to fighting back, a resting place, a refutation of the old hymn, "There's no hiding place down here." The Bowery offered a hiding place so secret that the fugitive could not be found even by himself.

The Jew is a rarity and a curio on the Bowery. On either side of the street are districts primarily Jewish. Until Puerto Ricans came in to share the East Side tenements with them, this was an area where Jewish life filled the air and flavored the stores and streets. But the peddlers, sweatshop workers, teachers, and rabbis looked upon the Bowery as beyond the pale.

Some Jews made Bowery history. Monk Eastman and his gang of thugs, almost all Jewish, were sponsored by Tim Sullivan who counted on them to deliver votes and loot from their side just as the Irish and Italians did. Jews also appeared in the Bowery theaters as producers, actors, directors, and impresarios.

They were part of the Bowery's history but not fully a

part of the Bowery until the depression. Then some of them
drifted down to the breadlines and the psychologists found
them in a bad way. These were the shattered, declassed
ones. They cropped up with skills that were unusual on the
Bowery. They were bookkeepers, teachers, musicians, tail-
ors, and salesmen; but temperamentally they were shot.

After the war Jews ran to about two per cent of the
Bowery population. Dr. Levinson has said that most of them
have deteriorated much further than the average non-Jew-
ish Bowery resident. Alcohol itself, said the Doctor, is outside the Jews' "cultural pattern," and presumably those
Jews who take to it suffer a cirrhosis not only of the liver
but of the psyche.

Perhaps it is only those disturbed Jews who end up on the
Bowery or else their fate disturbs them more than it does
the others. In any case, Dr. Levinson says, Jews on the
Bowery are more likely to be psychopathic or mentally
defective.

Even rarer than a Jewish Bowery Man is a Chinese.
Chinatown abuts the Bowery, and Chinese stores spill out
of the tight narrow streets of their quarter onto the Street,
but no Chinese panhandler works there.

Patrolman Leo O'Hea, who has walked the beat along
the Bowery for a quarter of a century, says the blotter is
clean of Chinese names. There are no Chinese vagrants.
The patrolman has no very fancy scientific notions of
"why," but he knows that when a Chinese boy breaks a
window all that a cop need do is to tell his brother or his
cousin or his uncle and the matter is taken care of. The boy
is likely to apologize.

In time the Chinese may become so Americanized that
the family will lose the antique function of mutual responsibility, of collective conscience. Until then, however, there
are not likely to be Chinese flophouses.

The only times when any police action was needed were
the days of the tong wars—a kind of bloody commercial
rivalry—and during the period when the exclusion laws
were so rigid that no Chinese man could hope to marry a
Chinese girl in New York. In those days, whores from the
Bowery would then come down to Chinatown to pay
the "house calls" of their profession, and now and then
the police would feel obliged to intervene.

The Bowery is above all American. More than three
quarters of its regular derelict population are white and

native-born, often tracing a native American lineage far back into their country's history. They come from all parts of the country to stand in front of the Salvation Army Building on an afternoon—cheerfully facing nothingness.

Dr. Levinson and his colleagues had these native-born Americans examine the telltale ink blots of the Rorschach test, and from their fancied images they pieced together this view of the personality type (which I have presumed to annotate):

"The homeless man has had a very poor psychosexual history, as a result of which he has developed a fear of either accepting or sharing affection," says Dr. Levinson.

(There is a musician who used to play with the Philadelphia Symphony. One day he came home and found a stranger in his wife's bed. He turned around, walked out, and buried his poor psychosexual history on the Bowery.)

The Doctor continues: "At some time, the mother figure had brought about a good deal of ambivalence and anxiety. To love meant to be hurt, to be rejected, to be deserted."

(A seaman, now permanently beached on the Bowery, says that he never had a home. He grew up in an orphanage. Sure, he had girls, but "you know the kind you meet on a waterfront. . . . Oh a nice girl would be something else again." So he never got married. He wouldn't make anybody a good husband, he says.)

"He now denies to himself his need for affection and tends to respond to the demands of the world of reality by repression. By withdrawing into passivity. . . . Since he replaces activity by passivity, he atones for his guilt. . . ."

("I didn't commit no crime, see," says Thomas Finn. "What I did, I did only to myself, right?")

"He is able to accept life and to continue existing on the Bowery because being there is a solution to his problems. His life on the Bowery is an acting out of his conflicts, an 'undoing' and assuaging of guilt, and is a replacement of his phallicism by castration."

(An old man says that he finds it hard to stay at the Muni—the Municipal Lodging House—because of the "queens." Disgusting, he says. The queens are young men who swing their hips and gather courts around them in secluded spots. Courtiers and courtesans vie for the queen's affections, and the old Bowery hands shrink to the wall in horror.)

Dr. Levinson concludes: "It is hypothesized that being

homeless has only exacerbated latent personality trends and that living on the Bowery is the solution of the emotional problems of these men and the natural outcome of the dynamics involved."

Psychologists agree that the Bowery Men need a place where an effortless going to hell is the accepted way of life.

They need a place where no one requires anything of them, where no one ever says: "You can do better." The institution the Bowery Men need is one where everyone agrees: "Mac, you can't do better."

They need the sweet delights of hopelessness, and anyone who seeks to energize them with hope betrays them, for he calls their spirit into action; calls them again to try, again to lose; calls them again to compare themselves with other men, to assert their worth—when all that they want is for the world to leave them alone, worthless and careless, beyond redemption or competition.

Where else could these men find such an institution? Where could they find a home in which all the talents and learning of psychologists are bent to give them the certainty they need that they have lost themselves? It is probably as difficult for a social worker or a missionary to let a man despair as it is for a doctor to oblige a patient with euthanasia. For that reason the Bowery Men have made their own community on the street.

Sociologists describe this institution—created by the men themselves, tailor-made for them and for no others—as a subculture. Prof. H. Warren Dunham, of Wayne University, gives the psychologists short shrift. It's all very well, he says in effect, to diagnose individuals as suffering from dependency needs ("inadequate personality" and so on), but the stubborn fact remains that a lot of men not on the Bowery fit that picture just as well.

Society, says Dr. Dunham, keeps producing "inadequately socialized types," and the skid rows are there to receive them. The world, after all, is full of opportunities for failure. A boy can flunk an exam or catch the look of scorn in a girl's eye. A man can lose a job, or possibly hold a job too long while his friends rise, perhaps stepping smilingly upon his neck as they go up. A businessman can lose his money and suddenly realize that he has nothing else.

And the world is scornful of failures. People persecute failures even by feeling sorry for them. Even when stretching out a helping hand, successful men make it clear that it is more blessed to give than to receive—though the receiver plainly stands in greater need of blessing.

Those who no longer aspire, who do not wish to rise on anybody's shoulders, who do not wish to sell more, make more, show more, even give more than others—these are among the "inadequately socialized" who have built the modern Bowery. There they need struggle no longer against the critics, the status-seekers and the status-markers who pigeonhole people.

The Bowery, it would seem, is a grotesque limbo beyond good and evil, where there is no first or last, no past or future—a death wherein one may have the delights and torments of being a spectator at one's own funeral.

In the quiet attitudes of the men in flops—the old ones often sit for hours with hands crossed in their laps—it is easy to read a prayerful solemnity. In the prim detached way in which sex is regarded there is something monastic. These men use the usual four-letter words, but this is a mere ritual and no more. Such words are expletives and no longer serve to recall the warmth of the fires below.

There is an air of finality on the Street. Each man thinks it is all over. He used to live some other way. There used to be another self. It's all gone now, as if he had taken holy orders, changed his name, and put on his rags as a sign. What they are a sign of is, of course, the crucial difference between the Bowery Man's retreat and that of a monk.

Learnedly, Dr. Levinson terms it "ego-devaluating, not a religious retreat."

Still it *is* a retreat, an escape into tranquillity. And here one is brought up short by the obvious bond linking the unshaved bum sprawled flat on his face in the street with the businessman, the advertising executive, the cocktail-drinking wife, the harried suburbanite—the whole organization, brief-cased, golf-and-bridge, scotch-and-soda set. All understand that the major objective of life is tranquillity freedom from tension, and an end to worry.

The parents who send their children joyfully off to life-adjustment courses do so with the notion that they will have fewer conflicts, fewer tensions. Life will be smoother.

But if life isn't smoother and the ideal is still tranquillity; if one is not fully adjusted to life and the objective is still to avoid tension; if the tranquilizers are too expensive or in the end fail to secure the all-important inner peace—then it may be a consolation to us all to know that there is a Bowery, a place where life is thoroughly anesthetized.

It is our brothers who have pioneered there.

DEPOSITION: TESTIMONY CONCERNING A SICKNESS
/William S. Burroughs

I awoke from The Sickness at the age of forty-five, calm and sane, and in reasonably good health except for a weakened liver and the look of borrowed flesh common to all who survive The Sickness. . . . Most survivors do not remember the delirium in detail. I apparently took detailed notes on sickness and delirium. I have no precise memory of writing the notes which have now been published under the title *Naked Lunch*. The title was suggested by Jack Kerouac. I did not understand what the title meant until my recent recovery. The title means exactly what the words say: NAKED Lunch—a frozen moment when everyone sees what is on the end of every fork.

The Sickness is drug addiction and I was an addict for fifteen years. When I say addict I mean an addict to *junk* (generic term for opium and/or derivatives including all synthetics from demerol to palfium.) I have used junk in many forms: morphine, heroin, dilaudid, eukodal, pantapon, diocodid, diosane, opium, demerol, dolophine, palfium. I have smoked junk, eaten it, sniffed it, injected it in vein-skin-muscle, inserted it in rectal suppositories. The needle is not important. Whether you sniff it smoke it eat it or shove it up your ass the result is the same: addiction. When I speak of drug addiction I do not refer to keif, marijuana or any preparation of hashish, mescaline, Bannisteria Caapi, LSD6, Sacred Mushrooms or any other drug of the hallu-cinogen group. . . . There is no evidence that the use of any hallucinogen results in physical dependence. The action of these drugs is physiologically opposite to the action of junk. A lamentable confusion between the two classes of drugs has arisen owing to the zeal of the U. S. and other narcotic departments.

I have seen the exact manner in which the junk virus operates through fifteen years of addiction. The pyramid of junk, one level eating the level below (it is no accident that junk higher-ups are always fat and the addict in the street is always thin) right up to the top or tops since there are many junk pyramids feeding on peoples of the world and all built on basic principles of monopoly:

1—Never give anything away for nothing.
2—Never give more than you have to give (always catch the buyer hungry and always make him wait).
3—Always take everything back if you possibly can.

The Pusher always gets it all back. The addict needs more and more junk to maintain a human form . . . buy off the Monkey.

Junk is the mold of monopoly and possession. The addict stands by while his junk legs carry him straight in on the junk beam to relapse. Junk is quantitative and accurately measurable. The more junk you use the less you have and the more you have the more you use. All the hallucinogen drugs are considered sacred by those who use them—there are Peyote Cults and Bannisteria Cults, Hashish Cults and Mushroom Cults—"the Sacred Mushrooms of Mexico enable a man to see God"—but no one ever suggested that junk is sacred. There are no opium cults. Opium is profane and quantitative like money. I have heard that there was once a beneficent non-habit-forming junk in India. It was called *soma* and is pictured as a beautiful blue tide. If *soma* ever existed the Pusher was there to bottle it and monopolize it and sell it and it turned into plain old time JUNK.

Junk is the ideal product . . . the ultimate merchandise. No sales talk necessary. The client will crawl through a sewer and beg to buy. . . . The junk merchant does not sell his product to the consumer, he sells the consumer to his product. He does not improve and simplify his merchandise. He degrades and simplifies the client. He pays his staff in junk.

Junk yields a basic formula of "evil" virus: *The Algebra of Need*. The face of "evil" is always the face of total need. A dope fiend is a man in total need of dope. Beyond a certain frequency need knows absolutely no limit or control. In the words of total need: *"Wouldn't you?"* Yes you would. You would lie, cheat, inform on your friends, steal, do *anything* to satisfy total need. Because you would be in a state of total sickness, total possession, and not in a po-

sition to act in any other way. Dope fiends are sick people
who cannot act other than they do. A rabid dog cannot
choose but bite. Assuming a self-righteous position is nothing to the purpose unless your purpose be to keep the junk
virus in operation. And junk is a big industry. I recall talking to an American who worked for the Aftosa Commission
in Mexico. Six hundred a month plus expense account:

"How long will the epidemic last?" I inquired.

"As long as we can keep it going. . . . And yes . . . maybe
the aftosa will break out in South America," he said dream-
ily.

If you wish to alter or annihilate a pyramid of numbers
in a serial relation, you alter or remove the bottom number. If we wish to annihilate the junk pyramid, we must
start with the bottom of the pyramid: *the Addict in the
Street,* and stop tilting quixotically for the "higher ups" so
called, all of whom are immediately replaceable. *The addict in the street who must have junk to live is the one ir-
replaceable factor in the junk equation.* When there are no
more addicts to buy junk there will be no junk traffic. As
long as junk need exists, someone will service it.

Addicts can be cured or quarantined—that is allowed a
morphine ration under minimal supervision like typhoid
carriers. When this is done, junk pyramids of the world
will collapse. So far as I know, England is the only country to apply this method to the junk problem. They have
about five hundred quarantined addicts in the U.K. In another generation when the quarantined addicts die off and
pain killers operating on a non-junk principle are discovered, the junk virus will be like smallpox, a closed chapter—
a medical curiosity.

The vaccine that can relegate the junk virus to a land-
locked past is in existence. This vaccine is the Apomorphine Treatment discovered by an English doctor whose
name I must withhold pending his permission to use it and
to quote from his book covering thirty years of apomorphine treatment of addicts and alcoholics. The compound
apomorphine is formed by boiling morphine with hydro-
chloric acid. It was discovered years before it was used to
treat addicts. For many years the only use for apomorphine
which has no narcotic or pain-killing properties was as an
emetic to induce vomiting in cases of poisoning. It acts
directly on the vomiting center in the back brain.

I found this vaccine at the end of the junk line. I lived in one room in the Native Quarter of Tangier. I had not taken a bath in a year nor changed my clothes or removed them except to stick a needle every hour in the fibrous gray wooden flesh of terminal addiction. I never cleaned or dusted the room. Empty ampule boxes and garbage piled to the ceiling. Light and water long since turned off for non-payment. I did absolutely nothing. I could look at the end of my shoe for eight hours. I was only roused to action when the hourglass of junk ran out. If a friend came to visit—and they rarely did since who or what was left to visit—I sat there not caring that he had entered my field of vision—a gray screen always blanker and fainter—and not caring when he walked out of it. If he had died on the spot I would have sat there looking at my shoe waiting to go through his pockets. Wouldn't you? Because I never had enough junk—no one ever does. Thirty grains of morphine a day and it still was not enough. And long waits in front of the drugstore. Delay is a rule in the junk business. The Man is never on time. This is no accident. There are no accidents in the junk world. The addict is taught again and again exactly what will happen if he does not score for his junk ration. Get up that money or else. And suddenly my habit began to jump and jump. Forty, sixty grains a day. And it still was not enough. And I could not pay.

I stood there with my last check in my hand and realized that it was my last check. I took the next plane for London.

The doctor explained to me that apomorphine acts on the back brain to regulate the metabolism and normalize the blood stream in such a way that the enzyme system of addiction is destroyed over a period of four or five days. Once the back brain is regulated apomorphine can be discontinued and only used in case of relapse. (No one would take apomorphine for kicks. *Not one case of addiction to apomorphine has ever been recorded.*) I agreed to undergo treatment and entered a nursing home. For the first twenty-four hours I was literally insane and paranoid as many addicts are in severe withdrawal. This delirium was dispersed by twenty-four hours of intensive apomorphine treatment. The doctor showed me the chart. I had received minute amounts of morphine that could not possibly account for my lack of the more severe withdrawal symptoms such as leg and stomach cramps, fever and my own special symptom, The Cold Burn, like a vast hive covering the body and rubbed with menthol. Every addict has his own special symptom that cracks all control. There was a missing factor in the withdrawal equation—that factor could only be apomorphine.

I saw the apomorphine treatment really work. Eight days later I left the nursing home eating and sleeping normally. I remained completely off junk for two full years —a twelve year record. I did relapse for some months as a result of pain and illness. Another apomorphine cure has kept me off junk through this writing.

The apomorphine cure is qualitatively different from other methods of cure. I have tried them all. Short reduction, slow reduction, cortisone, antihistamines, tranquilizers, sleeping cures, tolserol, reserpine. None of these cures lasted beyond the first opportunity to relapse. I can say definitely that I was never *metabolically* cured until I took the apomorphine cure. The overwhelming relapse statistics from the Lexington Narcotic Hospital have led many doctors to say that addiction is not curable. They use a dolophine reduction cure at Lexington and have never tried apomorphine so far as I know. In fact, this method of treatment has been largely neglected. No research has been done with variations of the apomorphine formula or with synthetics. No doubt substances fifty times stronger than apomorphine could be developed and the side effect of vomiting eliminated.

Apomorphine is a metabolic and psychic regulator that can be discontinued as soon as it has done its work. The world is deluged with tranquilizers and energizers but this unique regulator has not received attention. No research has been done by any of the large pharmaceutical companies. I suggest that research with variations of apomorphine and synthesis of it will open a new medical frontier extending far beyond the problem of addiction.

The smallpox vaccine was opposed by a vociferous lunatic group of anti-vaccinationists. No doubt a scream of protest will go up from interested or unbalanced individuals as the junk virus is shot out from under them. Junk is big business; there are always cranks and operators. They must not be allowed to interfere with the essential work of inoculation treatment and quarantine. *The junk virus is public health problem number one of the world today.*

Since *Naked Lunch* treats this health problem, it is necessarily brutal, obscene and disgusting. Sickness is often repulsive details not for weak stomachs.

Certain passages in the book that have been called pornographic were written as a tract against Capital Punishment in the manner of Jonathan Swift's *Modest Proposal*. These sections are intended to reveal capital punishment as the obscene, barbaric and disgusting anachronism that it is. As always the lunch is naked. If civilized countries want to return to Druid Hanging Rites in the Sacred Grove or to drink blood with the Aztecs and feed their Gods with blood of human sacrifice, let them see what they actually eat and drink. Let them see what is on the end of that long newspaper spoon.

I have almost completed a sequel to *Naked Lunch*. A mathematical extension of the Algebra of Need beyond the junk virus. Because there are many forms of addiction I think that they all obey basic laws. In the words of Heiderberg: "This may not be the best of all possible universes but it may well prove to be one of the simplest." If man can *see*.

POST SCRIPT . . . . WOULDN'T YOU?

And speaking *Personally* and if a man speaks any other way we might as well start looking for his Protoplasm Daddy or Mother Cell . . . . *I Don't Want To Hear Any More Tired Old Junk Talk And Junk Con.* . . . The same things said a million times and more and there is no point in saying anything because *NOTHING Ever Happens* in the junk world.

Only excuse for this tired death route is THE KICK when the junk circuit is cut off for the non-payment and the junk-skin dies of junk-lack and overdose of time and the Old Skin has forgotten the skin game simplifying a way under the junk cover the way skins will. . . . A condition of total exposure is precipitated when the Kicking Addict cannot choose but see smell and listen. . . . Watch out for the cars. . . .

It is clear that junk is a Round-the-World-Push-an-Opium-Pellet-with-Your-Nose-Route. Strictly for Scarabs— stumble bum junk heap. And as such report to disposal. Tired of seeing it around.

Junkies always beef about *The Cold* as they call it, turning up their black coat collars and clutching their withered necks . . . pure junk con. A junky does not want to be warm, he wants to be Cool-Cooler-COLD. But he wants The Cold like he wants His Junk—NOT OUTSIDE

where it does him no good but INSIDE so he can sit
around with a spine like a frozen hydraulic jack . . . his
metabolism approaching Absolute ZERO. TERMINAL
addicts often go two months without a bowel move and
the intestines make with sit-down-adhesions—Wouldn't
you?—requiring the intervention of an apple corer or its
surgical equivalent. . . . Such is life in The Old Ice House.
Why move around and waste TIME?

Room for One More Inside, Sir.

Some entities are on thermodynamic kicks. They invented
thermodynamics. . . . Wouldn't you?

And some of us are on Different Kicks and that's a thing
out in the open the way I like to see what I eat and visa
versa mutatis mutandis as the case may be. *Bill's Naked
Lunch Room.* . . . Step right up. . . . Good for young and
old, man and bestial. Nothing like a little snake oil to
grease the wheels and get a show on the track Jack. Which
side are you on? Fro-Zen Hydraulic? Or you want to take
a look around with Honest Bill?

So that's the World Health Problem I was talking about
back in The Article. The Prospect Before Us Friends of
MINE. Do I hear muttering about a personal razor and
some bush league short con artist who is known to have
invented The Bill? Wouldn't You? The razor belonged to
a man named Occam and he was not a scar collector. Lud-
wig Wittgenstein *Tractatus Logico-Philosophicus:* "If a
proposition is NOT NECESSARY it is MEANINGLESS
and approaching MEANING ZERO."

"And what is More UNNECESSARY than junk if You
Don't NEED it?"

Answer: "Junkies, if you are not ON JUNK."

I tell you boys, I've heard some tired conversation but no
other OCCUPATION GROUP can approximate that old
thermodynamic junk Slow-DOWN. Now your heroin addict does not say hardly anything and that I can stand. But
your Opium "Smoker" is more active since he still has a
tent and a Lamp . . . and maybe 7-9-10 lying up in there
like hibernating reptiles keep the temperature up to Talking Level: How low the other junkies are whereas We—
WE have this tent and this lamp and this tent and this
lamp and this tent and nice and warm in here nice and
warm nice and IN HERE and nice and OUTSIDE ITS
COLD. . . . ITS COLD OUTSIDE where the dross eaters
and the needle boys won't last two years not six months

hardly won't last stumble bum around and there is no class in them. . . . But WE SIT HERE and never increase the DOSE . . . never—never increase the dose never except TONIGHT is a SPECIAL OCCASION with all the dross eaters and needle boys out there in the cold. . . . And we never eat it never never never eat it. . . . Excuse please while I take a trip to The Source Of Living Drops they all have in pocket and opium pellets shoved up the ass in a finger stall with the Family Jewels and the other shit.

Room for one more inside, Sir.

Well when that record starts around for the billionth light year and never the tape shall change us non-junkies take drastic action and the men separate out from the Junk boys.

Only way to protect yourself against this horrid peril is come over HERE and shack up with Charybdis. . . . Treat you right kid. . . . Candy and cigarettes.

I am after fifteen years in that tent. In and out in and out in and OUT. *Over* and *Out.* So listen to Old Uncle Bill Burroughs who invented the Burroughs Adding Machine Regulator Gimmick on the Hydraulic Jack Principle no matter how you jerk the handle result is always the same for given co-ordinates. Got my training early . . . wouldn't you?

Paregoric Babies of the World Unite. We have nothing to lose but Our Pushers. And THEY are NOT NECESSARY.

Look down LOOK DOWN along that junk road before you travel there and get in with the Wrong Mob. . . .

STEP RIGHT UP. . . . Only a three Dollar Bill to use BILL's telescope.

A word to the wise guy.

FROM HANDICAP TO STRENGTH
/Donald Cory

There is an almost universal assumption that homosexuality is a personal tragedy. It is synonymous not only with the lonely life of the outcast, but it is destructive, the contention is made, of the socially and personally "good" forces in the individual. A symptom of a neurotic personality development, it manifests itself, some scientists contend, in combination with other sexual or personality maladjustments. The homosexual, whether for reason or not, is bitter against society, the social scientists believe, and his entire outlook is as a result anti-social. Finally, these people say, the homosexual hates his love-object and expends great energy seeking new partners for erotic pleasure, rather than utilizing his energy, time, and personality for individual or social betterment. All of this is meant to account for and perhaps justify the cultural attitude toward homosexuals in current and recent eras.

Some of the above statements bear a slight semblance to truth. Others are no more characteristic of the invert than of his brothers. Still others are clearly made because of the lazy thinking of the stereotype-minded, who note a single trait or group of traits in one or a few individuals and project the observed phenomena to an entire minority, whether it be racial, religious, or sexual.

The contention, however, that homosexuality can do the individual and society no good as a potent, imperious, driving, and ever-present force is contrary to historical truth, is inconsistent with the character and achievements of the homosexually-inclined geniuses, and is finally at complete variance with the subjective (albeit prejudiced) observations made by those who move within the homosexual groups in our society.

Characteristic of majority-minority group relations is the concept of superiority that the dominant group develops and that it attempts not only to utilize as justification for its terroristic repressions and as scientific foundation for its group attitude, but to impose even upon members of the minority. Thus within certain racial groups it is not uncommon to find at least unconscious acceptance of many of the tenets of the enemies of the particular group.

Throughout his life, from the moment that he awakens for the first time to the impact of the realization not only that he is a homosexual, but as such is part of a despised group of humanity, an individual is exposed to the propaganda that he is "not as good" as other people. He is told or hears that he (or his like, with whom he must identify himself) is "almost a man," is "half a man," and that he is a degenerate, a deviate, a pervert. He is exposed, in learned treatises no less than in the language of the streets, at the hands of the erudite no less than the ignorant, not only to contempt, but to a definite campaign to demonstrate and even convince him that his way of life is inferior.

From the time of my own high school days, I have heard these judgments and words, sometimes spoken by people I love, sometimes by those I despise. But, alas, I have heard the contempt of the world repeated by many of my gay friends. Gay despite themselves as are all those who inhabit this world of outcasts, they reflected, consciously or unconsciously, the propaganda of the dominant majority.

It is difficult to ignore this self-defeating invective. It took many years of experience in life, and some invaluable psychoanalytic therapy, for me to overcome such influences on my own attitudes. But even before I had succeeded in rebutting and then rejecting the hostile viewpoints, I had reacted to them. Since then, I have learned through observation that my reaction was not unusual.

The world considered me low, held in contempt my kind and therefore myself, believed me an inferior and unworthy specimen of mankind. The need for self-acceptance burned within me, and I could only throw off the influence of those who thought me beneath them by always striving, despite hardship and impediment, to excel even beyond my own capacities. My ethical standards must be above reproach, my honesty greater than that of others, my loyalty to friends and ideals firmer than that of other people, precisely because—knowingly or not—they thought so little of me, and precisely in order that I might think the more of myself.

The very doubts over my judgment of my personality— the very impact of the words: *I am a homosexual, I am a queer, I am a fairy*—forced me at each turn of life and at all moments of the day to convince myself that I was as good as the next person; in fact, better. It was necessary for me to believe in myself, as it must be for all persons. Because mankind made it so difficult for me to preserve my self-esteem, I found it necessary to hold aloft my own activities, to drive on with my own achievements in order that my faith in self could survive the impact of many crushing blows. And those who have studied the personality adjustments of people in other minority groups, whether of a racial or religious character, will recognize my own struggle as following a not uncommon pattern.

In my studies at school, I could not content myself with

doing the satisfactory work of which I was capable. I was always striving to excel over others. It would be my answer even to those for whom I wore the mask of anonymity, for they, too, reflected contempt for me, although they did not know that I was the object of their attitude. It would be my method of hurling back at them their smug opinion of their own selves as superior. I was spurred by a belief that if my learning were greater, my thinking deeper, my talents more creative, then the loftier would be the stature which I would assume in my own eyes.

Here is, perhaps, a phase of the laws of compensation. It is a counterpart of the bravado displayed by the cowardly, the overlording shown by the diminutive, the conceit by those who suffer from an inferiority feeling. In other fields, it is called a defense mechanism, or a Napoleonic complex. But it is not the origin that matters. We are concerned with the results, whether beneficial or destructive to society and to the individual. A small person is anti-social when he seeks to compensate, in his own image, for his inferior height by a display of dictatorial traits in which he uses other people as pawns. That his behavior stems from a factor beyond his control, and may be turned to other directions, does not make it the more palatable for society. And what of the homosexual? Many of his achievements may stem from the effort of the individual to excel in order to combat the influence of universal condemnation on his self-esteem. This is a beneficial consequence, even though it may (or may not) arise from an unfortunate source.

The homosexual, furthermore, is acutely aware of his lack of acceptance by society and of the difficulties (social, economic, and other) arising therefrom. Each moment of chagrin, each instance of humiliation, each act of rejection awakens a rebel spirit which is seldom antagonistic to society, but only to society's offensive and unjust attitudes. And, above all, the fact of being an untouchable provokes a solidarity with and understanding of other groups of individuals who may be in analogous positions in civilization.

"Being gay has taught me one thing," a social worker for whom I have the deepest respect pointed out to me, "and that is that 'tolerance' is the ugliest word in our language. No word is more misunderstood. We appeal to people to be tolerant of others—in other words to be willing to stand them. I don't want to be tolerated, and I can't see why anyone else should be struggling to be tolerated. If people are no good, they should not be tolerated, and if they are good, they should be accepted."

In the intergroup relations, particularly of Western culture, men are far from having attained acceptance of peoples other than themselves. Tolerance—in the sense of willingness to put up with the existence of others—is still to be achieved. But what is it but a miserable compromise? In the name of humanity appeals are made to various groups to tolerate each other, when tolerance is actually hardly more desirable than intolerance. The latter is only slightly more inhumane than the former.

The homosexual, cutting across all racial, religious, national, and caste lines, frequently reacts to rejection by a deep understanding of all others who have likewise been scorned because of belonging to an outcast group. "There, but for the grace of God ..." it is said, and the homosexual, like those who are part of other dominated minorities, can "feel" as well as understand the meaning of that phrase. The person who has felt the sting of repudiation by the dominant culture can reflect that, after all, he might have been of another religion or race or color, an untouchable in India, one of the mentally or physically handicapped. It is not for him to join with those who reject millions of their fellowmen of all types and groups, but to accept all men, an attitude forced upon him happily by the stigma of being cast out of the fold of society.

It is no wonder, then, that a true and genuine democracy so frequently pervades the activities of the homosexual group. Read the testimony of the trials of Oscar Wilde and you will find the prosecution repeatedly making sarcastic reference to the fact that a man of Wilde's social standing should have dined with a groom and a valet. In this circumstance, the prosecutor found an implication of an immoral (that is sensual) friendship. Intergroup mingling was not only unthinkable, but was suggestive of homosexual inclinations. A few years later, Edward Carpenter pointed out that it is not unusual for the employer and his clerk to cross class lines when they are united by their erotic temperaments. And today, the deeprooted prejudices that restrict marriages and friendships according to social strata—family, wealth, religion, color, and a myriad of other artifices—are conspicuously absent among the submerged groups that make up the homosexual society.

What are the sources of this democratic spirit? They are twofold: the similarity of activities and interests among those having similar sexual leanings, transcending their differences of ethnic and social backgrounds; and, secondly, a conscious rejection of the barriers and prejudices that divide humanity into innumerable antagonistic segments. It is in this latter category that we find a reaction to being gay that is strength born of handicap.

The sympathy for all mankind—including groups similarly despised in their own right—that is exhibited by so many homosexuals, can be a most rewarding factor, not only for the individual, but for society. The homosexual can—and often does—demonstrate that he harbors no bitterness, for he learns, of necessity, the meaning of turning the other cheek. He is forced by circumstance to answer hate with love, abuse with compassion. It is no wonder, then, that he can as a doctor, educator, or pacifist, show a tenderness to others, no matter how tragic their dilemma, that is seldom forthcoming from people who have themselves not deeply suffered. The humiliations of life can distill a mellow reaction, a warmth and understanding, not only for people in like circumstance, but for all the unfortunate, the despised, the oppressed of the earth.

Is the impact of being homosexual reflected in the realm of intellectual activities? The mere fact of belonging to this section of mankind, under the conditions prevailing in the current cultural milieu, compels a person constantly to search for the answers to his problems within himself. He must examine his motives, analyze his behavior. Reminded of the "baseness" and the "ugliness" of his acts, he wishes to understand what differentiates him from all others around him.

This introspective study is not limited to the sphere of sexual desires. It pervades the entire personality and all its activities. The great *why*, the infantile manifestation of curiosity that strives, in the less inhibited mind of the child, to gain the key to the ultimate riddle of man's life and its meaning, is typical of the homosexual's mentality. Unable, perhaps, to develop the extrovert qualities which require a receptive world in which to have free play; struggling to find a solution to the mystery of his own imperious desires; not suited for unquestioning acceptance of the facts of his self without an understanding of these facts—the invert finds much of his thought process consumed with inner projection. The flare-up of temper, the critical perception of a work of art, the basis of a broken friendship, the unfinished task at work, the daydream and the nightmare— whence come these facets of life, what are their hidden meanings, how do they tie in with the total personality? These perceptive abilities, sharpened by inner search, can be and frequently are applied to an understanding of all people. On the surface this seems to be confined to the ability to recognize hidden, latent, or well-disguised homosexuality behind the façade of respectability, but it also permits recognition of the concealed meaning of a poem, the delayed break of a handshake, even the condemnatory attitude of a hostile person. This ability is, in a sense, a form of self-protection.

Analytical abilities that are developed by introspection, sharpened by the search for a glimpse behind the anonymous mask, are extended to the understanding of all phases of human behavior. Because the homosexual learns that his activities, thoughts, philosophies, aspirations, are understandable only in the light of a full knowledge of the intricacies of the emotional structure; because he learns that the motives for an action may be camouflaged so thoroughly that it seems to stem from the very opposite of its actual source; because, in short, he is forced to obtain a wealth of knowledge about the personal psychological make-up, he can and frequently does apply this to the fuller understanding of others. And when to this understanding is added compassion for all individuals and groups, no matter to what tragic pass life has brought them, a rare combination of worthwhile traits is obtained.

Furthermore, the homosexual, not by inborn trait or coincidental development, but as a result of his anomalous position in society, is likely to become a skeptic and an iconoclast. Why? Because in that area of his life with which he is so vitally concerned, he is forced to reject an attitude which he finds so universally taken for granted by others. He learns that, except in a few rare spirits, the viciousness and the absurdity of homosexual practices are assumed beyond discussion. He sees that there is room neither for inquiry nor argument, and that even men who are otherwise of rational and scientific mind wish to dispose of homosexuality with rash invective or with scornful pity.

But he, the homosexual, is firmly convinced that the great mass of humanity is wrong in its judgment. Though his opinion grows out of necessity, its implications for his intellectual activity are widespread, for having come to reject a viewpoint held by so many to be beyond dispute, he must question whether many other tenets, similarly held to be beyond discussion, are not based on unthinking faith, blind passion, illogical reasoning, or lingering prejudices that at one time or another were part of the ruling mores of society.

Among many of my gay friends, no precept, no matter how dearly held, is allowed to rest unchallenged. No new thought, no matter how absurd it may seem to be, fails to receive its day in court. Whether one discusses politics or medicine, philosophy or literature, no matter how far removed from the field of sex, the homosexual brings a mind that is unusually questioning and skeptical.

Even the restlessness that permeates the homosexual's activities, his short-lived interests, his inability to complete many a task that is begun, are qualities that can be made useful both for the individual and society, for they are the characteristics of a versatile personality. If, during the course of short-lived interests and impatient investigation, an individual can acquire knowledge and develop talents in several directions, the combination of seemingly unrelated knowledge and talents becomes particularly valuable.

Indubitably, many of the qualities here so briefly outlined are absent in some homosexuals, just as they are present in many whose heterosexuality is above dispute. Not all homosexuals have been able to utilize their disadvantageous position for self-improvement in every respect and in all directions. I have pointed to the struggle to excel, but many gay people are easily defeated. Their resiliency in the face of the burden they carry is insufficient to meet the exigencies of life. I have outlined the understanding that is extended to other individuals and groups that struggle, each in its own manner, against exclusion. But many gay people are deeply rooted in prejudice. They have been unable to learn the lesson that should be so apparent to them in the face of the world's bigotry and persecution. I have depicted the individual turned compassionate toward his fellowmen, but there are those whose cruelty is lustful and murderous. Self-study and insight are not always present, nor is skepticism of necessity a constructive force.

The traits I enumerate, it is true, are not to be found in each homosexual. They are a few of the several possible beneficial results that are frequently reactions to the state of being gay, particularly under the prevailing social conditions. They are cited as a guide and encouragement to those, both the straight and the gay, who can see no good emanating from these passions. And it is in the light of the intimate relationship between the fact of being homosexual and the personality and intellectual characteristics derived therefrom that one can appreciate the genius of a Leonardo, a Whitman, and a Proust.

It is not, of course, my contention that the characteristics developed in homosexuals are confined to that group. Other minorities suffering from analogous exclusion, as well as many individuals with no minority status, display the qualities I find so widespread among homosexual groups. Desirable characteristics spring from many sources, group or personal. Homosexuality and social condemnation are merely the origins under consideration here.

If the homosexual drive is utilizable for ends that both the individual and society consider desirable, and if many or all of these characteristics arise, not out of the homosexual impulse, but out of the rejection of that drive by society and the stigma cast upon those who practice (or even wish to practice) this form of love, then is this not, in effect, a plea for a continuation of repressive attitudes? Would society not defeat its own ends by lifting its prohibitions or even by relenting in its hostility? The analogy with racial and religious minorities can again be drawn. It is to the fire of protest against post-slavery conventions and against anti-Semitism that many of the rewarding achievements of American Negroes and of the world Jewry can be attributed, but it would be absurd to distort this fact into an argument of justification for the Ku Klux Klan or for Hitlerism. And why? Because it is the very essence of democracy, the antithesis of totalitarianism, that justice and fair play are desirable ends in themselves. Repression and intolerance are to be condemned, no matter what lofty purpose may motivate them or what useful result may unwittingly issue therefrom.

The beneficial reaction that turns repression to the finer purposes in life is far from a justification of that course. In fact, the opposite is true, for it is a demonstration of the character, power, and intellect of the invert that gives the lie to the name-calling of his enemies and proves all the more his worthiness of acceptance by society.

The desirable ends which I have outlined must, in fact, be weighed against the needless sufferings, the dejection and humiliation, the blackmail and the court trials—all issuing from the same repressive character of modern culture. The great energy of those who have utilized the contempt of their fellows as an incentive to further creativity must be balanced against the energy expended and wasted in the struggle against this very same contempt.

There is a poetic irony in the future of the homosexual in society, for he will use the high attainments of character to struggle against the very injustices that are so largely responsible for these attainments, and the successful termination of repressive attitudes may erase the very achievements that were used to effect this termination. Nevertheless, I am convinced that there is a permanent place in the scheme of things for the homosexual—a place that transcends the reaction to hostility and that will continue to contribute to social betterment after social acceptance.

STREETWALKER
/Anonymous

I wake slowly and without enthusiasm, spinning out each moment as long as possible. Here, under the bedclothes, is the safety of the primeval cave, the womb-warmth of the animal's lair. All humanity loves the security and comfort of these slow, drowsy moments: to us, they are vital. More than sleep itself, they stoke up our energy, making unreal past and future, and all the present except the sweet laziness of muscle and the mind's soft meanderings.

It is, I suppose, about an hour before full consciousness crowds in on me and I can no longer lie in peace. I wish, I really wish, it were possible to prolong that state of trance indefinitely, to hibernate my way into eternity so that the world's events, great and small, passed unnoticed and unfelt. However, as I have gradually extended my sleeping hours from the normal eight to twelve or more, to fill in the long and empty days, I suppose I can't complain.

It is eight in the evening when I eventually get up, and dark outside. The gas fire has long since exhausted its shillings and the evening air through the open window is chill and damp. I put another shilling in the meter, light the fire, shut the window tight and get dressed, shivering, after a quick wash. Slacks, sweater, socks, mules—there is no need to own any more clothes than a few changes of these. Life, at present, does not demand of me that I wear skirts either in the evening or during the day, and I see no prospect of its doing so. I forgot months ago how to feel really feminine, though it would seem that to roving males I must appear so, despite the trousers.

Equally, I don't feel masculine, and I have no Lesbian tendencies, as far as I know. Very many of us develop them, possibly to counterbalance the cankerous revulsion that results from continual contact with male lust, and possibly because an affection which seems truer and surer than one has learned to expect from men, and a physical pleasure stronger because of its contrast to the robot love-making of business hours can be derived from an association with another woman. And perhaps it is because of the contempt we feel for the pasty white bodies and their owners who pass, like milk bottles on a conveyor belt, through our hands, that there are so many colored ponces, for after the pallid curds-and-whey of European flesh, warm sepias and ebonies must inevitably tickle our jaded palates. And then again, because they are different and strangers to our land, we can more easily find excuses for supporting them than we can the British riffraff.

For myself, though, I am content enough alone, although at times the need for emotional contact with another human being becomes hard to bear, and I feel sick with fear that my body will never again sing to the touch of a man's hand. As a rule, I feel sexless, unexcited and unexciting.

I can't be bothered to cook anything, so I make a pot of tea, have a slice of bread, switch on the radio, and attempt to read a day-old paper. Before long it begins to bore and annoy me. I don't really care about the situation in the Middle East, who gets in at the next by-elections, or what Society is up to. I don't even feel interested in the rising cost of living, or the increase in income tax. None of these things is likely to affect me, the way I live or the money I earn. A prostitute, after all, can make a living under any circumstances and in any town, without work permits or P.A.Y.E.,* or indeed any regulations except the payment of

* "Pay as you earn" (withholding tax).

the fortnightly fine, a ridiculous performance if ever there was one. A paragraph about a film starlet catches my eye, however. I have a slight fellow feeling for them. Then I read a nondescript short story quickly and put the paper down.

This is a pleasant room and well worth the money it costs. What I call a "flat" is really only a large bed-sitter with kitchenette attached, but it seems spacious enough to deserve the title. In it there is a large divan bed, the two armchairs I made up into a bed for the Irish hick last night which still embrace tumbled blankets and cushions, a table, a bookcase, and a chest of drawers—nothing more, and none of this expensive. Nevertheless, since the paint is fresh and the curtains and carpet attractive, as they are in the rest of the house, except for the basement where Mrs. Bligh, the landlady, leads her completely contrasting second life, I feel at ease in the place and it refreshes me to come back to it.

Mrs. Bligh and I, after a couple of weeks of conventional behavior as landlady and tenant, had a furious row resulting in something fairly like a friendship, though with no real depth to it on either side. In fact, I have had a daily cup of tea with her for two months now. It happened like this.

I rented the room from her late last July, explaining that I worked in a coffee bar at night and that therefore my hours would be a little unusual. She asked me whether I was unreliable, like all the rest of those Bohemians, and I said no, I would pay her well and regularly. I admired the cleanness of her house and of her person, and it seemed to me that if she did find out what I did she would, for her reputation's sake, tell me to go, quietly and with a certain dignity, garbed as she was with Earl's Court respectability. She showed me the flat, recited the many rules of which there were copious copies in sprawling violet ink at appropriate points, and took a fortnight's rent in advance, with meticulous care over the shillings involved, announcing that a week of it would be kept in hand in case of damage to the flat's contents. Then she disappeared into the bowels of the house, not to reappear until next rent-day, when she knocked on the door, inspected the place, took her money, and once more departed.

The day I stumbled upon her second life also heralded the tea-drinking ritual. I had been ill, and when she knocked for the rent I told her so, and that I could not pay till the next morning. Rigid with annoyance, she snorted, but went. Next morning I still could not pay, having been too sick to go out and earn—and that is very sick indeed. I got up early and went straight down to the basement to explain. I rang her bell, feeling confident that the aforesaid dignity would serve at least as a brake to her rage and prepared to offer her half of what I owed her, which was all I had.

At my ring, the door was jerked open and a scarcely recognizable Mrs. Bligh appeared. I was confounded. Forgetting her incredible state of dishabille, in such complete contrast to her former starched and suitable appearance, at the sight of me and the set look of apology I was bearing on my face, she became a monstrous, screaming virago. She clutched the dreadful orange silk kimono she was wearing to her heaving half-exposed bosom, thrust her be-curlered head into my face, and let forth a fusillade as vitriolic as any I have ever heard. I was on familiar ground then—I knew this type of old. I leaned against the wall and lit a cigarette, waiting patiently for the barrage to subside. There is something fascinating about a really furious woman, especially when she weighs two hundred and fifty pounds, and covers it with only an inadequate wrap, something as curious as coming across an electrocuted blancmange, and this transformed Mrs. Bligh was just such a sight. I noticed, detachedly, that her upper lip was stained with nicotine—a thing I had never spotted before—and that her breath reeked of a mixture of mutton broth and draught cider.

Somebody upstairs, one of the two probation officers who shared the flat above mine probably, must have heard the racket, for the next thing of which Mrs. Bligh and I became aware was one of those strangely penetrating knocks and super-audible authoritative voices which belong only to officials of some kind. At once the screeching trumpet of Mrs. Bligh's voice stopped dead and she crept along to the outside door, soundlessly, and peeped through the letter box. I peered over her shoulder and spotted an oblong of navy uniform and a silver button.

Immediately we were banded together, she and I, in consternation and alertness. She was definitely not what I had thought her at all, and not simply a virago, either, for I recognized that cat-padding to the door and that instant control and watchfulness: Mrs. Bligh was, or had been, one of us.

The whir of our brains working must have been practically audible, not because there could be much danger to liberty in the situation, but because of our instinctive wish to avoid contact with the law if possible, and, if not, to tackle its representative and deal with him as quickly and circumspectly as we could.

Mrs. Bligh wiped the sweat from her forehead, straightened her kimono, and opened the door. Now her mouth was stretched in a ghastly, conciliatory grin which could well have done with the teeth she wore on rent-day. Her Cockney accent, so recently come to light, vanished again and the Earl's-Courtese which she usually used slipped over her voice like a suedette glove.

"Is anything wrong, officer?"

"That's for you to say, madam. It certainly sounded like it from outside. Usually so quiet, this street, you know. The lady upstairs thought someone was being murdered."

"Oh no, sergeant, it was just my niece and I having a bit of a lark," said Mrs. Bligh, without a blush. "I daresay the lady thought we were arguing and acted for the best, but there was really no need to call you in. We were just going to have a cup of tea when she told me some joke she'd just heard, and my laughter's a bit loud, I suppose."

"That's right." I confirmed the statement. "Auntie and I don't see each other very often and we do make a bit of noise when we get together."

The policeman craned his neck to look behind us into the passage, searching for some unconscious unfortunate, no doubt. Mrs. Bligh and I moved politely aside to give him a good view. Disappointed at the empty passage and deciding against demanding to see the rest of the basement, he warned us about future noise of that volume and went truculently back up the steps, his fruitless journey obviously having poisoned his day. The probation officer, whose sturdy ankles were just visible, twittered through his basso-profundo as he set the mind of the lady upstairs at rest, and then they both went away, she to her Court, deprived of scandal, and he to his beat, and another dull day.

I waited for the next development. Would it be the landlady, the termagant, or the night prowler? It was none of these. She laughed, unexpectedly and hugely, in keeping with her size.

"We told 'im you'd come for a cuppa so a cuppa you'd better have. Wouldn't do to mislead the law, you know!"

We had the cup of tea in her room, which perfectly fitted these new sides of her personality. I was submerged in the enormous, overstuffed armchair whose cretonne covers were filthy with liquid stains and ash, into which she pushed me; and nearly choked by the sickly sweet tea she pressed on me. The atmosphere was stifling and, like herself at close quarters, tainted with cider and broth. Piles of dust-covered magazines sprawled on the floor, most of them open at the "Advice to the Troubled" page, for she wasted no time in telling me that her true vocation, she felt, was to help the unfortunate from her vast store of experience. Having since heard some of her comments on life, and knowing her core of granite, I think her following this vocation would have been disastrous.

This first tea session was short, but the invitation was repeated for the next evening, since she realized that I needed all the sleep I could get. Before very long it became a regular habit. She still arrives, starched and scrubbed, for the rent every week, but the disguise is for this expedition only, and in it she is the perfect landlady, never mentioning the fact that she and I have come to know each other extremely well, or suggesting in any way that either of us is more, or less, than we seem.

Despite this understanding with Mrs. Bligh and the easy, pleasant comfort of the flat, I have made no sort of home here. My possessions could be crammed within minutes into two suitcases, although this time last year I needed a pantechnicon to move my furniture and luggage. Now I can take up my roots and move no matter where at a moment's notice.

To be precise, I have no roots, and, apart from an African wood carving on the mantelpiece and a couple of books on the bedside table, the room is as impersonal as when I first took it. The carving is about all I have left of my childhood and family (from whom, obviously, I had to sever myself) and was collected by my grandfather, who specialized in African primitives. The books, relics of school-day enthusiasms, have remained unopened for months now, giving way to an endless stream of newspapers and periodicals.

However, I don't miss the trappings of the ordinary woman's home, the saucepans, the curtains, the vases, the linen. I am a nomad and want to be no more than just this. I have two suitcases and I am independent. I stand on my own two feet and need ask help from nobody, and this is compensation enough for the means I have chosen to achieve self-sufficiency.

Perhaps it is that people, through the medium of their possessions and the settings of wallpaper, paint, and upholstery they have provided for them, feel that they have impressed their personalities on the structure of their homes and the atmosphere therein, so that if they go away for a day, a week, a year, or even only an hour, this essence of themselves will steadfastly remain, passively attending their return, to strengthen and uphold them if they are weak or tired, and to complete them, if they are no longer complete in themselves. So if they must move from one house to another, they take their homes, snail-like, with them to be re-created without delay in their new stopping-place. Thus, if a man should die, yet his personality in his home is allowed to live on in that his possessions and choice of their settings are left as and where they are, his presence will continue to be felt, and more strongly so if he has passed his physical body and mental characteristics on to his children, and they continue to live in his home. But if he should leave a house, taking his home and declaring himself finished with the structure which once sheltered her, he will leave an empty shell, colorless and lifeless, a musty and dusty vacuum to have life breathed back into its lungs by the next comer.

Furnished rooms, though obviously not completely empty, have this same anonymity, so that the newcomer, feeling lost in the void, is indefinably cheered at the discovery of an old shoe in a cupboard or a mess of powder in a drawer, with their message that the vacant space has been filled in the past and can be so in their own share of its future.

And yet the most I personally can permit myself of this indulgence of self is the carving and the few books. Even if it were possible, no marriage of past or future to the present could hold comfort for me, and so home-making, which has such a marriage as a primary object, would be futile. If I were to concentrate my earnings and energies on making a home, which would necessitate blinding myself to this futility, I would be again defeated, but in a different way. The slight security I would be able to enjoy, by allowing myself to pretend that my personality was contained in something more than the shell of my body, would make the nights—which hold no safety and in which I must be constantly alert, constantly rootless—even more desolate.

Strangely enough, though, this rootlessness of day as well as night, engendered by possessing only the contents of two suitcases and living as a self-contained unit within four impersonal and alien walls, is in itself an antidote to dwelling on how time is, was, and will be spent. For I am afraid to look clearly on the passing of my time. I fear to look forward, lest I perceive nothing. I shut my eyes to all but the most immediate realities, lest I find in today, too, nothing. And I dare not look back, lest all I have lost should confront and confound me. I must see no more than the little, present moment, lest I perceive that there is nothing for me in the stars and nothing in the clockbound passing of each day.

I tidy the room hastily, spreading the divan cover smoothly over the tumbled blankets, clearing away the teacup, tidying the mess the Irish boy made, emptying the ashtray. There isn't a lot to do, since I spend most of my time in bed and never bother to cook here. Then I slap on some lipstick, pick up my duffel coat, lock the door and prepare for Mrs. Bligh. She opens the door to my knock, smiling broadly.

"Come in, come in, Jay! Got a nice bit of gossip to tell you today—I can't hardly wait to get started. Sit down and I'll make the tea, then we'll get down to it."

She practically runs out to get the tray and returns in a trice with it, laden with two odd cups, a bottle of sterilized milk, a bag of sugar, and an aluminum teapot. As usual, for my benefit, she has topped the kimono with an old gray coat, held together with a safety pin, and has taken out her front four curlers, leaving four black sausage curls in military formation across her forehead. But an uncommon touch is a rim of shocking-pink lipstick which she has applied to the outer edge of her mouth. From this addition I gather that the bit of gossip must be an exceptionally juicy tidbit. I know she won't divulge it, though, until she feels my curiosity is sufficiently titillated by her silence for me to appreciate fully the finer points of her story.

I've told her time and time again that I don't take sugar, but she refuses to believe me. I watch her resignedly, since protest has been of no avail, as she adds four spoonfuls to my cup now, making the tea thick, syrupy, and utterly loathsome. What a sordid, sloppy-looking woman she is! I've grown to like her, but never to trust her. For all the friendship she pretends, there is often a cold and calculating flicker in her eyes, as if she is trying to work out some way of making further use of me. Possibly she catches the same look in mine on occasions. It is an expression that belongs to neither the landlady nor the virago sides of her nature, but exclusively to the night-cat side, which she has never thrown off.

I noticed it for the first time on the occasion of the first cup of tea. Talking about this and that, she summed me up, face, clothes, bearing, even the pitch of my voice, with this same cold, watchful look, before she said what was in her mind and admitted us to be on the same level and able to understand one another.

"From the hours you keep—and giving me that coffee bar lark was a waste of time from the off—I'd say you were on the bash. That's nothing against you. I was myself once, till I got hitched up in a manner of speaking with a rich old geezer who left me this house and the cash to run it. Then I got out of the other as soon as I could. I was getting on, you see, and that's the time to stop—if you can. Not that some of my old mates have—I still see them, whenever I go along the Bayswater Road or through the Circus late at night, which I do sometimes, just for old times' sake, and there they are, knocking it out at their age. How they've got anything left to knock it out with beats me." She stared into space, visualizing those withered wrecks of women who didn't use their eighteenpence, or sense.

"Any rate," she went on, "I'm not giving you any advice. You go your own way—you'll either make it, or most probably you won't. I'm not chucking you out, either, for all that the rent's overdue. But I want it tonight, and on the dot every week in future. It's nice to have someone here who's one of my own, so to speak, but I know my own, and I don't want no liberties took because you and me know what each other are. Get that straight and we'll be friends. Muck me about and you're out, with the law after you if necessary, much as I hate their guts."

After making all this clear, and my telling her that I understood perfectly, the cold look vanished and she began to reminisce, fishing anecdote after anecdote from her bottomless well of experience, over the weeks. I have listened to dozens of stories about the old flush days immediately after the war, when even at fifty a nice little sum was assured you every night; to tales of liberties taken and her revenge upon the perpetrators; to stories of gaffs, brushes with the law, clients, the wide boys, affairs, successful cons, of all the fabric of her life. She's been off the game for over seven years now but it still obsesses her.

All she wants of me is my ready ear, my open-mouthed attention, my appreciation of the niceties of what she has to say, and to share my own small store of experiences when she has to pause for breath. I hope she doesn't sense the depression which comes over me, the occasional froth of panic which makes me get up quickly and wander to the window, as if to leave the fear in my chair. I hope she doesn't sense the occasional weakness in me, when I quail, wondering whether I can contend with the jungle she has managed to survive in and leave, at any rate physically, behind her. I belong, as she did and in so many ways still does, to the gray streets, the vagaries of the weather and of mankind, to streetlight and neon sign, to derelict, criminal, and pervert, to every shadow and to every other outcast under the night sky. There is no other life for me and no other place: so to admit fear and weakness to any living soul, even Mrs. Bligh who might, from the depths of her past, remember what they felt like, would be to reveal my unfitness for the life I have chosen, and since no other is now possible for me, to reach the limits of despair—and God knows what would happen then.

Apart from the extremes of fear and weakness of resolution, no softness of any kind must be shown or shared, for softness has no place in our world. It is at once shunned and despised when we come across it, because to be soft is to be constantly shamed and hurt, to lose illusions before others can be built up, to invite trickery, to open the door for the profiteer, the violent or the mad, to allow that vital and precious awareness to be dulled.

So I pretend to Mrs. Bligh tonight, as I always do, that my invulnerability is as complete as hers appears to be. The scandal she is so full of concerns a one-time friend of hers who has just been found huddled, unconscious and beaten up, near the warm vents of Charing Cross Underground Station.

"She's been doing it lately for five Woodbines and a cuppa, I hear," says Mrs. Bligh, between sips of tea. "I can't think how anyone'd touch her, really I can't. She used to be a real classy bit, too, which just goes to show. Earned a bomb, she did, even in the Slump—in the twenties, you know. She could have been well set up by now, if she'd used her loaf. But five Woodbines—well! I expect some bloke beat her up when he saw her clearly, out of them bushes, and realized what he'd been with. Can't blame him really, but I hope they get him for all that."

"Do you think they will?"

Mrs. Bligh swills the dregs in her cup round reflectively. "They might, if they happen to come across him, but they probably won't try very hard. They haven't got time for an old bag like her, except to lock her up for vagrancy every now and then, or for drunkenness. It makes you realize how lucky you are, though, to be out of all that. If anyone knocked me on the head, being a woman of property, so to speak, the law'd pretty soon get after them. But then, if they chased after everyone who beats up one of the girls, old or young, they wouldn't have much time left for anything else. Lucky we can look after ourselves, eh?"

"Doesn't look as if that woman was much good at it."

Mrs. Bligh dismisses her old friend with a podgy wave. "She should've had more sense—going around like that at her age. She could've got a job as a maid if she couldn't have managed to save. They earn good money, and all they've got to do is take the coats and hats, and say 'Yes, sir' and 'No, sir' for a fat tip. That's what I'd do, if I wasn't placed where I am."

I wonder how I shall end my days. Shall I be propertied, the concern of the police, or a beaten-up "case," pushed to one side as not worth seeking retribution for? Shall I end up hustling for Woodbines, or serving the new generation as a maid? Bang, goes the shutter against the thought in the back of my mind. Away, dwindling into the mist-clad hills in Mrs. Bligh's "Monarch of the Glen," goes the old girl, her Woodbines, and her battered head. The conventional farewell of one prostitute to another comes silently to me, and silently I say it to her, this drab I shall probably never know, "Be lucky!"

"How did you hear of it?" I ask, idly.

"Read some in the morning paper," she replies, "then I got the rest from old Willy this morning."

"Old Willy? I didn't know you knew him—you mean the contraceptive man?"

"That's right—didn't I tell you?" Mrs. Bligh smiles, almost tenderly. "I used to be with him, years ago, and we're still friends. He doesn't come here as often as he might, though—not unless he's got a bit of news to tell me, like today. He's scared his wife'll find out—I don't know why, after all these years. I often wished she would, before, in the days when he'd drop in, calm as you like, and give me a good tuning before he disappeared back home for another couple of days of respectable coffin-carrying. That's the nearest to a ponce I've ever had, and I never bunged him much, either. That's why he used to belt me—that, and to keep me faithful while he went home to wifey."

She laughs her jelly-roll laugh, straining the safety pin which holds the gray coat together beyond its capacity to hold, so that released bulges of flesh tumble on to her lap, greasy and gray against the garish orange kimono. Willy is such a tiny little man. I presume he still launches himself into this flaccid mountain occasionally. But it's not a pleasant picture.

Suddenly I feel I can't stand the sight of that stomach any longer, although she is now making some vague effort to get it under control. I can't stand the sight of her, or the smell of her, or the kinship with her. I get up hastily, pretending that I am late for some mythical date.

"I must go now—thanks for the tea, it was lovely. I'll see you tomorrow. Look after yourself."

"Be lucky!" she calls after me.

"Be lucky!" Round the corner I start to run as fast as I can, so that the wind buffets my face and the rain lashes me with a thousand biting thongs. I run so fast that I leave my mind and my dull heart behind me in the wind, becoming as timeless and unidentifiable as the leaves which whirl past me to the gutter.

JOEY: A "MECHANICAL BOY"
/Bruno Bettelheim

Joey, when we began our work with him, was a mechanical boy. He functioned as if by remote control, run by machines of his own powerfully creative fantasy. Not only did he himself believe that he was a machine but, more remarkably, he created this impression in others. Even while he performed actions that are intrinsically human, they never appeared to be other than machine-started and executed. On the other hand, when the machine was not working we had to concentrate on recollecting his presence, for he seemed not to exist. A human body that functions as if it were a machine and a machine that duplicates human functions are equally fascinating and frightening. Perhaps they are so uncanny because they remind us that the human body can operate without a human spirit, that body can exist without soul. And Joey was a child who had been robbed of his humanity.

Not every child who possesses a fantasy world is possessed by it. Normal children may retreat into realms of imaginary glory or magic powers, but they are easily recalled from these excursions. Disturbed children are not always able to make the return trip; they remain withdrawn, prisoners of the inner world of delusion and fantasy. In many ways Joey presented a classic example of this state of infantile autism.

At the Sonia Shankman Orthogenic School of the University of Chicago it is our function to provide a therapeutic environment in which such children may start life over again. I shall concentrate upon the illness, rather than the treatment. In any age, when the individual has escaped into a delusional world, he has usually fashioned it from bits and pieces of the world at hand. Joey, in his time and world, chose the machine and froze himself in its image. His story has a general relevance to the understanding of emotional development in a machine age.

Joey's delusion is not uncommon among schizophrenic children today. He wanted to be rid of his unbearable humanity, to become completely automatic. He so nearly succeeded in attaining this goal that he could almost convince others, as well as himself, of his mechanical character. The descriptions of autistic children in the literature take for their point of departure and comparison the normal or abnormal human being. To do justice to Joey I would have to compare him simultaneously to a most inept infant and a highly complex piece of machinery. Often we had to force ourselves by a conscious act of will to realize that Joey was a child. Again and again his acting-out of his delusions froze our own ability to respond as human beings.

During Joey's first weeks with us we would watch absorbedly as this at once fragile-looking and imperious nine-year-old went about his mechanical existence. Entering the dining room, for example, he would string an imaginary wire from his "energy source"—an imaginary electric outlet—to the table. There he "insulated" himself with paper napkins and finally plugged himself in. Only then could Joey eat, for he firmly believed that the "current" ran his ingestive apparatus. So skillful was the pantomime that one had to look twice to be sure there was neither wire nor outlet nor plug. Children and members of our staff spontaneously avoided stepping on the "wires" for fear of interrupting what seemed the source of his very life.

For long periods of time, when his "machinery" was idle, he would sit so quietly that he would disappear from the focus of the most conscientious observation. Yet in the next moment he might be "working" and the center of our captivated attention. Many times a day he would turn himself on and shift noisily through a sequence of higher and higher gears until he "exploded," screaming "Crash, crash!" and hurling items from his ever present apparatus—radio tubes, light bulbs, even motors or, lacking these, any handy breakable object. (Joey had an astonishing knack for snatching bulbs and tubes unobserved.) As soon as the object thrown had shattered, he would cease his screaming and wild jumping and retire to mute, motionless nonexistence.

Our maids, inured to difficult children, were exceptionally attentive to Joey; they were apparently moved by his extreme infantile fragility, so strangely coupled with megalomaniacal superiority. Occasionally some of the apparatus he fixed to his bed to "live him" during his sleep would fall down in disarray. This machinery he contrived from masking tape, cardboard, wire and other paraphernalia. Usually the maids would pick up such things and leave them on a table for the children to find, or disregard them entirely. But Joey's machine they carefully restored: "Joey must have the carburetor so he can breathe." Similarly they were on the alert to pick up and preserve the motors that ran him during the day and the exhaust pipes through which he exhaled.

How had Joey become a human machine? From intensive interviews with his parents we learned that the process had begun even before birth. Schizophrenia often results from parental rejection, sometimes combined ambivalently with love. Joey, on the other hand, had been completely ignored.

"I never knew I was pregnant," his mother said, meaning

that she had already excluded Joey from her consciousness. His birth, she said, "did not make any difference." Joey's father, a rootless draftee in the wartime civilian army, was equally unready for parenthood. So, of course, are many young couples. Fortunately most such parents lose their indifference upon the baby's birth. But not Joey's parents. "I did not want to see or nurse him," his mother declared. "I had no feeling of actual dislike—I simply didn't want to take care of him." For the first three months of his life Joey "cried most of the time." A colicky baby, he was kept on a rigid four-hour feeding schedule, was not touched unless necessary and was never cuddled or played with. The mother, preoccupied with herself, usually left Joey alone in the crib or playpen during the day. The father discharged his frustrations by punishing Joey when the child cried at night.

Soon the father left for overseas duty, and the mother took Joey, now a year and a half old, to live with her at her parents' home. On his arrival the grandparents noticed that ominous changes had occurred in the child. Strong and healthy at birth, he had become frail and irritable; a responsive baby, he had become remote and inaccessible. When he began to master speech, he talked only to himself. At an early date he became preoccupied with machinery, including an old electric fan which he could take apart and put together again with surprising deftness.

Joey's mother impressed us with a fey quality that expressed her insecurity, her detachment from the world and her low physical vitality. We were struck especially by her total indifference as she talked about Joey. This seemed much more remarkable than the actual mistakes she made in handling him. Certainly he was left to cry for hours when hungry, because she fed him on a rigid schedule; he was toilet-trained with great rigidity so that he would give no trouble. These things happen to many children. But Joey's existence never registered with his mother. In her recollections he was fused at one moment with one event or person; at another, with something or somebody else. When she told us about his birth and infancy, it was as if she were talking about some vague acquaintance, and soon her thoughts would wander off to another person or to herself.

When Joey was not yet four, his nursery school suggested that he enter a special school for disturbed children. At the new school his autism was immediately recognized.

During his three years there he experienced a slow improvement. Unfortunately a subsequent two years in a parochial school destroyed this progress. He began to develop compulsive defenses, which he called his "preventions." He could not drink, for example, except through elaborate piping systems built of straws. Liquids had to be "pumped" into him, in his fantasy, or he could not suck. Eventually his behavior became so upsetting that he could not be kept in the parochial school. At home things did not improve. Three months before entering the Orthogenic School he made a serious attempt at suicide.

To us Joey's pathological behavior seemed the external expression of an overwhelming effort to remain almost nonexistent as a person. For weeks Joey's only reply when addressed was "Bam." Unless he thus neutralized whatever we said, there would be an explosion, for Joey plainly wished to close off every form of contact not mediated by machinery. Even when he was bathed he rocked back and forth with mute, engine-like regularity, flooding the bathroom. If he stopped rocking, he did this like a machine too; suddenly he went completely rigid. Only once, after months of being lifted from his bath and carried to bed, did a small expression of puzzled pleasure appear on his face as he said very softly: "They even carry you to your bed here."

For a long time after he began to talk he would never refer to anyone by name, but only as "that person" or "the little person" or "the big person." He was unable to designate by its true name anything to which he attached feelings. Nor could he name his anxieties except through neologisms or word contaminations. For a long time he spoke about "master paintings" and a "master painting room" (*i.e.*, masturbating and masturbating room). One of his machines, the "criticizer," prevented him from "saying words which have unpleasant feelings." Yet he gave personal names to the tubes and motors in his collection of machinery. Moreover, these dead things had feelings; the tubes bled when hurt and sometimes got sick. He consistently maintained this reversal between animate and inanimate objects.

In Joey's machine world everything, on pain of distant destruction, obeyed inhibitory laws much more stringent than those of physics. When we came to know him better, it was plain that in his moments of silent withdrawal, with his machine switched off, Joey was absorbed in pondering the compulsive laws of his private universe. His preoccupation with machinery made it difficult to establish even practical contacts with him. If he wanted to do something with a counselor, such as play with a toy that had caught his vague attention, he could not do so: "I'd like this very much, but first I have to turn off the machine." But by the time he had fulfilled all the requirements of his preventions, he had lost interest. When a toy was offered to him, he could not touch it because his motors and his tubes did not leave him a hand free. Even certain colors were dangerous and had to be strictly avoided in toys and clothing, because "some colors turn off the current, and I can't touch them because I can't live without the current."

Joey was convinced that machines were better than people. Once when he bumped into one of the pipes on our jungle gym he kicked it so violently that his teacher had to restrain him to keep him from injuring himself. When she explained that the pipe was much harder than his foot, Joey replied: "That proves it. Machines are better than the body. They don't break; they're much harder and stronger." If he lost or forgot something, it merely proved that his brain ought to be thrown away and replaced by machinery. If he spilled something, his arm should be broken and twisted off because it did not work properly. When his head or arm failed to work as it should, he tried to punish it by hitting it. Even Joey's feelings were mechanical. Much later in his therapy, when he had formed a timid attachment to another child and had been rebuffed, Joey cried: "He broke my feelings."

Gradually we began to understand what had seemed to be contradictory in Joey's behavior—why he held on to the motors and tubes, then suddenly destroyed them in a fury, then set out immediately and urgently to equip himself with new and larger tubes. Joey had created these machines to run his body and mind because it was too painful to be human. But again and again he became dissatisfied with their failure to meet his need and rebellious at the way they frustrated his will. In a recurrent frenzy he "exploded" his light bulbs and tubes, and for a moment became a human being —for one crowning instant he came alive. But as soon as he had asserted his dominance through the self-created explosion, he felt his life ebbing away. To keep on existing he had immediately to restore his machines and replenish the electricity that supplied his life energy.

What deep-seated fears and needs underlay Joey's delusional system? We were long in finding out, for Joey's preventions effectively concealed the secret of his autistic behavior. In the meantime we dealt with his peripheral problems one by one.

During his first year with us Joey's most trying problem was toilet behavior. This surprised us, for Joey's personality was not "anal" in the Freudian sense; his original personality damage had antedated the period of his toilet-training. Rigid and early toilet-training, however, had certainly contributed to his anxieties. It was our effort to help Joey with this problem that led to his first recognition of us as human beings.

Going to the toilet, like everything else in Joey's life, was surrounded by elaborate preventions. We had to accompany him; he had to take off all his clothes; he could only squat, not sit, on the toilet seat; he had to touch the wall with one hand, in which he also clutched frantically the vacuum tubes that powered his elimination. He was terrified lest his whole body be sucked down.

To counteract this fear we gave him a metal wastebasket in lieu of a toilet. Eventually, when eliminating into the wastebasket, he no longer needed to take off all his clothes, nor to hold on to the wall. He still needed the tubes and motors which, he believed, moved his bowels for him. But here again the all-important machinery was itself a source of new terrors. In Joey's world the gadgets had to move their bowels, too. He was terribly concerned that they should, but since they were so much more powerful than men, he was also terrified that if his tubes moved their bowels, their feces would fill all of space and leave him no room to live. He was thus always caught in some fearful contradiction.

Our readiness to accept his toilet habits, which obviously entailed some hardship for his counselors, gave Joey the confidence to express his obsessions in drawings. Drawing these fantasies was a first step toward letting us in, however distantly, to what concerned him most deeply. It was the first step in a year-long process of externalizing his anal preoccupations. As a result he began seeing feces everywhere; the whole world became to him a mire of excrement. At the same time he began to eliminate freely wherever he happened to be. But with this release from his infantile imprisonment in compulsive rules, the toilet and the whole process of elimination became less dangerous. Thus far it had been beyond Joey's comprehension that anybody could possibly move his bowels without mechanical aid. Now Joey took a further step forward; defecation became the first physiological process he could perform without the help of vacuum tubes. It must not be thought that he was proud of this ability. Taking pride in an achievement presupposes that one accomplishes it of one's own free will. He still did not feel himself an autonomous person who could do things on his own. To Joey defecation still seemed enslaved to some incomprehensible but utterly binding cosmic law, perhaps the law his parents had imposed on him when he was being toilet-trained.

It was not simply that his parents had subjected him to rigid, early training. Many children are so trained. But in most cases the parents have a deep emotional investment in the child's performance. The child's response in turn makes training an occasion for interaction between them and for the building of genuine relationships. Joey's parents had no emotional investment in him. His obedience gave them no satisfaction and won him no affection or approval. As a toilet-trained child he saved his mother labor, just as household machines saved her labor. As a machine he was not loved for his performance, nor could he love himself.

So it had been with all other aspects of Joey's existence with his parents. Their reactions to his eating or noneating, sleeping or wakening, urinating or defecating, being dressed or undressed, washed or bathed did not flow from any unitary interest in him, deeply embedded in their personalities. By treating him mechanically his parents made him a machine. The various functions of life—even the parts of his body—bore no integrating relationship to one another or to any sense of self that was acknowledged and confirmed by others. Though he had acquired mastery over some functions, such as toilet-training and speech, he had acquired them separately and kept them isolated from each other. Toilet-training had thus not gained him a pleasant feeling of body mastery; speech had not led to communication of thought or feeling. On the contrary, each achievement only steered him away from self-mastery and integration. Toilet-training had enslaved him. Speech left him talking in neologisms that obstructed his and our ability to relate to each other. In Joey's development the normal process of growth had been made to run backward. Whatever he had learned put him not at the end of his infantile development toward integration but, on the contrary, farther behind than he was at its very beginning. Had we understood this sooner, his first years with us would have been less baffling.

It is unlikely that Joey's calamity could befall a child in any time and culture but our own. He suffered no physical deprivation; he starved for human contact. Just to be taken care of is not enough for relating. It is a necessary but not a sufficient condition. At the extreme where utter scarcity reigns, the forming of relationships is certainly hampered. But our society of mechanized plenty often makes for equal difficulties in a child's learning to relate. Where parents can provide the simple creature-comforts for their children only at the cost of significant effort, it is likely that they will feel pleasure in being able to provide for them; it is this, the parents' pleasure, that gives children a sense of personal worth and sets the process of relating in motion. But if comfort is so readily available that the parents feel no particular pleasure in winning it for their children, then the children cannot develop the feeling of being worthwhile around the satisfaction of their basic needs. Of course parents and children can and do develop relationships around other situations. But matters are then no longer so simple and direct. The child must be on the receiving end of care and concern given with pleasure and without the exaction of return if he is to feel loved and worthy of respect and consideration. This feeling gives him the ability to trust; he can entrust his well-being to persons to whom he is so important. Out of such trust the child learns to form close and stable relationships.

For Joey relationship with his parents was empty of pleasure in comfort-giving as in all other situations. His was an extreme instance of a plight that sends many schizophrenic children to our clinics and hospitals. Many months passed before he could relate to us; his despair that anybody could like him made contact impossible.

When Joey could finally trust us enough to let himself become more infantile, he began to play at being a papoose. There was a corresponding change in his fantasies. He drew endless pictures of himself as an electrical papoose. Totally enclosed, suspended in empty space, he is run by unknown, unseen powers through wireless electricity.

As we eventually came to understand, the heart of Joey's delusional system was the artificial, mechanical womb he had created and into which he had locked himself. In his papoose fantasies lay the wish to be entirely reborn in a womb. His new experiences in the school suggested that life, after all, might be worth living. Now he was searching for a way to be reborn in a better way. Since machines were better than men, what was more natural than to try rebirth through them? This was the deeper meaning of his electrical papoose.

As Joey made progress, his pictures of himself became more dominant in his drawings. Though still machine-operated, he has grown in self-importance. Now he has acquired hands that do something, and he has had the courage to make a picture of the machine that runs him. Later still the papoose became a person, rather than a robot encased in glass.

Eventually Joey began to create an imaginary family at the school: the "Carr" family. Why the Carr family? In the car he was enclosed as he had been in his papoose, but at least the car was not stationary; it could move. More important, in a car one was not only driven but also could drive. The Carr family was Joey's way of exploring the possibility of leaving the school, of living with a good family in a safe, protecting car.

Joey at last broke through his prison. In this brief account it has not been possible to trace the painfully slow process of his first true relations with other human beings. Suffice it to say that he ceased to be a mechanical boy and became a human child. This newborn child was, however, nearly 12 years old. To recover the lost time is a tremendous task. That work has occupied Joey and us ever since. Sometimes he sets to it with a will; at other times the difficulty of real life makes him regret that he ever came out of his shell. But he has never wanted to return to his mechanical life.

One last detail and this fragment of Joey's story has been told. When Joey was 12, he made a float for our Memorial Day parade. It carried the slogan: "Feelings are more important than anything under the sun." Feelings, Joey had learned, are what make for humanity; their absence, for a mechanical existence. With this knowledge Joey entered the human condition.

SUICIDE IN DENMARK
/Herbert Hendin

The Danish suicide rate is 22 in 100,000. It is twice that of the United States or England, over three times that of Holland, and there is evidence that it has been higher than that of most of the rest of Europe for the last hundred years. Although it is at present equaled by the suicide rates in Switzerland, West Germany, Austria, and Japan, one can say that, excepting the Japanese, the Danish suicide rate is the most publicized. Certainly it is only in Denmark that visitors on the tourist buses are told by their guides about silverware, Tuborg and Carlsberg beer—and the high local suicide rate.

The problem of suicide in Denmark had long been caught up in arguments pro and con about the social welfare measures that obtain in Denmark. Certainly suicide is a measure of social tension within a given society, and studying the motivations of suicidal patients in that society will throw a good deal of light on the sources of those tensions. But suicide is only one barometer of social tension. Crime, alcoholism, homosexuality and neurosis are equally such barometers. One cannot consult one such index without reference to all the others. For example, the Danish homicide rate is strikingly low. While their suicide rate is twice that of the United States, the United States' homicide rate is ten times that of Denmark.

Other questions about Danish suicide are of equal or greater interest than simply the question of its frequency. What motivates a Dane to suicide? Are his reasons different from those of an American or a German? What light do his reasons throw on the particular pressures and tensions within his country? The purpose of studying the motivations of individual Danish suicidal patients is also to answer questions like these. This leads to a consideration of what might be called national character and national psycho-social conflicts. Such study is an outgrowth of the work pioneered by Columbia's Abram Kardiner, who has for many years been concerned with correlating social institutions with individual character. My own research with suicidal patients in the United States brought me to this line of inquiry some time ago, and, when it came to studying the Danes, gave me a good basis for making comparisons. For the present purpose, I think it is possible to demonstrate that suicide is at least the likely form of expression that certain social tensions would take in Denmark, given the particular Danish character and circumstances.

Denmark lends itself well to a study of national character and institutions. Although the rural areas of Jutland and Zealand are as different from Copenhagen as rural Iowa is from New York City, nevertheless Denmark is homogeneous in her traditions, institutions and attitudes in comparison to the hybrid and diverse population of the United States. It was fortunate for this study that an extremely high percentage of the Danish people, including those of relatively little general education, speak English fluently, English being a compulsory language from the beginning of school in Denmark. It was additionally fortunate because my interviewing technique was for the most part psychoanalytic in nature; that is, it relied as much on what the patient unwittingly revealed as on what he actually said. And perhaps my own relative unfamiliarity with the institutions and attitudes of the country turned out to be more of an advantage than a disadvantage. Every day I would be struck by attitudes on the part of my patients remarkably different from attitudes common in the United States but which I would have taken for granted and overlooked had I spent my life in Denmark.

For example, one afternoon I heard a young Danish soldier at the Copenhagen Military Hospital, who had made a suicide attempt, threatening his Danish psychiatrist with a successful attempt if he were returned to camp. The doctor replied that he didn't believe the boy would actually kill himself. The boy in turn said that the doctor couldn't in fact be certain, and that if he did kill himself it would be on the doctor's conscience. Such incidents are extremely common in Denmark, and threatening suicide is perhaps the commonest way that a Danish boy will try to get out of the army. How different from the behavior of American servicemen. Not that our boys want to get out of the service any the less, but how different is the means they are likely to employ—vague psychosomatic complaints or difficult-to-diagnose syndromes (including, for instance, the famous low back pain), are probably the most common. Suicide threats are relatively infrequent. The American boy feels that the threat of suicide is futile for he has little expectation that those around him are going to take him at all seriously; and in a large measure he is right. The Danish boy, on the other hand, can be quite certain that such threats will arouse immediate concern and anxiety among his comrades and superiors. In the United States, one finds that suicide threats occur less among the military than among civilians. To be effective, a threat must have a receiver, and among Americans such threats are usually directed at mothers, fathers, wives and husbands. The American sergeant is none of these.

On another afternoon, while a rather sick Danish girl was telling me about her life and childhood, she stopped and said that she could go no further because to do so would only make me feel guilty. Why should it make me feel guilty? Well, she said, because I probably had had a happier childhood and I would feel guilty on that account. I assured her that since I did not feel responsible for her unhappy childhood, I would not feel guilty—that, at most, I might only feel fortunate to have escaped whatever she had gone through. She was then able to continue. But what was this girl doing? She obviously *wished* to make me feel guilty, and then felt guilty herself for wanting to make me feel so. What a refined, sophisticated and complex psychology of guilt! The behavior of this girl and the Danish soldier could be reiterated in a number of similar illustrations and was indicative of a particular and extraordinary knowledge of, use of, and ability to arouse guilt in others through one's own suffering or misfortune, and the expectation of being able to do so has important bearing on the whole question of suicide.

It also raises the question of where this is learned. Does the Danish mother use the arousal of guilt as a disciplinary technique and, if so, how much? It is one of many kinds of discipline that can be used with children. It is in fact used by many subcultures within the United States, and no one can say for certain how effective it is compared with other forms of discipline. But from interviews with Danish patients and talks with Danish mothers and Danish psychiatrists, particularly those working with children, it is evident that this is the principal form of discipline used in Denmark. The mother simply lets the child know how hurt she is and how badly she feels at his or her misbehavior. The child is thereby disciplined—and at the same time gets a lesson in the technique of arousing guilt which he can later put to his own uses.

Discussion of the problem of guilt leads naturally enough to the whole question of aggression and how it is handled, expressed or controlled. In general, far less overt destructiveness or violence is evident among Danish patients than will be seen among American patients. Even in the United States, patients of Scandinavian origin in a "disturbed ward" are more apt to be mute than actively enraged and throwing things. A disturbed ward in a Danish hospital is altogether a far quieter place than a similar ward in one of our hospitals. The strikingly low Danish homicide rate, in comparison with the American, is also relevant here. In a recent year there were only twenty-eight homicides in the entire country, thirteen of which were children killed in connection with their parents' suicides.

This control of aggression begins, of course, in childhood. The Danish child, while indulged in many ways, is not permitted anything like the aggressiveness toward his parents and siblings that is tolerated in an American child. Consequently, Danish children appear to Americans exceedingly well-disciplined and well-behaved, while American children often seem like monsters to the Danes.

If there is, by the way, a socially acceptable outlet for aggression among the Danes, it is their sense of humor. They are very fond of teasing and are proud of their wit. Their humor will often cloak aggressive barbs in such a manner as to get the point across without actually provoking open friction.

Now certainly a great deal has been written, with regard to suicide, about the importance of aggression turned inward. Yet, it is far from the whole story about suicide in general and very far from the whole story about suicide in Denmark. The English, for example, curb aggression in their children and have a low homicide rate without the high Danish suicide rate.

It is rather the forms of dependence in Denmark that are unique, in my observation, and equally important and fundamental to the whole Danish vulnerability to depression and suicide. As one Danish psychiatrist put it to me, you can, in a way, divide Denmark into two groups: those who are looking for someone to take care of them and those who are looking for someone to take care of. There is a good deal of truth in this epigram.

Here, too, it is best to begin with the child. The Danish child's dependence on his mother is encouraged far more than that of the American child. Danish mothers are most apt to boast of how well their children look, how well they eat, and how much they weigh—and far less likely to boast of those activities or qualities of the child that in any way tend to separate him from the mother: how fast the child can walk or talk or do things by himself. The child is fondled, coddled and hugged more often, and probably to a later age, than is general in the United States. The American mother may not curb her child's aggressiveness—out of the fear that she may damage his initiative. The Danish mother is much less ruled by this concern and the child's aggressiveness is strictly checked—is, in a sense, part of the price he pays for his dependence. Of course, the very checking of the child's aggressiveness serves, in turn, to increase and foster this dependence. Such behavior appears to make the separation from the mother, when it does come, all the harder to bear. Many seek a return to the maternal relationship either directly or through a mother-substitute, while others achieve this kind of gratification vicariously—through attending to the needs of the first group.

Of course, mixtures and alternations are common. Characteristic was the attitude of one 22-year-old Danish girl who was unable to manage her own life in Copenhagen and who yearned to return to her parents' farm in north Zealand and to be taken care of by her mother. In the next breath she expressed the idea that perhaps the solution to her problem was to go to England and live with a young artist she had met while there on a visit, since he was totally helpless and needed her.

The search for this dependence results in greater need of the sexes for each other, and more moving of the sexes toward each other, with less fear and more ease than is usual in the United States. Mutual attraction is not impeded, either, by the extensive competition between the sexes that is so common in the United States. Of course, these expectations of dependent gratification from the opposite sex are often disappointed and are a major cause for the ending of relationships and a major factor in Danish divorces.

The Danish husband is very often rather like a privileged

eldest child. He usually has little to do with the discipline
of the children. Resentment on the part of fathers at the
birth of children is quite common and is most strikingly
evident in the widespread loss of potency or loss of sexual
interest on the part of the husband after the birth of the first
child.

On the other hand, frigidity among Danish women appears to be as widespread as it is in the United States. This,
despite their very feminine manner, their non-competitive-
ness with men, and the fact that they are permitted somewhat more sexual freedom during adolescence than Americans are, though no more during childhood. (The attitude
of Danish mothers toward sexual activity in their children
is generally to prohibit it and at the same time to deny its
existence—very much as American mothers do.) Yet female frigidity does not appear to be of the guilt-ridden sort
common in the United States thirty years ago, or of the
competitive sort common today. Rather it seems to be
caused by the woman's dependent longings and by her
image of herself as a little girl rather than a grown woman.

It is only this dependency concern that can explain the
Danes' extreme vulnerability to depression and suicide following the ending of relationships. Both the protector and
the protected will be vulnerable in such a situation. Typical
was the attitude of one man who made a serious suicide attempt when his wife left him after twenty years of marriage.
He had not been happy with her and in many ways he had
precipitated her leaving; but three months later he said he
had no desire to live because there was no one to take care
of his apartment, to prepare his meals, and to attend to his
needs.

I have spoken of the manipulation of guilt, the control of
aggression, and the forms of dependency. My last observation on the subject of dependency is perhaps the most interesting. Related to the whole question of dependency but
important in its own right, are the Danish attitudes toward death and afterlife and suicide itself.

In working with suicidal patients in the United States, it is
not unusual for one to encounter fantasies of reunion
after death with a lost loved one. But in Denmark such
fantasies are so much more common as to be almost the
rule. This, despite the fact that most of the Danes I interviewed tended to stress their "not being religious," with an
overtone of pride. Yet, the Lutheran version of an after-

life is universally taught in the schools and the child often picks up the idea of reunion after death from his parents even before school. Even if formal religion ceases to be of interest in later life, the idea of afterlife and a reunion with loved ones after death remains. Such fantasies are not only more common among the Danes, they are more openly expressed; with American patients they generally have to be ascertained from dreams. Certainly the hold of such ideas is consistent with the dependency constellation of which I have already spoken.

I saw one Danish patient with such a fantasy following a serious suicide attempt in which he had turned on the gas. He was a 56-year-old man who had been separated for several months from his wife. When questioned, he expressed the idea that after death he expected to be reunited with his mother who had died eight years before—and eventually, following his wife's death, with his wife. He felt that he and his wife would not have the difficulties between them in an afterlife that they had had on earth. He recalled having held such a conception of an afterlife from his earliest school years, and perhaps before. When asked if he had not also been taught, as are Catholics in America, that, yes, you would go to heaven but, no, you would not get there if you killed yourself, he replied that he had been taught that but he did not believe this part of the teaching. He felt there was nothing one would not be forgiven if one repented. The last thing he had done before turning on the gas was to say a prayer in which he asked forgiveness for what he was about to do; with that, he felt confident that his admission to an afterlife was assured. His attitudes in these matters turned out to be quite typical of Danish patients.

And in fact the best and most perceptive prototypes of such reunion-in-death fantasies, apart from the dreams of individual patients, are to be found in that singular Danish literature, the fairy tales of Hans Christian Andersen. There is "The Little Match Girl" who, while freezing to death in the cold, lights her matches and sees the image of her grandmother, who is the only person who ever loved her and with whom she is reunited after her death. There is "The Steadfast Tin Soldier" who can only be united with the ballerina doll in the fire that destroys both of them. The Andersen stories are a mine of these fantasies of death, dying, and afterlife. Suicide itself is treated almost directly in "The

Old Street Lamp." The lamp fears decomposition, and it is relieved of this fear when it obtains the power to kill itself, so to speak, by turning to rust in one day. (Suicidal patients often feel a sense of mastery over all sorts of anxieties, including fears of death: their idea is that they can end their lives at will.) The lamp finally decides not to use this power, that even though a new existence might be better, it will not seek it, since there are others (the watchman and his wife) who care about it and whom it must consider.

Fantasies of rebirth are often associated with reunion after death. "The Ugly Duckling" appeals to the idea that while in the present life one may be unloved and unwanted, in some future existence one's whole state can be quite different, the duckling is "reborn" as a swan. While there is no dying in the story, the psychological idea of rebirth is there.

By and large, the love-death theme—the idea that without love there will be death, but that perhaps in death the desire for love will be gratified—runs through the Andersen stories. The boy who is in bondage to "The Snow Queen" is emotionally frozen: he has a "heart like ice" and can obtain pleasure in reason only. It is only by the strength of the love and faith of little Gerda that he can be returned to normal.

One should point out that these are by no means the universal themes of all fairy tales. Only consider that in the Andersen tales competition and performance are not important. Neither giants nor dragons have to be killed in order for the hero to succeed in whatever he is up to.

To be sure, death is as taboo a subject in Denmark as in the United States, if not more so. Parents are uncomfortable when their children bring it up. The Danes find funerals painful and wish them over as soon as possible, and they are often uncomfortable around a bereaved person. They expect a short period of grieving and then the subject is to be dropped. And such discomfort is in keeping with their anxiety about separation, loss, or abandonment by a source of dependency gratification. Several Danish psychiatrists, psychologists, and sociologists have expressed the idea that a longer period of grieving would probably be salutary, a sort of safety valve.

Suicide itself is less taboo than it is in the United States and is probably much less so than in Catholic countries. Patients who make suicide attempts and fail express less shame at having made the attempt than do such patients in the

United States. The Danish patient is more apt to express shame at not having successfully completed the act than he is over having made the attempt. While the wife or husband of the suicidal patient may feel some shame, the attitude of those around the patient is generally one of sympathy or pity. A Danish clergyman has admitted to me that the early church teaching that suicide is immoral has little effect, even in religious families, when suicide actually occurs or is attempted. Then, too, there is bound to be a weakening of such a taboo when so many Danes know personally friends and relatives who have killed themselves or made suicide attempts. Suicide does not have to become institutionalized, as it is in Japan, for it to be a known and almost acceptable expression of unhappiness.

I have dwelt on differences between the Danish and American characters. But it is certainly true that in studying suicide in the United States, one may observe any one of the character traits that I have described. American patients of English extraction or Puritan heritage will exhibit great control over the expression of aggression—but people of this background also discourage feelings of excessive dependency. Patients of southern or eastern European background often use the arousal of guilt to express hostility or to obtain obedience to their wishes; but, just as characteristically, they don't suppress aggression as do the Danes. It is the combination of traits we have examined that would seem to make the Danes liable to suicide rather than to other forms of discharge of aggression and frustration.

The study of suicide in Denmark (or elsewhere) throws light on the particular anxieties and preoccupations of the people in that country. Yet one pattern often associated with suicide elsewhere is important in illuminating Danish character by the very fact of its rarity among the Danes. And in speaking of it, we shall return to the question of socialism raised at the beginning.

The pattern I refer to is organized around performance and competitiveness—and it seems to have little bearing on Danish suicide. If only because of Denmark's proximity to Germany, and because part of her land area had once been controlled by Germany, I looked for the frequently described Germanic hyper-consciousness about performance. In this pattern, the individual has rather fixed, high, and rigid expectations of himself, and a great deal of aggression is tied up with the achieve-

ment of these expectations. Failure of achievement in such
a culture can be a direct cause for committing suicide.
And in such cultures the failure to achieve love will not be
interpreted, as in the Danish culture, as an emotional deprivation but more importantly as a poor performance in
which the individual gives himself, so to speak, a low mark
on love. I have noted that competitiveness and performance
do not figure significantly in the Hans Christian Andersen
fairy tales. But the conquest of giants and dragons is
crucial and decisive in the folklore of Germanic cultures
and the winning of the heroine at the end may be only incidental. In the light of all we have said about Danish
family life, upbringing, and attitudes, it is probably not surprising that this performance pattern does not have the life-
and-death meaning in Denmark that it appears to have in
Germany, Switzerland, and in Japan as well.

Although he finds his fair share of competition in school,
the Danish child is not particularly encouraged toward
competitiveness by his family, and in general it is understood among both children and adults that one should not
stand out too much in any direction, an attitude by no
means unknown among Americans, but which is more intense among the Danes. Anyone who violates this rule
against conspicuous high performance, whether it be the
child at school or the adult at work, is subject to a good
deal of envy and dislike.

What is the importance, then, of Danish socialism in
fostering the national attitudes toward competition and
dependency? Certainly most of these attitudes appear to
antedate the social and economic changes of the last few
decades in Denmark. All that can be said, I think, is that
Danish socialism may give expression to and reinforce these
qualities and attitudes in the national character, and these
qualities and attitudes, in turn, undoubtedly shape the particular form that social change has taken. Government
concern for the individual gives a kind of permission for
the overt expression of the longing to be taken care of.
Even the tone of the letters to the newspapers in Denmark
indicates a feeling of passively endured injustice, particularly under personal economic difficulty, and reflects a
lesser feeling of responsibility for one's personal destiny
than we are accustomed to.

The numerous social welfare agencies give opportunity
to those wishing to care for the dependent needs of others,

and there is a greater concern than in the United States on the part of those administering the help—whether it be medical care or financial aid—with the welfare of everyone; and there is a virtually unanimous tendency to feel personally responsible for all suffering. In discussing this at a seminar in Copenhagen, one doctor gave me as an illustration—with the aptness of which all agreed—that the entire country can experience a wave of guilt in reading a newspaper account of a man who died in his room and whose body went undiscovered for several days. It is assumed that he was lonely, uncared-for, and probably without friends; virtually everyone may feel personally responsible.

But this is all a far cry from equating socialism and suicide. The earlier-mentioned presence in Norway of equally developed social welfare measures together with a particularly low suicide rate demonstrates the falsity of the equation.

Let us look more closely at the Danish socialistic system. With its lack of natural resources, it is difficult to visualize Denmark as wealthy today under any economic system. Were she to lean toward more capitalistic practices, there would be no great amount of wealth for her to "capitalize." It is also hard to imagine Denmark surviving in the competitive international economy without a greater degree of internal economic cooperation and planning than we seem to find necessary.

Both the lack of wealth within the country and the high taxes required for Danish social welfare activities limit the accumulation of wealth by individual men. The very fact of this limitation may make for less competition. Individual initiative will accomplish less for someone trying to change his economic situation than it may, for example, in the United States or in Denmark's wealthier neighbor, Sweden. Thus, though in one sense economic life seems more difficult, in another sense Denmark appears to have escaped some of the pressure of the continuing chase for wealth and goods that is seen in so much of the rest of the western world. Living in Copenhagen, one can actually feel in a relatively short time the more relaxed pace of life there in comparison with the pace in cities like New York or Stockholm.

We do not know for certain how a particular people hit upon a particular set of institutions and attitudes with which to regulate their lives, bring up their children, and earn their bread—out of the several alternatives that may be available. We do know that once they choose a particular way it will have profound *further* effects upon character attitudes and institutions. Yet psycho-social studies are not developed highly enough to allow us to pass judgment as to better or worse ways of doing things or to make very definitive suggestions about doing them differently, either in our own country or elsewhere. For the present, we must gather more knowledge as to the ways in which different social institutions and customs produce individual characters and attitudes. It seems to me that the relatively greater homogeneity of the people in each of the Scandinavian countries would make the study of the differences among those countries and between them and ourselves a particularly fruitful source of information. Further, the Scandinavian countries are pioneering in several social and economic measures in which the rest of the world is interested; some of their ideas and plans have been and will be followed by other countries. If we can learn something from the inevitable difficulties they are bound to encounter in going first, we can only be grateful and trust that they will not begrudge the fact that our paths have been made easier.

VIII. INTEGRATION

To overcome the many forms of alienation various remedies have been proposed. To deal with any one of them fully would take a book many times the length of the present work. Here we can describe only a few such "cures." They range from individual psychotherapy at one extreme to "thought reform" and collectivization at the other. The question they raise is whether group solidarity can be achieved without sacrificing personal identity. If not, the cure will be fatal.

Our first selection, by Frederick A. Weiss, deals with the role played by psychoanalysis in treating neurotics suffering from self-alienation. Weiss describes for us the formative childhood experiences of such patients and the many devices they employ to escape from themselves. Thus in terms strikingly reminiscent of Joey, the "mechanical" boy, one of Weiss's patients tells him: "I am color-blind until somebody reveals the colors to me. Only when plugged into the wall-socket of 'the other' do I get the light, the energy, the reality of myself." But as Weiss observes (echoing Schachtel in our first section) most attempts at self-escape fail. Indeed, when psychoanalysis begins, the alienated patient hopes that the analyst will help him escape from himself and thus free him from anxiety. The analyst's task, however, as Weiss remarks, is not merely to remove anxiety and thereby perpetuate alienation, but rather to help the patient regain himself. But to do this, psychoanalysis must first overcome what Weiss calls its own alienated concepts of personality and its alienating techniques. What is called for is not just help in achieving self-awareness, not mere explanations, but emotional experience which will help the patient "to begin to feel himself and to permit himself more and more to be." In other words, he needs a warm, mutually trusting relationship in which for the first time he is accepted as he is, accepted with those characteristics which earlier in his life he had felt compelled to reject or repress.

Weiss's patients are "ordinary" neurotics who in trying to escape from themselves do damage chiefly to themselves. But what of those who express their alienation by destroying others? Such was the situation of the Swedish murderer, "Aake Horsten," as described by Giles Playfair and Derrick Sington. While the techniques of rehabilitation used in this case are extremely interesting, most striking here is the assumption by Swedish penologists that with proper treatment, including psychotherapy, even murderers can be restored to a fairly normal community life. Their approach may be contrasted with American practice, with its motives of revenge and retribution, which either executes the murderer or dooms him to life imprisonment. That civilized alternatives exist in the treatment of murderers is perhaps the most important lesson to be drawn from this case study.

The rehabilitation of disturbed persons is frequently an individual matter. But as we are beginning to learn, the community itself and its culture may affect the nature of mental disorders and their treatment. This is suggested in our third selection, a study of mental health among the Hutterites by Joseph Eaton and Robert Weil. An isolated and cohesive religious sect in the American mid-west, the Hutterites "live a simple, rural life, have a harmonious social order and provide every member with a high level of economic security from the womb to the tomb. They are a homogeneous group, free from many of the tensions of the American melting-pot culture. And they have long been considered almost immune to mental disorders." Contrary to such expectations, however, Eaton and Weil found a significant amount of mental illness. How explain this phenomenon in what is apparently so secure and stable a social order? To Eaton and Weil this "suggests that there may be genetic, organic or constitutional predispositions to psychosis which will cause breakdowns among individuals in any society, no matter how protective and well-integrated." But while the Hutterite culture does not prevent mental disorders, it has almost no violence, divorce, alcoholism, or other forms of social maladjustment. Moreover it provides a highly therapeutic atmosphere for treatment—the whole community showing sympathy and support for the disturbed individual and all patients being looked after by their immediate families. No stigma attaches to them and they are encouraged to participate in the normal life of family and community.

If the Hutterite community is more "therapeutic" than modern society, the explanation is not hard to find: the cohesion of that smaller and simpler culture extends to sick and healthy alike. Modern society offers no such solidarity and consequently no such therapy. There are exceptions, however. One is described by Richard Titmuss in his analysis of British civilian morale in World War II during the most terrible period of air raids in 1940–41. Although before the war government experts had predicted mass hysteria among civilians under air attack, when the attacks occurred there was no increase in the number of patients with neurotic illnesses or mental disorders. Furthermore, there was no indication of an increase of insanity, the number of suicides fell, the statistics of drunkenness went down by more than one-half, there was much less disorderly behavior in the streets and public places, while only the juvenile delinquency figures showed a rise (due largely to the forced breakup of families). The most positive expression of high civilian morale, as Titmuss relates, was that common danger "had brought a greater cohesion to society in general and to the family in particular." Thus most families, determined to stick together, refused to evacuate their homes, for that meant separation. For the first time in their lives and regardless of class, people felt a strong sense of solidarity. In the face of an external threat, social differences were forgotten and for a brief moment Britain was truly united.

This brings us back to our central problem: how can complex, modern societies achieve such solidarity in peacetime? This question has preoccupied a host of thinkers and planners. The four selections which end this section all deal in one way or another with this major theme.

In Murray Weingarten's description of individual and group life in the Israeli *kibbutz*, the problem is not how to achieve solidarity but how to preserve individual freedom in a highly cohesive group. A notable experiment in communal work and living, the *kibbutz* operates on the principles of common ownership of the means of production, the elimination of private property except for personal effects, and group responsibility for determining the social and economic needs of its members. As Weingarten shows, solidarity is achieved, but not without strain because of demands for conformity and especially because even private affairs are subject to group scrutiny and control. Sustained for some time by its powerful ideological appeal and by threats to Israel's very existence, the *kibbutz* is utopian socialism in action. But the restrictions which it places on individual expression and family unity raise the question whether group solidarity can be achieved only at the expense of these personal interests.

This problem arises not only in collectives such as the *kibbutz*, but in our own society as well. At first glance the suburbanites of Park Forest as described by William H. Whyte in *The Organization Man* would appear to be a far cry from the *kibbutzim* of Israel. But the organization men and their wives are no less the victims of powerful group pressures for conformity, no less the losers of privacy. As Whyte observes, "Privacy has become clandestine. Not in solitary and selfish contemplation but in doing things with other people does one fulfill oneself." The neighborly group becomes a kind of extended family and a most demanding family at that. On the positive side there is much friendliness in Park Forest, much sharing of interests and problems, in short, there is solidarity. But as Whyte makes clear, one pays a heavy price for such belongingness. Here we see precisely the kind of small group activity that so many social philosophers advocate, and we also see that "more" participation can become a trap.

Our last two selections deal with still more extreme forms of group control. The first of them, by Harriet C. Mills (who has herself experienced imprisonment in Communist China) describes the techniques of so-called "thought reform" in present-day China. A systematic process of reeducation and group control, thought reform is a method of securing conformity by group discussion, mutual criticism, and self-criticism. But to think of it merely as some devilish form of "brain washing" would be a mistake. While the group pressures for conformity are powerful, sometimes cruel, positive incentives also exist which encourage people to accept the group and to derive satisfaction, even happiness, from such acceptance. While thought reform is peculiarly Chinese, it has implications for other cultures as well, including our own. As Robert J. Lifton, another analyst of this technique, writes, thought reform "highlights the dilemma which we face in our own political, cultural and educational institutions. Every society makes use of similar pressures of guilt, shame, and confession, and of milieu control, as means of maintaining its values and its organization. We must ask ourselves where we—inadvertently, and in less extreme form—could also be applying these in excess, to mold uniform identities, and to make men think and act in conforming fashion. We are confronted with the problem of any democratic society—that of maintaining a balance which limits these forces sufficiently to allow its people a sense of individual freedom, creativity, and human dignity."

The last selection, by an American psychologist, describes Soviet techniques of "character training." Chief among these techniques are conformity to group norms and experience in collective living. As Urie Bronfenbrenner observes, the challenge of the "New Soviet Man" is that of a "potent social technology which renovates not only things but men themselves."

In all communities where solidarity is achieved men may escape from alienation, only to lose themselves in conformity to the group. Is there any way out of this dilemma? While it is important to recognize that belongingness and togetherness represent a new form of tyranny, it will not do to urge upon an alienated population a meaningless freedom. The task before us is to build group cultures that will satisfy man's yearning to reach his fellows without destroying him in the process. Who is to say that it cannot be done?

SELF-ALIENATION: DYNAMICS AND THERAPY
/Frederick A. Weiss

During the past decade, psychoanalytic therapy has become more difficult because more patients show an increasing degree of inner dissociation and emotional withdrawal. The age of hysteria was followed by the age of psychosomatics in which anxiety and conflict were mainly expressed in physical symptoms. In our times this has been followed by the age of alienation. The main characteristic of today's patient is his estrangement from himself. I am referring here not only to the extreme: the ambulatory schizophrenic so common today, whose automatized and mechanized shell personality enables him to function and survive surprisingly well in our present automatized and mechanized society. I am thinking of the majority of our neurotic patients. Here the alienation reveals itself—to use Horney's description— in "the remoteness of the neurotic from his own feelings, wishes, beliefs and energies. It is a loss of the feeling of being an active, determining force in his own life. It is a loss of feeling himself as an organic whole . . . an alienation from the real self."

Alienation has social and individual aspects which can be found in the two original meanings of the term. With emphasis on the social aspect, the estrangement from others and the environment, the concept of alienation was created by Hegel and later by Marx, who saw man become estranged from others and from his work under the impact of the Industrial Revolution. With emphasis on the individual aspect, the estrangement from the self, the concept of alienation was used in the last century and is being used now in some countries as connoting mental illness *per se*.

The pathogenic effect of social and cultural factors which reinforce and perpetuate the process of self-alienation is evidenced by comparative cross-cultural anthropological studies. However, to find the primary roots and the dynamics of self-alienation we have to study the early phases of human development and the "inner life history" of alienated patients. We have to use the methods of psychoanalysis.

The term "alienation" is not used by Freud. But in a letter to Romain Rolland, written in 1936, Freud reports about an *Entfremdungsgefuehl*, a feeling of alienation, which he had experienced on the Acropolis. He sees it as an aspect of depersonalization. "The subject feels that . . . a piece of his own self is strange to him. . . . The phenomenon is seen as serving the purpose of defense . . . at keeping something away from the ego."

Fenichel sees the alienation of one's own feelings as characteristic of compulsive neurotics and generally as the result of a long development, but it may also originate in specific traumatic experiences. He considers alienation as the effect of a reactive withdrawal of libido which serves as a defense against objectionable feelings.

Paul Schilder, as early as 1914, described the alienated patient as a person who observes his behavior from the point of view of a spectator. His "central ego does not live in his present and previous experiences. The self appears without soul." Later he stated that alienation can be not only part of depressive and schizophrenic psychoses, but that to some extent it occurs in almost all neuroses as an "unspecific result of the general shock of the psychic conflict. ... The individual does not dare to place his libido either in the body or in the outside world."

While still using the mechanistic concept of the libido theory in saying "the individual does not *dare*," Schilder already speaks in terms of motivation, of courage—or rather, lack of courage, the avoidance of anxiety and conflict and resignation, which we consider today basic aspects of self-alienation.

Schilder also states that the "amount of interest an individual receives in his early childhood is of great importance." This view is confirmed by my clinical experience, which shows that the most severe forms of self-alienation occur in patients whose early relationships were characterized either by lack of physical and emotional closeness, the fatal effects of which Spitz has convincingly demonstrated, or by symbiotic relationships fostered by anxious or overpowering mothers who deprive the child of the chance of growing up as an individual, and particularly by open or hidden over-expectations of compulsively ambitious parents who condition their love and make "shoulds" of performance or behavior a prerequisite for full acceptance of the child.

W. H. Auden describes this utterly destructive process in his poem, "The Average":

> His peasant parents killed themselves with toil
> To let their darling leave a stingy soil
> For any of those smart professions which
> Encourage shallow breathing, and grow rich.
>
> The pressure of their fond ambition made
> Their shy and country-loving child afraid.
> No sensible career was good enough,
> Only a hero could deserve such love.
>
> So here he was without maps or supplies
> A hundred miles from any decent town;
>
> The desert glared into his blood-shot eyes;
> The silence roared displeasure: looking down,
> He saw the shadow of an Average Man,
> Attempting the Exceptional, and ran.

This is the soil in which rebellious resignation grows. Here also grows compulsive non-conformism which, while it contains constructive strivings for freedom, distorts its meaning and perpetuates self-alienation as much as does compulsive conformism. The "beatnik" often is as alienated from himself as is "the man in the gray flannel suit."

The alienated patient is not born alienated, nor does he choose alienation. Lacking genuine acceptance, love, and concern for his individuality in childhood, he experiences basic anxiety. Early he begins to move away from his self, which seems not good enough to be loved. He moves away from what he is, what he feels, what he wants. If one is not loved for what one is, one can at least be safe—safe perhaps by being very good and perfect and being loved for it, or by being very strong and being admired or feared for it, or by learning not to feel, not to want, not to care. Therefore, one has to free oneself from any need for others, which means first their love and affection, and, later on, in many instances, sex. Why feel, why want, if there is no response? So the person puts all his efforts into becoming what he *should* be. Later, he idealizes his self-effacement as goodness, his aggression as strength, his withdrawal as freedom. Instead of developing in the direction of increasing freedom, self-expression, and self-realization, he moves toward safety, self-elimination, and self-idealization.

The alienated patient often is a good observer of himself. Together with the therapist, he looks at himself as though he were a third person in the empty chair. He seems not to care about anything, not to desire anything, particularly anything to which he could get attached. Experiences are dissociated from feelings, feelings do not reach awareness. Events "happen" to him, as they happen to Camus' *Stranger:* the death of his mother, the love of a girl, the fight, the murder. "It's all the same to me," he says again and again. No feeling is experienced, no joy, no longing, no love, no anger, no despair, no continuity of time and life, no self.

He has no active relation to life. This may be connected with an observation I have made several times. These patients often go first to an opthalmologist with complaints about visual disturbances for which no organic basis is found. Erwin Straus showed that in seeing we relate actively to the world around us, while hearing involves awareness of something which comes toward us. Physical symptoms, such as tiredness, dizziness, a general or localized numbness, various degrees of sexual anesthesia, headaches, or gastric disturbances, often are the only clinical evidence of a deeper emotional problem. The loss of primary feelings may be extreme, as in a patient who did not know how he felt until he had looked at his bowel movement in the morning. Such a patient often does not even experience his own feelings in a most intimate situation: when he has a date with his girl, or when he goes to a funeral. What matters to him is only whether he has the "right" attitude toward the girl or at the funeral—"right" meaning the attitude he is expected to have.

The absence of manifest anxiety, rage, or conflict in the clinical picture—Oberndorf spoke of "playing dead"—has led some psychoanalysts to diagnose this condition as an emotional or even constitutional defect, or as an irreversible end-stage of the neurotic process. Clinical experience, however, shows that below the apparently insensitive, frozen surface of these patients is a highly sensitive self, weakened and paralyzed by violent conflict. Underground there exist strong longings and feelings.

The alienated patient is by no means simply the other-directed radar type of Riesman. He is much more deeply blocked. He is dissociated from the active, spontaneous core of himself and his feelings and, therefore, from his incentives and his capacity for making decisions. Recently, a patient said: "I am color-blind until somebody reveals the colors to me. Only when plugged into the wall-socket of 'the other' do I get the light, the energy, the reality of myself." He could have added, ". . . and the feeling of being alive."

This explains the existence of what I call *"echo phenomenon"* in the alienated patient. His own inner voice often is so weak and unconvincing that he hardly hears it. A pertinent statement, a creative idea, a promising plan on which he has been working for weeks remains unreal and meaningless to him until, with much hesitation, he expresses it to another person. When, however, "the other," whom he experiences as an insider of life, repeats his statement, his idea, or his plan, this echo suddenly sounds real and convincing to him, while his own—usually much better—formulation of the same thought remains unreal. In his inner experience he does not count. He does not exist as an individual on his own.

He may say, "Nothing moves me," or "I cannot make any move." But should one follow his limited movements in life, one will notice that he moves for short spurts, like a car with a dead battery, which must be pushed by another car. It stops, however, not simply due to lack of power, but due to the action of an automatic built-in brake. The patient seems to say in a non-verbal way: "I *will* not move on."

The patient's paralysis reveals itself in psychoanalytic therapy in free associations, and particularly in dreams, as a "sit-down strike" against life. This is motivated in a passive way by feelings of deprivation and resignation, such as, "I don't want anything. If I don't want I cannot be hurt," or, in an active way, by violent feelings of bitterness, frustration, resentment, and rage against life and the world which has withheld love or recognition.

In both forms we find the same powerful, unconscious premise: "I shall not participate in the game of life, get emotionally involved, or make a move on my own, until there is a guarantee for the fulfillment of my needs." These by now have become "just" claims for total love or unique success which form part of the unconscious idealized image that has to be actualized.

The apparently static condition of self-alienation reveals itself as a dynamic and comprehensive attempt to avoid the painful experience of severe inner conflict, particularly between strong dependency needs and co-existing violent and hostile aggression. By remaining alienated from himself and detached from others, the patient avoids the anxiety connected with emotional involvement in conflict. But he pays for this with a steadily increasing restriction of his life, his feelings, and his wants; he pays with a loss of his self.

Self-alienation is an unavoidable result of the neurotic process. Simultaneously, however, it is an active move away from—or, rather, against—the real self:

1) Alienation prevents disturbing self-awareness. The alienated patient often complains of being "in a fog," but unconsciously he wants to stay in it. He welcomes *self-anesthesia*.

2) Alienation, in the sense of conforming like an automaton, protects him from the burden and the responsibility of commitment to himself and his identity. It permits *self-elimination*.

3) Alienation, in its most active form, is the rejection of being oneself and the attempt to become the other, the ideal

self. It means escape from the hated self through *self-idealization*.

These three ways, in which the "despair at not being willing to be oneself" finds expression, were already described by Kierkegaard, who gained insight from the experience of his own anxiety and conflict. He called loss of the self "sickness unto death." The first way is to avoid consciousness of the self:

> "By diversions or in other ways, e.g., by work and busy occupations as means of distractions, he seeks to preserve an obscurity about his condition, yet again in such a way that it does not become quite clear to him that he does it for this reason (that he does what he does in order to bring about obscurity)."

This is the overbusy person whom Tennessee Williams describes so well:

> "Mrs. Stone pursued the little diversions, the hairdresser at four o'clock, the photographer at 5:00, the Colony at 6:00, the theatre at 7:30, Sardi's at midnight ... she moved in the great empty circle. But she glanced inward from the periphery and saw the void enclosed there. She saw the emptiness ... but the way that centrifugal force prevents a whirling object from falling inward, she was removed for a long time from the void she circled."

This void, the "existential vacuum," as Victor Frankl calls it, is a main aspect of the neuroses of our time. Our culture is continuously providing new means for self-anesthesia through "shallow living" (Horney): social drinking, late and late-late shows on television, never-ending double features at the movies, Miltown taken like candy.

The second way "to avoid willing to be oneself" is "willing to be simply the conventional self":

> "By becoming wise about how things go in this world, such a man forgets himself ... finds it too venturesome to think, to be himself, far easier and safer to be like the others, to become an imitation, a number, a cipher in the crowd. This form of despair is hardly ever noticed in the world. Such a man, precisely by losing himself in this way, has gained perfectability in adjusting."

Kierkegaard here anticipates what today has become a

mass phenomenon: self-elimination through conforming "adjustment."

The third, most radical way "to avoid willing to be one-self" is "willing to be someone else." Binswanger emphasized the central role of this motivation for the schizophrenic in the "Case of Ellen West." I find the wish "to be someone else," in a decisive though modified way, also in most neurotic patients. They want to free themselves from the burden they experience their actual self to be, escape into fantasy, and try to become that ideal other self they feel they should be.

This process leads, in two ways, to steadily increasing atrophy and paralysis of the self and interference with its further growth. The first factor is the result of a kind of "inner deprivation." All available energy is used in the compulsive attempt to actualize the other, the ideal, self. Too little energy is left for the developing of the real potentials of the self. The second, much more active factor is the destructive force of contempt and hate which is generated incessantly by the omnipotent, idealized self-image and directed against the despicable, actual "self that failed." Early self-rejection and active self-alienation are the roots of masochistic and compulsive homosexual trends.

To get rid of his hated self is the pervasive motivation of the masochist. In Maugham's *Of Human Bondage:*

> "Philip would imagine that he was some boy whom he had a particular fancy for. He would throw his soul, as it were, into the other's body, talk with his voice and laugh with his heart; he would imagine himself doing all the things the other did. It was so vivid that he seemed for a moment to be *no longer himself.* In this way he enjoyed many intervals of fantastic happiness."

This self-elimination and identification with somebody else gives Philip "fantastic happiness" because he is temporarily freed from his hated self; but it also drives him into the self-destructive morbid-dependency relationship with Mildred.

Freud was right when he observed the close relationship between narcissism and homosexuality. The dynamics of compulsive homosexuality, however, become clear only when we recognize with Horney that "narcissism is an expression not of self love, but of alienation from the self.

... A person clings to illusions about himself because and as far as he has lost himself."

The narcissist lost vital aspects of himself due to early rejection which he internalized. He defends himself against this self-rejection by compulsive self-idealization. If the early rejection is experienced as directed particularly against aspects of the self connected with the sexual role, no clear sense of sexual identity can develop. It is a desperate search for a self and identity which drives him into the homosexual relationship. "I don't want to be me. I want to have his balls. I want to be him," a patient recently said.

Symbiosis seems to provide the solution in two ways: by merging with the partner he hopes to become the other, the ideal, self. This partner often is the externalized symbol of the lost, the repressed part of his own self, for example, of his "masculinity." The second function of the symbiotic relationship is what I have called the *magic mirror symbiosis*."

The alienated person exists, becomes at least partially alive, only in the mirror image reflected by others. Without it he feels emotionally dead, as Sartre shows in *No Exit*. A patient says it well: "I searched a way to me by drawing pieces of myself out of their eyes."

In the symbiotic relationship each partner functions as a mirror of the other's image. His "love" has to neutralize the acid of destructive self-hate in the other. The relationship immediately breaks when the mirror-function stops.

Phenomena such as so-called "penis envy," or a man's wish to be a woman, have to be seen as symbols of a partial or total rejection of personal and sexual identity. "If I had the chance of being myself, I would not be myself," a woman said. "I would be a boy. As a boy you are in control. You can do what you want; it is very depressing not to be a man." Such statements have to be analyzed as an expression of the total attitude the patient has toward himself and his life, as a characteristic of his very specific being in the world.

The wish not to be oneself often focuses on the body, fostering a negative body-image which may crystallize around tallness or shortness, overweight or underweight, face, skin, sex—and color. If self-rejection selects the focus on color or nationality, distorting attitudes not only of the parents but of the community have been in operation. We may well ask whether segregation does not foster as much self-alienation in the segregating person who glorifies body aspects, as in the victim.

Only when the unconscious attempts fail—be they self-anesthesia, self-elimination through conforming adjustment, or escape from the self through identification with the other, the ideal self—does the patient come to us. Something has "happened" to him which shows that his safety system is not so safe, his solution not so perfect as he expected. He hopes that the therapist will help him to correct his mistake, to improve his solution.

Thus a paradox is inherent in the therapy of such patients. In the beginning, patient and therapist seem to move in opposite directions. The therapist wants to help the patient to move in a "centripetal" direction, to reconnect him with the vital roots and the creative potential in him. But the patient is unconsciously divided. From the very beginning of therapy he is in search of his self and longs for a genuine relationship. But he still feels driven to accelerate his centrifugal move away from his self, which means to perfect his alienation. Or at least he expects to be freed from anxiety. He wants reassurance. Reassurance removes anxiety. But in so doing, it blocks awareness and destroys the patient's chance for growth and change. All too often the patient gets what he wants: the therapist complies with his expectations for a painless (because changeless) "cure."

The task of the psychoanalyst is not to remove anxiety and thereby to perpetuate alienation. He has to help the patient find the way back to himself. He has to help him face the anxiety generated on this road by self-confrontation and the surrender of cherished illusions. This can rarely be done by analysis in the orthodox manner, with the therapist sitting behind the couch taking notes and giving interpretations. The alienated, "shut-up" patient has all his life used words not to express but to hide his feelings.

Psychoanalysis has to outgrow alienated concepts of personality as well as alienating techniques in therapy. The image of man as an id harboring only libidinous, aggressive, and destructive drives, but no constructive forces; as a super-ego, functioning as an inner police force, not as a healthy human conscience; and as a more or less passive ego, which reminds one of a rather sick self—such an image of man in itself appears fragmented and alienated. The concept of a doctor-patient relationship which is seen as determined by the transference of a neurotic past but disregards the constructive impact of the creative "meeting" in the present is in itself alienating. Instead of lessening the patient's alienation, it is likely to prolong it.

Psychoanalysis, born as a child of the age of enlightenment, overestimated the therapeutic effect of knowledge in itself. Making the unconscious conscious is not, in itself, therapeutically effective. To know, for example, that I harbor strong, compulsive dependency needs, may increase rather than lessen my self-alienation. Self-knowledge becomes therapeutically active only when it is experientially owned, and generates the emotional shock which is inherent in the process of self-confrontation. Only such experience has the power to lead to change, choice, and commitment. Kierkegaard was aware of this:

> "'gnothi seauton' (know yourself) has been seen as the goal of all human endeavor . . . but it cannot be the goal if it is not at the same time the beginning. The ethical individual knows himself, but this knowledge is not a mere contemplation . . . it is a reflection upon himself which itself is an action and therefore I have deliberately preferred to use the expression 'choose oneself' instead of 'know oneself' . . . when the individual knows himself and has chosen himself he is about to realize himself."

Frequently at the end of an orthodox analysis, the patient has gained much knowledge. He could easily "present his own case." He looks with some interest at that stranger who happens to be himself. He may even reflect the image which the therapist expects. But he has not changed. The patient needs, as Ferenczi, Franz Alexander, and Fromm-Reichmann have emphasized, not explanations but emotional experience. To break through his alienation he needs to begin to feel himself and to permit himself more and more to be. The first step involves helping him to stop hating himself. "Any true psychotherapy," Binswanger states—and this is particularly true for the alienated patient—"is reconciliation of man with himself and thereby with the world, is a transformation of hostility against himself into friendship with himself and thereby with the world."

In the beginning of therapy, the patient who refuses participation in life will also refuse true participation in psychoanalysis, even though he may lie down on the couch or sit down on the chair with a compliant smile. He is deeply convinced that nobody cares, nobody understands him, and that communicating his true feelings, his sufferings, and his rage to anybody, including the analyst, is sheer waste.

To "defrost," to open up, to experience and to accept himself become possible for the patient only in a warm, mutually trusting relationship in which, often for the first time in his life, he feels fully accepted as he is, accepted *with* those aspects of himself which early in life he had felt compelled to reject or repress. Only this enables the patient gradually to drop his defenses. He will test the reliability of this acceptance again and again before he risks emotional involvement. He will need this basic trust especially when he begins to experience the "dizziness of freedom" (Kierkegaard). The road from self-alienation and self-rejection to self-acceptance and self-realization leads through steadily growing self-awareness, which is made possible by the new creative experience of acceptance and meeting. Thus, the main therapeutic factor becomes the doctor-patient relationship itself. Very much limited in the beginning by the patient's passive and active distrust, the relationship gradually becomes spontaneous and mutual. Binswanger expresses it like this:

> "The communication must under no circumstances be considered mere repetition, as orthodox analysts believe, that is to say, as transference and counter-transference in the positive case, as resistance and counter-resistance in the negative one; rather, the relationship between patient and doctor invariably constitutes an autonomous communicative novum, a new existential bond."

In the beginning of therapy, questions such as, "What do you feel now?" or "What would you really want?" may bring the patient close to panic. He becomes aware for a moment how deeply his capacity for spontaneous feeling or wanting is impaired.

The patient needs "emotional insight." Such insight is rarely verbalized. The patient may be silent or cry or laugh or do both at the same time. He may perspire, have palpitations, or breathe heavily. If he could verbalize his insight —it is characteristic that he cannot usually do it—he might

say, "Yes, now I see: it is me, not they. It is me, not fate."
In Kierkegaard's terms this changes the "aesthetical" person who experiences everything as coming from without to the "ethical" person, who, transparent to himself, knows that everything depends upon what *he* sees, feels, and does. In psychoanalytic terms it is the change from the feeling of being a victim of fate, constitution, the environment or "the unconscious," to experiencing one's conflicts within oneself, and oneself as an active force in one's life. It is a prerequisite for moving in the direction of freedom, choice, and responsibility.

Kretschmer compared alienated patients to Italian villas that have closed their shutters against the glaring sun. Inside, however, in subdued light exciting events are happening. It often is the dream that opens the shutters for a moment. As the pupil widens in the dark, the dream widens the scope of our self-awareness which, during the daytime, is restricted by compulsive focusing on emergencies, action, and defense. Self-alienation is temporarily lessened. The dream becomes a door to the larger self. It has access to aspects of our selves, neurotic as well as healthy, which we are rejecting or repressing.

With progress in therapy, the dreams of the alienated patient who appears emotionally dead often begin to reveal surprising aliveness and depth, passionate longings, strong feelings of loss and sadness, and conflict between moving into life and resignation. They may confront him with his emotional deadness, his unlived life, as in Ingmar Bergman's "Wild Strawberries," with the neglect of the growth of his real self, which may be symbolized by a plant that needs water, a kitten that needs shelter, a baby that needs food.

On the other hand, early in therapy—earlier than memories or free associations which here are often sparse—dreams reconnect the alienated patient, who is disconnected from his past and his roots, with his childhood when his feelings were more spontaneous and genuine, with his adolescence when he faced the conflicts of growing up, with times in his life when he was closer to his real self, when his heart was alive, and when he took a stand for himself. The past here enters the dream as a symbol of the potential present, as a symbol of the dreamer's own spontaneity, genuineness, and capacity for commitment. Originating in himself, such dreams often convince the patient that there is more strength, more courage, more "self" available in him than he was aware of.

Dreams may help him to move from alienation and self-rejection to genuine self-acceptance: acceptance of the self with its human limitations but with awareness of the potentiality as well as the responsibility for further growth. The patient may experience in a dream a new feeling of love and responsibility for a growing child that resembles him. Or he may meet and accept a person who symbolizes an aspect of himself he had violently rejected before. A Jewish immigrant, proud of his successful Americanization, met in his dream a strange-looking Ghetto inmate who reminded him of his father and, after initial hesitation, welcomed him warmly. A girl who had left the South, rebelling against parents and home, in her dream saw herself, to her own surprise, welcome cordially a girl whose Southern drawl revealed her own identity.

Therapy often is seen in dreams first as a molding procedure, a threat, a humiliation, an invasion of privacy. The patient experiences himself as a passive object resenting and rejecting the procedure. Whatever has to be done, he feels, will be done *on* him, *to* him, *for* or *against* him by the therapist. An alienated patient, unable to experience an intimate sexual relationship, saw himself on an operating table, anesthetized from the waist down. He felt nothing, but joined the surgeon in an intellectual discussion of the interesting operation. Later dreams reflect the patient more and more as an active partner in the analytic relationship. Medard Boss showed the lessening of alienation in a patient whose dreams first dealt only with inanimate objects, such as machines and cars. Then a plant appeared, and only much later, after many animals had entered the dreams, the first human being was encountered. I have seen the dreaming pattern in alienated patients change from dreams in which the dreamer himself is not seen—except perhaps as the symbol of a statue, a skeleton, or brain—to dreams in which the patient often appears, first, as a detached on-looker. Later, when the ice-wall of alienation is slowly beginning to melt, violent "split-image" dreams may occur, which show symbols of the emerging larger self in violent struggle with the old neurotic self, which often is idealized. Such dreams, if they are experientially "owned" by the patient, often are accompanied by that feeling of explosive rage and the sudden eruption of the long repressed hunger for life that Camus shows in the final crisis of *The Stranger:* "I started yelling at the top of my voice. I hurled insults. ... It was as if that great rush of anger had washed me clean—I felt ready to start life all over again." Total emotional involvement in rage and conflict often precedes acceptance of self.

This explains why, when the alienated patient first begins to "relate," there often are violent outbursts of rage. The therapist has to take hostility and contempt until the patient realizes that he has externalized his self-contempt onto the therapist.

An alienated patient whose key childhood memory was waiting in the rain for mother, in his first dream misses the boat—of life. Later dreams show him turning his back on life, running away from home where his parents are fighting, to follow his dog on a lonely road through the woods; living underground in a cellar, absorbed in monotonous, meaningless labor, trying to repair broken clocks (time has stopped for him), while upstairs in the daylight his wife, his life, are waiting. In a subsequent dream he is attracted to a warm, giving woman, but feels, "If I let myself be touched by her, I will get so involved that I will lose myself." Relating closely often contains for the alienated patient the threat of losing his weak identity. This is a fear that, in its greatest intensity, I occasionally have found expressed in fear of orgasm; emotional surrender, giving up control, here is experienced, as *"la petite mort,"* the small death.

Finally, the patient is shocked by a dream in which he sees himself actually touched by the therapist without being aware of it, an experience which he had fought but secretly wanted. Toward the end of his analysis, this patient said: "What helped me? Not so much your interpretations. It was the process of getting in touch, being touched by you, very much against my will, touching you, which I first did not like, and often disagreeing with you, during which I began to feel my own identity."

In such a patient, who is frightened of contact and longing for contact at the same time, the usual psychoanalytic technique often results only in a series of negative therapeutic reactions because for a long time the maintenance of the alienation appears to the patient as the only way to survive as an individual. Healing—to use Hans Trueb's words—here occurs mainly through meeting. But not just any meeting will be healing. The patient will misuse the relationship and the therapist for the satisfaction of his neurotic needs for love, for power, or for uniqueness. Only very slowly will the relationship change from what Martin Buber calls an "I-It" relationship to a truly mutual "I-Thou" relationship.

The therapist must have achieved in his analysis a lessening of his own alienation, which often is hidden behind a professional pseudo-identity. He must have gained a high tolerance for anxiety and hostility in the patient and in himself, an immunity against getting seduced by and neurotically involved with the patient. The authoritarian therapist fosters the development of a passive-rebellious pseudo-identity. The over-protective therapist fosters a weak, unconsciously still symbiotic pseudo-identity. The detached therapist often has the "meeting" with the patient so far out in the all that the boundaries between the self of the patient, the self of the therapist, and the cosmos become blurred. Here the patient has little chance to lessen his alienation and to gain true personal and sexual identity. Such a therapist, who himself is often afraid of a truly close and mutual relationship, deprives the patient of the experience of a genuine person-to-person meeting, which alone has the power of healing. Required is a truly mutual bipolar relationship. No "I" can develop without encountering a clearly defined, solid, but warm and spontaneous "Thou" in the therapist.

In the words of Buber, who wrote a beautiful introduction to Trueb's *Healing Through Meeting:*

> "If the psychotherapist is satisfied to 'analyze' the patient . . . at best he may help a soul which is diffused and poor in structure to collect and order itself to some extent. But the real matter, the regeneration of an atrophied personal center will not be achieved . . . This can only be attained in the person-to-person attitude of a partner."

SUMMARY

1. Self-alienation originates in an early childhood situation which deprives the child of the vital experience of feeling genuinely accepted as an individual. (Lack of physical and emotional closeness, symbiotic parent-child relation-

ships, over-expectations of compulsively ambitious parents).
Basic anxiety fosters compulsive needs for safety which
deflect the development of the child from spontaneity, self-
expression, and self-realization to self-rejection, self-elimination, and escape into the fantasy of self-idealization.
Cultural factors reinforce trends toward self-alienation.

2. Self-alienation is a result of the neurotic process. Simultaneously, however, by providing self-anesthesia and
self-elimination, it becomes a dynamic and comprehensive
unconscious attempt to avoid disturbing self-awareness,
anxiety, and interpersonal and intrapsychic conflict.

3. Active alienation from the self, unconscious rejection
of personal and sexual identity, and the wish to be the
other—the ideal self—are basic aspects of the neurotic
personality of our time. They foster self-destructive masochistic and homosexual trends and compulsive symbiotic
relationships.

4. To help the alienated patient, psychoanalysis has to
outgrow alienated concepts of personality and alienating
techniques in therapy. The basic change from alienation
and self-rejection to self-acceptance and self-realization requires steadily growing self-awareness gained in emotional
experience and emotional insight.

5. Dreams occur during a period of lessened self-alienation and become, therefore, an important mobilizing force
in the therapy of the alienated patient. They move him
closer to his real self and reconnect him with the vital
roots in his past and with the constructive potential he will
strive to realize in the future.

6. Therapeutic goals are genuine acceptance of self and
others, growing autonomy, a stronger sense of personal and
sexual identity, and commitment to further self-realization.
The main therapeutic factor is the new creative experience
of acceptance and "meeting" in a warm, truly mutual, trusting doctor-patient relationship.

AAKE HORSTEN
/Giles Playfair and Derrick Sington

In Sweden, murderers are not executed; nor, unless they are adjudged incurably insane, are they kept in confinement for the rest of their natural lives. Ten years is the maximum sentence they are likely to serve, and upon their release they are considered to have paid their debt to society in full. Regardless of how brutal and shocking their crime may have been, they carry with them the faith of the Swedish penal authorities in their capacity to lead fruitful and peaceful lives in the free world—a faith which statistics show is almost invariably justified.

But the Swedish penal authorities recognize that a released murderer's chances of rehabilitation, and of personal happiness, would be greatly reduced if he were obliged to live in a society that might still be hostile or antagonistic toward him, that might, at the very least, be distrustful of him. For this reason they usually advise him to change his name and to make his home in a different town, or part of the country, from the one in which his crime was committed. They regard it as part of their responsibility to find him a job and, if necessary, living accommodation. It is likely that the man for whom he eventually works will be the only member of the community aware of his true identity, and this man will be sworn to secrecy. In short, it is a cardinal principle of Swedish penal policy to protect the anonymity of released offenders, particularly of released murderers, and to make as certain as possible that their privacy will not be invaded by such as newspaper reporters.

We have gladly deferred to this principle in relating the case that follows. Hence Aake Horsten is not the real name of the murderer. Other names, too, that might lead to his being identified have been altered, as have, for the same purpose, the names of places and the dates of events. Even the events themselves have to some extent been disguised. Essentially, however, the story remains a true one. Though it did not happen exactly as we tell it, it could have;

and the actual crime was certainly no whit less brutal than the one we have partially invented.

On a cold, clear night in the winter of 1941 a man stood in a back street in Trollsborg watching a first-floor window. A scavenging cat brought an ash-can lid clattering down, and the man started and looked round; then he turned and walked fast down the street. Half running through a little square, he came into a brightly lit, silent thoroughfare—it was 1:00 A.M.—walked across it to the station, and bought a ticket to a place named Ornstad. On the platform he slumped down on a seat and slept. The hobnailed boots of night workers, boarding a train, woke him; and he climbed in too, sank back in a corner of the carriage and slept on. It was drizzling as he walked still short of sleep out of Ornstad station. Noticing his late-night reveler's face in a ticket-office window, he thought: I must get a shave. I look conspicuous. Outside he went into the first small restaurant in sight.

The only waitress was reading the morning newspaper over the shoulder of a solitary customer. By the cash register the owner was writing out a menu card. The man—his name was Aake Horsten—sat down and ordered herrings and coffee. He wished he could get a sight of the paper, but restrained himself from asking. As the waitress brought his coffee she spoke to the owner, who moved across to the other customer, glanced at the newspaper for an instant and then looked quickly at Horsten. Horsten ate his breakfast, went out across the square to a kiosk, bought a newspaper and opened it. Yes, there it was on the front page!

Ten minutes after Horsten left the little street in Trollsborg the light was still on in the first-floor window. It shone down on a bed–sitting room in some disarray—a few empty schnapps bottles, soiled linen on a chair, and bare boards because the carpet was rolled up and three men were busily unwrapping it, while a concerned-looking landlady looked on. The bundle came apart neatly as a parcel. First the outer wrapping, then a blanket, then a quilt with big brown stains on it. It took a little time to peel the quilt away from a heavy mass underneath. The center of the mass was a bare stomach which had been gashed in two directions so that it looked oddly like a hot-cross bun. The skirt had been pulled up over the face. One of the three lifted it away and uncovered a tangle of blond hair stained brown

with dry blood. Running his hand around the head, he felt
a deep cleft over the right temple.

"It's Inga Arvidsson, all right," he said.

He turned to the now pale and trembling landlady.

"Have you got a telephone here?"

As Horsten turned to walk away from the newspaper
kiosk a policeman standing at his elbow said, "Excuse me,
do you mind telling me your name?"

"My name's Stefansson."

"Have you some papers to identify you?"

Horsten started to move away. "This isn't Russia," he
blustered.

The policeman asked him to come to the station, and
Horsten went quietly enough. It was characteristic of him
that his little attempt to "cover up" did not last long. At the
police station he was talkative. In jerky sentences and gesticu-
lating with his arms he told the story of his meeting with
Inga Arvidsson and of the sequel.

"I didn't intend to kill her, but she made such an uproar,
screaming, and then she hit me with a bottle, and then it
was as if a thick vapor caught in my throat—that's what
it felt like—it got in my eyes and half blinded me."

"One moment!" said the police sergeant as he took out
his notebook and picked up a pen.

After two and a half hours the sergeant and his clerk
produced in their own dead style a confession which began
as follows:

"At 12 o'clock noon on December 19th I, Aake
Horsten, went to the Disconto Bank. I saw a girl at the
counter receive about 1,500 kronor in bank notes and
place it in a leather case. As she left the bank I followed
her and asked her what her name was. She said it was
Inga Arvidsson. I told her that her father had been taken
to my lodgings following a street accident and that he
wanted her to come to him. This was a device to induce
the girl to go with me."

Horsten then related how he had led Inga to his lodgings,
taken her inside and locked the door.

"I ordered her to hand over the money. I needed it to
buy a fur coat for my fiancée. She refused. She screamed
for help and struck me on the head with an empty bottle.
I picked up a hatchet which was lying near the stove

and swung it at her face. She collapsed on the floor and I saw she was bleeding from the head. I felt her pulse. After a little while it stopped beating. I made two incisions in her stomach with a penknife—I do not know why. I wrapped the body up."

At the end Horsten sat back wearily. The statement was read over to him but he hardly appeared to be listening. He signed it as a tired business executive signs the last letter in his tray.

The crime committed by Aake Horsten was, in many ways, an irrational one. He had accosted his victim in one of the most public places in Trollsborg, within earshot of a messenger boy who happened to know her. Before buttonholing the girl he had been greeted by a shopkeeper acquaintance of his who was also in the bank. When, therefore, the local radio station had broadcast an appeal for information about the missing Inga Arvidsson her messenger-boy friend had at once volunteered a description of the man in whose company she had left the bank. This in turn was broadcast, and the shopkeeper then telephoned to the police that Aake Horsten answered to the particulars given. The criminal had left behind a trail of clues almost as if he had been starting a paper chase.

There were other irrational aspects of the crime. Only robbery had originally been intended. To enlarge it to murder—even through fear of detection—was, considering how easy Horsten had made his identification, extraordinarily reckless. Moreover after the deed he made it appear more horrible by mutilation.

A good deal was known about Aake Horsten's career in certain Trollsborg circles before ever he came into court to be indicted for murder. It was not the first time he had disgraced the name of his father and of the family firm, Granquist & Horsten. The solid world of the businessmen's clubs and of the big villas by the fjords knew that old Gunnar Horsten had had to reimburse at least one employer to save his "young wastrel of a son" from the consequences of embezzlement. They knew too that Aake had lost several jobs in the years since his return from the Far East. After failing with a yarn agent in Trollsborg he had somehow picked up an assignment on a newspaper. But after a time the editor had wearied of reporting missions which turned into alcoholic incidents and failed to yield a line of "copy." After six months Horsten had been "fired."

In December 1941 he was free-lancing for advertising firms. His parents had lost track of him, though sometimes they were awkwardly reminded of his presence in Trollsborg. Once, as they were getting out of their car to enter a theater, they heard a loud, coarse laugh, and the swaying figure of Aake, supported by two ladies of the town, lurched into them. For a time Horsten stayed in touch with the harder-drinking reporters among his former colleagues. He went fairly often to a bar near the newspaper office. But when he became merely brooding and besotted, backs began to be turned ostentatiously at his approach; then his main haunt became a tavern which was reputed to purvey drugs. And yet, although they were aware he had gone pretty thoroughly to the dogs, people in Trollsborg who knew about him were dumfounded at the crime this man committed in an attempt to lay his hands on less than two thousand kronor.

The trial of Aake Horsten took place in February 1942. It was reported fully and straightforwardly by the Swedish newspapers but without sensational headlines or lurid feature articles. The street outside the courthouse looked as usual during the proceedings. No excited or hysterical queues of would-be spectators assembled. One of the positive results of the humanization of penal practice in Sweden is that the witch-hunting atmosphere and the man-hunting crowd that gather around so many murder trials in retentionist countries are virtually non-existent. In court Horsten pleaded guilty to the murder, and his counsel made no attempt to persuade him to put forward a plea of insanity. Under Swedish law—as under that of all abolitionist countries—the life of the accused never depends on such a plea, and therefore it is less frequent.

But there is another reason why there is in Sweden less urgency or inclination to put up a defense of insanity or diminished responsibility: no serious risk exists that an insane or abnormal murderer will be treated as sane and responsible, because in all murder cases the offender receives a thorough and systematic investigation by a special state-run psychiatric service—an investigation which may last up to two months. This is a very different matter from the practice in Britain and in most American jurisdictions. In Britain prison doctors, who are often not even qualified psychiatrists, pronounce on behalf of the State or of the prosecution on the mental condition of the accused; in both Britain and the majority of American jurisdictions expert psychiatric examination, when it takes place, is likely to be of very limited duration and thoroughness. In Sweden, on the other hand, decisions by judge or jury based on confused, unedifying wrangles in court between medical witnesses who may be both psychiatrically unqualified and insufficiently informed simply do not occur. Aake Horsten was sent, as soon as the court had satisfied itself that he had committed the deed of which he was accused, to Murrenholm, one of the 14 state clinics of forensic psychiatry in Sweden, for an extremely full report on his mental condition.

Murrenholm is a bungalow-type building in the garden of a large mental hospital. When Horsten entered it in 1942 it contained only a single ward for six patients. His four fellow patients were an arsonist, two housebreakers and a man who had attempted rape. During his first afternoon Aake was interviewed by the head of the clinic, Professor Friedrichsen. Seated in an armchair, he described, at the professor's request, his feelings and actions during the month before the crime, his early life, and his family background. The interview lasted two hours and was one of four he had with the professor; it was also the prelude to a series of meetings with doctors, social workers and psychologists. He was later seen by a social worker who had a transcript of the evidence at his trial and who asked him to tell her of former associates of his she might interview. He gave particulars of a friend on the newspaper he had worked for and of a clergyman who had tried to help him. During the following weeks the clinic's social workers also interviewed Horsten's parents, one of his schoolmates, the family doctor and two of his former business colleagues.

Two mornings at the clinic were spent at a writing table in the psychologist's office. Horsten was subjected to the standard intelligence tests; he then had to confront the queer-shaped ink blots of the famous Rorschach test and write down the associations and ideas which they conjured up in his mind. Personality and apperception tests followed. He had later to undergo the usual electroencephalographic brain test and to visit an outside hospital for a special X ray of his brain.

Not until he had been six weeks in Murrenholm was the

report on Horsten complete. It ran to 75 closely typed pages and, like most such case studies in Sweden, was a sort of skeleton novel.

Aake Horsten was born in Trollsborg in 1912. His father had succeeded his grandfather as chairman of the firm of Granquist & Horsten when Aake was fifteen. Several years earlier the boy had realized that he himself would one day sit in his father's paneled office facing a tall oil portrait of one of his ancestors and direct the firm.

From childhood Aake Horsten had been conscious of something called "the business" as his preordained future. It was not connected with the things that stimulated him, such as acting in plays at school; but "Granquist & Horsten," iron machinery and branded packing cases were part of the fabric of a "practical world" in which someday one would have to "sink or swim." At university some poems of his were published in an undergraduate anthology during a student phase he enjoyed, without, however, being very certain of himself or confident about the future. He took a fairly good degree in languages. At that time, as a photograph revealed, he had been a long-legged youth with plentiful dark hair, full lips and restless eyes. He plunged readily into debate or argument, in contrast to his father, who was apt to round off discussions between them rather irrelevantly with the pronouncement, "Well, at least you'll always have both feet on the ground. You're going into one of the soundest firms in the world, and one with a very great name in the Eastern trade."

When he was twenty-one Aake's father gave a glittering party for him. More than fifty of Trollsborg's leading business and professional men and their sons, daughters and wives raised their glasses to Gunnar Horsten's toast of "To Aake, on his last birthday before he goes out East!" At that time he was "going through the mill"—three months in each department of Granquist & Horsten, and similar periods of study with two famous engineering firms. Wherever he was apprenticed he was treated with the consideration due to Gunnar Horsten's son, as a young man who was later to be the head of a great family business.

In February 1934 the firm sent Aake to its branch in southern Asia. His father said he was to "flash his sword" and show his mettle. "Three years out East will prove if he has any stuffing in him," old Gunnar Horsten said to his chief clerk. And so Aake went to the tropics. His face had acquired a hail-fellow-well-met expression which, however, to those who knew him well, was a little masklike. In a colonial town he shared with two other young business-men a "chummery" with a long veranda. There were the exhilaration of tropical sunshine, dinner invitations from "old hands," and tennis at the club. At the office Aake read the reports of salesmen who were traveling in the hinterland and watched crates of goods being manhandled into and out of the company's godown. After ten months the local manager sent him on an "up-country" expedition.

Accompanied by a native servant, he had to make a river journey by outboard motorboat to a timber concession 300 miles from any other European settlement. He stopped the night at mission stations, or administrators' bungalows. His task was to investigate the chances of selling equipment to the sawmills. He stayed three months at the timber con-cession, which was called Kapang Kula. It was here he met Blanchard, a failed French actor whose uncle had paid for his training in forestry to get him a fresh start. Blanchard was assistant manager of the timber plant. He managed to dispose of a bottle of whisky most evenings after return-ing to his bungalow, and Horsten found him congenial company. The Frenchman amused himself with aboriginal women but willingly curtailed these distractions to drink with the young newcomer who, like himself, also had in-tellectual interests. Evening "sessions" in the bungalow grew frequent and lasted long. Aake acquired from Blanch-ard a curiosity about the tribes of the surrounding jungle. This was what took them to a distant area, officially to look at some timber but in reality to see what happened when two head-hunting tribes made war on each other. They reached a village at the exact moment when the wives and daughters of a defeated chieftain were being ritually butchered.

It was over a week before the two got back to Kapang Kula. Awaiting Aake was a message to return immediately to the coast. For lack of a report which he should have sent, a contract for equipment had been lost. That night the two young men got cheerfully drunk. Next morning Aake was laid up with his first attack of malaria. It was ten days before he could move off down the river. When he reached the coast he found a violently phrased letter from his father which spoke of his behavior as that of "a man of straw" and ordered him to pull himself together, "otherwise neither I nor anyone else will be able—or indeed will be inclined—to save you from going to the wall." As a postscript his father had added, "You are the first Horsten for three generations to have let down the firm and the family name."

Aake Horsten resumed the routine of the branch office. The staff treated him with wary politeness as his father's son, but the manager no longer asked him to tackle anything important. He developed an unnaturally "hearty" manner at the club; and he went on drinking heavily. There were buffoonish incidents. One morning he was found asleep and disheveled on the steps of the bank when the native clerks came to open it. Another time he brought into the office a Chinese woman, with whom he had spent the night in an opium establishment. His concentration and activity dwindled. Once when the manager was away, Aake was asked to draft and dispatch an important letter. He typed several naughts too many and a month later the company was landed with a consignment of canned goods far larger than it had intended to order. Gunnar Horsten telegraphed his son's recall at once. When they met again at home he told him that he was "finished" as far as any major role in the firm was concerned. If he preferred to take his chance elsewhere, an old family friend who had a cotton-yarn agency was prepared to employ him.

Such in outline was the first part of the Murrenholm Clinic's report on Aake Horsten, so much fuller and more penetrating than any that are normally forthcoming in the conventional prison systems of the world. The second part of Horsten's story has already been recounted. The following was the interpretation that the Murrenholm doctors sent to the judge and jury:

(1) Aake Horsten was not psychotic.
(2) He was a psychopathic personality.
(3) The degree of his responsibility for the crime was diminished because self-control and judgment had been undermined by the effects of alcohol and narcotic drugs.
(4) He deviated widely from the normal. He was a case of personality disorder accentuated by prolonged but unavowed inner conflict. Unsuited tempera-

mentally or intellectually to be "a captain of commerce," he had yet been cast for this role by a strong-willed father from the shadow of whose personality he had been unable to escape. The tension thus set up within him had resulted in a complete personality breakdown and finally resolved itself (or found an outlet) in the murder.

On April 20, 1942, Aake Horsten was taken from the clinic to Stockholm to hear the verdict of the court. They pronounced him "widely deviating" from the normal though "partly responsible" for his deed.

It would be hard to imagine a more repulsive crime than that of which Aake Horsten was convicted. On the surface it was committed for gain; the robbery which led up to it was premeditated; and, judging from the mutilation of the girl's body, there was an element of perversion. It is not difficult to imagine what would have been the verdict on him in the United States or Britain. In a retentionist American state Horsten's life would have been terminated in the execution chamber to the accompaniment of great public excitement, after almost ecstatic demands for the extinction of "a monster." In an abolition state of America the clamor for expiation would hardly have been less intense. Aake Horsten had not even the extenuating background of childhood poverty and parental neglect. It is unlikely that in the state of Minnesota he would have emerged from maximum-security prison before old age if at all. In Britain, where public pressures on the judiciary are less overt, he would have been led to the gallows against a background of tight-lipped public emotionalism, with a skilled but circumspect popular press "pointing the moral" of weakness and depravity in half a dozen titillating serial features by the relatives of murderer and victim.

The sentence of the court on Horsten was a minimum of ten years' confinement in a special institution. This is the so-called "indeterminate sentence" which means in Sweden that release on parole is *possible* after two thirds of a minimum period have been served or at any time subsequently. Confinement continues, however, unless and until a special review board, including laymen, lawyers and doctors, is satisfied that the convicted person has been sufficiently restored to normality to make it socially safe for him to be released. It means also that the offender, having been categorized as "abnormal," is viewed as a patient with potentialities of recovery, however dastardly his crime. And as we shall see provision is made in Sweden to record and assist such recovery in a planned and organized way.

In April 1942 Aake Horsten was taken to a prison called Grevebro, a maximum-security institution surrounded by high walls which was nevertheless a special prison for psychopathic offenders small enough—it contained only 100 prisoners—for its inmates to receive some individual observation and attention. At Grevebro Horsten, as an educated man, was given the most suitable work the institution could provide. He was made a clerk in the administrative office. For several months the warders had instructions to observe him closely and report frequently on him. The nature of his crime and the "psychopathic period" that had preceded it (several years of self-ruination, and occasional delinquency) dictated a cautious official policy toward any possibility of transferring him to a milder or more open institution, although, from the beginning, this was never ruled out. But it was by no means certain that Aake Horsten, as he appeared immediately after his sentence, might not prove a "difficult" inmate of Grevebro, an "escaper" or an unsettling influence on other prisoners.

Rather to the surprise of the prison staff, however, Horsten did not prove unco-operative or unwilling to adapt himself to the routine. At first he was irritable and taciturn, but after a short time the routine itself seemed to have a calming effect on him. He went about his tasks quietly and resignedly, ceased to brood, and made much use of the prison library. There were no complaints at Grevebro over any aspect of his behavior; and after three years of his sentence had been served both the institution officials and the Royal Prison Board of Sweden were satisfied that maximum-security confinement was no longer necessary and that Aake Horsten was a suitable subject for transfer to an open or semi-open "special institution."

And so in June 1945 he was taken from Grevebro to a place named Traspby. It is a country house, converted in recent years to fulfill its present function. That function is a remarkable one, for Traspby is a semi-open institution for abnormal criminals, including abnormal murderers. In few countries of the world is the public attitude toward crime and punishment yet enlightened enough for such an experiment. (In Britain, for example, "open prisons" are being increasingly used but only for "normal" or "star" offenders, including murderers, many of whom could, with perfect safety, be at liberty on parole.) Traspby is in beautiful country among fjords and pine woods. It is small, with only about 100 inmates and a staff half as numerous.

A determining factor in Horsten's progress at Traspby, was undoubtedly the influence of the governor and staff there. In so small an institution a governor-prisoner relationship becomes possible, indeed almost automatic. When Aake Horsten met the governer of Traspby his first impression was probably of a Bohemian, almost a dandy. The governor is a young man with an easy manner and an artist's interest in people. One of his articles of faith is that every criminal, like other human beings, has at least one constructive talent and inclination and that this "key interest"—though it often needs unearthing—can be developed almost without limit. He certainly went carefully into the question of Horsten's inclinations and hopes for the future. Among Horsten's numerous but mostly dilettante earlier enthusiasms he discovered a sustained interest in poetry and, rather unexpectedly, a more practical one in motor cars. The governor played an important part in persuading Horsten to take up motor engineering. Horsten did two years' technical reading, supplemented by practical work in the machine shop of the institution, and then worked happily in the garage. The governor had helped him to choose aright.

To those used to the comportment of most prison officials in Britain and the United States a surprising thing about the governor of Traspby's relations with the people under his charge would be the absence of any deferential or disciplinary element. He is punctilious in addressing each of them as "Mr." He does not expect himself to be addressed as "Sir" and makes this perfectly plain. When referring to his charges he talks about "the people," never about "the prisoners." The attitude is not personal eccentricity on his part but a normal part of Swedish prison practice. The underlying assumption is that enforced "respectfulness" impairs personal contact based on equality and sympathy and that the latter play an important part in any process of rehabilitation.

With only 100 inmates to supervise and a relatively large staff the governor of a modern Swedish special institution is in no sense overwhelmed with security problems—with possible escapes, outbreaks or mutinies. He has the opportunity and the environment in which to cultivate personal relations with every prisoner under his charge. Moreover, at Traspby—as indeed in most sectors of the Swedish penal system—all members of the staff are taught and encouraged to adopt a similar attitude and to become guides, counselors and friends to those in their charge, rather than watchdogs. In this kind of human atmosphere and in surroundings such as those of Traspby the reappraisal which a professional criminal has to make if he is to reform is clearly rendered less difficult than in the forbidding atmosphere of a maximum-security jail. Quite apart from the therapeutic attitude of governor and staff the institution is planned and constructed so as to offer hope to those who come there. There is a walled and guarded block (though the wall is not high); but in the neighboring fields stand two hostel-like unfenced buildings. One of them is guarded only at nighttime; the other has no guards by day or night. Each prisoner has the chance of graduating from the closed via the "semi-open" to the fully open block. The three buildings are—or can be—stages on the road back to freedom.

As we have seen, Horsten had never been a professional criminal. He was diagnosed as abnormal and probably psychopathic. We do not suggest that the "atmosphere of encouragement" at Traspby could have effected a direct cure of his abnormality. But that "atmosphere" certainly did not hinder, and it undoubtedly prevented a deterioration of his personality during imprisonment and—as we shall see—made his ultimate reintegration into society sure and successful.

Yet at Traspby, as in all prisons, however advanced and constructive, there were negative factors militating against the regeneration of offenders. Looking at the institution for a moment through the mind of Aake Horsten (a man of some mental caliber, however marked with psychopathy or neurosis that had preceded his crime), we see clearly that life there can have been only some degrees less enervating and demoralizing than in the closed prison from which he had come. His fellow inmates—as in the maximum-security jail—were mostly childlike or eccentric in the wearisome way of abnormal or psychopathic people of low intelligence. Most of them were egotistical or self-pitying.

Long confinement with such companions did not, however, erode Aake Horsten's personality, leaving him a passive or twisted creature; and this in the opinion of officials who knew him was due to the fact that regenerative influences outweighed demoralizing ones while he was in prison.

A particular cause of demoralization in captivity is broken contact with the normality of the outside world and one maiming by-product of this: sexual deprivation. Spiritual decay from these causes was averted in the case of Aake Horsten in rather dramatic fashion. In Sweden the system of leave and furlough for prisoners has for long been used exceedingly boldly. All people serving sentences, of whatever length, are automatically eligible for three days of leave or "furlough" after they have served six to ten months of a sentence. The furlough is then normally granted every four months. A prisoner can spend it anywhere he likes in Sweden. Traveling time is allowed, but prisoners have to save up part of their earnings* to pay for whatever journey they make. In the case of Horsten this furlough system made easier his eventual reintegration into society in a very direct and personal way.

He spent one of his furloughs at Upsala in the home of a professor under whom he had once studied. He had written to the professor from prison and been heartened by the kindly tone of the reply. It was in the professor's house that he met a Hungarian Jewish girl who was governess to the children. She had come to Sweden on a Red Cross transport three years earlier, after her liberation from a Nazi concentration camp. Swedish doctors had cured her of tuberculosis and she had since worked in Sweden, not wishing to return to Hungary under the Communists. Horsten had supper alone with her on the second evening of his "furlough," his host and hostess having been suddenly called away. The two got on well together. He did not tell her the facts about himself, but on his return to Traspby he wrote to her. Months later, when he was again on furlough, they met, by arrangement, in a small town and became engaged.

Sometime Horsten must have told the girl about his crime, for when the professor, having heard of the engagement, asked his governess in some perturbation whether she knew all about the man she smiled at his embarrass-

*Weekly earnings of $6 to $8 are normal.

ment and told him that she did. A year later Horsten was
granted twenty-four hours' leave from Traspby to get married in a neighboring village church.

Such engagements and marriages of offenders while they
are serving sentences are by no means uncommon in
Sweden. Public opinion has grown accustomed to them
and to the idea that, since they assist the social reintegration
of offenders, they are advantageous to society as well as
being humane.

I (Sington) met Horsten at Traspby not many months
after his marriage and five years after his admission into
the institution. It was a simple matter to arrange to talk
alone with him for nearly an hour in the office. In Sweden
no disciplinary regulation insulates the offender, like "an
infectious animal," against contact with people from the
outside world who try to see what happens to him in
prison. This is in contrast to Britain, where official rules
forbid interviews with prisoners except by difficult special
arrangement and under severe limitations. The assumption
in Sweden is that normal human intercourse is revitalizing
to the prisoner. The aim is to make normal, not to hurt,
humiliate or unnecessarily segregate.

Horsten shook hands with me with nervous friendliness.
He was a tall, burly figure in a brown leather windjammer
and the denim shirt and trousers of the institution. His
rather long, disheveled hair was gray. His nailed boots
clattered on the stone floor. He talked volubly but with
perceptible reserve. At that time he was obviously tense and
conscious of being "under observation." The parole board
was considering his possible release. I could see that he
was an intelligent man; and he talked readily about his
experiences in Asia twelve years before. He spoke, a
little excitedly, of Western contacts with aboriginal peoples and the resultant problems. He had none of the list-
lessness of the hopeless, worn-down prisoner broken by
captivity. He was not "beaten"; nevertheless, nine years'
loss of liberty can break a man's spirit. The governor of
Traspby was convinced that Horsten's personality had
remained unimpaired largely because of the furloughs or
leaves, and because these had led on to his engagement and
marriage.

When I asked him about his life in Traspby Horsten

rubbed his hand wearily across his eyes. "The worst of it is the sameness," he said. "It's not only the physical surroundings, but everyday listening to the same banal talk and obscene exchanges."

While we sat in the office the telephone rang. My tall interlocutor walked over to it eagerly and took a message for the governor. Obviously, this tiny exercise of responsibility was a rare and pleasurable assertion of personality.

Afterward he showed me the institution library. It is a very good one, stocked with scientific and technical works besides the literature of many countries. Horsten had been librarian for just over a year. He clearly enjoyed pointing out the different sections: Zoology, Astronomy, Russian novels, books by modern Swedish writers; but he was also tense and preoccupied—I suppose with the hope of freedom.

Horsten's room at that time was in the "fully open" cottage, a sanatoriumlike little building in the fields to which he had been promoted many months before in preparation for his release. His room was pleasantly furnished with vases of flowers, cushions on the chairs, a radio set and a shelf of books (prisoners are allowed to furnish their rooms if they choose to). He showed me a photograph of his "furlough wedding."

We strolled back across the fields to the institution office, past the bungalow area where the staff of the institution and their families live. A fair-haired child of about seven (I discovered afterward that she was the daughter of one of the warders) ran out and spoke to Horsten. Then she walked a short distance with us, holding his hand.

Horsten was indeed released eight months later, just one year before his minimum sentence had run (when he was told the news he wept for joy). The decision was not taken without very careful consideration by at least three bodies: the Traspby Institution Board, consisting of two prison officers and three outside experts; the Swedish Internment Board (made up of officials, a judge, a psychiatrist and a Member of Parliament); and the Ministry of Justice. The ultimate responsibility for such decisions in Sweden rests with the Minister of Justice.

The reports of the after-care workers who supervised and kept contact with Horsten during his first years of freedom show that he settled down satisfactorily. An uncle bought him a small garage shortly before his release and he is running it successfully. His marriage is to all appearances a happy one.

There are several morals to be drawn from the case. First and foremost, it contradicts the paradoxical assumption of those who, while they hold that a "mad dog" murderer should be considered sane and fully responsible for his actions, also maintain that he must forever remain a danger to society and on this ground demand either that he be executed or imprisoned under maximum-security conditions for the rest of his natural life. Aake Horsten is by no means the only murderer of the "mad dog" kind who has successfully re-entered society in Sweden. Out of ten psychopaths convicted of murder between 1930 and 1945, for example, seven had been released by 1953. Moreover—and this is of decisive importance—there has for decades been no instance in Sweden of a released murderer's repeating his crime.

How was Aake Horsten helped? It may well be—the majority of prison administrators seem to think so—that the sort of aggressive psychopathy that afflicted him sooner or later "burns itself out" automatically in captivity. But a mere "burned out" psychopath is likely to be a man broken in spirit, undermined in intelligence, hopelessly "institutionalized," of no further danger to society, but of no use to it, either, and of no use to himself. This is not, and never was, Aake Horsten. We may assume, therefore, that he made some effort to cure himself, and that he was encouraged and assisted in this effort by what might be described as a therapy of kindness. It was an effort which, if successful, was always bound to be rewarded not only by his release but by his planned reintegration in a free society.

We do not suggest that kindness, however imaginatively and intelligently applied by a prison governor in an attempt to build up the self-respect and develop the constructive drives of those committed to his charge, can in itself be regarded as a guaranteed cure for aggressive psychopathy or for any other sort of mental abnormality that makes a murderer. And we suspect that Aake Horsten's rehabilitation might have been achieved sooner had he received something more scientific in the way of treatment.

In this respect, indeed, the Swedish penal system falls considerably short of perfection, because its facilities for the psychiatric diagnosis of offenders are not, illogically enough, matched by facilities for the psychiatric treatment of such offenders afterward. Institutions like Traspby, for all that their administration is exceptionally humane, are still to a considerable degree punitive rather than curative in design or at least tradition. Nor—we might suggest resultantly—have they as yet had any marked success in solving the problem of non-homicidal recidivism, which is, in fact, their chief concern.

There are signs, however, that increasing use will be made of modern psychotherapeutic techniques to combat crime, and to prevent murder before it happens, alike in Sweden and in certain other European countries which are pursuing, broadly speaking, the same advanced penal policy. Further, it would seem only a logical development of this policy for all crime to be treated, eventually, clinically rather than punitively.

In this context it is worth drawing attention to a remarkable pioneering experiment that was started in Holland some two years ago. This is the Van der Hoeven Clinic at Utrecht, where seventy abnormal offenders, of both sexes, receive four or five hours of group therapy or individual psychoanalysis every week—an intensity of treatment which compares favorably with that offered in the world's most heavily endowed private institutions for mentally sick people. Conditions at the Utrecht clinic, moreover, are as free from restraint as possible. No prison clothes are worn, as they are still at Traspby, and no purely disciplinary regulations are in force. About half the inmates work in town. Any of them may be allowed to go out shopping, for recreation in the evenings, or on home leave, provided he or she is judged by the clinic staff to be fit and safe to do so.

Among the seventy inmates of the Van der Hoeven Clinic are eight murderers. One of them shot his homosexual partner; another strangled a twelve-year-old girl. There is also a patient there who, during the Second World War, worked for the German occupation forces as a concentration-camp guard and committed atrocities, including homicide, against his fellow Dutchmen. In Holland, apparently, it has now come to be realized that the proper approach even to so-called crimes against humanity is the curative one.

THE MENTAL HEALTH OF THE HUTTERITES
/Joseph W. Eaton and Robert J. Weil

Is modern life driving many people insane? Would insanity diminish or disappear if mankind could return to a simpler life? From Virgil to Thoreau the philosophers have had little doubt about the answer to these questions, and some modern anthropologists have offered data which seem to bear them out. They say they have found mental disorders rare among technologically primitive peoples. For instance, recent cursory studies of the people on Okinawa and of the natives of Kenya have suggested that these groups are virtually free of some psychoses. Contrasted with this picture is the civilized U. S., where some authorities have estimated that one person in 10 suffers an incapacitating mental illness at one time or another during his life.

Whether a culture can cause psychoses is not easy to discover, but one way to get at the question is to examine the mental health of a secure, stable society. The Hutterites, an isolated Anabaptist religious sect who inhabit a section of the North American Middle West, provide an ideal social laboratory of this kind. These people live a simple, rural life, have a harmonious social order and provide every member with a high level of economic security from the womb to the tomb. They are a homogeneous group, free from many of the tensions of the American melting-pot culture. And they have long been considered almost immune to mental disorders. In a study during the 1930s Lee Emerson Deets said that psychoses were almost nonexistent among them. The Manitoba Provincial Legislature received in 1947 a report which said that the Hutterites "do not contribute to the overcrowding of mental hospitals, since the mental security derived from their system results in a complete absence of mental illness."

Three years ago a research team consisting of the writers of this article—a sociologist and a psychiatrist—and the Harvard University clinical psychologists Bert Kaplan and Thomas Plant undertook a more intensive study of the Hutterites' mental health. The investigation was administered by Wayne University and financed largely by the National Institute for Mental Health. The Hutterite people cooperated generously. In the interest of science they opened their "family closets" and helped us to obtain a census of every person in their community who was then or had ever been mentally ill.

The Hutterites, whose origin as a sect goes back to 1528, are a closely knit group of German stock who had lived together in neighboring villages in Europe for a long time before they migrated to the U. S. from southern Russia between 1874 and 1877. The immigrants—101 married couples and their children—settled in eastern South Dakota. Their descendants have now spread over a wide area in the Dakotas, Montana and the prairie provinces of Canada. They live in 98 hamlets, which they call colonies. But they remain a remarkably cohesive group; each grownup is intimately acquainted with hundreds of other members in the settlements. The Hutterites believe it sinful to marry outside the sect, and all of the present descendants (8,542 in 1950) stem from the original 101 couples.

Cardinal principles of the Hutterites are pacifism, adult baptism, the communal ownership of all property and simple living. Jewelry, art and overstuffed chairs are regarded as sinful luxuries. Radio sets and the movies are taboo. Children are the only possessions to which there is no limit: the average completed family has more than 10. The Hutterites cling to their own customs and are considered "different" by their neighbors. But they are not primitive in the ethnographic sense. They get a grammar-school education and speak English fluently. They read daily newspapers, have a telephone in most colonies and own trucks. Since their own members are not encouraged to seek formal education beyond the primary grades, there are no doctors or lawyers among them, but they utilize such professional services from outside. Each hamlet engages in a highly mechanized form of agriculture. Their business with the "outside world," as Hutterites are apt to refer to their neighbors, usually exceeds $100,000 per year per colony.

On the surface it seemed that the Hutterites did indeed enjoy extraordinary freedom from mental illness. We did not find a single Hutterite in a mental hospital. The 55 outside doctors patronized by these people said they showed fewer psychosomatic and nervous symptoms than their neighbors of other faiths. But this appearance of unusual mental health did not stand the test of an intensive screening of the inhabitants, carried out colony by colony. Among the 8,542 Hutterites we discovered a total of 199 (one in 43) who either had active symptoms of a mental disorder or had recovered from such an illness. Of these illnesses 53 were diagnosed as psychoses, all but five of them of a functional (non-organic) character.

In short, the Hutterite culture provides no immunity to mental disorders. The existence of these illnesses in so secure and stable a social order suggests that there may be genetic, organic or constitutional predispositions to psychosis which will cause breakdowns among individuals in any society, no matter how protective and well integrated.

The distribution of symptoms among the Hutterites was quite unusual. There were few cases diagnosed as schizophrenia, although elsewhere this is the most common psychosis. Only nine Hutterites had ever manifested the pattern of delusions, hallucinations and other recognized symptoms of schizophrenia; the group lifetime rate was 2.1 per 1,000 persons aged 15 and over. On the other hand, the proportion of manic-depressive reactions among those with mental disorders was ususual; this disorder accounted for 39 of the 53 psychoses, and the rate was 9.3 per 1,000 aged 15 and over. The name of the disorder is misleading; manic-depressives often are not dangerous to other persons, and none of the Hutterite patients was. Their symptoms were predominantly depressive. There was much evidence of irrational guilt feelings, self-blame, withdrawal from normal social relations and marked slowing of mental and motor activities. Five of the patients had suicidal impulses. Two Hutterites had actually killed themselves.

The fact that in the Hutterite society manic-depression is more common than schizophrenia, reversing the situation in all other populations for whom comparable data have been obtained, suggests that cultural factors do have some influence on the manifestation of psychoses. A Johns Hopkins University team of researchers who recently made an extensive analysis of mental hospital statistics concluded that schizophrenic symptoms are most common among unskilled laborers, farmers, urban residents in rooming-house sections and other persons who are relatively isolated socially, while manic-depressive reactions are more prevalent among professional, socially prominent and religious persons, who have a stronger need to live up to social expectations. Our data fit this theory well. Religion is the focus of the Hutterite way of life. Their whole educational system, beginning with nursery school, orients the people to look for blame and guilt within themselves rather than in others. Physical aggression is taboo. Like the Catholic orders, Hutterites own everything in the name of their church. They eat in a common dining room, pay medical bills from the communal treasury and work at jobs assigned to them by managers elected by the males of the colony. The group, rather than the individual, comes first.

In projective psychological tests the Hutterites, like other groups, show antisocial and aggressive impulses, but in their daily lives they repress these effectively. Their history showed no case of murder, arson, severe physical assault or sex crime. No individual warranted the diagnosis of psychopath. Divorce, desertion, separation or chronic marital discord were rare. Only five marriages were known to have gone on the rocks since 1875. Personal violence and childish or amoral forms of behavior among adults were uncommon, even in persons with psychotic episodes. There were no psychoses stemming from drug addiction, alcoholism or syphilis, although these disorders account for approximately 10 per cent of all first admissions to state mental hospitals in the U. S. In general our study tends to confirm the theory of many social scientists and public health officials that a favorable cultural setting can largely prevent these forms of social maladjustment.

All this does not entirely rule out the possibility that genetic factors play some part in the unusual proportions of manic-depression and schizophrenia symptoms among the Hutterites. There is some evidence that these disorders tend to run in families. The Hutterites are biologically inbred. Three surnames—Hofer, Waldner and Wipt—accounted for nearly half of all families in 1950. It is possible that the Hutterite group has a disproportionate number of persons genetically prone to becoming depressed—if there is such a predisposition. A team of Harvard University workers is planning to make a follow-up genetic study of the Hutterites.

The question of the relation of mental disorders to culture is difficult to investigate quantitatively. No country has a really complete record of mental disorders among its population. Censuses of patients in mental hospitals are almost worthless for this purpose; they leave out patients who

have recovered and mentally ill persons who never come
to the attention of doctors.

The Hutterite study attempted to track down every case
of a mental disorder, past or present, hospitalized or not, in
the whole living population. It probably succeeded in finding virtually all the cases of psychosis. Similar studies have
been made of seven other communities in various parts of
the world.

On this basis the Hutterites apparently rank second highest among the eight populations in the rate of psychosis, being exceeded only by an area in the north of Sweden. But
there is considerable evidence that the count of mental disorders was less complete in the other seven groups; that is,
in those studies many cases were missed because their illness
was not a matter of public record, while the Hutterite population was thoroughly screened. It is probable that the psychosis rate among the Hutterites is actually low compared
with that in other populations. It seems to be only one third
as high as the rate in New York State, for instance, taking
into consideration the common estimate that even in that
State (where mental hospital facilities are among the most
extensive) there is at least one undetected psychotic person for every one in an institution.

The statistical comparison of mental disorder rates has
many limitations, but it does offer several promising leads
to the puzzle that the problem of functional psychoses presents to modern science. Among the Hutterites, as in all the
other populations, the frequency of psychoses increases
rapidly with age. Among those who showed manic-depressive reactions, females predominated. The social biology
of the aging process and of sex probably holds worthwhile
clues to some of the problems of cause and treatment.

Neuroses were more common than psychoses among the
Hutterites, as elsewhere. Four fifths of the 69 discovered
neurotics were female. Melancholy moods were regarded
by teachers as the number one emotional problem of Hutterite school children. Hutterite neurotics showed the same
tendency as psychotics to take out mental stress on themselves instead of on others. Self-blame and remorse were
common, as were psychosomatic headaches, backaches and
hysteric paralysis of a limb. There was little scapegoating or
projection of hostile feelings by imputing them to others.

There is no evidence of any unusual concentration of
hereditary mental defects in the Hutterite population. A

total of 51 persons was diagnosed as mentally deficient, and 20 normal persons had suffered epileptic attacks. These epilepsy and mental deficiency rates are not high in comparison with other groups.

How does the Hutterite culture deal with mental illness? Although it does not prevent mental disorders, it provides a highly therapeutic atmosphere for their treatment. The onset of a symptom serves as a signal to the entire community to demonstrate support and love for the patient. Hutterites do not approve of the removal of any member to a "strange" hospital, except for short periods to try shock treatments. All patients are looked after by the immediate family. They are treated as ill rather than "crazy." They are encouraged to participate in the normal life of their family and community, and most are able to do some useful work. Most of the manic-depressive patients get well, but among neurotic patients recovery is less common. Most of the epileptics were either cured or took drugs which greatly relieved the condition. No permanent stigma is attached to patients after recovery. The traumatic social consequences which a mental disorder usually brings to the patient, his family and sometimes his community are kept to a minimum by the patience and tolerance with which most Hutterites regard these conditions. This finding supports the theory that at least some of the severely antisocial forms of behavior usually displayed by psychotic and disturbed patients are not an inherent attribute. They may be reflections of the impersonal manner of handling patients in most mental hospitals, of their emotional rejection by the family and of their stigmatization in the community.

In the Hutterite social order people are exposed to a large number of common experiences. Their indoctrination begins in infancy and is continued by daily religious instruction and later by daily church-going. Hutterites spend their entire life within a small and stable group. Their homes consist only of bedrooms, all furnished in an almost identical manner. The women take turns cooking and baking for everybody. Everyone wears the same kind of clothes; the women, for example, all let their hair grow without cutting, part it in the middle and cover it with a black kerchief with white polka dots. The Hutterite religion provides definite answers for many of the problems that come up.

Despite this uniformity in the externals of living, Hutterites are not stereotyped personalities. Differences in genetic, organic and psychological factors seem to be sufficiently powerful to produce an infinite variety of behavior, even in a social order as rigid as this one. It appears that the nightmare of uniformity sketched in George Orwell's *Nineteen Eighty-four* is actually unachievable in a living society. At least our study in depth disclosed no simple standardization of personality structure among Hutterites.

There is considerable objective evidence that the great majority of Hutterites have a high level of psychological adjustment. Their misfortunes and accidents are alleviated greatly by the group's system of mutual aid. The sick, the aged, the widows and orphans are well taken care of. In the last three decades only about 100 persons (most of them male) have left the community permanently. During World War II about one third of the men between the ages of 20 and 40 served in camps for conscientious objectors; more than 98 per cent of them ultimately returned to their colonies.

There has not, however, been any rush of applicants from outside to join the Hutterite sect. Mental health involves value judgments and depends on what people want from life. Only 19 adults have joined the sect in America during the last few decades. The austere and puritanical customs of the sect impose restrictions which even the members, who learn to accept them, regard as a "narrow path." Their culture is therapeutic only for conformists. There are occasional rebels; the more able ones find a means of expressing themselves by becoming leaders, the less brilliant have difficulties.

The survival of this sixteenth-century peasant culture in the heart of the most twentieth-century-minded continent is a vivid demonstration of the power of values and beliefs. Although our data on the Hutterites' mental disorders clearly demonstrate the inadequacy of a purely cultural approach to the problem of mental health, they do show that culture has a large influence in shaping personality. Psychiatrists who work exclusively in hospitals or clinics cannot see the whole patient as he functions in his total environment. Our findings lead us to conclude that the social relations of the patient and his culture, including the things in which he believes, deserve more attention from psychiatric researchers and clinicians than is commonly given to them.

ARGUMENT OF STRAIN
/R. M. Titmuss

It is no exaggeration to say that in 1939 the leading mental health authorities in Britain feared a tremendous increase in emotional disorders and neurotic illnesses as soon as the Germans started to bomb. That was the essence of the advice which they voluntarily gave to the Ministry of Health. But the Government, while also taking a gloomy view—a view which found expression in many acts of commission and omission—did not go so far as the psychiatrists who, in fact, suggested that mental casualties might outnumber physical casualties by two or three to one.

It need hardly be said that what actually happened completely falsified not only the forecasts of the psychiatrists but the less pessimistic forebodings of officials. It is important, in trying to understand why these forecasts were wrong, to understand also how they came to be made. In attempting some tentative explanation, a generous allowance must above all be made for the oppressive atmosphere of the times in which these psychiatrists—along with everyone else—lived. They were as sensitive as other people to the pressures and persuasions of a world afraid of war. They may, indeed, have been more deeply affected than most people because the meaning and consequences of air bombardment to civilian society were to them a matter of great concern.

How powerful these contemporary forces were in molding opinion on questions relating to individual or group behavior may be illustrated by two simple examples taken from the early war years. During these years, when the life of the nation was in danger, values changed rapidly, yet the process was so imperceptible that many people were unaware of the effect it had on their attitude to other people and to questions of behavior in a society at war. For instance, what was regarded in one year as merely bad behavior was censured more severely in the next. Some evidence in support of this statement comes from the two examples. First, the proportion of civilian prisoners punished, particularly for "idleness," rose significantly after the outbreak of war, and again in 1941 after the air raids. Secondly, the proportion of boys aged under fourteen years who were ordered corporal punishment for offences of various kinds by magistrates' courts, which was falling before the war, rose during the two years of bombing (1940–41) by over six hundred per cent. Thereafter, the proportion declined rapidly.

These glimpses of the moral effects of a nation conducting war—conducting it alone and hard-pressed by the enemy—suggest that the aspirations and prejudices of the moment may have been reflected in the birching of more little boys. And so, in a similar kind of way, the national temper during the fateful months which preceded and followed the Munich crisis in 1938 may have influenced the psychiatrists. The events of this period forced a great many people to face as never before the possibility of air bombardment. Until then, it was something that could be avoided. Now the possibility had to be accepted. But emotionally the horror was still rejected, more especially by those with powerful imaginations. It was at this time that the leading mental health authorities in London expressed their worst forebodings in a memorandum to the Ministry of Health. These contemporary influences, while important, do not of course fully explain the origins of the alarm expressed by the psychiatrist and Government official alike. Other and even more complicated forces were at work which cannot, however, be discussed here.

Up to the end of 1948, no evidence was forthcoming to suggest that there had been any dramatic increase in neurotic illnesses or mental disorders in Britain during the war. The air raids of 1940–41 did not lead to a rise in the number of patients with such illnesses attending hospitals and clinics; in fact, there was a decrease. There was no indication of an increase in insanity, the number of suicides fell, the statistics of drunkenness went down by more than one-half, there was much less disorderly behavior in the streets and public places, while only the juvenile delinquency figures registered a rise. But these figures, it is well to remember, are not suitable for employment as an index of either juvenile or adult neurosis.

One criterion used to estimate the morale of a group during wartime was the amount of absence from work immediately after a city had been heavily bombed. It was thought that if the vast majority turned up at the factories and shops there was not likely to be much wrong with morale. There may have been more anxiety, more general depression, but attendance at work ruled out an immediate collapse in standards or resort to what the psychiatrists called "infantile security."

The Research and Experiments Department of the Ministry of Home Security studied this question in detail. The main conclusion of all the Department's investigations (which covered many raided areas) was that absence from work for personal reasons was closely associated with the amount of house damage. No other factor was important. A worker whose home was rendered permanently uninhabitable lost on the average about six days from his job. This does not seem an unreasonable amount of time to spend finding a fresh home, and gathering the family together again.

An outbreak of trekking, of nightly movements from target areas by thousands of people, which gave rise to much concern in the spring of 1941, was also investigated. It was found that, except for workers whose houses were seriously damaged, no more time (in absence from work) was lost by those who trekked as compared with those who continued to sleep at home. The fact that many people chose to trudge off into the country each evening did not, by itself, imply a deterioration in morale. These people were afraid of the bombs; of dark hours of wakefulness, of listening, sometimes tense and sometimes nodding, for the drawn-out whine, and then the rumbling murmur of a house collapsing in the blackness. Above all, they wanted sleep; for sleep was forgetfulness and rest. And to sleep—if only in a barn—was to behave normally; to lie awake was abnormal. So they "dispersed" themselves at night-time in much the same way as armies spread out their troops and transport as a precaution against air attack.

Trekking ensured for most of those who undertook it a good night's rest. The importance given to sleep during this period by the civilian population was sensible, for it was part of what Mr. Churchill called "making a job of this business of living and working under fire." The tubes and the public shelters in London were other means whereby many people were able to sleep soundly. They were to Londoners what trekking was to the inhabitants of Plymouth,

Hull and Merseyside. As dusk approached each evening, long queues of people, laden with bedding, filed toward the tubes and public shelters. Inside, a preference for informal organization, based on give-and-take and good behavior, manifested itself.

Yet, for many years before 1940, the place of the public shelter in civil defense policy had often been misunderstood. The Government feared to encourage a "deep shelter mentality"; it did not want a lot of "timorous troglodytes" on its hands. By 1940, the question of deep shelters had become so entangled with politics as a result of the activities of the Communists that few people could look at the problem objectively. The function of the shelter as a safety-valve for the badly housed, as a place to sleep in, and as a means of providing a feeling of warmth and security for those who found comfort in the actual presence of their fellows, was not properly grasped. This was partly because all-night raids were not expected, and partly because it was not realized that many of the poor of London did not violently object to sleeping together in rows; they had lived too long on top of one another to mind about any lack of privacy.

But, in fact, only a minority of people used these communal, underground refuges. At no period during the war did more than about one person in seven in Metropolitan London spend the night in a tube station or public shelter. This peak figure was reached some time during September–October 1940 when Londoners were being "battle-conditioned." In November, when the proportion had declined to one person in eight, the basements, railway arches, trenches and other public shelters were filled only to about forty per cent of capacity. At this time, eight per cent of the population were in public shelters, four per cent in the tubes, one per cent in surface shelters—making thirteen per cent in communal shelters—while twenty-seven per cent were in Anderson and other domestic shelters. Thus, among every ten persons six were sleeping in their homes in November 1940.

In heavily bombed areas like Bermondsey, with many old, decaying and shaky houses, one-quarter of the people stayed in their homes, and another quarter slept in Anderson or surface shelters. The remainder (except for five per cent on civil defense duties or night work) went to railway arches, tube stations and public shelters of various kinds.

After three months of the London raids, fewer people used these refuges. A survey of several South London boroughs, which were attacked in December 1940, showed that only about one-half of the number of people who had shelter accommodation within very easy reach actually made use of it, although they all had ample time to reach shelter between the sounding of the "alert" and the first fall of bombs. It was estimated by the Ministry of Home Security that if these shelters had been used by those nearby the number of people killed and seriously injured among those exposed to 250 kg. bombs would have been reduced by one-half. By the beginning of 1941, most Londoners had probably reached some sort of working, though no doubt uncomfortable, arrangement with the conditions of life imposed by nightly air raids. In April 1941, the report of a survey in Islington and Southwark by the Ministry of Home Security concluded that "very little notice is taken of an alert without noise." A number of persons moved from an upper to a lower floor, and a small number went to shelters.

It cannot be assumed because there was no panic, no rush to safety, that there was no anxiety. There was without a doubt a great deal, for fears and heartaches were inevitable in the circumstances, and many private terrors must have been stifled in the darkness. It was, as Sansom writes, "a time of raised eyes and apprehension, of ears opened to the lance-like descending whistle of high-explosives (a sound that made the sky seem so very high and wide) and the dull, smothered boom that had shattered some house somewhere away out in the darkened streets." If they were not to behave as the psychiatrists had expected, most people had therefore to come to terms with bombing. No community could withstand a warning of danger once (on an average) every thirty-six hours for over five years without coming to terms in some way or another.

For the family, one form of adjustment to the emergencies of air warfare was to divide, and for mothers and children to move to safer areas. For those members of the family left behind, at work, on Home Guard or Civil Defense duties, this allayed some of the anxieties. The great merit of the Government's evacuation scheme was that it did offer an outlet for a considerable section of the population, particularly the children. The Government was wise to retain the voluntary character of this conduit pipe to safety, despite the calls for compulsion from Parliament at the time of Dunkirk and again in the autumn of 1940. The scheme remained voluntary throughout all the raids, and it continued to function as a safety-valve for many Londoners. In such a war, safety-valves were indispensable to a society which placed more emphasis on cooperation than on compulsion. The evacuation scheme was one such outlet, shelters another, trekking a third, while the power of public opinion to force the Government to mend its ways and to clean up the rest centers and shelters, for instance, was the fourth and, perhaps, the most important.

People could use these temporary exits from danger—if they wanted to. That was the important fact for the majority of families; the knowledge that these facilities were available if the strain became unbearable; the knowledge that compulsion to stay in their homes and run the risk of bombing was not being enforced by the Government, by poverty or by other factors. That is why the Government was right to bow in acquiescence when Londoners took over the tube stations in September 1940. That is why the evacuation scheme was not a failure, even though the number who used it continued to fall as the months of bombing went by.

It has already been pointed out that a great many people chose not to make use of the public shelters or the tube stations during the winter of 1940–41. To this fact must be added the further fact that fewer people left London during the nine months of air attack than during the two or three weeks before and just after the outbreak of war. The area of Greater London lost about twelve per cent of its civilian population between June 1940 and June 1941, as against seventeen per cent between June 1939 and 30th September 1939.

The London population of September 1940 was not, of course, composed of exactly the same people as a year earlier. The comparison is not, therefore, of like with like; for there may have been a section who needed evacuation more than the rest. If this section—which, judging by the amount and speed of the return movement, seems to have been relatively small—left London in 1939 and stayed away, then it is arguable that the September 1940 population had already been, to some extent, sifted and selected as resistant to evacuation. But much of this is supposition. What does stand out is the order of magnitude of the two figures—the fact that 500,000 fewer people left Greater London during the bombing of 1940–41 than at the outbreak of war. In some senses, the fantasy of air attack may well have been worse than the reality, partly because fantasy seldom provides for the relief of tension through action. Moreover, to most adults the world of fantasy is a lonely world; unlike action, it does not usually permit cooperation and friendliness.

No objective or comprehensive explanation can be given of all the reasons, and combination of reasons, trivial and important, rational and irrational, which led so many families to decide during 1940–41 to stay where they were. There was no single or simple pattern of motives. A few good reasons may, however, be mentioned in general and more or less speculative terms.

Many parents knew that they could send their children away if they decided to change their minds. But some—and especially the mothers—had already experienced evacuation, and for many that was enough. For these and other parents, the shelters, both public and domestic, offered an alternative to evacuation and, what was particularly important, a way of keeping the family together. By the end of 1940, the stable base of the family seemed even more worth while when external danger had been experienced, for by then the comfort which the members of the family could give each other had been sensed and appreciated. Separation was harder to bear when familiarity with bombing had bred a certain philosophy of adjustment, and when danger to life had brought a greater cohesion to society in general and to the family in particular.

In the circumstances of 1940, the bases of sound morale among the civilian population rested on something more than the primary needs of life. Of course, the maintenance of food supplies, the provision and repair of homes, and security of employment were always of first importance. But other things vital in time of war mattered no less. Leadership was one, the sense of common effort and sacrifice was another. Self-control was easier when there was no awareness of injustice arising from the way in which the primary wants were met. The knowledge that large numbers of those who were privileged in the community were also carrying on with their work and facing the risks that ordinary people faced, the knowledge that such facilities as the evacuation and shelter schemes were available and were not limited to particular groups—here were important foundations of morale. The universal availability of services which often were not universally used had the function of "shock-absorption."

The rest centers, the feeding schemes, the casualty services, the compensation grants, and the whole apparatus of the post-raid services both official and voluntary occupied this role of absorbing shock. They took the edge off the calamities of damage and destruction; they could not prevent, but they helped to reduce, a great deal of distress. Like the civil defense services, these schemes encouraged people to feel that they were not forgotten. They rendered much less likely (in William James' phrase) an "unguaranteed existence," with all its anxieties, its corruptions and its psychological maladies.

What this period of the war meant to a great many people was less social disparagement. There was nothing to be ashamed of in being "bombed out" by the enemy. Public sympathy with, and approval of, families who suffered in the raids was in sharp contrast to the low social evaluation accorded to those who lost in material standards through being unemployed during the nineteen-thirties. The civilian war of 1939–45, with its many opportunities for service in civil defense and other schemes, also helped to satisfy an often inarticulate need; the need to be a wanted member of society. Circumstances were thus favorable to fuller self-expression, for there was plenty of scope for relieving a sense of inferiority and failure.

Looking back on these events after a lapse of many years, it could conceivably be argued that to some people the air raids brought security—not the security which spells passive acquiescence, but that which allows and encourages spontaneity. The onset of air raids followed a long period of unemployment. One thing that unemployment had not stimulated was an active body or mind. It might be suggested—though it cannot yet be asserted—that the absence of an increase in neurotic illness among the civilian population during the war was connected with the fact that to many people the war brought useful work and an opportunity to play an active part within the community. The proximity of death, the spread of physical hardship, and the ubiquity of destructive forces which were more intelligible to the ordinary man than the working of economic laws, gave existence a different meaning, and old fears and responsibilities less significance. In the transparency of life that marked the days of bombing, wrote Miss Bowen, "the wall between the living and the living became less solid as the wall between the living and the dead thinned." New aims for which to live, work that satisfied a larger number of needs, a more cohesive society, fewer lonely people; all these elements helped to offset the circumstances which often lead to neurotic illness.

Some of these elements had been manifest during the First World War. After 1918, a Government report drew attention to a remarkable fall in the claims for sickness benefit from the civilian population during the period of hostilities. This was attributed to a universal "will to work" which, under the stress of national necessity, dominated the people during the years when "the fate of the country hung in the balance." Lasswell, writing some years later on the significance and purposefulness of life in wartime, gave full rein to his imagination: "men with uncongenial spouses, wives with uncongenial husbands, youths with suppressed ambition, elderly men with their boredoms and faint yearnings for adventure, childless women and some wifeless men, the discredited ones who pine for a fresh deal in the game of life; all, and many more, found peace from mental fight."

The Second World War, while providing many opportunities for people to be useful members of a society with a single-hearted aim, was much less romantic than the first. It was also a longer war encompassing far more people; it dawdled intolerably between phases of action; it was more sternly and austerely conducted, and, except for some of the selfish ones, it was a more uncomfortable, physically upsetting war than 1914–18. In short, it imposed on a much larger part of the population the need to make a greater degree of adjustment in their personal lives for a much longer period.

The reaction to air raids by the mass of the people rested, in large measure, on this matter of adjustment. The capacity to adjust, and the extent to which people did in fact adjust themselves, depended on many factors. Some of the essential requirements for the development of sound morale have already been mentioned; leadership, an equitable sharing-out of food, shelter and social services, a job to do in a stable economy, and the provision of social safety-valves ranging from voluntary evacuation schemes to various mechanisms whereby public opinion could be effectively expressed. But these, by themselves, were not enough.

Many people were helped to withstand the grossly abnormal situation of continuous air bombardment by being among their families and friends. The individual's responsibility to his family, whose respect he valued, was thus encouraged to develop its maximum strength. This applied in particular to the poorer sections of the population, for among those with little property and social esteem, family members and family relationships are extremely important. With his own family the individual is, and what is more feels like, "somebody."

The maintenance of physical contact between the members of a social unit also helped to meet another imperative need in time of war; the need to be related to the world outside, to ideas, values and social patterns that bestow a sense of "belonging." When threatened with death, moral aloneness becomes to man even more intolerable than in peace-time, and perhaps more hurtful than physical isolation. In certain of these respects, the civilian had advantages over the soldier, separated as he was from his family and often from his social group.

Yet, before the war, some psychiatrists had considered that soldiers might stand the strain of air attack better than civilians. But the truth may be found to point in the reverse direction when all the evidence has eventually been sifted. The civilian was freer to adjust himself than the soldier; in his environment there was often more scope for individual responsibility to flourish, and he was not usually cut off, as the soldier was, from his family.

It was just this factor of family separation which had received insufficient attention before 1939 from the psychiatrists and those experts in mental health who advised the Government. The most prevalent and the most marked symptom of psychological disturbance among the civilian population during the war was not panic or hysteria but bed-wetting. Its importance as a social problem was demonstrated as a result of the evacuation of children, and observations showed that it was primarily caused by separation from the family.

Many people discovered for themselves during the raids that the best prescription for stability was to keep the family together. Resistance to evacuation grew in strength after the first few weeks of London's bombing until, by November 1940, almost as many children were returning to London as were leaving. And this was while London was still being bombed nearly every night. So poor was the response to the Government's repeated plea to "get the children away" that compulsory measures were thought, at one time, to be inevitable. The refusal of wives and mothers to be separated from their husbands and their older children was even more marked.

All this is understandable if it is accepted that a stable society rests on the basis of stable family life. A threat to society implies a threat to the family, and when the physical hazards of air attack were present, families naturally tended to close their ranks. Staying at home, keeping the family together, and pursuing many of the ordinary activities of life made adjustment easier. Men and women clung to these things, for they symbolized normal life, and helped them to minimize the abnormal situation.

Pessimistic views before the war about civilian morale were partly due to the assumption that air raids would tax the limits of potential adjustment. Events showed that most people had a greater capacity to adjust themselves than was thought possible: a tough resilience to the changed conditions of life imposed on them. Nor was it realized that there would be such a widespread and spontaneous development of ways of keeping up morale; friendliness, the constant talk about bombs, the attitude of "if it's got your number on it," and a preoccupation with apparently frivolous activities like going to the pub as usual or having a permanent wave.

There were also compensations about this civilian war, as Sansom noted in his story of Westminster. Certain responsibilities were pushed off or postponed. Others were assumed, but of a different, a more vivid, a shorter-lived nature. "There are sensations of new virility, of paradoxical freedom, and of a rather bawdy 'live-for-today' philosophy. New tolerances are born between people; offsetting the paleness of worn nerves and the lining of sorrow there occurs a marvelous incidence of smiles where smiles have never been before: an unsettling vista of smiles, for one wondered how unsympathetic life could have been before, one was ashamed to reflect that it had needed a war to disinter the state of everyday comradeship."

It was not altogether remarkable that people who were

dug out of the ruins of their homes first asked, not for food or safety, but for their false teeth. Nor was it just an odd streak of personality that made mothers in rest centers and shelters more worried about awkward behavior by their children than about death. The only possible way—as these mothers found—of dealing with death was to ignore it. Keeping ledgers up to date, worrying about false teeth, and correcting the manners of children affirmed the individual's confidence in life and, in the process, maintained morale.

While a few brief and hesitant reasons have here been offered to explain the absence of any breakdown in mental health during the air battles of the Second World War they do not rule out the possibility of some harmful psychological effects. Anxiety may have been temporarily suppressed; conflicts with "conscience" may have been masked, and it is conceivable that the effects of air bombardment could manifest themselves among some people after, and not during, the war. Moreover, and taking a longer view, it could be said that the neuroses of one generation may be an expression of the mental condition of an earlier one. But what form all these troubles would take, if they did appear, is not for the present writer to say; for the problem cannot be studied without reference, not only to air raids, but to all the other consequences of a long war and a difficult period of adjustment to peace.

THE INDIVIDUAL AND THE COMMUNITY
/Murray Weingarten

Community cooperation in the creation of goods and services and a framework of complete social and economic security are in themselves great advances over forms of society which sanction gross and unfair relations among men and which deprive some people of the minimum prerequisites for decent living. A modern philosophy of life, however, cannot content itself with equality and security alone. Our generation, perhaps more than all others, has witnessed the creation of chains of bondage and horror in the name of equality and economic security. An examination of the mechanics of kibbutz operation alone, therefore, offers an incomplete picture of the system, for these mechanics cannot be judged apart from the fundamental ethical and social principles which are part of kibbutz belief. This kind of dichotomy is impossible in discussing kibbutz government, work organization, education, and the system of distribution of goods and services. Particularly is it impossible in a discussion of the relationship between the individual kibbutz member and the community as a whole, and, continuing from there, of the relationship between the individual kibbutz and the kibbutz movement, the State of Israel and the Zionist movement.

Early kibbutz pioneers envisioned their project as the creation of an instrument of Zionist colonization and a socially just society, the epitome of Jewish national rebirth in Palestine, and a collectivist adventure—all of these aspects being as inseparable as man and the air he breathes. The rules and regulations were pragmatic, conforming to this synthesis of aims and ideals; the aims and ideals were not tailored to fit a predetermined set of rules. In the messianic society of which they dreamed, man would be freed of concern about his economic and social security. He would be at one with nature, free to develop culturally, free to develop his own personality. Israel in its entirety would be an independent Jewish state, its cultural and social physiognomy a mirror of an ethical socialism compounded of democracy and Jewish prophecy—and the kibbutz would be the main determinant of that Israel. Men would explore their own heritage and together create new values upon its foundation. The kibbutz, a voluntary democratic socialist community, in which men would submit to law for the sake of the group, would fulfill the prophetic vision of the "end of days."

This was and still is the vision of the kibbutz future. The exigencies of the moment, however, dictated by objective circumstance, have shaped the actual twists and turns of kibbutz evolution in equal measure with these long-range ideals. Throughout its history the kibbutz has been dominated by the dramatic pathos and tension of the Zionist effort. There were always reasons for calling upon the individual kibbutz member to sacrifice personal comfort, individual privacy, and some aspect of his long-range kibbutz dream—supposedly temporarily—the reasons for the sacrifice being in themselves of the essence of the dream. When tens of thousands of orphans and homeless children began to arrive from Nazi-devastated Europe, it was natural for kibbutz members to give up their housing in order to make room for them. When people were needed to work with Jewish underground forces in Europe, it was self-evident that the kibbutz movement should mobilize its best people for the purpose. The organizers of Hagana, the Jewish underground army in Palestine itself, automatically based their units on the kibbutzim, drawing upon kibbutz members for leadership cadres. During World War II thousands of kibbutz members joined the British Army's Jewish Brigade, responding to David Ben Gurion's call, as he put it, to fight the British White Paper as if there were no war against Germany and to fight Germany as if there were no British Paper. For decades kibbutz members lived with a constant feeling of emergency, a constant knowledge that they might be called upon in the dead of night, any night, to guard life and property, to help bring in "illegal" refugees or repel an Arab attack.

Many kibbutzim were actually established in places which the membership would never have chosen if the choice had been based merely on economic, agricultural, and environmental factors. They were deliberately established in places of military and strategic importance in terms of the total Zionist picture, with the full knowledge that they could not become economically independent on those sites for many years, if ever.

One natural result of this high pitch of idealistic tension was a tendency to ascribe possible failings in the kibbutz system itself to the stress and strain of the times.

"Our standard of living is low—wait until we can think in terms of economics alone and are free of other pressures." "People would like to live quiet, tumult-free lives, without the feeling of being continuously uprooted on one pretext or another—how can we think of such problems when so much needs to be done?" *"Haverim* (members) are interested in going to school, in studying arts and music, in thinking through unorthodox ideas—how can they, when all must be united every minute of the day for maximum Zionist effort?"

Actually these questions and answers never even became issues for debate. Interested members suppressed them at their own initiative. They were themselves engrossed in the common struggle and did not have to be given the answers. Responsibility for the immediate needs of the Jewish people was an overriding one, the responsibility of the kibbutz orange-picker as well as of the underground commander.

The questions themselves, however, were always there underneath the surface. Upon the emergence of the Jewish state, though the struggle for the continued buttressing of the newly won independence continued apace, though hundreds of thousands of new immigrants began to arrive in an historic ingathering of the exiles, the drama, nevertheless, began to lose much of its tense glamour. Kibbutz members began to examine the details of their own way of life more closely.

Small towns the world over have a specific character of their own—and the kibbutz is a small town. There is no such thing as anonymity. One cannot live—as one can for decades in a New York apartment house—without being on intimate terms with one's neighbors, without knowing, as the Yiddish saying goes, what is cooking in your neighbor's pot. Every small community has its share of gossips, its share of *nudniks* (bores), its share of pettiness, all accentuated by the hothouse atmosphere sometimes generated among a small group of people which can easily stew in its own juice if it permits itself the luxury of doing so. Every normal person, however, yearns for anonymity at some time or other, has some part of himself which he does not choose to reveal to others, desires to make his own decisions in certain spheres of life, needs some time to spend alone with himself in whatever form he chooses. Aside from the kibbutz structure, the very size of many kibbutzim and their cramped housing facilities make this very difficult. It is easier to find desired anonymity in a large kibbutz than in a smaller one. In such a community it is possible for a member to do his work and spend all his leisure time alone or with his family and close friends, never serving on a committee, never appearing at a meeting, and rarely having anything to do with the vast majority of his fellow members. Even here there are times when he will tire of eating in a dining room with a crowd—members, visitors, transient workers, and youth-trainees—and will want to eat alone, quietly, without the strain of social amenities. Small kibbutzim have sometimes disintegrated because the same thirty-five people could no longer bear living with each other in some difficult isolated spot.

The kibbutz movement as a whole, as a result of the increasing articulation of these desires on the part of the membership, has begun to realize that it must attend to the individual member and his needs—for in the last analysis the kibbutz idea will stand or fall with the extent to which he is convinced that it is a good way of life for him personally. People who decide to live in the kibbutz collective are powerful individualists in the first place, holding strong convictions and possessing developed tastes and often a high level of education. Otherwise they would not have the strength required to leave the way of life of the majority for this kind of social experiment. If such people do not have enough room to satisfy their own individual needs within the collective framework, they leave or else build up sublimated pressures within the community, which it sometimes cannot withstand. One reason, I am convinced, for the over-politicization of the kibbutz movement is the large number of people formerly active in politics who are seeking self-expression within the community. The momentum of this activity results in major rifts on issues which really have nothing to do with the kibbutz.

In another area one of the experiences which annoyed me most in my kibbutz was the necessity to explain personal matters to a large group of people, often including people with whom I felt no contact. The most difficult kind of kibbutz meeting is the one in which the whole group is called upon to decide whether a member's request to leave the kibbutz for a period of time in order to visit relatives in the United States, or to help solve family problems, or to study at the University, should or should not be granted. There are people who would prefer to leave the community rather than submit their problems to this kind of public examination.

In the December 1953 issue of the *Scientific American* two professors reported on a two-year study* made of the mental health of the Hutterites, a small collectivist religious sect of the Western United States and Canada. The distribution of psychotic symptoms among the Hutterites was radically different from that of the general community. Although schizophrenia is the most common kind of mental illness in the community at large, the investigators found very few such cases. The proportion of manic-depressive cases, however, was unusually high, though in no case

---

* [See pp. 498-504 this volume.—EDITORS.]

were they serious enough to be dangerous to other people. There was much evidence of irrational guilt feeling, self-blame, and withdrawal from social relations.

These data, according to the professors, confirm the theory that manic-depressive symptoms are most often found among professionals and other intellectual people who have a strong need to live up to social expectations. "Religion is the focus of the Hutterite way of life. Their whole educational system, beginning with nursery school, orients the people to look for blame and guilt within themselves rather than others. Physical aggression is tabu." In projective tests the Hutterites showed antisocial and aggressive impulses but in their daily lives these impulses were repressed. There were no cases of murder, arson, severe physical assault, or sex crime in their history.

The context in which the Hutterite community exists is completely different from the of that of the kibbutz. The Hutterites are a small, tightly knit, religious grouping whose ascetic way of life is basically at variance with the ideals, mores, and way of life of the general community. It deliberately isolates itself from the outside world, and this isolation makes for its inbred character. The kibbutz, on the other hand, over seventy thousand strong, is an open community, not religiously dogmatic, very much involved in the social and political life of the country, and part of a worldwide cultural movement. Nevertheless, some of the comments in the report have brought excited exclamations of recognition from every kibbutz member who has seen it.

This is perhaps one of the key dilemmas in the relationship between the individual and the kibbutz community. The kibbutz has successfully created an environment in which morality and ethics are the everyday standards of behavior. A case of stealing in the kibbutz is rare enough to be reported in general press. A case of one member hitting another is rare enough to be the subject of a special meeting which will attract every single member to it in horrified concern and sensational enough to provide material for the gossip among the women in the tailor shop for years. The community has succeeded in providing its membership with all-encompassing social and economic security. It does not discriminate in favor of particular people or against others. In its relationships with the individual member it is fair and considerate. In the country as a whole the movement has become synonymous with morality and social progress, actively interested in mobilization of its own resources in the development of Israel. The system in itself, however, brings with it the danger of forcing the individual to adopt compulsive behavior patterns without providing him with a private outlet for his own personality. Some people, as a result, feel consciously or subconsciously strait-jacketed and, consciously or subconsciously, chafe at this constraint, tending to self-criticism and depression. *Matzav ruah,* depression, is a very popular phrase in kibbutz circles.

Thinking kibbutz members, whatever their point of view on the specifics (and there are differences of opinion ranging from the diehards to the radical reformers), are very much aware of the problem. The trend of discussion on principle and structure within the movement is in the direction of providing the member with a greater sense of personal freedom and privacy. The kibbutz, like the United States of two hundred years ago, is a pioneering community. The immediate task of firmly establishing and developing the community outweighs the importance of gracious living. Presumably, many a descendant of highly literate Englishmen is now a Tennessee or Ozark backwoodsman; it was only possible for the United States to turn its attention to other matters after it had established a sound foundation of wealth and development. Kibbutz members, however, are twentieth-century people of complex cosmopolitan personality, and the community must find immediate compromise between limitations set by pioneering and the personality needs of the membership. It cannot afford to ignore either. Can it be done without disturbing the essential character of the kibbutz idea? Many kibbutz members believe it can.

The recognition of this problem is the real motivation behind the move in many kibbutzim to provide the individual with a "bill of rights," in order to assure the minima to which every member will be entitled automatically: a room to himself; a radio; an opportunity to have or to serve refreshments in his own room; books; sufficient pocket money for buying his children some toys, eating his fill of candy, or going to a concert in town without having to "request" a ticket; facilities for a decent vacation; opportunities for self-expression in art, music, or literature; chances for self-development through study—even in subjects which have no tangible relation to immediate kibbutz needs; and even an opportunity to eat in his room occasionally if he so desires. It is this recognition too which is one of the primary motives in the drive to provide wider latitudes of choice in clothing and home furnishings and greater opportunity for more family life.

In older, more experienced kibbutzim, an attempt is made to channel personal problems to a small committee, a committee which contains respected people in the community and which possesses wide powers, including the power to countermand decisions of other institutions without explaining its motives. A reservoir of precedent is built up which enables the individual member to acquire a fair idea of what the kibbutz is likely to agree to and what kind of request it is likely to refuse. Committee members, too, can then make decisions without subjecting the member and his motives to public discussion and scrutiny.

In Gesher Haziv a number of Americans requested permission to leave the kibbutz for specific periods in order to visit their families in the States. Their families were willing to cover expenses. Most of the other Americans, all of whom could see themselves in similar positions in the future, tended to agree. The non-American members, however, were vociferous in their opposition. The people could not be spared from the work program, they maintained. If we allowed such a precedent to be set, there was no telling how many people would be going at the same time, emptying out the kibbutz. What about all those who have no relatives abroad or whose relatives abroad are not wealthy enough? As luck would have it, several of the Israelis received similar invitations from their own relatives abroad—in America and in England. After that it was smooth sailing. Originally the committee had the right to grant a member one month's leave for whatever reason without bringing the matter to public discussion. Later this authority was expanded to three months, and now it is six months. There is some tentative discussion of making it possible for those whose families in the States do not have the means with which to finance their visit also to make similar trips. This is the way in which precedent and custom in the relationship of the individual to the group is created in many other matters as well.

One basis for measuring the maturity of a community is the degree of self-criticism and disagreement with established practice which it permits. There is perhaps no one as touchy about criticism or suggested change as former revolutionaries who have succeeded in creating a new framework for society. Many kibbutz members are no exception to this rule.

When David Maletz, a member of Kibbutz Ein Harod, wrote a novel about kibbutz life (translated into English as *Young Hearts*) which contained elements of self-criticism, he was bitterly denounced as a "renegade" and "traitor." Similar cries of "betrayal" sometimes greet proponents of reform at kibbutz gatherings or in kibbutz publications. When a member decides to leave the kibbutz, it is only the broad-minded colleague who can rise above the immediate needs of the community—to which every departure of this sort deals a blow—and consider the matter objectively. It is only the broad-minded colleague who can understand that perhaps from his own point of view his departing friend is doing the correct thing, that the kibbutz does not hold a monopoly on justice, and that there are other forms of life which are honest, just, and socially productive. The normal reaction is to feel deserted, to label the person involved a traitor to the cause, and to prefer the company of city people who have never even attempted the kibbutz to that of the former friend who did try and found that it was not for him.

Despite this touchiness, however, it would be a mistake to assume that these are the basic attitudes of the kibbutz population as a whole. They are not the majority attitudes, and the leadership is continually striving to maintain a truly free approach to ideas and to fight provincialism. This same David Maletz, for example, was elected to the steering committee of the recently held convention of the Union of Collective Settlements, and many former kibbutz members maintain cordial and intimate relationships with the communities of which they were once a part.

In the circles of the Stalinist-dominated left there exists a premise that all aspects of life are "political" and either directly advance or directly retard the cause of progress. Superficially stated, this means that a painting is either "proletarian" or "reactionary," a symphony is either written in the spirit of the revolution or is a betrayal of the revolution, and that every book, sociological study or murder mystery, is a political document. People who accept this doctrine cannot be eclectic about their beliefs. They cannot accept the "good" parts of religious belief and discard the "bad," cannot accept some aspects of Marx and reject others. Everything man does, from cracking jokes to playing bridge, must have a political overtone and is an instrument to be used in the furtherance of the cause. If this approach is to be applied to the kibbutz, then the individual is only an end in himself in the far distant future; until then he too is an instrument of the revolution. Not only does economics become collective, but thought also becomes collective; ideology too is collective.

No section of the Israel kibbutz movement identifies itself with the Communist Party. On the contrary, it took the extreme left-wing Hashomer Hatzair kibbutz federation, which is often pro-Soviet in foreign policy, 24 hours to expel 20 young members of one of its kibbutzim who had actually joined the Communist Party. They were removed bag and baggage. In Hashomer Hatzair, however, there is a tendency to speak in terms of "ideological collectivism." Alone among the kibbutz federations Hashomer Hatzair is, formally, not only a federation of communities in a common economic and social framework, but also, as a unit, part of a political party within the Zionist movement. Individuals who belong to other political parties are tolerated only so long as they do not attempt to organize adherents. Once the movement decides on a policy, in whatever sphere, there is no room for disagreement. The movement acts monolithically. Decisions have the force of unanimity.

This is not the case in the other kibbutz federations. The danger, however, of the individual's surrendering his right to his own opinion is the extreme form of a whole gamut of similar problems which occupy every kibbutz, and presented themselves to us in Gesher Haziv as well.

Reinhold Niebuhr in *Moral Man and Immoral Society* makes the point that moral values of individuals vary from those of groups made up of the very same individuals. On a very elementary level, it is a crime for a youngster to steal mimeograph paper from the office of a community center for the purpose of selling it; it does not seem to be a crime to steal the paper on behalf of one of the youth groups meeting in the center for the purpose of putting out the group newspaper. In his own life man thinks it wrong to cheat or to make a promise which he does not intend to keep. His political party, however, is free to do so, for the sake of the "cause." The same man who would never kill anyone, for whatever personal reasons, feels, once his ego has merged with the collective ego of a group, that it is then permissible to kill in the name of the group's ideals. The core of the problem facing those who would create a better society, according to Niebuhr, is the degree to which individual ethics and standards of behavior can be transferred to society as a whole.

The kibbutz meets this challenge in real terms—for this is specifically and exactly what it sets out to do. An individual in Tel Aviv will only rarely volunteer to work in an immigrant reception camp to the detriment of his own economic position. He will find it difficult to leave home and family on a community mission for an extended period of time and will be unable to open his own home to immigrant children. In the kibbutz this happens every day. The community acts as an ethical and moral entity, is concerned about its possible exploitation of other people working with it, is committed against speculation with its own produce.

In a movement comprising seventy thousand people and several hundred independent communities, however, there are bound to be groups that have arrived at different stages of comprehension of what such a transfer of ethical standards means in practical terms, and individuals who have reached different levels of maturity in the fulfillment of community responsibilities which have been entrusted to them.

During our first year at Gesher Haziv our treasurer once came to the secretariat with a proposal for alleviating the meat shortage. As all of Israel, kibbutzim too are rationed in their meat consumption. He had met an Arab who lived in the hills not far from the kibbutz. Since the control of Arab activities in this connection had not yet become effective, the Arab had offered to raise cattle in the hills on a black market basis for the purpose of supplying meat to the kibbutz. This treasurer, had he been living in the city, would not have made a practice of buying on the black market. Convinced, however, of the moral superiority of the kibbutz way of life and of the positive good it was creating in the country, it seemed to him somehow that for the kibbutz there might be some moral justification in taking such measures to ensure its food supply. It took an edict from the general meeting to convince him of the opposite.

There have, indeed, been some few cases of kibbutz treasurers marketing agricultural produce on the black market. Being members of pioneering communities in wild and desolate areas where the ordinary city dweller in Israel would refuse to live no matter how important it might be for the future of the country that he do so, it was relatively easy for these treasurers to find a rationalization for their activities. Once they were discovered, however, they were tried in a movement court of honor, disbarred from holding any further office in their kibbutz, and disenfranchised within the kibbutz for a long period of time.

Upon our arrival in Gesher Haziv the war was still on and government had not yet been effectively established, especially in our area. Not far from Gesher Haziv there was an abandoned army railroad camp, built by the British during World War II. It was winter. We were living in tents and had no cash intake except for loans. Our enterprising work coordinator thought it would be a good idea to send a group over to pick up bricks, tiles, tin-sheeting, anything which could be of use to us; under the circumstances there was almost nothing which did not fall into this category. Five of us were sent over, including myself. An equally enterprising policeman, driving by in a jeep, informed us that this was government property and that we had no right to take it. Being a neophyte in these matters, and having a hard enough time keeping up with my companions in the physical work itself, I looked to them, all experienced kibbutz members, for guidance. They talked to the policeman a while about the possibilities of Arab infiltration (the border was only half a mile away) and about common experiences in the army, and finally he drove away. After his departure they calmly began working again. I was too tired and felt too green to question them—and too uncertain in my own mind about Israel and the kibbutz in general to assert forcefully my own opinion. Sure enough, the policeman returned, this time accompanied by a sergeant. We were all arrested, and the fifty-seven large squares of floor tile which we had salvaged for our dining room were confiscated as Exhibit A.

The prosecutor asked us to plead guilty, but for some deeply innate reason of pride none of us could agree to do that, and we insisted on a trial. The trial was postponed three times and finally took place a year later. By that time everyone was keenly embarrassed, the police, the prosecutor, the judge, and certainly we ourselves. The judge got rid of the case as soon as he possibly could, saying that it had occurred in a twilight period when government had not yet been established.

I have often tried to estimate whether the same five people, had we been engaged in this activity as individuals, even in circumstances of poverty, would have continued our activity after that preliminary police warning. I haven't been able to give myself a satisfactory answer. One thing I know, however: after five years of kibbutz evolution, this could not happen in the Gesher Haziv of today. The crucial fact which must be understood is that in kibbutz society these two stories I have related are so rare and unusual that they bear telling as curiosities in discussing the problem. This is the kibbutz achievement.

In private society man has a direct personal incentive for work, and it is the emphasis on this personal incentive which is the core of modern efficiency engineering, whether in capitalist America or Soviet Russia. Methods of work and time and motion analysis are only important incidentals. The real basis for efficient production is the provision of a personal goal, whether monetary or in the nature of social prestige, for each and every worker. If this is lacking, no amount of technological efficiency will help. How, it is asked, can the kibbutz conduct its work efficiently and productively if it does not provide this kind of incentive?

There are people in the kibbutz whose actions are seeming evidence of the truth of this contention. There are members who really have their heart in their work; rising early, taking little time for lunch, returning late, reading technical and scientific literature, and participating in after-hours discussion and planning. Other members merely report to work on time, go through the motions of working until the official time is up, report sick at the first opportunity, and go home from work without being in the least concerned about its effectiveness. The second category will nevertheless receive the same kind of treatment in terms of services and consideration as will the first. The system thus makes it possible for some people to live a parasitic life.

The community has substituted group incentive for individual incentive. If the kibbutz succeeds in keeping the community goals alive—the ideal of a just society, the ideal of a recreated Jewish life in Israel—then it can fire the imagination of the individual member and can be as effective in productive accomplishment as is the present competitive economy. In the main the kibbutz has succeeded in doing this, to a greater or lesser degree, depending on particular periods in its history and particular kibbutzim. In this type of society it *is* possible for a person to "gold-brick," but if he is a sensitive person, he cannot keep it up for long. The reaction of his colleagues will make it well nigh impossible for him to continue in the community.

Of greater severity is "goldbricking" in such activities as the weekly group meeting. Some members are excellent and devoted workers who maintain, however, that they are not "politicians," or too ignorant to make decisions, or just indifferent to these meetings. In a report prepared by a committee on "Kibbutz Principle and Practice" of the Union of Collective Settlements it is stated that, of fifty-six representative kibbutzim queried, two have less than 25 per cent of the membership participating in weekly meetings, in sixteen less than half the membership partici-pates, twenty-eight have between 51 and 75 per cent average participation, and in ten only is the percentage higher than 75.

This leads to an obvious question: What actually drives the kibbutz community? Is it the weekly meeting? Is it a particular group within the community? In the last analysis it is particular people who do most of the driving and de-ciding, and they are often individuals who, because of the very character traits which make them the drivers, are difficult to get along with and are actively disliked by many of the rank-and-file members.

In Gesher Haziv there were for a long time two distinct groups which were very often at odds with each other, the Israelis and the Americans. Among the Americans we used to talk about the specific American contribution to Israel and about our desire for the kibbutz to have an American character. Very few people could actually spell out what they wanted. They knew only that they did not like things as they were and ascribed this to the fact that this Ameri-can character was lacking. Anyone entering Gesher Haziv can tell almost immediately that its membership hails in large part from the United States by the furniture in the rooms, the plaid lumberjack shirts to which even the Is-raelis have taken, and the clear tones of a long-playing record of *South Pacific* coming from an open window of a summer evening. Nevertheless, we were still vaguely dis-satisfied. The Israelis, in turn, were also dissatisfied. De-spite the imprint they were making on the way of life of the community, they also felt the same kind of group dissatisfaction.

But neither of the groups as a unit can lay claim to any kibbutz accomplishment. One person who happened to be elected secretary at a strategic moment did more toward stabilizing the community and putting it on its feet from the point of view of straightening out the problems of individuals and community structure than any group. The institution of educational reform depended on two or three energetic and talented people. The agricultural end of the kibbutz was driven by an excitable, moody, but capable and efficient production manager. Dissatisfaction with the state of affairs in any of these areas, without the fortuitous circumstance of being able to find a leader to point to positive effort, would not alone have produced anything. Some kibbutzim, consisting of many inarticulate people who happen to come from the same country of origin and have only vague ideas about what they want to see in the kibbutz, but lack leadership, disintegrate out of a feeling of purposelessness.

In discussing the question of women in the kibbutz it is important to bear in mind the atmosphere of Eastern Europe during the early decades of this century, in which the founders of the kibbutz movement received their political schooling. It was an atmosphere in which women were fighting for their elementary equality: the right to vote and to hold political office, the right to executive and administrative position in what had previously been strictly a man's world. It was the era in America and England of the women's suffrage parade and of woman sweatshop labor in the needle trades. In this context it was a revolutionary step for the kibbutz to declare that women were in all respects the equals of men in rights, privileges, and responsibility. Such equality was assumed from the first day of kibbutz organization and was carried out in practice. True emancipation of women, said kibbutz ideologists, moreover, depends on society's being so organized that women will actually be enabled to do the kind of work previously held to be man's work only, in addition to having merely the right to do it. When community services, therefore, were organized in such fashion that kitchen work, mending and washing of clothes, child care, and similar "women's work" became the responsibility of the central work co-ordination setup rather than of the woman of each family, this was not only hailed as a more efficient way of organizing this work but also as a step toward the emancipation of women from the yoke of household responsibility. It was then possible for women to work in the fields if they so desired, in town, or in executive and administrative work both in the kibbutz and in the general community.

Many kibbutz women have developed skills in various branches of agriculture and in other kibbutz fields of activity. To a degree unparalleled in the outside world, where women, unless they are wealthy, are unable to participate in community affairs because of household and child care responsibilities (American women's organizations, for example, are made up mostly of middle-class rather than working women and to a large extent of women whose children are already grown up), women in the kibbutz take an active part in all kibbutz affairs, in politics both in and out of the kibbutz, and in the life of the movement as a whole.

This philosophy is sometimes even carried to comic extremes. Hashomer Hatzair once went so far as to print a pamphlet for use in its youth movement affiliate, which later became famous in kibbutz *Kaffeeklatsch* small talk, entitled *The Biological Tragedy of Woman*. The theme of the pamphlet was that the only obstacle in the way of achieving true equality of the sexes was the unfortunate physical difference between women and men.

Aside from agreeing wholeheartedly with the classic French comment, *"Vive la différence,"* present day kibbutzim are finding that the goal of freeing women from household tasks is becoming increasingly unworkable. In a young community, where there are few children and where the accent is overwhelmingly on income-producing work to the neglect (temporary, it is hoped) of adequate food preparation, laundry, clothing, and education, it is possible to limit work in these fields to the barest minimum, thus freeing women for other activity. As the community grows older, a tremendous pressure develops to put more people to work in child care, to improve the dining room service, to provide more clothing and more adequate care of clothing, and graduate from tents to homes. The women, therefore, are pulled out one by one, often against their will, from whatever else they are doing and placed in the services.

By the time the kibbutz is fifteen or twenty years old only a small number of exceptional women are working in anything but services. As a result of the basic philosophy, however, though the work in services requires skill, training, and a sense of pride, and though no one questions its importance, there still remains among the women, and among many of the men as well, the sub-surface feeling that this work, because it is not income-producing, is inferior and is preventing women from the achievement of their true emancipation.

In this connection the movement has been facing the necessity for a considerable change in basic outlook, a change which has indeed already taken place in many kibbutzim and merely needs codification. Equality for women does not mean equal opportunity to do man's work. It means opportunity for women to do the work for which they are psychologically and constitutionally fitted and the elevation of this work to a status of equal importance with any other kind of work. When women decide to leave the kibbutz, and in a family situation it is more often the woman than the man who makes this decision, it is precisely because they want to be housewives. Kibbutzim, therefore, are beginning to understand that it is important to grant the work in the service areas the status of a career, that it is important to enable mothers to spend some time with their children, especially with infants, during the work day itself. Even in kibbutzim which do not have children sleeping at home mothers are now encouraged to come in early in the morning to help bathe and feed the infant and to feel themselves at home to drop in at the children's houses whenever they have the opportunity.

Some critics of the kibbutz have maintained that despite the status of full equality there are very few major leaders of the movement who are women, and that it is only rarely that women are placed in positions of central executive responsibility within individual kibbutzim. Within the limits of physical possibility this is not true. Many of the leaders of the Working Women's Council of the Israel Labor Federation are kibbutz members, kibbutz women have been members of Israel's parliament, kibbutz women are very influential in the field of kibbutz education and in Israel education in general. Within my own kibbutz, for example, women have been everything from coordinator of the educational system to work coordinator, to manager of our vegetable garden, a project which employs at times as many as forty people.

As in all pioneering communities there are more men than women in the kibbutz movement as a whole. This is especially true in younger kibbutzim. As the kibbutz develops, however, the percentage difference becomes normalized as does the position of the woman in general.

THE OUTGOING LIFE
/William H. Whyte

On the credit side the suburbanites have much to say about the group. One of the first points they make is how it has altered their personality—or how they and the rest of the group altered someone else's. For the good. "I've changed tremendously," says one typical transient. "My husband was always the friend-maker in the family—everybody always loves Joe; he's so likable. But here I began to make some friends on my own; I was so tickled when I realized it. One night when the gang came to our house I suddenly realized *I* made these friends."

The cumulative effect can be summed up in a word. One is made *outgoing*. If the person is too shy to make the first move, others will take the initiative. In almost every court, patio, or superblock there is usually someone who enjoys doing the job, and the stiffer the challenge, the more the enjoyment. "When Mr. and Mrs. Berry came, they wouldn't give you the time of day," one leader recalls. "But I knew they were real shy and unhappy beneath it all. I said to myself, 'I'm going to conquer them if it kills me.' I have, too. She was one of the organizers for the Mothers' March and he's gotten tremendously interested in the school. They're part of the gang now—you wouldn't know they were the same people."

Those who have been "brought out" bear witness to the transformation. They speak enthusiastically of it, and if their experiences had to be summed up in a phrase, it would boil down to one heartfelt note of joy: *they weren't introverts after all.* "One of the reasons I took technical training in college," explains one ex-introvert, "was that I thought

I wasn't the mixing type and wouldn't be much good with people. Well, here I am, leading meetings and what not, and, frankly, not doing too bum a job. It's changed a lot of ideas I had about myself."

In theory, one could keep entirely to oneself, and some people attempt to do so. It is not, however, an easy alternative. The court, like the double bed, enforces intimacy, and self-imposed isolation becomes psychologically untenable. People so ingoing that they have been proof against "bringing out" usually seem to be rather troubled people, and though the causes of their unhappiness may antedate their entry into the court, some leave at the first opportunity. The court checks off another failure. "At the very end the Smithers were beginning to come out of their shell," one outgoing resident recalls. "But it was too late; they'd already given up their lease. The night they left, you could tell by their faces, the way they tried to get friendly, they wished they weren't leaving. It was so pathetic."

On the matter of privacy, suburbanites have mixed feelings. Fact one, of course, is that there isn't much privacy. In most small towns there is at least enough living room to soften the shock of intimate contact, and, besides, there is usually some redoubt to which the individual can withdraw. In Park Forest not even the apartment is a redoubt; people don't bother to knock and they come and go furiously. The lack of privacy, furthermore, is retroactive. "They ask you all sorts of questions about what you *were* doing," one resident puts it. "Who was it that stopped in last night? Who were those people from Chicago last week? You're never alone, even when you think you are."

Less is sacred. "It's wonderful," says one young wife. "You find yourself discussing all your personal problems with your neighbors—things that back in South Dakota we would have kept to ourselves." As time goes on, this capacity for self-revelation grows; and on the most intimate details of family life, court people become amazingly frank with one another. No one, they point out, ever need face a problem alone.

In the battle against loneliness even the architecture becomes functional. Just as doors inside houses—which are sometimes said to have marked the birth of the middle class—are disappearing, so are the barriers against neighbors. The picture in the picture window, for example, is what is going on *inside*—or, what is going on inside other people's picture windows.

The walls in these new apartments are also dual purpose. Their thinness is occasionally a disadvantage; one court scandal, as a matter of fact, was provoked by a woman who chronically inverted a tumbler against the wall to eavesdrop. But there is more good than bad, many transients say, to the thinness. "I never feel lonely, even when Jim's away," goes a typical comment. "You know friends are near by, because at night you hear the neighbors through the walls."

Even the most outgoing, of course, confess that the pace of court life occasionally wears them down, and once in a while they reach such a point of rebellion they don't answer the phone. Such a purely negative response, however, is not enough. To gain privacy, one has to *do* something. One court resident, for example, moves his chair to the front rather than the court side of his apartment to show he doesn't want to be disturbed. Often a whole court or a wing of it will develop such a signal; a group in one Drexelbrook court has decided that whenever one of them feels he or she has finally had it, she should draw the venetian blinds all the way down to the bottom of the picture window. This lowered position is an unusual one, and the rest spot it as a plea to be left alone—for a little while, anyway.

But there is an important corollary of such efforts at privacy—*people feel a little guilty about making them.* Except very occasionally, to shut oneself off from others like this is regarded as either a childish prank or, more likely, an indication of some inner neurosis. The individual, not the group, has erred. So, at any rate, many errants seem to feel, and they are often penitent about what elsewhere would be regarded as one's own business, and rather normal business at that. "I've promised myself to make it up to them," one court resident recently told a confidant. "I was feeling bad that day and just plain didn't make the effort to ask them in for coffee. I don't blame them, really, for reacting the way they did. I'll make it up to them somehow."

Privacy has become clandestine. Not in solitary and selfish contemplation but in doing things with other people does one fulfill oneself. Nor is it a matter of overriding importance just what it is that one does with other people;

even watching television together—for which purpose, incidentally, several groups have been organized—helps make one more of a real person.

However one may view this responsiveness to the group, it is important to acknowledge its moral basis. That friendship in the new suburbia transcends personal characteristics so much is due in part to the increasing homogeneity of American middle-class values. But it is also due to a very active kind of tolerance, and unless this is recognized one cannot appreciate the true difficulty of the suburbanites' dilemmas.

Very consciously, they try to understand one another's backgrounds and prejudices. As the unresolved segregation problem indicates, the millennium is still some way off, but the fact remains that they make a great effort to meet one another halfway. If misfortune strikes a family, the neighbors are not only remarkably generous but remarkably tactful. If, say, the child of a couple in straits accidentally breaks someone's windshield, the group may not only chip in to pay for the damage but will try to conceal the fact that they have done so. Those in trouble are often irrationally antagonistic, but this the group takes in stride. They may have "a personality problem," and there is nothing so challenging to the others as its diagnosis and therapy.

In the more humdrum aspects of daily life, much of what could pass for lazy conformity is in fact a very energetic, and in many ways unselfish, quest for consensus. Just as the Bunco player may put his mind to mastering bridge, so the shy housewife makes herself have fun at a coffee party; just as the Fundamentalist unbends with a risqué story and a beer now and then, so his neighbors tone down their own stories.

For the intellectual also Park Forest is a melting pot. "When I first came here I was pretty rarefied," a self-styled egghead explained to me. "I remember how shocked I was one afternoon when I told the girls in the court how much I had enjoyed listening to *The Magic Flute* the night before. They didn't know what I was talking about. I began to learn that diaper talk is important to them and I'm not so highbrow about it now. I still listen to *The Magic Flute*, but now I realize that it's not wrong that most people care about other things."

In similar fashion, farm-bred Republicans learn to appreciate that not all urban Democrats are Communists. "The people who lived in the other half of our duplex," recalls one Republican, "were as different as could be from us. They were the kind who worshiped F.D.R.'s name. But we got to like them just the same. We just didn't talk politics. We used to go bowling together and that sort of thing. I didn't make him a Republican, but I think he appreciates my views a lot more than he did before, and I understand him better."

This seeking of common values applies markedly to religion. The neighborhood friendship patterns would be impossible unless religious beliefs had lost much of their segregating effect. And it is more than a passive, live-and-let-live attitude. Several people of other faiths, for example, have joined the National Council of Jewish Women; they like the intellectual content of its discussion programs, and they feel no conflict with their own beliefs.

Even where there is conflict, suburbanites lean over backward to see the other point of view. "When Will and Ada had to dash East last month—they're devout Catholics—I took care of little Johnny for them," recalls one non-Catholic. "It really tickled me. Here I was picking Johnny up at St. Irenaeus School every afternoon and seeing to it that he said his Rosary every night before he went to bed." Park Forest abounds with such stories, and the good will implicit in them is real.

Denominator-seeking is also illustrated in the commercial "parties" held in suburbia (Linda Lee clothes demonstrations, the Beauty Counselor, etc.). Stanley Home products demonstrators, for example, ask the hostess to serve only two refreshments, preferably coffee and doughnuts. If the choice is left to her, she may overdo it and others will fear to be hostesses lest their own offerings suffer in comparison. Similar care marks the games that precede the product demonstration. "The best kind of thing to start with," says one Park Forest housewife who has demonstrated Stanley products, "is something like the waistline game. That's where you lay a piece of rope on the floor and start making an ever-bigger circle; one by one the girls tell you when they think it's as big as their waistline. They always overestimate, because your waistline is oblong and not a circle. They get a big charge out of that. But if you do anything that shows up people's intelligence, it's tricky.

With a spelling game or naming states—you'd be surprised how many people can't name ten states—they just get uncomfortable."

The suburban group also has a strong effect on relations between husband and wife, and in many ways a beneficent one. The group is a foster family. In the transient organization life the young family has to take a good part of its environment with it; no longer is there the close complex of aunts and uncles and grandparents to support the couple, and when they come to their first crisis this absence can have a devastating effect. Thus the function of the suburban group. All the other young couples are in the same boat, and in a sort of unspoken mutual assistance pact they provide for one another a substitute for the big family of former years.

What unites them most are the concerns of parenthood, and this preoccupation with children is a potent factor in keeping marriages on keel. "The kind of social situation you find here discourages divorce," says United Protestant Church minister Dr. Gerson Engelmann. "Few people, as a rule, get divorces until they break with their groups. I think the fact that it is so hard to break with a group here has had a lot to do with keeping some marriages from going on the rocks."

So pervasive are the concerns of parenthood that adjustment to court life is almost impossible for childless couples. Unless the wife obviously loves children—unless she is the kind, for example, who keeps a cooky jar for the neighbors' kids—her daily routine is painfully out of kilter with the others'. Understandably, the recourse of adopting a child is sought very frequently. Complementing the social pressure of the group on the couple is the readiness of social agencies to give a Park Forest couple preference, for they look on the environment as ideal for adjustment. (Social workers' liking for Park Forest has been so strong as to force local authorities to yell uncle; so many problem children have been sent out that in several areas the problem children are having more impact on the normal ones than the normal ones on the problem children.)

Personal morals? The court is the greatest invention since the chastity belt. In company, young suburbanites talk a great deal about sex, but it's all rather clinical, and outside of the marriage no one seems to do much about it. There have been, to be sure, some unpleasant occurrences; in one court there was talk of wife-trading several years ago, and there have been affairs here and there since. The evidence is strong, however, that there is less philandering in the package suburbs than in more traditional communities.

For one thing, it's almost impossible to philander without everyone's knowing about it. One's callers are observed, and if neighbors feel there is anything untoward, suburbia's phenomenal grapevine will speed the news. This is not mere venom; in a web of relationships as delicate as that of the court an affair can harm not only two marriages, it can upset the whole court applecart. Infidelity, to put it another way, is an ethical as well as a moral problem.

More important, the neighborliness of court life fills a void in the life of the young wife that is not always filled elsewhere—and this is particularly important for the wife whose husband travels. "You don't find as many frustrated women in a place like this," says one young wife. "We gals have each other. A young girl who would get to brooding if she was in an apartment all by herself on the outside can talk things over with us. She's just too busy to get neurotic. Kitty, for example. She's married to a real creep—pardon me, but that's what he is—but when she's disturbed she comes over here for coffee and a little chat, and we have a fine old time yakking away. It helps, for people like her."

The participation also mitigates the "retrograde wife" problem that affects many corporation couples. If the husband is moving up rapidly this introduces a wedge between husband and wife, for while he is getting a postgraduate finishing through travel and exposure to successful older men, her tastes are often frozen at their former level by lack of any activity but child rearing. In the new suburbia this is somewhat less likely to happen. "Before we came here," one wife, typical of many another, says, "I was such a stupid little thing. I didn't think about anything except shopping and the babies and things like that. Now that I'm in the League of Women Voters and the school board I feel so much more worth while. When Joe comes home at night I have so many interesting things to talk to him about."

In this mutual seeking of denominators, to recapitulate, the young suburbanites have been re-creating something of the tight-knit group of old. It is an achievement not to be dismissed lightly. They have come together with many more differences in religion, background, and expectations to adjudicate than troubled communities of old. Tensions they suffer for the suppression of their differences, but the consensus that is the result bespeaks a pretty high quotient of kindliness and fundamental decency.

But there is another side to the coin. Contemporary prophets of belongingness point out the warmth and security the tight-knit group produces for the individual, but they generally stop short at diagnosing some of the other things it produces. The suburbanites are more troubled, for they experience the double-barreled effects of belongingness, and in highly practical, immediate ways. It is not the question of conformity, though many speak of it as such. It is, rather, the question of determining *when* one is conforming, when adjustment is selflessness, or surrender. It is a moral dilemma—the one, I believe, central to the organization man, and while the suburban group affords the most concrete illustration, the underlying problem will not be shed when he moves on.

Let's take a second look at that tolerance. There is one trouble with it. In the happy group, people are very intolerant of those who aren't tolerant. This is using the same word in two senses, I admit, but suburbanites are ambiguous about it too. Their tolerance, as they are so proud to point out, goes downward. It does not, however, go *upward* very far. The leveling process is just that—leveling—and those financially above the norm who let the fact be visible are risking trouble. Though neighbors speak kindly of someone who "has not had all the advantages," the phrase "they are more . . . fortunate than the rest of us" is likely to be spoken with a real bite.

Now let me make an important qualification. How much bite depends on how happy the group is. In the block which never quite jelled there is little of the belongingness, the mutual support characteristic elsewhere; for the same reason, however, there is not much pressure on the individual to adjust. There is no working group to adjust to. In the tight-knit group, however, each member feels an equity in others' behavior. With communication so intensive, the slightest misunderstanding can generate a whole series of consequences. If Charley ducks his turn at the lawn mower, if little Johnny sasses Mrs. Erdlick just once more, if Gladys forgets to return the pound of coffee she borrowed, the frictions become a concern of the group and not just of the principals.

The more vigorous the search for common denominators, the stronger the pressure to alikeness. Sometimes this extends even to house design. The architects have tried to vary the façades of each house, and one might assume that in putting up aluminum awnings, making alterations, repainting and the like, residents try hard to enlarge the differences. This is not always so; in some areas residents have apparently agreed to unify the block with a common design and color scheme for garages and such.

In such blocks an otherwise minor variation becomes blatant deviance; if a man were to paint his garage fire-engine red in a block where the rest of the garages are white, he would literally and psychologically make himself a marked man. So with fences; if they are obviously designed to keep the children safe, eyebrows are not raised. But if the height or elaborateness of the fence indicates other motives, there will be feeling.

An unkempt lawn is another symbol of malaise. The state of the lawn is an effect as well as a cause, and in talking to owners of neglected lawns one gets the suspicion that they have subconsciously used the unkemptness as a weapon to tell the others where they can head in. "I suppose I should do more about it," said one resident, waving to a rather weedy expanse outside, "but my wife and I think there are other things more important in life."

Reprisal is inevitable. The sanctions are not obvious—indeed, people are often unconscious of wielding them—but the look in the eye, the absence of a smile, the inflection of a hello, can be exquisite punishment, and they have brought more than one to a nervous breakdown. And the more social the block, the rougher it is on those who don't fit in.

In some areas it is questionable if the *Gemütlichkeit* of the gang compensates for the misery of the deviate. It is frightening to see the cruelty with which an otherwise decent group can punish the deviate, particularly when the deviate is unfortunate enough to be located in the middle of the group, rather than isolated somewhat out of benevolence's way. "Estelle is a case," says one resident of a highly active block. "She was dying to get in with the gang when she moved in. She is a very warmhearted gal and is always trying to help people, but she's well—sort of elaborate about it. One day she decided to win over everybody by giving an afternoon party for the gals. Poor thing, she did it all wrong. The girls turned up in their bathing

suits and slacks, as usual, and here she had little doilies and
silver and everything spread around. Ever since then it's
been almost like a planned campaign to keep her out of
things. Even her two-year-old daughter gets kept out of the
kids' parties. It's really pitiful. She sits there in her beach
chair out front just dying for someone to come and
Kaffeeklatsch with her, and right across the street four or
five of the girls and their kids will be yakking away. Every
time they suddenly all laugh at some joke she thinks they
are laughing at her. She came over here yesterday and
cried all afternoon. She told me she and her husband are
thinking about moving somewhere else so they can make a
fresh start." (The woman in question has since moved.)

Perhaps the greatest tyranny, however, applies not to
the deviate but to the accepted. The group is a jealous
master. It encourages participation, indeed, demands it,
but it demands one kind of participation—its own kind—
and the better integrated with it a member becomes the less
free he is to express himself in other ways.

Most of those who wanted to plan for more participation assumed there is a unity to participation—that is, a
layout that will stimulate neighborly social participation is
the layout that will stimulate civic and cultural participation. They saw no antithesis; their primary goal was to develop "citizenship" rather than social activity, but they saw
both kinds of participation as indivisible—parts of a satisfying whole.

When I first went to Park Forest I thought so too. The
courts and blocks that were most notable for the amount
of friendliness and social activity, I presumed, would be
the ones that contributed the greatest number of civic leaders, and as a check I plotted the location of all the leaders
in the principal community organizations. To my surprise,
the two did not correlate; if anything, there was a reverse
relationship. By and large, the people who were active in
the over-all community did not tend to come from the courts
that were especially "happy."

The cause-and-effect relationship is not too difficult to
determine. For some people, of course, it does not make
much difference whether the neighborly gang is a happy one
or not; they would be leaders in any event. But such people
are a minority. The majority are more influenced by the
good opinions of the group, and the cohesiveness of it has
a considerable bearing on whether they will become active

in community-wide problems. Where the group has never jelled enough to stimulate a sense of obligation, the person with any predilection for civic activity feels no constraints. The others would not be annoyed if he went in for outside activity; they don't care enough. If the group is strong, however, the same kind of person is less likely to express such yearnings. It would be divisive. There are only so many enthusiasms a person can sustain, only so many hours in the day, and the amount of leisure one expends outside the group must be deducted from that spent inside.

It is not merely that the group will resent the absenteeism. Again, on the part of the individual himself, there is a moral obligation, or, at least, the feeling that there should be. I recall how a young housewife put it to me. She had been toying with the idea of getting involved in the little theater, for she felt she and her husband were culturally very lacking. But she decided against it. "If we do it'll mean we'll have to spend more of our free evenings away from the gang. I'd hate to be the first to break things up. We've really worked things out well here. The two play areas for the kids—my, how we all pitched in on that! I know we spend too much time just talking and playing bridge and all. Frankly, Chuck and I are the only ones around here who read much more than the *Reader's Digest*. But have we the right to feel superior? I mean, should we break things up just because we're different that way?"

Is this simple conformity? I am not for the moment trying to argue that yielding to the group is something to be admired, but I do think that there is more of a moral problem here than is generally conceded in most discussions of American conformity. Let me go back to the case of the man who is wondering about something he knows would upset the group—like not painting his garage white, like the rest. He may have been one of the first settlers of a block where the people have suppressed potential dislikes in a very successful effort to solve their common problems. Quite probably, a piece of bad luck for one of the group might have further unified them. If one of the wives had come down with polio, the rest might have chipped in not only with their money but with their time to help out the family through the crisis.

In other words, there has been a great deal of real brotherhood, and the man who is now figuring about his garage faces a decision that is not entirely ludicrous. He knows instinctively that his choice will be construed by the others as an outward manifestation of his regard for them, and he does feel a real obligation to help sustain the good feeling.

If he goes along with them he is conforming, yes, but he is conforming not simply out of cowardice but out of a sense of brotherhood too. You may think him mistaken, but grant at least his problem. The group is a tyrant; so also is it a friend, and *it is both at once*. The two qualities cannot easily be separated, for what gives the group its power over the man is the same cohesion that gives it its warmth. This is the duality that confuses choice.

This duality is a very unpleasant fact. Once you acknowledge how close the relationship is between conformity and belongingness—between "good" participation and "bad" participation—you cannot believe in utopia, now or ever. But progress is not served by ignoring it. Many current prescriptions for a better society do ignore it, and thus are delusory. However shrewd their diagnosis of what is wrong, their precepts could intensify the very problems they are intended to solve.

Even so perceptive an observer as Erich Fromm has fallen into this trap. In his plea for *The Sane Society,* Fromm makes a searching diagnosis of man's desperate efforts to escape the burdens of freedom in group conformity. In documentation Fromm cites the conformity of suburbia. Appropriately enough, he singles out Park Forest as an example and dwells at considerable length on the baneful aspects of the group pressures found there. But what is his antidote? In conclusion, he advocates a "democratic communitarianism"—a society in which, through a multitude of small, local groups, people learn to participate more actively with others.

Well? Fromm might as well have cited Park Forest again. One must be consistent. Park Foresters illustrate conformity; they also illustrate very much the same kind of small group activity Fromm advocates. He has damned an effect and praised a cause. More participation may well be in order, but it is not the antidote to conformity; it is inextricably related with it, and while the benefits may well outweigh the disadvantages, we cannot intensify the former and expect to eliminate the latter. There is a true dilemma here. It is not despite the success of their group life that Park Foresters are troubled but partly because of it, for that much more do they feel an obligation to yield to the group. And to this problem there can be no solution.

Is there a middle way? A recognition of this dilemma is the condition of it. It is only part of the battle, but unless the individual understands that this conflict of allegiances is inevitable he is intellectually without defenses. And the more benevolent the group, the more, not the less, he needs these defenses.

For ultimately his tyranny is self-imposed. In earlier chapters on life within The Organization we saw how the increasing benevolence of human relations, the more democratic atmosphere, has in one way made the individual's path more difficult. He is intimidated by normalcy. He too has become more adept at concealing hostilities and ambitions, more skillfully "normal," but he knows *he* is different and he is not sure about the others. In his own peculiarities he can feel isolated, a fraud who is not what he seems.

Wives also. Like their husbands in the office, they are easily misled by the façades of those about them in suburbia, and a frequent consequence is the "superwoman" complex. Only a minority of wives are really successful at handling both a large agenda of social or civic obligations and their home duties, but everyone puts up such a good front that many a wife begins to feel that something is wanting in her that she is not the same. Determined to be as normal as anyone else, or a little more so, they take on a back-breaking load of duties—and a guilt feeling that they're not up to it. "I've seen it so many times," says Arnold Levin, Park Forest's overworked family counselor. "They may feel inadequate because they haven't a college degree, or haven't made the League of Women Voters, or can't be a 'model' mother like someone else in the court. 'I'm not worth *enough*,' they tell me."

The impulse to self-punishment sometimes takes a more pathological form. Barbiturate addiction and attempted suicides are not over average at Park Forest related to national statistics, but there is enough to mock the façade of well-adjusted normality. In the spring of 1955 there was a rash of publicity over the number of women found lifting groceries in the supermarket. Actually, the number was not really very high, the main reason for the excitement being the merchants' faith in publicity as a deterrent. The news about who the women were, however, was something of a shocker. The average shoplifter, the police chief told the newspapers, was not a low-income wife; she was the wife of a junior executive making $8,000, she belonged to a bridge club, was active in the PTA, and attended church. Usually she had about $50 a week to spend on food and sundries. Perplexed, the police chief and the village chaplain had to put it down as part of the "middle-class neurosis." Rarely was there any obvious motive; even the repentant of the wives could not explain. Perhaps, as some psychiatrists might venture, they stole to be caught— as if they were asking to be punished for wearing a false face to the world.

To bring the problem full circle, you often find wives in deep emotional trouble because they can no longer get understanding or help from their husbands on their social problems. The wife's talk about the court or the block is not just idle gossip; this is the world she and the children must live in, and the personal relationships in it are quite analogous to the ones that are the basis of the husband's worries. But husbands have a double standard on this: office politics they see as part of a vitally important process, but the same kind of relationships in the community they dismiss as trivia, the curse of idle female tongues. "I often wonder," says Levin, "does the husband look to the job in self-defense against his wife's lack of interest? Or does she go in for civic activity because he's withdrawn into the job? I don't know which cause comes first, but it's tragic how many couples have lost the ability to meet each other's inadequacies."

Those who seem best able to steer their own course care about the good opinion of the group, but they have this distinction: they are professionals. They know the conflicts of interest between themselves and others are natural; they have been through many environments and they have the intelligence to grasp this recurring feature of group life. To use Everett Hughes's phrase, they know how to routinize crisis.

Unlike the deviate, they pay the little surface obeisances to the group. Thus do they defend themselves. They have to. Usually, those who seek their friendships through civic or cultural interests have palpably different tastes than those who accept propinquity. Members of the League of Women Voters, for example, are apt to be somewhat absent-minded about their clothes and their housekeeping.

("Most of us League gals are thin," says one, after some comments on the Women's Club. "We're so busy, and we don't have time for coffee and doughnuts.") Such people, however, have much less friction with their neighbors than might be imagined. They do not give the group enough familiarity to breed contempt; although they may draw a firm line at intimacy, they are good about baby-sitting, returning borrowed lawn mowers, and the other neighborly graces.

Above all, they do not get too close. The transients' defense against rootlessness, as we have noted, is to get involved in meaningful activity; at the same time, however, like the seasoned shipboard traveler, the wisest transients don't get too involved. Keeping this delicate balance requires a very highly developed social skill, and also a good bit of experience. "It takes time," explains one transient. "I had to go through fraternity life, then the services, and a stretch at Parkmere before I realized you just get into trouble if you get personally involved with neighbors."

More basically, what they have is a rather keen consciousness of self—and the sophistication to realize that while individualistic tastes may raise eyebrows, exercising those tastes won't bring the world crashing down about you. "One day one of the girls busted in," one upper-middlebrow cheerfully recounts. "She saw I was reading. 'What you got there, hon?' she asked me. You might have known it would be Plato that day. She almost fell over from surprise. Now all of them are sure I'm strange." Actually they don't think she's overly odd, for her deviance is accompanied by enough tact, enough observance of the little customs that oil court life, so that equilibrium is maintained.

Just where the happy mean lies, however, still depends greatly on the degree of the group's cohesion. Relatively, the seasoned transient steers his course more intelligently than the others. But he too is not proof against beneficence. "Every once in a while I wonder," says one transient, in an almost furtive moment of contemplation. "I don't want to do anything to offend the people in our block; they're kind and decent, and I'm proud we've been able to get along with one another—with all our differences—so well. But then, once in a while, I think of myself and my husband and what we are not doing, and I get depressed. Is it just enough not to be bad?" Many others are so troubled. They sense that by their immersion in the group they are frustrating other urges, yet they feel that responding to the group is a moral duty—and so they continue, hesitant and unsure, imprisoned in brotherhood.

THOUGHT REFORM: IDEOLOGICAL REMOLDING IN CHINA
/Harriet C. Mills

For the past ten years the Chinese Communists have been conducting the greatest campaign in human history to re-shape the minds of men. No other Communist or authoritarian state, not even the Soviet Union, has ever equaled the scope and intensity of the Chinese Communist effort.

The Chinese Communists believe that thought determines action. Thus, if 650 million Chinese can be brought to think "correctly," they will act "correctly" along lines the Chinese Communist Party considers essential for the creation of its version of a socialist China, to become at some distant date a Communist society in a Communist world.

The Chinese Communists are attempting to remold the mind as well as the face of China. Their approach combines standard techniques of the authoritarian state with a system of their own invention. Like any authoritarian state, the People's Republic of China has the power to enforce its edicts and protect official ideology by absolute control of education and all regular mass media. A vast supplementary network of village radio receivers and loud-speakers, housetop megaphone recasts, and door-to-door agents of oral propaganda carries official news, slogans, rousing songs, and propaganda skits to the illiterate in re-mote rural areas. In the familiar pattern of modern au-thoritarian societies, the whole population is thoroughly organized. Virtually every individual belongs to one or more mass organizations built around his age, residential, trade, or professional group.

However, the Chinese Communists are well aware that, effective as such regimentation may be in conditioning hab-its of action and response, it does not necessarily achieve genuine reorientation. They know that only if people are truly persuaded of the justice and correctness of the Communist position will they release their spontaneous creative energy and co-operate, not from necessity but from conviction. To accelerate this persuasion the Chinese Communists have developed group study, or *hsüeh-hsi*, in which everyone must participate—peasant, ex-landlord, city dweller, artisan, worker, peddler, merchant, housewife, producer, industrialist, even the political prisoner. Group study is a unique means for achieving critical rejection of old ideas in favor of new ones and a powerful weapon for ideological remolding.

Two main lines of experience have gone into group study, one Chinese, one Communist. During their twenty-odd years as guerrilla fighters, the Chinese Communists stumbled, through necessity, on one basic element of what is now group study. In teaching uneducated peasant recruits to use weapons, obey commands, live together, and protect the country people, the Communists gradually found that small discussion groups were the best way to make sure each man understood not only how but why. These small groups went patiently over all questions, objections, or counter-suggestions until the best method had been found and agreed upon. To the peasantry, on whom the army depended for support and cover, the Communists likewise explained their rural improvement program, rent reduction, land redistribution, public health, and literacy. Thus, they persuaded the peasants that it was to their advantage to co-operate in resisting Japan or the Kuomintang. The high morale of the guerrilla areas justified the Communists' approach.

The second objective in group study—namely, the study of Marxist theory and the discipline of criticism and self-criticism—has long been standard practice in Communist cells around the world. Out of the gradual fusion of these two traditions—Chinese persuasion and Communist dogma —contemporary group study has evolved as the ubiquitous working mechanism of thought reform in China.

Today every office, factory, shop, school, co-operative, commune, military or residential unit in China is divided into ostensibly voluntary small study groups of about six to twelve persons. Under elected leaders, approved by the authorities, these groups are required to meet regularly to discuss government policies, Marxist theory, or whatever has been mapped out for discussion by the central Party and government organs directing the nationwide group-study program. The function of these small study groups is to persuade members of the validity of the official position by bringing their thinking into line with that of the Party. Complex interplay of psychological and personal factors gives the technique its special character and power.

First, the study group is official. The leader represents and reports to higher authorities. Every member knows that evaluation of his thinking as reactionary, backward, bourgeois, apolitical, progressive, or zealous materially affects his future for better or for worse.

Second, everyone must express an opinion; there is no freedom of silence. In a small, intimate group, whose members know each other well and work and sometimes even live together, it can be very embarrassing to express an incorrect idea, yet over a long period it is virtually impossible to dissemble.

Third, parroting theory or the official line is not enough. Nor is mere intellectual acknowledgment of the reasonableness of the stipulated position sufficient. The important thing is to apply correct theory so as to discredit one's previous incorrect conceptions so thoroughly in one's own eyes that one gladly discards them and accepts the new. It is not sufficient for one to come to the genuine intellectual position that landlords were bad for China, yet maintain that not all landlords, one's father or a friend, perhaps, were bad. This proves unresolved sympathy with the old order. Nor can one honestly believe that America had been aggressive in China and yet feel that the U.S. system of elections is more democratic than China's. This proves insufficient understanding of the nature of the capitalist-imperialist system, which, if predatory abroad, could hardly be benign at home. Likewise, it proves unresolved pro-Americanism, which by extension becomes general sympathy with the West and therefore hostility to the Communist Party in China.

For an intellectual to admit that labor—mental and physical—is the origin of all wealth, the root of all progress, and yet be reluctant to participate in an allotted span of agricultural work proves he still retains elements of bourgeois prejudice against manual labor and is therefore still bourgeois. Raising the level of one's political consciousness through group study is considered a lifelong process. Not even Mao Tse-tung is beyond improvement.

The weapon the group uses is criticism. The ideas of each member are criticized by the others against the correct standard. In this way, everyone is forced actively to apply that standard to someone else's problem and is not permitted simply to receive it passively. The individual who is co-operative, who satisfies his fellows that he is really examining and gradually modifying his views, is "helped" in a quiet, reasoned, and friendly manner, for his attitude is good. One who stubbornly insists on maintaining his original position, who says, if not overtly, at least in effect, "I know all your arguments, but I still think I'm right," is treated as an enemy of the group, subject to intense, prolonged criticism of his attitude as well as his thoughts. Helping him may even take the form of "struggle" or verbal assault (tou-cheng), a humiliating combination of loud criticism interlarded with sarcasm, epithet, and—very rarely—with minor violence. It involves ostracism by, but not escape from, members of his study group and even the threat of public verbal assault before several small groups or an entire organization. Nor can the one being helped find solace among other friends or relatives, for in China a thought problem is serious. Everyone must help to solve it. No one ventures to prolong the agony by dangerous sympathy.

Self-criticism is as important as, if not more important than, criticism. One cannot merely reveal his thoughts. He must detail convincing reasons why he thinks they are wrong. Only thus, it is argued, can he avoid continuing to think and therefore to act in the old, incorrect way. If his fellows feel his self-criticism is genuine, though not profound, they will—again with reason, quiet, and friendliness —help him to see more deeply into his problems. If, however, they feel his self-criticism is a ruse adopted to ward off criticism, the offender will be vigorously helped and, if necessary, subjected to verbal assault until his fellows are convinced that he has begun to see the light.

What are the factors which tend to make group study, tense and painful as it often is, effective? First, there is the essential human need to belong, to achieve and maintain emotional balance. To be unprogressive in China is not simply a political verdict; it is social suicide as well. Second, the constant repetition of correct ideas and particularly the application of them to the public analysis of one's own and others' problems mean that one is forced to give them detailed scrutiny. The Communists are conscious of the value of this. "From habit or pretense," they say, "it may become real." Third—and this is all too often neglected by outside observers—is the crusading idealism, the strong moral note, that runs through all discussion of political, social, and economic steps. Since it is obviously right that China should be made new and strong to assume its long overdue place as a major power, it is right to collectivize so as to mechanize and increase agricultural production. It is right to be Spartan and not demand higher wages so more effort can go into new plants, right to report opposition to the Party that is bringing medicine, schooling, and security to half a billion peasants, right to resist the "aggressive designs" of the United States in Korea, right that women should be emancipated. Fourth, there is the universal knowledge, as the highest spokesmen of the Party have frankly admitted, that in the long run no course but the correct one is open. Attempts to avoid the tensions of group study by tacit compact to go through the routine or to stick to pleasantries are blocked not only by the fact of the leader's relations with the authorities but by the ever-present possibility that some member, whether motivated by genuine change of heart or by a selfish attempt at winning official favor, might report the group. Thus, there is tremendous pressure both to fall in line and to want to fall in line.

Most important of all, however, is a sense of nationalism, a patriotic pride in China's new posture of confidence and achievement. That China, which in 1948 was economically prostrate under runaway inflation, maladministered by a weak and corrupt government totally dependent on American aid, incapable of producing motorcycles, much less automobiles, can now fight the United Nations to a draw in Korea, maintain the world's fourth largest air force, produce trucks, jet planes, even establish a nuclear reactor, is an intoxicating spectacle to the Chinese. This pride, in turn, has generated a remarkably effective and spontaneous code of public honesty, courtesy, and civic sense unknown in the old China. To be asked whether an incorrect idea is really worthy of the new China can make one feel guilty. Thousands have asked themselves, "What right have I to disagree with those who can achieve so much?" As a professor of English, remembering China's internal disintegration and international humiliation, explained to me in the spring of 1951, "Now we can again be proud to be Chinese!"

This man, a master of arts from Yale, had taught in an army language program at Harvard during World War II and knew and liked America. No left-wing enthusiast, he was slow in making up his mind about the Communists in the early period of their power, but as they brought the country under control, licked inflation, improved material conditions in the universities, and dared abrogate the unequal treaties, he proudly identified himself with the new China. For him, group study was stimulating. He looked on it as accelerating the weeding out of his undesirable bourgeois liberalism and promoting the growth of new socialist thinking. He had once enjoyed *Animal Farm*, but by mid-1951 he rejected *1984*, though his wife, a graduate of an American university in Shanghai, did not.

The valedictorian of the class of 1948 at the same university—the last class to graduate before the Communist take-over—was a brilliant student of international affairs. His English was good, his French and Japanese serviceable. His burning idealism had led him as a high school student into Christianity. Later, at the university, it led him into the student movement, which, in the last years before the fall of the Kuomintang, was dominated by the left. For months after the Communists came in, he was deeply troubled. His patriotism thrilled to the assurance and vitality of the Communists. Other aspects of his being cringed at their attack on habits and patterns of thinking which he subscribed to, including his Christianity.

One hot summer day he came to see me. "I have studied and studied," he said, using the Chinese term *hsüeh-hsi*, "and thought and thought. I have begun to feel there is more good in the Communist Party than in the Christian church. If I can satisfy myself on this score, I shall join the Party." Shortly afterwards he told me that he had. "Now that you are a Party member," I asked, "do you think group study is still worth your while?" "Oh, yes," he replied, his eyes burning with infectious enthusiasm, "it is indispensable."

Group study can even be exhilarating, particularly for those who, having been heavily criticized or struggled against, admit the error of their ways and are readmitted to the fellowship of the group. My good friend, a young former YWCA secretary, is only one example. Daughter of a Japanese-trained optometrist, she had graduated from the Catholic University in Peking about the end of World War II. A Protestant, she went to work for the YWCA and soon became close to young American students and diplomatic personnel who returned to Peking after the war. Transferred away for a while, she returned to Peking in early 1950 and joined the Central Relief Agency of the People's Government. She was miserable. She welcomed the material advances of the Government but felt that the price, in terms of regimentation, controlled thought, required group study, anti-Americanism, and the like, was too high. "I will go anywhere in the world," she used to remark, "where there is no group study."

Intrinsically honest, my friend's reservations about the regime were all too obvious. She could not fit into, and was therefore cut off from, the mainstream of Chinese life. Her Chinese friends pleaded with her to reconsider her attitude, particularly her relations with me, since by early 1951 I was known to be under suspicion. Her Western friends, knowing there was little possibility for her to leave China, were forced to urge her to compromise. But she remained fiercely loyal to her standards and her friends. For this she eventually landed, on my account, in the same prison cell with me.

In prison, as outside, she soon won the respect of wardens as well as prisoners for her honesty and courage. She did not pretend. Her kindnesses to me, whom the Communists had arrested as an American spy, were unobtrusive, but if discovered she courageously admitted them. For the first time in her life, she met people from many walks of Chinese life, people who, unlike herself, were uneducated, had had no contact with foreigners, people who were wholly and completely Chinese. Some had accomplished amazing things against incredible odds. She began to see a new dimension to her native land, to feel its hope lay within itself. She no longer felt that China was somehow inferior to the West. She began to discover her Chinese identity. But her habits of mind, her desire to look at both sides of a question, to undertake impartial inquiry, her reluctance to be regimented, and particularly her loyalty to her old friends died hard, and she was on one or two occasions briefly struggled against.

The result which I watched was a sort of catharsis. Her point of view changed, and with it her evaluation of past friends and associations. She remained as courageous, fair, and honest as ever, but her frame of reference was new. The joy and good feeling within the cell group that had helped her were enormous and vital. The helpers rejoiced at a black sheep brought home. She rejoiced at the psychological relief of having achieved spiritual integration. Very positive feelings of identification with and gratitude toward the small group and the larger society beyond followed.

From time to time, all means of state propaganda, including the group-study mechanism, focus the thinking of the entire nation on specific economic, political, or ideological questions in great campaigns or movements. These campaigns are building blocks in the monolithic orthodoxy which the Communists are determined to erect. Roughly, they fall into two categories. The primary purpose of one type is to discredit some existing idea, group, or system inimical to Communist ends. The second category aims to explain some program about to be enacted or some theory the Communists feel must be universally understood.

Campaigns usually begin with a series of articles and editorials in newspapers. Since newspaper reading is a political obligation in China and items of the day are often taken up in study groups, a subject which has received more than usual attention will begin to be discussed. Thus, a demand is created for further study, for which the materials and instructions are soon forthcoming. The campaign, which may last several months, is launched.

When the aim is to discredit, the initial articles will be exposés of the evil to be attacked. Some person, group, or catchword is made into a symbol. Every organization, office, factory, school, military unit, and so forth then embarks on an intense campaign of its own to find examples within its ranks. If concepts like bureaucracy, commandism, extravagance, timidity, and the like are under fire, flagrant manifestations of these are certain to be found in every organization, and most individuals will confess to similar tendencies in themselves. Serious offenders are required to examine their thoughts to uncover what causes them to act thus. Those whose examination is unsatisfactory are brought before a public meeting of the organization, which may turn into a struggle meeting. Depending on the nature of the campaign, the offense, and the outcome of organizational help, they may be remanded to a period of reflection, supervision, special full-time study, or, in serious cases where criminality is involved, to prison, where intensive thought reform and punishment are combined. The aim is *redemption through criticism*. Mass accusation meetings administering summary justice to landlords and counter-revolutionaries were used, particularly in the early years of the regime, in connection with campaigns to educate the public.

In campaigns like those against counterrevolutionaries, it is not suggested that every organization harbors a traitor. However, each study group will discuss not only the facts as presented by the Government but also what sort of thought could have produced such actions. The group will then proceed to look for traces of the same in themselves. Thus, a campaign against counterrevolutionaries provides education along many lines. Showing how counterrevolutionaries serve the exploiting classes raises the whole issue of class and the nature of the class struggle. Betrayal of the common good, as embodied in the state, by counterrevolutionaries becomes an object lesson in the meaning and duty of citizenship; enemies of the state, be they friends or relatives, must be reported. The difficulty of ferreting out counterrevolutionaries emphasizes the need to cultivate a high level of political consciousness. Promulgation of the statutes for dealing with counterrevolutionaries dramatizes the fact that harsh treatment and death are reserved for those who do not repent and reform. For those who confess and are penitent, there is leniency. So, too, the 1957–1958 anti-rightist and rectification campaign was used to educate the nation still further on the correctness of the Party in all things. Criticisms voiced during the Hundred Flowers period earlier in 1957 were refuted and discredited. A new movement to give one's heart to the Party followed.

Campaigns of explanation put the major emphasis on the Communist theory which makes impending economic or political changes both inevitable and just. A few movements, like the early campaign for the Stockholm Peace Appeal or the current Hate America campaign, are basically ideological in intent, unrelated to any impending change. Others, like the famous Resist America, Aid Korea movement, are designed both to discredit and to mobilize.

Physical labor plays a major role in thought reform in China. Invoking Marxist insistence on the dignity of labor as the origin of all value and wealth, the Communists strive to counter strong traditional Chinese scorn for manual labor. They are determined to negate a fundamental tenet of Chinese thinking formulated by Confucius 2500 years ago: "Who works with his mind rules; who works with his hands is ruled." Reform by labor goes hand in hand with reform through study in the rehabilitation of prisoners and landlords. In Peking political prisons, the right to labor comes only after a certain level of reform through study has been achieved.

Intellectuals, city office workers, and government cadres, merchants, capitalists, and students have long been urged to do voluntary labor on weekends and holidays. In a tremendous attempt to break down prejudice toward labor and increase appreciation of the leadership of the proletariat, during the past couple of years there has been regular assignment of large groups for extensive periods to agricultural and factory work.

How effective has ideological remolding been? No simple answer is possible, for it varies with and within different segments of the population. The Communists stress that thought reform is a long, arduous task which has just begun; even in theory, the perfect mentality which needs no reform must wait on a perfect society.

Particularly in the early years of the regime, the degree of organization for indoctrination through study differed sharply, from very loose among the peasants to very tight in well-defined bodies, like offices, factories, schools, and the military. Once the co-operatives were set up in the countryside, more intensive group study became possible, bringing peasants in many ways very positively into the pattern of national life. But, as a recent official summary admitted, many peasants did not clearly grasp the relation between the state, the co-operative, and the individual household; some still harbored "individual and group exclusiveness, which disregard national and collective interests." Some well-to-do peasants sabotaged or competed against the co-operative and resisted state grain policy. Unless a high level of political and social consciousness can be developed and maintained among the peasants, it is possible that, as communes are set up and proprietorship becomes more impersonal, they will be no more interested in working for the commune than they were for the landlord but will save their best efforts for their recently guaranteed private plots.

Among workers, the Communists claim—and reports tend to confirm—the ideological situation is generally good. But the influx of other than working-class elements into the labor force has led the Communists to call for a drive to help workers "recognize that they must, under the leadership of the Communist Party, constantly raise their own social consciousness . . . develop the excellent tradition of working hard, maintain the noble character of being just and selfless, work hard in production, save, and economize." Note that the word "raise," not "reform," is used, because under the theory that makes workers leaders of any Communist revolution, working-class mentality is, by definition, correct.

Resistance to ideological remolding has been strong among what the Communists call the "bourgeoisie" and the "bourgeois intellectuals." Both are very broad terms. "Bourgeoisie" covers roughly all private business above a one-man show, and well-to-do peasants. "Bourgeois intellectual" means not so much egghead as all students, technicians, and specialists beyond the high school level, scientists, professional men, and university personnel. From the beginning, the Communists, realizing that these groups, who generally had had the largest stake in the old order, would prove most troublesome, have given special attention to their reform.

Destruction of the bourgeoisie through the reform of its members has been declared a basic tenet of the revolutionary program. Thought reform, therefore, involves turning them into willing pallbearers at their own funeral. The 1951–1952 Five Anti Campaigns (against bribery, tax evasion, theft of state property, cheating on government contracts, and leakage of government economic secrets), designed to discredit the irresponsible selfishness of production for private profit, greatly weakened the economic position of the bourgeoisie. For many months they were required to study, examine, and confess with special intensity the errors of their thinking and conduct. Since 1953, a body established to deal with the bourgeoisie and pave the way for their compensated integration into the socialist economy has conducted thorough ideological education, urging the need to abide by law, the acceptance of socialist transformation, the teachings of Mao Tse-tung, and patriotism. The group has continually organized the bourgeoisie for participation in patriotic and social movements.

But though the bourgeoisie did not resist the socialist transformation of 1956, they have not been reformed, at least in areas touching on their economic role. The Communists candidly state that the majority have come to realize there would be no way out by opposing the proletariat. But they admit that those of the bourgeoisie and the bourgeois intellectuals "are unwilling to accept the leadership of the proletariat and the Communist Party."

Most difficult of all to refashion have been the higher intellectuals—scientists, professors, and the like. They have the knowledge and the skills which the Communists lack and need, but have little patience with Communist dogmatism and interference. Communist policy toward this strategic group in the past decade has consistently aimed at securing most effective utilization of its knowledge. Zigzagging steadily toward this goal, the Communists have now attacked, now united, now criticized. Meanwhile, they are recruiting their own Red intellectuals, but have not yet had time to train a new group both Red and expert.

The importance and recalcitrance of the intellectuals, largely Western-oriented and often American-trained, have subjected them to more intense and sustained reform than that applied to any other section of the population. Like everyone else, they have gone through a decade of group study. As many came from landlord families, they were sent to the countryside during land redistribution, an experience which for the most part appears to have decisively reformed their attitude toward landlords. Participation in such activities as the Resist America, Aid Korea campaign and the Sino-Soviet Friendship Association was supposed to help change their sympathy with the West to admiration for the Soviet Union. It is hard to assess just how successful these moves have been, but it should be noted in passing that the hardening American position toward China in the last ten years has not encouraged America's sensitive and nationalistic friends there and has unwittingly played into Communist hands.

After two years of gentle courting, the Communists stiffened the ideological remolding of the intelligentsia in late 1951. Thousands were concentrated in special centers for reform, and the group study of others was greatly stepped up. The hard line continued into 1955. By 1956, the Party had become seriously disturbed by the negative response of the intellectuals chafing under brusque dogmatism, the arrogance of ignorant cadres, and time-consuming group study and public meetings. Chou En-lai, admitting errors in handling intellectuals, estimated that only 40 per cent actively supported the regime. Relaxation followed. The Government materially improved living and working conditions of the intellectuals, treated them with polite respect, urged them to speak out—even to criticize—freely and frankly. The intellectuals were grateful but wary.

Finally, after more than a year of gentle prodding and watchful waiting, the Hundred Flowers of criticism bloomed wildly for one brief month from May 8 to June 8, 1957. One after another, intellectuals delivered scathing attacks on monolithic Party power, the identification of Party and state, the sham of coalition government with minor parties, the incompetence and arrogance of Party cadres. Intellectuals complained of high but powerless posts, of the damaging effects of Party interference with education and research, and of something not limited to Communist societies—denial of access to research data for reasons of security. They questioned the infallibility of Marx-Leninism. They called the Party incompetent to lead in science, education, and the arts. They declared that Party bureaucratism is worse than capitalism. Forceful as the criticisms were, they were not aimed at the overthrow of the Government. Rather, they aimed at making it genuinely democratic, with democratic safeguards and a sharing of political power. The intellectuals in essence demanded a separation of Party and government, of Party and technical endeavor.

Communist response was swift. Critics were automatically identified as rightists, and rectification campaigns were launched. In late 1957, prominent critics were forced to make public confessions and were dismissed from office, but apparently not imprisoned or executed. Lesser voices confessed and repledged their support of the Party. Nineteen fifty-eight brought a new and in many ways, unprecedentedly rigid orthodoxy. In January, 1959, a high official concluded that the intellectuals were dragging their feet, generally tired of self-remolding.

Because tired and resentful intellectuals do not release their full creative power, the tack in early 1959 veered once again toward persuasion. Many dismissed in 1957 were reinstated, although there have been recent indications of a new tightening up. "We must conduct long, recurrent, patient, delicate, and persuasive education." At least another decade—perhaps much longer—will be required, Party spokesmen emphasize, because bourgeois intellectuals are not just those left over from the old society whom the attrition of time could remove; men trained recently have acquired the same outlook.

What of the future? Mao Tse-tung has declared that there will be regular rectification campaigns. "Thought reform," he says, "is a protracted, gigantic, and complex task. As the struggle will continue to experience ups and downs, we shall have both tense and slack moments during our work and shall have to proceed in a zigzag."

To say that the Communists have not made complete Marxists out of the Chinese is not sufficient grounds for concluding that in the eyes of the Chinese people they have failed or that volcanic discontent smolders under the surface, straining to erupt. Certain expectations generated by a decade of Communist accomplishment will persist; certain attitudes have been permanently reformed by Communist education. The sense of national pride and dignity, the expectation of honest and efficient government will continue. Through group study and the experience of manifold collective living and working, the Chinese have become and will remain conscious of the interrelationship of various social elements. They may not agree with the Communist interpretation, but gone is the day when, in Sun Yat-sen's phrase, China was like a sheet of loose sand with no sense of cohesion. The thirst for modernity, for ordered, planned, and accelerated economic development by all levels of society, cannot be quenched. The farmer, who may not like the regimentation of the commune, desires not so much return to his unprotected position in the old order as more freedom to utilize for his personal profit the advantages which land redistribution, peace, market stability, and government technical assistance in seeds and fertilizer have brought. He wants to have his cake and eat it too.

Public demand for adequate health and welfare systems, for education will not abate. The shopkeeper, who may not be too happy about being socialized, nonetheless appreciates the fact that his son can finish school, and, with ability, even college. The woman who objects to placing her child in a state nursery so she may be freed for labor is still grateful for the genuine improvement in public health. As the Hundred Flowers movement showed, opposition and bitter criticism in many areas are not so much a demand for the return of the old order as for the revision of the new, under broader, not exclusively Communist leadership.

Observers recently back from China report that the crusading spirit of idealism and sacrifice so prevalent in the early part of the decade is gradually receding. There is a rising desire among the people for more material benefits *now*. Ironically, the Communists are trapped by their own success. Spectacular strides toward industrialization have unleashed tremendous, if premature, expectations, which the Communists will have to deal with both in their economic planning and their group-study program.

To date, success of group study has depended to no small degree on its invocation of moral and patriotic appeals. In the future, these may not be enough. If the system is to continue to be effective, the Communists will have to find a new focus for thought reform or resort to more pressure. How the inventors of history's most potent mechanism for ideological reform meet this challenge will be an important story of the next decade.

CHALLENGE OF THE "NEW SOVIET MAN"
/Urie Bronfenbrenner

Whatever course Mr. Khrushchev elects to follow in the development of world communism, its success or failure, so far as Russia is concerned, will depend on what Russian leaders call the "new Soviet man." Mr. Khrushchev has spoken about him in his speeches. We have seen his power reflected, so the Russian press tells us, in Soviet achievements in industry, athletics and science. And, of course, only recently the Russians introduced him to us in the flesh, in the persons of Major Gagarin and Major Titov.

The Soviet leaders give a double reason for their enthusiasm about the new Soviet man. They express pride not only in what he does, but also in what he is. For he is, as the Russians see it, a planned product of Communist society—the result of an explicit system of character training being employed daily in Soviet families, nurseries, schools and youth groups.

What is the nature of this system? One of the best ways to become acquainted with it is to examine some of the books and manuals for parents, teachers and youth workers that are published by the hundreds of thousands in the U. S. S. R. By far the most important of these are the works of the Soviet educator, A. S. Makarenko.

In the early Nineteen Twenties, Makarenko, then a young school teacher and a devout Communist, was given the task of developing a rehabilitation program for some of the hundreds of homeless children who were roaming the Soviet Union after the civil wars. The first such group assigned to him consisted of boys about 18 years old with extensive court records of house-breaking, armed robbery and manslaughter. For the first few months, Makarenko's school—an isolated, ramshackle building—served simply as the headquarters for a band of highwaymen who were his legal wards.

But gradually, through development of his group-oriented discipline techniques, and through what can only be called the compelling power of his own moral convictions, Makarenko was able to create a sense of responsibility and commitment to the work program and code of conduct he had laid out. In the end, the so-called Gorky Commune became known throughout the Soviet Union for its high morale and discipline and for the productivity of its fields, farms and shops. And in the years that followed Makarenko's methods came to be widely adopted not only throughout the U. S. S. R. but also in the satellites, notably East Germany, and in Communist China.

To get some notion of Makarenko's ideas, we might look first at what is probably the most widely read of his works, "A Book for Parents." Here is an excerpt:

Our [Soviet] family is not an accidental combination of members of society. The family is a natural collective body and, like everything natural, healthy and normal, it can only blossom forth in Socialist society, freed of those very curses from which both mankind as a whole and the individual are freeing themselves.

The family becomes the natural primary cell of society, the place where the delight of human life is realized, where the triumphant forces of man are refreshed, where children—the chief joy of life—live and grow.

Our parents are not without authority either, but this authority is only the reflection of societal authority. The duty of a father in our country toward his children is a particular form of his duty toward society. It is as if our society says to parents:

"You have joined together in good-will and love, rejoice in your children and expect to go on rejoicing in them. That is your personal affair and concerns your personal happiness. Within the course of this happy process you have given birth to new human beings. A time will come when these beings will cease to be solely the instruments of your happiness, and will step forth as independent members of society. For society, it is by no means a matter of indifference what kind of people they will become. In delegating to you a certain measure of societal authority, the Soviet state demands from you the correct upbringing of its future citizens. Particularly it relies on you to provide certain conditions arising naturally out of your union; namely, your parental love.

"If you wish to give birth to a citizen while dispensing with parental love, then be so kind as to warn society that you intend to do such a filthy thing. Human beings who are brought up without parental love are often deformed human beings."

From this it can be seen that paramount in Makarenko's thinking is the thesis that the parent's authority over the child is delegated to him by the state, and that duty to one's children is merely a particular instance of one's broader duty toward society. A little later in the book he makes this point even more emphatically. After telling the story of a boy who ran away from home after some differences with his mother, he concludes by affirming: "I am a great admirer of optimism and I like very much young lads who have so much faith in the Soviet state that they are carried away and will not trust even their own mothers."

In other words, when the needs and values of the family conflict with those of society, there is no question about which gets priority. And society receives its concrete manifestation and embodiment in the collective, which is any organized group engaged in some socially useful enterprise.

This brings us to the second major theme in Makarenko's

work—the focal role of the collective in the child's upbringing. In his view, only the collective can supply the necessary conditions for achieving what he describes as the
main aim of Soviet education—that of developing persons
who possess the ability, motivation and skill for working
together to attain the goals set for Communist society by its
leaders. Accordingly, in his voluminous writings, Makarenko devotes considerable attention to the principles and
procedures that are best employed for building the collective
and using it as an instrument for character education.

It is these same principles and practices which pervade
the manuals outlining the procedures to be employed for
the training of Soviet youth. The introduction to one typical example describes the work as a handbook for school
directors, class supervisors, teachers and Young Pioneer
(Communist youth organization) leaders.

The title gives one pause, for this book on how to conduct classroom activities is called "Socialist Competition in
the Schools." And the same idea is echoed in the titles of
individual chapters: "Competition in the Classroom,"
"Competition Between Classrooms," "Competition Between Schools," and so on. It is not difficult to see how the
Russians are led to the notion of competition between nations and social systems.

To turn to the text itself: In an early chapter we find
ourselves in the first grade on the first day of school. There
is even a photograph of the teacher addressing the class.
She is saying, "Let's see which row can sit the straightest!"

This approach, the book tells us, has certain important psychological advantages, for in response:

> The children not only try to do everything as well as
> possible themselves, but also take an evaluative attitude
> toward those who are undermining the achievement of
> the row. . . . Gradually the children themselves begin
> to monitor the behavior of their comrades and remind
> those of them who forget about the rules set by the
> teacher. . . . The teacher soon has helpers.

Nor is the emergence of such help left to chance, for the
teacher appoints row monitors for each activity—for personal cleanliness, condition of desks, conduct in passing
from one room to the other, quality of recitations in each
subject, and so on. Following the teacher's example, the

monitors are taught to evaluate the behavior and performance of their classmates and then to report their evaluations publicly or to "link" leaders. (A link is the smallest unit of the Communist youth organization, which reaches into every classroom, from the first grade on. Link members are commonly seated together and there are usually several links in each class.)

> Here is a typical picture [we read]. It is the beginning of the lesson. In the first row the link leader reports, basing his comments on information submitted by the sanitarian and other responsible monitors: "Today Valodya did the wrong problem. Masha didn't write neatly, and forgot to underline the right words in her lesson. Alyosha had a dirty shirt collar."
> The youngsters are not offended by this procedure; they understand that the link leaders are not just tattling but simply fulfilling their duty. It doesn't even occur to the monitors and sanitarians to conceal the shortcomings of their comrades. They feel they are doing their job well precisely when they notice one or another defect.

In the third grade, the teacher introduces a new wrinkle. She now proposes that the children compete with the monitors, and see if they can beat them at their own game through self-criticism. The results of this procedure are "spectacular," we are told. "When the monitor is able to talk about only four or five members of the row there are supplementary reports about their own shortcomings from as many as eight or ten pupils."

Evaluations come not only from teachers and classmates but also from parents, who are asked to report grades for their children's behavior and performance of chores at home. But how can one depend on parents to turn in truthful reports? Part of the answer was supplied to me in a conversation with a Soviet agricultural expert.

He explained that, no matter what a person's job, the collective at his place of work always took an active interest in his family life. Thus a representative would come to the worker's home to observe and talk with his wife and children. And if any undesirable features were noted, these would be reported to the collective.

Asked for an example, my informant said: "Well, suppose the representative were to notice that my wife and I quarreled in front of the children. That would be bad. They would speak to me about it and remind me of my responsibilities for training my children to be good citizens."

He agreed that the situation was different in America, and said: "That's one of the strange things about your system in the West. The family is separated from the rest of society. That's not good."

He paused for a moment and then went on. "I suppose if my wife didn't want to let the representative in, she could ask him to leave. But then, at my place of work, I should feel ashamed—'Ivanov,' they would say, 'has an uncultured wife.' "

But it would be a mistake to conclude that Soviet methods of character education and social control are based primarily on negative criticism. On the contrary, there is as much of the carrot as the stick. However, the carrot is given not merely as a reward for individual performance but explicitly for the child's contribution to group achievement.

The great charts emblazoned "Who Is Best?" which bedeck the walls of every classroom have as entries the names not of individual pupils but of rows and links. It is the winning unit that gets rewarded by a pennant, by a special privilege or by having its picture taken in parade uniforms.

Helping other members of one's collective and appreciating their contributions—themes that are much stressed in Soviet character training—become matters of enlightened self-interest, since the grade that each person receives depends on the over-all performance of his unit. Thus the good student finds it to his advantage to help the poor one. The same principle is carried over to the group level. There, champion rows and classes are made responsible for the performance of poorer ones.

This, then, is the process through which the Russians attempt to form the new Soviet man. Its aim is clear enough—to build a sense of commitment to and identity with the collective and, through it, with Communist society. How successful are the results of this massive endeavor? Here are some random impressions based on my own observations and those of other social scientists who have visited the U. S. S. R.

Like other observers, I was struck by the precociously adultlike behavior of Soviet children. By Western standards, they are remarkably well-mannered, industrious, serious and well-informed. But equally impressive to a social psychologist were certain aspects of the adult society. These features can be seen from two perspectives.

From one point of view, there is certainly, in the Soviet Union, a pervasive conformity to group norms, which is reinforced by social criticism—informal as well as formal. Deviant behavior, such as tossing a scrap of paper on the pavement, is promptly reprimanded by the nearest passerby as *"nyekulturno"* (uncultured). And when one requests anything that is the least bit irregular, there is a ready answer: "It is impossible" or "It is not my affair." Individual needs have no status. To have a request granted, one has to appear as a member of one's collective.

But there is another view of this same picture. Along with conformity, there is a common commitment to values, goals and ways of life. As I observed, listened to, and talked with many Russians, I was surprised by the strength and pervasiveness of what appeared to be genuine pride and faith in their system.

What is more, the commitment extended beyond mere words. On every side people were busily engaged in some form of productive activity, and they spoke enthusiastically of the progress they were making. Not only the newspapers, but the man on the street would proclaim proudly, "In a few more years, we shall catch up to you." Then, with a grin of confidence: "And a few more years after that, we shall be way ahead of you!"

Of course, not everything is going the Communists' way, even in the U. S. S. R. The apathy, corruption, disaffection and alcoholism which the Soviet leaders, in effect, acknowledge by their frequent denunciations are apparent to the visitor, especially if he takes the trouble to depart from the Intourist track and wander on his own.

In the face of such problems, the Soviet Government is placing more, rather than less, reliance on its methods of character education. A major aspect of the educational reform announced two years ago involves the development of several new types of educational institutions. The most important of these is the *internat* or boarding school, in which children are to be entered as early as three months of age, with parents visiting only on week-ends. (Surprising as it may seem to Americans, Russian infants are boarded out at this age.)

Recent statements in the Soviet press reveal that the Government is experiencing some difficulties with these schools. Construction is not proceeding according to plan and some parents object to sending their children to school in other cities or towns.

But the Government, apparently, has not modified its ultimate objective. Other types of schools will keep the youngsters from 8 in the morning until 8 at night. All types are designed not only to provide adequate care for children in a nation of working mothers, but also, in line with Makarenko's principles, to give maximum opportunity for training in practical education, character building and experience in collective living.

What are the implications of these developments for the West? Clearly, some central features of the Soviet approach, such as the denial of the right to deviate and the glorification of the "informer," are incompatible with what we regard as moral and right. But this does not mean that the Soviet methods are not effective. On the contrary, they may serve quite well for developing the motives and skills that make for progress and productivity in a Communist society.

Moreover, the Soviet social technology is exportable, and it *is* being exported on an extensive scale to other nations around the world. To cite but a minor example, a Russian educator told me that his latest book was the largest-selling psychology text in Mexico (and probably the cheapest in price). Finally, it is entirely possible that the recent Soviet achievements in industry, education, sports and science are merely the first fruits of an equally potent social technology which renovates not only things but men themselves.

What does one do in the face of such a challenge? Clearly, there is no simple, quick countermeasure that will remove the threat and relieve our anxiety. In fact, we have yet to learn to become anxious, to appreciate the full extent and nature of the danger we face. For it is not what the Communist world can and will do, but what we can and will not do that carries the threat to our Western civilization.

Our civilization challenges the Communist world with the revolutionary proposition that responsibility is not incompatible with freedom, and that the welfare of society and the dignity of the individual are inseparable. But the question of which thesis will triumph clearly depends not on ideas alone but on the actions these ideas inspire.

In the realm of education the Communists are giving

systematic attention and major emphasis to training in values and behavior consistent with their ideals. We can hardly claim we are doing as much or as well for our own value system. In American schools, training for action consistent with social responsibility and human dignity is at best an extra-curricular activity. Yet we are fond of saying that the American school is the bulwark of democracy. If this be true, we had better look to our defenses.

IX. EPILOGUE

THE HARE AND THE HARUSPEX: A CAUTIONARY TALE
/Edward S. Deevey

Biologists, of whom I am one, have been taking a lively interest in lemmings lately. These rat-sized hyperborean field mice were unknown in the ancient world, and even the sagas are strangely silent about them. They really began to draw attention only in Queen Victoria's time, and especially in England, when the notion somehow got about that Plato's Atlantis lay on the Dogger Bank, under the North Sea. The lemmings' efforts to emigrate from Norway were then explained as vain attempts to recover a lost homeland, now occupied by such thoroughly English creatures as the haddock and the sprat. The fact that Swedish lemmings march in the wrong direction, toward the Baltic, tends to undermine this theory, but science has not come up with a better explanation until very recently. Biologists always hesitate to impute human motives to animals, but they are beginning to learn from psychologists, for whom attributing animal motives to humans is part of the day's work. What is now suspected is that the lemmings are driven by some of the same Scandinavian compulsions that drove the Goths. At home, according to this view, they become depressed and irritable during the long, dark winters under the snow. When home becomes intolerable, they emigrate, and their behavior is then described by the old Norse word, *berserk*.

A lemming migration is one of the great eruptions of nature, and its reverberations, like fallout, are of more than local concern. Biologists like to picture nature in the abstract as a sort of irregular lattice, or Mondrian construction, composed of feeding relations, whose seemingly random placement is actually so tightly organized that every strut depends on all the others. The lemmings' place in this pic-

ture is that of a strut more easily fretted than most, because, like other vegetarians that nourish a variety of
carnivores, they are more fed upon than feeding. As Ca-
ruso's vocal cords, suitably vibrated, could shatter glass-
ware, the whole of animate creation sometimes seems to
pulsate with the supply of lemmings. In normal years they
live obscurely, if dangerously, in the mountains of Scan-
dinavia, and on the Arctic tundra generally. Periodically,
despite the efficient efforts of their enemies—which include
such mainstays of the fur industry as the marten and the
white fox—their reproductive prowess gets the upper hand,
and the tundra fairly teems with them. At such times, about
every four years somewhere in Norway, though any given
district is afflicted less frequently, the balance of nature goes
entirely awry, and the Mondrian composition seems to degenerate into parody. Sea birds give up fishing and flock far
inland to gorge on lemmings, while the more local hawks
and owls hatch and feed families that are several times
larger than usual. Foxes, on the shores of the Arctic
Ocean, have been known to hunt for lemmings fifty miles
out on the pack ice. The reindeer, which ordinarily subsist
on reindeer moss, acquire a taste for lemmings just as cattle
use salt. Eventually, faced with such troubles (but not necessarily *because* of them—I'm coming to that), lemmings
are seized with the classic, or rather Gothic, obsession,
and millions of them desert the tundra for the lowlands.

The repercussions then begin in earnest. As the clumsy
animals attempt to swim the lakes and rivers, the predatory
circle widens to include the trout and salmon, which understandably lose interest in dry flies. The forested lowlands, already occupied by other kinds of rodents as well as by
farmers and their dogs and cats, are not good lemming
country—the winters are too warm, for one thing—but
while the lemmings press on as though aware of this, they
show no sign of losing their disastrous appetites. When the
crops are gone, though seldom before, exorcism by a Latin
formula is said to have some slight effect in abating the
plague. Finally the vanguard may actually reach the sea,
and, having nowhere else to go, plunge in—sometimes
meeting another army trying to come ashore from a nearby
island. A steamer, coming up Trondheim Fjord in November 1868, took fifteen minutes to pass through a shoal of
them, but they were swimming *across* the fjord, not down
it to the sea. The landward part of their wake is a path of

destruction, strewn with dead lemmings, and an epidemic focus of lemming fever—which is not something the lemmings *have*, but a kind of tularemia that people get from handling the carcasses. As the Norwegians take up this unenviable chore their thoughts rarely turn to Mondrian or any other artist; the better-read among them may wonder, however, who buried the six hundred members of the Light Brigade.

American lemmings migrate too, but their outbreaks are observed less often, because no cities lie in their path. Knowledgeable birdwatchers are kept posted, nevertheless, by invasions of snowy owls, which leave the tundra when the lemming tide has passed its flood, and appear in such unlikely places as Charleston, the Azores, and Yugoslavia. Every four years or so, therefore, the lemmings affect the practice of taxidermy, and the economics of the glass-eye industry, as the handsome but unhappy birds fall trophy to amateur marksmen while vainly quartering the fields of France and New England. Closer to the center of disturbance, the cities of western Norway see lemmings before they see owls, and they are not unknown as far away from the mountains as Stockholm, though spring fever is reported to be commoner than lemming fever along the Baltic beaches of Sweden. Oslo is ordinarily too far south, but was visited in 1862, in 1876, in 1890, and again in 1910. The 1862 migration, coinciding with the Battle of Antietam, may have been the greatest of the century, and one of its episodes was touching, if not prophetic. The Norwegian naturalist Robert Collett saw them, he said, "running up the high granite stairs in the vestibule of the University" (of Oslo). Evidently they were begging to be investigated by professors. The Norwegian savants were busy, however, and scorned the impertinent intrusion. In 1862 the discoverer of the death wish, Sigmund Freud, was a six-year-old boy in far-away Freiburg, and if he ever saw a lemming or shot a snowy owl his biographers have repressed it.

That the lemmings are neurotically sick animals, at least during migration, has not escaped the notice of close, or even of casual, observers. For one thing, they wander abroad in the daytime, as small mammals rarely do. For another, when crossed or cornered they show a most unmouselike degree of fight; as Collett said, "they viciously drive their sharp teeth into the foot, or the stick advanced toward them, and allow themselves to be lifted high up by their teeth." Descriptions of the last snarling stages of the march to the sea recall the South Ferry terminal at rush hour, or a hundred-car smashup on a California turnpike. In his authoritative and starkly titled book, *Voles, Mice, and Lemmings,* the English biologist Charles Elton summed up "this great cosmic oscillation" as "a rather tragic procession of refugees, with all the obsessed behaviour of the unwanted stranger in a populous land, going blindly on to various deaths." Offhand, however, neurosis does not seem to explain very much of this, any more than shellshock is a cause of war, and in trying to understand the upheaval the experts have tended to set the psychopathic symptoms to one side while looking for something more basic.

That something, presumably, would be some property of the lemmings' environment—food, predators, disease, or weather, or perhaps all working together—that periodically relaxes its hold on the mournful numbers. Find the cause of the overcrowding, so the thinking has run, and you will find why the lemmings leave home. But this thinking, though doubtless correct, has been slow to answer the question, because it tends to divert attention from the actors to the scenery. The oldest Norse references to lemmings confuse them with locusts, and the farmer whose fields are devastated can hardly be expected to count the pests' legs and divide by four. More detached students know that mammals do not drop from the sky, but in their own way they too have been misled by the locust analogy, supposing that lemmings swarm, as locusts do, because of something done *to* them by their surroundings. The discovery that the migrations are cyclical, made only a few years ago by Elton, strengthened the assumption that some environmental regularity, probably a weather cycle, must set the tune, to which the lemmings, their predators, and their diseases respond in harmonics. Close listeners to nature's symphony soon reported, however, that it sounded atonal to them, more like Berg's opera *Wozzeck,* say, than like Beethoven's Sixth. Cycles of heavenly conjunctions were also looked into, but while the tides are pulled by the sun and moon, and the seasons are undeniably correlated with the zodiac, nothing in astrology reasonably corresponds to a four-year cycle.

If the lemmings' quadrennial fault lies, not in their stars, but in themselves, it is easy to see why the fact has been missed for so long. One reason, of course, is that most of their home life takes place under several feet of snow, in uncomfortable regions where even Scandinavians pass little time outdoors. The main trouble has been, though, as a quick review of thirty years' work will show, that the lemmings' path is thickly sown with false clues. Among these the snowy owls and white foxes rank as the reddest of herrings. The idea that the abundance of prey is controlled by the abundance of predators is a piece of folklore that is hard to uproot, because, like other superstitions, it is sometimes true. The farmers and gamekeepers of Norway have acted on it with sublime confidence for more than a hundred years, backed by a state system of bounty payments, and hawks, foxes, and other predators are now much scarcer there than they are in primeval Westchester County, for example. The result has been that while the grouse-shooting is no better than it used to be, the lemmings (and the field mice in the lowlands, where varmints are persecuted most actively) have continued to fluctuate with unabated vigor. A pile of fox brushes, augmented mainly every fourth year, remains as a monument to a mistaken theory, but their owners may take some gloomy pride in having furnished a splendid mass of statistics.

An even more seductive body of data exists in the account books of the Arctic fur trade, some of which go back to Revolutionary days. They give a remarkable picture of feast or famine, most kinds of skins being listed as thousands of times more plentiful in good years than in lean. Those that belonged to the smaller predators, such as the white fox and the ermine, rise and fall in numbers with the hauntingly familiar four-year rhythm, and the trappers' diaries (which make better reading than the bookkeepers' ledgers) show that their authors placed the blame squarely, or cyclically, on lemmings. Farther south there are periodic surges among such forest-dwellers as the marten and the red fox, whose fluctuating food supply is field mice. Lynx pelts, known to the trade under various euphemisms for "cat," show a still more beautiful cycle of ten years' length, which certainly matches the abundance of snowshoe hares, the lynxes' principal prey. The ten-year pulse of lynxes was extricated, after a brief but noisy academic scuffle, from the coils of the eleven-year sunspot cycle, and by the mid-thirties the theory of mammal populations had settled down about like this: the prey begin to increase, and so do their slower-breeding predators; at peak abundance the predators nearly exterminate the prey, and then starve to death, so clearing the way for the prey to start the cycle over again.

The simple elegance of this idea made it enormously appealing, not least to mathematicians, who reduced it to equations and found it to have an astonishing amount of what they call *generality*. In physics, for instance, it is the "theory of coupled oscillations"; as "servomechanism theory" it underlies many triumphs of engineering, such as remote control by radar; in economics, it explains the tendency for the prices of linked products, such as corn and hogs, to chase each other in perpetually balanced imbalance. Regardless of the price of hogs, or furs, however, some killjoys soon declared that the formulae seemed not to apply to rodents. Some populations of snowshoe hares, for example, were found to oscillate on islands where lynxes, or predators of any sort, were scarcer than mathematicians. Besides, the equations require the coupled numbers of predator and prey to rise and fall smoothly, like tides, whereas the normal pattern of mammal cycles is one of gradual crescendo, followed abruptly by a crashing silence. A Russian biologist, G. F. Gause, was therefore led to redesign the theory in more sophisticated form. The predator, he said, need not be a fur-bearing animal; it can be an infectious disease. When the prey is scarce, the chance of infection is small, especially if the prey, or host, has survived an epidemic and is immune. As the hosts become more numerous, the infection spreads faster, or becomes more virulent, until the ensuing epidemic causes the crash.

In this new, agar-plated guise the theory was not only longer, lower, and more powerful; it was testable without recourse to the fur statistics, the study of which had come to resemble numerology. Made newly aware of lemming fever and tularemia, pathologists shed their white coats for parkas, and took their tubes and sterilizers into the field. The first reports were painfully disappointing: wild rodents, including lemmings, harbored no lack of interesting diseases, but the abundance of microbes had no connection with that of their hosts. Worse, the animals seemed to enjoy their ill health, even when their numbers were greatest, and when they died there was no sign of an epidemic. Not of infectious disease, anyway; but there was one malady, prevalent among snowshoe hares, that certainly was not infectious, but that just as certainly caused a lot of hares to drop dead, not only in live-traps, but also in the woods when no one was around. Long and occasionally sad experience with laboratory rabbits suggested a name, shock disease, for this benign but fatal ailment, the symptoms of which were reminiscent of apoplexy, or of insulin shock. The diagnosis, if that is what it was, amounted to saying that the hares were scared to death, not by lynxes (for the bodies hardly ever showed claw-marks), but, presumably, by each other. Having made this unhelpful pronouncement, most of the pathologists went home. The Second World War was on by that time, and for a while no one remembered what Collett had said about the lemmings: "Life quickly leaves them, and they die from the slightest injury. . . . It is constantly stated by eyewitnesses, that they can die from their great excitement."

These Delphic remarks turned out to contain a real clue, which had been concealed in plain sight, like the purloined letter. An inquest on Minnesota snowshoe hares was completed in 1939, and its clinical language describes a grievous affliction. In the plainer words of a later writer,

"This syndrome was characterized primarily by fatty degeneration and atrophy of the liver with a coincident striking decrease in liver glycogen and a hypoglycemia preceding death. Petechial or ecchymotic brain hemorrhages, and congestion and hemorrhage of the adrenals, thyroid, and kidneys were frequent findings in a smaller number of animals. The hares characteristically died in convulsive seizures with sudden onset, running movements, hind-leg extension, retraction of the head and neck, and sudden leaps with clonic seizures upon alighting. Other animals were typically lethargic or comatose."

For connoisseurs of hemorrhages this leaves no doubt that the hares were sick, but it does leave open the question of how they got that way. Well-trained in the school of Pasteur, or perhaps of Paul de Kruif, the investigators had been looking hard for germs, and were slow to take the hint of an atrophied liver, implying that shock might be a social disease, like alcoholism. As such, it could be contagious, like a hair-do, without being infectious. It might, in fact, be contracted in the same way that Chevrolets catch petechial tail fins from Cadillacs, through the virus of galloping, convulsive anxiety. A disorder of this sort, increasing in virulence with the means of mass communication, would be just the coupled oscillator needed to make Gause's theory work. So theatrical an idea had never occurred to Gause, though, and before it could make much progress the shooting outside the windows had to stop. About ten years later, when the news burst on the world that hares are mad in March, it lacked some of the now-it-can-be-told immediacy of the Smyth Report on atomic energy, but it fitted neatly into the bulky dossier on shock disease that had been quietly accumulating in the meantime.

As a matter of fact, for most of those ten years shock disease was a military secret, as ghastly in some of its implications as the Manhattan Project. Armies are not supposed to react like frightened rabbits, but the simple truth, that civilians in uniform can suffer and die from shock disease, was horrifyingly evident in Korea. As was revealed after the war, hundreds of American captives, live-trapped while away from home and mother, had turned lethargic or comatose, or died in convulsive seizures with sudden onset. Their baffled buddies gave it the unsympathetic name of "give-up-itis."

Military interest in rodents was whipped up long before 1939, of course, but its basis, during more ingenuous ages, was not the rodents' psyches. Rats have fought successfully, if impartially, in most of mankind's wars, but the Second World War was probably the first in which large numbers of rodents were deliberately kept on active duty while others were systematically slaughtered. To explain this curious even-handedness, and at the risk of considerable over-simplification, we may divide military rodents (including rabbits, which are not rodents, but lagomorphs, according to purists) into two platoons, or squadrons. First, there are wild, or Army-type, rodents, which not only nibble at stores but carry various diseases; they are executed when captured. Then there are domestic, cabined, or Navy-type rodents; during the war these were mainly watched by Navy psychologists in an effort to understand the military mind. The story of the first kind was superbly told by the late Hans Zinsser in *Rats, Lice, and History*, a runaway best-seller in the years between World Wars. Conceivably as a result, there were no outbreaks of louse-borne typhus in the Second World War, but in the course of their vigil wild-life men continued to run into pathologists at Army messes around the world. The yarn of the Navy's rats has never been publicized, however (except, obliquely, in such studies of mass anxiety as William H. Whyte's *The Organization Man).*

The kind of nautical problem the psychologists had in mind was not the desertion of sinking ships, but the behavior of men under tension. The crowding of anxious but idle seamen in submarines, for instance, had had some fairly unmartial effects, which needed looking into. As subjects, when mariners were unavailable, the psychologists naturally used rats, which can be frustrated into states of high anxiety that simulate combat neurosis. So now, to recapitulate, there were *three* kinds of rodent experts in the Pacific theatre—zoologists, pathologists, and psychologists—and when they met, as they often did at the island bases, something was bound to happen. What emerged was a fresh view of rats, with which some of the lonelier islands were infested. These were no ordinary rats, but a special breed, like the Pitcairn Islanders, a sort of stranded landing-party. They were descendants of seagoing ancestors, marooned when the whalers had left; but, as the only wild mammals on the islands, they had reverted to Army type. It was soon noticed that when they entered messhalls and BOQ's they solved intellectual problems with great acumen, along with some anxiety-based bravado. Outdoors, on the other hand, their populations went up and down, and when abundant they terrorized the nesting seabirds or ran in droves through the copra plantations. Often, too, they simply dropped dead of shock. In short, they were rats, but whereas in confinement they behaved like psychologists, when at liberty they acted remarkably like lemmings.

If islanded feral rats contributed to the lemming problem, biologists could take wry pleasure in the fact, for most of the rats' contributions to insular existence—to the extinction of hundreds of kinds of interesting land birds, for instance—have been a lot less positive. Then, too, a back-to-nature movement led by psychologists promised to be an exhilarating experience, especially if it included an id-hunt through Polynesia. I have to admit, though, that it didn't work out quite that way, and my account of events in the Pacific theatre may be more plausible than accurate. The published facts are scanty, and my own duty as a Navy biologist was spent amid barnacles, not rodents, on the Eastern Sea Frontier. My first-hand knowledge of Pacific islands, in fact, is confined to Catalina, where rats are visible only on very clear days. What I *am* sure of is that startling things were learned in many countries, during the war years, about the capabilities of many kinds of animals besides rats. When these were added up it was not incredible that rodents might suffer the diseases of suburbia; some students would not have been surprised, by then, if bunnies were found to say "boo" to each other in Russian.

1. Bees, for example, were proved to be able to tell other bees, by means of a patterned dance like a polonaise, the direction and the distance from the hive at which food could be found, as well as the kind of flower to look for and the number of worker-bees needed to do the job. For compass directions they report the azimuth of the sun, but what they perceive is not the sun itself, but the arrangement of polarized light that the sun makes around the sky.

2. Navigating birds, on the other hand, take bearings on the sun directly, or on the stars, but when visual cues fail they fall back on an internal chronometer, conceivably their heart-beat, to reach their destination anyway.

3. Prairie-dogs in their towns pass socially accepted facts, such as the invisible boundaries between their neighborhoods, from one generation to the next; they do it by imitating each other, not by instinct, and European chickadees do the same with their trick, invented about 1940, of following milkmen on their routes and beating housewives to the bottled cream.

4. Ravens and jackdaws can count up to six or seven, and show that they can form an abstract concept of number by responding, correctly, whether the number is cued by spots on cards, by bells or buzzers, or by different spoken commands.

5. A Swedish bird called the nutcracker remembers precisely where it buried its nuts in the fall, and digs them up, in late March, say, confidently and without errors through two feet of snow.

6. For its sexual display, an Australian species called the satin bowerbird not only constructs a bower, or bachelor apartment, decorating it with flowers and *objets d'art,* as do other members of its family, but makes paint out of charcoal or fruit-juice and paints the walls of its bower, using a pledget of chewed bark for a daub.

7. Bats avoid obstacles in total darkness, and probably catch flying insects too, by uttering short, loud screams and guiding themselves by the echoes; the pitch is much too high for human ears to hear, but some kinds of moths can

hear the bats coming and take evasive action.

Made groggy by facts like these, most of them reported between 1946 and 1950, biologists began to feel like the White Queen, who "sometimes managed to believe as many as six impossible things before breakfast." Still, no one had yet spent a winter watching rodents under the snow, and the epicene behavior of bower-birds was not seen, then or since, as having any direct bearing on mammalian neurosis. If anything, the intellectual feats of birds and bees made it harder to understand how rodents could get into such sorry states; one might have credited them with more sense. Until new revelations from the Navy's rats laid bare their inmost conflicts, the point was arguable, at least, that anxiety is a sort of hothouse bloom, forced in psychologists' laboratories, and could not survive a northern winter.

As a footnote in a recent article makes clear, the United States Navy takes no definite stand on rodents. "The opinions or assertions contained herein," it says (referring to a report on crowded mice), "are the private ones of the writer, and are not to be construed as official or reflecting the views of the Navy Department or naval service at large." This disavowal is a little surprising, in that its author, John J. Christian, as head of the animal laboratories of the Naval Medical Research Institute at Bethesda, Maryland, can be considered the commander of the Navy's rodents. Ten years ago, though, when he wrote what may be thought of as the Smyth Report on population cycles, his opinions were temporarily freed from protocol. An endocrinologist and Navy lieutenant (j.g.), Christian had left the Fleet and gone back to studying mice at the Wyeth Institute, in Philadelphia. His luminous essay was published where anyone at large could read it, in the August, 1950 issue of the *Journal of Mammalogy*, under the title "The Adreno-Pituitary System and Population Cycles in Mammals." In it Christian said, in part:

"We now have a working hypothesis for the die-off terminating a cycle. Exhaustion of the adreno-pituitary system resulting from increased stresses inherent in a high population, especially in winter, plus the late winter demands of the reproductive system, due to increased light or other factors, precipitates population-wide death with the symptoms of adrenal insufficiency and hypoglycemic convulsions."

Dedicated readers of the *Journal* remembered the snowshoe hares' congested adrenals, and did not need to be reminded that shock is a glandular disorder. They also knew their scientific Greek, and easily translated *hypoglycemia* as "lack of sugar in the blood"; but what they found new and fascinating was Christian's clinical evidence—much of it reported by a young Viennese internist named Hans Selye—tending to show that rodents might die, of all things, from a surfeit of sexuality. Most people had thought of rabbits as adequately equipped for reproduction, but that is not the point, as Christian developed it: what does them in is not breeding, exactly, but concupiscence. Keyed up by the stresses of crowded existence—he instanced poor and insufficient food, increased exertion, and fighting—animals that have struggled through a tough winter are in no shape to stand the lust that rises like sap in the spring. Their endocrine glands, which make the clashing hormones, burn sugar like a schoolgirl making fudge, and the rodents, not being maple trees, have to borrow sugar from their livers. Cirrhosis lies that way, of course, but death from hypertension usually comes first.

In medical jargon, though the testy author of *Modern English Usage* would protest, the name for this state of endocrine strain is *stress*. As the physical embodiment of a mental state, anxiety, it is worth the respectful attention of all who believe, with mammalogists, that life can be sweet without necessarily caramelizing the liver. Despite its technicality, the subject is uncommonly rewarding. It is not only that seeing a lemming as a stressed animal goes far toward clearing up a famous mystery. And, though the how and why of psychosomatic ailments in wild rodents are undeniably important to tame men, the problems of gray flannel suits are not my main concern. The real attraction of stress, at least for a biologist, consists simply in the way it works: it turns out to contain a whole array of built-in servomechanisms. That is, the coupled oscillation of hosts and diseases, which Gause thought might underlie the fluctuating balance of nature, is mimicked inside the body, and may be said to be controlled, by mutual interaction between the glands. Biologists are impressed by abstract resemblances of this sort, which, after all, are their version of *generality*. In explaining stress by means of some fairly garish metaphors, therefore, I find it soothing to remember that what is called "imagery" in some circles is "model-making" in others.

As it happens, the master himself is no slouch at imagery. Selye's recent book, *The Stress of Life*, is notable, among other things, for its skillful use of the didactic, or Sunday-supplement, analogy. Without plagiarizing his exposition, though, it is possible to speak of vital needs as payable in sugar, for which the liver acts as a bank. Routine withdrawals are smoothly handled by hormones from the pancreas and from the adrenal medulla, which act as paying tellers; but the top-level decisions (such as whether to grow or to reproduce) are reserved for the bank's officers, the adrenal cortex and pituitary glands. Stress, in Selye's view, amounts to an administrative flap among the hormones, and shock results when the management overdraws the bank.

If the banking model is gently dissected, it reveals its first and most important servomechanism: a remarkably bureaucratic hookup between the adrenal cortex, acting as cashier's office, and the pituitary, as board of directors. Injury and infection are common forms of stress, and in directing controlled inflammation to combat them the cortex draws cashier's checks on the liver. If the stress persists a hormone called cortisone sends a worried message to the pituitary. Preoccupied with the big picture, the pituitary delegates a vice-presidential type, ACTH or adrenocorticotropic hormone, whose role is literally to buck up the adrenal cortex. As students of Parkinson would predict, the cortex, bucked, takes on more personnel, and expands its activities, including that of summoning more ACTH. The viciousness of the impending spiral ought to be obvious, and ordinarily it is; but while withdrawals continue the amount of sugar in circulation is deceptively constant (the work of another servomechanism), and there is no device, short of autopsy, for taking inventory at the bank. If the pituitary is conned by persisting stress into throwing more support to ACTH, the big deals begin to suffer retrenchment. A cutback of ovarian hormone, for instance, may allow the cortex to treat a well-started foetus as an inflammation to be healed over. Likewise, the glandular sources of virility and of maternity, though unequally prodigal of sugar, are equally likely to dry up. Leaving hypertension aside (because it involves another commodity, salt, which needn't be gone into just now), the fatal symptom can be hypoglycemia. A tiny extra stress, such as a loud noise (or, as

Christian would have it, the sight of a lady rabbit), corresponds to an unannounced visit by the bank examiner: the adrenal medulla is startled into sending a jolt of adrenalin to the muscles, the blood is drained of sugar, and the brain is suddenly starved. This, incidentally, is why shock looks like hyperinsulinism. An overactive pancreas, like a panicky adrenal, resembles an untrustworthy teller with his hand in the till.

Haruspicy, or divination by inspection of the entrails of domestic animals, is supposed to have been extinct for two thousand years, and no one knows what the Etruscan soothsayers made of a ravaged liver. Selye would snort, no doubt, at being called a modern haruspex, but the omens of public dread are at least as visceral as those of any other calamity, and there are some sound Latin precedents—such as the geese whose gabbling saved Rome—for the view that emotion is communicable to and by animals. More recently, thoughtful veterinarians have begun to notice that neurotic pets tend to have neurotic owners, and a report from the Philadelphia zoo blames "social pressures," on the rise for the last two decades, for a tenfold increase of arteriosclerosis among the inmates. If Selye seems to be playing down anxiety—the word is not even listed in the index of his book—I can think of two possible reasons, both interesting if not entirely convincing. Anxiety is an ugly word, of course, and using it can easily generate more of it, just as calling a man an insomniac can keep him awake all night; Selye, as a good physician, may well have hesitated to stress it in a popular book about stress. More important, probably, is the fact that Selye, like any internist, begins and ends his work with bodily symptoms, and only grudgingly admits the existence of mind. A curious piece of shoptalk, which he quotes approvingly and in full from a San Francisco medical man (not a psychiatrist), suggests that some of his professional colleagues, like too many novelists, have read Freud without understanding him:

"The dissociation of the ego and the id has many forms. I had an American housewife with dermatomyositis [an inflammation of skin and muscles] [the brackets are Selye's] who had been taught how to play the piano when she was little, and had continued for the entertainment of the children, but didn't get very far. When she started on large doses of ACTH she was suddenly able to play the most difficult works of Beethoven and Chopin—

and the children of the neighbors would gather in the garden to hear her play. Here was a dissociation of the ego and the id that was doing good. But she also became a little psychotic, and so her dosage to ACTH had to be lowered, and with every 10 units of the ACTH one sonata disappeared. It all ended up with the same old music poorly performed."

The false note here, of course, is that business about "the dissociation of the ego and the id." Whatever the id may be, it is not considered innately musical, and *my* professional colleagues would count it a triumph to be able to teach it anything, even "Chopsticks." Still, we may take the anecdote as showing *some* kind of mental effect of stress; what the psychologist sees as rather more to the point is the obverse of this: moods and emotions cannot be injected hypodermically, but their cost is paid in sugar, and their action on the cortex is precisely that of ACTH. Christian finds, for instance, that crowding mice in cages enlarges their adrenals, but fortunately, in experiments of this sort, it is not always necessary to kill the animals to learn the answer. A microscopic sample of blood reveals a useful clue to endocrine tension: college students at exam time show a shortage of the same type of white cell that is also scarce in the blood of crowded mice. (The skittish blood cells are called *eosinophils;* I mention this because the word is sure to turn up in detective stories before long.) The fact that tranquillizing drugs do their work by blocking various hormones opens up another line of evidence, as well as a fertile field for quackery. But the surest sign that anxiety is stress—and its most lurid property—is its ability to visit itself on the unborn. The maker of this appalling discovery, William R. Thompson of Wesleyan University, tells us nothing of the sins of his rats' fathers, but his report shows all too clearly that the offspring of frustrated mothers, part of whose pregnancy was spent in problem boxes with no exit, carried the emotional disturbance throughout their own lives. Nestling birds can learn the parents' alarm call while still inside the egg (as the nearly-forgotten author of *Green Mansions* was among the first to notice), but the mammalian uterus is more soundproof, and the only reasonable explanation of Thompson's results is that the aroused maternal hormones perverted the silver cord, and made it a pipeline to a forbidden supply of sugar.

Circumspectly, now, so as to forestall any harumphs

from the naval service at large, we may return to Christian's crowded mice. In outward demeanor the ordinary house mouse, *Mus musculus*, is the least military of rodents, but his dissembling is part of the commando tradition, and he would not have got where he is today without a lot of ruthless infighting. Nowadays house mice spend little time outdoors if they can help it, but in more rustic times they often scourged the countryside, like Marion's men, and the tenth-century Bishop of Bingen (who perished in the Mouse Tower) learned to his cost that country mice can be pushed too far. Recently, at some of our leading universities (Olso, strange to say, has *still* not been heard from), mouse-watching has proved informative, if not exactly edifying, and I cull a few tidbits from the notes of some shocked colleagues:

The first thing to notice is that the old murine spirit of mass emigration is not yet dead, despite the effeteness of modern urban living. Not long ago an outbreak was observed—provoked, in fact—at the University of Wisconsin, where the scientists had set up a mouse tower, or substitute patch of tundra, in a junkroom in the basement of the zoology building, and set traps (not enough, as it turned out) in the neighboring offices and laboratories. Nothing happened for a while, except that the food—half a pound of it a day—kept disappearing. Then, in Browning's words, "the muttering grew to a grumbling; and the grumbling grew to a mighty rumbling"; and the experiment, though publishable, became unpopular; the room was simply overstuffed with mice, like a sofa in a neglected summer cottage.

Chastened, yet encouraged by this experience, the zoologists fell back on emigration-proof pens, where they could keep tab on the mice. Taking census whenever they cleaned the cages (which was pretty often, at someone's pointed insistence), they noticed that the numbers went up and down, but, as there were no seasons or predators and food was always abundant, the fluctuations made little sense at first. Gradually, though, when one of the observers, Charles Southwick, thought to count the tiffs as well as the mice, the shiny outlines of a servomechanism came into sight: as each wave of numbers crested and broke, the scuffles averaged more than one per mouse-hour, and hardly any young mice survived to the age of weaning. Putting the matter this way lays the blame, unchivalrously, on the mothers, and in fact, as the tension mounted, their nest-building became slovenly and some of them failed to nurse their litters, or even ate them (proper mouse food, remember, was always plentiful). But the males were equally responsible, though for different hormonal reasons. Like chickens with their peck-order, the buck mice were more concerned for status than for posterity, and the endocrine cost of supremacy was sexual impotence. In one of the pens two evenly-matched pretenders played mouse-in-the-manger with the females, and suppressed all reproduction until they died.

While the Wisconsin mice were either suffering from stress or practicing a peculiarly savage form of moral restraint, mice at other centers were also made unhappy, or at least infertile, by being given plenty of food, space, and sexual access. It came as no great surprise, then, when the adrenals of Christian's mice were found to swell, as he had predicted eight years before, in proportion to the numbers of their social companions. The really arresting experiment, which dilutes the inhumanity of some of the others, shows that rodents—rats, at any rate—*prefer* to be crowded and anxious. At the National Institutes of Health, in Bethesda, John C. Calhoun allowed litter-mates to grow up in one large pen, where every rat had an individual food hopper. From the start, when eating, they huddled like a farrow at a single hopper; later, though free to roam, eat, and nest in four intercommunicating pens, these rats and their descendants spent most of their time in one of the four, and as I write this they are still there, paying for their sociability in lowered fertility and shortened lives. For his part, my friend Calhoun coined a phrase that deserves to outlive his rats, and is still musing on *pathological togetherness*.

At this point in the argument, explaining the lemmings' periodic dementia should be anticlimactically easy. I seem to have overstated the case, in fact, for it seems less Gothic than *gothick*, like some of the more unnecessary behavior described by the brothers Grimm. The cycle starts where population problems always do, with the lemmings' awesome power of procreation. Nubile at the age of thirty-five days, averaging seven or eight young at a cast, a female lemming may have worries, but barrenness is not one of them, and four litters is par for a summer's dalliance. Lemming life is more austere in winter, but not much. As long as food is plentiful under the snow, the winter sports of pullulation and fighting continue as at a disreputable ski resort. The wonder is—until we remember the owls and foxes above and the weasels *in* the runways—that it takes as long as four years for the numbers to become critical, like the mass of an atomic bomb. When the Thing goes off, then, it is the younger lemmings that emigrate, in search of a patch of tundra that is slightly more private than the beach at Coney Island; though less overtly anxious to begin with, presumably, their state of mind on reaching downtown Oslo is another matter entirely. The older, better-established residents, or those with stouter livers, stay home, and die of shock—having first passed on the family disease to the next generation. Before the epidemic of stress has run its course, it spreads to the predators, too (though *this* form of lemming fever is caught, ironically, from *not* eating lemmings). The snowy owl that died at Fayal, Azores, in 1928 may or may not have known that it had really reached Atlantis, but in being shot by an anxious man it provided a textbook, or postgraduate, example of a coupled oscillation.

If all this is true, and I think it is, the Norse clergymen who exorcized the lemmings in Latin were clearly on the right track, and what the Scandinavians need is a qualified haruspex. Before they hire one, though (I am not a candidate), or resort to spraying the tundra with tranquillizers (which would be expensive), there is one tiny reservation: there is not a scrap of *direct* evidence that the lemming suffers from stress. Come to think of it, no one has yet spent a winter watching lemmings under the snow. (Some Californian zoologists lived for several winters in Alaska, trying valiantly to do just that, but the runways are pretty small for Californians, and for most of the time there was trouble finding *any* lemmings). Except for some circumstantial lesions of the skin, which could be psychosomatic, like shingles (and which ruin the lemming's pelt), the case for contagious anxiety therefore rests on a passel of tormented rodents, but not as yet on *Lemmus lemmus*. That animal has baffled a lot of people, and I could be mistaken too. But if I am, or at least if the lemmings' adrenals are not periodically congested, I will eat a small population of them, suitably seasoned with Miltown. Fortunately, lemmings are reported to taste like squirrels, but better; in Lapland, in fact, with men who know rodents best, it's lemmings, two to one.

SUGGESTED READINGS

AMERICAN JOURNAL OF PSYCHOANALYSIS. *A Symposium on Alienation and the Search for Identity.* Vol. 21, No. 2, 1961.

ANGELL, ROBERT. *The Integration of American Society.* New York: McGraw-Hill, 1941.

ARENDT, HANNAH. *The Human Condition.* Garden City, N. Y.: Doubleday Anchor Books, 1959.

BARRETT, WILLIAM. *Irrational Man: A Study in Existential Philosophy.* Garden City, N. Y.: Doubleday Anchor Books, 1958.

BEDNARIK, KARL. *The Young Worker of To-Day: A New Type.* London: Faber, 1953.

BELL, DANIEL. *The End of Ideology.* Glencoe, Ill.: Free Press, 1960.

———— "The 'Rediscovery' of Alienation: Some Notes Along the Quest for the Historical Marx," *The Journal of Philosophy,* Vol. LVI, No. 24, November 19, 1959.

BETTELHEIM, BRUNO. *The Informed Heart: Autonomy in a Mass Age.* Glencoe, Ill.: Free Press, 1960.

BROWN, NORMAN. *Life Against Death: The Psychoanalytic Meaning of History.* New York: Vintage Books, 1961.

CAMUS, ALBERT. *The Rebel.* New York: Vintage Books, 1958.

DEAN, DWIGHT. "Alienation and Political Apathy," *Social Forces,* Vol. 38, No. 3, March 1960.

———— "Meaning and Measurement of Alienation," *American Sociological Review,* Vol. 26, No. 5, October 1961.

DOBRINER, WILLIAM (ed.). *The Suburban Community.* New York: Putnam's, 1958.

DUBIN, ROBERT. "Industrial Workers' Worlds," *Social Problems,* Vol. 3, No. 3, January 1956.

ECKARDT, MARIANNE H. "The Detached Person," *American Journal of Psychoanalysis,* Vol. 20, No. 2, 1960.

ERIKSON, ERIK H. "Identity and the Life Cycle," *Psychological Issues,* Vol. 1, No. 1, 1959.

———— "Identity and Uprootedness in Our Time," in *Uprooting and Resettlement,* London: World Federation for Mental Health, 1960.

ESSLIN, MARTIN. *The Theater of the Absurd*. Garden City, N. Y.: Doubleday Anchor Books, 1961.

FROMM, ERICH. *Man for Himself*. New York: Rinehart, 1947.

———— *Marx's Concept of Man*. New York: Frederick Ungar, 1961.

———— *The Sane Society*. New York: Rinehart, 1955.

GOODMAN, PAUL. *Growing Up Absurd*. New York: Random House, 1960.

GOULDNER, ALVIN (ed.). *Studies in Leadership*. New York: Harper, 1950.

HAJDA, JAN. "Alienation and Integration of Student Intellectuals," *American Sociological Review*, Vol. 26, No. 5, October 1961.

HALMOS, PAUL. *Solitude and Privacy*. London: Routledge & Kegan Paul, 1952.

HALSEY, MARGARET. *The Folks at Home*. New York: Simon & Schuster, 1952.

HAUSER, ARNOLD. *The Social History of Art*, Vol. 4. New York: Vintage Books, 1958.

HEINEMANN, F. H. *Existentialism and the Modern Predicament*. New York: Harper Torchbooks, 1958.

HOFFER, ERIC. *The True Believer: Thoughts on the Nature of Mass Movements*. New York: New American Library, 1958.

HORNEY, KAREN. *Neurosis and Human Growth*. New York: W. W. Norton, 1950.

HUSZAR, GEORGE. *The Intellectuals: A Controversial Portrait*. Glencoe, Ill.: Free Press, 1960.

INFIELD, HENRIK F. *Utopia and Experiment*. New York: Praeger, 1955.

JASPERS, KARL. *Man in the Modern Age*. Garden City, N. Y.: Doubleday Anchor Books, 1957.

KAHLER, ERICH. *The Tower and the Abyss: An Inquiry into the Transformation of the Individual*. New York: Braziller, 1957.

KENNISTON, KENNETH. "Alienation and the Decline of Utopia," *American Scholar*, Spring 1960.

KNIGHT, EVERETT. *The Objective Society*. New York: Braziller, 1959.

KORNHAUSER, WILLIAM. *The Politics of Mass Society*. Glencoe, Ill.: Free Press, 1959.

LANDECKER, WERNER. "Types of Integration and Their Measurement," *American Journal of Sociology*, Vol. LVI, No. 4, January 1951.

LARRABEE, ERIC and MEYERSOHN, ROLF (eds.). *Mass Leisure*. Glencoe, Ill.: Free Press, 1958.